Y0-BQU-446

ORB SCEPTRE THRONE

TOR BOOKS BY IAN C. ESSLEMONT

Night of Knives
Return of the Crimson Guard
Stonewielder
Orb Sceptre Throne

ORB SCEPTRE THRONE

A NOVEL OF THE MALAZAN EMPIRE

Ian C. Esslemont

A TOM DOHERTY ASSOCIATES BOOK
NEW YORK

This is a work of fiction. All of the characters, organizations, and events portrayed in this novel are either products of the author's imagination or are used fictitiously.

ORB SCEPTRE THRONE

Copyright © 2012 by Ian C. Esslemont

All rights reserved.

Maps by Neil Gower

Originally published in Great Britain by Bantam Press, an imprint of Transworld Publishers

A Tor Book
Published by Tom Doherty Associates, LLC
175 Fifth Avenue
New York, NY 10010

www.tor-forge.com

Tor® is a registered trademark of Tom Doherty Associates, LLC.

Library of Congress Cataloging-in-Publication Data

Esslemont, Ian C. (Ian Cameron)
  Orb sceptre throne : a novel of the Malazan Empire / Ian C. Esslemont. —
1st U.S. ed.
    p. cm.
  ISBN 978-0-7653-2996-7 (hardcover)
  ISBN 978-0-7653-2999-8 (trade pbk.)
  ISBN 978-1-4299-4324-6 (e-book)
  I. Title.
  PS3605.S684O73 2012
  813'.6—dc23

                                                                    2012001825

First U.S. Edition: May 2012

Printed in the United States of America

0 9 8 7 6 5 4 3 2 1

For Steve, once again

ACKNOWLEDGEMENTS

As always, my love and gratitude to Gerri and the boys for their support of my writing, which takes me from them more than I would ever wish.

CONTENTS

Darujhistan

LAKE

Maiten

BROWNRUN
BAY

DARU
BAY

Maiten River

TWO-OX
GATE

LAKEFRON
DISTRICT

GADROBI
DISTRICT

Gadrobi Road

1

DARU
DISTRI

CEMETERY

MARSH
DISTRICT

2

Foss Road

Ridge Road

Cutter Lake Road

Cuttertown

Ridge

Raven

River Foss

RAVEN

SCALE

0   ½   1m

AZUR

Lighthouse   Mole   TENDER ISLAND

Worrytown

Jatem's Worry

⑤   ⑥   ⑦

⑧

⑨   ⑩

⑪   ⑫

③   ⑬   ESTATE DISTRICT

④

SECOND TIER WALL   THIRD TIER WALL

GADAR QUARRY

Urs

Hinter Road

HILLS

N

Farms

❶ Arms Quarter
❷ Warden Barracks (City Watch)
❸ Quip's Bar
❹ Phoenix Inn
❺ Borthen Park
❻ Majesty Hill
❼ Despot's Barbican
❽ K'rul's Hill
❾ Orr Estate
❿ High Gallows Hill
⓫ Baruk's Estate
⓬ Simtal Estate
⓭ Hinter's Tower

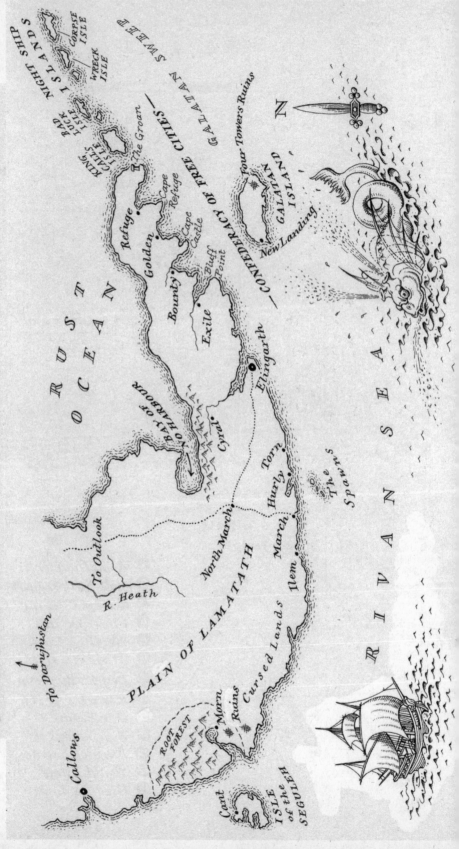

SOUTH GENABACKIS and environs

DRAMATIS PERSONAE

In Darujhistan

Coll	A Council member
Rallick Nom	A retired assassin
Krute	An assassin
Scholar Ebbin	An independent antiquarian/historian
Humble Measure	A native of Cat and rumoured power behind local underworld
Torvald Nom	A native of Darujhistan
Tiserra	Torvald's wife, and a potter
Jeshin Lim	A Council member
Redda Orr	A Council member
Barathol Mekhar	A smith
Scillara	Barathol's wife
Vorcan Radok/ Lady Varada	Head of House Nom and onetime Mistress of Daruhistan's assassins
Lady Envy	A visiting noble lady and mage
Leff	A guard
Scorch	A guard
Picker	A retired Bridgeburner and partner in K'rul's Bar
Blend	A retired Bridgeburner and partner in K'rul's Bar
Spindle	A retired Bridgeburner
Duiker	Once the Malazan Empire's Imperial Historian
Fisher	A bard, a regular at K'rul's Bar
Madrun	Colourful guard of Nom Manor
Lazan Door	Colourful guard of Nom Manor
Thurule	Lady Envy's guard
Studlock/ Studious Lock	A castellan

13

Of the T'orrud Cabal

Baruk	An alchemist
Taya	A dancing girl and assassin
Hister	A dead necromancer
Aman	An erstwhile shopkeeper
Derudan	A witch

The Phoenix Inn Regulars

Meese	Proprietor
Sulty	Server
Scurve	Barkeeper
Jess	A new server
Chud	Cook
Kruppe	A thief

At the Spawns

Malakai	A thief
Antsy	A Malazan veteran
Jallin 'Jumper'	A treasure-hunter
Orchid	A young woman
Corien Lim	Son of a noble Darujhistan family

Of the Seguleh

Jan	Second
Gall	Third
Palla	Sixth
Lo	Eighth
Oru	Eleventh
Iralt	Fifteenth
Shun	Eighteenth
Ira	Twentieth
Beru	Of the Thirtieth
Horul	Of the Hundredth
Sall	Of the Three Hundredth
Sengen	A priest

At the Shores of Creation

Leoman/Jheval	An agent of the Queen of Dreams
Kiska	An ex-Claw
Then-aj-Ehliel	An inhabitant
Maker	Inhabitant

14

Korus	A powerful demon
Then-aj-Ehliel/ Thenaj	An inhabitant

Of the Malazans

Aragan	Ambassador to Darujhistan, commander of Malazan forces in
Captain Dreshen Harad 'Ul	Aide to Aragan
Fist K'ess	Commander of Central Malazan provinces
Captain Fal-ej	Second in command to Fist K'ess
Fist Steppen	Commander of Southern Malazan forces
Sergeant Hektar	Sergeant of the 23rd squad, 3rd Company, 7th Legion, Second Army
Corporal Little	Squad healer
Bone	Saboteur
Bendan	New recruit, Darujhistan native
Tarat	Scout, Rhivi recruit

Further Players

Torn	Moranth attaché to the Malazans
Galene	A Moranth Silver priestess, member of their governing body
Yusek	An adventurer
Caladan Brood	Warlord of the north, an Ascendant
Jiwan	A new member of the Rhivi ruling council
Tserig	Also known as 'The Toothless', an old member of the Rhivi ruling council
Cull Heel	A mercenary most recently of the Confederated Free Cities
Morn	A ghostly visitor to the Spawn

PROLOGUE

Did we not look out together upon the dark waters of the lake
And behold there the constellations
Of both hemispheres at once?

Love Songs of the Cinnamon Wastes

THAT DAY OF DISCOVERY BEGAN AS ANY OTHER. HE AROSE BEFORE
the dawn and saw to his toilet aware that the toothless hag he
kept as camp cook was already up boiling water for the morning tea and mealy porridge. He checked in on the tent of the two
guards that he'd hired simply because he thought he ought to have
someone around to watch the camp. Both men were asleep; that
didn't strike him as proper guard procedure, but it was the Twins'
own luck he'd found anyone willing to work at all for the poor wages
he could offer.

'Tea's on,' he said, and let the flap fall closed.

He kicked awake his two assistants, who lay in the sands next to
the dead campfire. These were sullen youths whom he paid a few
copper slivers a month to see to the lifting and hauling. Like the
ancient, they were of the older tribal stock out of the surrounding
steppes, the Gadrobi; no citified Daru would waste his time out here
in the old burial hills south of the great metropolis of Darujhistan.
None but he, Ebbin, who alone among all the Learned Brethren of the
Philosophical Society (of whom he was charter member) remained
convinced that there yet lurked far more to be found among these
pot-hunted and pit-riddled vaults and tombs.

Sipping the weak tea, he studied the brightening sky: clear; the
wind: anaemic at best. Good weather for another day's exploration.
He waved the youths away from the fire where they huddled warming

17

their skinny shanks, then pointed to the distant scaffolding. The two guards drank their tea and continued their interminable arguing. Ebbin knew that at the end of the day he'd come back to camp to find them still gnawing on the same old bones from the first day he'd hired them. He supposed it took all kinds.

The lads dragged themselves down the hill to station themselves next to a wide barrel winch. Ebbin knelt at the stone-lipped well, opened the old bronze padlock, pulled free the iron chains, and heaved aside the leaves of the wood cover. What was revealed appeared nothing more than one of the many ancient wells that dotted this region, once a Gadrobi settlement.

But what might he find down at the bottom of this otherwise unremarkable well? *Oh, but what he could find!* Beginning some generations ago, a relative warming and drying period in the region's weather had resulted in a drain on the local water reserves and a subsequent fall in the waterline. A lowering of nearly a man's full height. *And what has lain submerged, hidden, for thousands of years may be revealed!* The subtlest of arcane hints and annotated asides in obscure sources had led him step by incremental step to this series of wells. As yet, all had proved unremarkable. Dead ends year after year in his research.

But perhaps this one. Perhaps this time all my work . . . vindicated!

He swung his legs out over the darkness, ran a hand over the lip's curved inner surface. Not for the first time did he marvel at these ancient artisans; the chiselled stone so smooth! The opening as near to a perfect circle as he could discern. How inferior and shabby contemporary construction now, with its eye to mere costs rather than the regal course of posterity!

He yanked down the board seat and wrapped an arm round its rope. After checking his bag of equipment, the lantern, oil, hammer, chisel and such, he waved a curt command to the youths. The winch screeched shrill and piercing as they let out slack and Ebbin swung out over the void.

The descent was eerily silent but for the occasional jangling of the bells attached to the rope – his means of announcing his intent to ascend, and calling the worthless youths back to the well from the shade to which they would always slink off during the heat of the day. He jerked the rope for a pause while he lit his lantern. This accomplished, he signalled for a continued slow playing out of the rope.

It was during these murky silent descents, as if he were submerging

18

himself, that doubts most vividly assailed him. What if the evidence were here, yet hidden from his eyes? He brought the lantern closer to his face while he studied the passing stones for any sign of structural elements. As before, he saw no hint of variation among the slime and dried algae scum.

Failure again. And yet this one had seemed to fit the clues perfectly . . .

Below, the surface of the water glimmered like night. Ebbin moved to shift the lantern to reach for the rope, but his fingers brushed the burning hot bronze and he yelped, dropping the light. It fell for an instant then was snuffed out. A distant splash reached him. He sat in the dark cursing his clumsiness and sucking his fingers.

Then weak shimmerings wavered before his vision. He squinted, dismissed the phenomenon as the stars one can see before one's eyes in the night. But the lustrous flickerings persisted. His eyes widened in the utter dark. Could these not be the remnants of Warren magics? Wards, and seals, and such?

And does not their very presence confirm the correlative supposition that follows?

Ebbin gaped, fingers forgotten. His grimed sweaty skin prickled with the sensation of . . . *discovery.*

Yet could these not be admonitions against meddling? Was it not whispered that it was from these very burial fields that the ancient Tyrant Raest returned (if indeed he had that night not so long ago, which was dismissed by many, and remains an incident completely undreamed of to most)?

He squeezed his hands to warm them in the cool of the well and made an effort to thrust aside such atavistic shrinking from shadows. Superstition! He was a scholar! He had no time for such mummery. True, the Warrens and their manipulation were real, but the efficacious power itself was not evil, not consciously malevolent. It was merely a natural force to be reckoned with, such as weight, or the life-essence.

Ebbin steadied himself in the cold damp dark and tentatively, almost reverently, reached out. His fingertips brushed cool eroded stone. He felt about for a sign of any opening and something brushed his fingertips – a curved edge. Luminescence flared then, limpid and fitful, and it seemed to him now that he must be mistaken, for no tunnel existed here down this thoroughly explored well: it was only the deceptive irregularities in the stone that had fooled him. He should abandon this wasted effort and signal the lads to pull him up.

Then his feet in their worn goatskin shoes suddenly plunged into frigid water and the shock made him flinch, almost tipping him from his narrow perch. He frantically signalled a halt.

The grip he kept on the lip of the curved wall steadied him. And it seemed to him that the tunnel had always been here, undiscovered and patient, as if awaiting him. He wiped a sleeve across his clammy face, swallowed his relief. He sat for a time immobile. His breath echoed in the enclosed space, harsh and quick.

I may have done it! Found what all others said did not even exist! Here may be the tomb of the greatest, and last, of the Tyrant Kings of Darujhistan.

And I can't see a damned thing. He shook the rope to signal retrieval. *Please, gods, please . . . let there be another lantern somewhere in camp!*

But there was no other lantern. After overturning all his equipment, his tent and that of his guards, Ebbin was reduced to having himself lowered clutching a single soft tallow candle. All through the descent he shielded the meagre flame as one might a precious gem. Just before his feet once more touched the frigid water he shook the rope to order a halt.

In the cool dead air he held out the candle. *Hadn't it been here? Was he mistaken?*

He squinted at the curved wall of eroded ancient stones, shifted the candle from side to side. *Gods, please! What a discovery this would be!* Then it was there. Not a sealed smooth barrier of bricks and mortar raised across a tunnel but a dark jagged hole of pushed-in stones.

Ebbin's heart broke.

Failure. Looted. Like all the rest. He was not the first. For a time he sat, hunched, wax dribbling down his fingers. Then, sighing, he roused himself to reach out. Leaning perilously far he just managed to clutch a stone and pull himself over. He raised the candle. A tunnel. Smooth-sided. And something ahead. Rubble?

Intrigued, he shifted his weight even further to lean upon the smashed opening. It was slow going, as he had to hold the candle upraised in one hand the entire time, but eventually, awkwardly, he slid forward into the tunnel and left the sling seat twisting behind. He edged onward through the dusty cobwebbed chute, candle held out before him.

It was a rockfall. A barrier of dirt and debris. *How old?* He glanced back to the hammered opening and his heart soared anew. *Did they get no further? Could what lay beyond as yet remain . . . inviolate?*

Perhaps. He would have to find out. He studied the packed dirt and rock with an assessor's eye. *Looks like this will call for some old-fashioned digging after all.* He began pushing himself backwards.

This could take some time.

* * *

In the surf of a shimmering sea of light a man struggled to push a creature four times his size free of the heaving waves. The liquid tore and ate at the creature like acid. Steam frothed and sizzled bubbling over its sides. Inhuman screams of agony and rage sounded. It flailed its limbs in terror, delivering desperate rock-shattering blows deflected from the man only by flashes of argent power. The brilliant waves crashed over them both as the man knelt, struggling to roll the creature.

Between waves he urged, 'Crawl! Crawl! You can do it!'

'I burn!' it shrieked, raging and crying.

'*Crawl!*'

'I die . . .'

'*No!*'

From rocks up the beach came running and limping a motley collection of mismatched creatures. They dashed into the surf, shrieking and gasping as the liquid burst into smoke around them. Their flesh sloughed off in strips, eaten by the acid light. '*No! Get back!*' the man bellowed, terrified. Together, all pulling and tugging, they heaved the giant figure on to the black sand beach. A number of the smaller ones sank from sight beneath the frothing waves and the man searched frantically, blindly feeling about. He dragged out two tiny smoking figures then fell, exhausted, on to the sands.

The huge creature snarled in an effort to gain its bird-like clawed feet. Its flesh was melted to the bone in places. Clear ichor ran from its wounds as it lurched to the man who lay gasping and knelt next to him.

'Why . . . ?'

The man rose to his elbows. The luminescent waters ran from him leaving no wounds. His long black hair lay plastered to his skull. 'You were cast out through no fault of your own. Cast out to dissolve into nothingness. That is not right. Not right.'

21

The creature's glowing furnace eyes blinked its wonder. 'You are unhurt. Immune . . . you are . . . *Eleint*?'

'No. I am just a man.'

A grunt of disbelief from the giant. 'You are more than that. I am Korus, High Born of Aral Gamelon. What is your name?'

The man lowered his gaze. 'I do not know it. It is lost to me. I was given a new one: Thenaj.'

Korus settled back upon his thick haunches, examined one clawed scarred hand where his armoured flesh had been scoured away entirely. Pale tendons shifted, exposed to the air. 'Well, Thenaj. Such as I am, I am yours.'

Angered, the man waved the offer aside. 'No. You are your own now. Free of all compellings. Free of all the summonings and abuse of exploiters of the Warrens, damn them all to dissolution! Free to do as you please.'

The huge demon cocked his armoured head, his golden eyes taking in the desolate shore of black sands. 'Then I shall remain.'

Thenaj nodded his gratitude. 'Good. Then help me with the little ones – their courage is greater than their wisdom.'

*   *   *

In the estate district of Darujhistan a tall, hook-nosed man returned to long-delayed work of drawing a new map of the city copied from an older version, one that bore upon it an obscuring rust-red stain. He worked bent over, face close to the vellum, the quill scratching patiently.

'The city ever renews itself, Master Baruk?' observed someone close to his elbow.

The High Alchemist jumped, his forearm striking a crystal inkpot and overturning it, sending an impenetrable black wash across the map. Baruk turned slowly to stare down at the squat rotund figure beside him, a figure so short as to barely see over the high table.

'Oh dear. Kruppe is most apologetic. If something should happen – as it cannot help but do – such will be looked back upon as a most portentous omen.'

Baruk cleaned the quill on a scrap of rag. 'It was only an accident.' He dropped the quill into its holder. 'And in any case, how did you . . . I doubled all the wards.'

Watery, bulging frog-like eyes blinked innocently back up at him. Baruk's shoulders slumped. 'We both know what is threatening.

There have been warnings enough. Death's death, for the love of all the gods. The green banner of the night sky. The shattering and rebirth of the moon. The breaking of Dragnipur . . .' He waved a hand. 'Choose any you wish.'

'As it is the proclivity of all to do.' The fat man sighed contentedly as he settled into a plush chair. 'In the ease of hindsight . . . or is that behindsight?' The bulging eyes seemed to cross and the man held a white silk handkerchief to his face. 'Gods wipe such a sight!'

From his high stool Baruk studied the man. He pressed steepled fingers to his chin, his gaze sharpening. 'I fear you will not fare as well this time.'

A demon waddled up to sit at Kruppe's slippered feet – one even more squat and obese than he. It struck Baruk that had Chillbais possessed a tail, it would most certainly be wagging. From one voluminous sleeve, rather dirty and threadbare, it must be said, came a stoppered sample jar. Baruk's gaze sharpened even further as he recognized the jar. Kruppe uncorked it and fished out the sample, which itself was a fish, a small white one. This he held out over Chillbais, who snapped up the offering. Kruppe petted the demon's knobbled bald head.

'That was a rare blind albino cave fish from the deserts of the Jhag Odhan, Kruppe.'

'And tasty too. I highly recommend them. On toast.'

'And to what, other than the raiding of my sample shelves and the bribing and suborning of my servants, do I owe this visit? I am reminded of your earlier call not so long ago, and I am not reassured.'

The fat man sniffed the jar's milky fluid, wrinkled his nose, and set it aside. 'Kruppe wonders now, in the presentsight, as it were – or is it is? – what pedestrian activities or seemingly innocuous events will, in the hindsight of the future, be seen to be foreshadowings of the grievous event which may, or may not, come to pass, and which, by the forewarning, may thusly be headed off.' He set his pale hands under his chin and beamed up at Baruk who blinked, frowning.

'Such as?'

A fluttering of the oversized handkerchief. 'Oh, who is to say? The subject is quite picked over. Perhaps if one dug deeper, though – who knows what might be uncovered? Things long hidden from the bright glare of the sun heaving up gasping and blinking unseeing orbs yet somehow managing to be preserved, perhaps for all foreverness, thereby outlasting even you and me?'

Baruk turned the quill in its carved soapstone holder. 'Now

you are making me damned uncomfortable, Kruppe. The circle remains broken,' and he inclined his head, 'thanks to . . . whoever. Its hoped-for eternity of perfection was smashed. And all my time and resources are spent in ensuring that it remain so . . . yet the perturbations of these powerful events of late . . .' He rubbed his brows and his back hunched, betraying an uncharacteristic infirmity and exhaustion.

For an instant the little man's brows pinched in concern, unnoticed. Then he puffed out his chest – though to nowhere near the protrusion of the straining lower buttons of his waistcoat.

'Do not despair, my High Alchemicalness. The Eel has eyes like a hawk! And had it any limbs, why, they would be the thews of a panther! No pale wriggling albino cave fish is the Eel! Er . . . that is . . . unlike said fish, no pickling jar could ever be quick enough to capture it!'

*   *   *

All through the alleys of the bourse of the dancing girls, beneath its multi-coloured awnings and drifting fumes of burning prayer sticks, the gossip of the day was fixed upon the unprecedented arrival of a bright new star among the constellation of its most talented practitioners.

The heart of the bourse was the narrow Way of Sighs, a length of shadowed alley not incidentally overlooked by the open window alcoves of the dancers' quarters. Here in the cool of the twilight the girls often gathered in their window seats to take in the pleasant night air, observe dusk prayers, and to receive the admiration of suitors lingering below. This eve the courtiers and young bravos talked among themselves, comparing rapturous descriptions of the new dancer's goddess-like grace and classical beauty; while, above, tortoiseshell combs yanked rather savagely through midnight manes of hair.

She had appeared out of nowhere, this diminutive captivating sprite whose confidence so far surpassed her apparent age. No school could boast of having trained her, though many wished they had. A secretive rise of her painted lips and a flash of her green-tinged sloe-eyes easily deflected even the subtlest of questioning and left would-be interrogators speechless. Schooling at home by her mother, herself once a very famous dancer, was all she had admitted so far.

Then the romance began. How the alleyways resounded, the

awnings fluttered, with twice the usual wistful sighs of admiration! The dedicated, brilliant dancer (no doubt of the lowest of family origins) and the awkward son of a noble house (and that house in poverty and decline). Why, it was like the stories of old! Jeshin Lim, the bookish, unpromising son of the once great Lim family, cousin to councilman Shardan, himself cut off so tragically, madly in love with a dancing girl of no family and no connections. What other explanation could there be but pure unadorned love?

In their window nooks some clenched perfectly manicured nails to palms and muttered through pearl teeth of *bewitchment*.

Then the unlikeliest of strokes. The cousin vaulted to a seat on the Council! All nod sagely at the obvious tonic to a man of the love and devotion of a gifted woman. And the path to said Council seat no doubt paved by the freely given gold bangles and anklets from those very shapely limbs!

Yet inevitably must come the tragic and tearful end. All know the conclusion to such star-crossed affairs. Lim, having achieved the vaunted rank of councilman is far too prominent for such a low entanglement.

And so, in the cooling breezes of the window nooks, brushes now slid smoothly through long black hair, and kohl-lined eyes were languid and satisfied in the certain knowledge of such pending devastation.

Now he came, this very eve, drawn in a hired carriage to the apartment houses near the dancers' quarters where so many girls were similarly kept at the expense of their, shall we say, patrons.

Lim's carriage pulled up at the private entrance and he stepped down wrapped in a dark hooded cloak, a delicate gold mask pressed to his face, obscuring his features. The guard bowed respectfully, eyes averted, and pulled the sliding bolt. The councilman slipped within.

He came to one specific door along the second floor hall and knocked four quick raps: their agreed secret code. Yet the door did not open; no smooth naked arms entwined him. The gold mask edged right and left, then a hand rose to try the latch, and found it unlocked. He stepped within, pushed the door shut behind. 'My love?'

No answer from the cluttered darkened room. Layered carpets covered the floor in heaps, cushions lay about draped in abandoned gossamer clothes. He edged forward tentatively. 'My dear?'

He found her at the window – no open seated alcove here: bars sealed these small openings. She was peering out to where the blue-tinted night flames of the city seemed to battle the green-tinged night sky above.

'I am sorry, my dear . . .' he began.

She turned, arms crossed over her small high breasts. For a moment her eyes seemed to flash with a green light akin to that of the night sky. 'And who is this who comes intruding upon my privacy?'

Jeshin stared, confused, then lowered the mask and examined it wryly. He pushed back the hood, revealing his long black hair, his narrow scholar's face. He tapped a finger to the gold mask. 'You see? Even now I come as you request. Though why this façade of anonymity when everyone seems to know of . . . well.' He tossed the mask aside.

'You should not have come,' she said, hugging herself even tighter, as if struggling to keep something in.

Jeshin turned away, pacing. 'Yes, yes. Now that I am a councillor. Even now you shame me in your concern for my *reputation*.' He spun upon her. 'Yet perhaps there *is* a way. I no longer need the blessings of my family . . .'

Slipping forward, she silenced him with a finger to his lips. 'No.' She spoke soothingly, as if to a child. 'I'll not have you weakened in any way. Your opponents will use it against you. Paint you an impetuous fool. You must not be compromised.' And she peered up at him, her gaze almost furtive. 'Your great vision for the city, remember?'

He squeezed her to him. 'But without you?'

Dancer that she was, she somehow easily eluded his grasp to put her back to him. 'We . . . both . . . must make sacrifices,' she said, facing the window once more.

He shook his head in awed admiration. 'Your determination is a lesson to me.'

She turned, finger at her chin. 'Yet there is one last thing I can do for you, my Jeshin, my noble councillor.'

He waved the suggestion aside, still shaking his head. 'You have done enough – too much. Your advice, the things you knew . . . As they say: all secrets are revealed beneath the feet of the dancer.'

Her henna-lined lips drew up, pleased. 'That is a very old saying. And very true. No, one last word that has come to me. There is an extraordinarily wealthy man in the city who shares your vision of a strong Darujhistan that commands the respect it deserves.' Her lips drew down, dismissive. 'True, he is a northerner, from Cat. But he should support you. His name is Humble. Humble Measure.'

Jeshin frowned. 'The ironmonger?'

'He is more than that. Trust in me.'

The young councillor held out his hands as if in surrender. 'If you say so, dearest. I shall contact him.'

'Excellent. With his resources your ascent will be assured.'

Jeshin stared, almost awestruck. 'I do not deserve you, my love.'

Smiling once more, she pressed a palm to his chest and gently urged him down to a heap of cushions. 'You shall, my love. You shall.'

Standing above him she struck the opening pose of *Burn Awakening*, one leg raised, toe just brushing the floor, one hand lifted to face as if warding off the harsh glare of a primeval dawn. From this pose she flowed into the first four devotional motions, one to each corner of the world, bowing, hands raised in supplication, palms inward.

Then she danced.

Staring, mesmerized, his pulse racing, Jeshin could only moan, 'Oh, Taya . . . Taya . . .'

*   *   *

The retreat had been established in the coastal mountains south of Mengal generations ago. Some named it a monastery, others a school. Those who entered did so in the understanding of a voluntary abandonment of the world, with all its diversions and deluding ambitions.

Why the legendary Traveller, slayer of Anomander Rake, the very son of Darkness and Lord of Moon's Spawn, would come here was a mystery to Esten Rul. If *he* had defeated the most feared and powerful Ascendant once active in the world he would not be squatting in some dusty monastery full of mumbling priests and acolytes.

And that was not what he planned on doing after he in turn defeated this Traveller.

Even now, assured by numerous independent sources, he could not quite believe that this squalid mountain-hugging collection of huts and open-air temples was the retreat of the great swordsman. Entering the main sand courtyard he paused, eyed the passing robed priests on their unhurried ways. None even cast him a single glance. This was not the sort of treatment to which Esten Rul, master duellist and swordsman of three continents, was accustomed.

27

These shaven-headed wretches obviously did not possess the wit to understand that the man who stood before them was acknowledged a master on Quon Tali and Falar. And that he had taken the measure of the current crop of talents here in Genabackis and frankly thought them rather second-rate.

One oldster was dutifully sweeping up the leaves that littered the courtyard and this one he approached.

'You. Old man. Where can I find the one who goes by the name Traveller?'

In what was obviously a deliberate insult the fellow had the effrontery to continue sweeping. Esten stamped his foot down on the bundled straw of the broom. 'I am talking to you, grandfather.'

The man peered up at him, very dark, not a local, his scalp freshly shaven, the face scarred and graven in lines of care. Yet the eyes: utterly without fear, deep midnight blue like ocean depths.

The weight of that gaze made Esten look away, uncomfortable. So, not a servant after all. A broken-down veteran perhaps, shattered by battle. 'You know of him?'

'The one those here call Master? Yes.'

Esten grunted. So, their master, was he? Of course. What else could such a man be? 'Where is he? Which of these pathetic huts?' The old man looked him up and down. Esten saw his eyes casting over the quillions of his sheathed rapier.

'You would challenge him?'

'No, I'm here delivering flowers from Black Coral. Of course I'm here to challenge him, you senile fool!'

The old man closed his eyes as if pained; lowered his head. 'Go back to Darujhistan. The one called Traveller has . . . retired . . . from all swordplay.' He returned to his sweeping.

Esten barely restrained himself from cuffing the insolent fool. He set his hand instead on the grip of his sword. 'Do not try me. I am not used to such treatment. Take me to Traveller or I will find someone else who will – at sword-point.'

The old man stilled. He turned to face him: the eyes had narrowed now, and darkened even more. 'Is that the way of it? Very well. I will take you to Traveller, but before I do you must demonstrate your worthiness.'

Esten gaped at the man. '*What?* Demonstrate my . . . *worthiness?*' He peered about in disbelief. A crowd of the robed monks, or priests, or whatever they were, had gathered silent and watchful. Esten Rul was not a man to be spooked but he found their quiet regard a touch unnerving. He returned his attention to the old sweeper, gave a vague gesture of invitation with one gloved hand. 'And pray tell how do I do that?'

'By defeating the least of us.'

Esten bit down on his impatience and took a slow calming breath. 'And . . . that would be?'

A sad slow shrug from the man. 'Well . . . that would be me.'

'You.'

'Yes. I'm very new here.'

'You . . .' He stepped away as if the fellow were a lunatic. 'But you're just cleaning the court!'

A rueful nod. 'Yes. And I've yet to get it right. It's the wind, you know. No matter how careful you are the wind just comes tumbling through and all your plans and care are for naught.'

Esten snorted his disgust and turned away. He raised his hands to his mouth to bellow: '*Traveller!* Can you hear me? Are you hiding here? Come out and face me!'

'Defeat me and they will bring you to him.'

Having turned full circle Esten faced the man again. 'Really . . . just like that.'

'Yes. Just like that. It is an ancient practice. One remembered and honoured here.'

Esten opened his hands as if in a gesture of futility. 'Well . . . if I must . . . You *do* have a weapon?'

The old man merely shrugged his regretful apology once more and raised his broom.

From the gates to the monastery an acolyte watched the foreign duellist walking down the zigzag mountain trail. The swordsman's hands were clasped behind his back and his head was lowered as if he had just been given a great deal to think about. The acolyte bowed to the man at the gate where he leaned on his broom, the wood of the haft nicked and gouged.

'Will he return, Master?' the acolyte asked.

'I keep telling you lot not to call me that,' sighed the man who had given up the name Traveller. He shrugged. 'Let's hope not. He's been offered a lesson. We can only hope it will be heeded.' He shifted his grip on the broom. 'But . . . life is nothing more than a series of lessons and few learn enough of them.' He looked to the courtyard and winced. 'Gods – you turn away for one moment and everything goes to the Abyss. I'm going to have to start all over again . . .'

29

'As we all should, Master.'

For an instant a small smile graced the man's pain-ravaged face, then the mouth eased back into its habitual slash of a grimace. 'Well said. Yes. As we all should. Every day. With every breath.'

*　　　*　　　*

In the nameless shanty town rambling westward of Darujhistan, an old woman squatted in front of her shack carving a stick beneath a night sky dominated by the slashing lurid green banner of the Scimitar. Her hair was a wild bush about her head tied with lengths of string, ribbon, beads, and twists of leather. Her bare feet where they poked out beneath her layered skirts were as dark as the earth the toes gripped. She droned to herself in a language no one understood.

An old woman living alone in a decrepit hut was nothing unusual for the shanty town, peopled as it was by the poorest, most broken-down of the lowest class of tannery workers, sewer cleaners and garbage haulers of Darujhistan. Every second shack seemed occupied by an old widow or grandmother, the menfolk dying off early as they do everywhere – the men claiming this proves they do all the hard work, and the women knowing it's because men aren't tough enough to endure being old.

And so this woman had lived in her squalid hut for as long as anyone could remember and none remarked upon it, except for all the surrounding old widows and grandmothers who amongst themselves knew her as 'that crazy old woman'.

Squatting in the mud before her hut she brought the thin stick she was carving close to eyes clouded by milky cataracts and studied the intricate tracery of curve and line that ran end to end. She crooned to herself, 'Almost, now. Almost.' Then she glanced fearfully, and rather blindly, to the starry night sky and its intruding alien banner, muttering, 'Almost now. Almost.'

The stick went into a sack at her side. From a smaller bag she drew a pipe and a pinch of a sticky dark substance like gum that she rolled into a ball then pressed into the pipe. She lit the pipe with a twig from a low fire, drew the smoke in deep and held it down in her lungs for a long time before leaning her head back and letting the great plume blow skyward.

She blinked her watering eyes. 'Almost, now. Almost.'

BOOK I
Orb

CHAPTER I

The problem with paths is that once you have chosen one,
You cannot choose the others.

Attributed to *Gothos' Folly*

O N THE SOUTH COAST OF GENABACKIS THE FORMER FISHING village of Hurly was a mess. Nearly two years before, its original inhabitants had drowned without warning in tidal waves that inundated it when the last fragments of the titanic floating mountain named Moon's Spawn crashed into the Rivan Sea. Then, when the flood waters receded, a motley army of treasure-hunters, scavengers and looters had descended upon its corpse like a swarm of flies, and soon after that came an even worse plague: the thieves, conmen and other swindlers who preyed upon them.

Representatives of the Southern Confederation of Free Cities were the first to arrive at the scene of devastation. Wreckers and pirates from way back, they salvaged everything they could, namely the surviving boats of the region, and established a concession out to the newly born isles. A few months later transport fees and tariffs were settled upon and four separate armed challenges to their monopoly had been successfully put down.

Now, after more than a year of trade, the Southern Confederation had firmly established itself as the sole representative of the islands, which they named, with characteristic directness, the Spawns.

Jallin, nicknamed the Jumper for his habit of ambushing from the rear, had to admit that the good times in Hurly were officially over. He and all the other hustlers and scavengers could feel the pinch of lean times. The one-time flood of fortune-hunters had thinned to a trickle of ragged men and women no better off than those who'd already clawed out a spot in the festering town.

Jallin the Jumper knew this well. He'd seen the cycle play itself out in town after town up north, where the Malazan wars had fuelled the rabid, cannibalistic economies of scarcity and demand. He sensed that here the frenzy of fortunes won overnight and even more quickly lost would never reach the pitch it had seasons ago. And it was ending before he'd made his big strike. Just as it had at Pale, Kurl and Callows. Only this time he wouldn't let that happen. Couldn't. Because Hurly was the end of the road. As far south as all these losers and dregs could slide. Everyone's last chance.

So he paid close attention when yet another new arrival came tramping down the town's muddy main track. The newcomer was a wiry ragged veteran, a foreigner by his ruddy hair and ginger moustache – a Malazan. He wore army-standard sandals and cloak, and carried battered leather panniers over one shoulder. That the man was a veteran didn't worry Jallin; almost all the loser fortune-hunters who came down that road had once marched in any number of armies up north – and usually deserted from every damned one. To him they were pathetic in their willingness to get maimed or killed for the promise of a handful of coin or a scratch of land.

This one appeared to have fared even worse than most. A single shortsword hung at his side, but other than that all he carried was the panniers slung over a shoulder and kept tightly gripped in one scarred and sun-browned hand. Those wide bags interested Jallin. What, he wondered, would an old soldier, cashiered or deserted, think vital enough to drag with him all the way down here to the Spawns?

The veteran stopped where so many of the other hopeful Spawn-looters had halted: where the cart-track ended at the strand of slate-black gravel that sloped down to the Rivan Sea. Here, the observant among them usually noticed two important things: that the Spawn Isles were those distant faint dots far out to sea, and that there wasn't a single boat in sight.

These discoveries often left even the hardiest and most resilient feeling lost, and so here was where Jallin preferred to approach his targets. As he came alongside, the fellow was still squinting out to sea, and so he murmured: 'There they are, hey? Pay-dirt.'

The old guy grunted something, eyed the wreckage-strewn gravel beach. 'I'm lookin' for a boat.'

Jallin smiled. 'Isn't everyone here, friend? And it just so happens I know a man who might have room for one more on his.'

That got a look. He could tell from the man's blunt gaze that he'd seen a lot. Most veterans had an odd hard stare that Jallin couldn't quite understand – himself not having ever been stupid enough to set foot on a battlefield. It could make a man think twice about giving them trouble. But despite this he'd gone ahead and robbed, cheated, rolled, and even murdered some. All from behind, or from a position of trust, of course. Which was why he considered their toughness and fighting skills irrelevant. After all, peacetime was a very different sort of war.

'How much?' the fellow asked. He relaxed his grip to shade his eyes against the western sun. Whatever was in those bags, it looked heavy. Jallin wet his lips then gave his friendliest chuckle.

'How much? Oh, it'll cost. I won't insult you by pretending I can get you some kinda special deal or some such shit. It'll cost. *That* we got to negotiate, right?'

Another neutral grunt. Jallin pointed back up the track to where it cut between slapped-up inns, stores and taprooms. 'The Island Inn maybe, hey? What d'you say? You look like you could use a drink.'

The fellow turned, squinted up the track, even chewed at an edge of his moustache. After one last lingering stare out to sea, his tensed shoulders fell and he sighed. 'Yeah. Could use a drink.'

Jallin showed the way. He kept up a constant distracting chatter about all the adventurers he knew who'd struck it rich out at the Spawns – which in truth was no one. None who had ever returned, that is. All the while he was thinking: we'll settle a price for tonight, not too low, not too high. Nothing to arouse suspicion. Then down at the beach he'd introduce him to his 'friend'. All the razor-sharp pointed length of it. His misericorde – the weapon he used to put old soldiers where they belonged: out of their misery.

The Island Inn was unique among Hurly's new buildings in that it possessed stone walls. It occupied all that remained of a temple to Poliel, goddess of disease, pestilence and plague. It seemed the old population of Hurly had been particularly anxious to appease her. Perhaps it had to do with all the neighbouring marshes. The new owner of the structure, Akien Threw, liked to joke that they would've been far better off appeasing the cult of Elder Dark, of which the Moon's Spawn had been a holy artefact.

As Jallin entered, guiding the old soldier to a table in the rear, he caught Akien's eye. All the town's touts and hustlers had an understanding with the man: a meal and a floor to flop on in exchange for heading clients his way. Plus a percentage of any take, of course.

Two tall tankards of beer arrived almost the instant they rested their arms on the tabletop of silvery-grey driftwood slats. The veteran's eyes narrowed and his mouth turned down. 'What's this?'

In the relative darkness of the inn Jallin was struck by the scars that lined the fellow's face and how his mangy ginger hair, grey in places, grew patchily one side as if over burns. But he'd seen old soldiers before and almost all carried scars. They all parted with what little coin they'd gathered over the years as easily as anyone, and more swiftly than most. 'So what's your name then, friend?'

After a time the man growled, 'Red. Red Dog.'

Jallin raised a brow at that but said nothing: he didn't give a damn what the fellow's name was. 'Well, Red, this is Elingarth ale. The good stuff.' He touched a finger to the side of his nose. 'The owner's a friend of mine.'

'I'll bet he is,' the soldier muttered darkly. But he lifted the tankard and took a long pull. Jallin noted the nest of white scar ridges up and down the man's forearm. He decided he'd be a touch worried if the fellow wasn't obviously so far past his prime. He also noted how the fellow kept a tight grip on the panniers on his lap.

The veteran wiped his mouth and grimaced his distaste. 'I doubt that's from Elingarth.'

Jallin gave an easy shrug. 'I wouldn't know. Another?'

'Abyss, no.'

'Sure. It's early yet.'

In keeping with the diminishing flow of treasure-hunters, the inn's common room was deserted. A pair of guards, no more than old-hand hustlers like Jallin, sat by the door. Two men sat hunched almost head to head at a table nearby, both staring sullenly out into the day's last slanting yellow rays. One elegantly dressed young man, a scion of some aristocratic family or other, commanded another table. He was with three others, all of whom Jallin knew as local thugs and would-be guides, like himself.

The young man leaned back suddenly and announced: 'Then there's no sense heading out. It's too late by far. The place has been picked clean by now.'

The old soldier, Red, turned to watch him.

One of the local guides said something to which the nobleman answered, dismissively, 'Well, who's come back recently? Has any-one?'

Another of the companions offered, 'If I found anything out there I sure as death wouldn't come back *here*.' They all had a good laugh at that, except the noble youth.

Jallin leaned forward, murmured, 'That's all just sour talk. He's afraid to head out.'

'So,' the veteran drawled, 'where are all the ships?'

Two more tankards arrived care of a shuffling serving boy. 'Anchored off shore. Launches put in at dawn and you buy your berth. But,' he added, lowering his voice, 'it's possible to slip out past them at night. For a fee.'

The soldier nodded his understanding. 'At dawn, when the boats put in. Why doesn't everyone just rush 'em?'

'Southern Free Cities Confederation soldiers, my friend. They got things wrapped up.'

'So what's to stop others from showing up with their own boats?'

Jallin laughed. 'Oh, they've tried. They've tried. But these Confederation boys are pirates and wreckers like none other. Sank the lot of them.'

'But a warship maybe? Malazan?'

Jallin drained his tankard. 'Yeah. A couple months back. A Malazan warship bulled its way through. Ain't been seen since.' He grinned toothily. 'Maybe they all got done in.'

The old soldier took a long pull from his tankard. 'Just like the guy said. No one's come back. Is that right?'

Jallin did his best to laugh good-naturedly. 'What? You want someone else to get out with a boatload of loot? Listen, the main isle is damned huge. It takes a lot of time to search through all that. You don't just arrive and trip over some kinda chest of gold.' He pretended to take a deep sip of his second tankard, unconcerned, but damned the loudmouth, whoever he was. Anyway, all that mattered was that the old guy accompany him down to the shore to meet his 'friend'. He would meet him all right.

The veteran sucked his teeth then brushed at his moustache. 'Right. Well, that's about all I need to hear. Thanks for the drink.' He stood, draped the bags over one shoulder.

Jallin stood with him. 'But I could get you out tonight. My friend—'

'Would bash me over the head,' the soldier finished.

Jallin caught Akien's eye, spread his hands. 'Fine. You don't want my help? To Hood with you.'

From the bar, Akien nodded to his two guards, who stood and blocked the door. The soldier pulled up short. He glanced to the big bull-like owner who was crossing the floor, tapping a truncheon in one hand. 'What's the problem?' the old guy asked.

'The problem, sir, is of the bill.'

Jallin had kept his distance, waiting for his chance, and the veteran motioned directly to him. 'This one here. He'll pay.'

Akien stopped before his guards, which put Jallin directly to the soldier's rear. Jallin curled his fingers around his belt, close to the worn grips of his daggers. 'No,' Akien said, slow and stubborn, like the bull he resembled. 'It is plain to me that you ordered the drinks, sir.'

The old soldier bit back any further argument; everyone knew he hadn't ordered the drinks but the claim had to be made for the sake of appearances. It was the dance of the clip joint – free to enter, but damned expensive to leave. 'All right,' he growled, resigned. 'How much is it then?'

Akien raised his bows, figuring. 'Four tankards of Elingarth ale, sir? That would be two Darujhistani gold councils.'

An awed whistle sounded through the inn. Everyone looked to the young nobleman. He had an arm hooked over the rear of his chair, leaning back. 'That, good innkeeper, is a ruinous price.'

Akien hunched his fat rounded shoulders, glowering. 'Cartage.'

The nobleman eyed the veteran, cocked a brow.

The soldier grasped a nearby chair to support himself. 'I don't have that kind of money!'

Jallin touched his shoulder to indicate the bags. Akien nodded. 'Then your bags, sir, in payment.'

The soldier's other hand went to the pannier. 'No.'

The two guards started forward, their truncheons ready. At that instant the soldier exploded into action: the chair flew into one guard while a boot hammered into the second. The veteran's speed surprised Jallin but he knew he was faster. Akien's bulk in the doorway caused the man to ease his rush and Jallin had him.

A voice barked: 'Your rear!' and the veteran twisted aside. Jallin's razor-honed friend missed the artery in a shallow slice. Then a blur at the edge of Jallin's vision smacked his head backwards and he fell. The last he heard was Akien's bellow of pain and outrage as the soldier dealt with him.

*   *   *

'The Moranth attaché awaits you, Ambassador.'

Ambassador Aragan of the Imperial Malazan delegation in Darujhistan held his head and groaned over his steaming infusion of koru nut. 'Burn's mercy, man. Can't it wait?'

His aide, Captain Dreshen Harad 'Ul, being one of the noble houses of Unta, stood spear-straight, his maroon and black Imperial dress uniform enviably crisp. 'The attaché is most insistent.'

Aragan tossed back the thimble of black liquid and winced. *Gods, I should never have tried to keep up with those visiting Barghast. They just don't know when to quit.* He blinked gritty eyes at Dreshen, picked up a knife and oven-roasted flatbread. 'Invite him to breakfast, then.'

His aide saluted.

He spread Rhivi honey on the bread. *Haven't even found my footing yet and I'm supposed to negotiate with the Moranth? What do they expect in Unta – bouncing me all over? Damned cock-up is what it is. I'll probably never even* meet *this new damned Emperor Mallick what's-his-face.*

The Moranth attaché was shown into Aragan's chambers, the outer of which he chose to use as a meeting room and office. He liked the view from the terrace overlooking the estate's rear gardens. The attaché was a Red veteran. His blood-hued chitinous armour bore a skein of scars and gouges from combat. Aragan rose, dabbed at his mouth. 'Commander Torn.'

The attaché bowed stiffly. 'Ambassador.'

Aragan sat, gesturing to the chair opposite. 'To what do I owe the honour?'

The attaché declined the invitation with a small wave of a gauntleted hand. He straightened and clasped those armoured gauntlets behind his back. 'We of the Moranth delegation request a favour from our old allies.'

Aragan's brows rose. *Oho! Old allies is it now? When did this come about? They've been denying troop requests for the last year.* 'Yes?'

It was hard to tell with the man's full helm and body-hugging armour, but the attaché appeared uncomfortable. He paced to the threshold of the double doors that opened on to the terrace, his back to Aragan. 'We request that you press the Council into interdicting the burial grounds to the south of the city.'

Aragan choked on his mouthful of toasted flatbread. The aide rushed forward to pour a glass of watered wine, which Aragan gulped down. 'Gods, man!' he gasped. 'You do not ask much!' He cleared his throat. 'I suggest you press them yourself.'

'We have been. For months. They will not listen to us. There is a . . . history . . . between us.'

Aragan raised the glass to his aide, who nodded and exited. He edged his chair round to face the attaché's stiff back. 'So, what is it? Why the burial grounds?'

'There are those among us—' The attaché stopped himself, shook his helmed head. 'No, that will not do.' He turned, took a long bracing breath. 'You name our colours clans, so we understand. Yet "guilds" would really be a more accurate description. In any case, among us those you name the Silvers you could think of as closest to your mages. Though they are more like mystics, in truth.'

Aragan could only stare. This was more than he'd ever heard from all the Moranth he'd ever spoken to before. There were scholars in Unta who could establish careers on the information he'd just been afforded on these ferociously secretive people.

Attaché Torn crossed his arms. 'For some time disquiet has spread among the Silver. They are anxious regarding the burial grounds – and the things that many believe they hold.'

Captain Dreshen returned with the tiny cup of koru-nut infusion. Aragan took it, then signed for privacy. 'Torn, those ruins extend for leagues across the Dwelling Plain. An area larger than the city itself! Do you have any idea how many troops it would take . . .'

'I'm told to point out your garrisons and the majority of the Fifth in the north. Elements of Onearm's Host in the south—'

Aragan threw his hands in the air. 'Hold on!' Grimacing in pain, he gulped down his infusion. 'I can't bring that many troops so close to the city! Think about it. It would be seen as tantamount to a Malazan putsch! An act of war.' He waved it aside. 'No. Out of the question.'

Torn dropped his arms, the keratin plates grinding. 'I thought not.' He almost sighed. 'However, my superiors commanded that the request be made. So be it. I ask, then, that you at least gather your most skilled mages and task them to delve into any activities out on the burial grounds.'

Aragan frowned, considering. 'I can probably do that, yes. But, think of it. What your Silvers are sensing is probably just the disturbances in the Warrens from what happened here . . . Anomander Rake's sword broken, so they say. Hood cultists claiming *he* was here and died himself – if you can credit that. My cadre mages are still groaning from those shocks.'

'Be that as it may . . . will you indulge me in this?'

'Of course, Torn. Of course. As a favour to you.'

The Moranth inclined his helmed head in thanks. 'Very good. Please pass on any intelligence. Until then, Ambassador.'

Aragan crossed to the door. 'Attaché.'

Once the Moranth had gone, Aragan waved in Captain Dreshen and returned to his breakfast. He ate staring out of the open twinned doors of the terrace. When he'd finished he sat back, sipping his watered wine. He raised his gaze to his aide. 'Pass word down south to Fist . . . who is it down there?'

'Steppen.'

'Yes, Steppen. Tell her to send up all the troops she can spare. And who's Central Command, the Free Cities garrisons?'

'That would be Fist K'ess, in Pale.'

'Right. He should be able to knock together at least a few companies. They can rendezvous to the west, somewhere south of Dhavran.'

Dreshen merely cocked a brow. 'And when there are questions . . . ?'

'Just a training exercise, Captain. Nothing more. The usual hurry up and wait.'

'I understand. Very good, Ambassador.' He turned to go.

Aragan gulped down the last of his watered wine. 'And whom do we have in the city whom we can rely on to do some quiet work for us, off the books?'

A smile crept up Captain Dreshen's lips. 'We keep a list, Ambassador.'

*　　　*　　　*

She was getting used to the strangeness of this bizarre realm so far from the world she knew. And she wondered whether that was a bad sign. Her companion, Leoman of the Flails, had named it the 'Shores of Creation'.

Firstly, there was the dawn – if such a term could be applied. It seemed to emerge from beneath the sea of molten light. It began as a brightening in one direction, call that the east if you must, though any magnet and needle brought here probably would not know what to do. The glimmering sea of energy seemed to give up some of its shine and this bright wash, or wave, swelled over the dome of the starry sky, obscuring it in a kind of daylight that, in its turn, faded back into starry night.

Of their route of entry, the Chaos Whorl, she could find only the faintest bruising against the horizon in one direction, and that fading like the last traces of twilight. Perhaps the army of Tiste Liosan with Jayashul and her brother, L'oric, had overcome the magus who sustained that gap, or tear, in creation.

Or perhaps he'd simply fled. Who knew? Not she. Not trapped here in this eternal neverplace. Which was just as well, since yet again she'd failed. Even with the help of her witch aunt Agayla and the Enchantress, the Queen of Dreams herself, she'd failed. And now it was over, everything, over and done. No more striving. No more seeking. No more self-recrimination – what was the point?

It was, she decided, in one way deliciously liberating.

She laid her head on Leoman's bare arm. Was it then desperation that finally drove them together? Or mere loneliness? They were, after all, the only man and woman in all creation. And this man: one of the Malazan Empire's deadliest enemies. He had been body-guard to the rebel leader Sha'ik. Then he'd commanded the Seven Cities Army of the Apocalypse and delivered to the Empire one of its bloodiest maulings at the city of Y'Ghatan.

Yet no ogre. Harsh, yes. Calculating, and a survivor. In the end not too unlike her.

His breathing pattern changed and she knew he was awake. He sat up, ran his gaze down her naked flank and thigh and smiled from beneath his long moustache. 'Good morning to you.'

Gods how she ached to tell him to get rid of that moustache! 'If it is a morning.'

Grunting, he crossed his legs and set his arms on his knees. 'We can only assume.'

'So, what now? Do we build a hut from driftwood? Weave hats from leaves and raise a brood of savages?'

'There is no driftwood,' he said absently, eyes narrowed to the south.

She sifted a hand through the fine black sand they lay upon. 'I'd always wondered how those old creation of the race myths ran. Populating the land was one thing, but what about the second generation? I suppose if you're all for polygamy and incest in the first place it wouldn't strike you as a problem . . .'

She glanced up: his narrowed gaze was steady on the distance. 'Burn take it! You're not ignoring me already, are you?'

His mouth quirked. 'Not yet.' He raised his chin to the south. 'Our friend is gone.'

She rolled over, scanned the sky over the shore. Gone indeed, their titanic neighbour. A being so immense it seemed as if he could hug the entire floating mountain of the Moon's Spawn within the span of his arms. Now there was no sign of him. And she hadn't heard a thing.

She sprang to her feet, began dressing. 'Why didn't you say something, dammit!'

He peered up at her, still smiling. 'I didn't want to interrupt. You don't like it when I interrupt you.'

She threw her weapon belt over a shoulder. 'Very funny. C'mon.'

He pulled on the silk shorts he wore beneath his felt trousers – for the itching, he'd explained. 'Something tells me there's no hurry, Kiska. If there's any place to abandon haste, this is it.'

She continued arming herself. 'Your problem is you're lazy. You'd be happy just to lie here all day.'

'And make love to you? Certainly.'

'*Leoman!* You can turn off the charm, yes?'

He pulled his stained quilted gambeson over his head, yanked it down. 'With you, Kiska? No charm. It's the moustache – the moustache gets them every time.'

'Gods deliver me!' Kiska headed off down the beach. *If he only knew.*

Three rocky headlands later Kiska stood peering down on yet another long scimitar arc of black beach. The clatter of jagged volcanic rocks announced Leoman's approach. He sat with a heavy sigh, adjusted the leather wrapping over his trouser legs. 'He'd have a hard time hiding, Kiska.'

She bit back a snarl of disgust. 'Don't you want to find out what's here?'

A disinterested wave: 'There's nothing here.'

She eyed the broad smooth expanse of the beach, noted something there, something tall. 'Over there.'

Closer, she saw now why she'd missed it. The same dull black as the sands, he was. Now about her height, since he was sitting. As they approached, feet shushing through the sands, he stood, towering to twice that. He reminded her of a crude sculpture of a person carved from that fine-grained black stone, basalt. His hands were broad fingerless shovels, his head a worn stone between boulder-like shoulders. He was identical in every detail to the mountain-sized titan they'd watched these last weeks digging in the sea of light, apparently building up the shoreline. Leoman stepped up next to her, hands near his morningstars, but those weapons still sensibly strapped to his sides. 'Greetings,' she called, her voice dry and weak. *Gods, how does one address an entity such as this?*

Stone grated as it cocked its head aside as if listening.

'My name is Kiska, and this is Leoman.' She waited for an answer. The entity merely regarded them – or so she imagined, as now she could see that it had no eyes, no mouth, no features at all that could be named a face. 'Do you understand—'

She flinched as a voice spoke within her mind: *'Do you hear me? For I hear you.'* The wonder in Leoman's widened eyes made it clear that he had heard as well. 'Yes. I – we – can hear you.'

'Good. I am pleased. Welcome, strangers! You are most welcome. For ages none have visited. I have been alone. Now even more come! I am gladdened.'

At that she could not suppress an eager glance to Leoman. *More! It said more!* His answering gaze held warning and caution. She brushed them aside: if this thing wanted to kill them there was little they could do about it. She took a steadying breath. 'And your name? What should we call you?'

'No name such as I understand your term. I carry what you would call a title. I am Maker.'

She stared, speechless. *All the gods above and below.* Maker. The Creator? No. It did not say *Creator*. It said *Maker*. Muttering distracted her: Leoman murmuring beneath his breath. She almost laughed aloud. The Seven Cities invocation of the gods! Cynical Leoman thrown back on to his roots! Yet the prayer seemed mouthed more in wonder than devotion.

She tried to speak, couldn't force words past her dry throat. Her knees felt watery and she stepped back, blinking. Leoman's hand at her shoulder steadied her. 'There are others, you say?' she managed to force out. 'More of us?'

'One other like you. One other not.'

'I see . . .' *I think.* 'May we meet them? Are they here?'

'One is.' An arm as thick and blocky as a stalactite gestured further down the beach. *'This way.'* Maker turned, stepping, and when the slab-like foot landed the sands beneath Kiska's feet shuddered and rocks cracked and tumbled down the surrounding headlands.

Now we hear him? Perhaps he has made himself somehow

different in order to communicate. Walking alongside, she saw no one else on the sweep of the black sands. Yet some object did lie ahead. A flat polished flag of stone, deep blood-red veined with black. Garnet, perhaps. And on the slab what appeared no more than a wind-gathered pile of trash: a fistful of twigs and leaves. Kiska gasped and ran ahead.

Their guide.

She knelt at the stone. Maker towered over her, his featureless domed head bent to peer downward. Leoman came walking up behind, his hands tucked into his wide weapon belt.

'Is it . . . dead?'

'For this creature, a curious distinction. What essence animated it before was not its own. And now, though that vial essence might have fled, an even greater potentiality yet remains within.'

'It was with us.'

'I thought as much. You arrived soon after.'

Kiska swept the remains into its small leather bag. Struggling to keep her voice steady, she asked, 'And the other? The one like us?'

'The other is gendered as this one,' Maker said, indicating Leoman. *'He came to me out of the Vitr.'*

She blinked up at him. 'The Vitr?'

Maker's blunt head turned to the restless surging sea of light. 'The Vitr. That from which all creation comes.'

'All . . . creation? Everything?'

'All that exists. All distills out of the Vitr. And all returns to dissolution. You, I. All life essence. All sentience.'

Kiska felt her brows rising higher and higher. '*All*? Everything? All races? Surely not the dragons . . . the Tiste . . . or the Jaghut.'

Maker's shovel hands clenched into fists with a grinding and crackling of rock. The sands at his wide feet hissed and glowed, sintering into black obsidian glass. The beach shuddered and a great landslide of rocks echoed among the distant headlands. Kiska found herself on the ground, and rolled away from the searing heat surrounding Maker.

'Speak not to me of the meddling Jaghut!'

The juddering of the ground faded away. She had covered her face to shield it from the radiance and now her leather sleeve came away red and wet. She coughed and spat out a mouthful of blood. Leoman was daubing at his nose. 'My apologies, Maker,' she managed, coughing more.

The entity had raised his fists before his blank stone face and seemed to regard them as if astonished. The hands ground open. *'No – it is I who must apologize. I am sorry. My anger . . . they have done me a great wound.'* The arms fell to hang loose at his sides. *'As to those you name dragons, the Eleint. I myself have assisted beings who emerged fully formed from the Vitr. Some took that form. I do not know whether they were the first of their kind, or if others came into existence elsewhere. As to the Tiste . . . the Andii emerged from eternal night, true, yet what of the vital essence which animates? I believe the underlying energy which moves all originates here, in the Vitr. And for that some would name it the First Light.'*

Kiska regarded the great shifting sea, awed. First Light? Yet who was to say otherwise? Could this 'sea' be nothing more than a great reservoir or source of energy – power, puissance, call it what you would. It was theology, or philosophy, all far beyond her. She returned her attention to Maker. 'And this other? The one like us?'

'I aided him in his emergence from the Vitr . . .'

Kiska laughed, and winced at the note of hysteria. 'Then I assure you, Maker, he is nothing like us.'

'He is. He is formed as you, and mortal.'

'Mortal? His name? Does he have a name?'

Maker shifted, glass crackling, and started a slow lumbering walk down the beach. Kiska moved alongside. *'Understand, little one, those who have experienced the Vitr first hand emerge as if freshly born. Newly formed, or re-formed. His mind carries nothing of his prior existence. And he has proved a great help in my work and a balm to my loneliness. I named him Then-aj-Ehliel, Gift of Creation.'*

'Your . . . work?' Leoman asked from where he trailed behind.

Stone grated as the great domed head turned to Leoman. *'Why, the bolstering and maintenance of the edge of existence, of course, against the constant erosion of the Vitr.'*

Kiska found that she'd stopped walking. Her hands covered her face, where they brushed dried flakes of blood. The ground seemed to waver drunkenly and there was a roaring in her ears. *Gods below! This was . . . this was . . . impossible!* What was she doing here? What could she possibly . . .

Hands supported her: Leoman. 'Kiska. You are all right?'

She laughed again. *All right!* 'Did you hear that? What Maker said.'

'Yes. Maintaining the shores. I understand.'

Yet the desert nomad sounded unimpressed. Queen of Dreams!

Was there nothing that could ruffle this man's reserve? She brushed away the rest of the dried blood, straightened.

'Kiska,' Leoman began gently, 'the odds that this one could be . . .'

She pulled away. 'Yes, yes.'

Maker raised an arm to gesture down the coast. *'Follow the shore on further. He is there, helping in my work.'*

She bowed. 'Our thanks, Maker. We are in your debt.'

'Not at all. It is I who am indebted. It is good to see others. Good to speak to others.'

Bowing again, Kiska headed off. As she walked, the sands pulling at her boots, she made every effort to keep her legs from wobbling and gasps of suppressed tears from bursting forth. This was impossible. She had wandered too far. The urgent unanswerable needs that drove her on now seemed . . . gods, she could hardly even recall them! Oponn's jest! Even if she found the man she no longer had anything to say to him. No compelling case to make for his return. She had nothing to offer save . . . herself. And now . . . now she was no longer so certain of that either.

*   *   *

It took nearly a month of digging. Ebbin worked entirely alone. He trusted no one else with the secret of his discovery; and, in truth, the youths and his two hired guards were quite content to spend their days lazing in the shade while he sweated underground. The dirt and stones he loosened from the blockage he pushed behind him to dump straight down to the water below.

With more funds from his backer he'd bought supplies, including two new lanterns. One lit his work now as he succeeded in clearing a narrow gap through the rockfall to peer beyond. To his enormous relief the tunnel continued onward. Ebbin wiped a grimed sleeve across his face, picked up the lantern, and wriggled ahead. He clawed his way through the dirt, then raised the light within the half-choked narrow confines. The flame burned as straight as a knife-blade. No air movement at all. He peered up the pipe-like length of the tunnel. Ruled straight, perfectly circular. Angling upwards as well. And no vermin, no detritus, no cobwebs. It was strange that the fall should have been so localized, but he shrugged off his concerns and began shuffling forward on his elbows and knees.

The tunnel debouched on to a circular chamber that in the poor light appeared smoothly domed. Shattered stone littered the floor. He

stepped in carefully over the sharp shards. As his vision adapted to
the gloom, openings emerged from the dark: smaller side chambers,
all broken open, circled the circumference of the main tomb.

*Beaten after all! Cheated! Yet how could someone have preceded
him? Not one word in the records hint at such a tomb!* He wiped the
cold sweat from his face. *Damn them!* The looting was most likely
done almost immediately after completion. Cousins of workers, or
sharp-eyed locals spying upon the construction. He kicked through
the wreckage. Something uneven under his feet. He knelt, cupped
the lamp-flame.

A skull stared back up at him. He flinched; then, recovering,
brushed aside more of the pulverized stone. More. A row . . . no . . .
a circular band of human skulls set almost flush with the floor. And
more bands. Ring upon nested ring of them. Rising, he closed upon
a large shadowy object ahead.

At the centre, a mystifying sculpture-like construction: twin arches
intersecting to create four triangular openings. Within, resting upon
an onyx plinth, a cloaked corpse. And upon that corpse, glittering
amber in the lamplight, a hammered mask of gold, plain, embossed
with a face. And the mouth sculpted into the faintest of smiles like
an aggravating, knowing smirk of superior knowledge.

Ebbin almost stepped in to reach for that exquisite object, but
something stopped him. Some instinct. And perhaps he was mistaken, but was that a ghostly, whispered *not for you* . . . so faint he
might have imagined it there in the dead silence so far underground?
He pulled back his hand. Odd . . . these chambers looted, yet this
crowning prize untouched. Why so?

He backed away, raised his lantern to the outer walls. All of the
smaller side niches broken open, their plinths empty. No, not all.
One remained, its sealing door unscathed. He crossed to it. The
door consisted of a single carved granite slab, unmarked, without
any sigil. No hint of who, or what, lay within.

He tapped the solid rock. An aristocrat of the legendary Imperial
Age? He eyed the central dais-like installation.

Or loyal retainer thereof.

He ran his hands over the cold polished slab. He did not have the
chisels to cut through this. And there was no way he was going to let
his cretin assistants down here. No – to do this properly would take
tools and resources currently beyond his reach.

He'll have to see his backer. And with this breakthrough the man
will have to grant him further monies. He's bankrolled him this far,

after all. Remarkable foresight and vision this businessman from One Eye Cat has shown. Even if others murmur against the man and spread ugly rumours of criminal interests. He of the odd northern name: Humble Measure.

Returning to the tunnel an instinct, or irking detail, made him pause. Something about those sub-chambers. He counted them: twelve. Why always this mystical number? The legends? The old folk tales of the twelve fiends? Mere mythology handed down from ancient practices? Or a homage from the builders? He shook his head. Too tenuous as yet.

Perhaps an answer would be forthcoming.

*   *   *

Word had spread across Genabackis that the great Warlord of the north had for a time established a camp in the hills east of Darujhistan, the city that had taken his friend and sometime enemy, Anomander, Lord of Moon's Spawn and Son of Darkness. Emissaries from across the north, the Free Cities and the Rhivi Plains came and went from his tent. They came asking for adjudication of land rights issues or title inheritances, and to settle territorial disputes. The great hulking beast of a man spent his days and evenings sitting cross-legged on layered carpets, drinking interminable cups of tea while city representatives and tribal elders argued and complained.

One such night, when the issue of Sogena's unfair taxation regime had degenerated into reminiscing of the old days before the arrival of the hated Malazans, Brood arose and went from the tent. Jiwan, son of one of the Warlord's trusted old staff of Rhivi, and now making a name for himself within the great man's council, took it upon himself to follow and intrude upon the Ascendant's solitude.

He found him standing alone in the night, staring west where the blue glow of the hated city softened the night. And perhaps the great man stared even further, beyond the city, to the barrow raised by his own hands in honour of his friend.

Jiwan thought of the rumours circulating that the tomb was actually empty. After all, how could any darkness contain the one known as the Son of Mother Dark herself? But he neither knew nor cared about the truth of that. He did know that only fear of this man kept war from flaring in the north once again. A peace that held the Rhivi's place upon the plains. The peace of the Warlord.

A peace that may now be slipping. He cleared his throat to announce his presence. 'You are troubled, lord?'

The man swung his heavy beast-like gaze to him, then away, to the distant glow. 'I allowed myself the luxury of thinking it was all over, Jiwan. Yet they rest uneasy. In the south. The Great Barrow of the Redeemer. And the Lesser, his Guardian. And this one of my friend. There is a tension. A stirring. I feel it.' He voice softened almost into silence. 'I was fooling myself. Nothing is ever finished.'

'The sword is shattered, is it not?'

'Yes, it is shattered.'

'And the Lord of Moon's Spawn is gone.'

'Yes, he is gone.'

Jiwan was uncertain. 'You fear, then, the Malazans shall be emboldened?'

The Warlord glanced at him, surprise showing on his blunt, brutal features. 'The Malazans? No, not them. With Rake gone . . . It is his absence that troubles me.'

Jiwan bowed, taking his leave. He knew it was right and proper that the Warlord should mourn his friend, but he, Jiwan, must think first of his people. An enemy was encamped on their borders to the north and the south, an enemy that was solid and real, not the haunted dreams of some troubled old man. The damnable Malazans. Who else would be emboldened by the fall of Anomander? They might seize this opportunity. But he was reluctant to speak of it yet. Loyalty and gratitude to the Warlord still swayed too many hearts among the elders. This too he understood. For he was not of stone; he felt it as well. Yet times move on – one must not remain a captive of the past.

He came to a decision. Changing direction, he headed instead to the corral. He would send word to the north for more warriors to gather. They must be ready should the Warlord call upon them . . . or not.

*　　*　　*

The nights in Darujhistan were far more hushed now than he could ever remember. Muted. One could perhaps even call the unaccustomed mood sombre. Ill-fitting airs for the city of blue-flame, of passions, or, as that toad friend of his named it, the city of dreams.

For his part Rallick hoped the mood was not one of tensed expectation.

It was past the sixth hour of night by the Wardens' bells. He stood at an unremarkable intersection in the Gadrobi district. Unremarkable but for one very remarkable thing: here, Hood, self-appointed godhead of death, met his end. Followed shortly thereafter by his destroyer, Anomander Rake, Lord of Moon's Spawn.

Events dire enough to shake the confidence of anyone.

No second- or third-storey lights shone in any window facing this crossroads. All forsook it. Patrons refused to enter the shops facing the site, and so the surrounding blocks progressively became abandoned. For who would live overlooking such an ill-omened locale? Weeds now poked up through cobbles. Doors gaped open, the empty shop-houses looted. In the heart of the most crowded and largest metropolis of the continent lay this blot of abandonment and death.

The thought caused Rallick to shift uneasily. *Dead heart.*

Yet not completely lifeless; another figure came walking up, boots kicking through the litter, his hands tucked beneath his dark cloak. Rallick inclined his chin in greeting. 'Krute.'

'Rallick.'

'Survived the guild bloodletting, I see. I'm pleased.'

A soft grunt. 'Too few of us old-timers did. Gadrobi's my parish now. Shows you one way to get promoted.'

'Congratulations.'

'Thanks.' The man peered about. The wrinkles framing his small eyes tightened. 'But . . . I gotta wonder . . . who's really in charge?'

Familiar cold fingers brushed Rallick's neck. 'Vorcan's not interested, Krute,' he said, his voice flat. 'As the guild now knows, she has a seat on the Council.'

'That talking shop? Sounds like a front to me.'

'She's moved on. As have I.'

The man gave an exaggerated nod. 'Oh, so you say. So you say.' He laughed, more like a grunt. 'There're some in the guild who say you *have* moved on – body and soul. Those who hold to the Rallick Nom cult.' He laughed again, as if at the stupidity of people. 'And yet . . . got something to show you.' He edged his head aside. 'This way.'

After a measured glance all round, Rallick followed. To his ears his boots crackling on the gravel and debris of neglect sounded startlingly loud.

They crossed to the poorest, lowest-lying quarter, bordering on the Marsh district. Here the most squalid of what could hardly be called businesses occupied rotting row-houses and shacks. Rag and bone shops, pawnshops, manure collectors, small family tanneries. In the soggy alley of an open sewer lay two bodies.

Krute invited him to examine them. 'What do you think?'

An eye on the assassin, who backed up a reassuring distance, Rallick bent over the first. 'Professional work. Straight thrust through the back to the heart. Complete surprise – no twisting or turning in the wound.' He pushed over the second, hesitated, then studied the neck. 'First-rate cut. Thin razor blade. Straight side to side. Right-handed, with a slight upward angle – attacker was shorter than victim.'

An angry grunt from Krute. 'I missed that.'

Rallick straightened. 'What's your point?'

'What brings two ex-Warden guards down here to this shit-hole street, Rallick? You recognized them, didn't you?'

'I recognized them.'

'But you didn't say . . .'

A thin shrug from Rallick. 'You're inside now, Krute.'

'Dammit, man! I'm doing you a fucking favour! Everyone's accounted for! Everyone!' He pulled savagely on his stubbled chin. 'Who could pad up on two veteran guards, take 'em both without a peep? Without even a struggle? It's a short list, Rallick. And your name's on it . . . along with hers.'

'Like I said already, Krute. What's your point?'

The man let out a long tight breath, almost like a growl. 'Always gotta be the hard way with you, hey, Rallick? Well, okay. Here's my point – Vorcan's short.'

Rallick let his head fall as if studying the rank gutter, was quiet for a time, then began backing off. 'My advice to your superior is stay away. She's out of your class.'

He'd exited the alley, now ripening with something far beyond garbage, when a trick of the acoustics brought Krute's ghostly voice: 'Yours too, Rallick. Yours too.'

*

Impatient banging brought the new waitress, Jess, lumbering to the doors of the Phoenix Inn. She unlatched the lock to peer out, blinking and wincing, into the glaring morning light. A tall dark figure brushed round her, imperious.

'Not open, sir,' she said, surprised, still blinking. Then, eyeing the retreating back, she relaxed. 'Oh.' And she shuffled to the kitchen to wake up Chud.

Rallick peered down at the fat man sprawled in his chair, head slung back, snoring. Amazement warred with disgust. Crushed pastries littered the table along with empty bottles, smears of exotic mustards and pâté. The rotund figure snored, mouth slack. Rallick had a good view of the bristles of his unshaven bulging neck and the ridiculous vanity of the scruffy braided rat-tail beard. He gave a table leg a light kick.

The man snorted, jerking. Pudgy hands patted vested stomach, the ruffles of the silk shirt. The head rolled forward, lips smacking. Beady eyes found Rallick, widened. 'Aaii! Thought grim graven friend new apparition of death come for modest Kruppe. Most discomfiting and shocking wakening. Kruppe has not yet seen to his toilet.'

'Don't let me stop you.'

'Friend Rallick is always so civilized.' A large stained handkerchief appeared in one hand, brushed flakes of pastry from the man's wide midriff. Then he wound a fold of the cloth round one finger and daubed daintily at the corners of his mouth. 'Done!' He sighed contentedly and slipped his hands into the black silk sash that circled his crimson waistcoat. 'Now Kruppe can only respond in kind.' He raised his chin: 'Dearest Jess . . . We die of famishment! Bring biscuits, tea, Elingarth blood sausages and honeyed bacon, flatbreads and Moranth cloudberry syrup.' He lowered his voice. 'Not sure how she'll fit in, you know.'

Jess's voice bellowed from the kitchen. 'Chud says we ain't got none o' that crap!'

'She'll serve just fine, I think,' Rallick murmured under his breath.

The squat man's brows wrinkled, pained. 'Oh, dear. I must have been dreaming . . .' A quick shrug. 'Oh well. Biscuits and tea, then. Oh! And a crust of burnt toast for my friend here.'

Rallick could hear his clenched teeth grinding. 'Kruppe, I just—'

A raised hand forestalled him. 'Explain not, old friend! No need for explanations . . . please sit!' Growling, Rallick pulled a chair out with his heel, eased down and leaned back, hands on his thighs. 'Kruppe understands. Why, it is on everyone's sighing lips these days, dear friend. The city's two most deadly killers tamed by love's soothing embrace!'

Rallick's front chair legs struck the floor with a bang. 'What?'

'Do not worry! Kruppe's feelings shall recover.' He peeled a sliver of wrinkled dried fruit from the table, sniffed it, then popped it into his mouth. 'Sustenance, Jess! We are positively expiring here!' He shook his head, sighed dreamily. 'It is an old story, yes, friend? Love is found and old friends are forgotten. Kruppe does not wonder why you have been neglectful of us these last months. The two of you haunt the rooftops in flighty trysts, no doubt. Like bats in love.'

'Kruppe . . .' Rallick ground out.

'Soon a brood of baby killers to follow. I see it now. Knives in the crib and garrottes in the playpen.'

'*Kruppe!*'

The fat man lifted his eyes to blink innocently up at Rallick. 'Yes?'

'I just want to know if Cro— Cutter is in town.'

'Kruppe wonders . . .' Something strangled the man's voice and he choked. Pudgy fingers fished in his mouth, emerging with the mangled stringy sliver of fruit, which he then carefully smeared back on to the table. 'Jess! One need not cross the Cinnamon Wastes for tea!'

The big woman emerged from the kitchen, tray in hand. Her white linen shirt had been hastily laced, revealing a great deal of flesh. She glared at Kruppe, thumped the tray down, nodded to Rallick. 'Good to see you, sir.'

'Jess. How's Meese doing these days?'

'She comes round most evenings.'

'You manage?'

She pushed back her hair, waved to the empty tables. 'I'm worked off my feet.'

Rallick also eyed the empty common room. He frowned as if struck by a new thought. The woman walked back to the kitchen doors, her hips rolling like ships at sea. Rallick cleared his throat. 'Just who does own this place anyway, Kruppe?'

'Friend Rallick was asking after young Cutter . . .'

Rallick slid his gaze back. 'Yes?'

Kruppe peered into the depths of the teapot. 'Kruppe wonders why.'

Snarling, Rallick stood, pushing back his chair. 'Is he here or not?'

Lifting a knife and a biscuit, the little man peered up with a steady gaze. 'Kruppe assures friend Rallick that equally loved young vagabond is most assuredly not in our fair city.' He raised the biscuit. 'Crumpet?'

Rallick's chest, which had been clenched in one coiled breath the inspection of certain wounds hours earlier, eased in a long exhalation, and he nodded, 'Good . . . good.'

Kruppe's eyes had narrowed in their pockets of fat. 'Again – Kruppe wonders why.'

But Rallick had turned away. 'Doesn't matter.' He called to the kitchen. 'Jess.'

Kruppe threw his arms wide. 'But breakfast has only just arrived!'

Rallick pushed open the door in a bright wash of sunlight and walked out, the door swinging closed behind.

Shrugging, the fat man scooped up a smear of jam. 'And to think Kruppe named impatient friend civilized. Kruppe was egregiously in error!'

*　　*　　*

In the harsh morning light Scholar Ebbin trudged up the muddy unpaved street of the pure-gatherers in the Gadrobi district. A dusty leather bag pulled at one shoulder and he wore a wide-brimmed hat yanked down firmly on his head. He stopped at a shuttered storefront of age-gnawed wood on worn stone foundations, banged on the solid door and waited. Across the street, between the cart traffic and crowds of market-goers, he noted the blue uniform of the Wardens. The sight was a surprise to him; while crime was endemic in this district, attention from the Wardens was rare. They had a wagon with them and appeared to be moving something.

The door vibrated as bars and locks were removed. It grated in its jambs to open a sliver. Darkness lay within. 'Ah,' a thin voice breathed, 'it is you, good scholar. Enter.'

Ebbin edged in sideways and the door ground shut. In the relative dark he was blind for the moment but he could make out a hunched dark figure securing bars and bolts again. 'You are ever mindful of thieves, Aman. Yet . . . rather a barrier to commerce, I would imagine.'

'Darujhistan has fallen very far, good scholar,' the bent man answered in his breathless voice. 'Very far indeed. It is not like the old days of peace and strict adherence to the laws of its rulers. As for commerce . . . I service a select few who know where to find me, yes?' He chuckled drily.

The unease that his visits here always engendered within Ebbin was not relieved by these comments. He thought of how his own whispered and circumspect enquiries into the subtleties of wardings, Warren-anchored barriers and the avoidance thereof led him step by step and source by source to this one man and his seemingly unpatronised shop. Yet to maintain appearances he answered genially enough, 'Of course, Aman. Very select,' and he laughed modestly as well.

Aman ushered him into the shop proper, one foot dragging in his crippled walk, back twisted from some accident of birth. His hands too were crippled – malformed and bent as if having been caught within some mangling instrument. He shuffled behind his counter where a raised platform allowed him to peer over it, looming like some sort of gangly bird of prey.

Ebbin's vision was now adjusting to the permanent gloom in the shop, and he gently set his satchel on the counter.

'You have something for me?' Aman asked, cocking a brow already higher than its fellow.

'Yes.' He untied the leather strapping, eased out a wrapped object. 'From the lowest I've gone so far.'

Setting the package between them, Ebbin carefully parted the thick felt outer wrappings then a sheer inner layer of silk to reveal what appeared to be nothing more than a fragment of eggshell, albeit one from an egg of impossibly huge dimensions. Aman bent forward even further, his canted nose almost touching the object. Seeing him up close Ebbin was struck by the deformed shape of his knobbly skull beneath its patchy pelt of filmy grey hair. Perhaps sensing his attention, Aman pulled away.

'A magnificent specimen, good scholar. Beautiful.' The shop-keeper lit a lamp from a wall-sconced lantern, set it on the counter. 'May I?' Ebbin gestured an invitation. For all his bent root-like fingers, the man lifted the fragment smoothly, held it before the flame. Ebbin crouched to peer: the flame was visible as a blurred glow through the fragment, which was astonishing enough, but the entire piece had somehow taken up the light and now glowed, warm, soft and luminous, like the dawn in miniature.

Aman sighed, almost nostalgically it seemed. 'I invite you to imagine, if you would, good scholar, entire structures of such stone, carved and polished to near pure translucency, glowing with the cold blue flames of the city. A magnificent sight it must have been, yes?'

'Yes. Darujhistan in the great Imperial Age of the Tyrants. At least, so it has been conjectured.'

The bulbous eyes moved to his, blinked. 'Of course.'

'Is it treated?'

Aman returned the piece to its cloths and began rewrapping it. 'We shall see. It will have to be tested. Should it prove a fragment from a container utilized in certain, ah . . . esoteric . . . rituals from that age, then it may be resold for a great deal to those eager to reuse it for their own . . . well . . . similar research.'

Ebbin cleared his throat, uncomfortable. 'I see.'

Aman tucked the package under the countertop. 'And how may I help *you*, good scholar?'

'I've come to a chamber. One still sealed.'

The shopkeeper's fingers, which had been tapping the counter like spiders, stilled. 'In truth?' he breathed in wonder. 'Sealed as yet? Astonishing. You must take care, good scholar. The traps these ancients set upon their interred . . .' He shook his misshapen head. 'Deadly.'

'Of course, Aman. I know the risks. I am no amateur.'

'Of course,' the shopkeeper echoed, smiling to reveal a mouthful of misaligned teeth. 'The barrier?'

Ebbin cleared his throat once more. 'Stone. A flat slab. Unmarked in any way.'

'Unmarked, you say? No sigils of any sort? Not even the faintest of inscriptions?'

Ebbin frowned, impatient. 'I know my work. I've been excavating for decades.'

Aman raised his hands. 'No disrespect intended, good scholar. Please. It is just very . . . unusual.'

An uncomfortable shivering took Ebbin then and he rubbed his chest, nodding his agreement. 'Yes. It is . . . unusual.'

'An unimportant personage, perhaps. A minor court retainer.'

Ebbin thought of the figure laid out on its onyx bier at the chamber's centre. The beaten gold mask with its eerie mocking smile, and the bands of skulls encircling the plinth. Nested councils of death. He nodded, shivering. 'Yes. My impression exactly.'

Aman appeared to be studying him somehow, his gaze weighing. Then the man quickly turned away to his shelves. 'I may have just the tools for you, good scholar. Moranth alchemicals . . . acids, perhaps? Or chisels. Not your everyday sort of tool, no, not at all. Hardened iron, alloyed with that Malazan mineral otataral. If you give me a few days I will have them for you.'

'You have nothing like that here?'

A dry laugh from the man. 'Oh my goodness no. That mineral would have a most deleterious effect upon . . . upon my wares.'

Ebbin could only agree. 'If you say so, sir. A few days then. I have to consult with my backer in any case.'

'Excellent, excellent.' And he bobbed his head, his knotted fingers tapping incessantly on the counter.

Once every bolt had been shut and every bar replaced, Aman shuffled back into his shop. Here he found a beautiful young woman, her long black hair braided and coiled atop her head, awaiting him. His mouth tightened into a sour pucker. 'Your *intrusion* into my affairs is most ill-advised. Most unwelcome.'

The girl merely cocked a shapely hip to lean against the counter where she turned the wrapped package in slow circles. 'Why are we relying on this cretin?'

'We? There is no *we*. You are deluded. Your uninvited meddling will complicate matters most stressfully.'

'They were watching the shop, Aman.'

The man hobbled back up on to his platform behind the counter. 'Watching the shop? Of course they were watching the shop. They are always watching the shop! These agents of my one-time allies have proved most persistent. But because I remain within, and am *circumspect* . . . they have been none the wiser.' He gently touched his fingertips to the wood countertop. 'Needless to say, said circumspection has now been shattered . . .'

'They are dead, Aman.'

The shopkeeper started to speak, caught himself, rubbed his hands over the countertop as if stroking it. He began again, slowly, 'Yes. However, the one who hired them now knows he, or she, is close to something. Best to have maintained the aura of mystery.'

The girl's pale thin shoulders lifted in an unconcerned shrug. She began unwrapping the package. 'Then I will kill whoever that person is.'

'Ah yes. Speaking of mysteries. No one knows the identity of the circle-breaker. Many poseurs have surfaced pretending to the title, but no one knows for certain. It may have even been one of my old allies – even your mother.'

The girl's coquettish gaze hardened. 'Never mention her to me, Aman.' She peered up from half-lidded eyes. 'Anyone, you say? But not you, of course.'

Aman shook a bent finger. 'You *are* learning.'

She made a face, then indicated the carved fragment. 'Is this thing really as valuable as you say?'

He raised it between them, his gaze holding her eyes. 'Ahh . . . beautiful, yes? Slender, striking. A magnificent specimen. On the outside. But within, flawed. Worthless. A piece of useless trash.' He crushed it in his hand.

The girl flinched away as if slapped, bumping something in the dark. Her full lips tightened to a pale slash and a molten light blazed within her eyes. The man studied her quite calmly, his head cocked, fingertips lightly touching together. The golden light faded from her eyes as she stood quivering in suppressed rage. She drew a shuddering breath and raised her chin in defiance. 'You are *quite* finished, I hope?'

He bowed. 'Quite.'

'And what is this monstrosity?' she demanded, waving at the tall figure she'd struck.

Aman raised the lamp, revealing an armoured statue. The light reflected green and blue from an inlay of semi-precious stones. 'Magnificent, is it not? From distant Jacuruku. One of their stone soldiers.'

She peered closer in an almost professional evaluation. 'An automaton?'

'Not . . . *quite*.' He set the lamp on the counter. 'In any case, m'lady, since you have returned, I suggest you make yourself useful and shadow our friend. Nothing untoward must happen to him. Be ready to intervene. He is close, Taya. Very close.'

'Why him? Why don't you go down?'

The man did nothing to hide the condescension in his answering chuckle. 'My dear. You are most diverting. The countless protections, wards and conditions imposed by my erstwhile allies are most exacting. Almost without openings. Only those who do not seek may pass. They must be innocent of bloodshed, possess no lust for personal gain . . . the conditions go on and on. Mammotlian contrived them. And so, since Mammotlian, a scholar, built the tomb, perhaps only a fellow like-minded spirit may possess the instincts to follow. If you see my reasoning.'

'And should he fail – like all the others?'

A crooked shrug from the man. 'Well, they're nearly out of floor space down there, aren't they?'

Her eyes constricted to slits and she tilted her head, unsure of his meaning.

*　　*　　*

On the street of the whitesmiths in the Gadrobi district, Barathol Mekhar inspected his latest consignment of iron ore. It was of unusually good quality. There was a useful variation of softness and brittleness within the clumps. He closed the box and went to the forge, held a hand over the bed of coals. Still needed more time. He left the shop to cross a small open court to the rear of his row-house. Dusting his hands, he climbed the narrow stairs to his rooms above. Dawn was just brightening the sky outside the shuttered windows. For a time he stood next to the bed where his wife Scillara still slept. Then he went to the other side of the bed to the tiny crib fashioned by his own hands. Kneeling, he studied the infant within, curled and plump.

Never had he ever imagined such a treasure would be his. It seemed too defenceless for the world. Too tenuous. Its fragility terrified him. He feared even to touch it with his coarse blackened hands. He did however gently ease one into the crib to let the child's quick hot breath warm those fingers.

Smiling, he rose to see Scillara watching him. 'Not run off yet, I see,' she said, stretching.

'Not yet.'

'Not even with a squalling brat and a fat wife?'

'I guess I must have done something terrible in a prior life.'

'Musta been pretty damned awful.' She looked about as if searching for something. 'Gods, I miss my pipe.'

'You'll live.'

She pointed to the door. 'Throw me my gown. Don't you have work to do? Money to earn? Enough to hire a cook. I'm getting sick of your burnt offerings.'

'You could try lending a hand, you know.'

She laughed. 'You don't want to eat my cooking.'

'I'll be out back then.' He threw the gown. 'Could use some tea.'

'We all could.'

On the way down the stairs he looked forward to another day standing at the forge where he could look over to the courtyard and see Scillara sitting on rugs laid out on the ground there, nursing little Chaur.

Life, it seemed to him, was better than he'd ever hoped it could be.

CHAPTER II

Turn not thine hand against thy father; for it is sacrilege

Inscription upon stone fragment
Dwelling Plains

T HE CHALLENGE BEGAN AS THESE THINGS ALWAYS DO: WITH A LOOK. A glance held a heartbeat too long. In this case lingering across the beaten dirt of the practice grounds at the centre of Cant, the marble halls of the Seguleh.

Jan, in the act of turning away to call for a slave, noted the glance, and stopped. Those of the ruling Jistarii family lineage out exercising that morning also instinctively sensed the tension. The crowd parted and Jan found himself staring across the emptied sparring fields and wrestling circles to Enoc, the newly installed Third. He watched while the young aristocrat's friends and closest supporters within the rankings crossed to stand at his side. Without needing to turn his head Jan knew his own friends had come to his. He held out his wooden practice sword. It was taken from his hand.

'Give him your back,' Palla, the Sixth, hissed from behind. 'How dare he! This is not the place.'

Jan answered calmly: 'Does not our young Third claim that daring is just what is lacking these days among our ranks?' A snarl of clenched rage answered that. Jan allowed himself a slight raise of his chin to indicate the seats of the amphitheatre across the way. 'Look . . . the judges of the challenge assembled already.'

'They are all of his family!' Palla exclaimed. 'This is the work of his scheming uncle, that fat Olag.'

Jan's sword appeared, offered hilt-first from behind. He took it and began securing the sheath to his sash. Across the field Enoc's coterie of supporters, ambitious young-bloods mostly, did the same for him. Someone handed Jan a gourd of water and he sipped. His gaze did not leave Enoc's mask: a pale oval marred only by two black slashes, one down each cheek.

So, a year already, is it? He was surprised. Time seemed to pass ever more quickly as he became older. Not that he intended to get older – it was merely the byproduct of his extended wait for someone to manage to defeat him. Enoc obviously thought his chance had come. And he had to acknowledge that the daring youth seemed to have chosen his moment quite well: Enoc himself was yet fresh, merely having stretched and warmed up, while he had just completed a very gruelling series of sparring matches and was even now still sweating with exertion. It would appear that this cunning new Third had the advantage.

But Jan was where he wanted to be. His blood was hot and flowing fast. His limbs glowed with heat and felt strong. Practice did not drain him as it seemed to so many others. Rather, it enlivened him. Yet . . . a challenge during exercise . . . a time when by tradition all members of the Jistarii aristocracy were welcome to mix freely, practising and training. This was very bad form. An assembly of impartial judges wouldn't even countenance it.

Yet there was no question he must answer. It was his duty. He was Second.

He set the tips of his fingers on the two-handed grip of his longsword and walked out to the middle of the amphitheatre sands. Over the years he had lost count of the many Thirds who had come and gone beneath him. The ranks of the Agatii, the top thousand, were like a geyser in this manner – ever throwing up new challengers. And this one was an impatient example of a notoriously impatient ranking. Long ago it was always said that Second was the worst ranking to attain. Ever Second, never First. But with the death of the last ancient to achieve First, it was Third that was now so regarded. The itchiest ranking; the briefest rung . . . in one manner or another. *And this one seems to think me tired. Very well. Let him do so. Let him challenge now, so very early. So very . . . precipitously. So be it. I can only do my part and accept.*

Enoc strode out to meet him. The Jistarii backed away, leaving the field clear, while slaves removed equipment. The wind was calm, and the sun was far enough overhead not to be an issue. Jan waited, head cocked. When the Third was close enough to allow private conversation, he offered the ritual exchange: 'I give you this last chance to reconsider. Form has been obeyed. No shame would accrue.'

The gaze was scornful behind the white mask with its two black lines. 'Waiting is not for me, Second. I do not plan to cling to my perch – as you have.'

Jan's breath caught momentarily. 'You covet the *First?*'

'It is time. If you will not lead, then stand aside for one who will.'

So that is what they are whispering in the dormitories . . . How they have all forgotten. One does not claim First. It cannot be taken. It can only be given. And I – even I – was not judged worthy. Anger beckoned now, and with a supreme effort he allowed it to flow past. No. There must be no emotion. No thought. This one thinks too much – it slows him. One must not think. One must simply act. And he, Jan, had always been so very fast to act.

Pushing with his thumb, he eased the blade a fraction from its sheath. 'Very well, Third.' He inhaled, and exhaling whispered the ritual words: 'I accept.'

Their blades met crashing and grating even as the last syllable left Jan's mouth. Jan deflected several attacks, noting subconsciously how the lad relied too much on strength as a bolster to a form not yet quite at ease with itself. He knew instinctively he had the better of him, and that any of the rankers above the Tenth would see this as well. But the judges. They would not be convinced. Something much more irrefutable would be needed.

The poor lad. In stacking the assembly his uncle has left me with no alternative. And now this one will pay the price.

Still he delayed, parrying and circling. Among the highest rankings, actually being sloppy enough to spill blood was considered very poor form. The best victories were those achieved without such crudity.

The storm of the Third's unrelenting aggression washed over him in a constant ringing of tempered, hardened steel. Yet he remained calm – an eye of tranquillity surrounded by a blurred singing razor's edge. That storm had first been one of blustering overbearing power. But now it carried within it a discord of confusion, even recognition.

And a coiling frantic desperation.

Jan chose to act. Best to end the testing now, lest he acquire a reputation for cruelty. In the midst of their entwined dance of thrust, feint and counter, Jan's blade extended a fraction of a finger's breadth further as his shift inward allowed Enoc's own movement to close their distance more than intended and the tip of his blade licked the inside of the right elbow, severing tendon.

Enoc's right arm fell limp, the longsword swinging loose. The lad froze, chest rising and falling in an all too open display of exertion. His fevered gaze through his mask of was one of disbelief now crashing into horror.

The lad was crippled. Oh, it would heal, and in time he would probably regain use of the arm. But with that wound he would be hard pressed even to maintain a position within the Agatii. He would retain the right to carry a blade, of course. But there would be no more challenges for him.

Jan considered a whispered apology now while they held this fragile intimate moment between challengers, but the youth would probably take it as an insult. And so he said nothing.

That moment, the onlookers' caught breath of aesthetic appreciation of the beauty of a single cut perfectly executed in power, timing, accuracy and form, passed.

And the gathered Jistarii all bowed to their Second.

Later that evening Jan sat cross-legged at dinner with his closest friends among the ranked: Palla, the Sixth, and Lo, Eighth these many years, but recently, with the reported death of Blacksword, under consideration for promotion to the long empty rank of Seventh. With them also was an old friend of his youth, Beru, one of the Thirtieth.

'Will Gall reclaim the Third?' Jan asked Palla.

She laughed, and, ducking her head, lifted her mask to take a pinched morsel of rice and meats. 'He will. And with gratitude to be back on his old rung again.'

'Gratitude? I did not act as I did for his benefit.'

She bowed, all formal, but her voice held humour: 'Gratitude for reminding everyone why he has remained Third for so long.'

Jan motioned gently to close the subject. He turned to Lo, seeing the seven lines of soot that radiated out from round the eye holes of his friend's mask. 'And what of you? Will you take the Seventh?'

Lo bowed stiffly from the waist. 'If commanded. But I do not seek it. It is . . . distasteful . . . to step up in this manner.'

From Beru's tense pose Jan could tell he had something to say. 'And you, Beru?'

The man bowed, and kept his gaze averted. 'With respect, Second. There is talk of this swordsman, whoever he may be, who slew Blacksword, the Lord of the Moon's scion. Some say he must be regarded as the new Seventh. Some suggest a challenge.'

Jan had been reaching for a pinch of meat, but stilled. 'You know I am against such . . . adventurism. I opposed the expedition of punishment against the Pannions. What did that gain us? Mok's skills wasted against rabble and unworthy amateurs.'

His three companions ate in silence for a time, for all knew Jan's feelings regarding Mok, his elder brother, who volunteered to silence those disrespectful Pannions. And who returned . . . changed. Broken.

It fell to Palla to speak, the one who shared the greatest claim to intimacy with him, as the lovers they had been. Until both had climbed too high in the rankings and the tensions of the challenge intervened. 'And yet,' she began, cautiously, 'you supported Oru's venture.'

Jan made a deliberate effort to soften his tone. 'Oru claimed to have had a vision. Who am I to dispute that? I allowed him to call for any who would voluntarily accompany him.'

'And twenty answered! Our greatest expedition ever mounted.'

'True.' And for the greatest goal of all. For only to him, as Second, did Oru reveal the truth of his vision . . . the belief that somehow, in some manner, he would regain the honour of the Seguleh stolen from them so long ago. A mad, desperate hope. But one he could not oppose.

His gaze fell on Lo, face turned away as he raised his mask to drink. Perhaps he should allow the challenge. Any man who could defeat Blacksword . . . if he could better Lo then he could have the rank.

A gentle tap at the door broke into Jan's thoughts. He nodded for Beru to answer. On his knees, one hand on the grip of his sword, Beru cracked open the door and spoke in low tones to whoever was without. After a short exchange he opened it.

It was an old man, an unmasked honoured Jistarii who had chosen the path of priest. The man shuffled in on his knees and bowed, touching his brow to the bare hardwood floor. 'My lord. You are requested at the temple. There is . . . something for you to see.'

Jan inclined his mask fractionally. 'Very well. I will attend.' The priest bowed again. He shuffled backwards on his knees and stepped out of the low threshold without turning his back upon them. Jan took a sip of tea to cleanse his mouth.

Palla bowed in a request to speak.

'Yes?'

'May we accompany you?'

'If you wish.'

The main temple of Cant was a large open-sided building of columns and arches. It was constructed entirely of white marble veined with black. Lit torches hissed in the evening wind, casting shadows among the eerily pallid white stone of the columns, floor and ceiling. The High Priest, Sengen, awaited them. He wore the plain tunic and trousers of rough cloth that were the customary clothing of the Seguleh. He was cleanly shaven, as most Seguleh males of the Jistarii tended to be, and his long grey hair was oiled and pulled back tightly in a braid. He bowed to Jan.

'Sengen,' Jan acknowledged, thereby granting him permission to speak.

'Only the Second may accompany me,' the old man commanded, stepping forward.

Palla and Lo stiffened, exchanged outraged glances. Jan raised a hand for patience. 'That is your right here within the temple.'

Sengen bowed again, beckoning Jan forward.

He led him to the very rear. To the altarpiece: a single pillar of unearthly translucent white stone, waist-high, its top empty. Sengen regarded the pillar reverently, his hands crossed over his chest. Jan stared at him, puzzled by his odd behaviour. Then his gaze moved to the pillar, and he started forward, amazed. Beads of moisture ran down the white stone, and a thin vapour, as of a morning mist, drifted from it.

'It sweats, Second,' the High Priest breathed, awed. 'The stone sweats.'

'What does this mean?'

Eyes fixed on the pale stone, Sengen answered, 'It means that what we have been awaiting all this time may come. Our purpose.'

Shaken, Jan stepped away. Yet the pillar was empty . . . was this right? How could this happen?

'It is your duty to make ready,' Sengen said sharply.

Jan nodded. Turning, he caught his reflection on a nearby polished shield. A pale white mask distinguished by a single blood-red smear across the brow. A mark put there by the last First, so long ago. 'Yes,' he answered, his voice thick. 'I shall.'

His three friends waited on the steps of the temple. Coming to them Jan stood silent for some time while they shifted, uncomfortable, gazes averted. 'Lo,' he said at last. 'I give you permission to seek out this Seventh. We may have need of him.'

'Need?' Lo echoed, glancing up in startlement, then quickly away.

'You may take one other with you. Who would that be?'

Lo gestured. 'Beru here, if he would.'

'No. I would have him remain. Choose another.'

Lo bowed. 'As you command.'

'What is it?' Palla asked, inclining her head. 'You are . . . troubled.'

Jan regarded her. For a moment he allowed himself the pleasure of taking in her lithe limbs, her tall proud bearing, and wished she had not pursued the Path of the Challenge. But that was selfish of him; she deserved her rank. 'Gather the Agatii, Sixth. We must make ready. The altarstone has awakened.'

The three glanced to the temple, their eyes behind their masks widening in awe. 'We thought that just a legend,' Palla breathed.

'Before he passed, the First imparted to me a portion of what was handed down to him. It is no legend. Now go, Palla. Tell the first half of the Agatii to gather here.'

Palla jerked a swift bow and dashed down the steps. Jan turned to the Eighth. 'A vessel will be placed at your disposal.'

Lo bowed and backed away down the stairs. Watching him go Beru spoke, wonder in his voice. 'And what can this lowly Thirtieth do to help?'

'I would have you remain among the ranks, Beru. Listen to the talk in the dormitories. A difficult time may be coming. We will all be tested. Let us hope we are not judged . . . unworthy.'

'I understand, Second.' Jan did not answer, and, sensing that his friend wished to be alone now, Beru bowed and departed.

Jan stood for some time in the chill air of the evening. He looked out across the paved white stone Plaza of Gathering to the houses and the mountains of this, their adopted homeland. That adoption was itself no secret. They knew they'd come from elsewhere; all their old stories told of a great march, an exile, although none named their mythical place of origin. That was another truth the First had confirmed: their homeland was to the north. And he had named it.

Precious little more guidance had the ancient yielded, though. When pressed for more the old man had simply peered up at him from where he lay and shaken his head. 'It is best you do not know these things,' he had said. 'It is best for all.'

Ignorance? How could ignorance be best? Jan's instincts railed against such a claim. Yet he was raised and trained to obey, and so he had submitted. He was Second. It was his duty. Perhaps it was the old man's tone that had convinced him. Those words had carried in them a crushing grief, a terrible weight of truth that Jan feared he may not be able to endure.

*   *   *

'You smell that?' Picker asked. She looked up from where she sat with her feet on a table in the nearly empty common room of K'rul's bar., chair pushed back, cleaning her nails with a dagger.

Blend, chin in hand at the bar counter, cocked a brow to Duiker in his customary seat. 'That a comment?'

Picker wrinkled her nose. 'No – not you. Somethin' even worse . . . Somethin' I ain't smelt since . . .' The chair banged down and she cursed. 'That hair-shirted puke is back in town!'

Blend straightened, peered around. 'No . . .' She lunged for the door. 'Get the back!'

The door opened before Blend reached it. She tried to push it shut on a man with a shock of unkempt salt and pepper hair and a weather-darkened grizzled face, wearing a long ragged hair shirt. He managed to squeeze in as she slammed it shut. 'Good to see you too, Blend,' he commented, scowling.

Blend flinched away, covering her nose and mouth. 'Spindle. What in Hood's dead arse are you doing here?'

Picker ran in from the rear: 'Back's locked. There's no way he can— Oh. Damn.'

A toothy smile from the man. 'Just like old times.' He ambled over to sit at Duiker's table, nodded to the grey-bearded man. 'Historian. Been awhile.'

The old man's mouth crooked up just a touch. 'Nothing seems to keep you Bridgeburners down.'

'Shit floats,' Picker muttered from the bar on the far side of the room.

'So how 'bout a drink then?' Spindle called loudly. ''Less you're just too damned busy with all your customers an' all.'

'We're out,' Blend said. 'Have to try somewhere else. Don't let us stop you.'

Spindle turned in his chair. 'Out? What kind of bar has no alcohol?'

'A very grim one,' Duiker offered so low no one seemed to hear.

'Hunh.' The man pulled on his ragged shirt at its neck as if it were uncomfortable, or too tight. 'Well, I think maybe I can help you out with that.'

Picker and Blend exchanged sceptical glances and said in unison, 'Oh?'

'Sure. Got some work kicked my way. You know, paid work for coin. For drink and food. And to pay the rent.' Spindle studied Blend more closely. 'Who do you pay rent to here anyway?'

The women shifted their stances, squinting at the walls. 'Why us?' Blend asked suddenly and Picker nodded.

'They just want people they can count on to keep their damned mouths shut.'

'People have given up on the assassins' guild, have they?' Picker commented.

'If there's any of them left . . .' Blend added, aside.

Spindle rolled his eyes to the ceiling. 'Not that kinda work!'

'What in Fener's prang is it then?' Blend demanded.

Sitting back, booted feet straight out before him, the veteran clasped his hands over his belt. He smiled lopsidedly in what Picker imagined to be an effort at ingratiation, but looked more like the leer of a dirty old man. 'Right up your alley, Blend. Plain ol' low-profile reconnaissance. Observe and report. Nothin' more.'

'How much?' Picker asked.

'A gold council per day.'

Blend whistled. 'Who's worth that much? Not you, that's for damned sure.'

Spindle lost his smile. 'They're payin' a lot to make sure the job gets done.'

'Who's paying?' Duiker suddenly asked in a low hoarse voice. 'Who's the principal?'

All three regarded the old historian, amazed.

'Damned straight!' Blend said.

'Yeah,' Picker said. 'Could be a trap. Fake contract to draw us out.'

Spindle dismissed that with a wave. 'Ach! You're soundin' too much like Antsy.' He peered around. 'Where is that lunatic anyway?'

Blend leaned back to set her elbows on the bar. 'Went south. Said he was . . . ah, antsy.' She scowled. 'Stop changing the subject! Who's payin'?'

Spindle just waved again. 'Never you mind. I know. And I know we can trust 'em.'

'Them?' Picker said, arching a brow. 'Who're *them*?'

Spindle threw his hands up. 'All right, all right! Trusting as Jags, you lot are. Okay!' He leaned forward and tapped the side of his gashed and battered nose. 'You could say it's our old employers.'

If Picker had had something in her hands she would've thrown it at the man. 'You great idjit! We're deserters!'

He got that knowing smirk once more. 'Exactly. That makes us free agents, right?'

'It makes political sense,' Duiker said, and he brushed a hand across the tabletop. 'Aragan can't have the Council accuse him of meddling, or spying.'

Spindle's brows rose. 'Aragan? That old dog's here?'

Blend and Picker both swore aloud. 'Spindle!' Blend managed, swallowing more curses. 'You brick-headed ox! He's the Oponn-cursed ambassador! You said you knew who you were working for!'

Spindle's face reddened and he stood, heaving back his chair. 'Well he hardly stopped me on the damned street, did he!'

The old historian eyed the three veterans glaring each other down across the room. He raised a hand. 'I'll mind the shop.'

All three blinked and eased out tensed breaths. Picker gave a curt nod. 'Okay then.'

'Where?' Blend asked.

Spindle was frowning down at the historian. 'South of the city. The burial fields. People want to know what's goin' on there.'

'Everyone says that's all tapped out,' Picker said.

'The past never goes away – we carry it with us,' Duiker murmured, as if quoting.

Brows crimped, Spindle scratched a scab on his nose. 'Yeah. Like the man says.'

Blend was behind the bar. She pulled out a set of scabbarded long-knives wrapped in a belt. 'We should head out tonight. Before the Ridge Town gate closes.'

A wide sideways grin climbed up Spindle's mouth. 'Spot their campfires, hey?'

'Just like old times.'

*   *   *

They walked the desolate shore of black sands, over coarse volcanic headlands, and along the restless glowing waves of the Sea of Vitr. Beach after beach stretched out in arcs of pulverized glass-like sands.

As they walked one such beach Leoman cleared his throat and motioned to their rear. 'Do you think he really is what he claims?'

70

Kiska shrugged her impatience. 'I don't even know what it is it claims to be.'

Leoman nodded to that. 'True enough. Not for the likes of us, perhaps.' He stretched, easing the muscles of his shoulders and back.

How like a cat, Kiska thought again. *With his damned moustache – like whiskers!*

'I had a friend once,' he said, after a time of walking in silence, 'who was good at ignoring or putting such questions out of his mind. He simply refused to dwell upon what was out of his control. I always admired that quality in him.'

'And what came of this admirably reasonable fellow?' she asked, squinting aside.

The man smiled, brushing his moustache with a finger and thumb. 'He went off to slay a god.'

Kiska looked to the sky. *Oh, Burn deliver me!* 'Are your companions always so extravagant?'

He eyed her sidelong. The edge of his mouth crooked up. 'Strangely enough, yes.'

Kiska had stridden on ahead to where an eroded cliff blocked the way. They would have to climb.

At the top Kiska could see far out to the empty sea of shimmering, shifting light. Nothing marred it. Behind, the shadowy figure of Maker had re-joined the sky. The entity had returned to what Kiska mused must be an infinite labour. Was it some kind of curse? Or a thankless calling nobly pursued?

She turned her attention to the next curve of beach and her breath caught.

Leoman found her like that, sitting on her haunches, staring, and drew breath to ask what was the matter, but she raised her chin to the beach ahead. He looked, and grunted a curse.

An immense skeletal corpse lay sprawled across the beach. Half its length narrowed down to the glimmering surf where it disappeared, eaten away by the Vitr.

The corpse of a dragon.

They approached side by side. Leoman clutched his morningstars and Kiska her stave – though she knew neither would help them should the beast prove some sort of undead creature. But no sentience animated the dark sockets of its eyes. The flesh of its great snout, itself of greater length than she or Leoman, was desiccated, curled back from the dark openings of its nostrils. Yellowed curved teeth, an alchemist's horde, grinned back at them.

Who had this Eleint been in life? Had it been known to humans? Or was this the extent of its life . . . this one brief titanic struggle to escape the Vitr? The idea made her very sad.

Leoman cleared his throat but said nothing. She nodded, swallowing. As they walked away his hand found hers but she pulled it free. She covered her reaction by walking impatiently ahead to where the beach ended at a tumble of the loose porous volcanic rocks.

After a time, Leoman called after her: 'There's no hurry, lass.'

She hung her head, pausing on the uneven rocks jutting out into the glowing waves of the Vitr. She glanced back to the man; he was coming along slowly, taking great care with his footing.

'We don't know for certain—'

'Yes, yes! I know. Now hurry up.'

He came up beside and offered a wink. 'Wouldn't do to get yourself killed this close, would it?'

'This close to what?'

He brushed his moustache. 'Well, to an answer. One way or t'other.'

'Leoman,' she began, slowly, as she hopped from rock to rock, 'promise me one thing, won't you? Should I fall into the Vitr and get myself burned to ashes.'

'And what is that, lass?'

'That you'll shave off that idiotic moustache.' She jumped down on to the black sands of the next long stretch of beach. 'And stop calling me "lass".'

He thumped down next to her, ran a finger along the moustache, grinning. 'I'll have you know the ladies always love it when I—'

'I don't want to know!' she cut in. 'Thank you.'

'So you keep sayin'. But I promise you you'll—'

Kiska had snapped up a hand. She knelt and he joined her.

Tracks in the sands. Unlike any spoor she'd ever seen, but tracks all the same. When they'd yet to see any at all. Some kind of shuffling awkward walk. She pointed to cliffs inland that the beach climbed to. Leoman nodded. He freed his morningstars to hold them in his hands, the chains gripped to the hafts. Kiska levelled her stave.

They kept to the edge of the rocky headland, slipping inland, keeping an eye on where the beach ended at the cliffs. She saw the dark mouths of a number of caves. She looked at Leoman, pointed. He nodded. Reaching the cliff, she dodged ahead from cover to cover. Behind, a strangled snarl sounded Leoman's objection. The first opening was narrow and she slipped within, stave held for thrusting. The cramped space was empty. But packed sand floored it, and depressions showed where people, or things, may have sat or lain. A population? Here? Of what nature? A sound raised the hairs on the back of her neck. A high-pitched keening. Leoman's morningstars, which he could raise to a blurred speed greater than any she had ever seen or heard tell of.

She leapt out of the cave to see the man facing off a crowd of malformed creatures. Daemons, summoned monstrosities, all somehow warped or wounded. They grasped with mangled clawed hands. The faces of some were no more than drooling smears. Some raised limbs far too crippled to be any danger. Leoman held them off, his back to the cave mouth.

'What do you want?' she yelled. 'Speak! Can you understand me?'

Then the ground shook. Kiska tottered, righted herself and peered up. A gigantic creature had joined the crowd. It appeared to have jumped down from the cliff. It straightened to a height greater than that of a Thelomen. Great splayed clawed feet, like those of a bird of prey, dug into the sands. Its broad torso was armoured like that of a river lizard. It brushed aside its smaller kin with wide, blackened, taloned hands. A huge shaggy mane of coarse hair surrounded red blazing eyes and a mouth of misaligned dagger-like teeth.

She sent one quick glance to Leoman, who nodded, and they both leapt backwards into the cave. In the narrow chute of the entrance she took the forefront; there was no room for morningstars.

A shadow occluded the opening. A deep voice of stones grinding rumbled, 'Who are you, and what do you wish here?'

'Who are you to attack us!'

'We did not attack you – you trespass! This is our home.'

'We didn't know you lived here . . .'

'So. Even when you knew you were the strangers here, you assume *we* are the interlopers. How very typically human of you.'

Kiska looked at Leoman, who rolled his eyes. A lecture on manners was the last thing she expected. 'So . . . this is a misunderstanding? We can come out?'

'No. Stay within. We do not want your kind here.'

'*What?* Now who is being unfriendly?'

'You have proved yourselves hostile. We must protect ourselves. Stay within. We will discuss your fate.'

'Let us out!' Kiska stood still, listening, but no one answered. She edged forward a little and saw a solid wall of the deformed creatures blocking the exit. She slumped back inside against a wall, slid down to the sand.

Leoman eased himself down next to her. He glanced about the narrow cave. 'Damned familiar, yes?'

Arms draped over her knees, she only grunted her agreement.

'We could fight our way out,' he mused.

'That would only confirm their judgement, wouldn't it?'

'I suppose so. I wonder how much time we will have . . .'

She cocked a brow. 'Oh?'

'Because we might as well spend it profitably . . .'

'*Leoman!* Can't you keep your mind off that for one minute?'

He shrugged expansively. 'You need to learn to relax when you have no control over a situation. There is nothing you can do, yes? Now I will rub your back.'

She snorted, but fought a rising grin. 'Leoman . . . you can rub my back if you promise me *one* thing . . .'

*   *   *

Early in the morning Scholar Ebbin approached the main gates of the Eldra Iron Mongers in the west end of Darujhistan. Under the bored eyes of the door guards he waited as wagons and carts came and went, all stopped and inspected by tablet-wielding clerks, their contents counted, itemized and graded. Ebbin stood waiting. Smoke from the foundries belched overhead. A steady rain of soot added to the layers already blackening the helmets, shoulders and faces of the guards.

After waiting what seemed like half the morning – the guards staring ox-like at him the entire time – Ebbin thrust himself forward into the path of one of these soot-smeared scurrying clerks. 'I'm here to see the master,' he blurted out.

Sniggering laughs all around from the youthful clerks. 'Hear that, Ollie?' the addressed one said, turning his back on Ebbin to examine a wagonload of crates. 'Here to see the master.'

The fellow Ebbin presumed to be Ollie answered with a mocking laugh. 'I'll just summon him then, shall I?'

More laughter answered that. Ebbin pulled a scroll from his shoulder bag. 'He gave me this.'

The nearest clerk simply continued his tally. Finishing, he swung an exasperated glare to Ebbin. 'What's this then? You'd better not be wasting my time.' He snatched the scroll from Ebbin's hand and yanked it open, scanned it. He paused, returned to the top to go through it again, more slowly. After finishing the entire letter he raised his eyes to Ebbin; a kind of guarded resentment now filled them. 'Follow me,' said.

With the clerk leading, Ebbin wound his way across the busy yards of the ironworks. They crossed rails guiding wooden cars pulled by soot-blackened sickly mules, past great hangars where smoke billowed and sparks showered like glowing rain. They reached a building that looked to have once been a handsome estate house, but now stood almost entirely black beneath countless years of soot. Dead, or nearly dead, vines clung to its façade, some still bearing leaves thick with ash.

Just within the main doors they met some sort of reception secretary, or higher-ranked clerk. 'Yes?' the pale fellow asked without so much as glancing up. In answer Ebbin's guide shoved the letter in front of him. The receptionist's lips compressed and he took the now soot-smeared vellum between a forefinger and thumb as if it were a dead animal. He gave it a cursory glance, even in the act of tossing it away, then stopped suddenly and slowly flattened it before him. After reading the letter he said, 'You may go.' It was not clear to Ebbin whom the man meant. But the young clerk immediately turned on his heels and left without a word. The man blinked up at Ebbin. 'Follow me.'

The receptionist led him up a wide set of ornate stairs of polished stone. Soot smeared the balustrade and the steps were black with ground-in dirt and ash. The man knocked at a set of narrow double doors then pushed them open. Here in a slim but very high-roofed room waited another cadaverous fellow just like this one. The receptionist set the vellum sheet on the man's desk then returned to the doors. He bowed to Ebbin and made a curt gesture that was somewhat like an invitation to enter. Ebbin did so; the man shut the doors behind him.

The secretary glanced at the letter as he continued writing. The scratching of the quill was quite loud in the upright crypt-like room. 'You are lucky,' he said without glancing up. 'The master is rarely in. If you wait here I will announce you.'

Ebbin hardly trusted himself to speak. A breathless 'Certainly' was all he could manage.

The man set down his quill and blotted the document before him, then pushed back his chair. He knocked on the door beside the desk then went through and quickly shut it behind him. Ebbin waited, rubbing his fingers nervously over the sweat-stained leather strap of his shoulder bag.

The door opened and the secretary brusquely waved him forward. Smiling and nodding, Ebbin edged in past the fellow, who closed the door so quickly he almost caught Ebbin's fingers. The room within was quite large – it might have originally been a main bedroom, or private salon. Tables cluttered it, each burdened by great heaps of documents and folders. Maps covered the dark-grimed walls. Ebbin recognized schematic drawings of mineworks and street maps of Darujhistan, some very old indeed. One map on a far wall appeared remarkably ancient and he was about to head for it when someone spoke from where light shafted in from a bank of dirty windows. 'Scholar Ebbin! Over here, if you please.'

'Master Measure,' he replied, squinting and bowing. 'Good of you to see me.'

The master of Eldra Iron Mongers, rumoured to be the richest man in all Darujhistan, stood at one of the tables, his back to a window, studying a folder. He was rather short, going to fat. His northern background was evident in his black curly hair, now thin and greying. Ebbin recognized the folder in the man's hands as his original project proposal.

'So,' the master announced, 'you are here to request further funding, I take it?'

Ebbin's throat was as dry as the dust swirling in the light shafts that crossed the room. His heart was hammering, perhaps reverberating with the pounding of the forges. 'Yes, sir,' he gasped weakly.

'This would be your . . .' he sorted through the papers, 'third extension.'

'Yes . . . sir.'

'And what do you have to show for my investment?'

Ebbin struggled with the clasp of his shoulder bag. 'Yes, of course. I have some shards that hint at decorative styles mentioned in the earliest accounts . . .' He halted as the master curtly waved a hand.

'No, no. I'm not interested in your knickknacks, or your odds and bobs. What have you *found*?'

Ebbin let go of his shoulder bag. *Gods, dare I say it? What if I am laughed out of this office? Well, no more funding regardless . . .* He took a deep breath. 'I believe I have discovered a vault that may contain proof of the Darujhistan Imperial Age.'

Humble Measure dipped his head in thought, pursed his lips. He started out from behind the table. 'A brave claim, scholar. Isn't it orthodoxy that such an age is mere myth? Whimsical wish fulfilment of those yearning for some sort of past greatness?'

The master had walked to the centre of the room. Looking back at Ebbin, he added, 'As the honoured members of the Philosophical Society point out: surely there would be evidence?'

'Unless it was expunged with the last of the Tyrant Kings.'

The ironmonger crossed to a table bearing great heaps of papers, yellowed maps and dust-covered volumes. He picked something up and turned it in his hands, a card of some sort. He spoke while peering down at it. 'One and the same, then? Scholar? The Tyrants and the city's place as the true power of these lands?'

Ebbin nodded, said, 'I believe so, yes. Back then.'

'And what gives you reason to believe you may be close to such proof?'

'The artistic style of the décor. The architecture of the cenotaph itself. Associated artefacts above from the earliest of the Free Cities period. All evidence points to this conclusion.'

'I see. And this vault?'

'It looks undisturbed.'

'And . . . just the one?'

Ebbin's brows rose in surprise and appreciation at the astuteness of the query. 'Why no. One of twelve, in fact.' *And the thirteenth? The central figure? What of him? Shall you mention him? And the floor of skulls? No! Mere excesses of funerary devotional offerings, nothing more.* He drew a handkerchief from a pocket and wiped his face and the palms of his hands. He felt almost faint with thirst. The slanting yellow rays cut at his eyes.

'Twelve,' the master repeated. 'Such a weighty, ill-omened number for Darujhistan. The twelve tormenting daemons come to take children away.'

Ebbin shrugged. 'Obviously some ritual significance of the number goes back even to the time of the Tyrants. Those old wives' tales of the twelve fiends merely reveal how far we've fallen from the truth of the past.'

The Cat native glanced sharply back at him then, over a shoulder. 'Indeed, scholar. Indeed.' He returned to studying the card. 'You shall have your funding. I will provide labourers, draft animals, cartage. And, because what you find may be valuable, armed guards as well.'

Ebbin now frowned his confusion. 'Master Measure, there is no need for such measures – ah, that is, for such expenditures. Such a large party would only attract the attention of all the thieves and pot-hunters on the plain.'

'Thus the armed guards, good scholar. Now, I own a warehouse close to the Cutter Town gate. My guards will know it. You will bring whatever you find there.'

'But sir. Really, it would be best if I made the arrangements—' The ironmonger had raised a hand, silencing him.

'I will protect my investment, scholar. That is all. Wait without.'

Over the years Scholar Ebbin had not begged and scraped for monies from this man, and many others like him, without learning when to argue and when to obey. And so in an effort to salvage some modicum of dignity, he bowed and left.

Alone, the ironmonger Humble Measure returned to studying the card. It was an ancient artefact of the divinatory Dragons Deck. The single surviving example from an arcania of an age long gone. He held it up to the light and there, caught in the slanting afternoon rays, it blazed pearly white, revealing an image of one of the three major cards of power, rulership and authority . . . the Orb.

*

There is a steep gorge amid the hills east of Darujhistan that all the locals know to avoid. To some it is the lair of a giant. To those who have travelled, or spent time talking to those who have, it is merely home to a displaced Thelomen, or Toblakai, of the north.

Here he had lurked for nearly a year. And though several people had complained to the tribal authorities, no one had organized a war band to drive him out. Perhaps it was because while sullen, and an obvious foreigner, the giant had not actually killed anyone as yet. And the woman who was sometimes with him did eventually pay for the animals he took. And he did seem gruffly affectionate towards the two children with him. Or perhaps it was because he was a giant with a stone blade that looked taller than most men.

In any case, word spread, and the gorge came to be avoided, and developed an evil reputation as the haunt of whatever anyone wished to ascribe to it. The local tribes became comfortable with having someone conveniently nearby to blame every time a goat went missing or a pot of milk soured. A few unexplained pregnancies were even hung upon him – charges the foreign woman with him laughed off with irritating scorn. As she also did their subsequent angry threats to skin the creature.

78

In time, some locals claimed that in the dim light of the re-formed moon they had seen him crouched high on the hillside, glaring to the west, where one could just make out the blue flames of Darujhistan glowing on the very horizon.

Had he been cast out of that pit of sinfulness? Or escaped the dungeon of one of the twelve evil magi whom clan elders claimed secretly ruled that nest of wickedness? Did he plot revenge? If so, perhaps he deserved their tolerance; for the destruction of that blot of iniquity was ever the goal of the clan elders – when they weren't visiting its brothels, at least.

And so an accord of a sort was established between the clans of the Gadrobi hills and their foreign visitor. The elders hoped that flame and sword was what the giant held in his heart for Darujhistan, while the war band fighters were secretly relieved not to have to face his stone blade.

As for the creature himself, who could say what lay within his heart of stone? Had he been thrown out of the city as an irredeemable troublemaker and breaker of the peace? Or had he turned his back on that degenerate cesspool of vice and nobly taken up station in the hills, far from its corrupting influence? Who could say? Perhaps, as some elders darkly muttered, it merely depended upon which side of the walls one squatted.

*

In the estate district of Darujhistan a grey-haired but still hale-looking man walked through an ornamental garden, but he hardly saw the heavy blossoms, or registered their thick cloying scents. His hands were clasped behind his back and his path was wandering. He was a bard who went by the name of Fisher, and he was wrestling with a particularly thorny problem.

He was struggling with his growing impatience and lack of respect for his current lover. In the past such a falling away of allure would have proved no complication. All it took was a tender chaste kiss, a last lingering look, and he was on his way.

No, the problem was that his current lover was Lady Envy. And Envy did not take rejection well. He paused in his pacing, wincing in memory of their last parting. At least he had gotten away alive.

A woman's voice rose in the distance, cursing, and Fisher ran for the white pavilion that graced the middle of the gardens. Here he found Envy sitting cross-legged before a low table of polished imported wood. A scattering of cards lay on the thick rich grain and Envy was cursing a streak of invective that would make a dock porter blush.

'An unhappy future?' he asked in mock innocence, then winced again.

'This is nothing for you to joke about,' Envy answered, imitating his tone. Thankfully she did not look up to catch his pained features.

He made an effort to pull his expression into one of serious concern. 'What is it?'

She held up a card. 'This bastard.'

The Orb. He frowned. 'Yes?'

She eyed him aslant. A smile that hinted at oh so many secrets raised one edge of her lips. 'You have no idea, do you?'

Fisher struggled to hide all signs of his exasperation. Keeping his voice light, he asked, 'Perhaps you would be so kind as to inform me?'

Envy tapped the card to her lips – lips that she had taken to painting a pale blue after the current fashion. She lowered her green eyes. 'No. I think not. This could be . . . diverting.'

Fisher lurched to a sideboard to pour himself a crystal flute of wine. 'A drink, m'lady?' he asked, ever courtly.

'No. Nor should you, I think. I note you are drinking more lately. You should stop. I find it . . . unflattering.'

Turning from the sideboard he leaned back against it and downed the entire glass in one long pull. He crossed his arms. 'Really?'

Lady Envy pursed her sky-blue lips and began shuffling the Deck of Dragons. 'Dearest Fisher,' she said after a time, 'you are a talented man . . . but still just a man. These are matters far beyond you.'

He carefully set the delicate flute on the table. 'Well, then. Perhaps I should ask around.'

Already into a new casting, Envy was quiet for some time. A vexed frown creased her powdered white brow and she bit her lip. She had paused at the final card, which when turned would be the centre of her field. 'Ask around?' she echoed, distracted. She laughed throatily. 'Oh yes. Do so. If you enjoy playing the façade of usefulness.'

Instead of the anger that ought to have answered such a dismissal, Fisher felt only sadness; an ache for what briefly had been, and for the fading promise of what might have been. He bowed to Envy. 'I shall go and play then.'

She did not answer as he walked away.

Envy sat alone for a long time, unmoving, hand poised over the card that would lock the swirling pattern of futures before her. Orb high, of course. Card of authority and rulership. And Obelisk near. Past and future conflating. But what of her? What of Envy?

Shadows crept across the faces of the cards. The sky darkened. At long last Envy steeled herself sufficiently to slide the card from the top of its fellows and hold it over the centre position.

She turned it and immediately let go as if burned. Her hands flew to her throat. She gasped, unable to speak. A great inhuman gurgling yell exploded from her and a burst of power erupted, blowing off the top of the pavilion. Out of the billowing flames stalked Envy. She walked stiff-legged up a garden path, her rich robes scorched and smouldering. Heavy flower blossoms beamed and nodded at her. Snarling, she batted one into an explosion of crimson petals.

A rain of cards came fluttering down around the estate district that afternoon. Aristocratic couples out for a promenade watched, puzzled, as blackened rectangles fluttered down on the roads. Servants pocketed many, recognizing the gold and silver paints and the exquisite, though ruined, quality of production. A tutor hired to knock some sense into the spoiled scions of one noble family saw a card lying on a back servants' way, and bent to pick it up. Having some touch of access to the Mockra Warren, he immediately dropped the thing as accursed.

The focal card, the axis of the casting, fell into the deep shadows next to a hothouse where it lay half-burned on the cool wet earth. It bore on its face the barely discernible remnants a hooded dark figure, crowned in jet night.

The King of High House Dark.

*

The guard walked his rounds of Despot's Barbican as he did every evening. In the dusk the clamour of Darujhistan, the calls of the street merchants and the braying of draught animals, was dying down, although it was still too early for the grey-faces to start on their silent rounds from gas jet to gas jet lighting the blue flames that would pierce the night.

Arfan expanded his chest, taking in a good breath of the cool air wafting in from the lake. It was a good sinecure, this post. If certain parties wanted an eye kept on these dusty ruined monuments to the city's past, then so be it. This retired city Warden was happy to offer his services. There was nothing here to tempt any thief. The hilltop was abandoned. Not like Hinter's Tower. Those ruins gave him chills. Everyone was right to think that place haunted. But not here. The tumbled weed-dotted white stone foundations were silent. On the darkest of nights he could even sometimes see the distant glow of the blue flames flickering through parts of the white stone walls. It was actually rather pretty.

This evening the weather was unusually chill. He hugged himself, shuddering. Very unseasonal. He paced his rounds, stamping his sandalled feet to warm them. In the twilight, over the hilltop ruins, the air seemed to shimmer. Stopping, he rested his spear against the base of a broken wall to rub his hands together. The air seemed to be full of vapour, as after a summer's rain. Yet it hadn't rained in days. He retrieved the spear, then yelped and dropped it. The wood haft was as chill as ice.

Tatters of clouds now flew overhead, sending a confusing riot of shadows over the hill and the city beyond. He squinted in the shifting glow of starlight, seeing something. His wanted to flee but also knew it was his duty to remain, and so he crouched, advancing behind the cover of a ruined curving wall. Up close he saw how condensation beaded the wall, running in drops down the smooth flesh-like stone.

A sudden wind blew up, lifting a storm of dust and litter. Arfan shielded his eyes; it was like one of those sudden dust-devils that arise in the summer's heat. He peered up, eyes slit, and in the shifting shadows and blowing dust he thought he saw something . . . a ghostly image, a watery shimmering mirage: it was as if he stood next to an immense structure. A building, a palace, tall and ornate, which overlooked the city there on the next mound, Majesty Hill. All overtopped by what appeared to be an immense dome.

Then a stronger gust of air and the ghost-image wavered, shredding, to waft away into tatters that disappeared like mist. And he ran . . . well, jogged really, as fast as he could, puffing and gasping, down the hill to bring word to his contact, an agent of the one who styled himself 'circle-breaker'.

Nearby in the old city estate district, among the ruins of Hinter's Tower Hill, the arched entrance to said ruined tower glowed with a ghostly presence. The image of a tall man in torn clothes. His eyes were nothing more than dark empty sockets yet they stared, narrowed, towards Majesty Hill. He mouthed one short word. Only someone within a hand's breath would have heard his cursed, 'Damn.'

His empty gaze edged slant-wise to where a fat winged demon lay snoring among the stones, a half-eaten fish in each thorny claw. The ghost raised a gossamer hand to his chin and tapped a finger to his lips.

*　　　*　　　*

Antsy jerked awake to surf rustling over smoothed shingle, the cawing of seabirds, and a poke in the ribs. He lay among tall rocks just up from the shore of the Rivan Sea. Two kids, a boy and a girl, peered down at him. The boy held a stick.

'See,' the boy announced, triumphant, 'he *is* alive!'

'G'away,' Antsy croaked, and he coughed up a mouthful of phlegm and spat aside. His clothes stuck to him, chilled and wet with dew, and he shuddered. *Too damned old for this bivouacking crap.*

'You want food? I got fish – one crescent each!'

He probed the crusted bloodied cloth he'd pressed to the side of his neck. That had been one damned thin and sharp blade. He wondered whether he'd ever see the young nobleman again. He certainly owed him one.

'Where you from? Darujhistan? You heading out to the Spawns?'

'Why's your hair red?' the girl asked.

''Cause I'm half demon.'

That quietened them. He decided to try to stand. First he leaned on the knuckles of one hand. Then he got to his knees. Next, he brought up a foot and pushed up to lever himself erect. His ankles, fingers and wrists all burned with the morning joint-fire. *Too damned old.*

The girl said in a sing-song voice: 'If you're heading out you're gonna be too late.'

He was scratching the bristles of his chin. 'What?'

'They're already linin' up.'

'*Shit* . . . ah, pardon my Malazan.' He headed for the beach.

The kids trailed him. 'I have vinegared water too. You sure you don't want any fish?'

A crowd had gathered on the far end of the curving strand. Launches rested there, pulled up from the surf. He angled that way while chewing on a slice of smoked meat taken from one pannier bag.

'I got a map of the Spawns too,' the lad said, jumping up in front of him.

Antsy eyed the boy in complete disbelief. 'Thanks, kid, but I can't read.'

The boy shrugged. 'That's okay. The map's still good.'

Antsy barked a laugh. Had he any coin to spare he might've purchased the rag as reward for the lad's salesmanship.

Confederation soldiers guarded the boats. A table stood aslant on the gravel beach. The crowd consisted of men and women apparently waiting their turn to pay the transport fee. Most, Antsy figured, couldn't and were just hanging around. He decided to join the spectators for a while to get a feel for how things worked.

Here, a simple picket of soldiers was barrier enough to keep everyone back. An armed man, he reflected, might be able to fight his way to the boats, but then what? It took at least ten people to handle such huge launches. An armed party then. Ten to twenty to take the boat and oar it out through the surf. But again, then what? Free Cities Confederation ships waited beyond the bay. Your own ship then. But that had been tried. Four private armies had apparently made the attempt – and failed. Only a Malazan warship had forced its way through, and none had seen it since.

A party of five pushed through the crowd of onlookers. They were well accoutred in cloth-wrapped helmets, banded iron armour. They carried longswords, crossbows, and large bags and satchels presumably containing supplies. Four carried large round shields, their fronts covered in canvas slips. The leader wore a long grey tabard over his mail coat. He had a commanding presence, with a great beak of a nose, broken, and a mane of wild blond hair that whipped in the wind.

'You're going?' someone said to Antsy.

He looked over, then up. A dark-skinned young woman stood at his side, slim, and a good two hands taller than he. She wore a dirty cloak over layered shirts and skirting that might have once been fashionable but were now shredded and grimed. Her thick black hair hung in kinked curls, unwashed and matted. Her dark eyes were bruised from hunger and lack of sleep.

'What's the price?' he asked. The girl stiffened and her dark eyes flashed in shocked anger until Antsy raised his chin to indicate the table and the fee-collector.

She relaxed, almost blushing. 'Oh. I thought . . . never mind. About fifty gold councils a head.'

Antsy gaped. 'That's . . . that's pure theft! How can they ask that much?'

She indicated the party. 'Because they get it.'

A price appeared to have been agreed as the fee-collector gestured to the guards. The party of five was allowed to pass.

'Mercenaries from the southern archipelago,' the girl sneered.

'You're from Darujhistan?'

The sneer disappeared and she hunched self-consciously. 'No. The north.'

Her manner struck him as very young and very sheltered. A rich kid out of her element. 'And you don't have the price . . .'

She gave a wry grin. 'You've wangled the truth out of me.'

'You came down on your own?'

'Yes.'

'To find your fortune?'

She hesitated. 'Sort of. You see, I'm a student of ancient languages. I speak Tiste Andii. And I read the script.'

'Bullshit,' was Antsy's gut reaction.

The girl grimaced and tucked long strands of the greasy hair behind an ear. 'That's what everyone says.'

The mix of naïveté and worldly adolescent disgust touched something in him. He wondered how on earth she'd lasted this long among such a lawless bunch. 'Listen. What's your name?'

'Orchid.'

'Orchid? That's your name?'

Another grimace. 'Yeah. Not my idea. Yours?'

'Red.'

'Must be a common name where you're from.'

Antsy just grunted, chewed on the end of his moustache. The man behind the table shouted, 'Anyone else? Anyone else for today's party?'

No one answered. It occurred to Antsy that the girl might have just made a joke. Gathered at one launch, the day's complement of treasure-seekers consisted of the party of five plus four other individuals. The Confederation soldiers began packing up.

'Another day's waiting,' Orchid sighed.

'I'm gonna have a chat with that fellow taking the coin.'

Orchid's hand closed on his wrist. 'Take me with you, please. If you go.'

He gently twisted his arm to free it. He failed. 'I don't know.' He stared at her hand. She followed his gaze and pulled her hand away.

'I'm sorry. It's just that I *have* to go. I don't know why. I just know.'

He stood rubbing his wrist: damn, but the tall gal had a strong grip. How old *was* he getting? 'I'll see what I can do.'

'Thank you.'

The pickets let him through. The two guards at the table merely cradled their crossbows and watched while he stood waiting for the clerk to deign to notice him. Eventually, the man looked up.

'Yes?'

'The price per head is about fifty gold Darujhistani councils?'

The man sighed, started packing his scales and record books. 'Yes. And?'

'What would you give me for this?'

The man didn't stop packing while Antsy placed a leather-wrapped object on the table. It was about the size and shape of a flattened melon. The man gave another vexed sigh. 'No bartering. No trades. I'm not a merchant. I don't want your silverware or your chickens.'

Antsy ignored him. He pulled back a portion of the quilted padding and the man couldn't help but look. He paled, jerked away, then covered his reaction by closing an iron-bound chest behind the table.

'How do I know whether that's real?' he asked after a time.

'You saw the seal,' Antsy growled.

Disassembling the scales the man said, 'Yes . . . but seals can be counterfeited. Replicas can be made. I'm sorry.'

'It's real enough to pulverize everyone on this Hood-damned beach.'

His back to Antsy, the man paused in his packing. 'That may be so. But then you wouldn't get out to the Spawns, would you?' And he turned to study him over his shoulder with a cool stare.

Antsy decided that maybe there were good reasons why these Free Cities Confederation boys had managed to keep hold of the isles. He gave a sigh of his own and eased the object back into the pannier.

'I suggest,' said the man, 'that you sell that to Rhenet Henel.'

'Who's this Rhenet?'

'Why, the governor of Hurly and all the Spawns, of course.'

Antsy just rolled his eyes.

Orchid caught up with him at the cart track. 'Turned you down, hey?'

'Yeah. He didn't like the look of my chickens.'

She frowned, prettily, he thought, then let the comment pass. 'So, where to now?'

He stopped, faced her. 'Listen, kid. I can't get you out to the Spawns. I can't even get myself out. There's nothing I can do for you.'

She bit at her lip. 'Well, maybe there's something I can do for you?'

He had to take a long breath to safely navigate that minefield. *Gods, girl! How naïve can anyone be?* He cleared his throat. 'Yeah. I suppose there is. You wouldn't know where I could get a decent meal round here, would you?'

She took him a few leagues down the shore to what appeared to be nothing more than a camp of refugees squatting among the driftwood of dying overturned trees. 'Welcome to New Hurly,' she said, waving an arm to encompass the ramshackle huts and tents.

'New Hurly? What's wrong with the old one?'

'This is the real Hurly,' she explained, waving to kids and oldsters nearby. She was obviously well known here. Antsy spotted his two would-be guides among a horde of running children. 'This is what's left of the original inhabitants.'

'Here? Why not in town?'

'Driven out by those vulture hustler scum.' She sat on a driftwood log before the smouldering remains of a cook-fire and invited him to join her. 'They have no money so they'd just get in the way, right?' Her tone was scathing.

He grunted his understanding. He'd seen it before: these natural disasters were not so different from war. An old woman ducked out of a nearby wattle and daub hut and Orchid signed to her. She grinned toothlessly and returned to the hut. A moment later she emerged carrying two wooden bowls which she filled from a cauldron hanging over the fire. It was some kind of fish stew. He blew on it.

While they ate the old woman squatted before them, grinning and nodding. He studied the girl. Skin the hue of polished ironwood, slim, hands unblemished and smooth. Educated. A pampered upbringing in some large urban centre. Tutors, fine clothes. All this spoke of a great deal of money yet here she was sitting on a log pushing boiled fish into her mouth with her fingers.

'Good, yes? Good?' the old woman urged.

'Yeah, sure,' he said, uncomfortable under her manic stare. 'Good. Thanks.'

She grinned lopsidedly then took the bowls and returned to the hut.

Orchid watched her go, her gaze sad. 'Lost her husband, three married children and eight grandchildren in the flood. Never recovered.'

Antsy grunted again, this time in sympathy. He'd seen a lot of that too. He cleared his throat. 'So, what do I owe . . .'

'Nothing. You owe nothing. I healed one of her last remaining grandchildren. Had an infection and fever.'

'You're a healer?' That put a whole new perspective on things.

She shrugged. 'A little training and reading. All mundane. I just kept the wound drained, threw together a poultice of some herbs and moss and such.'

He eyed her anew. All this made her a great deal more valuable. Why hadn't she marketed her skills? Hood, they could use her in Hurly. Then he realized: she chose not to offer her services there.

The old woman ducked out of the hut carrying a small water bucket. She offered Orchid a dipper and the girl drank. Antsy had a mouthful as well – it was clean, mostly. 'Orchid,' he began, awkwardly, 'you've hitched yourself to a broken cart. I'm going nowhere fast right now.'

'You'll get out there.'

'How do you know?'

'I have an intuition,' she said, completely without any hint of embarrassment or reserve. 'A feeling. I know you will go.'

He just raised a brow. *Crazies. Why do I always get the crazy ones?*

'So,' she said, breaking the silence. 'What's your next move?'

He studied the blasted tumbled landscape. 'Where can I find the governor of this fair land?'

The governor, it happened, occupied a fort under construction up the shore in the opposite direction. Fort Hurly. Walking to it they crossed an eerie post-flood landscape of dead uprooted trees flattened like grass where stiff seaweed hung from the bare limbs. Skeletal carcasses wrapped in dried flesh lay tangled in the wreckage. Flies were a torment. They quickly became muddied up to their thighs. Orchid's layered skirts hung like wet sails.

Antsy knew they had been followed since leaving Hurly. The fellow wore a dirty brown cloak and made no secret of tagging along at a discreet distance. Antsy had the troubling sensation of being dispassionately studied. Finally, as they clambered over an enormous pile of fallen tree trunks, he decided he'd had enough of the game. He pushed Orchid down behind cover at the natural fortress's peak, whispered, 'Quiet,' and moved off.

From his panniers, waist and leggings, he drew together the

components of his Malazan-issued heavy crossbow. Since he'd spent years field-stripping and reassembling the weapon, he did not have to look at his hands while crouched behind cover, keeping watch. Orchid remained quiet and didn't move and because of this he felt better about possibly taking her with him – should he ever manage to get out.

The man came into view at the base of the heaped logs. He paused as if sensing something. Antsy grinned: a canny devil. He shouted down, 'What do you want?'

The fellow appeared to be considering the climb.

'Don't move! We can have us a little chat just like this.'

'Talk is what I wish.' The voice was soft and low yet carried easily over the distance. The tone bothered Antsy: much too assured given the situation. He stood up, the crossbow levelled.

'All right. Talk.'

The man peered up, his hood shadowing his face. 'That object you showed the fee-collector. I'd like to examine it. I may want to purchase it.'

'Not for sale.'

'How about fifty Darujhistani gold councils?'

Antsy raised his gaze from sighting down the stock, considered. 'I don't trade with someone who hides his face.'

'Sorry,' the man answered, amused. 'Force of habit.' He threw back his hood. His face was scrawny and thin, like a cat's. A small trimmed beard sat on his chin like a smudge of dirt and his black hair hung in thick oiled curls.

A Hood-damned fop. Antsy didn't like him already. He raised the weapon to rest it on a hip. 'All right. Back away. I'm coming down.'

Gloved hands out from his sides, the man backed away. Closer, Antsy was struck by the fellow's wiry leanness, his knife-like slash of a mouth. A cruel mouth, he decided. And small eyes that seemed to glitter like polished obsidian stones.

The fellow pointed to the crossbow. 'No need for that.'

'That's my call and I've decided to keep it.' Raising his voice, he shouted, 'Orchid! Bring down my bags. Bring them here.' She carried the bags down and laid them next to him. 'Careful now, take out the wrapped package there. Set it between us – gently.'

A sideways smile on the man's mouth seemed to be calling attention to how silly all this was. 'You're a careful man, soldier. I want you to know I respect that.'

Antsy didn't bother answering. Orchid had stopped rummaging and now peered up at him, uncertain. 'The largest one,' he told her.

Nodding, she drew out a wrapped packet, set it between them, then backed away. The man knelt, unwrapped and studied the dark green oblong. Without looking up he asked, 'You are trained in its use, I presume?'

'Aye.'

The man straightened. 'Then I would like to hire you for my expedition to the Spawns.'

Orchid's breath caught.

'And how many are there on this expedition of yours?' Antsy asked.

The man smiled again. 'Two, now.'

'Three.'

The smile fell away. The man edged his head aside. 'Three?'

'The girl here. She's a trained healer and claims she can read the Andii scribblings.'

'Really? Read the language? Hardly possible. Let me see you, girl.'

Orchid raised her chin, a touch nervously.

'You say you can read the Tiste Andii script?'

She nodded.

'Answer carefully, girl. If I find that you've lied then I'll leave you out there to die. Do I make myself clear?'

Orchid nodded again, barely. 'Yes.'

From his demeanour Antsy knew the man would do just that. And so, rather belatedly, he hoped the girl wasn't overstating her skills.

They returned to Hurly. Antsy made sure the fellow walked ahead all the way. He led them to another of the many inns and taverns that dotted the boom town: the Half Oar. They took a table and the man excused himself to go to his room above.

As soon as he'd left the table Orchid whispered, fierce, 'I don't trust him at all.'

Antsy chuckled. 'Damned good that you don't.'

'He's a killer.'

'Probably. But is he an honest killer?'

'How can you joke like that? He makes me shiver.'

Antsy pulled his hands through his tangled hair. 'Look, you want to get out to the Spawns and he's willing to take us. One thing you can be sure of – there'll be a lot more like him out there already. And I get the feeling it's better he's with us than against us.'

They ordered tea and shortly after that the man returned. The cloak was gone, revealing a vest of multicoloured patches over a black, billowy-sleeved silk shirt. The black matched his hair, beard and eyes. 'So,' Antsy asked, 'what's your name?'

'You can call me Malakai. Yours?'

'Red.'

Malakai smiled thinly. 'And the girl is Orchid, I understand,' he said, his eyes not leaving Antsy's. 'An interesting name.'

A serving boy offered vinegared water to drink, then a mid-day meal of roasted waterfowl. They tore the carcasses apart with their hands. 'We'll leave on tomorrow's boat,' Malakai said. 'You, Red, will be my guard. And you, Orchid . . . well, just look imperious.' The girl seemed to shrink under his gaze. 'Speak and read the language, do you?'

She straightened her shoulders. 'Yes.'

'How came you by this rare gift?'

The girl visibly braced herself, pushed back her unruly mane of hair. She seemed to be taking his questions as some sort of test administered before fifty gold councils were thrown away. 'I was raised in a temple monastery dedicated to the cult of Elder Night. Kurald Galain, in the ancient tongue. The nuns and priests taught me the language, the rituals and the script.'

'And are you a talent in that Warren?'

The girl deflated. She shook her head, 'No. That is . . . sometimes I *feel* as if something's there. But no, I could never summon the Warren.'

Malakai frowned his exaggerated disappointment and Antsy squirmed, uncomfortable with the enjoyment the fellow took in baiting the girl. The man set his chin in his hands. 'Tell me, then, what you know of the history of Moon's Spawn.'

Orchid nodded, took a drink of water. Her gaze lost its focus and she spoke slowly, as if parsing some text visible only to her. 'No one really knows the origins of what we call Moon's Spawn. It emerged from Elder Night, but what was it before then? Some argue it is the remnant of a K'Chain Che'Malle artefact that ventured into Kurald Galain and was taken by the Andii. Perhaps. Others suggest it was found abandoned and empty deep within the greatest depths of Utter Night. In any case, Anomander Rake brought it into this realm together with a legion of his race, the Tiste Andii, who followed him as he was the son of their sole deity, Mother Dark.'

Antsy gaped his amazement. He'd heard all kinds of legends and tales touching upon these ancient events, but this girl spoke them as if they were the literal truth!

She resumed after another sip. 'For ages the Spawn floated over the continents, roving everywhere. We know this to be true as it figures in almost every mythology in every land. During these ages its inhabitants rarely involved themselves in human, or Jaghut, or K'Chain affairs. All that changed however with the rise of the Malazan Empire and its ruler, Kellanved. For some reason the Emperor gained Anomander's enmity. Some suggest a failed assault upon the Spawn by Dancer and Kellanved.'

She shrugged, clearing her throat. 'In any case, Anomander opposed Malazan expansion here in Genabackis. From that fell out the engagements up north, the siege of Pale, the Spawn's fracturing and fall, and all the unleashing of Elemental Night at Black Coral.'

Listening to this litany a memory suddenly possessed Antsy: staring up at the dark underside of that suspended mountain while below Pale burned, a city aflame. Then, the ground shuddering, his ears deafened, as all the old Emperor's High Mages summoned their might against its master . . .

He shivered, blinking and wiping his eyes.

Neither Malakai nor Orchid seemed to have noticed. The man was nodding, his gaze distant as if in meditation. 'He would've won, I think, had not the Pale Hand thaumaturges betrayed him and gone over to the Malazans.

'You wanted him to win?' said Orchid, outraged.

Malakai continued nodding. 'Oh, yes.'

'You'd support the inhuman over the human?'

The man's smile was a knife blade. 'I admired his style.'

Antsy cleared his throat. 'So, tomorrow. Supplies? Equipage?'

Malakai leaned back, swung his lizard gaze to him. 'In my room. I have rope, oil, lamps, dried food. We need only purchase water.'

'And crossbow bolts. I'll need more of them.'

Malakai shook his head. 'I think you'll find that more than enough of them have already been taken out to the island. Those and other things.' His dark gaze fixed on the gouged tabletop. 'There's probably continual warfare on the isle. We may be attacked the moment we land. For our food, our supplies. The ruins have been a lawless hunting ground for over a year. The stronger parties have probably carved out claims, territory. There might even be a form of taxation for passage. Very probably slavery. I've heard that no one has returned for over two months now. It may be that newcomers are simply killed out of hand as useless mouths to feed.'

Orchid stared, plainly shaken by this calm assessment.

'And you were prepared to step into the teeth of that alone?' Antsy said.

The man smiled as if relishing the prospect. 'Of course. Weren't you, too?'

Antsy took a drink to wet his throat. 'Well . . . I suppose so.' Truth was, he hadn't really given much thought to what might be awaiting him on the islands. All his plans had been fixed on just getting out there. After that, well, he imagined he'd see which way the wind was blowing. Stupid, maybe. But he had his shaved knuckles in the hole and rare skills to offer. Besides, things may not be as bleak as this morbid fellow would have it.

'Friends of yours, Red?' Malakai whispered into the silence.

Startled, Antsy looked up from his scarred knuckles. Three men now crowded the table. His friend from last night, Jallin, and two toughs. The Jumper sported a large purple bruise on his temple where Antsy knouted him. Antsy rolled his eyes. 'For the love of Burn, lad! What is it now?'

Jallin carried a truncheon tight in both white-knuckled hands. His lips drew back from his small sharp teeth. 'Three councils is what it is now.'

'Three?'

'Interest.'

'What's this about?' Orchid asked.

Jallin's eyes, sunken and bloodshot, flicked to her. His lips twisted into a leer. 'Seen you around. Finally broke down and sold the last thing you got left, hey?'

Antsy cut off Orchid's shout. 'Call it a day, lad. Don't push this one.'

The youth's laugh of contempt was fevered. Antsy wondered when he'd last had a meal. Jallin glanced at his companions. 'Hear that? The man arrives yesterday and all of the sudden he's the governor. Well, I'll tell you, old man – you hand over them bags and we're even and no one gets hurt.'

'That I cannot allow,' said Malakai.

Jallin jerked a glance down to the man as if seeing him for the first time. He gave a twitched shrug of dismissal. 'Stay out of this if you know what's good for you.'

Malakai's slash of a mouth spread in a big wide smile. Antsy noted that Jallin's companions were nowhere near as confident as he. One licked his lips nervously while the other eyed Malaki with open unease.

Malakai raised his gloved hands, palm down. He turned them over and suddenly both held throwing knives. He turned them over again and the knives disappeared. He did this over and over again, faster and faster, the blades seeming almost to flicker in and out of existence. The two thugs stared, fascinated, almost hypnotized by the demonstration. For his part, Antsy wondered whether what he was watching was the product of Warren manipulation or pure skill.

Finally, jarring everyone, a blade slammed into the table before each of the two hired toughs. Both flinched back, and then, sharing a quick glance, continued their retreat leaving Jallin standing absolutely still, his mouth working. All eyes shifted to the youth, whose chest heaved as if winded. 'Damn you to Hood's paths. I swear I'll have your head!' He threw the truncheon, which Antsy deflected with a raised forearm. Then he marched out after his companions.

Orchid clearly wanted to ask what all that had been about, but instead her gaze swung to Malakai and Antsy watched her begin to wonder just who this was she'd entered the service of. As for himself, he now understood why the man was willing to venture out to the Spawns alone: there were probably damned few out there who could trouble him. The fellow struck him as a cross between his old army companions Quick Ben and Kalam. He wondered who he was and what he wanted out there. And just what he had sold himself into for fifty gold councils.

Malakai simply returned to studying the tabletop as if he'd already forgotten the incident and was unaware of their quiet regard.

CHAPTER III

In ancient times a Seguleh came shipwrecked to the shores near Nathilog. The local ruler, thinking to impress upon him the strength and power of his city state, took the warrior upon a tour of the ringed-round cyclopean walls, the thick towers, and the deep donjons that was the fortress of Nathilog of that age. When the long detailed demonstration was finished the ruler turned to the man, saying, 'There! Now you may return to your home and convince your fellows of our impregnability and might!'

The Seguleh replied: 'I have but one question.'

'Yes?' the ruler invited.

'Why do you live in a prison?'

Histories of Genabackis
Sulerem of Mengal

A S WAS HIS HABIT, SCHOLAR EBBIN ROSE EARLY AND WAS THE FIRST to have tea. He found that the old hag was three times as sullen as before now she had to cook for three times the men. One of Humble's new guards was also up, pacing over the beaten dusty ground of the Dwelling Plain, a cloak wrapped tightly about him. The two guards Ebbin had hired weeks ago lay snoring next to the smouldering remains of a bonfire. He sighed.

Still, somehow he'd felt safer with just those two incompetents watching camp. Captain – and he doubted the man really *was* a captain – Drin had made it very clear that he worked for Humble Measure, just as did he, Ebbin. This uncomfortable truth rankled as he'd always thought of himself as a free hand, more independent iconoclast than employee.

Also, from time to time he'd seen the guards watching inwards towards camp as much as outwards towards any potential thieves or marauders. Sometimes Ebbin felt more like a prisoner than a client. Shrugging, he tossed away the rest of his tea and went to collect his equipment and to wake the two Gadrobi youths.

At the well, he unlocked the cover and shoved it aside. Captain Drin was there with his four men. Ebbin's two guards had also tagged along uninvited. Ebbin almost laughed. Seven guards! For what? A few potsherds. A handful of votive funerary offerings. Nothing of any true monetary worth. Some silver perhaps, but little gold. It was the artistic style and the subject matter that would be explosive. Potential proof of an erased, or systematically suppressed, Darujhistani Imperial Age.

The captain peered down into the dark pit. He motioned to his men. 'Strap your gear.'

Ebbin eyed the man while he secured his helmet and tied his shield to his back. 'Ah . . . Captain. Only I need go down.'

'No longer.'

An almost speechless panic gripped Ebbin. He wiped his sweaty hands on his thighs. 'It's dangerous – the rope. The youths are not strong enough . . .'

The captain yanked on the rope, grunted his satisfaction. He pointed to Ebbin's guards. 'You two – you can man the winch.'

Ebbin's panic turned to a sudden possessive anger. He stepped up before the hired sword. 'My find, Captain,' he said, low and firm. 'There's no need for you or your men. You'll only get in the way. You'll unknowingly damage or trample precious artefacts. You would be interfering in a delicate excavation.'

A lazy smile crooked up behind the man's beard. He touched a finger to the point of a long iron chisel protruding from Ebbin's shoulder bag. 'Delicate. Right.' The man was peering down with oddly veiled eyes, as if he were not really seeing him at all. 'It's settled, scholar. Humble Measure's orders. We come along to oversee his interests. Whatever you find – it's his.' He motioned to the sling seat. 'Now, if you please . . . you first.'

Down in the tunnel opening Ebbin crouched, lit lantern in hand, awaiting the captain. His dread was now like a caged rabid animal racing round and round his skull. What of . . . *it*? The figure? What if they . . . disturbed it? Yet what if they did? Gold held no fascination for him. Humble Measure was welcome to all the loot he wanted. Why should this alarm him?

Yet it did. He felt an unreasoning dread of that supine waiting figure. So exposed, so . . . inviting. He wanted to cringe from it in terror.

When the captain arrived Ebbin helped him find his footing in the tunnel, then backed up a ways to make room for the others. Drin had picked two of his men to accompany him, leaving two at the well-top – along with Ebbin's men, of course.

'Captain,' he said, whispering in the dark, 'there's a figure in the tomb . . . I don't want you or your men touching it . . . disturbing it. Do I have your word?'

The man squinted at him, his face wrinkling up in scepticism. 'What d'you mean?'

'A body, lying on a plinth. It's not to be disturbed.'

'Whatever you say, scholar.'

Somehow Ebbin was not reassured.

When the next two had entered the tunnel, Drin motioned for Ebbin to go on. Lantern raised high before him, the scholar edged his way forward on hand and knees. Once within the large round burial chamber the three guards stood stock still for a long time, hands on strapped sword hilts, their eyes bright and big in the gloom. Eventually their gazes found the figure lying exactly as before, at the very centre of the chamber, within the arches that resembled two large rings carved of stone. The beaten gold mask gleamed in the lantern light. The graven smile seemed to welcome them. Their gazes rarely left the figure as Ebbin led them to the remaining sealed side-niche. He set down his shoulder bag, began getting out his tools.

'Since your men are here, Captain,' he said, 'I could use some help.'

Peering back over his shoulder at the figure, Drin grunted his agreement. He motioned to one of his men. Ebbin handed the guard one of the special alloyed chisels supplied by Aman. 'If you'll hold this steady . . .' He showed the man where he wanted the chisel on the door slab, then raised the hammer he'd packed down the tunnel.

While Ebbin carefully tapped, the captain stood behind, watching. 'Twelve,' Drin mused, sounding much more subdued now in the dark confines of the tomb. 'Like the stories my old grandpa used to tell. The Twelve Fiends . . .' He shook his head in remembrance. '"Be good", the old guy used to warn, "or they'll come steal ya away."'

'This one's still sealed,' Ebbin said, and he blew on the scarring now visible on the face of the slab.

'Aye. The others all looted. But not this one . . . nor him,' and he jerked a thumb to the chamber's centre. 'Like they was interrupted, maybe.'

Ebbin swept at the face of the slab with a fine horsehair brush. It looked as if a crack was developing. 'Perhaps they meant to return to finish the job – but never made it back.'

'Maybe.' The captain sounded unconvinced.

A desperate urge to hurry was on Ebbin, yet at the same time he was painfully aware that this was his one chance, his gods' sent opportunity to salvage his reputation. To make a name for himself and overturn many past insults. And so he took his time despite the guard's wandering attention and the heat that gathered in the confines of the tomb sending drops of sweat down his nose and neck, and making his hands slick.

Boredom had driven the captain and the second guard from his side. They poked through the other chambers only to report them all empty, as Ebbin knew.

A crack now ran horizontally across the slab, close to the top. He planned to take off the upper section then reach behind to pull or strike the rest outward, thereby avoiding damaging any artefacts which might lie near the entrance. He grunted his frustration as a few shards fell within. The guard with him could not suppress a flinching retreat as the seal was broken. 'It's okay,' Ebbin murmured. He raised the lantern to peer within, but couldn't make out anything defining. The niche appeared no different from the eleven others. 'Could you . . .' He mimicked a yank on the remaining section of stone slab.

The guard reluctantly put down the chisel. Behind, the captain came from where he'd been leaning against one of the stone arches, staring at the figure on its black onyx plinth.

'Go ahead,' Drin said to his man. The fellow took hold and pulled. The stone ground and scraped. The man tried again, jerking, pushing against the wall with one booted foot. He grunted, cursing, but the slab would not budge.

'Let me.' Drin pushed the man aside and took hold, tensing. Ebbin was impressed by the breadth of his bunched shoulders, his thick roped forearms. The man snarled, his breath hissing from him as he pulled. A crack shot through the slab like the strike of a slingstone. Dust billowed from the seal round its edges, then it juddered outwards to fall crashing to their feet.

Studying the fallen rock, Ebbin suddenly recognized the pattern. All the other niches shared it. All their doors had been pulled outwards to fall into the chamber. Pulled out . . . or pushed. Sudden renewed panic clenched his throat. He could not swallow; his heart seemed to be bashing against his ribs. He raised the lantern to reveal something lying on the plinth within. A corpse.

It was nothing like the figure behind them. This thing was quite obviously dead. And not human. It was massive, its bones far thicker and more robust than those of any human. Its desiccated fingers ended in bear-like yellowed talons, as did the toes of its naked feet.

'Demon,' Captain Drin breathed.

Ebbin stepped within for a closer look. He was confused. This was not what he'd expected. Not at all. Where was the artwork? The funerary offerings?

Something caught his eye: a cold white gleam shone from deep within the cadaver's hollow chest cavity. Ebbin bent closer. It was a pale stone bearing the oily shimmer of the insides of shells. Perhaps it was a pearl itself. Ebbin reached for it.

'Find something?' the captain warned, his voice suddenly tense.

Startled, Ebbin snatched his hand away, glanced over. 'I'm sorry . . . ?'

Drin was reaching out one hand while his other closed on the kit of his drawn weapon. 'No, scholar. It's me that's sorry. Measure's orders, y'see . . .'

A yell of warning from behind snapped the man's attention round. He gaped, '*Shit!*' and ran, drawing his sword.

Ebbin ducked from the niche to see the two guards struggling with the figure from the plinth beneath the spans of the arches. The two mouthed yells and screams yet no sound reached Ebbin. The captain was running for them.

'*No!*' Ebbin shouted too late. The captain swung a great two-handed blow that appeared to have no effect on the cloaked and masked figure, which had lashed out and caught one of the guards. While Ebbin watched, petrified, it gripped the man's neck with one hand and with the other pulled the gold mask from its own face. Ebbin glimpsed a ruin of sinew and rotted flesh over bone, and stood rooted to the ground in horror as the fiend ignored the increasingly frenzied attacks of Drin and the other guard and slowly, inexorably, pressed the mask to its victim's face.

The guard fell to his knees, pulling frantically at the mask, but he was unable to move it. Transfixed, Ebbin watched as the cloaked figure disappeared in a great swirling cloud of dust and the dark cloak fell empty to the floor.

Some sort of invisible barrier held the captain and the remaining guard beneath the intersecting arches. They screamed unheard commands at Ebbin, who could only shake his head in mute appalled terror, while behind the two men the corpse of their fellow climbed to his feet. The gold mask shimmered brightly in the lantern light, its mysterious graven smile now horrifying in its promise. Ebbin pointed, his other hand covering his mouth.

The two men turned. It seemed to Ebbin they both leapt in shock, dismay and terror as they realized what awaited each in turn. The captain swung a huge two-handed blow at his ex-guard's neck but the corpse took it on an arm. Though the strike slashed along the bone, flensing that arm, no blood flowed, and the revenant was not slowed.

The captain danced away out of reach. The remaining guard punched at whatever barrier it was that held him captive. Falling to his knees he held out his arms to Ebbin, pleading, begging, as if this were somehow all the scholar's doing. From behind, his dead companion wrapped an arm round his neck, and tearing the mask from his head – in the process pulling away the flesh which brought up Ebbin's gorge in a gasping heave of vomit – clamped the mask over the other's face.

When Ebbin looked up, wiping his mouth, coughing, only two figures remained within the arches. The captain and his last guard. Drin was retreating round and round the onyx plinth, always giving ground before the slow relentless advance of the masked fiend.

Ebbin could only sit and watch, fascinated, helpless. As time passed he decided that there must have been good reasons why this man Drin was a captain. How long had he held out? How many hours caught there in the confines of his inescapable prison, avoiding his unkillable foe? He himself would not have lasted more than the first minute. Yet for what seemed half a day this man had ducked and flinched aside, postponing his end. Occasionally he would dash in to aim a blow at his enemy's neck, perhaps in the hope that decapitation would end the curse. But Drin faced something extraordinary – blades damaged it, but it seemed that none could bring it down. No blow could dismember it, or slow it.

Finally, after hours of that macabre dance around the raised plinth, Captain Drin turned his strained, sweat-sheathed face to Ebbin. He mouthed something, perhaps 'Remember me'. Ebbin wasn't sure. Though no soldier, he roused himself to salute the man.

The captain nodded in bleak acknowledgment and then, throwing aside his sword, launched himself upon the creature. Legs clamped around the renevant's waist, he clasped both hands on the mask and worked to yank it free. Ebbin's heart leapt in admiration: *Yes! If he can dislodge the mask before it is set upon his face! Perhaps then this curse will somehow be broken . . .*

Though a bear of a man, Drin was no match for the fiend. One by one, his fingers were prised from their grip on the gold, and the fiend took hold of the mask himself.

Ebbin looked away. *Gods! Was there no escape for anyone? Was this to be his end as well?*

After waiting a time, his limbs twitching in dread, he could not help but glance up.

All was as it had been before under the arches. A figure lay upon the black stone plinth, dark cloak wrapped tight, gold mask covering its face. But Ebbin knew that Captain Drin, or at least his body, now bore that mask. As for the others, all the countless others who preceded him, well, there was plenty of dust on the floor of the chamber.

The scholar staggered to his feet, gathered up his shoulder bag. There was nothing here. This whole tomb was just one gruesome trap. A trap for those foolish enough to come digging up the past. Everything he had ever hoped for was now shattered. He stumbled for the exit. On the way he froze and his gorge rose again in a wrenching dry heave.

Set in the stone floor of the chamber lay three fresh skulls. The bare bone of two still gleamed wet with gore.

*

After the guards descended, Scorch and Leff peered down into the darkness of the well for a time before wandering over to the shade of a lean-to to return to teaching the two Gadrobi youths how to play troughs. The boys didn't seem able to grasp the basic arithmetic; or perhaps the problem was their own disagreements over the rules. Humble's remaining two guards sat down to lean against the stone lip of the well.

Leff tucked an arm under his head, sighed, 'If only we were still with her ladyship, hey? Too bad . . .'

Scorch threw the carved knuckle dice so hard they bounced from the board to disappear into the dirt. The two youths hunted for them. 'What was that?' he answered, his voice low.

'What was what?'

'Was that an impercation? 'Cause it sounded like maybe you was makin' an impercation!'

Leff pushed himself up on his elbows, rolled his eyes. 'Gettin' all huffy won't change the facts, Scorch.'

'*Facts*? And just what facts might those be?'

'That it was you that lost us the job with Lady Varada.'

'I did not—' Scorch threw up his arms. 'Tor explained it. The lady didn't want so many guards no more. So who gets the axe? Why, us outside guards, right? Plain and simple. That hierarchy thing, right?'

Leff waved that aside. 'Didn't you see through all that bullcrap? I did. Tor was just coverin' up the truth. Sparin' our feelings.'

His shoulders falling, Scorch frowned, uncertain. 'Really? Then ... what was he really sayin'?'

'That it was you lost us the job.'

Scorch threw himself aside to sit facing the opposite direction.

Towards noon the old hag came limping up to the lean-to. She shooed the youths away, gabbling in Gadrobi, then turned on Scorch and Leff. 'You two, get out!' she spat. 'You go! Bad things come. I see in the sands. In smoke!'

Scorch and Leff shared a knowing look. 'Better stay off that fermented goat's milk,' Leff said. 'That kefir can sneak up on ya.'

The old woman waved an angry dismissal. 'Die then . . . Daru dogs!' And she scuttled off.

Leff stretched out, yawning. 'Keep a watch, Scorch,' he said, and closed his eyes.

Around mid-afternoon Leff awoke to the screeching of the winch. The guards were raising it. He and Scorch wandered over. It was the scholar, Ebbin. Scorch leaned over to help him out, then lurched as the man seemed to fall into his arms. Leff helped to yank him over the lip of the well and set him down in the dirt where he lay panting, his face gleaming pale as milk.

'Where's the captain?' one of the guards asked.

'Water,' Ebbin gasped, and Leff helped him to sit up while Scorch went to fetch a skin. The scholar took a long drink, then splashed his face and pulled out a cloth to wipe it dry. 'Down below,' he breathed, hoarse. 'A trap. They were taken.'

'Taken?' the guard echoed.

Ebbin nodded. He appeared on the verge of tears.

'Show us,' the guard said.

Ebbin gaped up at him. 'What?'

The guard stepped back and drew his longsword. Scorch and Leff eyed one another, set their hands on the grips of their shortswords. Ebbin struggled to his feet. '*Show you?*' He laughed. Rather unnervingly, Leff thought. 'You have no idea—'

The second guard raised a cocked crossbow. 'You show us, old man. Or die now.'

Ebbin looked from one to the other, pressed his hands to his face and moaned from behind his fingers: 'Gods forgive me . . .' Then he brushed Scorch's hand from his weapon. 'You wish to see?' he asked the guard. 'Truly *see?*'

The man gestured to the well with his longsword. 'You first.'

'If you must.' Ebbin looked at Scorch and Leff. 'You two. Lower us.'

Leff scratched his cheek, bemused. 'Well – if you say so, scholar.'

'Those are my orders.' He swung his feet up over the stone lip of the well, began readying the sling seat.

'We come back up first,' the guard warned.

Ebbin gave a long slow nod. 'Yes. You first.'

It seemed to Leff that no sooner had the second guard descended than the rope shook with a signal to be raised. He and Scorch rewound the barrel winch to bring it back up and were surprised to see that the occupant of the sling seat was Ebbin. Scorch helped him out.

'And the guards, sir?' Leff asked. 'They saw?'

The scholar was sickly pale and panting once again. He drew a cloth and wiped at his sweaty face. He nodded. 'Oh yes. They found out what happened to their captain.'

'So . . .' Scorch began, 'we wait for 'em?'

'No. They won't be coming back up.' Ebbin held his brow, looking faint.

'You all right, sir?' Leff asked.

'No. I . . . I don't feel well. I need to get back to Darujhistan.' He nodded with sudden vigour. 'Yes. That's right. I must go to Darujhistan.'

'We'll pack up the camp then,' Leff said.

'No! You two wait here. Guard the camp. Wait for me. Yes?'

Leff frowned, doubtful. 'Well . . . if you say so.'

Ebbin took his forearm. 'Excellent. Thank you.' He paused, blinking, then glanced about as if confused. 'Now, you'll close up here, yes? You won't go down?'

Scorch and Leff eyed one another: *the man's mad!* 'No, sir. You don't have to worry about that. We ain't goin' down there.'

'Good! Good. I knew I could trust you. Now, I must go.

'Go? Now?' Leff raised a brow. 'Night's comin', sir. We really shouldn't let you go all alone. Can't you wait till tomorrow?'

Ebbin jerked as if stung. 'No! I must go! It is important . . . I feel it.'

Scorch and Leff exchanged looks. Scorch inclined his head, indicating that Leff should accompany the scholar. Leff flinched, offended, and pointed back. Scorch gestured angrily that Leff should go. Leff's hand went to his sword grip and he glared his defiance.

'Uncle!' a voice called from the gathering dusk and both guards spun, hands at weapons.

A slim girl was suddenly quite close. She wore loose white robes that rippled in the weak evening wind. Her feet were bare. Rings glinted gold on her toes.

Ebbin stared at the girl in utter incomprehension. 'Uncle?'

'Yes,' she answered, smiling. She took the man's arm, leaning against him. 'May I call you that? I feel there is some sort of connection between us, yes? You feel it too?'

Scorch cleared his throat. 'Ah, miss? You lost?'

She ignored him so completely it was as if he hadn't spoken. She whispered something into Ebbin's ear and the scholar's brows rose. 'Really? From *him*?'

She nodded eagerly. 'Oh yes! And he is ever so keen to hear what you have found.'

Ebbin passed a hand over his eyes. 'Gods! What I have found! Yes. Of course.' He turned to Scorch and Leff and rubbed his eyes, squinting, as if trying to focus on them. 'Ah, you two. I will go with this girl here. You two stay.'

The guards shared another look. 'I think,' Scorch began respectfully, 'you should both come back to camp with—' He stopped because the girl had flicked out an arm and a knife blade appeared in her hand. Its razor tip hovered a finger's width from his throat.

'You have seen and heard enough,' she said.

'No!' Ebbin shouted, rousing himself. 'Ignore them. They have no idea . . .'

The girl's kohl-ringed eyes, now touched by a deep smouldering crimson, slid to the scholar. The arm flexed and the blade disappeared. She bowed her head. 'As you command, Uncle.'

But Ebbin had staggered off. 'Darujhistan,' he was muttering. 'There's something . . .'

The girl remained a moment, eyeing the two men. A smile played about her full lips as she enjoyed their extreme discomfort. Then she winked and blew a kiss at each, and sauntered off after Ebbin.

Leff let go a long tensed breath.

'Gods below,' Scorch murmured.

'Reminds me of the Mistress.'

Scorch cocked his head. 'Yeah. Don't she just. Now what?'

'Now?' Leff kicked at the lid of the well. 'Now I'd say we're out of work again.'

'*Shit.*'

*

Lying flat on the crest of one of the low rises of the Dwelling Plain, Picker watched the white-robed girl escort the old man north. If they kept going in that direction they'd make the trader road to Raven Town, then on to Darujhistan. A long hike, but if they didn't stop at an inn they'd make Darujhistan near dawn.

A noise from the dark behind her announced Spindle's presence and she slid backwards down behind the rise.

'See that?' Spindle hissed from the dark.

'Yeah,' she answered drily. 'I was watchin'.' Struck by a thought she raised her chin to the north, asking, 'What does your mum say about that girl?'

Spindle reflexively rubbed his shirt. 'My mum tells me to watch out for girls like that.'

Picker grunted her agreement. 'Well . . . she was right.'

'Course she's right! She's a witch!'

Picker paid no attention to the tense in that statement since the man's shirt was woven from his mother's hair, and that shirt was the main reason he was still alive.

'Now what?'

'Now?' Picker gave a slow shrug in the dark. 'Maybe we should eyeball that well.'

'Hunh. Well, I ain't goin' down.'

She raised a hand as if to slap him. 'Course no one's goin' down! Six go down. One comes up! They ain't payin' us enough for that!'

'Where's Blend anyway?'

'She's around. C'mon. Let's see if those two guards are gone yet.'

Blend joined them at the well. She just appeared out of the dark, as was her way. Picker examined the wooden lid and the lock. 'All back like nothin' happened.'

'Mark it,' Blend said. 'We may have to describe its location.'

Picker used a rock to scrape the side – a mark that would only mean something to a Malazan marine.

Spindle had been standing motionless as if listening, and now he raised a hand for silence. He pointed frantically to the well. Picker stilled, listening. A blow from down below. Falling stones, rubble. A muted splash. Another strike, like a punch. Closer. She raised her stunned gaze to Spindle who was now backing away, a hand pressed to his chest over his shirt. Picker signed a *retreat* and scrambled for cover.

Moments later some sort of blast sent the wooden lid erupting into the night sky where it turned over and over, hung for a moment, then fell with a crash.

A figure climbed from the well. He wore a long dark cloak and a mask. The mask caught the moonlight and for an instant it glowed like a moon in miniature. Then the man turned away to walk off north, calmly and regally, as if out for a stroll in his own pleasure garden.

'Did you see that?' Picker breathed. She eyed Spindle behind their pile of stones. 'What does your mum say about *him*?'

'I think she would've shat herself.'

'Well, I nearly did.'

Spindle drew his crossbow from beneath his cloak. 'I say we give him lots of room.'

Picker nodded. 'Oh yeah. Plenty.'

*

It was all very confusing for Ebbin. He knew that he had to get back to Darujhistan – though *why*, he didn't really know. It was some sort of instinct, or overwhelming certainty. Then a girl appeared in the middle of the plain and claimed to have been sent by Aman. Even more strangely, somehow he recognized her, though he was sure he'd never seen her before in his life.

Then they set out on a damnably trying walk. His legs ached beyond anything he'd ever experienced. The soles of his feet felt as if they'd been hammered all over by truncheons. And he was having hallucinations. Sometimes it seemed as if the entire Dwelling Plain was one huge urban conglomeration of square flat-roofed mud-buildings all jammed together. Smoke from countless hearth fires rose into the night sky while he and Taya walked the giant city's narrow crooked ways.

Of course, Ebbin realized . . . the *Dwelling* Plain!

Far ahead, glimpsed through the narrow gaps in the tall mud walls, there sometimes reared some sort of domed edifice like a monument, or immense temple. Its pallid stone glowed with a pale blue luminescence that seemed somehow familiar. At other times the great urban sprawl lay smashed in flaming ruins all around, the victim of some sort of titanic upheaval.

When they entered Raven Town he wanted to stop rest, but somehow he couldn't bring himself to demand that they stop. And the girl, Taya, was pushing him along like some sort of draught animal and constantly shooting quick looks behind. It seemed as if she was actually frightened of something.

Could it be . . . *him*? No, that would be too terrible to imagine. Too awful.

And there, on the main street through town, within sight of the closed city gate, who should stand waiting wrapped in a shabby cloak but Aman himself? Ebbin stared — he'd never seen him stick his head outside his shop, let alone leave it.

The man waved Taya onward then wrapped one crooked arm round Ebbin as if supporting him. Ebbin tried to tell him what he'd seen, all the horrors, but somehow he couldn't force the words past his throat. Aman started force-marching him along in his own slow crablike limp. Ebbin glared ferociously at him as if he could somehow send his thoughts to him but the man just patted his arm. 'There, there, good friend. It'll all be over soon enough.'

What would be over? This nightmare of a night? Or far more than that? Ebbin dreaded the answer. As they closed on the gates the great iron-bound leaves improbably swung open to greet them, and there was Taya. She waved them in.

Aman frog-marched him onward. Like Taya, he too was glancing behind, squinting with one eye, then the other. What was back there? Ebbin tried to look but the shopkeeper forced him on. They passed through mostly empty streets. In one of the market squares the early morning vendors were busy setting up their stalls and arranging their goods. Ebbin and Aman marched through with no one paying them any particular attention. Taya was still with them. Sometimes she shadowed them closely and Ebbin caught sight of her glowing white robes. At other times she was nowhere to be seen.

They reached the main east-west thoroughfare that ran alongside the Second Tier Wall. Aman hugged Ebbin closely, as if afraid he would run off, but the scholar was too confused to muster any sort of resolution. At times he didn't recognize any of the streets they walked. Tall white-stone buildings faced the roads, great estates, their façades richly decorated with scrollwork. Fanciful miniature creatures, some winged, peeped out amid the scrolls and stone forests.

And Ebbin recognized the style. It was the fabled Darujhistani Imperial baroque.

But perhaps this was all nothing more than his own deluded wish fulfilment. He wondered, terrified, whether the horrific events in the mausoleum had finally driven him over the edge. Perhaps he *was* mad. His peers, the scholars and researchers of the Philosophical Society, had already dismissed him as such.

He remembered a chilling definition of insanity he'd read in some wry old commentator's compendium: when you think everyone around you is mad, that's then you should start to suspect it's actually you.

They reached the ruined old gates to the estate district and here another figure awaited them. This one appeared to be no more than a dark shadow, a tall man in tattered clothes, a ghost. Ebbin flinched away but Aman marched him right up to the wavering, translucent shade.

Taya, now with them, curtsied to the ghost. 'Uncle,' she murmured.

Aman bowed mockingly. 'Well met, Hinter.'

The shade arched a brow in lofty disparagement. 'Aman. We'd thought you dead.'

The hunched shopkeeper waved to indicate his bent body. 'Who could have survived, yes?'

'Indeed.'

'All is in readiness?' Aman enquired.

'All is ready,' the shade responded tartly, 'since I am left with no alternative. He comes?'

Aman shook Ebbin by his shoulders. 'Oh yes. *He* comes. Always a way, scholar. There is always a way. If it is nearly impossible to break in – then perhaps one must reverse one's thinking, yes? I am sorry, scholar. But no one has ever escaped him.'

The shade turned away. 'Not true,' it murmured. 'One did.'

Aman sniffed and rubbed his lopsided face. '*Him*. I never did believe that.'

*

Spindle and Picker followed the masked man up the Raven Town trader road, all the way into town. It was eerie the way no one was about. Dogs ran before it. Early morning merchants and farmers turned sharply to take side streets, or quickly entered shops and buildings lining the way. The man had the entire road to himself. Picker passed men and women crouched in the dirt beside it, hands covering their faces, shuddering. She yanked a hand away from the face of one old farmer only to provoke gabbled terror and tears.

The fellow strode majestically along right up to and through the open Raven Town gate. A city gate that should not be open. Picker signed to Spindle to check out the west gatehouse then slipped into the east. Blend, she knew, would keep tabs on their friend. Inside she found the guards dead, thrust through with swift professional cuts. Their young little sprite? Or another? An organization? Their guild friends?

She exited to see Spindle, who signed that on his side all were dead. She did the same. Together they trotted on after Blend. They found early risers in the streets but all were silent, all turned to face the walls. Picker pulled one burly labourer round but only to find him weeping, his eyes screwed shut.

At the spice-sellers' square they found the morning market already set up in a maze of carts, mats laid out and stalls unfolded, but utterly silent and still. People crouched, hiding their faces, or lay on their sides as if asleep. Picker swallowed to wet her throat, tightened her sweaty grip on her long-knife. Then Spindle touched her shoulder and pointed up to the paling clear night sky.

'Would ya look at that.'

*

Ambassador Aragan awoke with a start and a curse. He flailed about searching for a weapon.

'It's all right, sir!' a familiar voice yelped, alarmed. 'It's me sir!'

Aragan sat up, blinking in the dark. 'Burn's teats, man! What hour is it?'

'Just dawn, sir.'

'This better be good, Captain.'

'Yes, sir. It's the Moranth mission, sir. They're fleeing the city.'

109

Aragan gaped at the captain then shut his mouth. '*What?*' He threw himself from his bed, searched the floor. Captain Dreshen held out his dressing gown.

'This way, sir.'

Dreshen led him to what had originally been a front guest bedroom but was now an office of trade relations. Here night staff crowded the windows looking over the city. Aragan pushed his way through to the front. The pre-dawn was a paling violet in the east, the brightest stars still blazing above. His heart sinking, Aragan saw the obscene green streak over the setting, mottled moon. He made a sign against evil, though he knew the gesture was meaningless. After all, every escaped cow and dead chicken was blamed on the damned thing, so there was no way of knowing what influence, if any, it may be exerting on anyone's life.

Movement caught his eye. Winking, glimmering, flashing high over the city. Quorl wings – a flight of the giant dragonfly-like creatures taking their Moranth masters west, to the Mountains of Mist, which some called Cloud Forest. Aragan was reminded of the Free Cities campaign to the north and similar night flights and drops over Pale and Cat.

Even as he watched, another wing took flight, heaving up from rooftops around the quarters of the Moranth embassy. The quorls turned through the air, wings scintillating like jewels in the pre-dawn light, and arced to the west. Aragan watched them go, feeling both terrified and exhilarated. He pushed away from the window, faced his aide. 'Rouse the garrison, Captain. Order full alert.'

The aide saluted. 'Yes, sir.'

'And fetch my armour.'

*

Picker ducked reflexively as quorls swooped overhead sending stalls toppling and garments and powdered spice flying.

'Dammit to dead Hood!' Spindle swore. 'Is it a drop?'

Picker covered her eyes from the stinging spice. 'No. A pick-up. They're runnin'.'

'Fanderay . . . maybe we should too.'

'Not yet. We've been hired to recon. So—' She broke off as a whistle sounded. 'That's Blend. This way, c'mon.'

They halted at the corner of a wide boulevard. Blend stepped out of shadows to meet them. 'You lose him?' Picker asked.

'Hood no. Walkin' right up aside the Second Tier Wall, plain as day. Headed for the estate district.'

'You see them quorls?' Spindle asked.

Blend eyed him as if he were demented. 'You two hang back. I'll tag along.'

Picker nodded. 'Right.'

Spindle handed over a satchel. 'Take this . . . insurance.'

She held the bag away from herself. 'This what I think it is?'

'Yeah.'

She shot him a dark look. 'Been holding out on us?'

'No more than anyone else.'

'That's not an answer,' Blend growled.

'I know.'

*

An old woman was shouting herself hoarse in the narrow crooked paths through the Maiten shanty town west of Darujhistan: 'Pretty birdies! Pretty birdies! Look all at the pretties!' In the twilight before dawn the garbage-sorters, beggars and labourers groaned and pressed their thread-thin blankets to their heads.

'For the love of Burn shut up!' one fellow bellowed.

The women, already up preparing the meals for the day, fanned their cook-fires and watched the old woman pointing to the lightening sky as she staggered up and down the alleys. They looked at one another and shook their heads. There she went again. That crazy old woman – proving all the clichés their men kept mouthing about old women who lived in the most rundown huts at the edges of towns. Someone should let her know what an embarrassment she was.

And where did she come by all that smoke, anyway?

'Almost now! Almost!' the old woman shouted. Then she fell to her knees in the mud and streams of excrement and loudly retched up the contents of her stomach.

The women pursed their lips. Gods, the menfolk would never let them live this one down! Someone ought to guide her to the lake and set her on a walk up a short pier.

Problem was – the women knew she really *was* a witch.

*

The fat demon, who was about the size of a medium breed of dog, sat dozing amid the tumbled broken rock of the ancient ruins. Grunting, it coughed, then choked in earnest, flailing. Clawed fingers thrust their way into his mouth, seeking, then withdrew holding a long pale fishbone.

The demon sighed its relief, adjusted its buttocks on the rocks and cast a cursory glance to the stone arch opposite. It froze.

Oh no. Nononononono. Not again!

It launched itself into the air. Its tiny wings struggled to gain purchase, failed. It bounced tumbling downhill, gained momentum, succeeded in lifting its dragging feet from the weeds and took off slowly and heavily across the city like an obscene bumblebee.

Once more it had that word for its master. That most unwelcome word.

*

She'd been irritable of late. Distracted. Short-tempered. If Rallick was the type of man to be dismissive of women he might've characterized her as catty. Not that he would dare intimate such a thing to Vorcan Radok, once mistress of Darujhistan's assassins. And so it was some time before he finally worked up the determination to mention the topic of the professional killings in the Gadrobi district. He alluded to it over dinner. Her gaze in response had been withering. She sipped her wine.

'And you think I'm responsible. Taken work on the side?'

'I don't know who did it,' he responded, honestly enough.

But that had been enough to break the spell between them. She retired alone and he sat up late into the night in turn damning her as an unreasonable prickly woman and damning himself for allowing anything to come between them. When he finally lay down she was asleep – or pretending to be.

She'd been sleeping poorly lately. Tonight she tossed and turned, even murmured a language he'd never heard before. So he was not surprised when she rose naked and padded across to the open terrace doors to stare into the blue radiance that glowed over Darujhistan. He came up behind her, set his hands on her shoulders. 'What is it?'

'Something . . .' she breathed, head cocked as if listening to the night.

'Should I—' She lifted a hand for silence. He stilled, trusting her instincts.

Then, astonishingly, the skin beneath his fingers flashed almost unbearably hot. For an instant it was as if he held the spiny, gnarled back of a boar, or a bull bhederin, and Vorcan flinched backwards, brushing him aside like a child. '*No!*' she ground out. 'How could . . .'

112

She went to the bed, began throwing on clothes.

'What is it?'

Dressed, she stopped before him. Something new was in her dark eyes. Something that stole his breath, for real fear swam in those deep pools. 'Leave the estate now,' she told him. 'Do not return. Do not try to contact me. Go.'

'Tell me what it is. I'll—'

'No! You will do *nothing*.' She pressed a smooth dry palm to the side of his face. 'Promise me, Rallick. No matter what happens, what comes, you will not act. No contracts, no . . . attempts.' She rose on her toes to brush her dry hot lips to his. 'Please,' she whispered.

He nodded, swallowing. 'If you insist.'

She backed away from him into the darker gloom of the bed-chamber, those dark eyes holding his. He dressed quietly while listening to the night, trying to hear what she might've heard. But he detected nothing – as far as he could tell it was just unusually still and quiet.

Downstairs, Vorcan's one servant, the butler-cum-castellan Stud-lock, who never seemed to be off duty, let him out. Rallick listened to the many locks being ratcheted back into place behind him, then set out into the night.

*

In the tallest tower of his grounds, Baruk stood looking out over the estate district of Darujhistan. For a moment he looked not upon the night-sleeping buildings as they lay now but upon another city, one of a profusion of towers much like his, all aglow with a flickering ghostly blue illumination. And amidst all the towers, rearing far more immense, a great dome encompassing Majesty Hill. Then he passed a shaking hand before his eyes and glanced aside, down to where a shivering, whimpering Chillbais crouched, terrified, but not quite so terrified as to not be chewing on a loaf of old bread.

'Was he waiting?' Baruk mused. 'Waiting for Anomander to be gone?' He drew his hand down his chin. 'I wonder.' He went to the door, turned as a final thought struck him. 'You are free to go, Chillbais. Your service is done.' He pulled the door shut behind him.

Fat loaf of bread jammed in his mouth, the demon peered about the empty room. *Free? Free to go where? Free to do what? Oh dear, oh dear. Free perhaps to be enslaved by something far worse? No no no. Not I.*

Chillbais waddled to a clothes chest, struggled up over the side to tumble in, then pulled the top closed.

*   *

Aman dragged Ebbin to the ruins atop Despot's Barbican. Here, he turned to face the way they'd come, a fist tight on Ebbin's shirt.

'Why are you doing this?' Ebbin asked in a plaintive whisper.

Aman slapped him. 'Quiet. Your turn will come.'

'He is near,' the shade of Hinter said.

Aman tilted his crooked head in order to look skyward. 'The moon is not right,' he warned.

'Soon,' answered the shade.

Taya ran up. Her gossamer silks blew behind her like white flames. 'He is here.'

Aman pushed Ebbin to his knees then lowered himself on to one knee. He shook Ebbin, snarling, 'Bow your head, slave.'

Ebbin could not have kept his head erect if he tried; something was hammering him down. Some unbearable pressure like the hand of a giant was squashing him as if he were an insect. A whimper slipped from him as he glimpsed the dirty bottom edge of a dark cloak before him.

'Father,' Aman murmured. 'We remain your faithful servants.'

Ebbin whimpered, shaking. This was not for him. Such scenes were not to be witnessed by such as he. The pressure – the iron hand grinding him into the dirt – eased, and he caught his breath.

Aman straightened, yanked him up. 'Stand now.'

He complied, but would not raise his gaze beyond the mud-spattered edge of the cloak. *So, now it was his turn. A hand would clasp his arm or shoulder and the mask would be pressed to his face. He would be blind behind it, unable to breathe. He would die choking. And then . . . and then . . . what? What was this thing before him? Would he then become . . . it?*

Some force compelled Ebbin's gaze upwards. His eyes climbed to the oval gold mask, now a glowing circle of reflected light. The mysterious mocking smile engraved there was sly now, as if he and it shared some hidden knowledge unguessed at even by those surrounding them.

The cloaked figure raised a hand, gesturing, and Aman bowed again. 'Yes. Spread out. Guard all approaches. Let none interfere.'

Ebbin was left alone with the creature. What had they named it? *Father?* In truth? Perhaps the title was merely honorific. Now would

114

it do it? Take him? His knees lost their strength and he fell to the ground. *Gods! Why this agonizing delay? Won't it just end things?*

Standing above him the creature held out its right hand, pointed to Ebbin's. Mystified, Ebbin looked at his own right hand. It was fisted, the knuckles white with pressure. *When did . . .* His breath caught. He remembered the tomb. He remembered reaching . . .

Oh no. Please, no . . .

Something was in his fist. It was hard and round. Ebbin's heart lurched, skipping and tripping, refusing to beat.

Oh no. Oh no, no. Please no.

He held out his hand. It was oddly numb, as if it were someone else's. He unclenched his fingers and there on his palm rested the gleaming white pearl from the last niche of the sepulchre. Moonlight shone from it like molten silver.

Please! I beg of you . . . do not make me do what I think you will demand. Please! Spare me!

The creature raised its head to the night sky, and for an instant Ebbin had the dizzying sense that the moon was no longer in the sky but on the mask before him.

A pale circle. A pearl . . . of course! It was so obvious. He would have to warn everyone! He—

The creature raised a hand above that smiling uplifted mouth. The fingers were pinched together as if holding some delicacy, a grape or a sweet, then opened there above the mouth. The moon lowered to regard him. Its enigmatic smile was now one of triumph.

Oh no.

*

At Lady Varada's estate its two remaining guards, Madrun and Lazan Door, were engaged in their timeless ritual of tossing dice against a wall when one bone die refused to stop spinning. Both watched it, wonder-struck, as it turned and turned before them.

Then screaming erupted from the estate. They ran for the main hall. Here they found the castellan, Studlock, in his layered cloths as if wrapped in rags, blocking the way down to the rooms below. The continuous howling was not just one of fear. It sounded as if a woman was having her hands and feet sawn off.

Studlock raised open hands. 'M'lady gave commands not to be disturbed.'

The two guards peered in past the catellan. 'Would you listen!' said Madrun. 'Someone's got her.'

'Not at all,' soothed Studlock. 'M'lady is experiencing an illness. Nothing more. You may characterize it as something like withdrawal. I will prepare suitable medicines this moment – if I have your word not to go below! M'lady values her privacy.'

Madrun and Lazan winced at a particularly terrifying scream. 'But . . .'

Studlock shook a crooked finger. 'Your devotion is commendable, I assure you. However. All is in hand. Oil of d'bayang, I believe, is called for. And alcohol. A great deal of alcohol.' The castellan shuddered within his strips of cloth. 'Though how anyone could consume such poison is beyond me.'

Lazan stroked his face and jerked as if surprised when his fingers touched his flesh. He tapped his partner on the shoulder and the two reluctantly withdrew.

Behind them the tormented howling continued throughout the night.

*

In the deepest donjon beneath his estate High Alchemist Baruk knelt before a large diagram cut into the stone floor and inscribed in poured bronze, silver and iron. In one hand he held out a smoking taper with which he drew symbols in the air, while with the other he flicked drops of blood from a cut across the meat of his thumb.

In mid-ceremony the locked, warded and sealed iron-bound door to the chamber crashed open and a gust of wind blew out the taper and brushed aside the intricate forest of symbols lingering in the air.

Baruk's shoulders fell. '*Blast.*'

He lunged for the middle of the concentric rings of wards but something seemed to yank on his feet and he fell short. His arms, which crossed the rings of engraved metal, burst into flames. The robes fell to ash, revealing black armoured limbs twisted in sinew. His hands glowed, smoking, becoming toughened claws. The yanking continued. He scrabbled at the stone floor, gouging the rock and the metal bands.

'*No!*'

He flew backwards, stopped only by his clawed hands grasping the stone door jamb. He hung there, snarling, while the stone fractured and ground beneath his amber talons. The stones exploded in an eruption of dust and shards and he was whipped away up the hall to disappear.

Rallick entered the Phoenix Inn to find the common room uncharacteristically subdued. The crowd was quiet, the talk a low murmur, tense and guarded. He nodded to Scurvy, the barkeeper, as he crossed to the back. Here Kruppe sat at his usual table. A dusty dark bottle stood before him, unopened. Rallick pulled up a chair and sat, noted the two glasses.

'What are you celebrating?'

The fat man roused himself, blinking as if returning from some trance. 'I? Celebrating? Neither. I invite you to join me in giving witness. *We* shall drink to the inevitable. The unavoidable. The relentless turning of the celestial globes in which all that was before shall be again. As it must.' He took up the bottle and began picking at its seal.

'What are you going on about?'

Tongue pressed firmly between his teeth, Kruppe answered, 'Nothing. And everything. Chance versus inevitability. How those two war. Their eternal battle is what we call our lives, my friend! Which shall win? We shall see . . . as we saw before.'

For a time Rallick watched his friend wrestling with the bottle, then, sighing his impatience, snatched it from him and began picking with his knife at the tar-like substance hardened around the neck. 'What drink is this?' he asked. 'I've not seen the like. Is it foreign? Malazan?'

'No. No foreign distillation is that. It is sadly entirely of our own making. And very sour it is too. It was set aside long ago for just this foreseen occasion.'

'And the occasion?' Rallick managed to remove the last of the old wax.

Kruppe reached for the bottle but Rallick jammed his blade into the cork and twisted. The fat man winced, yanking back his hand. He studied his fingertips as if burned. 'Nothing important,' he murmured. 'Everything is connected to everything else. Nothing is of more significance than any other thing.'

Twisting and twisting, Rallick drew out the cork. He handed back the bottle. Kruppe took it, gingerly.

'So we're celebrating nothing?' Rallick said, arching a brow.

Kruppe raised the bottle. 'You are most correct. This is nothing to celebrate.' He tilted the bottle to pour. Nothing appeared. He tilted the bottle even further. Still nothing emerged. He held the bottle upside down over the glass, shook it, and not one drop fell. Rallick took it from him and held it up to one eye. He handed it back.

'Empty. Empty as death's mercy. What kind of joke is this, Kruppe?'

Kruppe frowned at the bottle. 'An entirely surprising one, I assure you, dear friend.'

Rallick raised a hand to Jess. 'If you're too tight-fisted to spring for a bottle you just have to say so, Kruppe. No need for cheap conjuror's tricks.'

The squat man suddenly grinned like a cherub, his cheeks bunching. He raised a finger. 'Ahh! Now I have the way of it. The bottle was not empty at all!'

Rallick grimaced his incomprehension. 'What?'

'No. Not at all, dear friend. What you must consider, my dear Rallick, was that perhaps it was never full to begin with!'

Rallick just signalled all the more impatiently for Jess.

*

In the slums west of Maiten the old woman sat slouched in the dirt before her shack and inhaled savagely on a clay pipe. The embers blazed, threatening to ignite the tangled nest of hair that hung down over her face. She sucked again, gasping, her face reddening, and held the smoke far down in her lungs, her eyes watering, before releasing the cloud in a fit of coughing. She wiped her wet lips with a dirty sleeve and staggered uncertainly to her feet.

'Now is the time,' she murmured to no one. 'Now it is.' She reached for the open doorway to her shack, tottering. She managed to hook a hand on either side of the ramshackle wattle and daub edge to heave herself inside then fell, fighting down vomit.

She felt about in the dirt until one hand found a bag which she clutched to herself and curled around, sometimes giggling and sometimes weeping. The weeping became a sad song crooned hoarsely in a language none around her understood. She lay cradling the bag for some time.

*

Atop Despot's Barbican, Aman, Taya and the shade of Hinter made their way through the maze of ruined foundations to return to their master's side. Aman fell to his knees in obeisance, saying, 'Yes, Father?'

118

Hinter bowed, as did Taya. Her eyes shone with wild exhilaration as she peered up at the masked figure. She noted the body of the scholar lying nearby and kicked it. The man grunted, stirring. 'This one lives?' she asked aloud.

The masked creature gestured. Aman grunted his understanding. 'He will speak the Father's will.'

The girl sneered. 'This one? Him? He is nothing.'

'Exactly,' Hinter said. 'A slave. He will never be a threat.'

'And speaking of slaves!' Aman suddenly crowed, peering down the hill.

Among the ruins some *thing* was clawing its way to them. Blackened, smoking, it made its agonized crippled slither all the way up to the mud-smeared edge of the masked creature's cloak. There it lay, face pressed to the dirt. Aman cackled his enjoyment of the sight. Hinter merely shook his head. Taya's face lit up with avid glee. She knelt to prod the sizzling body, raw and crimson where cracks revealed deeper flesh. 'Is this . . . *her*?'

'No,' said Hinter. 'It is Barukanal.'

The grin inverted to a pout. She searched the hillside. 'No others?'

'They appear to have eluded the Call,' Hinter mused, thoughtful. 'For the moment.'

Taya straightened from the smoking body. 'What is to become of him then?'

'He is to be punished,' came a new voice and the three turned to regard Scholar Ebbin who was now sitting up, a hand over his stomach, the other over his mouth, horrified shock on his face.

After a moment of silence, the city eerily still beneath them, Taya cleared her throat. 'So,' she asked Aman, 'is that it? Is it done?'

'It has merely begun,' Hinter said. And he pointed an ethereal arm to the sky.

Taya looked up and her face lit with child-like pleasure. 'Ohhh . . . Beautiful!'

*

At first Jan thought he dreamt. A voice was calling him. Distant at first, it seemed faint, gentle even. He saw his old master, the last First, sitting cross-legged before him. On his face was not the pale oval mask of all other Seguleh, painted or not. Instead he wore coarse wood, unpolished and gouged, worn to remind its bearer of the imperfection and shame of his people.

As always, the dark sharp eyes behind the mask studied and

weighed him. Then, alarmingly, the mask tilted downwards as if in apology. *I am so sorry*, the wiry old man seemed to say.

Then the image exploded into smoke and a far more distant figure now stood in the darkness, cloaked, tall and commanding. Upon his face was not the crude wooden child's mask, but a beaten golden oval that shone cold and bright, like the moon. And in his dream Jan bowed to the mask.

Yet it was not the bended knee and lowered head of devotion freely given to his old master. In his dream Jan was sickened to find that he had no choice.

He awoke, his body shivering in a cold sweat. A light tap at his door sounded again. He reached out and drew on his mask. Rising, he picked up the sword that lay next to his bedding and crossed to the door. A servant was waiting, head lowered.

'Yes?'

'The Third and Fourth await without, sir. And . . . others.'

'Thank you.'

Jan slid the door shut and threw on a shirt, trousers and sash. He went to the front. There in the night, their servants holding torches aloft, waited his fellows of the Ten, the ruling Eldrii. They bowed.

'You felt it?' Jan asked.

Six masks inclined their assent.

Jan answered their bow. 'We are called, my friends. As was promised us so long ago. Ready the ships.'

And they bowed once more.

CHAPTER FOUR

And he who knew many conflicts
spoke these words:

Where have the swordsmen gone?
Where is the gold giver?
Where are the feasts of the hall?

Alas for the bright dome!
Alas for the fallen splendour!

Now that time has passed away,
dark buried in night,
as if it had never been!

Where lay the servants,
wound round with wards?
Brought low by warriors
and their cruel spears.

Now storms beat
at rocky cliffs,
the bones of the earth
harbingers of storm.

All is strife and trouble
in earthly kingdoms.
Here men are fleeting.
Here honour is fleeting.

All the foundation of the world
turns to waste!

Song of the Exiles
Cant

NTSY SPENT THE NIGHT ON THE COMMON ROOM DIRT FLOOR. Malakai paid for that and a room for Orchid. Money, it seemed, wasn't an issue for the man. She woke him up in the morning bleary-eyed and hung over; he'd brooded far too long into the night over far too many earthenware bottles of cheap Confederation beer. That the ale went on to Malakai's bill made the drinking all the easier, and his funk all the greater. His friend Jallin made no reappearance and Antsy decided that maybe he'd seen the last of that skinny thief.

Malakai brought down six fat skins of sweet water, two bulging panniers and a coil of braided jute rope, and piled the lot beside Antsy and Orchid. Antsy took the majority of the waterskins, the rope, and one pannier to balance his own. He wondered resentfully whether the man had taken them on merely to serve as porters. Malakai wore his thick dirty cloak once more, but now, in his black waist sash and on two shoulder baldrics, he carried as many knives as you could collect from shaking down an entire bourse of Darujhistani toughs. Each was shoved into a tight leather sheath so it wouldn't fall out or rattle. The man caught Antsy eyeing the hardware and smiled, waving a leather-gloved hand. 'For show,' he said.

Orchid took the second pannier. She too was unable to look away from all the pig-stickers. Malakai led the way, and though Antsy listened he didn't hear the faintest rattle or tap. The man still moved as silently as a shade. Antsy shivered, reminded of certain assassin-types he'd served beside over the years; then he shrugged and thumped along behind: better with him than against him. Leaving the inn he winced as the bright morning glare stabbed his eyes.

The day's fee-collecting had already begun. They entered the crowd, but unlike yesterday, when Antsy had had to push his way through the press, it parted before them as if everyone sensed that something was up. The faces he passed betrayed hostility, curiosity, resentment, and even smug smiles as if some knew what waited out at the Spawns – and it wasn't pretty.

Malakai handled the transaction. Antsy experienced a moment of light-headed avarice when the man tipped a stream of cut rubies on to the tabletop. Whatever this man was after out at the Spawns, riches could not be it. He probably already possessed enough to purchase a title in Darujhistan. Free Cities Confederation troops escorted them to the launch.

'So you made it safe and sound, I see,' a voice greeted Antsy when he jumped up and swung his legs into the tall boat. Malakai, already within, turned to the voice, his eyes narrowing dangerously. There, ensconced at the stern, sat the young Darujhistani nobleman from the Island Inn who'd probably saved Antsy's neck.

Antsy touched Malakai's arm. 'It's okay. I met him here.' Malakai just turned away to occupy the prow.

Antsy leaned over the side to help Orchid up. She tried to clasp his hand but he avoided that to show her the wrist grip. He hauled but barely raised her; the girl was surprisingly heavy. *Must be her damned height.*

'Wait,' said the young sword who had moved next to him. He jumped over the side and knelt before Orchid. 'You may stand on me, m'lady.'

Orchid stared at his bent back as if it were some sort of cruel trick – he would tumble her into the surf or move aside at the last instant. 'Go ahead, lass,' Antsy growled. 'Give the damned fool your boot.'

She planted one muddy shoe on his back and, steadied by Antsy, swung the other over the side. Looking rather embarrassed, she sat down among their equipment. Antsy helped the nobleman back up. 'Thanks,' he told him. 'And thanks again.'

'Yes. Thank you,' Orchid added, her flushed face turned aside.

'It was nothing,' and the young man bowed.

'Anyone else!' a guard bellowed from the beach. 'Anyone else for today?'

'So, what's your name?' Antsy asked.

The lad bowed again, brushed back his long brown hair. 'Corien. Corien Lim. Honoured, sir.'

Antsy cocked a brow. 'Honoured? What in the Abyss for?' He touched his neck. 'It's me who's grateful.'

The lad smiled. 'Honoured to meet a veteran. I am a great admirer of your, ah, military organization.'

Antsy lost his ease and frowned, glancing about. 'Yeah. Well. Keep that under your damned hat.'

The youth laughed. 'It is quite obvious to everyone, sir, I assure you.'

Confederation guards began pushing the launch out. Antsy steadied himself. 'Sir? I ain't no Hood-damned officer.'

'Your name, then. If you would?'

'Red.'

Corien's gaze rose to his hair. 'Admirable alias.' Grinning, he bowed to Orchid and returned to the stern.

Antsy sat amid the coiled rope and piled panniers. 'Thanks for all your help,' he muttered aside to Malakai. But the man continued to ignore everyone, his gaze on the horizon and the black dots of the distant Spawns.

Glancing back, Antsy watched the crowd diminishing on the beach. He caught eyes glaring daggers at him. It was Jallin sending doom and destruction upon his head by way of the evil eye. The youth drew a finger across his neck in a universal gesture. Antsy simply turned aside: he was on his way while the thief was stuck in Hurly. And that, he decided, must lie at the root of the youth's fanatical hatred.

The crossing took most of the day. First, the twelve guards rowed them out to a waiting double-masted Confederation coaster. Here they were offered smoked meats and kegs of water at outrageous prices. They declined. The sails were raised and they headed south, crossways to the prevailing easterlies.

Antsy watched Corien strike up conversations with the sailors. Easy charm, that one had. Boundless confidence that seemed to flow into anyone he addressed. Had to watch out for that. Confidence got you killed. Better to be careful. Better to be . . . suspicious.

He settled into the deepest shade he could find on the coaster's deck. He unwrapped his grinding stone, spat on it, and set to work on the edges of his long-knives. He knew they thought he was crazy, all his buddies in the army. They sure looked at him askance whenever he gave his opinion. But he was also just as sure he'd long ago come to the deepest truest secret about how to stay alive . . . and it was one most people either didn't want to know, or couldn't face up to.

The truth is that the goal of existence is to kill you.

Once you grasped that essential truth it was pretty much everything you needed to know in a nutshell right there. He'd learned that the hard way, growing up working Walk's fishing fleet and then in the army. Of course, the world always won in the end. The only real question was just how long you could hold out against all the infinite weapons and tools and stratagems at its disposal. The only way he'd succeeded so far was in always expecting the worst.

'Look at him,' Orchid snorted from where she leaned against the ship's railing. 'The peacock fool. Can't he see they're just stringing him along – laughing at him?'

Antsy turned an eye on Corien, still joking with the sailors. 'Maybe. Where's our employer?'

She peered round the deck. 'Don't know. He sort of disappeared the moment we got on board.'

'Good.'

She pulled her wind-tossed long hair from her face, peered down at him, puzzled. 'Why?'

He let out a long breath, brushed a thumb across the long-knife's edge. *Good enough for hack 'n' slash work.* "Cause who's to say these Confederation boys are gonna deliver us to the Spawns?' Now the girl looked completely thrown. *Poor lass . . . not fit the world, you are.*

'Whatever do you mean?'

He shrugged. 'No one's come back, right? So who's to say they don't just dump us over the side?'

'But – that would be murder!'

He winced. 'Keep your voice down, lass. And yeah – it would. But these boys are pirates and wreckers for generations. Nothing new for them.'

'No. I don't believe it.'

Like always. Denial of the discomfiting truth. He hugged his pannier to his lap. 'Yeah. Well. Let's just hope so.'

The Spawns grew to the south. They became a collection of jagged black-rock islands. The only signs of life were wheeling cawing seabirds and faint tendrils of smoke rising here and there amid the peaks. They didn't look all that big, only the main island, which at sea level looked as wide as a mountain. From there it climbed steep and saw-edged into a series of knife-like crags. He wondered why it hadn't sunk lower. Could it have landed on shoals? Surely the Rivan Sea wasn't so shallow this far out. It also struck him that the entire mammoth structure listed to one side. Antsy canted his head as he followed the angle down to where the waves crashed in a distant white surf at the waterline. *Burn preserve him! Was it floating?*

At last a reef-like collection of black rocks reared ahead, sharp-edged and spotted with bird-droppings. The sea hissed and the muted roar of surf reached Antsy. At a yell from the mainmast the anchor was dropped. Men ran for the sails, taking them in. Their bare feet thumped over the deck timbers. Some readied the ship's boat, a flat-bottomed punt.

Malakai appeared at Antsy's side. 'We'll disembark now.'

'Aye.'

The punt was lowered into the rough waters and four sailors climbed down to handle it. Their equipment was lowered by rope.

Antsy climbed down first then called for Orchid. She was lowered in a sling that he helped guide from below. Next came Malakai. Last, Corien swung down on one of the punt's ropes. The sailors pushed off using long polished poles. Everyone crouched as low as possible as the tiny punt yawed alarmingly.

Poling from rock to rock the sailors made good time. Soon the ship was lost to sight behind a maze of stone shards that varied from man-height to ship-size. The farther they penetrated into the eerie reef the smoother the water became until it was as if they were crossing a land-locked lagoon.

'Look there,' Orchid cried, pointing.

To one side a pointed stone shard resembling an immense fang reared at an angle from the waters. Its contours troubled Antsy until he recognized its features: a circular staircase cut from the very rock spiralled upwards, ending at empty air. The sight brought home the outrageousness, the impertinence, of their intentions. Orchid sobered, losing her excited grin, and she rubbed her arms as if chilled. Even the sailors grew quiet. They peered everywhere at once and Antsy didn't think it was from the difficulty of the passage. Only Malakai and, surprisingly, Corien appeared unaffected by the atmosphere of alien grandeur.

Every little sound echoed into distorted noise: the harsh cawing of the seabirds, the crack of the poles against rock, unseen falling stones, and the constant slap of the waves. Beneath the water Antsy caught the glint of the day's dying light glimmering from sunken metal, possibly even silver or gold. Multicoloured fish darted, nibbling at the first growth of algae and seaweed.

Orchid began humming a slow dirge-like tune. The humming became words that she whispered to the passing shattered basaltic rock.

> Mother Dark he forswore
> Death's own blade he bore.
> Dragon's blood course his veins,
> Immortal,
> He walks till end of Light:
> Anomander,
> Night's own fickle Knight.

Everyone turned to her. Even the sailors stopped poling. Blinking as if returning from a long daydream she blushed furiously, her dark features flushing, and she lowered her head. 'From an epic poem composed during the Holy City period of the Seven Cities region,' she said.

Corien cleared his throat. 'Thank you. Very appropriate.'

The sailors eyed one another but none commented. They returned to their poling, following a route known only to them. The main island reared over them now, rising sheer from the surf as a cliff. The sailors started edging the punt round it. Between the shards, off to one side, Antsy spotted an anchored ship rocking in the waves. It was long and low-slung in the water, single-masted. A war galley. Shields hung all along its side just above the oar-ports. In the dying light it was hard to tell, but the shields appeared somehow decorated. Then it was gone in the maze of rocks. Antsy turned away shaking his head; it was almost as if he'd imagined it.

The punt yawed dangerously now, threatening to capsize. The waves batted it like the toy it was. A number of times it was almost swamped as the surf threatened to suck it against the rocks of the cliff. A darker shadow, the mouth of a cave some way above the waterline, came into view round the curve ahead and as they drew near Antsy spotted a rope ladder hanging from it into the surf. The sailors poled the boat to just beneath. 'Get your gear,' one yelled over the crash of the waves.

'Get closer!' Antsy demanded, but started gathering the equipment. Corien grabbed one set of waterskins and Antsy silently thanked him.

'Now, go!' a sailor shouted.

'Wait just a damned minute!'

When the punt dipped in the surf Malakai suddenly leapt to land on a tiny stone ledge. He trailed the rope behind him. Antsy pressed it into Orchid's hands. 'Hold on.'

'I can't swim!'

'Then hold on, dammit!'

The poles cracked against the rocks as the sailors desperately fended the boat from the cliff. Orchid yelled something lost in the crash of waves and jumped for the end of the rope ladder. The punt nearly tipped over. She disappeared into the foaming blue-black waves. Malakai hauled on the rope. Antsy remembered the girl's amazingly strong grip. She appeared again, thrown up by the surf, driven against the rock wall, to which she clung. Malakai began making his way to her, dragging the rope ladder with him.

Corien took the punt's side next. While the man timed his jump

Antsy belted the two panniers he had been carrying to himself. 'How do we get off the damned island?' he yelled to the nearest sailor.

The man waved him away. 'Go, damn you!'

Antsy pointed to the cave. 'Is this where we get off, too?'

Corien leapt and hit the side where he hung by both hands. He clambered up the uneven cliff face.

'Jump or we take you back with us!' a sailor barked, and swung his pole at Antsy.

All right – we'll have to do this the hard way then. Antsy drew a dirk and yanked the nearest sailor down into the bottom of the boat. All four screamed insults. The punt bounced like a cork. Antsy shoved two fingers' length of the dirk blade into the man's side. The sailor jerked, then held himself utterly still. The other three were too busy holding the punt off from the cliff to come to his aid. 'You know!' Antsy yelled. 'What's the story on getting out?'

'Let me go or we're all dead!'

'Answer!'

'All right! Hood's grin, man!'

Then the bottom of the punt launched up into Antsy, clouting him in the mouth, and there was a shout of warning, a snapping of wood, and the water sucked him down into its cold embrace. The sailor he still had by the belt kicked at him; the two panniers of equipment dragged him down like stone weights. He cut the straps of one, hoping it was the right choice. A wall of black stone veined with bubbles flew at him. The collision knocked out his remaining breath and he gulped in a mouthful of water. He scrabbled for a grip over the slimy rock. He knew he was drowning and it outraged him that there wasn't a damned thing he could do about it. It wasn't god-damned fair.

It seemed that the world, with all its infinite traps, had finally caught up with him.

He came to coughing and vomiting up seawater. Someone held him upright in chest-high surging waves: Malakai. The man was shouting something: 'Did you lose it! Where is it?'

Still dry-heaving, Antsy dug at the remaining pannier; it was his. He grinned his relief to Malakai who grunted, nodding. The man also had a grip on the rope ladder and he swung Antsy to it. 'Damned fool.'

At the back of the cave was a flight of ascending steps cut into the rock, barely as wide as his shoulders. It was pitch black but for the light from the cave mouth. Antsy felt his way on all fours. Seawater dripped from him on to the stairs, which were cold beneath his hands, and as slippery as polished marble. He kept almost falling until he realized that the stairs tilted crazily to one side. He smelled something, an old familiar smell – it came from something smeared over the stairs, and because it had been some time it took him a moment to recognize the tang of dried blood.

'Almost at the top,' came Orchid's voice from above.

Hands took his shoulders and she led him to a wall. He leaned against it, grateful. She seemed to be having no trouble in the absolute black. 'Corien?'

'Gone ahead.'

'How far?' from Malakai, sharp.

'Not far,' came Corien's voice.

Antsy couldn't take it any longer: 'I can't see a goddamned blasted thing!'

Silence, the muted roar of the surf. 'Anyone else?' asked Malakai.

'I've always had excellent night vision,' said Orchid.

'Before I came I visited an alchemist. He gave me an unguent,' Corien said.

'Can you give some to Red?'

'Ah. Sorry. There's really only enough for one.'

Antsy felt his way along the wall to the top of the stairs. He squinted down; there, dull grey, a glimmering.

'Don't we have *any* light?' Orchid asked.

'Yes,' Malakai answered, reluctantly. 'But I'd rather not announce our presence by shining it everywhere.'

'Well, you should've thought of that when you hired us.'

Corien chuckled his appreciation of the point.

A long silence followed that. Antsy peered about the black, which seemed to him no longer absolute. His vision was adjusting; he could make out blobs of greater and lesser darkness, catch hints of movement. Someone slid down one wall to a sitting position. 'We'll wait,' said Malakai. 'We're wet and it's night. 'We'll have more light in the morning.'

Everyone sat. Equipment banged to the floor. 'What was that about, Red?' Corien asked. 'There on the boat?'

Antsy debated not bothering to answer but decided that since they were all stuck together he might as well make the effort. 'I wanted some information so I put a knife to one of them. We capsized.'

Corien laughed a loud barracks-room bray. 'Remind me not to withhold information from you in the future.'

Antsy allowed himself a sour half-smile. He hugged his pannier to his chest. He was soaked, cold, and his mouth hurt like the devil. This was not going the way he'd imagined. Then he laughed, thinking of something: 'I'm sure as Hood not keeping watch tonight.'

Orchid and Corien chuckled.

'I will. Everyone get some sleep,' growled Malakai.

No one spoke again that night.

＊　　　＊　　　＊

Kiska had no idea how long they sat imprisoned in their cliff-face cave. Or even that such concepts as days or hours even mattered here at what now truly seemed to be the 'Shores of Creation'. Leoman practised with his morningstars at the widest point of the cave-fissure. Kiska had her chance to practise close work with the stave. She tested herself until her arms burned then threw herself down to sleep.

But sleep would not come. Instead, her thoughts wandered to one of her last assignments within the Claw. One of a team pursuing indigenous leaders in Seven Cities. Assassination, disruption of nativist movements, the seeding of spies and provocateurs. Ugly work. Murder, torture, extortion, blackmail. That was where she fell away from the Claw. Not out of squeamishness, or adherence to any sort of misplaced moral philosophy – if they weren't doing it to others then others'd be doing it to them, after all – no, it was purely professional disgust. The politicking within the Claw. The careerist lies and backstabbing. The toadying and outright favouritism in promotions. At first it only disgusted her and she kept her distance.

But then it happened to her.

It had been a routine operation. The target was an entrenched anti-occupation movement gaining strength around Aren. She'd been second in command of the Hand assigned the clean-up. They were lucky to have two locally recruited agents: Seven Cities natives who favoured the Malazan mission of suppressing the wasteful feuding, the opening up of the culture to the wider world.

These two were tasked with infiltrating the movement.

During this time the Hand waited and watched. Buildings were noted. Members were marked. The Hand held off until word was passed of a major meet or gathering. The night was set. Kiska's Hand was positioned; the sign was given; they moved.

They stepped right into an ambush.

Somehow, these Seven Cities patriots had gotten word of the attack. A number proved to be hardened veterans from the first war of invasion. When it all was over the small dank cellar was a bloodbath. Only she and the Hand commander remained standing.

On searching the side rooms she found their agents. Both had been monstrously tortured. Mauled and carved almost beyond recognition as human. Bound and hanging like meat. Unbelievably, one still lived. Though eyeless, his stomach eviscerated, the innards dangling in loops, he mouthed that the insurgents had been tipped off. That he'd overheard their boasting of a source within the Claw itself.

Both Kiska and Lotte, the Hand commander, immediately knew who it probably was. The man was Lotte's rival for promotion to the regional directorate. Kiska was all for murdering him that night. Right then and there with the blood still wet on their boots and gloves. But Lotte demurred. He was willing to grant his rival this round. The operation would be reported as botched, a black mark on his record, and the other fellow would get the directorship.

But with Kiska's help he vowed to see to it that the man's tenure would be one long series of failures and setbacks in the region. He would be removed. And then, Lotte proposed, himself and Kiska could potentially rule the Seven Cities holdings from behind the scenes. In the dark of the cellar, the stink of blood and bile a miasma in the air, the dead a carpet round their feet, and Lotte's gaze bright upon her weighing, guarded, Kiska thought it prudent to agree.

But her faith in the virtue of her calling had been shaken – no, more than shaken . . . it had been stabbed through the heart. Lost among the self-promotion and careerist manoeuvring within the order was any concern or responsibility to their larger mission serving the Empire. It seemed that the entire Malazan goal of subduing the Seven Cities region could go down in flames so long as one Claw operative managed to sabotage his rivals. And also dead were two infinitely valuable local agents, loyal and dedicated to the Malazan cause. Betrayed for a cheap leg-up in one bureaucrat's career. Kiska was sickened beyond disgust by the utter short-sighted selfishness of it.

Shortly after that she abandoned the Claw and fled to the service of High Mage Tayschrenn. There they dared not touch her, and there she remained until *that* day: the day that saw not only the Empress's fall, but Tayschrenn's disappearance. The fall of the Empire's greatest High Mage to this Yathengar, a Seven Cities priest-mage, crazed with the desire for revenge for the occupation of his lands and the insults to his city gods. To destroy his enemy the man had actually summoned raw Chaos to drive a hole in creation itself. And the two had been sucked within.

So now she sought him. Across all the face of creation, it seemed, she sought her master. Again she scoured among her feelings for the reasons for such pursuit. The most uncomfortable suspicion was of course that she longed for his attention, his embrace as a man. She studied that urge as ruthlessly as possible to come to the conclusion: no. She no longer dreamt of such a liaison – the stuff of some syrupy courtly romance. When she'd been younger she'd allowed herself the illusion. But no longer. Perhaps some scholar would argue she sought him as the father figure she'd never truly known as a child. Perhaps. What she thought far more germane was that she considered him possibly the only one left who could enforce some sort of standard of behaviour, or moral direction, upon the Empire. If that were at all possible.

All very high-sounding in purpose and aspiration.

But the suspicion pricked her: perhaps the truth was far less noble. Perhaps she was here because she was afraid the Claw would eventually come for her. The organization was famous for never forgetting. But no, all that was so long ago and far away. They had much bigger things to concern themselves with. And she had leverage. She knew things about the Empire. Things no one wanted whispered.

Yet was that not another good reason to see you gone?

She opened her eyes to the familiar narrow cave. Something was different. She heard whispering, a murmuring out beyond the cave mouth. Leoman lay asleep, his breath even, the pulse at his neck steady. Thinking of Seven Cities: this man had served in the resistance against Malazan occupation alongside Yathengar, or at least in sympathy with him. And in that region he had delivered a heart-thrust to the Empire with the conflagration at Y'Ghatan.

The dizzying idea came to her that in her actions she was some-how aiding him in some hidden goals against the Empire. Perhaps she should take the opportunity now to slay him in his sleep, or regret it later. Yet she knew she could not bring herself to commit murder. She was no assassin, though trained in their techniques.

She rose and glided soundlessly to the opening.

It was unguarded. The lumpish beings who had barricaded them in had moved off. They were whispering – well, croaking, belching and lisping – among themselves. It was the gloomy dusk of night. Alien stars glimmered overhead. It occurred to her that if she wished she could make up new constellations among them. The Stave and the Morningstar perhaps.

The lumpy guards squealed and burbled as they caught sight of her, and they came limping up to surround her. It seemed to her that she could smack them to pieces with her staff, but she felt only pity for them. Pity and sadness. She couldn't bring herself to strike any one of them.

At least not yet.

One of the malformed creatures edged up closer before her; it struck her that they were even more wary of her than she of them.

'You are understanding of me?' it asked.

'Yes. Yes I am.'

'We are decided to allow you go. You go if you wish. Imprisonment is hurtful. We are many victims of cruel imprisonment. We would not impress it upon any other. We are not like you.'

Kiska thought it rather convenient of them to allow her to leave after she'd already escaped. But she let that pass. Instead she asked, 'Like me?'

'Yes. Like you. Those who summon us, imprison us, use us cruelly, send us melt among the Vitr. Those like you.'

Kiska understood. Human mages. Summoners. Theurgical researchers. Her breath caught as she realized: *like Tayschrenn*.

Steps behind her and Leoman emerged. 'Labour problems?' he asked.

'They are lowering the blockade.'

The Seven Cities native nodded sagely. 'Sieges are a test of patience.'

Kiska didn't say that she thought these things could easily outwait them if it came to that. She addressed them: 'I am looking for the one known as Thenaj. Do you know where he is?'

A flurry of hissing and burbling among the dun-brown creatures answered her. Their spokesman pointed the longer of its blunt limbs. 'It is as feared. You are come to take him away. You mustn't! The Great One is much pleased by him. He was very sad all alone for so long.'

'The Great One. You mean Maker?'

'Names are dangerous things. To us he is the Great One.'

'I understand.' She set her hands on her hips. 'May we go then?'

'We will not close the way . . . but we will not help either.'

Kiska sighed. 'Fine.' She waved Leoman forward. 'Let's go.'

They walked in silence for a time. The malformed creatures were left behind at their caves. Leoman, she noted, paced warily, hands on his weapons. 'You're nervous?' she asked.

'I'm wondering how the big one will take this.'

'Sounds like he was outvoted.'

'Ah, voting. Such a political arrangement is fine on paper, or among philosophers. But it tends to break apart upon the rocks of application.'

Kiska cocked a brow. A revolutionary political philosopher? 'Oh? How so?'

'Inequity. Disparities in power. For some unknown reason our big friend chooses to play along with the delusion of egalitarianism. But believe me, when the wishes of the powerful are thwarted they will set aside any communal agreements and pursue their own plans regardless. Because they can.'

'You sound bitter.'

'No. Not bitter. Realistic.' He waved a gloved hand. 'Oh, because no one likes to think of themselves as a despot they will cloak their actions in high-sounding rhetoric. Announce that he – or she – sees the situation more clearly. That everyone will thank them in the end. That it is for the better. And so on.'

She eyed him where he walked next to her, hands on the hafts of his weapons, his gaze somewhere else. The Sea of Vitr glimmered ahead. Lazy waves came hissing up the black scoured strand. 'You *sure* you're not bitter?'

Beneath his moustache the man's lips curled up in a rueful smile. 'The curse of an unflinching eye.' He froze. 'And here comes the test.'

Kiska glanced over and tensed. It was the big demon hurrying up to them on its broad ungainly bird's feet. It stopped a short distance off, glowered down at them. 'You are out,' it growled after a time.

Kiska decided to forgo any sarcastic response. She levelled her stave before her. 'Yes.'

It looked over them to the cliff face. 'I disapprove. But it is their decision.' It held out an amber-taloned hand and clenched it as if crushing them within. 'If you hurt anyone you will answer to me.' And it stalked off.

Kiska caught Leoman's bemused gaze. 'And what do you say to that?'

He stroked his moustache, frowning thoughtfully. 'I would say this place seems to have rules of its own.'

She could not argue with that.

CHAPTER V

What is the Deck of Dragons
But where one bends to look
For reflections
Of all things unseen?

Verse attributed to the Seer of Callows

SPINDLE COULD NOT SLEEP AFTER HE AND BLEND AND PICKER
dragged themselves back to K'rul's bar. It was dawn in any case,
and his nerves were shot. They'd witnessed something they
shouldn't have; they all knew it. No one said a thing all the way back
from the base of Majesty Hill – which wasn't very far in any case, as
K'rul's old temple stood on its own hill in the estate district.

Blend and Picker thumped up the stairs to their room. Spindle
slouched into a booth. The common room was empty. The historian
was upstairs asleep. After dozing for a short time, Spindle was
driven by a full bladder to shamble out of the rear kitchen exit.
Facing the yard, looking out over the chicken coop, the woodpile
and the pigsty, he untied his trousers and relieved himself in the
chill air.

In mid-stream he gaped, jerked, traced a warm stream down his
leg, then stumbled back inside struggling with his trousers.

'Picker! Blend! Burn's own tits, would you come and look at this!'

'Shut up!'

'No, really! This is amazin'! You gotta see this.'

Shambled footsteps sounded from above. Picker's voice called
down: 'If it's just you findin' your little soldier then I'm gonna be
real mad.'

'Ha, ha! No. I'm fucking serious here.'

136

'All right, all right.' Picker appeared tucking in her shirt and tying her trousers, boots clumping. 'What is it?'

'Out back. Take a look.'

'What? Has Moon's Spawn returned?'

'Somethin' like that.'

Picker sobered, eyed the man, doubtful. She hiked up her trousers and headed to the kitchen. Spindle followed.

At the open doorway Picker stopped, peered right, then left. Behind, Spindle hopped from foot to foot, brushed at his wet pants. 'Do you see it? Do ya?'

'What? The amazin' chickens? They dancin'? Singin'?'

'No! Not . . .' He squeezed his way round her, stared squinting into the distance. 'But there was . . .' He turned back to the big woman, hunched his shoulders. 'There was this huge dome-like thing there. Over the hilltop . . .'

Picker just shook her head in a slow heavy dismissal. She rubbed her arm where scars marked a ring round the flesh, eyed the distance one more. Then she pushed him aside, muttering, 'Fuckin' moron. Can't believe I'm beginnin' to miss Antsy.'

Spindle was left alone in the chill air. He turned back to the view across the hills of the Estate district, snorted to himself.

'What did it look like?' someone asked from behind.

He spun, jumping. It was Duiker, the old historian. He nodded a greeting. 'It was pale. Kinda see-through. Big. Like the moon. It looked like the moon.'

The historian frowned thoughtfully behind his thick grey beard. His gaze fixed on Spindle. 'You lot been gone days. What happened?'

'I'll tell you over some hot mulled wine.'

'We don't have any.'

Spindle cast another pinched glance over the hilltops. 'Then I'm gonna go get some.'

*

Torvald Nom awoke to a cat's claws sinking into his chest. He jerked upright with a gasp, heard something ricochet off the shelves under the open window, then sat tensed, limbs trembling with startled awareness.

'What is it?' Tiserra murmured, still mostly asleep.

'For a moment I thought you'd thrown yourself upon me and sunk your nails into my chest in an ecstasy of passion, dear. But it was the cat.'

'That's nice,' she murmured into her pillow.

Torvald sighed, peered about the shadowed room. 'Well. I'm up now. Might as well head out.'

'Hmph.'

'Don't trouble yourself. Don't bustle about with tea and bread and such for your working man.'

'Hmm?'

'Never mind.' Torvald got up.

Passing through the streets on his walk to the estate district it struck him that the city was very quiet this morning. He felt that sense of suspended expectation, the atmosphere that some described as 'holding one's breath'. And he had had the strangest dreams just before awakening so very painfully. He did hear one noise that was very out of place indeed. He recognized it only because of his travels so far from this city of his birth. For it was a sound utterly unfamiliar to Darujhistan: the ordered stamp of marching soldiery. He hurried to where the marching echoed, the Second Tier Way.

He joined a press of Darujhistani citizenry turned out to watch this once in a lifetime sight. The tall cross-piece hanging banner preceding the column declared their allegiance: the white sceptre on a field of black, the sceptre much like an orb clasped in an upright three-toed predatory bird's foot. The naked clawed grip of the Malazan Empire.

Elite heavy infantry. Campaign stripes marked them as veterans of every engagement on these, to them, foreign Genabackan lands. They carried broad rectangular shields blackened and edged in burgundy. Shortswords swung belted high at their sides. Crossbows and javelins rode strapped to their backs. The Malazan delegation honour guard, some two hundred strong. Withdrawing?

'What's goin on?' he asked one fellow in the crowd.

'The Empire's invading!' the man bellowed, half drunk.

Torvald grimaced at his bad luck. 'They're headed in the wrong direction,' he pointed out.

'Ha ha!' the drunk yelled. 'We beat them! Good riddance, y'damned foreigners!'

Torvald walked away just in case the appropriately feared Malazan mailed fist should make itself felt. The rear of the column came marching up. Mounted officers rode just before a train of wagons and carts and strings of spare mounts. Torvald noted that he did not see the bald and rather fat figure of the ambassador among the

138

officers. He hurried on to bring the news to his employer, the head of his family house and thus councilwoman, Lady Varada.

Madrun let him into the compound. 'Captain,' the man said, bowing. Torvald always listened carefully to this welcome but so far he'd yet to detect even the slightest tinge of insincerity. More than ever he regretted the absence of his old partners, Scorch and Leff, who used to guard these doors.

At least then *he* wasn't the obvious weak link in the estate's personnel.

The castellan Studlock met him at the open front doors of the house. 'I have orders from the mistress,' he lisped as Torvald hurried in past him.

'Lady Varada?'

'The mistress is . . . ill,' Studlock murmured. 'Yes. That is it. Quite ill.'

Torvald sniffed the air. 'What is that I smell? Is something burning?'

'Just my preparations. The singeing of rare leaves. An infusion gone wrong.' The strange man crept up close, the tatters and strips of gauzy cloth he wrapped himself in dragged long behind. Torvald flinched away. 'You appear tired, malnourished,' Studlock went on. 'Are you having trouble in your sexual performance? Perhaps a mineral poultice to rebalance your animus?'

'Rebalance my *what*? Ah, no. Thank you.'

'A pity.'

'Ill, you say? Where is she?'

'The mistress is . . . indisposed.'

'Indisposed . . .'

'Yes. Quite. She did however leave detailed instructions regarding you.'

'Me?'

'Yes. None other.'

'I see. And these instructions?'

The man edged closer, his watery green eyes narrowed upon Torvald. 'There is a worrisome choleric tinge to you. Have you evacuated lately?'

'Evacu what?'

'Evacuated. Discharged your bodily wastes.'

'Ah! Yes.'

'And your bowels? How are they?'

'Sacrosanct, thank you.'

'Regretful. How am I to continue my practice?'

Torvald was surprised. 'You're a physicker?'

The man blinked his confusion. 'No.'

Torvald regarded the unnerving hunched figure for a time, cleared his throat. 'So . . . these instructions?'

'Yes. You are now head of House Nom. Congratulations.' The castellan shuffled away.

Torvald stood motionless in the receiving hall for a long time. Then he ran up the stairs for his employer's office. He was in the process of ransacking her desk when he looked up to see the gauzy apparition of Studlock before him once again.

'There must be some mistake.'

'None, I assure you.'

'What of Bellam?'

'Young Bellam remains an eventual heir.'

'But . . . it can't be official. There has to be paperwork. Certificates and such.'

The castellan drew a scroll from within the folds of cloth at his chest. 'I have them here. Sealed and authenticated.'

He slumped down into the chair. That had been his last hope. He straightened, his brows rising. 'Aha! I appoint another. Someone else. *Anyone* else.'

'Rallick Nom will support m'lady's choice. So then will the majority of the House.'

Torvald slumped once more. *Damn him! He would, too – if only to avoid being appointed himself!*

He set his elbows on the desk, cupped his head in his hands. 'But this is terrible . . . Tiserra will kill me! One day I leave for work and when I come home it's hello dear your husband has a seat on the Council! Rather a shock.'

The castellan cocked his head. 'Will she not be pleased?'

'You don't know her.'

'You are correct. I do not. Are introductions in order? Some tea? My special brew . . .'

Torvald threw up his hands. '*No!* No, no thank you. That's quite all right.'

Studlock's shoulders fell. 'That is regrettable. Who will I test it on?'

Torvald frowned. 'So, now what? What do I do?'

'You should register your appointment with the clerk of the Council, I imagine.'

'Ah. Thank you. How very . . . practical.'

The castellan bowed. 'My only wish is to serve.'

Torvald had never been to Majesty Hill; indeed, had never dreamed he'd have cause. The Wardens at the lowest gate stopped him to have his paperwork inspected. Before him rose the stairs that switched back and forth up the flank of the hill, lined all the way by monuments, family shrines, plaques commemorating victories – real and invented – and other grandiose pronouncements meant to impress the reader with the virtue and generosity of their sponsors. All no more than base self-aggrandizement, Torvald reflected, once you boiled it all down.

He clasped his hands behind his back and rocked on the worn heels of his old boots. Perhaps such an attitude was precisely what was not welcome on yon prestigious hilltop.

A clerk bowed as he handed back the scrolled paperwork. 'Welcome, sir. My apologies for the delay. We do not see many councillors here at the gate.'

'No? You do not? Just what do you see, then?'

'Petitioners mostly. Appellants and other claimants summoned, or hoping, to address the assembly. And minor functionaries, of course.'

'Ah. I see.' Torvald wondered, vaguely, whether he'd just been insulted in some very sophisticated indirect fashion. Considering where he was headed, he decided that he'd better get used to it. 'So, just where do the Council members enter?'

The man bowed – unctuously, it seemed to Torvald. 'These days most take the carriageway from the south.'

'Ah, well. Perhaps many would benefit from coming in this way occasionally, don't you think?'

'Oh, beyond a doubt, sir,' the man agreed smoothly, his face straight.

Good at his job, this one, Torvald reflected. This gate must be where most of the squeezing of petitioners takes place. A coveted post. He bowed a farewell. 'I'd best be going then.'

'A sound decision, sir.'

Torvald walked away, wincing. *Damn, drubbed by a bureaucrat. It's going to be a long day.*

Eventually, after rather a boring walk up an unnecessarily long set of stairs, he entered what appeared to be a main reception hall lined by many doors. It was . . . deserted. *Is the place closed?* Yet someone *was* here: noise reached him, a muted roaring as of many voices shouting. But where was it coming from?

A door slammed and a robed clerk appeared, sheaf of papers in hand, reading as he scuttled quickly across the hall.

Torvald cleared his throat. 'Excuse me – could you tell me . . .'

The man disappeared into another side door. Torvald lowered his arm. A gods-damned rabbit warren. He poked his head into that door to see another hall, also lined by doors, albeit far less ornate. It occurred to him that a rather large old friend of his would know exactly what to do to a place like this. The sound of another door opening pulled him away. Another functionary was walking the hall. He planted himself before her.

The plump woman nearly ran into him before halting to blink up confusedly. 'Yes?'

He wordlessly offered his paperwork. She examined it, then bowed. 'Welcome, House Nom. I shall see to it that these are registered with the proper offices. You are no doubt come for the assembling of the emergency steering committee.'

It was now his turn to blink his confusion. 'I'm sorry?'

'This way. If you would, sir.'

Torvald followed the woman down the long hall, round a series of turns, to a tall set of double doors. Two city Wardens barred the entrance. From behind the doors came a riotous roaring such as Torvald imagined must prevail before the gates to Hood's old realm.

The guards' hands went to their shortswords. 'This is a closed emergency session,' pronounced one in what sounded like a carefully rehearsed line.

The woman bowed her agreement. 'And Councillor Nom is here to participate.'

The guard's brow furrowed. He licked his lips while he appeared to be frantically digging through options. The brows unfurled and he smiled, reciting, 'Chambers are closed.'

'Open those doors!' a bull-roar echoed from behind Torvald, who spun.

A great bhederin of a fellow was hurrying up, unshaven, finery askew, a hand to his forehead, grimacing in pain. The clerk bowed. 'Councillor Coll.'

Torvald stared despite himself. Great gods, *the* Councillor Coll? The man was a legend among those who've served on the Council.

The councillor cocked a bloodshot eye at Torvald. The clerk

murmured, 'Councillor Coll, may I introduce Councillor Nom, newly invested.'

The bleary, watering eyes widened. 'Indeed . . . may I ask after the mesmerizing Lady Varada, whom I have seen only from a distance, across the assembly?'

The stale bite of cheap Daru spirits wafted from the man and Torvald struggled not to change his expression. 'Ah . . . her health precludes her participation . . . I am come in her stead.'

'My regrets to your family, Nom. And may she soon recover.'

Torvald frantically cast about for something equally well mannered and sophisticated. 'Ah, our thanks.' *Wonderful! Off to a dazzling start, you are.*

But Councillor Coll's attention had shifted to the closed doors and the guards. 'You're still here?' he demanded.

'Of course you may enter, Councillor. But this other . . .'

Coll snatched up the sheaf of papers held by the clerk: Torvald's documents. He waved the flapping pages, complete with wax seals and coloured ribbons, before the faces of the guards. 'You see these certificates? This man is as qualified to sit as I!'

The guards eyed the sheaf, all in the tiniest spidery penmanship, the way those manning a wooden palisade might dread the approach of a siege onager. Resistance collapsed and they stood aside.

The clerk pushed open the twin leaves. And as they passed within, it occurred to Torvald that an impenetrable bureaucracy was in truth more powerful than any sword.

They stood high in a semi-circular amphitheatre of seats. The view reminded Torvald of a depiction of one corner of Hood's realm: an immense prison for kings and despots, all arguing over who was in charge, when in truth none of the dead outside cared what went on within its tall walls.

The floor of the amphitheatre was crowded with the cream of the city aristocracy. All were standing talking at once, many red-faced, some waving their exasperation. Occasionally thrown papers fluttered over the crowd, or some particularly loud yell penetrated the din, but mostly it was an unintelligible gabbling of voices.

'Welcome to Council,' the woman said, shouting to be heard though she stood right next to him.

'How very inspiring,' he answered, to himself of course, as none could have possibly heard, or cared to hear, for that matter.

The woman backed out, pulled the doors closed. Councillor Coll took his arm and hurried him down the stairs. 'My thanks,' Torvald offered.

'You can thank me by swearing to give me your first vote.'

Such a vow struck Torvald as extremely dangerous, but he also knew that honour would dictate that he had no choice. Best to pretend that such was the case, then.

A loud, exceptionally sharp knocking sounded which Torvald identified as coming from a slim man standing on the raised speaker's platform, banging a stone on the lectern.

'Order!' he bellowed in a surprisingly commanding voice. '*Order!*'

The clamour slowly diminished and the councillors stood silent, leaving only a single old fellow waving his arms and shouting, 'I tell you, everything would go so smoothly if only everyone would just do as I say!'

'Hear, hear!' someone shouted in answer and they all burst into applause.

The old fellow peered about myopically then hurriedly turned away, red-faced.

'The floor recognizes Councillor Lim,' a clerk announced into the silence.

It now occurred to Torvald that crowding about the central lectern were only some fifty or so members of the Council, yet the amphitheatre held seats for hundreds. 'Where is everyone?' he whispered to Coll.

'It's a damned trick,' Coll answered, low and fierce. 'There *is* a little-known emergency steering committee that can be called to meet in case of fires and such. Just those close enough to participate. Quorum is thirty. Thankfully I was nearby . . . sleeping in my chambers.'

Passed out, you mean. So, an emergency sub-committee of Council. But to decide what?

At the lectern, Lim stood tall and pole-thin, his dark expensive silk shirt and trousers accenting his figure. He raised his arms for silence.

So, Lim, is it? Torvald believed he'd heard that Shardan Lim was dead.

'Thank you,' the fellow began. 'My fellow councillors, fair Darujhistan has weathered astounding events of late. Many of you, myself included, no doubt wish that history would be so good as to pass us by for once, allow us our well-earned peace to quietly tend our fields and watch our children play . . .'

Torvald snorted: the man looked as peaceful and compassionate as a viper. Coll chuckled. Torvald glanced over to see him offer a wink. 'What's going on?'

In answer, the man gestured to the front. 'Let us hear from Lim.'

'That's not Shardan Lim, is it?'

'Ah. You *are* new. No, this is Jeshin Lim. His cousin.'

Torvald grunted. He'd never heard of a Jeshin Lim. But then, he'd probably never heard of most of the men and women in the hall. The young man had been talking all the while, offering some long-winded soothing introduction to the course of action he wished to suggest. In time, the meat of the speech arrived: '. . . and so it is clear that this abrupt, unannounced flight by the all Moranth present within the city, combined with the equally sudden withdrawal of their allies, the Imperial Malazan elements staining our fair city, can amount to only one thing: the first stage in a pre-planned, coordinated initiation of hostilities against the freedom and independence of Darujhistan!'

The hall erupted into chaotic noise once more. Most cheered, calling out their support of the claim. Only a few shouted their dismissal.

Torvald and Coll remained silent. Torvald leaned to Coll. 'Why is he saying everything twice?'

'Ah. An older style of rhetoric. Something of a traditionalist, our Jeshin. New to assembly, he is. But there's a great deal of money backing him.'

Closer to the man, Torvald noted that while he was impressively large, it had all gone to fat. And though a strong miasma of Daru spirits surrounded him, he did not appear to be drunk.

'And what do you propose?' an old man's sarcastic voice cut through the shouting.

The raucous arguing died down as everyone waited for Lim's answer.

Coll gestured aside, indicating the speaker: an aged fellow, thin and straight, his hair a grey hedging round his skull. 'Councillor D'Arle.'

'Will you marshal the troops?' the old man continued scathingly. 'Assemble the navy? But wait . . . we have none! And the Malazans know this! If they wanted to occupy us they would have done so long ago.'

Councillor Lim was shaking his head. 'With all respect to House D'Arle, that is not so. The truth is that the Malazans *have* tried to annex us to their Empire but that said efforts have to this time failed, or been defeated by circumstance, or the intervention of diversionary challenges – such as the Pannions to the south. Now, however, with said threat crushed, and Moon's Spawn also eliminated from the field – *now* it appears clear that the Malazans see that it is time to bring our fair city to heel.'

'You *do* have a proposal,' Councillor D'Arle demanded, 'lurking somewhere within all that puff and wind?'

'I like this fellow,' Torvald whispered to Coll.

A taut smile from Coll. 'Sad family history there.'

Showing surprising patience, Councillor Lim inclined his head in assent. 'I do. I propose that this emergency assembly of the Council now vote upon the investiture of the ancient position created precisely for such rare crises. I am speaking, of course, of the temporary and limited post of Legate of Council.'

Coll's meaty hand closed painfully on Torvald's shoulder. '*The bastard!*' he hissed, giving out a cloud of stale alcohol. 'You can't do that!' he bellowed into the hall.

Lim's thin brows rose. 'I see that we are fortunate in this time of threat to have Councillor Coll with us. You have a proposal for the floor, do you?'

'Only that the office of Legate was abolished centuries ago because of its abuses!'

'Hear, hear!' called Councillor D'Arle.

'And short-sighted and mistaken that was too,' Lim answered. 'For how else can the city respond quickly and authoritatively to sudden emergencies?'

A cheer went up from the gathered councillors. Coll slowly shook his head. 'A stacked deck, as they say,' he murmured to Torvald.

'We will now vote upon the reinvestment of the position of temporary Legate of Council,' called out the clerk. 'All in favour raise hands.'

Almost all raised their hands. Coll and Torvald did not.

'Proposal carried,' announced the clerk.

A great cheer answered that pronouncement. The councillors congratulated one another, slapping backs and shaking hands. The celebration seemed premature to Torvald as they had yet to actually *do* anything.

Councillor D'Arle pushed his way forward. 'And I suppose you would tender your name for this post?' the man's voice was icy with scorn.

Lim bowed. 'Yes. Since Councillor D'Arle has been good enough to mention it.'

The old councillor's jaws snapped shut.

'Seconded!' another councillor shouted.

It occurred to Torvald that the man with him was probably the only councillor who could boast of any direct military training or experience and that time was running out. He shouted, 'I nominate Councillor Coll!'

'What in Oponn's name are you doing?' Coll ground through clenched teeth.

Silence answered the shout. Councillor Lim squinted down at Torvald, a look of distaste upon his pale fleshless face. 'And you are . . . ?'

'Nom, Torvald Nom.'

'*Councillor*,' Coll hissed.

'Councillor! Ah, Nom.'

Lim inclined his head in greeting. 'I see. Welcome, then, to House Nom, so long absent from these proceedings. We have a nomination on the floor. Does anyone second?'

Silence, then a young woman's voice called out, 'I second.'

Torvald sat to find Coll glaring at him. 'I don't know whether to thank you or call you out,' the man growled.

'Don't you think you should be Legate?'

'If reason and logic ruled the world no one would be Legate. But it doesn't rule. Power and influence does. And I have neither. I am sorry to say that you have made yourself some enemies this day my friend.'

'Well, we're off to a good start then. Who was that who seconded?'

'Councillor Redda Orr. Most say she is too young to sit on the Council, but she has a sharp political mind and grew up in these halls.'

'Friend of yours?'

'No. She just hates House Lim. Blames them for her father's death.'

'Ah.' Rather belatedly it occurred to Torvald that he had just leapt into a kind of gladiatorial free-for-all without knowing any of the rules or the players. But then, why should he change the habits of a lifetime? He'd always run a very fast and loose game. Never mind the poor record scattered in his wake – he was alive, wasn't he? There were many others who couldn't boast as much.

'Very good,' announced the clerk. 'We will now vote upon the nomination of Councillor Lim to the position of temporary Legate of Council. All in favour?'

Almost all hands rose. The clerk did a quick count. 'We have a majority of forty-two votes. Nomination carried.'

This time a stunned silence answered the announcement, as if those gathered could not believe that they'd actually succeeded. Then an enormous cheer arose, councillors laughing, reaching up to clasp Lim's hands, hugging one another.

'I wonder just how much all this cost,' Coll murmured into the clamour. 'A family fortune, I imagine.'

Speaking of money, it occurred to Torvald that he still had to break the news to Tis. Perhaps he should visit the bourse of the flower-sellers before heading home. And on the subject of costly items, just how huge was his new income from this prestigious post?

'Excuse me for being so ill-mannered, friend Coll . . . but what is the pay for sitting on this assembly?'

The big man frowned. His thick greying brows bunched down over his eyes, almost obscuring them. 'Pay? There's no pay associated with a seat on the Council. It's a service. One's civic duty. However,' and here the man strove to keep his face straight, 'monies do flow to members . . . in direct relation to their power and influence upon the Council . . .'

Torvald slumped into a nearby seat. In other words, his earnings would amount to the impressive sum of zero. Perhaps for the immediate future it would be better if he avoided returning home altogether . . .

*

Impatient banging brought Jess lumbering once more to the doors of the Phoenix Inn. She unlatched the lock to peer out into the glaring morning light. A tall dark figure brushed in past her, imperious.

'Not – oh, it's you,' she said, blinking. She shuffled to the kitchen to wake Chud.

Rallick crossed to the rear table, which stood covered in clumps of old wax, stained by spills of red Rhivi wine. Empty wine bottles crowded it, and crumbs lay scattered like the wreckage of war.

Jess came shuffling up to offer a glass of steaming tea. Rallick took it. 'Thank you.' He blew on the small tumbler, then sipped. 'So . . . where is he?'

Jess cocked a brow at the man – a man rumoured to be the lover of Vorcan, once head of the city's guild of assassins. And thus to her a man commanding a great deal of physical . . . tension. She kept her eyes on him. 'Where's who?'

'The toad . . . self-proclaimed Eel. The fat man.'

She swept an arm to the table. 'Why, he's right—' She stared, gaping. 'Fanderay's tits! He's not here! He's buggered off! Where's he got to?' A hand closed over her mouth. 'Oh, Burn's mercy . . . who's gonna cover his tab? Have you seen the size of his tab?'

Rallick handed over the glass. 'No. And I don't care to, thank you.' He headed for the door.

'Where are you going?'

Without stopping Rallick answered, 'Looks like maybe it's up to me to settle accounts, Jess. I seem to be the only one around here willing to do it.'

Of all the men and women she'd seen in the Phoenix Inn it had always appeared to Jess that Rallick was the one who could close any debt. But this was a damnably huge one.

*

Rallick pushed open the ornamental wrought-iron gate that allowed entrance to the grounds of the alchemist Baruk's modest estate. He walked the curving flagged path past subdued plantings of flowering shrubs. A small fountain tinkled spray from the mouth of an amphora held at a boy's stone shoulder. Leaves cluttered the surface of the pond, as did something else: a piece of litter, or wind-tossed garbage. Rallick's long face drew down, accentuating the deep lines framing his mouth.

Baruk's grounds were always immaculate.

He pulled on a pair of leather gloves and extracted the litter from the sodden leaves. A card. A card from an expensive custom-made Dragons Deck. Soaked now, and flame-scorched. Turning it over, he grunted. A card of rulership: Crown. He dropped it back into the glimmering water.

The front door was unlocked. He lifted the latch and pushed it open. Inside lay destruction. Shards of ceramic urns and expensive glassware littered the carpet of the entranceway. Paintings had been thrown down; furniture overturned.

Rallick crouched to his haunches just outside the threshold. He drew pieces of wood and metal from his pockets and waist until he'd assembled a medium-sized crossbow, its metal parts blued. The sort of weapon that would immediately have you arrested should anyone catch sight of it.

He loaded it, then cocked it by slipping a foot into its stirrup and straightening up. Then he crossed his arms, cradling the weapon across his chest. He called out, 'Roald? Hello? Anyone?'

No answer. He heard the wind brushing through nearby boughs; a carriage made its noisy metal-tyred way down one of the alleys bordering the estate. In the light of the sun he studied the weave of the carpet lining the way.

Smooth well-worn slippers. The foot narrow, gracile. Yet the impression very heavy. Female. Slim but hefty? Entering then leaving. Trod over some shards as she left. Agent of the vandalism? No other recent traffic . . . except . . . the ghostliest of hints. A brushing across the rich weft as of broad, splayed moccasined feet slipping side to side, never lifting, entering and exiting also. And before the woman arrived, as her tracks obscure these others. An interesting puzzle.

He rose, edged inward. Over the years he'd done occasional work for Baruk; non-assassination jobs, gathering intelligence, trailing people, collecting rare objects, and such like. As had Kruppe, Murillio, and sometimes Coll. Indeed, it was this very work that had thrown the lot of them together. Four as unlikely associates as one might imagine. In any case, he knew enough to be very wary of crossing this particular threshold.

But others had entered already, to no ill effects he could discern. He peered into the nearest room opening off the foyer. Some sort of waiting room. Complete carnage and wanton devastation. Everything broken, thrown to the floor. Vandalism. Plain juvenile vindictiveness.

He moved on. Up the narrow tower stairs he found chambers similarly ruined. So far he couldn't tell if the intruder had come deliberately searching for something and was venting her frustration upon failing to discover it, or whether such destruction, or insult, had been the prime purpose of the visitation from the start.

He glanced into what appeared to have been some sort of workroom. Delicate glass fragments of globes covered the bare stone floor, as did the tattered remains of torn books and scrolls. Workbenches had been swept clear of their clutter, which now lay in tangled heaps on the floor.

His foot crushed a glass shard and a chest flew open across the room. Rallick's crossbow snapped out, seeming to point of its own accord, only to fall again – a squat toad-like familiar, or demon, was peeping out, its amber eyes huge with fear. 'Gone!' it croaked. 'Out! Oh my!'

Rallick frowned, his mouth drawing down even further. 'Who? Who's out?'

'Hinter gone! Out. Oh my!'

Hinter? As in the old ghost story Hinter of Hinter's Tower?

'Where's Baruk?'

'Gone! Oh my!'

'And the place ransacked,' Rallick muttered, more to himself.

'Not all,' and the demon's clawed hand flew to cover its mouth.

With a jerk of the crossbow, Rallick motioned the creature from the chest.

The demon led him down the narrow circular staircase, which continued on past ground level, passing floor after floor of quarters, storerooms, and workrooms. Rallick had had no idea the place was so extensive. It seemed so small from the outside. The creature stopped at what appeared to be the lowest floor. Rallick lit a wall-mounted lantern and raised it to peer around. The room was bare, almost completely empty. *Nothing to vandalize here.* Old inscriptions covered the floor in ever-narrowing circles. Old metal-working tools lined the walls: tongs, hammers, a small portable forge, twinned anvils. The demon waddled to a heavy metal chest against one wall, only to recoil as if struck.

'Oh no!' it gibbered. 'Out! Out!' It slapped its bald head with its tiny under-sized clawed hands and hopped from foot to foot.

'What's out?'

'Scary big man squash us with hammer for this! Oh no!'

Hammer?

Rallick crossed to the chest. It was constructed of thick metal plates. A lock at its front hung open. He pulled on the lid, failed to budge it. He set down the crossbow, clasped a hand at either side of the lid and lifted. It grated, edging upwards. He strained, gasping, managed to lever it up to clang back against the stone wall. It was a full hand's thickness of dull metal.

'A lot of lead,' he muttered.

'Not lead!' the creature answered. 'Magic-killing metal!'

Rallick flinched from the chest. *Otataral! An entire box of the metal? Beru fend! Why, an ounce of this would bring a man a fortune!*

Within, a length of white silk lined the bottom, empty.

The demon was blubbering, hands at its head. 'Scary big man mustn't know! He will flatten us all!'

Something lay scattered on the dusty stones of the floor next to the chest. Rallick bent to study the mess. Crumbs? And next to that, a ring-stain – as of a wine glass? He pressed a finger to the crumbs, touched it to his tongue. *Pastry crumbs?*

He straightened, asked almost absently, 'What was in the chest?'

The demon's hands were now squeezing its own neck. 'The master's most awful terrible possessions of all!' it choked, throttling itself. 'Flakes. Slivers. Little scary slivers.'

'Slivers of what?'

The creature's already red face now glowed bright carmine. Its amber eyes bulged. 'Slivers of death!' it gurgled in a seeming last gasp, and fell, fat stomach heaving.

Rallick regarded the empty otataral chest. *Slivers of death?*

* * *

Went, Filless and Scarlon, the three cadre mages assigned to Ambassador Aragan's contingent of the Fifth, were busy in the embassy cellar sorting through files for destruction. None noticed the presence of the slim young girl until she cleared her throat. Then all three looked up from the folders and string-bound sheaves of orders and logistical summaries to stare, dumbfounded, at what appeared to be a dancing girl in loose white robes with silver bracelets rattling on her wrists.

'Are you lost, child?' Filless demanded, first to recover her wits.

'You three do constitute the last full Imperial mage cadre in this theatre, do you not?' the girl enquired, and she smiled, demurely.

The three exchanged wondering glances. 'You are a guest of the ambassador . . . ?' Scarlon offered, tentatively.

The pale girl drew up her long mane of black hair, knotted it through itself. 'No. I am the last thing you will ever see.'

All three summoned their Warrens; none lived long enough to channel them. Filless died last, and hardest, as she was not only a mage of Denul but the last Claw of the contingent as well.

It was half a day before the mess was discovered.

Ambassador Aragan kicked through the wreckage of singed papers, destroyed tables, blood and gore-smeared folders cluttering the cellar. His aide, Dreshen, stood at a distance, as did the hastily assembled bodyguard of marines.

The ambassador was in a filthy mood.

'No one heard a thing? Not a damned thing?' he demanded, turning on them.

'No sir,' Dreshen answered, wincing.

'Someone enters the estate, happens to find all three of our cadre mages together in the same room, and kills them all without so much as a peep?'

'Yes, sir.'

'And of course the only ones who could be counted on to sense anything happen to be the very three lying here!'

'Yes, sir.'

Dreshen swallowed to settle his stomach as the ambassador squatted on his haunches next to the ravaged body of Filless: the woman's face had been torn as if by jagged blades and her midriff had been slashed open, her looped entrails spilt out over her lap. Aragan stared down moodily at the corpse, drew a hand across the woman's staring eyes to shut them. Dreshen felt his knees going weak at the sight of all the ropy blue and pink viscera.

Aragan used some of the scattered papers to wipe the blood from his hands. He stood, and started to pace again. 'An act of war, Captain. An Osserc-damned act of war.'

'Yes, sir.'

'In the Academy this is what you'd call a "pre-emptive strike".'

'Sir?'

'We're effectively cut off now, aren't we, Captain?'

'Ah. Yes, sir.'

'Communications neatly severed. No cadre mages to contact Unta. No access to the Imperial Warren.' Aragan turned. 'There must be *some* talents among the rankers, surely?'

'Minor only, sir. None trained in cadre protocols.'

The ambassador stood still, apparently thinking. He had that wide-legged stance of big men, when in fact most of his size was a broad circle around his middle. He pulled on his lower lip, his mouth drawn down in a moue of angry disgust. 'An act of war . . .' he mused. 'Someone's made their opening moves against us and we don't even know who we're facing yet! We are too far behind.' He pointed to Dreshen. 'What about Fist K'ess? He must have cadre.'

Dreshen nodded thoughtfully. 'Yes . . . but none to spare, I'm sure. There's still fighting in the north.'

Aragan grunted, accepting this. 'And Fist Steppen?'

His aide cocked his head. 'I don't believe there are any active cadre in the south.'

Aragan looked to the low ceiling. *Ye gods! That the Empire of*

Nightchill, Tattersail and Tayschrenn should be reduced to this! It would be laughable if it weren't so damned tragic! Very well. If it's to be war . . . then war it shall be.

He crossed to the stairs. His bodyguard parted to make way for him. He stopped before his aide. 'Get the box, Captain.'

Dreshen frowned, uncertain. 'The box, sir?'

'Yes. *The* box.'

Dreshen's pale thin brows rose. 'Ah! *The* box. Yes, sir. Here?'

The ambassador peered about the cellar, shook his head. 'No. Upstairs.'

Aragan waited in his office, hands clasped behind his back. Eventually Captain Dreshen entered, followed by two marines carrying a small battered travel trunk which they thumped down heavily on a table. Aragan motioned the marines out. He reached for the buckles securing the leather straps around the iron box but hesitated at the last moment and looked to Dreshen. 'Well, let's just hope I'm allowed to open this.'

The captain offered a stained smile. 'Of course, sir.'

Aragan undid the buckles, opened the latches, and swung up the lid. Within lay a long thin object wrapped in oiled leathers. Captain Dreshen studied the item, mystified. The truth was, he had no idea what was in the box – other than that the cadre mages all considered it the most important artefact the Fifth Army possessed.

Aragan pulled off the oiled wrap and Dreshen caught his breath, stepping back. *Burn, Oponn and Fanderay protect him. No. It couldn't be . . .*

His mouth drawn wide in satisfaction, Aragan hefted the thing in one hand. It was about the length of a long-knife. One end was a blade, the other sculpted into a three-toed bird's foot gasping a black orb of glass or jet.

An Imperial Sceptre.

Aragan slammed the artefact blade-first into the table. The gleaming point bit deep into the wood and the sceptre stood upright, at a slight angle. Aragan set his fists to the table on either side, studied the orb. Despite his awe, Dreshen edged forward as well.

Aragan cleared his throat. 'This is Ambassador Aragan in Darujhistan. I do not know whether anyone is listening, or if this message will reach anyone, but I must report that all the remaining mage cadre of the Fifth have been murdered. Assassinated. Cadre Filless may have also reported that our allies, the Moranth, have fled the city – terrified, as far as I can see. Something is stirring here in the city and it has moved against us. This is our only remaining communication channel to command. If Unta values Darujhistan then some sort of help must be sent. That is all.'

The ambassador pushed himself from the table, stood with arms crossed regarding the sceptre. Dreshen watched as well, though for what he had no idea.

After a protracted silence during which nothing apparently changed in the state of the sceptre, Dreshen coughed into a fist. 'How long,' he began, 'until . . .'

'Until we know? Until they answer – or if anyone's going to answer at all?' Aragan shrugged his round shoulders. 'Who knows.' He peered round the room. 'Until then I want this room sealed and guarded. Yes, Captain?'

'Yes, sir.'

They shut and sealed all the doors, locking the last one behind them. While Aragan waited Captain Dreshen went to find two marines to post on the door.

Behind, in the gloom of the office, the only light was the glow through the slats of the folding terrace doors, now barred from within. And it may have been a trick of that uncertain light, but deep within the black depths of the orb a cloudy glimmering awakened and the darkness, like a pool of oil, began to churn.

* * *

When Spindle finally started awake, fully clothed on his cot, he lay back and held his head, groaning. No more Barghast mead. Never again. Even warm, as he'd had it with Duiker. Though come to think of it, the historian had drunk little more than one tumbler from the jug.

Holding his head very still for fear that it might fall off, he carefully edged his way down the stairs to the common room. By the light streaming in through the temple-bar's few windows he saw that it was late afternoon. *Damned well slept most of the day – a bad sign. Discipline's goin' by the wayside.*

Now that the bar was wet once more a few of the regulars had returned to sit by themselves among the tables and booths. Irredeemable souses all, they spent the day expertly maintaining a steady state of numbness bordering on unconsciousness. Watching them, Spindle sometimes worried that that was where he was headed.

Somehow, though, the abstract dread was not enough to stop him from getting hammered whenever possible.

He was surprised to see some tall well-dressed fellow sitting with the historian, and slowly eased himself down into a chair at the table. The two older men shared a knowing, amused glance.

'Care for another to chase that one away?' Duiker asked.

Spindle showed his teeth. 'Evil bastard.'

The historian – a dour grim man at the best of times – offered a death's head grin. He motioned to the man, 'Fisher, Spindle.'

The bard nodded his greeting, his face held tight – Spindle recognized this as the politest possible reaction he could get to his hair shirt, which he never washed. He was surprised that this was the fellow Picker and Blend had spoken of: he had thought he'd be more imposing, more . . . mysterious. And they said he didn't come round much any more. Taken up with a witch, or some such thing. He turned to the historian. 'Remind me to never buy mead again.'

'I've heard that before,' Duiker answered.

Spindle blew out a breath, rubbed his face. 'Damned strange night last night.' He tried to get the attention of Picker behind the bar.

'They have been strange, lately,' Fisher affirmed, his gaze distant.

'Last night?' Duiker asked, a grey brow arching. 'You mean two nights ago, don't you?'

Spindle stared, amazed. *Damn, but time flies when you finally have coin in your pocket!*

'Spindle, why don't you tell Fisher here what you thought you saw *two* nights ago.'

Spindle waved to Picker, who looked right through him. 'Does a man have to get his own tea and a bite around here?' he murmured absently. Then he stiffened and half started up from the table, only to groan and sink back down again, holding his head. 'Beru take it!'

The historian lost his amused half-smile and studied him, uncertain. 'What is it?'

Ye gods! Two days and I haven't reported in! What was that woman's name? Fells? Fillish? Damn! The saboteur's bloodshot eyes darted right and left and his face took on a pale greenish hue. 'Nothing,' he said. 'Think I'll get me some soup.' He nodded a curt goodbye and ran.

After Spindle had darted out of the bar Duiker said to Fisher, 'There goes one of the last remaining Bridgeburner cadre mages. Or rather, a mage who thinks he's a saboteur.'

Fisher touched a long thin finger to his nose and nodded thoughtfully. 'Yes, there was a certain air about him.'

*　　*　　*

The papers in Humble Measure's hands did not so much as quiver when the double doors to his office were kicked open and his secretary was pushed in before an armed and armoured knot of the city watch. His brows, however, did climb his pale forehead as he peered up from the accounts. 'And to what do I owe this interruption?' he asked from across the darkened room.

'They wouldn't—' the secretary began only to be hushed by a wave from a man accompanying the guards. This fellow wore plain, rather cheap dark woollen robes.

'The business of the ruling Council of Darujhistan does not wait for appointments, nor sit patiently for the pleasure of a mere merchant.'

Measure nodded to himself, setting the papers down on the cluttered desk before him. 'Ah, yes. Council business. Pray tell, what business could the Council have with this mere merchant?'

The young man produced a sealed scroll from his robes. 'By order of the ruling Council of Darujhistan, as countenanced by its newly elected City Legate, this business is seized as property of said Council as a strategic resource vital to the defence of the city.' He swallowed as if out of breath, or awed by the significance of what he had just blurted out.

Humble Measure cocked one brow. 'Indeed?'

'It is of course your prerogative to dispute the Council's decision. You are free to appeal the judgement with the relevant sub-committee—'

'I am not disputing the Legate's decision,' Humble said calmly.

The young man continued: 'All petitions must be reviewed before any hearing . . .' He blinked, faltering. 'Not disputing?' he repeated as if uncomprehending.

Humble waved to dismiss the very possibility.

'Not – that is – there will be no appeal?'

'None. I've been expecting this, truth be told.'

The young clerk of the council wet his lips then cleared his throat into a fist. 'Very well. You are free to remain, of course, in a purely supervisory role, as the entire production capacity of these facilities is to be immediately given over to the manufacture—'

'Of arms and armour,' said Humble.

The clerk frowned at the scroll in his hands. 'No . . . to the manufacture of construction matériel. Namely chain, bars, quarrying implements and such.'

Humble Measure stared at the fellow as if he hadn't spoken, then said, very softly, 'What was that? Construction matériel?'

'Yes. And half your labour force is to be transferred to the salvage works at—'

The clerk broke off as Humble stalked round the desk to snatch the papers from his hand. The Watch guards pressed forward, wary. Humble read through the official pronouncement, and looked up to blink wonderingly. 'This was not our – that is, I will take this up with the Legate.'

The clerk found himself on familiar ground and this emboldened him to gently take back the nested scrolls. 'You are of course free to register for an appointment with the city court.' He waited for a response, but the burly merchant seemed to ignore him as he returned to his position behind his formidable desk. 'Official copies of this notification will remain on file with the court.'

The merchant waved him away. His job completed in any case, the clerk found no difficulty in bowing and withdrawing. He was relieved: he would now have time to stop at a street stall for steamed dumplings.

Humble Measure sat for some time staring off at the empty darkness of his shadowed office. His secretary watched from the shattered doors, not certain whether he should withdraw or not. Then the man let go a long hissed breath as if releasing something held deep within, something held for a very long time indeed. His hands were fists on the desk before him.

The secretary bowed, tentatively, 'Your orders, sir?'

'Cancel today's schedule, Mister Shiff. I am . . . planning.'

'Perhaps I should request an appointment with the office of the Legate, sir?'

'No. No need for that, Mister Shiff.'

'You do not desire an appointment?'

'Oh, he'll see *me*,' said Humble. 'You can be assured off that. He will see me.'

*　　*　　*

Out on the Dwelling Plain the wind snapped the tattered edges of the awning Scorch and Leff huddled beneath for protection against the glaring sun. In all directions scarves of dust and sand blew about the low, desiccated hills. Leff raised the earthenware jug he was holding to his cracked lips.

'Ain't no more water,' Scorch said, watching him. 'Ran out day b'fore yesterday.' He blinked his eyes sleepily. 'I think.'

Leff looked at the jug as if just noticing it. 'Oh – right. F'got again.' He heaved a tired sigh and set down the jug in the sand next to him, though he retained a firm grip at its neck. 'You know,' he mumbled, forcing himself to swallow, 'I don't think they're comin' back.'

'Who's not comin' back? The lads? That Gadrobi hag?'

'Naw. Not them. They stole everything they could carry, didn't they? Naw . . . I mean what's his name. The chubby guy. Our employer.'

'Not comin' back?' Scorch repeated, his face revealing his customary astonishment. 'But he ain't paid us!'

Leff's long face paled in surprise. 'Whaddya mean he ain't paid us? Y'r supposed to take care of all that paperwork an' such.'

Scorch shook his head in vigorous denial until he blinked, dizzy, and nearly toppled over. 'That's your side of the partnership.'

'No. I clearly remember—' Leff stopped because he discovered he'd once more raised he jug to his mouth. He let it fall. 'Damn. Well, I guess we gotta find him.' He took a deep breath. 'Right. Find him.' Then a sly look came to his bleary eyes and he touched a finger to the side of his nose. 'But . . . come to think of it, he didn't really fire us neither, did he?'

Scorch's expression was its usual utter lack of comprehension. He slowly blinked again. 'Hunh?'

'I mean every day that passes he has to pay us for, right?'

Scorch drew breath to speak, stopped himself. His eyes widened and his lips formed a silent O of understanding. He eyed Leff, who nodded.

They started chuckling. Then they started laughing. They guffawed and slapped their thighs for a long time before they quietened down.

A shepherd minding his flock across the hills nearby heard the wind-borne crazy laughter of evil spirits and hurried his charges on with swift strikes of his staff. The fat gourds of water slung over his shoulders sloshed and rubbed his back raw.

He swore to the Mother Goddess he would never try this short cut through the hills again.

Ephren was by trade a fisherman in a nameless village on the coast where the Mengal mountains sweep down to the shores of the Meningalle Ocean. He was inspecting the caulking of his skiff which he had drawn up in the strand when six long vessels eased silently into the bay. He was curious, but not alarmed, since pirates and raiders were hardly known on this coast. While he watched, the vessels stepped their masts and sweeps ran out to drive them, with surprising speed, to shore.

As they drew closer he saw that the vessels' lines were unlike those of any he knew: very long and low open galleys, their sides lined by rows of shields. These were not from Mengal, Oach, or distant Genabaris. Nor were they the fat carracks of the distant south, Callows, and the far off Confederacy beyond.

When the shields resolved into oval painted masks Ephren's skin shivered as if he had seen a shade and his heart lurched, almost failing. Once before he'd seen a similar vessel. He'd been trading in the south and such a ship had been drawn up on the shore for repairs. Its crew had been the talk of Callows; everyone stared though none had dared approach.

Seguleh, they'd whispered. *Disarm yourself to approach – wait for one to address you then speak only to him or her.*

And there had been some trading; the strangers' amphorae of rare oils for food, sweet water, and timber. No one was wounded or killed. Indeed, the Seguleh had seemed just as curious as their hosts, wandering the markets and walking the fish wharves, if extraordinarily prideful and utterly aloof.

Others further up the shore were pointing now; word of the vessels' arrival was spreading. Ephren studied the hammer and awl in his hands, then set them down and walked – *never run!* – to the hamlet to warn everyone.

All six longships were drawn up side by side. Ephren made certain everyone in the settlement was unarmed and warned them to just go about their normal business. But of course none did. Everyone gathered on the edge of the small curve of beach the Seguleh had landed upon.

There were more of them than he'd ever heard tell of. Down in Callows there'd been some four, together with a regular crew of hired Confederacy sailors – many of the latter outlawed men and women with blood-prices on their heads and nowhere else to turn. Here, all hands and crew were masked Seguleh; hundreds of them. It was an army. An invading army of Seguleh. Ephren almost fainted at the thought. *Hoary Sea-Father! Who could withstand such a force?* Why had they come? Was it in response to these other invaders – the foreign Malazans from across the sea? Perhaps that was the answer; the legendary Seguleh ire, finally provoked.

In any case they ignored Ephren and his family and neighbours. And instead of trading, or setting up camp to overnight, out came the amphorae of rare oils, which to Ephren's astonishment and growing dread they upended over their vessels, splashing the contents all over the open holds and over the sides.

A single torch was lit. One of their number silently held it aloft. From a distance this one's mask was very pale. He, or she, touched it to the nearest of the vessels and the yellow flames leapt quickly from one to the next. A great cloud of black smoke arose and billowed out to sea. The gathered Seguleh stood as still as statues, and as silent, watching.

Then, just as silently, they set out, two abreast, running inland. They took the track Ephren, his neighbours and their parents and grandparents before them had tramped up into the Mengal range, onward to Rushing River pass, then even further, twisting downslope towards the dusty Dwelling Plain far below.

The last to go was the one who had set flame to the vessels. After the last of his brethren had jogged off he remained, motionless, torch still in hand. Finally he dropped the blackened stick and walked up the beach to come within an arm's length of Ephren. And as he passed, his walk so fluid and graceful, Ephren saw that a single smear of fading red alone marked the man's otherwise pristine pale oval mask. He knew enough lore of the Seguleh to know what that should indicate. But still he could not believe it. It was unheard of. Unimaginable. And if in fact it *was* true – then perhaps this was not an invasion as he had thought.

It was, perhaps, in truth more . . . a migration.

CHAPTER VI

They who go out into the world see the wonders wrought by
the gods
And return humbled

Wisdom of the Ancients
Kreshen Reel, compiler

NTSY DREAMT OF THE NORTHERN CAMPAIGNS. HE WAS BACK IN
Black Dog Woods. He lay flat in the cold mud and snow
as auroras and concatenations of ferocious war-magics
flickered and lanced overhead. Mist clung about the trees like
cobwebs. His squad was hunched down around him, toothy grins
gleaming through the camouflaging muck. Downslope, along a
track of churned mud and ice, a column of Free Cities infantry
filed past. He gave a ready hand-sign, he timed his move then leapt
up, aimed, and fired his crossbow. A hail of bolts lanced down
from either side of the road. The column became a churning mass
of screaming men.

The contingent's leader ignored the missiles. Wearing armour of
blackened plates over mail, and a helm beaten to resemble a boar's
head, the man charged the slope. Behind him, soldiers scattered,
struggling in the rime and iced mud. The commander was headed
straight for him. Antsy threw aside his crossbow, knowing it was
useless as every bolt rebounded from the man's virtued armour. The
Sogena City officer swept up a blade that resembled a cold blue shard
of ice. *No choice now but to pull a Hedge.* Antsy threw a Moranth
munition point-blank at the man's iron-armoured chest.

His world shattered into white light as a giant's fist slapped him
backwards. He lay staring up at snow drifting over him like ash. He

felt nothing, just a vague lightness. Faces crowded into his vision. Unending thunder reverberated in his ears.

'Sarge? Antsy? You alive, man?'

He swallowed hot blood mixed with bile. Countless gashes stung his face, and his chest was cold with wet blood. He grabbed one trooper, a woman, and tried to raise himself. 'Did I get the bugger?'

'Yeah, Sarge. You drove him off good.'

Something was stabbing at his arm. Antsy snatched the hand, twisted it, and got a girl's surprised squeak. He looked up, blinking, into darkness. A weak bronze light was shining up the stairwell of the Spawn, and in its glow he saw Orchid glaring at him. 'Sorry.' He released her hand.

'Your neck bled in the night. Did you cut it on the rocks?'

'Something like that. Where're Malakai, Corien?'

'Malakai went further in, exploring. Corien went down to the water. Now take off that armour. I have dressings and a balm.'

He pulled at the laces of his hauberk – more of a jack, really, what some might call a brigandine. Mail over layers of leather toughened by bone and antler banding glued between them. Beneath this he wore a quilted aketon padded with hessian, and under that a linen shirt. When he pulled the shirt over his head Orchid let out a hiss – he presumed at all the scars of old wounds and the crusted blood from his dash against the rocks.

'Corien told me you were a professional soldier. I've never met one before. What's this?'

She was pointing to the tattoo on his shoulder of an arch in front of a field of flames. He thought about lying, then decided it really didn't matter any more. 'That's my old unit. The Bridgeburners. All gone now.'

'Disbanded?'

'Dead.'

'Oh.' She lowered her gaze. 'Is that why it's glowing and the flames are moving?'

'Glowing?' He raised his arm to study it. 'It ain't glowing.'

The girl was frowning, but she shrugged. 'I thought it was.' She handed him a wet cloth. 'Clean yourself up. I guess that makes you my enemy,' she added, musing, watching him wipe away the blood.

'Oh? From the north?'

She glanced away, biting at her lip. 'Sort of. Anyway, you sacked the Free Cities.'

'Sacked ain't the word. Most capitulated.'

She took back the cloth, began cleaning the wound on his neck, rather savagely. 'Who wouldn't in the face of your Claw assassins? Your awful Moranth munitions?'

He winced. 'Careful there, girl.'

'You use them, don't you? Bridgeburners? Siegeworkers, sappers, saboteurs?'

'Yeah. That's right.'

She pushed herself away. 'It's not deep, and it's clean now.' She dug into her shoulder bag then suddenly looked up. 'Those are the things in your pannier bags, yes? The things Malakai wants?'

'That's right.'

'You would have used them against Darujhistan, wouldn't you? Razed the city?'

'I suppose so. If it came to a siege.'

She threw a leather pouch at him. 'Put that on the wound. You Malazans are nothing more than an army of invading murders and bullies. Barbarians.'

Antsy saluted. 'Yes, ma'am.'

They sat at opposite ends of the tilted chamber in silence the rest of the time. Antsy pulled on his shirts and hauberk then set to oiling his weapons and tools. Orchid wrapped herself in Malakai's cloak, which was dry; the man must have thrown it before diving into the water. Digging through the equipment Antsy found a lamp: a simple bowl with a wick. Utterly useless. And without a light he was useless. What a way to pull together a cache for his retirement.

Oh well, he'd probably just have died of boredom anyway.

Corien returned first. He climbed the stairs carrying an armload of flotsam: broken boards, lengths of rope, pieces of broken furniture cut from some dark wood. He dropped the lot in the lowest corner of the chamber then brushed at his brocaded finery.

'What's all this?' Orchid demanded.

He bowed. 'Well, we are wet and the air in here is chill. That calls for a fire.'

'That won't burn. Half of it is wet.'

He looked to Antsy. 'Would you care to do the honours?'

'Certainly.' Antsy crab-walked across the canted floor. He dug in the equipment for a skin of oil from which he poured one precious stream over the refuse, before pulling out his flint and iron.

'Uh-oh,' said Orchid, and clambered to the opposite side.

All it took was a few strikes at the driest length of old rope and the hairs began to sizzle. Blue and yellow flames enveloped the pile. 'Excellent,' said Corien. 'Now, Orchid, you first.'

'Me first what?'

'Your clothes. We ought to dry your clothes. You have that big cloak to wrap yourself in.'

She snorted. 'Tell you what – *you* two wander up the hallway to take a look while *I* dry my clothes.'

Corien bowed again. 'Your wisdom is as unassailable as your beauty.'

She scowled at the courtly praise as if suspecting she was being mocked.

Antsy pushed Corien up the tunnel.

A cloud of sooty black smoke climbed with them. They shared a worried glance in the uncertain light of the fire before a leading edge of the cloud caught an updraught and the smoke was sucked deeper into the complex. Antsy eased out a tensed breath.

Corien led the way. Round the first corner it became almost instantly dark. Even for Antsy, trained and experienced sapper that he was, comfortable in any mine, it was unnervingly close and black. *Like feeling your way through ink.* He resisted the urge to call for Corien. The lad was just ahead, he could hear him: the scrape of the bronze end-cap of his sheath, his slightly tensed breathing, his gloved hands brushing the stone walls as they advanced like blind fish through the murk.

Beneath Antsy's fingers the cut and polished stone walls were as smooth as glazed ceramic. He kept stumbling as the passage not only tilted upwards but canted a good twenty degrees. The walls slid by slick and cool under his fingertips. He glanced back and could just make out a slight lightening of the absolute black – a hint of the fire far behind. 'How far on does this go?' he asked.

'I don't know.'

'Can't you see? I thought you had that unguent thing.'

He thought he glimpsed a bright grin in the gloom. 'I do. I just haven't used it yet.'

'So we're *both* blind as bats?'

'Looks like it.'

'This is useless – not to mention damned dangerous. We should stop here.'

'I agree.'

Antsy slid down one wall. Examining the dark, it appeared that an intersection lay just ahead. Corien was a shadowy shape on his right. He pulled out a scrap of dried meat and chewed for a time. He felt as disheartened as he could ever remember. And for him, a career paranoiac, that was saying something. 'So . . . this is it. The Spawn.' He spoke in a low whisper. The darkness seemed to demand it. He wondered where Malakai had gone off to. He speculated, briefly, that the man had simply abandoned them all as useless baggage. But probably not yet. Not before getting his fifty gold councils' worth.

'Indeed. The Moon's Spawn,' Corien echoed after a time.

'So . . . why'd you come then? No insult intended, but you look like you got money.'

'No offence taken. Yes, the Lim family's been prominent in Daru-jhistan for generations. We practically own a seat on the Council. But money? No. Over the years my uncles have bankrupted us. They've pursued all sorts of reckless plans and political alliances. I think they're taking the family in the wrong direction.' He sighed in the dark. '*But* . . . if I'm to have any influence I must have some sort of leverage . . .'

'So . . . the Spawn.'

'Quite.'

'I understand. Well, good luck.'

'Thank you. And you? The same?'

Antsy shrugged, then realized neither of them could see a thing. His personal reason for coming here to the Spawn was just that, personal. So he fell back on the obvious and cleared his throat. 'Pretty much. I never expected to get old. Didn't think I'd live long enough. Hood's grasp, none of my friends have. Anyway, a man starts to think about his final years. Retiring from soldiering. I need a nest-egg, as they say. Buy some land, or an inn. Find a wife and have kids and be a cranky burden to them. And—' He stopped himself as he seemed to sense something close, watching them, though he could see nothing in the dense murk of shadows.

'Hear that?' he whispered. He listened and after a moment's concentration began to hear the background noises of the Spawn. Groaning seemed to be emerging from the very stone – the conflicting strains and forces of tons of rock held somehow in suspension, as if waiting, poised, ready to drop at any instant. Antsy suddenly felt very small. *A roach in a quarry and the rocks are falling.*

Or was it his sense of not being alone: that this darkness was no ordinary lack of light? After all, the Spawn had been an artefact holy

166

to Elemental Night. He'd heard stories that Mother Dark herself lingered on in all such shrines. He cleared his throat, whispered, 'You don't think there're any spooks 'n' such, do you? Here in the dark?'

'Well, now that you mention it, Red . . . of all the places I can imagine being overrun by your spooks 'n' such, this would have to be it.'

Antsy shot the young man a glance and saw his teeth grinning bright in the gloom. 'Burn dammit, man! You really had me going there.'

'I agree with our fancy friend,' said another voice from the dark.

Corien flinched upright, his long duelling blade coming free in a swift fluid hiss. Antsy's hand went to his pannier. He squinted into the murk; the voice had been Malakai's but the hall seemed utterly empty. It wasn't just that he couldn't see, it was that the hall felt vacant. 'Malakai?'

Then he saw it against one wall: an oval pale smear that was Malakai's face, seemingly floating over nothing, so dark was his garb. Eyes that were no more than black holes in the oval shifted to glance up the hall.

'What's this?'

'We're all wet and cold,' Corien offered. 'I thought that called for a fire.'

'The girl?'

'Presently availing herself of it to dry her clothes.'

The face grimaced, perhaps at the delay. 'Fine. I'll continue to reconnoitre.'

'What have you found so far?' Antsy asked.

Malakai answered, slowly, as if resenting having to share anything at all. 'This area has been emptied of everything. All valuables, all possessions. Even every scrap of furniture. Fuel for fires, I imagine.'

'Any lanterns? Lamps?'

The ghost of a smile touched and went from the pale lips. 'What need would the Children of the Night have for those?' Then he was gone in the dark, utterly without a sound.

Snarling, Antsy fell back against the wall. 'Hood on a pointy spike! No lamps at all? Nothing? What am I supposed to do?'

'There are other people here. They'll have lanterns and such.'

Antsy eyed the youth, who was grinning his encouragement. He shrugged. 'Yeah. I suppose so.'

They sat for a time in silence, Antsy's vision gradually adapting to the dark. He caught Corien waving after Malakai. 'Your employer seems one to prefer working alone.'

'Yeah. I get that feeling too.'

'Then, may I ask . . . why did he hire the two of you?'

Antsy cleared his throat while he considered what to say. 'Well, me he hired as a guard. An' Orchid, she's a trained healer and says she can read the Andii scribbles.'

After a time Corien said, 'If she really can read the language then I can see how she would be valuable. And you are this fellow's guard? In truth, he strikes me as the sort one should guard against.' And he chuckled at his witticism.

Not wanting to dig himself in any more, Antsy added nothing. Corien, ever polite, refrained from further questions. They sat in silence. As the time passed, Antsy became aware of more sounds surrounding him. He could hear the waves of the Rivan Sea shuddering up through the rock like a resting giant's heartbeat. Other noises intruded: the fire crackling and popping, and faintly, once or twice, what sounded like voices from far away, further into the maze of halls and rooms ahead.

He heard Orchid coming up the hall long before she called, tentatively, 'Hello?'

'Yes?' Corien answered.

She walked up to them with the ease of one completely unhindered by the dark. 'All done. Or good enough, anyway. Help yourselves. The embers are hot.'

Antsy let out a thoughtful breath. 'I'm thinkin' I'm gonna dry my footgear. You should too, Corien. We could be facing a lot of walking, and believe me, there's nothin' worse than blisters and sore feet on a march.'

'Very well. I bow to your superior experience.'

Antsy wasn't sure how to respond to that; he didn't detect any hint of sarcasm at all. The lad seemed to be one of those rare ones who could actually take advice without resentment or sullenness. Maybe he wouldn't be such a burden after all.

They dried what gear they could while the embers lasted. Corien re-oiled his weapons. Watching, Antsy thought him too liberal with his oil: it was damnably expensive stuff, but the lad could probably afford it.

'So where is Malakai?' Orchid asked.

'Reconnoitring,' Corien answered.

The girl made a face in the dimming orange glow. 'I hope he never comes back.'

'Our chances are better with him,' Antsy said.

'Very true,' Corien added. 'Red and I are blind in the dark.'

'I thought you had some sort of preparation.'

'That is true. However, it is only good for a short time.'

'So you lied to Malakai?'

'Not at all. He didn't ask how long it would be effective.'

She let out a frustrated growl. 'So this is it? You two come all this way just to sit and wait for Malakai to hold your hands?'

'Hey now!' Antsy protested. 'Just a minute there, girl.'

'Well? What are you going to do about it?'

Antsy took a long breath, thinking. 'You can see fine?'

'Yes. Never better. My vision seems even stronger than before.'

He nodded, then remembered Corien might not see. 'Okay. We'll pack up, then.'

They shared out the waterskins, the panniers of food, and the equipment. Antsy wondered where in the Abyss Malakai had gotten to but there was nothing he could do about the man's absence. And anyway, there was nothing the man could do about his blindness either.

Leaning close, Corien murmured, 'Very strong-willed, our lass.'

Antsy merely grunted his assent. *Tongue like a whip dipped in tar and sand.* The girl's jibe had gotten under his skin. Were they malingering here on the doorstep because they were afraid to venture in? He'd always pulled his weight; he was proud of that. He might not be crazy brave, but neither did he ever shirk. Was he loosing his edge?

They felt their way up the hall. Antsy had Corien leading, sword drawn, himself next, and Orchid bringing up the rear. As they walked, awkward and slow over the tilted floors, he assembled his crossbow. That at least he could do blind.

At an intersection of four halls he whispered for a halt. 'All right,' he said to Orchid. 'Which way? What do you think?'

'Let's ask Malakai,' she said.

'Okay . . . just where in the Abyss *is* he?'

'Right over there.' She must've pointed but he couldn't catch the motion. 'I see you skulking in that doorway, Malakai. Enjoying yourself?'

Silence. Not a brush of sleeve or cuff of booted heel. Then Antsy flinched as directly in front of him he heard the man say, 'Well done, Orchid. I'd thought you the least of the party. But perhaps you and I could manage things on our own. These two don't seem to be of much use.'

'What of Red's munitions?'

'There's much less structural damage than I'd feared. Perhaps they won't be needed.'

Antsy had had enough of them talking as if he wasn't standing right there and cleared his throat. 'Listen, if there's no light then I *will* turn round and leave. There's no point in me going on.'

Silence. Malakai murmured, 'Leave? It seems plain there's no going back.' He sounded as if he was enjoying giving this news far too much.

'What do you mean? I'll just wait for another boat.'

'I overheard they drop people off at different places each time.'

Antsy wanted to punch the bastard. He squinted so hard stars burst before his light-starved eyes. 'But a pick-up? There must be a pick-up!'

'Yes. A place called the Gap of Gold, apparently. Just where that is I have no idea.' From the man's tone Antsy could imagine him arching a brow there in the darkness. 'We'll just have to poke around . . .'

Antsy managed to bite back his yelled opinion. He almost exploded so great was the wash of rage and frustration that coursed through him. No wonder no one had returned in so long! This island was a death trap – and he'd walked right in like a lamb! *You damned fool. You should've known better than this.*

He realized that the others were talking and that he had no idea what they'd been discussing. 'What's that?'

'Some way ahead,' Malakai said. 'People. I spotted them earlier. They have a few lights burning.'

That was all Antsy needed to hear. 'Why didn't you say so? Let's go!'

'I'll go first,' Malakai cautioned. 'Give the crossbow to Orchid.'

'She can't use it. She'd put one in your back.'

'At least she'd have a better view of her target than you would. What do you say, Orchid? Will you take it?'

'Yes,' she agreed, reluctantly, her voice sour with distaste. 'I suppose so.'

Antsy held out the weapon, felt her take it.

'Okay. Red, Corien, you two are in the middle. Orchid will follow, guiding you.'

Antsy growled.

They advanced in that order for some time. Orchid would whisper what was ahead, giving directions. Antsy trailed his left hand along a wall, his shortsword out. Malakai led them on through hallway after hallway, round corners, past open portals that gaped as blind emptiness to Antsy's questing fingers. It seemed to him that the air was steadily getting warmer. And he was completely lost. Then a familiar stink offended his nose. To Antsy it was like a veteran's homecoming: the pungent miasma of an old encampment. Smoke, the stale stink of long unwashed bodies, noisome of latrines. He heard snatches of exchanged words, echoes of footsteps, wood being broken and chopped.

Ahead, his light-deprived eyes beheld what seemed like a golden sunset far overhead. He stopped, squinted his disbelief. The apparition resolved itself into light reflecting off a high domed ceiling. Silver paint or perhaps actual gems dotted stars and wisps across the dome in constellations completely unfamiliar to him. The night sky of true Night? Something for philosophers to get into fistfights over.

Orchid whispered, 'Malakai's at some kind of low wall or balcony ahead. He's signalling for you . . . wants you to crawl over.'

'Straight ahead?'

'Yes.'

Grunting, Antsy sheathed his shortsword and got down to crawl along the cool polished stone floor until his hand hit a wall.

'To your right,' Malakai hissed. Antsy shuffled along until he touched the man.

'Okay. Take a look.'

He felt up to the lip of the wall and peered over. At first he saw nothing; the glare from what was only feeble lamplight blinded him. Then, slowly, he began to make out details. He was looking down about three or four storeys on to a city, or village, cut from solid rock. Light shone from a small huddle of buildings near its centre. People walked about, in and out of the light's glare. Muted conversations sounded. A woman's harsh laugh broke the relative quiet. He'd seen eight people so far.

'What do you think?' Malakai asked.

'There's a lot of them.'

'At least twenty.'

'Damn. Too many.'

'I agree.'

'There might be a watch up here somewhere.'

'On the other side right now.'

'Hunh. Time's running out then. What do you have in mind?'

'Parley for information.'

'I agree. Who?'

'You and Corien. I'll shadow. Orchid stays out of sight.'

Antsy ran a thumbnail over his lips. 'Okay. Rally to here?'

'Might as well.'

Antsy waved for Corien and Orchid to come up.

It was a village sculpted from stone in every detail. Antsy and Corien descended a street of shallow stairs that ran between high walls cut with windows, doors, and even planters. All now was wreckage, tilted and uneven. Litter covered the street; fallen sheets of stone choked some alleys. Jagged cracks ran up the walls. And everywhere lay the remnants of water damage; they breathed in the stink of mouldering and mud. The stairs opened on to the main concourse of the houses the people occupied; they'd obviously just found the place and moved in.

Antsy felt naked. He couldn't remember the last time he'd been without his munitions. He'd hated leaving them behind, but Malakai had been right: no sense in risking these people getting their hands on any. He carried only a dirk; Corien his parrying gauche. They advanced side by side down the middle of the street, careful to step over rubbish, broken possessions and scatterings of excrement. The population seemed to just squat wherever they wanted. Up ahead four men stood within the light of a single flickering lantern. Since Antsy and Corien stood in the dark the men could not see them – so much for having a light with you on guard.

'Hello,' he called.

Three of the men yelped, diving for cover. A woman screamed and was roundly cursed. Only one man remained standing in the light. 'Yes?' he called, squinting. 'Who's there?'

'Newcomers.'

'Ah! Welcome, welcome. Please, come right up to the light and let's have a look at you. You gave us quite a start there.'

'We'll stay back here for now, if you don't mind.'

The man held up his empty hands. 'Fine, fine. Whatever you wish. *We*, you say? How many are you?'

'My friend and I. We speak for a larger party. We'd like some information.'

The man motioned towards the houses as though beckoning

172

his companions. 'Come on, come on! No sense hiding. It's not hospitable.' He turned back to Antsy and Corien, bowing and holding out open empty hands. 'Sorry, but we're a harmless lot, I assure you. My name is Panar. We're just poor stranded folk, like yourself.'

'Stranded?' Antsy echoed. Something churned sourly in his gut at the word.

The man nodded eagerly. 'Oh, yes.' He raised his arms to gesture all about. 'This is it. All there is. The Spawn. Utterly emptied. Looted long ago. The Confederation sailors might as well have knocked us all over the heads and pitched us into the drink.'

Antsy gaped at the man. 'What?' And a voice sneered in his mind: *Fucking knew it! Too good to be true.* He tottered a step backwards.

Corien steadied him with a hand at his back. 'I don't believe it,' the lad whispered.

'Believe it,' Panar answered. 'The Twins have had their last jest with us. All the gold, all the artwork, whatever. All gone. Looted already. Come, come! Relax. There's nothing here for anyone to fight over.'

Corien leaned close to Antsy. 'This smells as bad as a brothel.'

'Yeah.' Antsy raised his voice: 'What about the Gap of Gold?'

Panar's brows furrowed. He rubbed his chin. 'The gap of what? What's that?'

'Bullshit,' Antsy muttered. He noted that none of the men from the fire had reappeared. Nor any others, for that matter. 'Let's get out of here.'

Corien began edging backwards. 'Yes. Let's.'

'There's no other way forward!' Panar shouted. 'This is it. The end of the road . . . *for you.*'

A screaming horde disgorged from the surrounding doorways and engulfed them. Antsy went down like a ship beneath a human wave. He was trampled, bitten, punched and scratched. Broken-nailed fingers clawed at his eyes, his mouth, pulled at his moustache. Hands fought to slide a rope over his head. The stench choked him more than the slick greasy hands at his neck. Somehow he managed to get his dirk free and swung it, clearing away the hands from his eyes and mouth. He pushed his feet beneath him and stood up, slashing viciously, raising pained howls from both men and women. He reached out blindly to find a wall, put his back to it. They screamed and shrieked at him, inhuman, insane. It was as savage a close-quarter knife work as any he'd faced in all the tunnel-clearing he'd done. He slid along the wall searching for an opening, slashing and jabbing, ringed round by glaring eyes and dirty grasping hands.

His questing left hand found a gaping doorway and he slid into it, able now to face his attackers without having to defend his flanks at the same time. His face, arms and legs stung from cuts and slashes. His leggings hung torn.

A shout sounded from the dark and the mad frenzied faces backed away, disappearing into the ink of utter night. Antsy stood panting, his heart hammering, squinting into the gloom. '*Corien!*' he bellowed.

'Here!' came a distant answering call.

'Here! Here! Dear!' other voices tittered from the dark, mocking and laughing. Antsy himself was frankly surprised to hear the youth's response; he hadn't thought the dandy could've withstood such a savage onslaught.

'You're trapped,' Panar said from somewhere nearby in the murk. 'Maybe you are with others. Maybe not. But I wonder . . . just where are they?'

Antsy said nothing. He'd been wondering that too. Earlier Malakai had hinted at his and Orchid's going it alone. Now the two had all the supplies – and his munitions as well! And Malakai had neatly manoeuvred him and Corien down here. Had he and Orchid simply sauntered off leaving them to keep these people busy?

But he was being unfair to the girl. Surely she wouldn't go along with that. And the munitions were useless without him to set them. Still . . . where *were* they?

'The way I see it you have only one choice,' Panar continued from the cover of the gloom, 'give up now. You can't guard yourself for ever. Eventually you'll weaken. Or go down in some desperate rush into the dark. But where would you rush to? Believe me, there's no escape. Best just to give up now.'

Noises sounded from the street and dim light blossomed. Antsy peered out – a lantern had been lit. Rocks clattered from the walls around him and he flinched back. Where in the Abyss was Malakai? 'Hey, Corien,' he shouted, 'what do you say we link up and kill the lot of these rats?'

'Gladly! I got two, I believe.'

Two. Out of how damned many? Too many. Had Malakai written them off?

Then the light went out. Shouts of alarm and fear all around. Feet slapped the stone floor, running. A woman asked from the dark, her voice tremulous, 'Is it the fiend?' Someone cursed her to shut up. It seemed to Antsy that these people were uncommonly scared of the dark. He started to wonder if perhaps he should be too.

Was it Malakai? Antsy considered a rush to the far side of the street – Corien sounded as if he was there.

'Red?' Malakai's disembodied voice spoke from just outside his doorway.

'Yes?'

'Cross the street then go four doors to the right.'

'Aye.'

No answer. The man was gone – Antsy wasn't even sure he'd been there at all: just a voice in the dark. He dashed out into the street. Part of the way across he tripped over a body and fell, knocking something hot that clattered off across the stone street. Cursing, he chased after it, only to bash his head against a wall. He knelt, squeezing his head in his hands, biting his lip. Someone ran by in the absolute black; Antsy had no idea who it might've been. Panicked shouting sounded all around.

Feeling about blindly Antsy found what he'd sought and burned his hand in the process: the snuffed lantern. With its handle in one hand and his shortsword in the other, he felt his way down the wall. Feet thumped and scuffed in the dark. Someone was crying far off in one of the houses. He reached what he thought was the fourth doorway. 'Corien?' he whispered.

'Here.'

Antsy recognized the voice. He slipped in, covered the doorway behind him. 'Malakai speak to you?'

'Yes. And—'

'I'm here,' Orchid cut in from the blackness.

'What's the plan?'

'I'll lead you out,' Orchid said. 'Malakai said he'll keep them busy.'

'Okay, but listen. Malakai seems to know his business, I admit, but these people scattered like chickens. He's not *that* good. One of them mentioned some *thing* . . . a fiend.'

'I don't know anything about that,' Orchid snapped. 'We just have to get out of here. Take these.'

The panniers hit Antsy in the chest. He arranged them over his shoulders. Orchid pushed out past him. Someone else, Corien, bumped him and squeezed his arm. 'How'd you fare?' the lad asked.

'Okay. Scrapes. You?'

'Just between us . . . I took a bad one. Someone stuck me. I rubbed in something I purchased. We'll see.'

'*Hurry,*' Orchid hissed.

She led them each by the arm through the narrow canted streets. Light now shone from a few high windows. Everything was quiet, hushed. Antsy imaged everyone huddled in their rooms, waiting. What was out there in the dark? What were they afraid of? The dark itself?

'These are quarters for servants, guards, and others of lesser status,' Orchid whispered as she yanked them along. 'Mostly abandoned for centuries. The Moon's population was always low. The Andii have few children.'

Antsy wondered whether she spoke to distract herself from the fear that surely must be writhing in her guts. They twisted and turned up the narrow tilting stone streets. Antsy was completely lost. Then Orchid slowed, hesitated, came to a halt. 'Where are we going?' Antsy asked.

'I don't know,' she hissed, low. 'Just away from there for now. I thought . . .'

'What?'

'I thought I saw something. A dark shape.'

Antsy barked a near-hysterical laugh. '*Dark?* Isn't it all dark?'

'No. Not at all. I can't explain it. I can see well enough. Textures, shapes, even shadows. But that one seemed . . . deep.'

'Deep,' Antsy echoed, uncomprehending. 'Where is it?'

'Gone now.'

Totally blind, Antsy felt as if he was about to be jumped at any instant. He gripped the still-warm lantern as if he could squeeze comfort from it. 'Well, where will you meet Malakai?'

'Nowhere. Anywhere. He said he'll find us.'

'Then let's just get into cover. A small room. Defensible.'

'Yes,' Corien said in support, his voice tight with pain.

'Well . . . okay.'

A shriek tore through the blackness then, echoing, trailing off into hoarse gurgling. A chorus of terrified screams and sobbing erupted in response as the locals broke into a gibbering panic.

'I don't think that's Malakai's doing,' Corien said.

'No . . .' Antsy agreed. He sheathed the shortsword and took a tight grip of his pannier.

Orchid rushed them into a room. Antsy wanted to light the lantern so badly he could taste the oil and smell the smoke. But he set it aside; the light would only bring their pursuers like flies. They waited, he and Corien covering the open doorless portal. No further screams lifted the hair on his neck, though he did hear distant voices raised in argument.

Then, down the street, the scuff of footsteps. 'Company,' he hissed, crouching, drawing his shortsword.

'Red?' came Malakai's voice, whispering.

A nasty suspicion born of years of warfare among the deceptions of magery made Antsy ask, 'Red who?'

'Red . . . whose name that isn't.'

Antsy grunted his assent, backed away from the portal.

Orchid gasped as Malakai came shuffling noisily into the room. Antsy and Corien demanded together: 'What? What is it?'

'Company,' Malakai said, the familiar acid humour in his voice. 'Your friend Panar. And Antsy, I like that counter-sign. Speaks of a sneaky turn of mind. I like it. We'll adopt it.'

'Fine,' Antsy answered, impatient. 'But what's the idea dragging this guy off? Now they'll come after us.'

'No they won't. They're too busy fighting over who's in charge now. Isn't that so, Panar?'

A pause, cloth tearing, then Panar's voice, rather blurry and slurred: 'They'll ransom me.'

'No they won't. You're dead and buried to them.'

'They'll ransom me with information. Just go back and ask.'

Malakai laughed quietly at that. 'You'll give us all the information we need.'

'I won't talk.'

'Then,' Malakai whispered, 'I'll have to do . . . *this*.'

From behind a hand or a balled cloth erupted a gurgled muted scream of agony. Feet kicked against the stone floor.

Orchid gagged. 'Gods, no! Stop him! Stop him, Red!'

Then silence and heavy breathing. Antsy imagined Orchid covering her eyes. Malakai's voice came low and cold – as when they'd met and he warned her he may leave her to die: 'If you don't like it, Orchid, then I suggest you step outside.'

'Red?' she hissed. '*Do* something! You aren't going to let him torture this poor man, are you?'

Antsy fumbled for words. 'I'm sorry . . . I've questioned men myself. Has to be done.'

'Oh, you've *questioned* men, have you? Her voice dripped scorn from the darkness. 'Barbarian!'

She had his sympathy. He'd lived his entire adult life in the military and he'd long ago been hardened to brutality. But men – and women – like Malakai left him squeamish.

'What do you say now, Panar?' Malakai asked. 'Tell us what we want. After all, what does it matter? We're all dead anyway, yes?'

Silence in the room's darkness. Then a groan, someone shifting. 'Fine. Yes. What do you want?'

'Let's start at the beginning,' Malakai said conversationally. 'Who are you?'

'Panar Legothen, of March.'

Antsy grunted at that: March was one of the so-called Confederation of Free Cities.

'How did you get out here?'

A laugh full of self-mockery. 'You won't believe me, but I was one of the first. I came out in my own boat.'

'And?'

Silence, followed by a long wistful sigh. 'What a sight it was then. A glittering mess. Everywhere you looked pearls, moonstones, tiger-eye, sapphires, gold and silver. Silver everything! You could scoop it up by the armload.'

Antsy stopped himself from barking at the man to go on. Where was it all? What happened? He wanted to take the fellow by the shirt and shake him, but Malakai was obviously just letting him talk himself out.

'There were others, of course. Sometimes I fought – most times I just ran. Where could I keep it all though? We all had too much to carry, so we started to strike bargains, band together. Stake out territories. This here, this town – Pearl Town, we call it – is just a little place. The bottom of things. Where I've ended up.'

'What happened?' Orchid prompted gently.

Another groan from the dark. 'Me and a few partners, we'd cleaned out our stake. When we saw more dangerous fortune-hunters arriving we knew things would be goin' downhill fast. So we made for the Gap. But we'd waited just a touch too long. Got greedy. I caught that particular fever when I arrived. I think if I'd just picked up the first thing I found . . . a beautiful statuette in silver, such a sweet piece . . . if I'd just climbed back down to my boat and left right then and there I'd be a rich and happy man right now.'

'But?' Orchid prompted again after a long silence.

Stirring, the man roused himself. 'Well . . . first we met the Malazans. They controlled about a third of the isle then. We bribed our way past them. Then a band of other looters jumped us. I guess they waited there for fools like us to go to all the effort to bring the riches to them. I got away with a bare fraction and reached the Gap.'

'What is it?' Malakai demanded.

'It's just what it says – an exit. A big series of terraces open to the outside. I guess the Andii used them to view the night sky or some such thing. The water comes right up to them now. They pull their boats up there, take their cut then take you out. Least, that's what everyone said happens . . .'

'But . . . that's not what happened,' Corien said.

'No. That's not what happened.' The man's voice thickened, almost choking. 'I handed over all my best pieces, the cream of the riches – and do you know what they said?'

'It wasn't enough,' Malakai said.

'That's right. It wasn't enough. I threw them everything I had, even my weapons. They still claimed I was short of the payment for passage.' The man sounded as if he was on the verge of tears. 'You've all probably figured it out, haven't you? But only then did I realize what was going on. Up until that moment I truly believed they would take their cut and let me go. God of the Oceans, what a fool I was.'

'They just sent you back to collect more,' Malakai said.

'Yes. This is their gold mine and they need the labour. They said they'd keep what I'd brought as a down payment on my exit fee. Ha! That's a joke. I had nothing left, just the shirt I'm wearing. I simply wandered off and ended up here.'

That mailed fist of rage brought stars to Antsy's vision once more. *Trapped! Fucking knew it! A joke? Oh yes, because all Oponn's jests are bad news!*

Orchid was saying, 'How do you survive down here?'

'Oh, we scrape together enough to buy food and water from the Confederation crews. At astounding prices, of course. Water is truly worth its weight in gold.'

'We want up,' Malakai cut in. 'Which way do we go?'

'There are stairs . . . it's the only way. It's—'

A second scream exploded in the night, making Antsy flinch and raising an answering cry from Orchid. It wailed, rising in terror and agony until it cracked as if the throat carrying it had been torn out.

In the long silence following that terrifying sound Malakai asked mildly, 'And what was that?'

'Ah. That. The Spawn is an ancient place, you know. Full of inhuman spirits and sorcery. Some claim it's a curse on all of us.

Humans aren't welcome here. Myself, I believe it to be an escaped demon. Every few days it comes to feed. I was rather hoping it would show up here.'

'That's enough,' Malakai said. 'Let's get going.'

'And . . . what of me?'

'You we leave behind. Congratulations. Maybe you'll be the last off this rock.'

'But – as I told you – there's nothing left.' The man sounded genuinely puzzled. 'What could you possibly be looking for?'

A long awkward silence followed that seemingly simple question. Antsy wasn't looking for anything beyond someone to pay him handsomely for his skills. And to look into rumours he'd heard about this place. Corien wanted riches and the influence they could bring. Malakai similarly so, he imagined. He had no idea what Orchid wanted.

Malakai spoke into the silence: 'Myself, I'm searching for the gardens of the moon.'

Antsy blinked in the night. There was no such thing; it was just poetic – wasn't it? But Orchid's gasp of recognition told him she knew something of it. As for Panar, he started laughing. He laughed on and on and would not stop. It seemed the man was laughing not so much at Malakai's gallows jest as at them, and himself, and at the entire absurd fate they'd all so deftly manoeuvred themselves into through greed, and ambition, and short-sightedness – all the classic character flaws that lead men and women to their self-inflicted dooms.

And he kept on laughing even after Malakai threw him aside.

*   *   *

Nathilog had been among the first of the settlements of north-western Genabackis to fall to the Malazans. It had been a notorious pirate haven before that, ruled by might of fist under a series of self-styled barons. Now, after decades of Malazan occupation, its aristocracy was thoroughly Talianized. Trade across the top of the Meningalle Ocean was heavy as the raw resources and riches of a continent passed across to the Imperial homeland, and troops and war matériel returned.

Agull'en, the Malazan governor, resided in the rebuilt hall of rulership once occupied by his robber baron antecedents. It was here at the end of his daily reception that a mage suddenly appeared in the hall. His picked bodyguard of twenty Barghast surged forward to interpose themselves between him and the interloper. His own mage, a Rhivi shaman, stared frozen at the apparition, clearly stunned.

Remind me to fire the useless sot, Agull'en snarled to himself, then turned his attention to the mage. Tall, regal-looking with his long hair pushed back over his skull. A greying goatee. Plain brown woollen robes, though a wealth of rings on the fingers. The man's face was badly lined – red and blistered with livid scars as if he had recently been severely wounded, or lashed.

The governor steeled himself and hardened his voice: 'What is the meaning of this? Who has sent you?'

The man bowed low, hand at goatee. 'Greetings, Agull'en, governor of north-west Genabackis. I am come with salutations from my master, the newly installed Legate of Darujhistan.'

Agull'en frowned, puzzled. 'Legate? Darujhistan has a Legate?'

'Newly installed.'

'I see.' Agull'en peered around, thinking. His mage, he noted, was nowhere to be seen. Had the man fled? Damn him! He'd see him flogged! Then the instincts that had guided his path these many years over so many rivals and up so many rungs asserted themselves and his lips eased into a knowing, rather condescending smile. 'You wish to renegotiate trade agreements. Very well. A trade delegation may be sent.'

'No, Governor. My master does not wish to renegotiate details of trade.'

'No? Treaties then? This "Legate" must speak with the Malazan ambassador there in Darujhistan regarding any treaties.'

'Be assured that my master will deal with the ambassador when his time comes. No, I am come as the mouthpiece of the one who is the rightful spokesman for all Genabackis. And he demands, my good governor, that you swear allegiance to him.'

Agull'en sat forward in his chair. 'I'm sorry? Swear allegiance to this Legate of Darujhistan?' He laughed his utter disbelief. 'Are you mad? Is he mad?'

The mage bowed once more. 'No, sir. I assure you he is not.'

'And what if I refuse this demand? What will this self-styled Legate do should I decline his invitation? You may be an accomplished practitioner in your field, mage. But I offer a lesson in stark politics for your consideration. Malazans have thousands of troops. Darujhistan has none.'

'If you do not swear, then we will find someone who will,' the mage answered simply.

181

Agull'en's face darkened as his rage climbed beyond his control. He waved his guards forward. 'Flay this bastard!'

The guards did not live long enough to draw weapons. And the hall of rulership at Nathilog was once more in need of rebuilding.

Similar scenes played themselves out across the north of the continent from one ex-free city to the next: Cajale, Genalle, and Tulips. Last of all was a visitation within the temporary wood hall of mayorship in Pale. The mayor was dining with guests when an apparition wavered into view before the long table. The guests started up in panic, raising eating daggers. Guards were called. The ghostly figure of a tall man opened his hands in greeting. 'I would speak to the Lord Mayor,' he called.

Guards came scrambling in, crossbows raised. A portly bearded man raised his arms, bellowing, 'Hold!' The guards halted, taking aim. 'Who are you and what do you wish?' the man demanded of the apparition.

The figure bowed. 'Lord Mayor of Pale. I am come as the mouth of the newly installed Legate of Darujhistan.'

The mayor frowned behind his beard, clearly astonished. He glanced aside to another guest, a balding dark man in a black leather jerkin. 'Is that so? A Legate in Darujhistan?'

'Yes. Newly installed. As such, he claims his traditional position as spokesman for all Genabackis. And in such capacity he demands your allegiance.'

The mayor's tangled brows climbed his forehead. 'Indeed. My allegiance in . . . what? May I ask?'

'In Darujhistan's enlightened guidance and protection.'

'Ah. How . . . appealing.' The mayor shot another glance aside to the balding dark fellow who had sat forward, chin in fists, eyes narrowed to slits. The Lord Mayor wiped a cloth across his brow and cleared his throat. Then a thought seemed to strike him and his thick brows drew down together. 'All Genabackis, you say? What of Black Coral? Does this claim of suzerainty extend over the Tiste Andii?'

The shade's haggard features twisted in distaste. 'Black Coral is no longer part of Genabackis.'

'Ah. I see. How . . . unfortunate.' The Lord Mayor drew breath, raising his chin. 'We in Pale wish his excellency to know that we consider it an honour to be so invited. We convey our salutations, and beg time to give this offer the serious consideration it demands.' The man sat heavily, gulping in breath, his face flushed.

The apparition straightened; it did not bother to disguise his disapproval. 'Consider carefully, then. You have two days.' It disappeared. The Lord Mayor and his guests sat in stunned silence. The dark balding man pushed back his chair and stood, revealing the sceptre inscribed on the left of his chest.

'You are leaving us, Fist K'ess?'

The Fist wiped his hands in a cloth and threw it to the table. His gaze remained exactly where the casting had once stood. 'My apologies, Lord Mayor,' he grated. 'Duty calls me away.'

'We understand.'

The Fist stalked from the hall, followed by two officers, male and female.

A woman beside the mayor whispered, fierce: 'Who is this Legate? Who is he to challenge the Empire?'

The mayor raised a hand for silence. 'We will wait and see.'

'And if two days pass and we are none the wiser?'

The mayor shrugged. 'Then we will agree.'

'And the Malazans?'

'We will tell them we agreed only to buy time.'

Another guest smiled his approval. 'Which is true – time to discover which of them is the stronger.'

The mayor picked up his crystal wine glass, studied the muddy red liquid. 'Of course.'

Outside the hall, Fist K'ess turned to the male officer with him. 'Cancel all furloughs, restrict the troops to garrison. Have we no one capable of raising the Imperial Warren?'

'None.'

The Fist pulled savagely at his chin. 'What a gods-awful state of affairs. Going to the dogs, we are. Go!'

The man saluted, ran off.

The Fist started walking again, striking a stiff marching pace. The other officer, the woman, hurried after him. 'Might I remind you we are at half strength, Fist,' she said. 'Half went south at Ambassador Aragan's request. Now we know why.'

'Yes, yes. Your point?'

'We are under strength. In case of an uprising I suggest we withdraw.'

The Fist halted. Next to him lay a stretch of buildings still in ruins from the siege of years ago. Squatters now occupied it, living in huts of wood and straw among the fallen stone walls. 'Withdraw?' he repeated, outraged. 'Withdraw to where?'

'West. The mountains.'

He rubbed his chin. 'Throw ourselves on the mercy of the Moranth, you mean? Aye, there's some merit there. I'll keep it in mind. Until then, no. Too much Malazan blood was spilled taking this city. We'll not withdraw.' He started off again, his pace swift.

Captain Fal-ej, of the Seven Cities, struggled to keep up.

K'ess barked at her: 'Send our swiftest rider south, Captain. I want to know from that fat-arse Aragan what in the name of fallen Hood is going on!'

Captain Fal-ej saluted and ran off.

K'ess massaged his unshaven throat. He spat aside. 'What a gods-damned time to choose to quit drinking. Just when things were getting quiet . . .' He shook his head and hurried on.

*   *   *

As was his habit of late, the Warlord spent time in the evening in silent solitary vigil overlooking the valley leading west to the glow of Darujhistan. Yet perhaps his gaze passed over the city, even beyond, to the barrow of Anomander Rake, once Lord of Moon's Spawn. This evening was dark and close. Thick clouds massed from the north, over Lake Azur and the Tahlyn Mountains beyond.

Something troubled the Warlord; this everyone spoke of, though none knew what it was. The castings of the shamans hinted at blood and violence to come. Word of war against the Malazan invaders swept like wildfire across the wide plains – though the elders them-selves had not raised the White Spear. All this was might have been part of the weight the Warlord carried. For though he was so named, some now whispered that he was too old, too grief-stricken, and perhaps his time had passed.

He may or may not have been aware of these whispers within the assembly as he stood his solitary evening vigils out upon the hillside. Some said that in truth it was his distaste for it all that drove him from the tents to begin with.

In either case, late into one such evening the Warlord suddenly knew he was no longer alone. He glanced about to see standing a short distance off a man he'd thought his friend. A single glimpse, however, was enough to convince him that that was no longer the case. He shifted his weight to face the man, slid a hand over the grip of the hammer at his side. 'Greetings, Baruk. What brings you from the city?'

The man certainly was Baruk, but not the Baruk the Warlord knew, with that avid hungry light in his fever-bright eyes, the fresh scars that traced a map of pain across his face. 'The one you called Baruk is gone. Burned away in the cleansing flames of truth. I am Barukanal, restored and reborn.'

Gossamer flames of power burned like auroras at the man's hands, where forests of rings now gleamed gold. Caladan's grip tightened upon his hammer. 'Truth? Which truth would that be?'

'The truth of power. One I know you are intimately familiar with. The truth that power will always be used. The question only being by whom.'

'Then you know enough not to tempt me.'

A gleeful mockery of a smile twitched the man's mouth. 'I recall enough to know that to be an empty threat, Warlord.'

In answer Caladan's lips pulled back over his prominent canines. 'Then you presume too much. If the . . . presence . . . I sense makes any effort to reach beyond Darujhistan, I will not hesitate to remove the city from the face of the continent.'

The one he once knew as Baruk gave a sham frown of sorrow. Backing away, he gestured to the west. 'More deaths, Warlord? How many more must die . . . ?' The figure dissipated into the night, leaving Brood to pull his clenched hand from the hammer and massage its stiff knuckles. He let out an animal growl and headed back up the hill to the distant lit tents. Baruk taken, he mused. That one will be a dangerous opponent. Yet he wondered at the constant stream of tears that had glistened on the man's scarred cheeks. And the eyes – that feyness could just as easily have been torment and horror trapped within.

Before he reached the tent the flap was pushed aside and a Rhivi elder hurried out. 'The shamans bring amazing news from the north, Warlord.'

Something in Caladan's expression caused the elder to flinch aside. 'Why am I not surprised?' Brood rumbled as he stalked past.

*   *   *

It was the most difficult act he had ever had to force himself to commit. Every step deliberate, stiff, reluctant, he approached the squat, ominous house that stood alone in the woods of Coll's estate. Every beat of Rallick's pounding heart screamed at him to flee. For not so long ago, when the Jaghut Tyrant Raest returned to the city only to be entombed here in this Azath construct, so too was he. And perhaps the house would not give him up a second time.

But he did not flee. He understood necessity. He alone in this city seemed to understand that there were things that simply had to be done. Reaching the door he paused, hand outstretched. Someone had been digging in the yard. A trail of dirt led across the grounds. He knelt to study the spoor. Two sets of tracks. One in rotted leather sandals. The other naked bony feet. Very bony, and very definitely inhuman in shape. Shedding dirt as they came.

While he crouched there before the door it opened and Rallick found himself staring up at the grim, emaciated figure of the ancient Jaghut Tyrant Raest, prisoner to the house, and now its . . . guardian? Or perhaps more accurately its interpreter or spokesman. Or doorman.

'Not even if you beg,' the Jag breathed, his inflection completely dead.

Rallick straightened. 'May I speak to you?'

The unsettling vertical-pupils of the eyes rose to encompass the night sky over the estate district; narrowed. 'We already have a boarder. I am not taking in more. No matter how awful it will get.'

A shiver ran its fingers down Rallick's spine. He clenched and unclenched his sweaty hands. 'That is the last thing I would want.'

The Jag shuffled out of the doorway back up the hall. 'That is what they all say – then there's no getting rid of them.'

Rallick forced himself up the hall. Behind, the door swung shut, enclosing him in almost utter gloom. On one side, in a narrow corridor a large man lay blocking the way, snoring loudly and wetly. Raest passed this strange apparition without comment and Rallick was forced to follow. Murky light shone ahead; a sort of limpid greenish underwater glow cast down as if from a skylight. Here he found the Jag seated at a table and across from him sat another creature – an Imass. Or at least so Rallick assumed. He was no expert. Half-rotted flesh over bones and those bones stained dark. Battered armour of leather, furs and bone plates. And over all clumps of dried dirt. The entity held wooden slats in ravaged hands of bone and ligament. It raised its empty sockets to regard Rallick for a moment then returned its gaze to the slats in its hands.

In that brief regard a cold wind had brushed Rallick's face. He heard it moaning, carrying the call of large animals far in the distance. He shivered again.

The Jag, Raest, took up his own slats.

Cards, he realized. They were playing cards. Now. With so much hanging over the city.

On the table between them sat the corpse of a cat.

Rallick cleared his throat. 'What is going on?'

'I am up ten thousand gold bars,' Raest breathed. 'My friend here is having troubles with the changes in the rules.'

The Imass's voice came as a low creaking of dry sinew: 'I am better at mechanisms.'

'No,' Rallick insisted. 'The city. What's going on outside?'

'The neighbourhood is fast deteriorating. I am considering a move.'

'A move? You can move?'

The Tyrant turned his ravaged features to study him wordlessly for a time.

Rallick swallowed. *Ah. I see.*

The Jag laid down one wooden card from his hand.

The Imass edged its blunt skeletal chin forward to study the card then sat back to return to the contemplation of its own. Rallick also leaned to squint at the face; he saw nothing more than a crudely scratched image he couldn't make out.

'No,' the Jag continued, 'I've put too much work into the place.' Rallick eyed the walls of rotting wood, the hanging roots, the dust sifting down through the cascading starlight. 'Besides, Fluffy here would be devastated.'

Fluffy? Please be referring to the cat – my sanity won't survive otherwise.

'Can you give me any hint of what is to come?'

'I serve the House now. Only it. However, I can tell you what sort of game we are playing.'

Game?

From his mangled leathery hand the Imass slowly slid a wooden card on to the table.

Raest leaned forward to study the image scratched upon its face. He sat back shaking his head. 'No – not her. She's out of the game. For now.' He brushed the card aside. The ligaments of the Imass's neck creaked as it followed the card to the far edge of the table. It growled.

Rallick found he was holding his breath. 'What sort of game . . . is it?' he asked, hardly able to speak.

'It's a game of bluff. Bluff on both sides. Remember that, servant of Hood.'

'Hood is gone.'

'The paths remain.'

'I see.'

'Do you? It would be astounding if you did.'

Rallick clenched his lips. *I can't settle my aim here.* He turned his attention to the Imass. *Those are not his leg bones.* He looked away 'Is there anything more you can tell me?'

The Jag remained immobile, his slashed and battered face a mask, long grey hair like iron shavings hanging to his shoulders. 'I can tell you that you are distracting me from the game. Go away.'

Rallick decided that he should not wait to be told twice. He edged back out of the room, not turning away from the oddly mismatched, yet so utterly matched, couple.

He reached the closed door.

Now for the hardest part of all.

But the door did open.

*   *   *

When someone entered his office, Legate Jeshin Lim's first thought was that a councillor had requested an unscheduled meeting and his staff had ushered him or her through. He was surprised therefore upon peering up from composing his next speech to see the merchant Humble Measure standing before him.

He stifled the urge to leap from his chair. *Burn's mercy! Who allowed the man in! Someone will lose their position over this.* He transformed his twitch of mouth into a rigid, if rather strained, welcoming smile. *Well . . . one can hardly complain. This man's money allowed me entrance to this office . . . why not the man himself?*

He stood, smiling, and came round the desk. 'Humble Measure! This is a surprise!' He motioned to a chair. 'Please, sit. May I offer you some tea?'

The big man sat stiffly and ponderously. 'None, Legate . . . thank you.'

How odd to see him outside the offices at his works. He looks . . . diminished. Jeshin poured himself a tiny thimbleful of tea and retreated once more behind his desk. 'What can I do for you, old friend?'

'First,' the man ground out, 'congratulations upon the renewal of the ancient honoured position, Legate.'

Lim waved such formalities aside. 'It is *our* victory, Humble. Our shared vision led to this. We achieved it together.'

Humble inclined his head in acknowledgement. 'The Legate is too generous. Yet I wonder, then, why, with this victory in your grasp, you have not gone on to move Darujhistan towards the position of pre-eminence we once agreed it deserves?'

Jeshin frowned, cocking his head. The tea sat forgotten before him. 'How so?'

'Legate – Darujhistan must have an arsenal. Arms, armour, siege engines. The matériel of war—' He stopped himself, because the Legate had raised a hand to speak.

Back to this old argument. Should've anticipated it. The man's a fanatic. 'Humble . . . your point is well taken. Arms and armour are needed, yes. Yet look at what we have accomplished! We are in accord on so much. Darujhistan shall be set once more on a course of pre-eminence. We only differ in this one small matter – you believe that putting weapons and armour on every citizen will accomplish this, while I believe the city's defences must first be addressed. The walls, Humble—'

The merchant interrupted. 'Darujhistan has walls, Legate.'

Jeshin waved this aside. 'Hardly worth the name. Playgrounds for the city's children. Neglected and pillaged for centuries. They must be rebuilt, strengthened.'

'It's not the *walls* of Darujhistan that must be strengthened, Legate . . . it is the will.'

Jeshin stilled, hands pressed to the cool marble surface of his desk. 'The discussion is closed, Humble. I thank you for your concern. I know I can count on your cooperation in our efforts to bring prestige and influence to our city.' And he stood, smiling once more. He motioned to the door.

Humble Measure levered his bulk from the chair. He glowered from under his thick brows. Without a word he turned and lumbered to the door.

Jeshin watched him go, stiff smile still fixed on his lips. *A guard. Guards, today. Unbribable guards. Am I not the damned Legate of this ridiculous city?*

Humble's closed carriage rocked as he settled his weight within. He sat hunched forward, elbows on knees, as if examining someone seated opposite. The carriage started its twisting way down Majesty Hill. The man's heavy-lidded eyes were narrowed, almost closed, as he lolled back and forth. Indeed, another passenger might have thought him asleep.

But he was far from asleep. Like the ponderous presses of his foundry his mind was slowly working, inexorably turning, and with crushing irresistible weight. And the conclusion he reached was that he did not sacrifice so much to put a Legate in charge of this city so that the holder of the position could cower behind walls.

Fortunately, however, ways exist to resolve this temporary hindrance.

* * *

The Mengal mountains ran as a backbone along the west coast of the Genabackan continent. They were for the most part a dangerous unsettled wilderness. A trader mud track twisted along the skirts of their inland eastward slope, unkept, swept away in places by erosion, crossed by fallen trees. Mule trains, two-wheeled carts and backpacks were the only way to make the trip. And even then in places the track was practically impassable. Far quicker and easier to ship any goods, livestock or people up and down the coast by water. But there were always those for whom the up-front expense of such cargo space or berths was unaffordable. For these petty traders, tinkers, travelling smiths, would-be homesteaders, or plain adventurers off to find a new horizon there would always be the mud track through the tall evergreen forest, their breath pluming in the cold wet mist cascading down the slopes, and their own rag-swathed feet and bent, burdened backs.

And so, too, there were always those who preyed upon them.

Yusek's people were out of the east, Bastion way. During the Troubles they'd packed up and headed west. By the time they crossed the Dwelling Plain the way of life had become habit and they just kept on moving. Eventually Yusek raised her head and looked around and realized that all her family's starving and slogging hadn't gotten them anywhere worth going. So she packed up everything useful and did the only thing she knew how to do: she moved on.

She'd fallen in with Orbern's crew, or rather they'd taken everything she had and given her the choice to join them or starve in the cold. Being young and new they'd tried using her, of course, but she'd grown up defending herself and had discovered early on that she didn't mind the shedding of blood half as much as those around her. So they made her a scout, or a runner, or whatever you damned well wanted to call it, on account of the fact that she could walk all their fat drunken arses into the ground. And they had no armour worth the name to give her anyway.

Orbern claimed to be from Darujhistan. From one of the city's noble families. Kept going on about being cheated of his position, unappreciated, or driven out by idiots, or some such. Not that anyone gave a damn. Fancied himself 'Lord of the Western Mountains'. Even had a horse, a sickly lonely-looking thing that he insisted on riding through the dense brush. Stupidest spectacle Yusek had ever seen.

In any case, Orbern ran things because at least he had some kind of claim to an education. Knew how to build. He'd had them put up a palisade across the gorge they occupied. Raised log cabins that didn't leak. Even got a crude sort of forge up and running for their metalworking needs. It used a big ol' flat stone as an anvil.

And because of all this the man's rule was tolerated, even if he was a pompous ass.

Today Yusek was 'scouting'. Which consisted of crouching under the cover of a tall evergreen watching the rain misting down the mountainside. The Mengal mountains were tall enough to gather clouds to themselves, but here they were not tall enough to completely shadow the leeward slopes, and deep valleys cut through to the coast. As a result, a portion of the mist always reached inland – not that any ever touched the Dwelling Plain.

She was keeping an eye on the trader track where it came winding up from the south. And this day, sure enough with the damned cold rain and all, there came two figures tramping through the mud, stepping over the trunks of fallen trees, pushing through the channels of run-off that charged across the path.

Damned fools. Out in this weather. Now she had to get soaked too!

She went down to meet them.

They were a couple of the sorriest travellers she'd ever seen. Carried no goods or packs as far as she could make out; they wore big loose hooded cloaks pulled close against the rain. At least they were armed, as she could see the polished bronze heels of sheaths hanging down beneath their cloaks.

As she stepped out on to the track they stopped and exchanged looks with each other from under their deep hoods. 'Where you headed?' she asked.

One stepped forward. 'North,' he said in a strange accent.

'I'm with a settlement just—'

'Do you know of a monastery here in these mountains?' the fellow demanded, cutting her off.

'A what? Monastery? No. Like I said, I'm with—'

But the two had walked on right past her. She watched them go, dumbfounded. *What in the name of Mowri . . .*

She caught up with them. 'Listen. There's a settlement near here. Orbern-town.' *Stupid damned name. Orbern-town! Damned ass. Ha! Ass-town!*

The two stopped. Even this close Yusek couldn't see into the deep hoods. One spoke again, the same one as before – the other had yet to say anything at all. 'There are people there who would know these mountains well?' he asked.

Yusek wiped the cold mist from her face, shrugged. 'Yeah. Sure. You bet.'

'Very well. You may lead us there.'

She snorted, waved for them to follow. *Listen to that!* 'You may lead us there . . .' *Who do these two think they are?*

Yusek wouldn't have denied she'd grown up in the middle of nowhere and knew next to nothing, but even she would've run off when the sharpened logs of the palisade hove into view. She especially would've panicked when the heavy log door was pushed shut behind them and the great cross-piece was set into place and all the hairy unwashed mountain men of Orbern's crew came shambling out to see what was up.

But not these two. They followed her right in, meek as lambs to the axe. Some people, she reflected, didn't have the sense to be allowed to live.

She led them straight up to the main log 'Hall' as Orbern called it, pushed open the door. The two followed her in. A bunch of the crew pushed in behind.

Orbern was eating; he spent a lot of time doing that, hanging around the table. Yusek guessed this was his way of playing 'Lord of the manor'. He looked up, surprised, set down his knife and wiped his hands on the layered robes he wore to demonstrate his 'Office'. He had a great head of straggly hair and beard that Yusek figured he cultivated, again as part of his image as some kind of great master of the wilderness, like those of the ex-free cities of the north.

'And who do we have here?' he asked, all arch and loud.

'Travellers, sir,' she answered, addressing him, as he kept telling them to.

Orbern pulled on his beard, nodding. 'Excellent! Greetings, sirs! Welcome to Orbern-town – such as it is at this time. Admittedly no Mengal yet. But we are growing. Soon we hope to become a regular waystop on the trader road. What may we do for you? Beds for the night, perhaps?'

Some of the boys behind the travellers chuckled at that. The two didn't even turn round.

'Do you know of a monastery in these mountains, north of here?'

Orbern made a great show of stroking his beard and studying the cross-beams above. 'A monastery, you say? Are you on a devotional pilgrimage? Are they expecting you?'

'If none here knows it then we will move on.'

A lot more of the men laughed at that. Yusek couldn't hide her disbelief. *How dense can you be?*

Orbern merely raised a hand for silence. 'There's no hurry. Perhaps we *do* know of such a place. Perhaps—'

'Do *you* know?' the traveller asked, interrupting.

Orbern was thrown for a moment but recovered smoothly. 'I? No. But for a contribution to Orbern-town's—'

'Then who?'

Orbern glared from beneath his tangled brows. Yusek laughed, and none too gently. Now this was funny . . . this was a good show. 'A contribution to Orbern-town's future will gain you our good will,' Orbern ground out sounding far from friendly.

As if by way of answer, the spokesman of the two pushed back his heavy hood.

Yusek heard gasps of hissed breaths. Almost as one the crowd of outlaws and murderers, hunted men all, flinched several steps backwards, clearing a circle round the two. She stared surprised: the man wore a mask, a painted oval, all complex swirls and bands. Oddest thing, she thought. Then she glanced to Orbern.

The man was frozen, eyes huge. He appeared to be struggling to take a breath to speak but failing. Yusek made a disgusted face. *What's this? So the fellow's wearing a mask? So what?*

No one moved or spoke; it was as if all were too terrified. A few like Yusek were peering about, confused; mostly men from the north.

Since no one was saying anything she stepped forward, hands on the knives at her belt. 'Hand over everything you have,' she demanded.

A strangled high-pitched laugh burst from Orbern. He waved his hands frantically. 'Don't listen to her!' he spluttered, almost squeaking. 'You are free to go, of course!'

'What's this?' called out Waynar, a great hairy fellow from the north who claimed Barghast blood. He uncrossed his thick arms and stepped forward. 'Free to go?'

'Would you shut up!' Orbern snarled at him, then offered the two guests a nervous laugh.

'You ain't our king or anything,' Waynar countered. He loomed up so close to the visitors that his out-thrust chin almost touched the masked forehead of the much shorter and slighter of the two. 'Who in Hood're you? An' why're you wearin' that stupid mask?'

Damned straight! Yusek added silently. *'Bout time someone took charge. Looks like Orbern might be on the outs.*

The spokesman tilted his head to peer past Waynar's shaggy bulk. 'Is this one in defiance of your orders?'

Orbern's shoulders fell. He clasped his head in his hands and let out a long shuddering breath. 'I am very sorry, Waynar,' he said. 'But . . . yes. He is.'

The spokesman shrugged. Or appeared to shrug. *Something* happened. Yusek wasn't sure; she didn't quite catch it. His cloak moved, anyway. Waynar's eyes bulged. His mouth opened but nothing came out. Then a great torrent of blood and fluids came gushing down from the man's waist, down over his legs, splattering amid falling wet glistening coils and viscera. The man almost split in half.

Yusek screamed, jumping backwards. Even the strangers stepped away from the spreading pool of gore.

Some went for their swords but others in the crowd stopped them, grabbing their arms. Orbern threw up his hands for calm. 'Do not move!' he called. To the travellers he offered a small bow of his head. 'There will be no further challenges. Your demonstration is most . . . pointed. North of here you will find a handful of small settlements, homesteads and such. And I *have* heard rumours of a temple of some sort.'

'Who knows this region best?' the spokesman asked, his voice still mild and uninflected.

Orbern's brows drew down once more. 'Well, Yusek here has covered most of the slopes.'

Yusek tore her gaze from the pile of viscera and saw that the spokesman stranger was now regarding her through his painted mask. His eyes were hazel brown.

'What?' she snapped.

'You will guide us.'

'Sure as the bony finger of the Taker I will not.'

The spokesman turned away. 'It is decided. We require food and water.'

Orbern exhaled his relief. 'Shel-ken, find them some supplies.'

'No! It is *not* decided!' Yusek snarled. She glared at Orbern. 'I won't go with these murderers!'

'Is this one also defying the hierarchy?' the spokesman asked of Orbern.

Yusek backed up until her shoulder blades pressed against a wall. Orbern eyed her, one brow arched as if to ask: *well?*

All eyes swung to her. A few of Orbern's men licked their lips as if eager to see her sliced from throat to crotch. 'No,' she said.

Yusek confronted Orbern after the two visitors had left the hall to wait outside. 'What are you doing?' she demanded while he watched, pulling on one fat lip, as the mess that had been Waynar was hauled away. Fresh sawdust was thrown over the stained dirt floor. He returned to picking at the greasy bird carcass. 'Well?'

His tired gaze flicked to her. 'You're hardly really a member of this little community of ours, are you, Yusek? You take every excuse to range over the slopes for days on end. It's as if you've just been waiting for an excuse to cut and run anyway.'

She couldn't find it in herself to deny any of what he said. 'But with these two murderers? You saw what they did to Waynar! You just want to get me killed.'

Orbern pushed aside the bones. 'Yusek . . .' He rubbed his brow, sighing. 'Firstly, dear, Waynar asked for it. He challenged the Seguleh. So, lesson number one – do not challenge them! Now, secondly, contrary to what we all just saw, in their company you will be the safest you've been in years.' He sat back, opening his hands. 'Thirdly, almost everyone here is a murderer – since when has that been a problem for you? And lastly, frankly, it has been a royal pain in the arse keeping everyone off *your* arse this last year.'

'If they can't control themselves that's their problem, not mine. They can go hump animals.'

'Oh, don't fool yourself – some do. Or each other. In any case, I agree, yes. Why women get blamed for men's callousness and lack of respect for others is beyond me. But it becomes your problem when it's you they're attacking. Yes?'

'I'll kill anyone who tries that. They know that.'

'So I'm down yet another man.'

'It's not *my* damn fault they're arseholes!'

He pulled savagely on his beard. 'Yusek! The reason they've been driven out of all other towns and villages and families – any community of cooperative people – is because they *are* murderous, selfish, short-sighted, impulsive, cruel arseholes!' He pointed to the door. 'I'm doing you a favour.'

She didn't move. 'I can take care of myself.'

'The fact that you're still alive proves that, Yusek. But the odds are stacking up. Eventually, you'll disappear and Ezzen, or Dullet, will have a self-satisfied smirk on his face for a few days . . . and that would be the end of it.'

Yusek lowered her chin. 'I'm not asking you to do me any favours.' She hated how sullen that sounded, but it was the truth.

Orbern sighed again. 'I know. But I am anyway. Osserc knows why. Must be my civilized conscience.'

She went to pack the rest of her meagre belongings. *Queen's throw! I may as well just ditch 'em.* She spotted Short-tall, out of the south, and raised her chin to him. 'So who are these Segulath anyway?'

'It's Seguleh,' he corrected her, then drew a slashing line across the air. 'Swords, sweetmeat. Walking swords is what they are. Watch yourself or they'll do you as they did Waynar.'

She gave him a face, threw her tied bedroll over her shoulder.

She found them waiting in the muddy garbage-strewn grounds that Orbern called the 'Marshalling field'. A pack of gathered stores sat with them.

The spokesman indicated it. 'Carry this.'

'I ain't no one's pack mule.'

'None the less.'

'No. You can fucking carry it.'

Something whipped past her face – a silvery blur. Her bedroll fell from her shoulder into the mud, its rope tie cut. The man straightened, his cloak falling back into place.

Yusek stared. *How in the name of Togg did he do that?* She raised her gaze to the painted mask and the eyes behind: these studied her, narrowed, as if gauging her reaction. It was not the swaggering superior look she was used to from all those who'd bested her in the past.

She spat to one side – 'Fine!' – yanked up the pack, which was damned heavy, adjusted it on her back. 'You *do* have a name . . . ?'

The spokesman motioned for her to walk with him. The silent partner followed, hood still raised. As they approached the palisade door she spotted fat Orbern up on the catwalk. He waved for the solid log cross-piece to be pulled aside and the door pushed open. They exited into the woods with almost the entire crew of Orbern-town at the palisade watching them go.

'My name is Sall,' the spokesman said. Now, in the silence of the woods, he sounded rather young.

Yusek jerked a thumb to the other. 'And him?'

Sall was silent for a time, perhaps searching for the right words. 'In the rankings of the Seguleh I am of the Three Hundredth—'

'Three hundredth what?' she cut in.

Again, he was silent for a while. The rain had let up and now the streams of run-off trickled across the track. Heavy drops pattered amid the woods. The morning's mist was gone with the rain.

'The Three Hundredth I refer to means among the Seguleh fighters,' Sall said, his tone now quite icy. It seemed he wasn't used to being interrupted.

She eyed him sidelong. He'd raised his hood again. 'So . . . you mean that you're among the top three hundred fighters of all you Seguleh?'

'Among all those who choose to pursue the rankings, yes. Not all need do so.'

Among the three hundred best fighters of these Seguleh? Damn! She jerked her thumb to the other. 'And him?'

'Yusek' – he spoke much more quietly now – 'I can give you his name . . . but it will be of no use to you. You might address him but he will never speak to you. He is Lo. And he is Eighth.'

Eighth? Like in eighth best of all of 'em? Burn's embrace! And they're out here in the middle of nowhere? 'What're you two doing here?'

'As I said. We are looking for a monastery that is supposed to be somewhere here in these mountains.'

Yusek snorted. Damned foolishness. Here she was guiding a couple of fanatics off to some temple so they could bow to some dusty piece of bone, or a sacred statue on a wall, or have a senile old man wave his hand over their heads. What a fucking waste of her time!

She decided to ditch them right away.

She simply didn't stop walking. So far that tactic had never failed her. She'd lost everyone she'd ever walked away from. As the day progressed, sure enough they fell back just as everyone always did. Once they were far enough behind on the trail she shucked the pack from her shoulders, took the best of the dried staples and a skin of water, and just kept right on going without looking back. In fact, she decided to run.

She made for an overhang she knew of, a kind of unofficial way-station along the trail. It was much further than an average day's travel but she'd push on into the night.

For all the rest of the day, into the long twilight of evening, until the light failed entirely and she couldn't make out the track ahead, she saw no more sign of them. The combined light of the mottled moon and the ill-omened green night sky visitor allowed her to find the narrow path up the rocks to the overhang and here she crouched down on her hams, in the dirt and rotting leaves, and chewed on a strip of dried venison. Her legs were trembling and numb, her chest aflame, but she'd made it. And she was rid of them. She was rid of them all! Fat Orbern, leering Ezzen, slow-witted Henst with his clumsy paws. She'd done it again! Shaken the useless dust from her heels. Just like her ma and pa that day in the worst stretch of the Dwelling Plain when it was them or her and damned if it was gonna be her!

I'll head for Mengal just as I've always wanted. Make a name for myself there. Must be plenty of opportunities for a girl like me . . . I'll be—

She stiffened, listening. Rocks were falling down on the trail. She slowly straightened, a hand going to the fighting knife at her hip, her heart thudding.

The hooded and cloaked figure of Sall climbed up into the over-hang. He brushed dirt from himself. He dropped the pack to the dry dust and leaves. She lowered her hand. *I don't fucking believe it!*

'A fair first day's travel, Yusek.' The hood rose as he peered about. 'I approve. You may rest. I will take first watch.'

Lo joined them, rising as silently as a ghost from the murk. He crossed to the rear of the overhang and sat without a word.

'Who are you people . . .' she breathed, awed despite herself.

'We are the Seguleh, Yusek. And all these lands will soon come to know us again.'

*　　*　　*

Spindle sat on a stone bench in the Circle of Faiths. It was a paved plaza in the Daru district that through the years, building by building and yard by yard, had been invaded then annexed by the worshippers of foreign, emerging, or even discredited religions. A sort of unofficial bazaar to any god, spirit or ascendant you'd care to name. Tall prayer sticks burned next to him as votive offerings to some obscure northern deity, possibly Barghast ancestor spirits. He waved the thick smoke from his face. Across the plaza a tiny stone building looking unnervingly like a sepulchre housed a priest of the new cult of the Shattered God. The man sat gabbling on to all who passed but was rather hard to understand, speaking as he was through broken teeth and a swollen jaw from the many beatings the local toughs meted out. Spindle had to hand it to the fellow, though. The man was undeterred. He even seemed to relish the extra challenge to his devotion and perseverance.

Some people just want to be persecuted . . . it proves they're right.

But then, he knew all about persecution. He and his ma together had watched the world succeed in its persecution of his father, uncles, brothers, aunts, sisters and uncounted cousins. 'Ain't gonna lose you, little 'un,' she'd always told him. She repeated it yet again when word came of the loss of his last brother, fallen overboard in rough seas off the coast of Delanss. 'That's my sworn vow, that is.' And he'd looked up from where he sat next to her chair to watch her brushing her hair – hair so long it would drag along the ground behind her should she ever let it down. 'Hold you in my arms, I will. Bind you up in protection. Keep you safe. Your mama's gonna keep you safe. You'll see.'

He rubbed his shirt over his chest. She was close now. He could feel her next to him the way he could when trouble was coming.

Been three days and no contact yet from any of the cadre mages. Should've been contact by now. Ain't right.

'You look like a brother,' someone addressed him in Daru.

Spindle shaded his eyes to blink up at a young swell-sword all done up in mock Malazan officer gear complete with torcs and Quon-style longsword. On his silk surcoat the lad bore the sword symbol of the cult of Dessembrae. 'Whazzat? Brother?'

'One of the initiate. The Elite. Recognized by Dessembrae.'

'What in Osserc's smothering warmth are you going on about?'

The young man's ingratiating smile slipped into a stung haughtiness as he looked Spindle up and down. 'My apology. Clearly I am mistaken. Obviously you not possess the requisite dignity.'

Spindle hawked up a mouthful of phlegm and spat. 'Dignity my arse. If he saw you now he wouldn't know whether to laugh or cry.'

'So those found unworthy may grumble.'

Spindle considered rousing himself to teach the pup a lesson, but he was feeling at ease on the bench and decided not to let the ignorant fool ruin his day. He waved the lad away. 'Take your rubbish elsewhere.'

The aristocratic youth actually tossed his head as he walked off. Spindle snorted at the absurdity of it all, then realized he was no longer alone on the bench. He eyed the fellow sidelong: tall and rangy, wrapped in an old travelling cloak. Long black wavy hair. Looked Talian in profile.

'If that lad knew he was talking to a Bridgeburner he'd have pissed himself,' the man said.

Spindle cursed under his breath. 'Took your own damned time, didn't you?' He rubbed his hand over his chest, listening for guidance, heard nothing. This man was no mage. 'Who are you anyway? Where's Filless?'

'Filless is no longer with us. Someone's made a sport of hunting Imperial mages and Claws.' He turned to address him directly. 'If I were you I'd keep my head down.'

'Hunh. That's me. Question still stands. Who're you?'

'I'm with the Imperial delegation.'

Spindle snorted again. 'Military intelligence. Shoulda known.'

'We learned long ago not to depend entirely on the Claw.'

'Hood's cautionary finger to that, my friend.'

'So – your report?'

'Some kinda spook's entered the city. Drug his arse outta the burial grounds to the south. Wasn't alone neither. Has servants. And they ain't entirely human, if you know what I mean.'

The intelligence officer let out a faint whistle, fingers tapping on his lap. 'And the Moranth flee . . . Damned scary, that.'

'As did we. You lot marched out.'

'Just a training exercise,' the fellow answered, his mind elsewhere. 'I want you to try to track him, or it, down.'

Spindle gave him his best glare. *The feller tells me to keep my head down, then he has the nerve* . . . He spat again. 'Not me. Just a bystander, remember?'

The young officer murmured, 'Might I remind you the punishment for desertion is still death?'

Stretching out his legs, Spindle took out a handful of nuts he'd purchased from a street vendor, began cracking them and tossed them one by one into his mouth. 'Amateurish bluff, lad. I'm the last asset you got left in this whole Queen-damned city.'

The officer studied his tapping fingers for a time. 'I wouldn't count on that. When the Fifth came to this continent an Imperial Sceptre was sent with High Fist Dujek. It's with us now. Here in the city. And it's awakened.'

Spindle missed his mouth with a thrown nut. *Gods all around. A line straight to Unta. Anything could be sent through. An army of Claws. A High Mage.* He cleared his throat, shrugging. 'Well, then, you don't need me.'

The young intelligence officer pursed his lips eloquently. 'Until then – we'll just have to put up with you.'

Damned Empire! Never lets you go. Always drags you back in. Sons a bitches.

Then he squeezed the nuts in his sweaty hand. *Oh no. Picker's gonna kill me!*

*   *   *

Stooped and shuffling, Aman picked his way through his wrecked shop. Taya followed in his wake. Her steps were dainty and soundless against his noisy dragging of boots through the broken wares.

She wrinkled her nose at the churned-up dust. 'Revenge?' she asked. 'A warning?'

Aman picked up a relatively whole glass urn, turned it in an errant ray of sunlight that penetrated the shutters he kept locked. 'No, my dear. Neither.' He dropped the urn to smash to pieces alongside its fellows. 'Irrelevant. All too irrelevant.'

Taya studied his gnarled profile. She blew a hair from her face. 'Then why are we here?'

'Tone, dear. Watch your tone. Petulant. It is not becoming.'

She raised her full painted lips in a smirk that was almost a leer. 'Depends upon what you're looking for.'

After a moment Aman tilted his head to acknowledge the point. 'True. It has served you in the past. But things are changing now. And you must change as well.'

She snorted her opinion of that. '*Nothing* has changed! Still we skulk in the shadows.' Her gaze slid sideways to Aman. 'Perhaps you're too used to living like rats?'

He was examining the glittering jade-encrusted statue, running his mangled hands over its strange crusted armour of stone. 'You are wasting your breath, young one. Too long among those who can so easily be stung. Whereas I possess no vanity to be plucked like a thin rich robe. No fragile self-image so readily chipped or shattered.' He regarded her, his gaze weighing. 'No. The die is cast . . . as they say. We merely wait while the ripples spread outward – if I may be permitted to tweak my metaphors. We must wait for we are yet vulnerable, yes? But soon . . . soon we shall be unassailable. Never you doubt, child.' He clasped his hands together under his uneven chin as if praying. 'So. What happened here?'

She shrugged her thin bare shoulders. 'Someone broke in and ransacked the place. Probably offended by your housekeeping.'

Aman touched his fingertips to his mouth. His mismatched eyes, one brown, the other a sickly yellow, seemed to peer in two directions. 'No. That is not what happened at all. Observe.' He indicated the floor next to the statue. Taya looked: near where it stood the floorboards clearly showed the dark outline, free of dust, of its carved stone armoured boots.

'It moved,' she breathed.

Aman smiled lopsidedly – the only way he could. 'Yes.'

'So . . . it's alive?'

He patted the statue's chest. 'No. It is not. Makes it even more formidable, truth be told. No, this is what happened. Someone entered undetected, bypassing all my considerable wards, spirit guardians, and Warren-keyed traps. An accomplishment all by itself. He was in the process of examining the premises when the one guardian he did not anticipate acted.'

'And the mess?'

'The clumsy efforts of my foreign friend to corner the pest . . . who, with breathtaking insolence, continued his search even while being chased.' He shook his misshapen head, awed. 'Such effrontery! It will be his downfall.'

Taya raised an expressive, elegant brow. 'Whose downfall?'

Aman tugged at something clasped in one stone fist. He pulled again, grunting. Cloth tore. He raised a dirty shred of material: a stained handkerchief. 'An old friend. Slipped greasily away . . . yet again.'

CHAPTER VII

The scholar and traveller Sulerem of Mengal writes in his journals of a distant land to the south where every man and woman is as a sovereign unto themselves. It is a wasteland where in over a hundred years not even one fallen tree has been moved.

Letters of the Philosophical Society
Darujhistan

KISKA HAD LONG LOST TRACK OF HOW MANY LEAGUES OF SHORELINE she and Leoman had walked when, eventually, as she knew he would, the man cleared his throat in a way that told her he had something to say – something she would no doubt not want to hear.

She stopped on the stretch of black sand, the sun-bright surf brushing up the strand, and turned to regard him. He stood some paces back. His hands were at his weapon belt; his long pale robes hung grimed and ragged at their bottom edge over his chain coat. He was growing a beard to match his moustache and his hair hung long and unkempt from beneath his peaked helmet.

She knew she must present no prettier a picture. She waved for him to speak. 'What is it?'

He gave an uneasy shrug, not meeting her eyes. 'This is useless, Kiska. If he wanted to be found he'd have come to us long ago.'

'We don't know that . . .'

'Stands to reason.'

'And I suppose you have some brilliant alternative?'

'I suggest we strike inland. Perhaps we'll find something. A way . . .' He tailed off, seeing Kiska's change of expression. She was no longer looking at him, but above and beyond. He turned round. A moment later he cursed softly. She came up to stand next to him. 'It's closing,' he said.

'Yes. Definitely smaller.'

The dark smear in the slate-grey sky that was the Whorl had faded to a fraction of the size it had once been.

'Looks like the Liosan have put an end to it.'

'I suppose so. Two offspring of Osserc ought to be enough.'

He studied her, his gaze oddly gentle. 'That could be our way out closing before us.'

She turned away to keep walking. 'All the more reason to track him down.'

'Kiska,' he called, a touch irritated. 'We could be walking in the wrong direction.'

'Go ahead! I'm not keeping you! I'm sure all the ladies are missing your moustache.'

She walked on in silence. Part of her wondered whether he'd answer, or whether he was following along at a distance. She refused to glance behind.

Then his voice came, shouting from far off: 'What if I told you I could find him?'

She stopped, let out a long angry breath. *Ye gods! Was this all just some sort of game to the fellow?* She turned round, eyed him. He was standing as before, hands still at his belt, rocking back and forth on the heels of his boots. Shaking her head, she retraced her tracks back up the stretch of beach and planted herself before him, hands on hips.

'This better be good.'

His brown eyes held the usual glint of amusement. He brushed at his now enormous untrimmed moustache so very pleased with himself. *Like the damned cat that has the mouse.*

'You seem to have a soft spot for these local unfortunates, don't you?'

She flinched away, eyeing him warily. 'I'll not let you harm any of them.'

The man looked positively pained – or made a great show of it. 'Never. What do you think I am?'

A murderous self-interested callous prick? Yet didn't there seem to be something more to the man? He did appear to have a surprising gentleness. A kind of unpredictable fey compassion. *His problem is that he hides it too well.* 'Your point?'

A nod. 'My point is that your pity for them seems to have blinded you to how they could be of use in your . . . well, quest.'

She felt distaste hardening her mouth. 'And that is?'

He sighed, opening his hands. 'Think, Kiska. There is some kind of connection there. All we need do is keep an eye on them. And eventually . . .' He gave an evocative shrug.

She felt a fool. *Yes. Stands to reason. Simple. Elegant. Why didn't I think of it?* Because it was passive. She much preferred action. Yet Leoman was hardly the retiring type. Perhaps it was because he must have grown up hunting and thought like a hunter, whereas she had not. For her, just sitting and waiting for something to happen, well, it grated against all her instincts.

Yet she had to agree. And so she allowed a curt nod and headed back up the curve of shoreline. Leoman followed at a discreet distance. Perhaps to spare her his supercilious smirk and self-satisfied grooming of his moustache.

✳   ✳   ✳

Barathol was slow to answer the loud persistent knocking at his door. It had a suspiciously arrogant and officious sound to it. Finally opening up, he found that he'd been right. A clerk faced him, a great sheaf of scrolls tucked under one arm and another in his hand. Behind him stood three Wardens of the city watch, and behind *them* stood a wrinkled pinch-faced woman he recognized as a representative of the city blacksmiths' guild.

He crossed his thick arms, peered down at the clerk. 'Yes?'

'Are you . . .' the young man consulted the scroll he was hiding, 'the smith known as Barathol Mekhar, a registered foreigner?'

'I'm not foreign where I was born.'

The clerk blinked up at him. His brows wrinkled as he considered the point. Then he shrugged. 'Well, Barathol, as a tradesman and a resident you are hereby conscripted to the city's construction efforts.'

'I'm not a mason.'

'Metalworking is also required,' the woman observed from the rear.

Barathol jerked a thumb to her. 'Then why isn't she conscripted?'

'Members of the blacksmiths' guild in good standing are exempt,' the woman replied, prim and flushed with triumph.

Barathol nodded. 'I see.'

'I'll give you a good exempting,' Scillara spat from behind Barathol and tried to push past him. He threw an arm across the doorway.

'Is it paid service?' he asked.

The clerk allowed the thick paper of the scroll to snap back into a cylinder. 'It will count as taxation.'

Barathol had yet to pay any tax whatsoever on any of his income but decided that perhaps it would be best not to raise the point at this time. 'Starting when?'

'The morrow. Report to the site foreman in the morning.' The man hurried off, clearly relieved to be done. The woman threw Barathol a haughty glare then hastened in his wake. The three Wardens ambled off, hands tucked into belts. Barathol closed the door.

'How can you go along with that?' Scillara demanded.

Barathol peered around the small apartment, which was barely furnished at all. The only domestic touches were those he'd added: a cloth at the table, utensils he'd made. 'Have to,' he murmured. 'No choice.'

'No choice,' she echoed, disappointed. 'No choice. I thought I'd picked one with a spine.'

He flinched, but eased his shoulders. 'They would arrest me. You'd be on the street.'

She sniffed, dismissing that. 'I've been there before. I'll do it again.'

'Not with the little 'un. Not with him. I'll not see that happen.'

Scillara gave a great rolling of her eyes. 'Gods! Back to that. Martyr for the children.' She waved him off and headed up the stairs. Barathol watched her go.

Only thing worth martyring for, I'd say.

*   *   *

'You a friend o' that rat?'

Rallick looked up from his usual seat in the Phoenix Inn. He blinked, widening his gaze at the astounding apparitions before him. Two men, twins it seemed, embalmed in dust. Clothes ragged and torn. Dirt-pasted faces cadaver hollow. Hair all standing wind-tossed and hardened in grime. 'What rat might that be?' he asked, though he sat at the man's table.

Each pulled out a chair and sat, stiffly. One coughed into a fist and managed, croaking, 'While we hash that out how 'bout standing two thirsty men a drink?'

Rallick signed to Scurve for a round.

The two let out long exhalations as if cool cloths had just been pressed to their brows.

207

'And who are you?' Rallick asked.

'Leff.'

'Scorch.'

Ah. In the flesh. He leaned back, nodding. 'I see. What can I do for you?'

'We're at the rat's table but we don't see no hide nor tail,' said the one who gave his name as Leff.

'And for the immediate future let's keep it to rat – shall we?'

'Oh?' said the other, Scorch, his expression puzzled. Or at least so it looked beneath all the pancaking of dust and grit and untrimmed beard. 'Why'zat?'

Subtlety, Rallick decided, would be lost upon these two and so he allowed himself an exaggerated frown and lift of his shoulders. 'Well . . . let's just say that everyone's name is on a list somewhere . . .'

The two stiffened, their gazes flying to one another. One touched a dirty finger to his nose; the other touched a finger just beneath his left eye. Both gave Rallick broad winks.

'From your lips to the gods' ears, friend,' said Leff.

The drinks arrived care of Jess: two tall stoneware tankards of weak beer. The two men stared at them as if they were miraculous visitations from the gods. Each reached out shaking dusty hands to wrap them round a tankard. Each lowered his mouth as if unequal to the task of raising the vessel. Each sniffed in a great lungful then sighed, dreamily. They took first sips by sucking in the top film then coughed, convulsing and gagging. When the fits had subsided they returned to the tankards to rest their noses just above them once more.

All this Rallick watched wordlessly, his face a mask. *And so it is for men. What we lust after almost kills us yet we always return for more . . . we never learn.*

Rallick waited while the two addressed the tankards. It took some time. The surrounding tables changed over during the wait. Rallick overheard talk of Lim, this new Legate, and of vague building plans. Right now operations were beginning at the mole to recover stone blocks dumped into the harbour. Finally, after much sighing and swallowing, the two wiped their mouths, leaving great smears of wet dirt across their faces.

Leff pointed to Scorch's face and laughed. Scorch pointed to his and he scowled. He cleared his throat and spat on to the straw and sawdust scattered across the floor. 'We're lookin' for a man,' he told Rallick.

'I'm happy for you.'

Both frowned and canted their heads as if thinking they'd misheard him.

Rallick sighed and waved his comment aside. 'What's that got to do with the rat?'

'We've done *work* together. Him 'n' us. Might be a percentage in it all for him. If you know what I mean.' And he touched a finger under his eye once more.

'I'm listening.'

'This feller owes us a lot o' money—'

'And countin'!' Scorch interjected. 'And countin'!'

Leff nodded his profound, rather drunken agreement. 'And counting too. A scholar. Ain't been seen for a long time – so his landlady says. Overdue on rent too.'

'Maybe he's skipped.'

Scorch shook his head, unsteadily. 'Naw. All his books 'n' old broken pieces 'n' such is still there. He'd never leave them behind.'

'All right. So, when did you last see him?'

'Ah. Well . . .' The two blinked at one another, their heads sinking lower and lower. 'We'd rather not say at this juncture of time . . . kinda confuse the issue . . . if you know what I mean.'

'Fair enough.' Rallick eyed the two slumping in their chairs. *Full tankards on empty stomachs. They'll be under the table in moments.* 'There're rooms upstairs, you know. You can maybe use a rest.'

Leff gave a vague wave as he tottered to his feet. 'Naw. You tell that rat. We're lookin' for the scholar.'

Scorch banged into the neighbouring table, righted himself. 'Look out for that dancing girl, though! That minx. Got a temper like a she-devil. Wouldn't even give us a kiss.'

Rallick watched them go. *I'll no doubt see them in the gutter later tonight. And dancing girls? Where'd that come from?*

*   *   *

Kenth, out of Saltoan, had graduated quickly to full Hand membership. He'd always heard the old-timers grumble that the winnowing of the ranks that had been going on for a while now had also thinned their quality. He was determined to prove them wrong. He was of Golana's clan and they had been given the biggest contract of recent times, one guaranteed to restore the reputation of the guild in Darujhistan.

The target was Jeshin Lim, the new self-styled Legate.

The Hand moved in as soon as the coming dawn allowed enough light. The Lim estate was well known to the guild. And this Lim was inexcusably negligent in not hiring more guards now that he was Legate.

Kenth's particular talent was climbing and so he was assigned to help secure the second-storey rooms while the main party assaulted the Legate's chambers. Their watchers had reported that the man was not taking any particular extra precautions such as sleeping in different rooms, or even securing his doors and windows.

Kenth and his brothers and sisters stole across the estate grounds, dark shadows slipping from cover to cover. No challenges arose from roving guards; no dogs barked or attacked; no Warren-laid traps or alarms burst forth with claps of thunder or blazing lights.

It seemed to Kenth that this city's ruling class had forgotten their fear of the guild. Tonight, he decided, would restore that ancient and time-tested balance of power.

The estate's ancient brick and stone wall was simplicity itself to scale. He found a small window terrace and popped the thin wood shutters sealing it. Within, the false dawn's glow through the shutters revealed the room to be made up as a child's nursery. It was empty. From here he gained the second-storey main hall. He went from room to room finding all unsecured, and all empty. It seemed that their watchers' report was accurate: the Legate had sent all the Lim family members to another of their many residences scattered about the city and surrounding countryside.

Presumably, one would think, for their safety.

Yet at the same time all to the guild's convenience.

Having secured the east wing of the rambling building, Kenth signed to his opposite number covering the west wing, then padded to his assigned post guarding the narrow servants' stairs. Here he waited, tensed, fingertips on the top stair feeling for the slight vibrations of footsteps below, his ears pricked for the telltale creak of old dry wood. He waited, and waited.

And still his superior did not show to sign the all-clear.

A pink and amber dawn brightened perceptibly in the east-facing rooms.

Should he check in? But, gods, abandoning his assigned post! He would be lucky to be kept on as message-runner! Not to mention whipped to a bloody pulp. *Still . . . so much time!*

Dread and the insect-crawling passage of minutes won out and

Kenth padded off to check on his opposite number across the main stairs. He leaned out to glance across the broad balustraded marble expanse. *And the woman was not there!*

Something lay in a dark heap at the top of the stairs.

He darted out, knelt, blades ready. It was Hyanth, dead. No sign of a wound. *Magery! No doubts now – time to report.*

He ran for the main chambers. The tall twin door leaves were open. He slid in, a hand raised in the alarm sign, only to halt, stunned. Everyone was dead. That is, the entire assault team lay sprawled as corpses. And on the bed, sheer sheet rising and falling in calm sleep, the Legate.

Kenth did not even hesitate then. He went for the target, blades out.

Before he reached the big four-poster something slammed into his back, sending him tumbling forward to hit the base of the wall. He peered up dazed at a slim lithe figure wrapped in black cloth. The figure stepped over him to open the shutters of a nearby window, then grasped his shoulders and, with astounding strength, levered him out and held him there. He scrabbled frantically for handholds.

She whispered close to his cheek, 'Take this message to your superiors, good soldier,' and released him.

Kenth half fell, half scrambled from stone to stone, snapping latticework and grasping at vines, and crashed to the ground. He lay groaning, his vision flashing with blazing lights. Fortunately, he'd managed to avoid landing on his back.

Report, he told himself – or thought he did. *Report!*

He lurched to his feet, muffling a cry of pain. Then he staggered, hunched, arms wrapped around his torso, across the grounds to the rallying point.

*

Rallick sat in his room in an old tenement building of the Gadrobi district. He sipped the morning's first cup of tea while considering all that he'd learned – or, rather, what little he'd learned.

Baruk missing. Vorcan secreting herself away. Both reputed members of this half-mythic T'orrud Cabal. And in the Council an old forbidden title renewed.

A power struggle. It all adds up to a power stuggle. Yet with whom? This upstart Legate?

And Vorcan's words: No matter what happens, you will not act.

Then there's what Raest said. Bluff. It's a game of bluff. And what is bluff but lies, deception, misdirection?

And who does that *remind him of?*

He stilled, hands wrapped around the warm cup. He cocked his head, listening; the building was silent. Not in all the years he'd kept this room was the building ever silent. He stood, pushing back the chair, hands loose at his sides.

'Who's there?'

The door swung open revealing the empty hall beyond. Someone spoke, and Rallick recognized the voice of Krute of Talient. 'It's all come clear now, Rallick.'

'What's clear, Krute?'

'No longer in the guild, you said . . . aye, I'll give you that. But it's all in the open now. No need to play the innocent.'

'What are you talking about, Krute?'

'She's backing the Legate, ain't she? And maybe you are too. We lost six of our best this night. But one made it out. What he brought with him made everything clear. I'm sorry you chose to go your own way on this, my friend.'

Something came sliding in along the floor. A blade: blued, slim, needle-tipped, good for close-in fighting and balanced for throwing. An exquisite weapon exactly like those commissioned by only one person he knew.

The old floor creaked in the hall: a number of men on both sides of the door. Rallick considered the window and the sheer three-storey drop.

Damn. Done in by my own precautions.

He serried through a number of other options, none particularly promising. Then he noticed a smell. A strong sewer stink.

'Gas leak, lads!' Krute shouted from the hall. 'Damn you, Rallick! A trap! Make for the roof.'

Rallick remained frozen, hands close to the heavy curved knives beneath his loose shirt. The floorboards of the hall creaked and popped, then were silent. He edged towards the door, leaned to peer out. It was empty.

Gas? None can afford gas here.

He returned to his room, froze again. Something was on the table that was not there before. A small leaf-wrapped object. He pulled open the greasy package to reveal a rolled crepe. A breakfast crepe with a delicate nibble taken from one end, as if the purchaser couldn't bear to part with the treat without a taste and hoped no one would notice.

Lies, deception and misdirection.
So be it.

*

'So you are saying that your timely arrival scared them off? Is that what you're saying?' Lim eyed the two estate guards, both retired members of the city watch, standing uncomfortable, and extremely nervous, before him. Somehow he was not convinced. He pulled his dressing gown tighter about himself. 'And the mess outside?'

'Ah! Well, in their haste to flee – one appears to have fallen.'

'Is that so? A clumsy assassin. It's standards that appear to have fallen.'

The guards shared embarrassed glances. One swallowed while the other clasped and reclasped a hand on the shortsword at his side.

Sighing his disgust, Lim turned away. He faced the small desk he kept in his room for correspondence and composing his memoirs. He picked up a slim gold mask among the mementos there and turned it in his hands. 'I suppose I should hire more guards.'

'We strongly recommend it, sir.'

He turned, favoured the two with an arched brow. 'Well . . . do so. Take your leave. Hire as many as you deem appropriate.'

They snapped salutes. 'Yes, sir. Right away, sir.'

Incompetents. It's a miracle I'm alive. Someone had taken out a contract on me and I slept right through it. And frankly, who it is I suspect is no mystery. The Abyss has no fury like a patron scorned, as they may say. I'll have to respond. Hit him where it hurts. In the moneybelt.

Lim crossed the room to dress then paused, confused. *Hadn't there been a rug here? The servants appear to be taking great liberties with the furnishings. They ought to let me know when they take things away to be cleaned.*

*   *   *

Torvald Nom and Tiserra eyed one another other across the table of their house. Her gaze was a steady unswerving pressure while he shot furtive skittish glances her way between long perusals of the various ceramic bowls, jars and cups arrayed about the room. A breakfast meal of tea, honey and flatbreads lay untouched between them.

'I'm not moving,' Tiserra said.

213

'No one has mentioned such a thing.'

'Well . . . I'm not.'

'As you say.'

She sipped her tea. Torvald shifted in his seat. 'Did you say something?' she demanded.

'No – nothing at all.'

'I suppose you'll be receiving all sorts of petitions to intervene in this or that. Ladies throwing themselves at you, bosoms heaving, panting how they'll do *anything* to have your support.'

'No bosoms heaved my way yet, dear.'

Tiserra glared. Torvald cleared his throat, reached for a flatbread.

'And I'll attend none of those damned fancy parties, or gala fetes.'

Torvald withdrew his hand. 'Perish the thought.'

'Won't have those harridans whispering behind their hands about the cut of my dress or the state of my hair.'

'Who would do such a thing?'

'Won't have it.'

'Quite.'

'I like it here!'

'Absolutely.'

She raised the cup to her mouth, set it down untouched. 'So we're agreed, then.'

'Yes.'

'All right then.' She shifted in her seat, tore a flatbread. 'Good.' She nibbled at the bread. 'So . . . what has this Legate proposed?'

'Nothing too shocking yet. Various construction and maintenance projects. All long overdue, really.' He spread honey on a flatbread.

'And how much does the position pay?'

The rolled flatbread paused before it reached his mouth. *Damn.*

*   *   *

In his private room in the Malazan garrison at Pale, shouts of alarm and banging awoke Fist K'ess. He leapt up from his piled furs and blankets already gripping the sheathed shortsword he always slept with and thumped barefoot to unlatch the heavy wood door. Captain Fal-ej stood waiting there, fully armed and armoured, torch in hand.

'What is it, Captain?' he demanded.

The Seven Cities officer took in her Fist standing in the open doorway and quickly looked away. 'Fire, sir. Kitchens and barracks.'

'Kitchens *and* barracks?'

A weary nod. 'They abut each other.'

'Who in the name of Togg built . . .'

The captain raised a forestalling hand. 'Be that as it may – perhaps the Fist should get dressed.'

K'ess frowned, then remembered that he was naked. 'Well . . . if you think it would help.' He gave the captain a courtly nod and slammed the door shut. Facing the adzed wooden slats Captain Fal-ej let out a silent breath of awe and headed down the hall on weak knees. *By the great stallions of Ugarat. This puts the man into a different perspective.*

Fist K'ess caught up with Fal-ej where the captain stood shouting commands to a bucket-brigade vainly tossing water on the burgeoning flames consuming the barracks. Studying the conflagration, a hand raised to shield his face from the heat, the Fist shouted: 'Never mind! It's a loss! Just try to stop it from spreading.'

Fal-ej saluted. 'Yes, sir.' She jogged off, shouting more commands.

After the captain had reorganized the soldiers K'ess waved her to him. 'Anyone hurt?'

'No, sir.'

A roar as the roof collapsed silenced any further talk and drove everyone back a step, coughing and covering their faces. Fist K'ess wiped a smear of some sort of air-borne grease from his face – the larders up in smoke.

'What happened?' he asked. 'An accident?' He asked but he didn't believe it: the fire had spread far too swiftly. The shake of her head confirmed his suspicions. *Sabotage, act of rebellion, call it what you will. They never wanted us here.*

And now this new Legate down in Darujhistan to goad them on.

He waved the captain further back to talk. 'Any suspects?'

She'd pulled off her helmet and now ran a hand through her matted dark hair. K'ess noted how her features seemed to glow – a combination of sweat from the heat and the grease of the smoke. He realized she had a strange look in her eyes even as he studied them.

She glanced away, clearing her throat. 'One of the kitchen staff, probably. Or one of the local servants.'

'You have them?'

'A few. They all claim innocence, of course. What do you want done with them? We could . . . send a message.'

'I very much doubt that the one who set this hung about to get caught.'

215

'I agree, Fist.'

'So . . . let them know what we *could* do with them should we be so inclined. Then let them go.'

Her thick black brows rose. 'Let them . . . go?'

'Yes. We're soldiers, not executioners, or some sort of police. It's subjugation that requires brutality, and I'm not willing to stoop to that yet. Do you understand, Captain?'

The woman's face hardened as if struck. 'I am from Seven Cities, Fist.'

K'ess cursed himself for his obvious misstep but kept his expression blank. He inclined his head in acknowledgement. 'My apologies – then you more than understand.'

A lieutenant arrived, rescuing the Fist from his discomfort. 'A mob at the gates, sir. Blocking the exit.'

'Armed?'

'Haphazardly so. Though there may be veterans mixed in among 'em.'

K'ess turned to Fal-ej. 'My apologies again, Captain. You were correct. Perhaps we should have withdrawn earlier. It seems we're always underestimating Pale.' He motioned to the lieutenant. 'Have the entire command salvage what they can then form up before the gates. We're evacuating.'

The lieutenant saluted. 'Aye sir.' He ran off, bellowing.

'North, sir?' Fal-ej asked.

They flinched at another thundering reverberation accompanied by curtains of sparks from the collapsing barracks. *Did we have any Moranth munitions stored there? Well, I understand they aren't flammable anyway.*

Their few horses, pulled from the stalls, began screaming their terror as the flames drew nearer the mustering square. 'No, Captain. South. We'll catch up with the twenty-second.'

'Aye. And the gates?'

'I understand they're designed to be unhinged, if need be.'

The Captain's full lips drew up in a feral grin of anticipation. 'I'll see to it.'

'Very good.' K'ess saluted. Fal-ej jogged for the gates. He wiped his sweat-slick face. *Now to toss everything from my office into these damned flames.*

A short time later, mounting amid the column, K'ess slapped his gauntlets against his cape to put out drifting sparks. Then he nodded to the bannerman, who dipped the black, grey and silver standard of the Fifth. At the gates Fal-ej oversaw the saboteurs who struck the hinges. At her wave, K'ess motioned that the banner be pointed forward and the entire garrison charged into the broad timber doors. For an instant the gates wavered, creaking, then shouts of alarm from beyond signalled their leaning outwards.

K'ess drew his longsword, bellowing, 'Onward, Fifth!'

The entire column leaned forward, shields to backs, pressing. The gates groaned, gave, toppled. Screams sounded beyond. The broad timber leaves crashed down – but they did not lie flat – far from it, in truth. The front ranks stepped up on o the planks, ignoring the cries beneath. The garrison marched out, stamping over a good portion of the crushed mob while the rest fled. Even halfway back in the column when K'ess urged his mount up on to the planking the flattened gate still settled slightly.

Watching from across the square, the Lord Mayor stared in utter horror at the slaughter done by the Malazans in one murderous gesture. He turned to the shadowy figure next to him. 'This is unspeakable! What have we done?'

'We?' intoned the shade of Hinter. 'As yet I have done nothing. This is all your doing, Lord Mayor.'

The man's plump hands clasped the furred robes at his neck as if he were strangling himself. 'What?' he spluttered. 'But you assured me . . .'

The shade made a gesture as if to remove dust from one translucent sleeve. 'All I assured you was that you would be rid of the Malazans. And behold – am I not good to my word?'

'But . . . these deaths!'

'Not nearly so many as when they arrived, I understand.'

That comment, so calmly delivered, touched something in the Lord Mayor and he clenched his fists around the rich material. 'You will fare no better! Darujhistan has no more army than we!'

The tall shade's regard seemed to radiate an almost godlike disinterest. 'We shall see. In any case, I suppose we do owe you our thanks for sending them off. Therefore – you are now on your own.' The shimmering figure bowed mockingly, murmuring, 'Better luck to come.'

The Lord Mayor's eyes bulged. 'You are . . . leaving? But what of the Rhivi raiders? Barghast war bands? The Moranth? You said you would protect us!' The mayor, nearly breathless, ceased his objections when he saw he was alone; the shade had faded from view. He glanced terrified at the shadows surrounding him in the empty night, then quickly scuttled away.

*

The Malazans had not entirely abandoned southern Genabackis. After the crushing of the Pannion Seer Dujek embarked with the battered remnants of his Host for some distant continent, while Captain Paran collected his remaining columns and also departed. Not all elements withdrew, however. A small portion consisting mainly of the last under-strength legion of the Second Army was left behind. Its mandate, straight from Dujek, was to maintain order while the surviving inhabitants of the region rebuilt their lives, their cities, and their defences. Command of this garrison fell to a veteran who had risen through the logistics and supply side of campaigning. Her name was Argell Steppen and she was awarded the honorary rank of Fist.

What she was entrusted with some thought no honour. Many soldiers muttered that these last fragments of the Second, Fifth, and Sixth Armies were shattered, if not irrevocably broken. Whether the blunt-talking, short, and some thought rather unattractive woman agreed with this estimation she never said. What she did do was order a general withdrawal from the festering wrecks that were the one-time urban centres of the south – Bastion, Capustan and others – to a hillock near the headwaters of the River Eryn, close by the verges of the Cinnamon Wastes. And here she ordered a fortress built. Most of her command thought her mad to be constructing a redoubt in the middle of nowhere so far from the coast.

Then the raids began.

Bendan, son of Hurule, had grown up among the huts, open sewers and garbage heaps of the Gadrobi slums west of Darujhistan. Being a young lad kicking about the alleys with no income or any likelihood of it he naturally joined together with other youths of his background to form a brotherhood for mutual support and protection. And for the generation of gainful profit. An organization that the city Wardens and ruling Council of Darujhistan denounced as a gang.

After a successful run of thefts, beatings and a few murders, the ire of the wealthier class of merchants was finally roused and the city Wardens were spurred to corner Bendan and his fellows in the abandoned two-storey house they used as their base. By this time he had acquired a nickname, the Butcher, of which he was inordinately proud, but which stood him in no stead against the armour and shortswords of the Wardens.

He escaped the encirclement, unlike most of the brothers and sisters of his gang, the last remaining friends of or ties to his youth. Hunted, with nowhere to turn, he naturally sought out the final option available for someone without any attachments to his homeland: enlistment among the invading Malazans.

He watched now, under the cover of night, from the crest of a shoreward dune on the coast just north of Coral, close to Maurik, while four ships stole quietly up on to the strand. He glanced to his right, down the line of his fellow squad-members, anxious for the signal. Eventually, the sergeant, a giant of a man with skin so black Bendan had thought it paint, gave the sign.

As one the squad slithered down the rear of the crest then jogged for the narrow streambed the raiders had been using. Here, under cover of the scraggy brittle brush, they readied crossbows and javelins. Somewhere in the dark across the steep-sided cut waited the 33rd. Once his squad, the 70th, opened fire and engaged the raiders, they'd charge in from the rear. Meanwhile, the 4th was perhaps even now coming up the shore, ready to cut off retreat to the ships.

'Like herding sheep,' the corporal, Little, had told him, winking. 'Just keep them from breaking out.'

'More like wolves,' the oldest of the squad had warned, a hairy and very dirty fellow in tattered leathers everyone called Bone. 'These Confederation boys are pirates and slavers. Been raiding this coast for generations. Think it's their gods-given right. This'll be right sharp.'

'I'm not afraid of no fight,' he'd said.

'Right, Butcher,' Bone had answered.

He'd given that name when asked. And surprisingly, they used it. Only when they said it they used the same tone they used for *arse*, or *idiot*. And somehow there was no way he could call them on it. So he'd shrunk back, glowering, determined to show them what fighting was all about. After all, it was the one thing he'd had to do every day of his life, and since he wasn't dead yet he was obviously good at it.

'Let none escape,' had been bald Sergeant Hektar's last rumbled instruction. 'This is our warning stroke. Our last chance before we go.'

Before they left. Marching out! Bendan had seen everyone's reaction to that stunning news. Crazy as one of them Tenescowri!

Abandoning the fortress before it's even finished. Who was this ambassador to order them out? Couldn't Steppen have just sent ten or twenty for that marionette to inspect?

Everyone in his squad was disgusted at this typical army stupidity. All except Bone, who'd muttered through a mouthful of the leaves he chewed, 'The ways of officers is a mystery to regular people.'

Bendan thought it an improvement – he was damned sick of hammering rocks and humping dirt. He'd take a bit of marching over that backbreaking work any time.

Now, it seemed, was their last chance for any real action and everyone was eager to make it count. Beneath them, tracing the bed of the dry cut, came the Confederacy raiders jogging along to their target, another defenceless farming hamlet. He struggled with his crossbow in the disorienting light of the silvery bright reborn moon, and the greenish glow of the swelling arc of light in the sky that some named the Sword of God – though just which god varied.

The mechanism of the crossbow defeated him once again. He couldn't seem to master the damned foreign thing. He set it down and readied one of the wicked barbed javelins he'd brought against just such a possibility. And just in time as well, as the whistled signal came to fire.

Everyone straightened, letting loose. Crossbows thumped, soldiers shouted, tossing javelins. Bendan hurled his, then without waiting to see whether he'd struck anyone or not started down the slope readying his shortsword and shield. What he glimpsed below worried him. Instead of the milling chaos he'd been told to expect the line of warriors had simply knelt behind large shields, taken the initial barrage, and even now was counter-charging up through the rock and brush.

And damn his dead and gone ancestors but there were a lot of them.

No more time to think as his headlong run brought him smack into the first of the raiders. He shield-bashed the man and knocked him backwards off his feet. That shock absorbed almost all his inertia and now he traded blows with two others. His squad was ridiculously outnumbered. Bendan released all the ferocity he'd learned in life or death fights before he'd even grown hair on his chin. He gave himself into the blazing rage completely, whirling, screaming, attacking without let-up. Raiders backpedalled before him, overborne. Blades struck his hauberk of leather hardened with mail and iron lozenges but he ignored the blows in a determination to carry on until dead. Only this complete abandon had seen him walk away from all his fights – bloodied and punished, but upright.

Then in what seemed like an instant all that stood before him wore the black of Malaz and he lowered his arm, weaving, sucking in great ragged breaths, near to vomiting. The other squad had pushed through from the other side. The column of raiders had broken and men were running for their ships. Bendan and his squad mates left them for the others.

Someone offered him a skin of water and he sucked in a small mouthful and splashed one spray over his face. The blows he'd taken were agony and he knew he'd be hardly able to move tomorrow but he'd been lucky: none was serious enough to take him down.

Sergeant Hektar came by and cuffed his shoulder. 'Damn, Butcher,' he rumbled. 'I can see we're gonna have to rein you in some.'

Nearby Bone had a cloth pressed to his blood-smeared face, still grinning. 'Lookin' forward to a full day's march tomorrow, lad?' He laughed.

Bendan waved that off.

'What about these wounded, Hek?' someone called.

The massive Dal Hon ran a hand over his gleaming nut-brown scalp. 'These are slavers . . . give them a taste of it. We sell them.'

'Can't do that,' Bone shouted from where he was rifling the bodies, one-handed. 'Empire don't sell slaves.'

'Indentureship is so much better, is it?' the Dal Hon muttered, and shrugged. 'So we give them away to the Coral merchants.'

Bone's answering laugh was genuine, but it wasn't pleasant.

Later that night as he was walking back to camp it occurred to Bendan that when Hektar had called him 'Butcher' he hadn't used *that* tone. The sergeant had seemed to mean it. He felt grateful, but also a little embarrassed. Because for the entire fight he'd been so terrified he'd pissed himself.

*   *   *

Awareness came to Ebbin in brief disconnected instants. Like startling flashes of lightning in an otherwise terrifying pitch black landscape of lashing, spinning winds. Each illuminated an instant tableau frozen in stark contrast of light and shadow: he huddled among the bones of a hilltop sepulchre, its stone door shattered; he chiselling layers of barnacles and sea-growths from a stone revealing it white and pure as mountain snow; he being kicked aside by Aman while the girl Taya danced frenzied before a cloaked figure with the face of the sun; his hands held before his face cracked and bloodied, sleeves in tatters.

At other times, the worst times, he was called to writhe in abject terror before that cloaked figure. During these times, lost in the eternal storm that now raged in his mind, the being's face shone silver like the moon. At other times he raged insane against this monster, shook his fists, swore himself hoarse.

All his tormentor ever gave in return was lofty mocking amusement. As if not only his life and ambitions were meaningless, puerile, but the hopes, struggles and dreams of everyone in the city and beyond were nothing more than puffery and self-important vacuousness. This god-like overview of the entire sweep of human civilization on the continent sent Ebbin once more into the eternal raging storm within his mind.

Yet the stones are important. He is worried about the stones. Will there be enough to complete the base?

At other times they shook him from his tortured nightmare trance to perform tasks for them. The girl – though hardly a girl, Taya – always accompanied him. He helped oversee the salvaging of these very stone blocks being taken from the city mole. He hired craftsmen, answered queries. In short, was the human face before the operations these fiends wished to complete.

And all the while he was powerless to speak of any of it. He tried – gods, how he fought to utter any word of objection or defiance! But the moment he contemplated such rebellion his mouth and throat constricted as if throttled. Not even his hands would cooperate to scrawl a plea for help. And so, like a prisoner within his own skull, he could only watch and speculate.

Whatever these fiends planned, it reached back all the way to their internment. A resurrection of their rule as one of the legendary Tyrants. Yet why the elaborate charade? Why wait to declare their return? Why the mask? Ebbin was frustrated beyond measure by the mystery. He felt that he had almost all the pieces, yet arranging a meaningful pattern defied him.

One strange moment seemed to almost shock him out of his fugue. He was working in the tent on the salvage site near the shore at the base of Majesty Hill when someone stopped before his table and spoke to him. He looked up from the wage lists, blinking, to see a dark muscled fellow with a wide mane of black hair peering down at him; startling honest concern creased the man's features. 'Yes . . . ?'

'Are you sure you are all right?' the fellow asked.

Something squeezed Ebbin's chest painfully – and it was no outside coercion from the masked fiend. He fought to find his voice. 'Yes . . . yes. Thank you.' Emboldened, he took another breath. 'Your name . . . ?'

'Barathol Mekhar.'

Ebbin searched his mental lists, found the man. *Foreigner, skilled, unregistered blacksmith*. Something in that sketch moved him to lurch forward, saying, 'You have to—' Then came the clenching fist at his throat. He struggled to continue, even to breathe.

The man's puzzled concern returned. 'Yes?'

Then Taya was there at his side to wrap an arm about his shoulders, and squeeze, painfully. 'My uncle has a lot on his mind,' she explained sweetly. 'He is ashamed. He gambled, you see. And he lost. He lost everything.' She squeezed him again, digging in the nails of a hand. 'Isn't that so, Uncle?'

Ebbin could only nod his sunken head.

'Well,' the man said, his voice gruff but gentle, 'I understand. I was just saying that I could set up a smithing station here for your needs. Sharpening tools, forging items.'

'Yes,' Taya said. 'That would be excellent. Thank you. I believe we will have need of that.'

After one last warning clasp she watched while the man moved off, then she left Ebbin to pick up his stylus and return to his record-keeping.

*   *   *

Antsy and Corien led the way out of Pearl Town, as Panar had named it. Malakai immediately slipped away without a word. Ashamed to be seen with the likes of us, Antsy grumbled to himself. Progress was slow, as they elected to travel with no light at all. Orchid murmured directions from close behind. Despite the girl's descriptions of the way ahead Antsy kept crashing into walls in the pitch black. And Corien limped, unsteady, grunting his pain, his breathing wet and laboured.

'I see them,' Orchid announced after they'd walked a maze of narrow streets. 'Stairs, ahead.'

Antsy let out a snort of disgust. *Just great – climbing blasted stairs in the dark!*

'They're very broad. Open on the right. They climb a cliff up and up . . . Great Mother – so high!'

In the dark Antsy rolled his eyes. *Wonderful. Absolute night all around and a drop-off. Couldn't get any better.* 'Malakai?'

'No sign.'

Gettin' too casual, he is. Antsy's right foot banged up against the riser of the first stair and he tumbled forward on to them. He dropped his sword and scraped a shin, cursing. The blade clanged from the stone steps like anvils falling in the dark.

'Sorry, Red,' Orchid offered, sounding embarrassed.

Antsy just cursed under his breath. Corien almost fell over him as he felt his way forward in the black ink. *Fucking band of travelling harlequins, we are. Just missing the floppy hats.*

Orchid grasped his arm to help him up and he almost yanked it free.

'Keep tight to the left,' she suggested. 'Single file . . . I guess.'

'I'll go first,' Antsy said. Then he froze, his lips clenching tight. 'Orchid – where's my Hood-damned sword?'

'Oh! Sorry.' She pressed it to his hand. He snapped it up, grated a sullen, 'Thanks.'

Can't even find my own damned sword! Useless! Completely useless!

Up they went, sliding along the smooth left wall. The staircase was quite broad, with shallow risers only a hand's breadth or so in height. Luckily the natural list of the Spawn tilted forward and to the left. If it had leaned the other way he didn't think they could have managed. A gathering warm breeze dried the sweat on the nape of his neck and pressed against his back as the air pushed in around him, rushing up this access. Just warm air rising? Or something more . . . worrisome? He couldn't be sure.

'Feel that wind?' Corien asked from the dark.

'So pleasant for a change,' Orchid answered.

Antsy said nothing.

Finally, Orchid ordered a stop. 'Something's ahead. Doors. Broken doors. Stone. Very thick. Looks like we can get through, though.' Antsy grunted his understanding. 'Careful now. Slow.'

Antsy and Corien felt their way over shards of shattered rock, ducked under leaning eaves of larger fragments. The Darujhistan swordsman was stumbling more and more and Antsy found himself helping him constantly now. He whispered, 'How're you doing?'

'Not so well, I'm afraid. Feeling weak.'

Antsy touched the back of a hand to the lad's forehead: hot and slick with sweat. Maybe an infection. That blade or sharpened stick couldn't have been too clean. 'We have to stop,' he said, louder.

'Corien?' Orchid asked. 'It's bad?'

'My apologies. Not what I had in mind.'

'Why didn't you say so?' she demanded, outraged. 'I asked earlier!'

'We couldn't very well have stayed there,' he said, tired and patient, 'could we?'

'There are rooms ahead,' came Malakai's voice from far to the fore.

Despite himself Antsy flinched at the sudden announcement from the dark. *Hate it when he does that!* 'What've you been doing!' he yelled back angrily.

'Scouting,' came the answer, much closer now. 'Orchid, the hall goes on straight then there are multiple rooms to either side. Take one. We need to rest anyway.'

Antsy started forward, still helping Corien. 'Any sign of the Malazans?'

'No. None. No sign of anyone at all.'

'Perhaps we should've brought that fellow Panar with us,' Orchid said.

Antsy snorted. 'What could he do for us?'

'He knows his way around the Spawn. He could direct us.'

'Almost all of what he told us was lies,' Malakai said, dismissive.

'How do you know?'

'His story's full of holes. How did he get away from the attacks he described? I wager he betrayed his comrades. Sold them out to save his skin.'

'You don't know that,' said Orchid, outraged. 'You weren't there. Why assume that?'

'Because of his other lies.'

'What do you mean his other lies?' she demanded, her voice getting even louder. 'Stop making empty accusations. Either you know or you don't.'

'Leave it be,' Antsy murmured. 'I agree with him.'

'No! I will not be shut up by this man's airs and knowing hints.'

'Very well,' Malakai answered, sounding grimly pleased. 'These poor starving men and women you seem to feel such sympathy for. These scrapings of the would-be treasure-hunters who came scrambling for easy riches. They can't buy food and water from any Confederation boats. They've nothing left to sell. They didn't even have the weapons left to stab our two friends. Now, there's only one thing left down here to eat – which is why they attacked us in the first place, and why they didn't pursue us afterwards. We killed or badly wounded a number of them, and – for the time being at least – they have enough to eat.'

Orchid's breath caught in the dark. 'No,' she said, her voice strangled. 'I don't believe you.'

Malakai didn't answer; he didn't need to.

Antsy remembered those snarling rat-like faces, the bared teeth, the frenzied glistening eyes, and thought he'd vomit right then. Instead, he took a bracing deep breath of the sea-tinged air. 'So this is not the way?' he asked, dizzy.

'*The* way?' Malakai answered. 'It's *a* way – at least that. And that's what I want. We'll reconnoitre after a rest.'

Antsy grunted his agreement and he and Corien continued shambling up the hall.

They took turns keeping watch, or in Antsy's case listening very hard indeed. And the titanic fragment of Moon's Spawn spoke to him. A saboteur, he understood the deep groans that came shuddering up through the stone beneath his thighs and hands. The sharp distant poppings of snaps and cracks. He'd spent a lot of time underground. It reminded him of something . . . something from his youth. But for the life of him he couldn't quite place it just then.

Even Malakai stayed with them to lie down and to stand a watch. It seemed he wasn't the sort to pretend he needed less sleep than anyone else.

In the 'morning', when Malakai woke everyone, Orchid came to Antsy and set a hand on his arm to crouch down next to him. 'Corien's getting worse,' she whispered. 'I've done everything I can, but that weapon, whatever it was, must've been filthy.'

'How bad—'

'I can still walk,' Corien interrupted loudly. 'The quiet and dark, you know. Sharpens the hearing.'

'You'll have to walk on your own,' Malakai said flatly.

'Your concern is a soothing balm,' the youth replied.

Antsy smiled in the dark: he would've just told Malakai to go fuck himself.

'Red, you lead then,' Malakai said, ignoring the sarcasm. 'Corien . . . walk with Orchid.'

'And you?' Orchid demanded. 'Wandering off gods know where? You should stay with us in case there's trouble.'

'If there's trouble I'll be more use as a hidden asset.'

Orchid just snorted at that. Antsy imagined her throwing up her hands in the dark.

As they readied, Antsy asked Orchid over and held out his pannier. 'You're sure?' she said, surprised.

'Yeah – no use in a fight. An' I'll need both hands. Corien? The use of your sword perhaps?'

'Yes, Red.' There came the unmistakable sound of polished iron brushing wood as the blade cleared the mouth of the sheath. 'Orchid?'

'Oh, yes.' Fumblings as Corien handed Orchid the weapon. 'Ach!'

'What?' from both Antsy and Corien.

'Cut my hand on the edge.'

'Don't hold it by the blade!' Corien exclaimed. 'Both edges are razor sharp.'

'So I see,' she answered, scathing. 'Here.'

The grip was pressed to Antsy, who took it and readied his own sword in his left hand. 'Okay. Which way?'

'To the right.'

Antsy edged to the right. He held the blades before him, off slightly to each side. Occasionally a tip grated against a wall and he would adjust his direction. Behind, Corien grunted his effort. His boots slid heavily over the smooth stone floor and every breath was tight with pain. Antsy knew Orchid was doing her best to help him along.

After a time turning corners and crossing large chambers – meeting places, or assemblies, Orchid thought them – she sent them climbing up against the Spawn's slant to what she said was a large building front across a broad open court. 'Do you even know where you're going?' Antsy finally complained.

'Malakai is there, waiting,' she said; then, rather impatiently, 'I've been keeping us to the main ways, you know!'

Antsy now said aloud what had been bothering him for some time: 'Then where *is* everyone? The place is deserted! Where're these Malazans? Where's *anyone*?'

'How in the name of—' She stopped herself. 'How should I know?'

Antsy just grumbled. Again it seemed the constant straining to see in the utter dark was giving him hallucinations. Lights blossomed before his eyes. Shapes of deepest blue seemed to waver in his vision like ghosts. He silently fumed against it all. *What a fool I was for throwing myself into this. A bad start before a worse end! I'm gonna die in the dark like a blasted worm.*

'You made it,' Malakai said blandly from the dark. Antsy pulled up sharply. The observation was neither a compliment nor a complaint. 'This looks to be some sort of large complex. We should take a look.'

'I'm not so sure we should go in there,' Orchid said, sounding worried.

'Not for you to say. Corien, perhaps you can sit down inside, in any case.'

The lad managed a tight, 'Certainly. That would be . . . most welcome.'

'We are agreed then.'

'Which way?' Antsy rasped, his throat dry – already they were getting low on water.

'There are stairs up,' Orchid said.

He slid his foot ahead until he bumped up against the first, then he carefully felt his way up until Orchid told him he was on the last. 'This is a very wide doorway, tall too,' she murmured. 'Open double doors. Inside is a kind of arcade with many side openings and corridors.'

Shit. This could take for ever. 'Look, Malakai,' he grumbled, 'it would help if we knew what we were looking for . . . Malakai . . . ?'

'He's gone.'

Osserc-damned useless whore's son! That's fucking well it! He pulled off his rolled blanket and began rummaging through it.

'What are you doing?' Orchid asked.

'I'm getting the lantern.'

'Malakai said—'

'Malakai can dick himself with his own—' Antsy bit off his words, cleared his throat. 'Sorry, lass. Malakai isn't here, is he?'

He set the lantern on the stone floor, pulled out his set of flints and tinder and began striking. The sparks startled him at first, so huge and bright were they. *Light deprivation – seen it before in the mines. Have to shield the lantern.* In moments he had the tinder glowing: that alone seemed light enough. He took up a pinch of the lint and shavings and held them to the wick and blew. Once the wick caught he blew again, steadily, pinched out the tinder and shoved it away back into its box, which he snapped shut.

The lantern's flame blossomed to life and he had to turn his face away, so harsh was the golden light. Blinking, squinting against the pain the light struck in his eyes, he could eventually see and what he saw took his breath away.

Everything was black, yes, but not plain or grim. The walls, the columns of the carved stone arcades, all writhed with intricate carving. Stone vines climbed the walls, delicate stone leaves seemed to wave before his eyes. Bowers of trees, all carved from the glittering finely grained black stone, arched over a second-storey walkway above.

Then he saw the smooth polished floor and he frowned. Dust covered it, but so too did a litter of broken pots and scattered furniture. *No looting here. Why?*

In the light, Corien shuffled over to a side alcove of carved benches and sat down, hissing his pain. Antsy set the lantern on the bench next to him. The lad squinted his puzzlement. His face gleamed sickly pale, sheathed in sweat. 'You keep the light,' Antsy told him. 'I'll have a poke around.' Corien drew breath to object but Antsy held out his sword, pommel first. Offering a tired smile, Corien took it. 'Look after Orchid here while I'm gone.'

Orchid had the sense not to object to that bit of chauvinism.

Shortsword out, Antsy picked his way through the litter. It was a large main entrance hall, or gathering chamber. Halls opened off it all around. Stairs led down and up from it on both the right and the left. The stairs were intricately carved, the balusters with vines and blossoms. His light-starved eyes made out much more in the weak light than he knew he could've normally; as on a night of a full moon or a fresh snow. In places the floor bore carved designs like grille-work or lattices bearing foliage.

Far off across the chamber the lantern glowed like a star. Next to it Orchid paced restlessly. Antsy found an overturned chest or travel box, its contents of cloth spilled across the floor. He kicked through the dark rich robes. *Damn me if I don't know what's valuable or not! A Togg-damned waste of time this is.*

Something about the nearby stairs caught his attention and he crossed to them. The dust was disturbed here. Not by tracks, but brushed aside, as if disturbed by a wind or the dragging of a wide cloth. He decided to follow as far the light extended. The stairs brought him to a floor just beneath the main one. Here light streamed down through the carvings in the floor above, casting illuminated scenes of bowers of trees across another smooth floor. An intended effect; Antsy wondered? Did lamps or such like burning above cast the same shadows when this place was occupied? He walked out on to the floor.

An object gleamed in the light streaming down. A stick of some kind. Antsy walked up and crouched over it. A bone. A leg bone. A human tibia. And not clean, either. Tangles of ligaments and dried meat still clung to its ends.

He straightened, swallowed the bile churning sickly in his stomach. A dense glow now shone from the far end of the chamber. Fascinated, unable to turn away, he edged closer until the light was sufficient to reveal a carpet of similar remains choking the far side. The shadows of alien blossoms streamed down upon a mass of human carcasses. Many still wore their helmets. Their feet remained in boots. The meat of calf and thigh was gone, as were the viscera from empty gutted chests and abdomens. Ribcages gaped like open mouths hanging with desiccated strips of flesh and meat. Antsy had seen similar remains after battles where scavengers had picked over the dead, taking the choice bits and leaving the rest.

He choked back a yell of alarm and ran for the stairs.

Not looted. Avoided! Everyone else knows better! And Panar sent us here! To our damned deaths.

He came pelting back to Orchid and Corien who stared, tensing in alarm. 'What is it?' Orchid demanded, rising.

'We have to get out of here – *now*!'

'What—'

'That – *thing* – everyone was scared of below. I think this is its lair. We have to go.' He snatched up the lantern, took Corien by the arm. 'Come on.'

He chivvied them back up the hall to the doors. Here Orchid suddenly let out a cry and froze. Antsy let go of Corien, drew his shortsword. He squinted, seeing nothing. 'What?'

Hand at mouth, the girl stammered, 'The door.'

Antsy peered at the doorway anew. What of it? Dark, yes, but . . . Dark. The light did not penetrate. *Something* was blocking the entrance, something utterly black like a curtain of night. 'What is it?'

But Orchid could not speak. She merely jerked her head side to side, appalled, eyes huge.

Shit. Antsy hefted his shortsword. Somehow he didn't think it would do him much good. And munitions? Probably not them either. He looked to Corien; that finely curled hair now hung down sweat-plastered. The lad met his eye and nodded, hand tightening on his swordgrip.

'It is a creature of Elder Night,' said Malakai, stepping out from an alcove next to them. 'Call it what you will. A daemon, or a fiend. Night animate. No doubt to it *we* are the invaders, the monsters.'

'Spare me your sophistry,' Antsy grated. 'What can you do against it?'

'I?' The man cocked a brow. 'Nothing. We are trapped. It would seem Panar has the last laugh after all.'

Antsy almost threw his shortsword at the man. 'Fine,' he snarled. 'Everyone back! I'll try my munitions.'

'Red . . .' Corien warned, touching his arm.

Antsy spun: Orchid had advanced upon the creature.

Shit! 'Orchid!'

The girl ignored, or couldn't hear him. One hand was at her throat, the other reaching out as if entreating. She spoke, and Antsy started for now she uttered another language. One completely unfamiliar to him. Sing-song, it was. Not unpleasant to his ears.

She spoke at length, pausing from time to time as if awaiting an answer. Antsy, Corien and Malakai waited, silent, scarcely breathing.

Despite his anticipation Antsy jerked when a reply came at last. Words murmured from the night, deep and resonating, as if enunciated by all the immeasurable dark surrounding them. Orchid shuddered as if burned – Antsy wondered if she was even more surprised to hear an answer than they. Her breath caught and she looked aside, head bowed as if searching for something, grasping after memories.

Come on . . . Do it, girl. You can do it . . .

She nodded then, her gaze distant, and returned her attention to the doorway in front of her. Both hands went to her neck, as if she would throttle herself, and she spoke slowly, haltingly, for some time. The speech ended in a gasp, Orchid wrung out, breathless.

Silence followed. The barrier across the doorway seemed to waver in the lantern light like a wall of hanging velvet. The thing spoke again, a brief response, and Orchid launched into some sort of recitation. Antsy squeezed the grip of his shortsword, his hand wet with sweat. A biting cold now filled the hall. His breath plumed before him.

She finished again with a gasp as if barely able to squeeze out the words. In the silence that followed Antsy wiped the ice from his hands then examined his fingers: blue and numb with cold. An answer rolled out of the dark: a speech in slow measured tones, a chant almost. The coal-black curtain wavered, then disappeared or slipped away like a shadow exposed to light.

A hissed exhalation escaped Orchid and she would have toppled but for Antsy rushing forward to steady her. He guided her to a bench. Her skirts rattled ice-stiff and rimed with hoar frost. Her skin was burning cold to the touch. Corien sat beside her, holding the lantern close.

'Malakai . . .' Antsy said, gesturing to the entrance.

After a moment the man answered from beyond, 'It's gone.'

A distant shout sounded from the darkened halls beyond: a frenzied cry of frustration and rage, and Antsy barked a laugh. 'So much for Panar's vengeance. I'm tempted to slit his throat.'

'No!' said Orchid, struggling up. Antsy helped her stand. 'Let's just go.'

'And just which way do we go?' Malakai asked, appearing from the dark.

'Any way,' she answered, annoyed. 'Right. Left. It doesn't matter. Just find a way up.'

'Why?'

'Because what you seek is in the upper levels.'

Malakai froze, astonished. His eyes widened with new appreciation, and he gave a bow of his head – though shallow and tinged by irony. 'Very well. I will be back shortly.'

Orchid turned to Corien where he slouched on the bench, a hand pressed to his side. She knelt before him. Gently, she set her own hand over his and he hissed at the touch. She spoke again in that same eerie tongue that raised the hairs on the small of Antsy's neck. It sounded like an invocation or recitation.

A great sigh escaped from Corien and the man would have fallen forward if Antsy hadn't steadied him. Antsy let him slide down on the bench, unconscious.

'What was that!' he demanded, far more harshly than he'd intended. *Fear. I'm hearing fear in my voice.*

Orchid held her hands out before her, studying them. She stood, wiped the wet condensation from her face. 'Strange, isn't it?' she said dreamily. 'To be told stories all your life, to read them, study them, then suddenly discover it's all *true* . . .'

Antsy was looking at a line of empty pedestals. Someone had set a rusted helmet on one. It looked just like a decapitated head. 'Yeah. Life's full o' twists and turns,' he breathed, uneasy.

She sat, folded her graceful dark hands primly on her lap. Like a priestess, Antsy thought. She looks like some kinda damned ancient priestess with her thick mane of tousled black hair, tattered skirts, and torn lace. Who was she?

He cleared his throat. 'So . . . what happened there?'

Her gaze was tired, half-lidded, directed at the entrance. 'I'm not sure myself. It surprised me, answering like that. Probably was just as amazed as I was to hear the old tongue.'

'Yeah. The old tongue. Imagine that. And?'

An exhausted lift and fall of the shoulders. 'I invoked the Rite of Passage as recorded by Hul' Alanen-Teth, a Jaghut who claimed to have travelled the Paths of Eternal Night. The guardian honoured the formula.'

Beside her Corien stirred groggily. Antsy nodded to her, accepting her words. 'Well, thanks for saving our lives.'

A wry smile twisted her lips. Head lowered, she peered up at him. 'I did not save *your* life, Antsy. You it called . . . "Honoured Guest".'

He frowned at her. 'What . . . ?'

Corien sat up. He held his head, touched his side. His brows rose. 'The pain is gone.'

Orchid nodded. 'Good. That was an Andii invocation of healing. You will be weak for a time, but you should mend.' She stood. 'Now, if you will excuse me. I . . . I want to be alone for a time.'

As she passed Antsy touched the cloth of her sleeve. He tried to catch her gaze but she would not meet his eyes. 'And what did it call you . . . ?'

She flinched away. 'Not now.'

Antsy eased himself down next to Corien. They exchanged wondering glances. Antsy blew out a breath. 'Well . . . what d'you know.'

The lad gave a long thoughtful nod.

When Malakai returned he found them still sitting side by side. He cocked a brow. 'What's this? Why aren't we moving?'

'Orchid's resting,' Antsy said, smiling up at him.

'And what are you so pleased about?'

Antsy tucked his hands up under his arms. 'Oh, I'm always in a better mood when the squad has its cadre mage.'

The man wrinkled his dark brows, uncertain what to make

of that. But Antsy just smiled. It seemed to him that everything had changed. As in battle. Things had reversed themselves as they can in any close engagement. There'd been no announcement, no horns blowing to signal it. Everyone involved just knew it, sensed it. The energy had shifted. Earlier, the party had been Malakai's. Now, it was Orchid's. And he and Corien? Well, they were *her* guards now.

BOOK II

Sceptre

CHAPTER VIII

Madrun and Lazan Door –
From distant lands they hail.

One day Door did announce:
'Tis time my hair to cut.

Yet no shear would tear
No blade would part
No scissor snick nor sever

And so it grew –
this bounteous mane.
Wenches plotted
Knives were sharpened
Yet no helm nor hat could tame
These wilful, prideful curls.

When last Door heard
His hair had fled
Fighting pirates off far Elingarth!

attributed to Fisher

I N THE MORNING BROOD PUSHED ASIDE THE HEAVY CLOTH FLAP OF HIS
tent to find the Rhivi warriors in the process of breaking camp.
He frowned then, feeling a chill premonition, and crossed to
where one of the Elders stood wrapped in a blanket warming himself
at a fire. It was one of the more amiable of them, Tserig, called the
Toothless. The Warlord inclined his head in greeting. 'Word from
the north?'

Looking unhappy, the old man gave a shallow bow. 'Yes, Great One. A rider came in the night. The Malazans are in disarray. They have been driven from Pale and are retreating to the south-west.' He shrugged, apologetic. 'The circle of war leaders decided to act.'

Without consulting me. 'I see. Since when did the Rhivi chase after war?'

The old man seemed to consider one answer but clamped his lips tight against it. He adjusted the folds of the horse blanket, indicated the embers dying before him. 'War is like a grass fire, Great One, is it not? Once sparked it cannot be controlled. It will burn and burn until it has consumed everything it can reach.'

'Its fuel is blood, Tserig.'

A gloomy nod of agreement. 'I know, Ancient One. I was against it. But I am old – and toothless.'

Brood smiled his appreciation. 'And so your reward is to be the one who has to break the news that my, ah, *leadership* is no longer required.'

The old man offered another half-bow. 'I am sorry, Warlord . . . perhaps they merely did not wish to disturb you in your mourning.'

'That's putting about as pretty a face on it as anyone can manage.' He eyed the embers for a time, rubbed a forefinger along his jaw. Tserig, he noted, was cringing away and Brood realized the old man must think he was scowling his displeasure at him, so he turned to face the west.

'What will you do now, Great One?' the old man ventured after a time.

Around them the last of the burdened asses, carts, and travois and herded bhederin made their way north, following the track through the Gadrobi hills. Riders bowed to Brood as they passed, or saluted, raising spears and loosing their war calls. 'If the Mhybe was still with us, or Silverfox, none of this would be happening . . .' he murmured, but distractedly, his thoughts elsewhere.

'I agree, Warlord. But they are gone from us. The Mhybe was given her great reward. And Silverfox has departed. Gone to another land, some say.' Like Brood, the old man did not mention the other who was gone from them as well.

The Warlord cleared his throat, profoundly uncomfortable. *How to broach this without insulting this man, his people, and all they have sacrificed these last years?*

'Would you share the morning tea with me, Warlord?' Tserig said suddenly, his gaze oddly gentle, as if he were addressing a youth rather than someone incalculably older than he.

'Yes. Thank you, Tserig. I would welcome that.'

The old man motioned aside to an attendant who hurried to ready the tall bronze pot and the tiny thimble-sized cups, and the two stood in silence waiting for the leaves to steep. Both watched the ragged columns of the Rhivi snaking their way north through a cut in the hills. Behind them Tserig's servants struck his tent.

'You'll make much better time now with the herds returned to the north,' Brood observed.

'Yes. Mostly it is those fearful of the Malazans, or anxious to prove themselves as warriors, who have remained. Is it any wonder then that they should have found their excuse? And Jiwan had at his service a most convincing weapon.'

'And what is that?'

'An earnest belief in his cause.'

Brood found himself again appreciating the old man. He allowed himself a grin.

A servant handed each a tiny bronze cup then poured tea in long hissing streams from the slim pot. Tserig raised his cup to the Warlord. 'To wise council.'

'Wise council.'

The old man smacked his lips, sucking in the tea. 'I ask then, again. What will you do?'

Brood grimaced his awkwardness. He looked off to the west. 'I've become convinced that we shouldn't confront these Malazans any longer. It will be a disaster for the Rhivi, in the long run.'

Distaste wrinkled Tserig's pursed lips. 'Yet they hem us in on all sides. Trespass across our lands. Kill all the animals they find. They are like a plague. Are we to abandon our way of life?'

'Tserig,' Brood's voice was low and hoarse with emotion, 'that will happen anyway. It is inevitable. Question is, then, how best to mitigate the damage of it all? The answer is ugly and brutal, but it is plain . . . You get better terms in a peace treaty than you get when you're conquered – which is to say, no terms whatsoever.'

That stung the old man's pride and he straightened, offended. 'You question our spirit!'

The Warlord raised a placating hand. 'No. Never that. I am not talking about the brief season of war . . . I am talking about the generations that follow.'

Tserig's gaze sank to the fire. His face was pained as if he were studying such a future within the dying embers. 'Treaties,' he finally spat. 'Never honoured by the powerful. I place no faith in such agreements.'

'They will be honoured,' Brood grated, 'if *I* witness them.'

Tserig's greying brows rose as he considered this, then he bowed his head almost in salute. 'I accept your plan, Warlord, as the best course for my people. How then do we proceed?'

Brood, who had been eyeing the west before, raised his chin to the distant horizon, the brown hills, and Lake Azur beyond. 'Have you ever been on a boat, Tserig?'

The old man shuddered. 'Ancient hearth-goddess, no. My feet have never left touch with our Mother.'

The Warlord's beast-like eyes swung to him, held steady.

Tserig hunched beneath the weight of that gaze, gummed his lips. 'Please . . . Great One. Have mercy on an old man.'

* * *

In Darujhistan's guild hall of guards, sentinels, wardens and gatemen, Captain Soen of the Legate's bodyguard looked these two most recent applicants up and down and didn't bother hiding his disgust. Clothes no better than rags, dirt-smeared faces, cracked sandals. Not even a scrap of armour or a weapon showing anywhere. *Must have pawned the lot to buy booze. And must be alive with fleas. Trake's tail, I'm here to hire guards – not beggars.*

'Names?' he demanded, and grimaced as a wafting hint of their stink reached him.

'Scorch, sir,' said one.

'Leff.'

'You're in the lists, I assume?'

The two appeared to pale where they stood before him. They exchanged terrified glances. 'Ah, beggin' yer pardon,' said the one who had given his name as Scorch, 'but did you say list, sir?'

Soen rolled his eyes. 'Gods, man. Yes. The lists. The record of all certified members in good standing with the guild in the city!' At their expressions of complete blankness the captain leaned forward to explain, more slowly, 'Your references.'

The one named Leff made a great show of understanding, nodding vigorously. 'Oh sure, Cap'n sir. O' course.'

His friend goggled what resembled complete surprise. Unconvinced, but required to be thorough, Soen walked over to the

240

record keeper where he sat in the rear of the hall. 'Scorch and Leff,' he said.

The clerk immediately began scrolling through a long rolled sheet, winding the document down and down. 'Now *there's* a list,' one of these new applicants murmured to his companion.

After searching for a time the clerk appeared to have found his place, for he stopped and began to read. His brows shot up and he went back to the beginning once again. His brows continued to rise, almost touching his slicked-flat hair. He looked up, amazement plain on his face. 'Their references are impeccable!'

Soen, who had leaned his elbows in the counter, flinched straight. 'What?'

'These two are in excellent standing.'

'Let me see that.' He reached for the scroll.

The clerk backed away, hugging the roll to his chest. 'This is proprietary information, I'll have you know! Try that again and you'll be blacklisted.'

Soen turned on the two applicants who stood shifting from foot to foot like eunuchs in a brothel. *Gods. Guild rules are that I have to hire them now. Damn their stranglehold.* He marched up to them, as close as their stink would allow. 'Okay. Your references are in order. Fine.' He held up a finger. 'But before I see you tomorrow you'd better be cleaned up and fit for duty – or I'll have some ex-Urdomen I know scrub you all over with rayskin brushes. How would you like that?'

The one who had given his name as Scorch raised a hand.

'Yes? What?'

'Ah . . . does this mean we're hired, Captain, sir?'

'*Does this* . . .' Soen dragged a hand down his face, took a deep breath to calm himself. 'Yes,' he hissed, 'you're hired. Report to the Legate's manor tomorrow.' He eyed them up and down once more. 'Mind you,' and he raised a warning finger, 'you two report to the servants' gate – is that understood?'

Scorch nodded vigorously. 'Oh yes sir. Understood.' He saluted multiple times.

Soen waved a dismissal and stalked off, muttering. *Elder gods look away! How standards have fallen from the old days. Damned embarrassing it is. Still, these two could free up a couple of good men I could use elsewhere . . .*

Once the Captain was gone Leff cuffed Scorch. 'There! Y'see? Wasn't so hard, was it?'

'I thought I said we should try here.'

Leff appeared not to have heard. 'Let's go.'

'Where?'

Leff made a great show of looking to the sky. 'Well, you heard the Captain! It's as obvious as Moon's Spawn in full-on daylight, o' course.'

'What is?'

'Where we have t'go!'

'An' that's . . .'

'To the lake, man!'

Scorch's permanent scowl of uncertainty deepened into stunned incomprehension. 'The lake?'

Leff sighed his impatience. 'Yes! Can't you hear? The man told us to get cleaned up. So it's a wash in the lake for us.' He stomped out.

Scorch was slow to follow. He scratched the thick grime caking one cheek, muttering, bemused, 'People do that? They wash? In the *lake* . . . ?'

*   *   *

Yusek guided her two charges north up the slopes of the coastal Mengel range. She was aware that these peaks were also known as the Mountains of Rain and she mused, bitterly, that they were damned well living up to that title. This wide pass in particular led all the way to the coast. Her leathers were rotting off her; the skin of her toes was peeling off like bark; and she had a constant raking cough, spitting up great wads of thick green catarrh.

She took out her frustrations on the two Seguleh. Their silence and impenetrable calm only sharpened her tongue. *Think they're so damned superior. Nothing more than smug assholes is what they are!*

This day she was off ahead alone, if only to give herself a break from her constant snarling and sniping. She studied the lower slopes where the banners of sinking mist were burning away leaving shallow rivulets and gullies that would eventually come together to form the headwaters of the Maiten River.

She glanced back and her shoulders fell as she saw that the two had stopped far back up the rocky path and were awaiting her return in their typical complete silence. *Brainless idiots! Could at least give me a shout.* Retracing her steps, she reached them standing where a major fork led off into the higher slopes.

'What, dammit?' she demanded, rubbing the wet mist from her cheeks and shuddering with cold.

The one called Sall gestured up the other trail. 'It occurs to us that you are leading far to the east when we wish to go north. This trail appears to lead north.'

Yusek gave a curt wave gesturing them on. 'Well, go ahead, by the Queen's tits! What do you need me for then? I'll just go my own damned way, shall I?'

Deep within the shadows of his hood, Sall's masked face revealed no emotion. It did look as if he frowned, though, as he squinted up the rocky trail. 'This will not get us north?'

'Look. You took me on to guide you, right? Well, that's what I'm doing. Guiding. I don't go telling you how to be all stiff as a board, okay? So don't question my choices. It just so happens that we have to swing around easterly here for a few days to avoid the valleys just north of us.'

'Why?'

'Why what?'

'Why must we avoid the valleys to the north?'

Yusek snarled her annoyance, coughed, and spat. Throughout all this the third member of the party, Lo, remained his usual silent self. Only his hood shifted as he glanced behind from time to time, watching, always scanning about. 'Listen,' she began again after clearing her raw throat, 'Dernan the Wolf controls these valleys. My old boss is a pup compared to him. He might squeeze a few coins where he can from travellers, but Dernan wipes out entire caravans. He even beat back soldiers from Kurl sent to smoke him out.' She shook her head and hugged herself against the chill, shuddering. 'No. We go round.'

Lo's hood dipped then as he spoke close to Sall and the lad gave one quick nod. 'Presumably this Dernan has shelter of some sort. A building or retreat. You are ill. In need of warmth, dry clothes. We will go north.'

Yusek gaped her disbelief. 'What? Go north? Are you fucking stupid or something? Haven't you listened to a word I said? Dernan will kill us for the gear on our backs. Or maybe just sell us as slaves down south.' Panting, her chest aching, she glared from one to the other. Both remained unmoved, mute in the drifting rain like grey ghosts. Drops pattered on them and a hidden stream hissed down a nearby cliff. *Fucking foreigners! Don't know a damned thing! Gonna get me killed.*

She cursed them, waved them to the Abyss, and turned away. 'I'm not going—' She froze as cold iron suddenly lay against her neck.

'Do not worry, Yusek. You will not be harmed.' The blade tapped her in a signal to turn round. She faced him. From behind the mask his mild brown eyes, though guarded, seemed to hold amusement. 'You can hardly guide us if you are dead, yes?'

Two days later, deep within the thick woods of the valley, next to a small stream, Sall and Lo froze in their steps and Yusek's heart sank. *Gods spare us!* She gripped her long-knife under her sodden cloak and crouched, seeking cover among the moss-grown wet boulders.

'Don't move!' a harsh voice bellowed from the woods. 'You're covered and surrounded!'

Peering over a rock, she watched a number of men and women closing in among the trees. They wore battered mismatched armour like the tattered remnants of some defeated mercenary army. Two had beads upon her over the stocks of crossbows. *An army! An entire fucking army!*

The voice called out again: 'Hands out! That's right. Don't move.'

She glanced back to see Lo and Sall standing motionless in their loose cloaks, hoods up, hands held out a slight distance from their sides. Men and women, crossbows raised, took up positions while others approached, swords drawn.

'Hand over your weapons,' the hidden voice ordered.

Sall and Lo remained immobile, hands at their sides.

'Drop them, or we fill you full of quarrels. Now.'

The two shared a glance then reached under their cloaks to produce their swords, still sheathed, offering them one-handed. Yusek dropped her long-knife. A scraggy-bearded fellow came scrambling down to her.

Two of Dernan's soldiers – and she was quite sure these must be they – warily approached Lo and Sall. A woman reached out a free hand to take Sall's sword, her own blade held ready to stab. She wore torn hunting leathers and tall moccasins that came up to her knees. A great fat fellow in a banded hauberk too small for him came swaggering up to Lo and reached out to snatch his sword.

Then a number of things seemed to happen all on their own. The woman reaching out to Sall tottered to her side. The wide fellow in front of Lo now had a blade thrusting out from his back. Crossbows thumped, firing, and bolts hissed but Sall simply seemed to

244

roll aside and the missiles snapped past. He disappeared among the trees. Crossbow bolts hammered into the fellow standing before Lo but somehow the great wide bulk of him didn't fall. Lo even seemed to be manoeuvring him, turning this way and that, intercepting the missiles. Everyone was shouting; the bearded one in front of Yusek was watching all this, mouth agape. Then he turned to her. 'A *mask*? Is that guy wearing a Hood-damned mask?'

She tried to dodge past him but he smacked her back down among the rocks. Her right hand found a stone and she swung, catching him on the side of his head, making him stagger. She dodged again but somehow he tripped her up. Standing over her he touched a hand to the blood streaming down his temple and into his beard. He gave her a gap-toothed grin. 'I'm gonna tear you from crotch to gullet for that.' He drew back his blade for a thrust.

A shadow arose behind the man and something hummed in the air, and then his head flew from its neck. The corpse tottered forward to fall gushing a great hot flow over Yusek, who screamed and screamed. All she remembered after that was scrambling on all fours for the stream, crying, utterly revolted, desperate to clean herself. The blood stained the icy water red.

When she stood, water dripping from her, it was silent. Only the stream hissed and gurgled around her. The woods were dark and still. She struggled over the slick wet rocks out of the water. Bodies lay everywhere. The amount of blood and fluids was terrifying, as were the wounds: many men were decapitated. Movement caught her eye and she glimpsed Lo throwing on his cloak. He appeared to be wearing beneath it some sort of light leather gambeson, possibly sewn with blued iron rings.

Sall appeared. His cloak was open as well, revealing nothing more than a plain shirt and sashed wide trousers. His sword was sheathed and he was escorting one of Dernan's people, a woman. Her long sandy hair was a tangled mess but she appeared unharmed.

'Did you . . .' Yusek began, but could only motion to the dead man who had threatened her.

'Yes.'

'Well, thanks. Who's this? A prisoner?'

He cocked his head, considering. 'I suppose you could say that.' Then he walked off, leaving the two of them together. Yusek eyed the woman; she couldn't take her stunned gaze from the Seguleh. Disgusted, Yusek went to find her knife. The woman followed.

'How is it you're still alive?' Yusek asked.

'I've spent time on the south shore – I threw down my blade. I've never heard of them this far north.'

'So you gave up? Just like that?' The woman wore a long coat of scaled leather armour, was tall and rangy. She appeared competent. Her awed gaze shifted to Yusek. 'You travel with them and you say that?'

Yusek felt her face flushing. 'It's different, okay? They – they hired me to guide them.'

'Hired . . .' the woman echoed, clearly sceptical. She gazed off to the north and her brow clenched in pain as she seemed to contemplate what was to come. 'Gods, girl . . . why didn't you take them round.'

Yusek thrust herself close. 'Listen,' she hissed. 'I *tried*, all right? Now we're stuck with it, ain't we.'

'Find a way. All this blood . . . it is on *your* head.'

'No it Hood well isn't!'

Lo and Sall approached.

'What do you want here?' the woman demanded.

Neither answered. Sall cocked his hooded head to Yusek. She eyed them in return, uncertain of their silence.

'Well?' the woman asked her.

She hugged herself, shuddering with the cold. 'There's a path I know west of here. It's a short cut. We should take it.' She thought she glimpsed Sall's eyes wrinkle, perhaps in a small smile.

'We go north,' he said.

'North? Why?' Yusek stepped closer, almost reached out to the youth's arm. 'Look at all this. We should go round.'

The hooded head shook a negative. 'They shouldn't have challenged.'

'Challenged?' the woman spat suddenly. 'No one here knows anything of your ways. How can you hold them responsible?'

Sall's hood did not shift from Yusek as the youth said mildly, 'So among you here in the north it is customary to murder travellers? People should be allowed to do so at will?'

'We didn't – that is . . .' The woman fell silent, turning away.

Despite her dread of more bloodshed, Yusek had to give this one to Sall. His point, though, gave her an idea. 'You want to go north, hey? To this monastery? Well, how will chasing some feud help that?'

The youth was still for a time, then he stepped over to Lo, who had kept his usual distance. The two conversed very briefly. Lo made a cutting hand gesture and Sall bowed. He returned to them. 'The challenge stands – and must be answered.'

'This is ridiculous!' the woman burst out. 'More bloodshed? And for what?' She pointed at Lo. 'Now I understand your reputation. *Seguleh*. No better than butchers! You enjoy it!'

'We are the test of the sword!' Sall answered hotly. 'Those who chose to pursue the path of the sword should be prepared to be challenged. And if they should fall' – he turned away – 'they have no grounds for complaint.'

'I understand,' Yusek breathed in wonder. Something in that outburst spoke directly to her heart.

The woman eyed her warily. 'You have been too long among them,' she said, then bent to begin rooting through the clothes of one of her dead companions.

Yusek followed the woman as she went from corpse to corpse, taking a pouch here, a ring there. On an impulse Yusek collected a longsword and sheath from one body. 'What is your name?' she finally asked, breaking the long silence between them.

'You can call me Lorkal,' she said, not looking up from her grisly work. 'You?'

'Yusek.'

'Where are you from then?'

'My family's from around Bastion.'

Lorkal stilled. She peered up, wonder in her eyes. 'Were you . . .'

'No. We fled.'

The woman grunted her understanding. She would have spoken, but Sall approached.

'We must move on,' he said to Yusek, ignoring Lorkal. 'Tell the woman to journey ahead and contact Dernan. We have a message for him. We are not bloodthirsty. We have decided that if he will provide us with food and shelter we will not trouble him.'

Lorkal straightened from a body to face Sall. 'No,' she said, loudly and firmly.

Sall's hood did not turn from Yusek. He was silent for a time; a deep breath raised and lowered his shoulders. 'Tell the woman it would be best if she complied . . .'

'Or what? You'll cut off my head?' Lorkal held out her open hands. 'I'm unarmed. What does your precious path of the sword say to that?'

'Tell the *prisoner*,' Sall began again, his voice tight.

But Yusek stepped away, waving to Lorkal. 'Tell her yourself – she's right here.' Lorkal chuckled, shaking her head and grinning. 'What's so damned funny?' Yusek demanded.

'Speaking to outsiders is your responsibility,' Sall told her.

'Speaking to . . . who? Outsiders? Aren't I an outsider?'

'You have entered into patronage with us. You are *Eshen-ai*. An outsider with countenance.'

'That means they're willing to consider you a potential human being. For a while.' Lorkal explained.

Yusek eyed Sall up and down. 'Well thank you so very fucking much!'

Lorkal laughed anew but quietened as Lo approached. These Seguleh seemed to specialize in hiding all hint of their emotions and intent, but it appeared to Yusek that a new tension and discomfort had taken hold of Sall's stiff posture. He took another long slow breath. 'Before I departed on this trip,' he began, 'my father told me this would be the greatest test I would ever face.' The hood rose to the sky. 'I did not believe him at the time. It seemed to me then that no test could be greater than facing the challenges of my brothers and sisters. But I see now that I was wrong. My father was not speaking of the rankings. He was speaking of greater trials. Of challenges to everything I have been taught. I understand this now.' He pointed to Lorkal. 'Tell this woman that if she cooperates and speaks to Dernan then there is a chance that further bloodshed can be avoided. However, should she refuse, it is very certain that a great many more lives will be lost.' And with a small bow of his head for emphasis, he walked away.

Yusek let go a long breath, impressed. *Probably the longest speech of his life.* She cocked a brow to Lorkal.

The woman was studying the pouches and gold ornaments in her hands. 'Shit.'

They advanced north up a side-gorge of the valley for a time until Lo sat down where boulders as large as huts choked the stream. His sitting announced that they would wait there. Saying nothing, Lorkal walked on alone, taking a higher path. Sall crouched down on his haunches where he could keep an eye on the approach up the valley. Yusek came and sat near him, hugging herself for warmth. She felt exhausted yet she could not stop shuddering. Her fingers were numb and blue and she clenched them as hard as she could. What would she do, she wondered, if she were in Lorkal's position right now?

Would she just keep on walking?

It was one option. Who was to know? Except for you. That was the thing. And she suspected it was somehow similar to this test of the sword Sall mentioned. What would you do when no one would ever know of your actions? The easy thing? Shrink away? Bend? But one shouldn't bend too much. A sword that bends too easily is useless; yet one that is too rigid will shatter. These Seguleh did not strike her as the type who would bend. What they must watch for, then, was shattering.

She must have drifted off soon after. Dozing, or perhaps sinking into hypothermia, for she thought she heard voices. 'She won't last another day,' one said.

'There are others with this Dernan,' said a second, a voice she had never heard before.

'She has held to our agreement – we can hardly do less,' said the first.

'Do not forget she is merely a servant.'

'How we treat others is the measure of how we should expect to be treated.'

'Straight from the teaching halls, Sall. Let us hope all such obligations prove as easy to cut.'

She was shaken, gently, but could barely rouse herself. She found Sall's cloak over her. 'We're going,' Sall said. 'Lorkal has had time enough.'

Blinking, she waved him off. 'I'll stay here,' she mumbled.

'If you sleep any longer out here you will never awaken.'

She heard the words but somehow they didn't mean anything. She shut her eyes. 'Tired.'

Disjointed images followed. She became aware of being carried. Of crossbows firing and Lo before them, his sword a humming blur. Next she was jarred awake briefly to find herself lying sprawled on the ground while before her Sall and Lo fought side by side facing a score of armed men and women emerging from a steep cliff path. Then she was carried in Sall's arms while he stepped over bodies sprawled across the rock steps and, from far ahead, she heard panicked yells and the dash of iron.

She awoke to daylight shining in upon a crude circular dwelling of piled rocks. She was lying among hides and blankets. A low fire in a central hearth sent tendrils of blue smoke up through a hole in a roof of laid branches. Two small figures, a boy and a girl, leapt to their feet from next to the hearth and brought her bread and a bowl. 'Eat,' said the girl.

She took the flat unleavened bread, tore off a piece. 'Where am I?'

'You see,' the boy hissed to the girl, '*she* can speak.'

Yusek thought she might know what the lad meant by that. 'Where am I?' she repeated.

'Dernan's—' the boy began, then flinched as if terrified. 'Well, that is . . . your camp, I guess.'

She eyed them, frowning, while she chewed. 'What do you mean – mine?'

'Are you their princess?' the girl asked, her eyes huge.

Yusek coughed on her bread. She forced it down, her eyes watering. 'Their *what*?'

'Are they your servants? They carried you in. Are they Ascendants? They killed everyone.'

'Not *every*one,' sneered the boy.

'Well, not us slaves.'

'*Slaves*?'

The light was occluded as someone ducked into the hut. It was an old man, pole slim and dressed in a threadbare linen shirt that hung to his bony shins. He bowed his head to Yusek. 'You are awake. Excellent.'

'Who're you?'

'Bo'ahl Leth. They call me Bo. You may too.'

'Bo?'

The man raised his sharp narrow shoulders in a sort of apology. 'It amused Dernan.'

'Where's he?'

'Dernan?' Bo raised his greying brows as if he himself could not believe what he was about to say. 'Well, searching for his head thanks to your friends.'

A coiled band that Yusek did not even know was wound around her chest loosened. She let out her breath. 'So – it's over. They won.'

The man's expressive face clouded with distaste. 'Won?' he repeated. 'That is a rather coarse way to put it. Many men and women lost their lives yesterday. No one wins when so many die.'

'Those standing do.'

He regarded her now in disappointment. 'Ah, I see. My mistake.'

Yusek found that she cared nothing for the old man's disapproval. She pushed herself to her feet; she was weak and dizzy but she could stand. 'Where are they?'

'Keeping watch.'

'Take me to them.' He gestured to the exit.

Outside lay a circle of stone huts atop a bare hillock surrounded by what appeared to be steep cliffs on most sides. Bo led her up a path. Then Yusek remembered: 'Lorkal! You know her? Where is she?'

Bo halted and turned back to her, pained. 'Ah . . . Lorkal.' His gaze lowered. 'Yes, I knew her.'

The band of iron returned to Yusek's chest. She found it difficult to breathe. 'Take me to her.'

'It would do no good . . .'

Yusek's jaws clenched. 'Take me to her.'

He lowered his head. 'This way.'

The bodies had been collected to one side of the village, next to a rocky field where men and women, all ex-slaves or bondsmen, were at work digging a trench. They paused at Yusek's approach, peering at her in curiosity. A few bowed. It did not take her long to find Lorkal. Like all the bodies hers had been stripped of arms and armour and wore only a long linen undershirt, stained with blood. Yusek studied the bruising, the cuts, the flesh of the wrists torn and bloodied. Tortured to death.

She turned on the skinny old man. Cold wetness chilled her cheeks. 'Did you stand by and look on disapprovingly while *this* happened?' She was hardly able to grind out the words.

He would not meet her gaze. 'I'm sorry. Dernan didn't believe her. Who would have? They never come this far north. What do they want? Why are they here?'

Yusek had knelt at Lorkal's feet. She adjusted the shirt to cover the woman's legs. *What lesson am I to take from this, Lorkal? Were your actions brave? Stupid? I suppose all that can be said is that you held to your convictions. Perhaps that's the best that can be said of anyone. Yet now here you are, dead. Am I the coward, then, for always walking away? Well – at least I'm still alive.*

She fought down the tightness in her throat. 'They're looking for a monastery. One that's supposed to be north of here.'

The breath hissed from the old man. 'Gods, no . . .'

Yusek looked at him sharply. He gripped his neck. Something like panic had entered his eyes. She straightened. 'You know what they're looking for.'

'I . . . can't say.'

Yusek found her hand had gone to her long-knife. 'Can't? Or won't?'

His gaze took in her tensed grip. 'What is your name, child?'

'Do not call me child.'

251

He searched her face. 'No . . . I suppose not. My mistake again. Would you give me your name?'

'Yusek.'

He nodded. 'Come, Yusek. Let us talk.' He invited her back to the huts. After one last glance at Lorkal, she followed.

'What do you know of the Ascendants?' he asked as they walked along, his breath pluming in the frigid early morning air. They were higher up here and Yusek shuddered anew – her leathers and under-clothes were still damp and they were sucking the warmth from her once again. 'Ascendants?' she answered, bemused. 'Just what I've heard in stories and such. Why?'

He led her back to the hut she awoke in. The two children jumped away from the hearth where the plate and bowl now sat empty. He clapped his hands. 'Go gather a selection of clothes.' The pair bowed to Yusek and dashed from the hut. He sat next to the hearth, began rebuilding the fire. She sat as well, willing to grant the man a few moments before she left to find Sall.

'Ascendants,' he began. 'I mention them because they are very few and far between, yes? Yet so many must arise in potential or power, only to fall short. We know of how many? The Warlord, the Lord of Moon's Spawn, one or two others. Why do so few achieve such heights?'

'What are you? Some kind of scholar?'

A small shrug. 'Scholarship is a hobby only. I am a mage.'

Yusek stared at him; this was the first man or woman she'd ever met of any self-admitted talent. 'A mage? Really? Why didn't you blast Dernan to ash?'

Tolerant amusement twitched his mouth. 'Mages whose, ah, *aspects* are useful in warfare or in combat are a very small minority, I assure you.'

Yusek wasn't sure what to make of him or all this talk. 'You have a point? Because I'm not in the mood to chat.'

He raised a hand to beg her indulgence. 'The children are gone to gather you warm clothes. Surely I have until then.'

She merely grunted to urge him on.

'I believe there are many more Ascendants out there in the world, of course. Most are far less – how shall I put it? – *blatant* in their activities. Such as the Enchantress, the Queen of Dreams. Now, why should that be among such powerful entities? Anyway, who dare oppose them? Well, each other, of course. I believe Ascendancy is something of a struggle. A constant effort to assert one's identity.

An eternal reinscribing of what one is. And why? Because there are others out there, rivals, all vying for what are, after all, in the end, a very limited set of roles or identities.'

'The Dragons Deck?' Yusek said, drawn into the man's discourse despite her impatience.

Bo nodded, impressed. 'Yes. I believe the cards serve as *one* expression of these identities. There are many others, of course. And they are by no means exhaustive either. So too with godhead, I believe.' He waved a stick as if to encompass the entire lowlands to the east. 'Look at this ferment over the god of war. Who will it be in the end? Will its face be that of a beast? A wolf? Or some other? Who is to say? Only time will tell. But I digress.'

He set his elbows on his knees, examined the stick. 'I say all this because there is a small retreat in these mountains. A monastery or sanctuary, call it what you will. Very small, very remote. There, it is rumoured someone has taken up residence. Someone who may count among those few thrown up every hundred years or so who could achieve Ascendancy. Think of that!' he breathed, almost in wonder. 'An Ascendant of our age. Just as the Warlord, Caladan Brood, is of his distant age. A stunning thought.'

'So where is it?'

'Ah! Well. We have arrived at the crux of the problem.' He squeezed the thin stick in his hands. 'I don't know if I should tell you.'

Yusek snorted her impatience. 'You'll tell *them* when they get here. Believe me.'

He blinked up at her, calmly. 'No I won't, Yusek. What will they do? Do you think they will torture me the way Dernan did Lorkal?'

The idea disgusted her; as if he'd asked whether she would. He dared ask that after what happened to Lorkal? She stood to wave her dismissal. 'Fine. We'll just ask someone else.' He started to speak but the boy and girl came bustling in carrying armloads of clothing. Bo dusted his hands, bowed to her, and left her to it.

Later she emerged warm and well insulated. Tall hide moccasins, their fleece turned inward, rose to her knees over leather trousers. She had also put on multiple layers of shirts. Of what armour fit her, the best she could find was a heavy leather gambeson sewn with bands of what looked to be shaved horn and antler. Over that she'd pulled a thick wool cloak. A sheepskin hat and toughened hide gloves finished it all off.

She took a path at random, meaning to track down Sall. As she went she belted on the longsword she'd scavenged, leaving the two knives at her waist as well. Armed to the teeth now, she thought, adjusting the strange new weight on her left hip. *Not that it'll do me any good – don't know how to use the damned thing.*

She found Sall, his hood down, at a high point in the village, keeping watch. 'Where's Lo?'

'On the path.' Sall gave the slightest inclination of his masked head – the closest he came to pointing. 'This village possesses an excellent defensive position. The path is its only entrance.'

So? 'What now?'

The mask shifted; brown eyes examined her. 'You are recovered?'

'A hot meal and I will be.'

'Very good. Collect supplies and we will depart.'

She turned to go but stopped, thinking of something. 'You saw Lorkal?'

'Yes. We saw her.'

'And – you killed Dernan?'

The mask tilted ever so slightly. The light played over its complex lines. 'Which one of them was he?'

Great Goddess . . . Yusek waved it aside. 'Never mind.' She went to find Bo.

The mage was speaking to the rag-tag remnants of slaves and bondsmen Dernan had kept: youths, oldsters, a few women fat with child. People probably dragged off from all the caravans and traders he'd slaughtered. Bo appeared to be organizing them into packing everything up.

'What's this?' Yusek asked.

The mage gave her an impatient look. 'We can hardly just hang about waiting for the next gang of thuggish swordsmen to claim the place. Thanks to your Seguleh we're utterly defenceless.'

'Thanks to them you're free!'

'Free to be enslaved. Free to starve. Free to be abused or murdered at a whim. Yes. Freedom – rather more complicated in the concrete than the abstract, yes?'

Yusek just curled a lip. 'Don't play your word games with me. I'm not interested.'

'The fate of someone unarmed, or alone, or unprepared, in this lawless wilderness is hardly a game.'

'Fine. Whatever you say. Listen . . . I don't know why I'm doing this because I really don't give a damn . . . but take your troop south. You know Orbern's hold? Orbern-town, he calls it.'

'Yes? What of it? Why should I deliver these people and myself to yet another murderous petty warlord?'

Yusek exploded in laughter. 'Old man . . . calling Orbern a warlord is like calling a grandmother a courtesan. He's just not the right material. Go to him and say you're settlers. Settlers come to Orbern-town. I swear, he'll hug every one of you.'

Bo looked doubtful. 'You're quite certain . . .'

'Absolutely. Now, we need two packs of supplies ourselves.'

'I will see to it. We can manage that at least, I suppose. You are determined to head north, even further into the mountains?'

'Yes.'

'I see.' The man was obviously struggling with something. He raised his face to the snow-clad mounts biting off the northern horizon, sighed, and nodded to himself. 'Head north-west. Keep going higher, towards the coastal range.'

'Thank you.'

Bo still appeared troubled. He ran his fingers through his thin beard. 'Do you know who he is? This man?'

'No.'

'You would only know of him in one way, I think.' He shifted his gaze, studying her. 'As the slayer of Anomander Rake, Lord of Moon's Spawn, and Son of Darkness.'

Yusek snorted her denial. 'That's impossible.'

'No. It is he. They are seeking him. And for one purpose only that I can imagine.'

'What?'

'To challenge him, of course.'

*　　*　　*

Jeshin Lim, the Legate, was in special session together with his closest advisers and supporters among the councillors when yet another urgent communication arrived from the north. This newest information of events in Pale sent yet another round of confusion, denials and recriminations through the assembly. Jeshin, for his part, withdrew from the arguments, sitting back and turning in his hands a small curio, a delicate gold mask.

'M'lord,' Councillor Yost called, his voice deep and rumbling up from his great bulk. Then, louder, 'Legate.'

Jeshin peered up, startled. 'Yes?'

'M'lord, this latest news is above reproach. A relation of our

255

family who minds our interests there in the city has cultivated long-standing sources—'

'*Your* interests,' another councillor shouted.

Yost continued through gritted teeth: 'These accounts corroborate earlier rumours. Some impostor is fomenting hostility, perhaps even war, between us.'

'We cannot be certain,' Jeshin said, eyeing the gold mask. 'Who would gain from this?'

Yost swung out his thick arms. 'Why, any number of parties! Even the Malazans—'

'The Malazans have apparently been driven from Pale,' cut in Councillor Berdand. 'And they fled from here.' He gave an exaggerated farewell wave. 'Their star is falling. We have seen the last of those invaders.'

'Are you drunk *and* stupid?' Yost barked.

Berdand leapt from his chair. 'How dare you! You push your family interests here at this table then insult us?'

Jeshin raised a hand for quiet. 'Gentlemen! Accord! Obviously we require more complete intelligence. I suggest a – well, not an *envoy* now, obviously, but something rather more covert. Someone to travel north and ascertain conditions first-hand and report back. I suggest . . .' Jeshin eyed Councillor Yost who shrank an involuntary step backwards under his speculative gaze, a hand going to his throat. 'What was the name of that new upstart Nom?'

Yost's wide frame eased in relief. 'Ah, Tor – something or other, Legate.'

'Yes. I designate Councillor Nom as emissary of this body to investigate conditions and developments at Pale and its environs.' Jeshin raised the gold mask to his face and spoke from behind it. 'He is to travel north at once.'

The assembled councillors shared barely suppressed smiles. Councillor Berdand laughed aloud, saluting Jeshin. 'Excellent stroke, Legate.'

*

Torvald sat, head clasped between his hands, at the tiny kitchen table in the cramped main room attempting yet again to dredge up any excuse, no matter what, to rid himself of his appointment to the exalted, but unpaid, position of councillor. Tis had taken the news of its non-compensatory nature with a steely unsurprised silence that only made him feel all the more guilty – though over

256

just what he wasn't sure. *He* hadn't done anything. None of this was *his* fault.

It was simply an inconvenient circumstance. That was all.

A tentative knock sounded on the door. Torvald frowned; it was late in the evening. Surely not the debt collectors already? How could word have travelled that fast? Since Tis was in her workshop in the rear he unlatched the door and opened it a crack. 'Yes?'

It was a clerk of the council escorted by three city Wardens. Torvald opened the door wider. 'Yes?'

'Is this . . .' the clerk ran her disbelieving eyes over the plain front of the row-house, 'the residence of Councillor Nom?'

'Yes.'

'May I speak to him?'

'I'm he – that is, he is me, myself.'

The clerk's brows arched even higher. 'Indeed. How . . . refreshingly informal of you, Councillor.'

One day I'll get the better of one of these bureaucrats, I swear. 'You have a message?'

'Indeed.' She held out a sealed scroll.

Torvald read it by the uncertain light of a torch carried by one of the Wardens. Then he read it again. When he looked up there was an expression upon his face that made the clerk eye him more closely, puzzled.

'You are quite well, sir?'

Special emissary! Travel to Pale and environs. Report on state of affairs. Torvald restrained himself from hugging the clerk. *A gift from the gods!* He managed to hold his mouth tight, nodding curtly. 'Yes. Thank you. Thank you. I will leave at once, of course. The Legate can be assured of my cooperation.' He moved to close the door but stopped, thinking of something. 'Ah – there wouldn't be a travel stipend associated with this position, would there?'

Later, retracing her steps to Majesty Hill to finish her report and retire for the night, it occurred to the clerk that never before had she ever seen any councillor so happy to be sent from the city.

*　　*　　*

Barathol worked only at night. Long after sunset armoured chests arrived at the tent containing his makeshift forge set up close to where the harbour mole began. The chests contained silver to be melted down and poured into moulds. And not raw silver: finished jewellery, utensils, ornaments and coin. A great deal of silver coin. All destined for the ceramic crucible supplied to him to be heated on the forge.

Once the metal was melted he poured it into sand moulds, two at a time. Plain forms they were, shaped exactly like the iron pins used to hold stone blocks together. Except these would be of silver and thus far too soft to secure anything. And he'd told them that as well, the two who took over the process once he'd poured. Neither gave a damn what he thought. One was a tall scarred fellow with a great mane of hair and a ferocious hooked nose. The other was some sort of hunchback, or cripple, even worse-looking, all mismatched in his broken features and mangled hands. Both stank like mages to him.

They would curtly gesture him out then work some sort of sorcery over the still soft metal. Later, he would be allowed back into the tent to knock the pins from their black sand moulds and polish them up. Each time he found them inscribed in symbols and script utterly unfamiliar to him. In the morning the men would pack up the finished items and carry them off. He never saw either of them during the daytime excavations.

Shortly after the morning shift began work he would stagger home to get some sleep. Unfortunately for him this was a rather rare commodity. Scillara was disinclined to rise before noon and so he watched little Chaur until she came downstairs. Then he made lunch for them. After that she often had little chores for him; repairing this, or replacing that. Sometimes she went out, leaving him to mind Chaur for the rest of the day.

Then there was dinner to be made.

Often he did not lie down in the cot downstairs until close to dusk. Only a few hours later it would be time to rise to work the night through once again. For Barathol time began to pass in a dazed fog of utter exhaustion. Fortunately the work was not demanding. He was tempted to sleep in the tent next to the forge but was haunted by what might happen to little Chaur in his absence. Scillara was not cruel; she was simply not interested and he did not hold this against her. It seemed to him that frankly *most* people by temperament and character should not be thrust into the role of parents. She was simply uncharacteristic in admitting it. He was at a loss to know how to resolve the trap life had set for him. The most attractive answer was to take little Chaur and walk away. He wondered, idly, his mind barely on his work, whether Scillara would even complain.

As the days passed, and his shambling dazed existence extended into a near hallucinogenic stupor, he would take breaks from the heat of the forge to stand outside in the cool night air. Here, he was sure the lack of sleep was affecting his mind, because he was seeing things. Sometimes the night sky would be occluded by the arc of an immense dome that glowed like snow. It would be gone when next he blinked. At other times flames seemed to dance over the entire city. Once he saw the taller of the mages standing out among the salvaged stones. The man was weeping, his hands pressed to his face, his body shuddering in great heaving sobs.

Am I going mad? Perhaps we both are.

* * *

A smooth warm hand brushing his cheek brought Lim to consciousness. He smiled, remembering similar nights long ago – then his eyes snapped open.

He stared at Taya crouched on his bed. 'What in the name of Gedderone are you doing here!'

The girl's full lips puckered into an exaggerated pout. 'Don't you want me, dearest Jeshin?'

'Well, yes. But – no! You mustn't . . . how did you get in here?'

She uncoiled herself from the bed, walked round it. Jeshin could not take his eyes from her. 'Never mind that, dearest. I am here to congratulate you.'

He rose and threw on a silk dressing gown. He eyed the door to his chamber – closed. 'Congratulate . . . me?' he said as he edged towards the door. A shape emerged from the shadows next to it, a ghostly wavering figure of a man in tattered finery. The spectre raised a finger to its lips for silence.

Jeshin found that his voice had fled.

'You've played your part magnificently, dearest. Even better than we could have hoped. But now . . .' She sighed. Jeshin pulled his gaze from the apparition to her. She was shaking her head in mock sadness. 'Now it is time to move on to the second act.'

Jeshin tried to shout but something had a fist at his throat. He could barely draw breath. Taya was at his side. Her soft lips brushed his cheek. 'There is someone here I want you to meet,' she whispered, her voice thick with passion.

Through tears he saw a new figure emerge from the gloom. A man in loose obscuring robes and on his head, bizarrely, an oval mask that shone pale in the starlight like a moon. Terror drove a knife into his heart and he would have collapsed but for Taya supporting him by one arm.

'You wished to be a great ruler and for Darujhistan to rise anew,' Taya breathed in his ear. 'Well, you shall have your wish, my dear! You shall be the most magnificent ruler Darujhistan has ever seen. And under your hand the city will be reborn. All Genabackis shall bow before it, as before.'

She grasped his hair to wrench back his head. His cheeks ran with tears. The figure raised a hand to the mask, lifted it from its head.

When he saw what was revealed beneath Jeshin managed one soul-shattering scream before the suffocating metal was pressed to his face.

Scorch and Leff paused in their card game at a table next to the rear servants' entrance of Lim manor. Leff cocked his head. 'Hear that? You hear something?'

Scorch took a stiff sip from a jug of cooking wine, set it down with a grimace of disgust. 'Hunh?'

'I said, did you hear something?'

Scorch listened fiercely, cocking his head.

Leff raised his eyes to the ceiling. 'Not now! A minute ago – anything?'

Scorch shook a negative. He set a hand on the crossbow leaning against the table. 'Should we . . . you know . . .'

'Should we what?'

'I dunno. 'Vestigate?'

Leff examined his cards. Tower, magus, mercenary. It was a good hand. 'Naw. Not right now.' He eyed the pot. 'Raise you ten copper crescents.'

Scorch made a face. 'I don't got ten crescents. You cleaned me out.' He threw down the cards crossed his arms and eyed the great mound of copper on the table. 'Where's all our silver gone, anyway?'

*   *   *

Spindle sat cradling a tankard from the last barrel of beer in K'rul's bar. The former Imperial historian, Duiker, sat with him. Fisher was at another table, leaning back, tuning a long-necked instrument. Blend and Picker were at the bar staring at the door as if willing customers to enter.

It seemed to him that he'd done quite enough to answer the Malazans' request for intelligence. He'd told them all they'd discovered that night out on the Dwelling Plain. He'd even poked around where they were salvaging stone blocks out of the harbour. He saw the scholar there, the one who'd been down the well. He seemed to be working for these scary mages. And weren't they a hair-raising lot, too. Reminded him of the old gang who used to work for the Empire. It was enough to make his shirt squirm. He wasn't going to tempt their notice, no sir. *Ma told me 'bout mages like that.*

Everyone was quiet, as they had been for the last few nights. Even Fisher's plucking was subdued. *Waitin'. Waitin' for the storm to break.* The historian had been frowning at his glass of tea for some time and now he raised one cocked eye to Spindle.

'Did you get a good look at these stones?' he asked.

Spindle nodded, frowning thoughtfully. 'Pretty good. They got masons cleaning them. Chisellin' off growths and barnacles and such, then polishing them. The stone's white beneath. Like purest marble.' He paused, his brows crimping. 'But not like any marble I ever seen. Not hard white like solid. Kinda clear, smoky almost . . .'

Everyone flinched at a discordant jangle from the instrument in Fisher's hands. All eyes turned to the bard, who was watching Spindle, his brows raised. 'Smoky?' he repeated. 'As in see-through, or translucent?'

Spindle nodded eagerly. 'Yeah. That's it. Like you said, see-through.'

From the bar Picker's voice sounded, low and warning. 'What is it, bard?'

Fisher lowered his gaze to the instrument and strummed a few idle bars. 'Has anyone noticed how among all the towers and buildings and temples here in the city, none uses white stone?'

'I'm not a damned architect,' Picker grumbled.

Spindle had noticed, but he'd put it down to some sort of local shortage. 'Well, those're building stones awright. And they're digging a trench there too, come to think of it. A foundation.'

Fisher shrugged, returned to his tuning. 'It's a local superstition. White stone's considered bad luck here – even a symbol of death. It's only used in sepulchres or mausoleums . . . And then there are the old songs too . . .'

The bard's voice trailed away and no one spoke for a time. Finally

Blend ground out from where she leaned against the bar, chin in hands. 'What songs?'

Fisher shrugged as if uninterested. 'Oh, just local folk tales, really. Rhymes and sayings.'

Blend shifted to return her attention to the door again. Picker, arms crossed, hands tucked up under her armpits, nodded to herself for a time. Spindle took a small sip from his tankard. He watched her over its rim. 'Like?' she finally asked, almost resentfully.

'Well, there's one titled . . . "The Throne of White Stone".'

'Wonderful,' Picker snorted.

'Not our fight,' Blend muttered, facing the door and hunching her shoulders higher.

'It exists only in fragments,' Fisher continued, apparently unaware of their reactions, or unconcerned. 'It's very old. Thought to date back to the Daru migrations into the region. It tells of tormented spirits imprisoned in an underworld of white stone ruled by demons and guarded by . . .' The bard's voice trailed away.

'All right!' Picker snapped. 'We get the picture.'

'Not our fight,' Blend repeated, her jaws set and eyes fixed on the door.

Neither saw Fisher's expression turn to one almost of alarm as he sat upright. Spindle noticed the man's change in mood but didn't know what to make of it. Duiker's gaze, however, steady upon the man, narrowed suspiciously.

Much later that night only Fisher and the old Imperial historian remained within the bar's common room. Fisher, it seemed to Duiker, appeared to be waiting for him to retire for the night. He finished his cold tea and turned a speculative eye on the tall bard, who had appeared preoccupied all evening. Perhaps even worried.

'I've not heard that lay,' he said.

'It's not local,' Fisher said, his gaze on his hands. 'It's a travellers' tale, told of a distant land.'

'A land distant from where?'

Fisher offered a wry smile. 'A land rather distant from here.'

'And who is it that guards those tormented souls?'

The bard took a troubled breath, glanced down once more. 'A prison of white stone guarded by . . . faceless warriors.' He stood, brushed his trousers. 'I'm . . . going for a walk.'

Duiker watched the man go. The lock of the door fell into place behind him. He returned his attention to the empty teacup, its leaves drying on the bottom. He swirled the dregs, studying them. *There are patterns here. The trick is in being able to identify them.*

Faceless warriors . . .

*

Fisher had prepared himself but he could not quell his start when the masked figure of Thurule opened the door to Lady Envy's manor. 'I wish to see the Lady,' he said. 'I take it she is up.'

Silent, of course, Thurule motioned him in.

Fisher knew he hadn't given the fellow much thought before, other than that he was Seguleh, and a rarity. Now, however, with fresh suspicions gnawing at his mind, he could not help but distance himself slightly from the man as walked along. Though he knew that even a Seguleh would find in him a far from easy challenge. The manor house was dark, and, it must be said, still almost entirely unfurnished. Thurule guided him to the rear terrace where Fisher glimpsed Envy standing at a short brick wall overlooking the unkempt grounds, peering up into the night sky. She was shimmering bright in some sort of glowing sheer pale-green dress.

'Bored with your simple-minded friends already?' she said without even turning round.

He noted that she held a drink in one hand, elbow on her hip.

Fisher took a steadying breath. 'You know what is coming . . .' he began, and then a new thought struck him. 'You've known all along . . . that's why you're here.'

She flashed a satisfied smile over her shoulder. 'A proper court at last. It's been ages. I'll finally be able to get a decent wardrobe.'

The callousness, the monumental self-interest, struck him dumb. He realized there was nothing he could possibly say to change her mind. He spoke his anger instead. 'It does not matter to you then that untold thousands must be ground into the dirt so that you can wear fashionable dresses and attend your damned balls?'

She slowly turned. The smile was still there, but it was as brittle as crystal. An emerald fire simmered in her eyes. 'Really, Fisher, such hypocrisy. If you cared so much why are you not beating your chest already? There are poor in the city now. There will always be those who rule and those who are ruled.' She gave the faintest shrug of her bare, shapely shoulders. 'And come now, be honest. If you could choose, which would you really prefer?'

What he saw saddened him. He'd seen how Anomander's death had touched her, yet he knew now it registered only because it was

263

personal. Sympathy for any other's loss or suffering was beyond her. He should have said nothing then, simply left. But his own anger was up – or was it bitterness and disappointment? 'I would choose rulership that generated wealth rather than that of a parasite sucking blood and contributing nothing. Rather like a leech.'

The thrown glass struck him on the side of his face, shattering. 'Said the *bard* – who contributes nothing save hot air! Thurule!' she called. 'See this man out. And never admit him again.'

Fisher touched his face where warmth ran down to his neck. His fingers came away wet with blood. Then Thurule was there, silent, one arm indicating the way out. He bowed his exit to Lady Envy though her back was turned.

There is nothing for me here anyway.

CHAPTER IX

For ages the citizens of Darujhistan were amazed by the riches
dug from the tunnels and vaults beneath the region known as
the Dwelling Plain. Yet while sitting in a tavern this visitor did
overhear one fellow opining the following: 'Is it not so that better these ancients had been men and women of worth than to
possess things of worth?'

Silken Glance, traveller, of One Eye Cat

A KICK TO HER FOOT WOKE KISKA AND SHE BLINKED UP TO SEE
Leoman kneeling next to her. He motioned her to follow.
'They're on the move.'

He led her up the slope of one of the dunes of black sand. Together
they lay down just short of the crest and peered over. The troop of
misfits and malformed survivors of the Vitr were shuffling off round
a headland of jagged tumbled stone. Back the way she and Leoman
had come.

Kiska pushed herself away from the crest. 'We missed him?'

'Perhaps he crossed back when we were in the cave,' Leoman
suggested, thoughtfully brushing at his moustache.

The sight irked Kiska and she climbed to her feet, taking care to
remain crouched. 'Let's circle round inland.' She jogged off without
waiting to see whether he followed or not.

Soon the faint metallic jingle of armour and the chains of morningstars sounded just to her rear and she knew he'd caught up. *Please
Oponn and the Enchantress – let this be it! This is no place for me
. . . or even Leoman. This is a land for gods and Ascendants, not
plain old mortals such as us. Let us please complete our mission and
meekly slink away!*

Keeping to the highlands and cliff-tops, they shadowed the file of waddling creatures as they made their slow awkward way along the shore. Against the sky she could just make out the mountain-tall shadowy figure of Maker as he continued his unending labour. Some, she knew, would consider his task a divine curse. For her own part she had yet to decide. After all, he *was* holding back the Vitr – wasn't he?

Below, the creatures had gathered on a stretch of shallow beach where a broad strand ran out to the glimmering sea of light – what on any body of water would be called a tidal flat. And she wondered, could this ocean of seething energy even be said to have a tide? She'd seen no sign of any.

The creatures faced the shallow waves, perhaps waiting for something, or someone. Kiska shaded her gaze into the blinding brightness, but saw nothing.

'Anything?' she asked Leoman.

The man shook his head, his eyes slitted against the glare. 'We'll wait.' He sat down, his back to the rocks, and stretched his legs out before him. 'Kiska,' he began after a time, tentatively, 'if he wanted to return . . . don't you think—'

'Quiet,' she hissed, not even glancing down.

She heard him shift impatiently, exhale his irritation, then ease into a reluctant silence. She kept watch. He had to be out there. Why else would these outcasts be waiting?

Eventually, after staring into the stabbing brilliance, her eyes came to water so furiously she couldn't see anything at all and she had to cuff Leoman to signal him to take over. She sat down blinking and rubbing her gritty eyes. *Please all the gods come and gone, let this be it.*

After a time there came a tap on her shoulder. 'Movement.' She leapt up – the hand on her shoulder pressed her back down. 'Let's wait and see, shall we?'

Crouched, she scanned the expanse of scintillating shimmering glare. At first she saw nothing: the stunning intensity of the sea of brightness blinded her to all else. 'On the left,' Leoman murmured. She edged her gaze aside, shaded her eyes. Movement there: a shadowy flickering among the silver-bright waves. A shape approaching like a dark flame almost lost amid all that brightness.

Over time the figure resolved itself into a tall man pushing his way to shore through the knee-high waves of liquid Vitr. Kiska surged to her feet. 'It's him!'

'We don't know . . .' Leoman began, then some instinct made him throw himself round hands going to the morningstars at his sides, and at the same time someone else spoke.

'Yes. I do believe it *is* he.'

The hair on Kiska's head actually rose. *I know that voice!* Slowly, dreading what she would find, she willed herself to turn round. There stood a haggard battered man in torn robes, his face scalded livid red and swollen. The Seven Cities mage and holy Faladan, Yathengar.

Ye gods – he was supposed to have been destroyed by the Liosan! How could he still live? The man who summoned the Chaos Whorl to avenge himself against the Malazan Empire and in the end consuming him and Tayschrenn, flinging them both to this edge of creation. 'You live!' she gasped in shocked disbelief.

The rabid gaze swung to her. 'So I wished you to never suspect. Ingrates! Did you not consider that I could follow where you—'

Leoman leapt upon him, his morningstars keening, only to fly aside, the weapons clashing together about his head. Kiska lunged as well, stave flashing in a thrust, but Yathengar merely tilted his head and the weapon flashed searingly hot and she cast it away yelling her agony. Hands useless, she spun a backward kick. Her foot rebounded from the man's torso, which seemed as hard as oak. He scowled his irritation, gesturing, and a vice-grip took her at the neck to lift her from the ground. He gestured with his other hand and Leoman lurched upright. The morningstars hung wrapped about his neck.

Starting forward, Yathengar marched the two of them along, each fighting for breath. 'Let us go and say hello to our old friend, shall we? I'm sure he will be very pleased to see the two of you.'

They descended the rocks. Kiska fought to yell a warning. Leoman's face darkened alarmingly, the veins at his neck swelling. At the shore the pressure eased off a touch. Perhaps Yathengar was worried they would expire before he could torment them any further. However, the grip at Kiska's throat was still too fierce for any shout. The shambling creatures caught sight of them and scattered gabbling their panic and terror. Kiska had no time for them: her gaze was fixed upon the slim man slowly advancing through the last of the shallow surf.

It was Tayschrenn, former High Mage of the Malazan Empire.

He'd changed, of course, as would be expected of anyone who had endured the passage he had experienced. His hair was now almost entirely grey, and short, as if growing out from having been shaved, or burned off. He'd lost weight. A simple shirt was loose upon him, hanging down over ragged trousers. Oddly he wasn't wet. The glimmering Vitr merely ran from him in beads, like quicksilver.

But what troubled her was his expression: it was all open puzzlement. Not one hint of recognition touched his night-dark eyes.

'Tayschrenn! You have eluded me for the last time,' Yathengar called out.

The lean aristocratic head tilted to one side, apparently bewildered. 'You are from my past then, are you?'

'He is your enemy!' Kiska managed to grind out, feeling as if her throat were tearing.

Snarling, Yathengar threw her and Leoman down, punching them into the sands.

'So . . . I had enemies,' Tayschrenn said, speaking almost to himself.

'Do not take me for a fool! No play-acting will help you now.'

'You are harming those two.'

'This is as nothing compared to what I will do to you.'

'What will you—'

But Yathengar had had enough of talk. He thrust with both hands. A storm of roaring energies engulfed Tayschrenn, who fell back into the Vitr bellowing his pain. In the sands Kiska struggled to draw her long-knife.

Yet the smoking blackened figure that was Tayschrenn arose from the Vitr. 'Why . . .' He spat aside through blistered bleeding lips.

A howl of rage took everyone by surprise and Kiska snapped her head round to glimpse the giant demon launching itself upon Yathengar. An eruption of puissance threw the fearsome entity to the ground where it lay groaning, the fur on its armoured torso smoking.

'So . . .' said Tayschrenn, agony making his voice faint, 'you are a mage.'

Yathengar scowled, disbelief obvious on his ravaged face. 'What is this . . . ?'

Tayschrenn advanced a step. 'Then you *are* my enemy . . .'

The mage's hands fell, so startled was he by the statement. Tayschrenn lunged at him just as his huge friend had. This time the Seven Cities mage was too slow to react and the two went down grappling.

Kiska could only stare, baffled. *What was he doing? Fighting? Why didn't he just . . .*

Then she realized – the man must have forgotten everything about his prior life. *Everything.* Perhaps he no longer even knew how to channel power. *Gods! How could he defeat this madman? By punching him?*

Perhaps strengthened by his insanity, Yathengar managed to raise his hands. Power rippled there, sizzling in Tayschrenn's grip. At the same time the fist at Kiska's throat eased and she sat up, drawing her knife. Leoman also rose. The morningstars hissed to life in his hands. But neither dared strike while the two mages squirmed in the sands.

Then Kiska realized even more. 'The Vitr!' she shouted to Tayschrenn. 'He hasn't touched the Vitr!'

Understanding, Tayschrenn heaved himself to one side. The two struggled while power lashed, searing the flesh of the ex-High Mage's arms. They rolled into the thin anaemic surf. Tayschrenn fought to press Yathengar down while the mage wrestled to free his arms. Finally Tayschrenn managed to force the man into the wash.

Immediately, the silvery liquid burst into foaming hissing froth. Yathengar howled, jerking free of Tayschrenn. He lunged for the dry shore; the former High Mage yanked him back by his robes. Leoman saw an opening and moved to close, but Kiska shouted a warning. Leoman leapt back but not fast enough, and his sandals smoked. He dug his feet into the sands, almost dancing in panic.

Meanwhile Yathengar had fallen again into the Vitr and now writhed screaming and flailing. Tayschrenn grimly took hold of a leg to drag him further out. The writhing and screaming went on for a long time. The great demon arose, groggy, to stand to one side, and Kiska stood panting, shuddering with suppressed energy. The continuous distant shrieks and hoarse pleading mixed with vile threats made her wince. She sat heavily in the sands and Leoman joined her.

They had found Tayschrenn. Succeeded in an apparently impossible task. Followed him through the Whorl to the very edge of existence. And now he did not even recognize them.

Eventually, the tall figure re-emerged from the glare of the Vitr. Kiska climbed to her feet. The man favoured her and Leoman with a harsh, unforgiving gaze. Kiska couldn't trust herself to speak; she was afraid that anything she might say would be wrong. 'So,' he began at last, musing, 'you are from my past.'

Kiska swallowed to wet her throat, managed a faint, 'Yes.' Then, stronger, 'You are needed—'She stopped as he raised a hand to silence her. He examined that hand, and the other, turning them over before his face. Kiska noted that his flesh was healed. The Vitr appeared to have somehow restored him.

He continued to study his hands, flexing them. 'And I take it that I, too, was a mage.'

'Yes,' Kiska breathed, knowing that she could not lie.

Leoman, to his credit, remained silent, his narrowed dark eyes travelling between them, observing, gauging. The demon was also silent, watching, its great taloned hands clenched, the lenses of its bulbous eyes flashing as it blinked.

At Kiska's whispered *yes* the man shuddered as if struck. His eyes squeezed shut and his hands fisted rigid, then fell to his sides. He exhaled through clenched teeth, made a sweeping gesture with one hand as if cutting the air between them. 'Well, you can keep that past. I want nothing to do with it.' He motioned to the demon. 'Come, Korus. We have work to do.'

Kiska could not read the demon's alien face but the massive tangle of fangs at its mouth seemed to curve in a grin of triumph.

'But Tayschrenn!'

The man paused. He turned back, his expression unchanged. 'If that was my name it is no longer. You can keep it as well . . . and take it with you when you go.'

She could not think of anything more to say. The ex-High Mage walked away, trailed by the demon Korus. She turned to Leoman; the man gave a long slow shrug. 'Kiska, I'm sorry . . .'

Snarling, she turned and stalked off along the shore. *I've not come all this way . . .*

The gentle metal jingling of Leoman's armour announced his following. 'Kiska, listen . . . you've done everything that could be expected. If he does not want to come then that is his choice . . .'

Kiska kept walking. *I'll convince him. He's needed.*

'You may not believe me but I've been through something rather similar before.'

Did he really say that? She spun on her heel. 'Yes – you're right. I do *not* believe you've followed a quarry to the edge of creation only to have him walk away!'

Leoman gripped his belt in both hands, rocked ever so slightly under her glare. 'I was bodyguard to Sha'ik. You know that.'

Her rage abated and she hesitated, interested despite her doubts. 'Yes?'

His narrowed gaze was on the middle distance, perhaps unwilling to meet her eyes. 'I was with the uprising from the start. Rose through the ranks to become her bodyguard. She dragged my partner and me out to the deep desert, claimed she was going to be reborn. She had her blasted Holy Book with her. She'd consulted it, the divinatory deck, the astrological signs, everything. All to be at the right place at the right time to be reborn . . .'

'And?' Kiska prompted.

'The Malazans put a crossbow bolt through her head at that very moment.'

Queen preserve me! She turned away, furious. 'There is a point to this?'

Stung, his voice hardened. 'The point is that what happened was not what I thought was supposed to happen – that's the point!'

She stopped, glancing back. 'But she *was* reborn . . .'

'A – girl – showed up just then to take on the mantle. She became the new Sha'ik.

'Ah-ha! So eventually you did succeed! Your determination paid off.'

'No. Actually, that's not my point at all. I was thinking more that we should strike inland, see what turns up.'

'Well, I'm staying. His memory might return.' She waved him away and walked on after Tayschrenn, yelling over her shoulder: 'Did you think of that!'

Leoman stood kicking at the black sand. He sucked a breath in through his teeth. 'Yes,' he said, all alone. 'I thought of that.'

*   *   *

After they left the temple quarters Malakai scouted ahead as usual. Antsy was content to let him range about as before. Frankly, part of him hoped he'd never return. Orchid was subdued. The lass had been handed a lot to think about. Corien was still weak and so he carried the dimmed lantern and the crossbow while Antsy led.

The way up was an ornate hall, or tunnel, broad and gently rising. More like a covered boulevard, with openings off it, perhaps shops or private dwellings. These chambers gaped empty, stripped of furnishings but for a litter of broken pots, trampled torn cloth, and shattered glass. The avenue opened to what appeared to be an open square, and beyond this, just hinted at by the weak lantern light, marched street after street of another underground city.

Shit. Now what? He turned to Orchid. 'Which way?'

She was eyeing the buildings, her lower lip clenched in her teeth. Clearly, this was not what she'd been expecting.

'Well?'

'I don't know. We should explore . . . I guess.'

'Where is Malakai, I wonder?' Corien murmured, keeping his voice down.

'Exploring, I guess,' Antsy said, rather more acidly than he'd intended. 'C'mon. This way.'

He led them up a narrow alleyway where the tilt, or cant, of the entire structure was uncomfortably evident. Antsy had to push off occasionally from the right-leaning wall.

'We should make for one edge of the town,' Orchid finally announced, perhaps having regained her bearings.

'Why?' Antsy asked, and stopped for her answer. Both spoke in subdued tones, almost whispering; the quiet emptiness and gaping doorways seemed to demand a reverent, or at least sombre, response. *Gone*, the silent stone streets and alleys seemed to sigh. *They are gone from us.*

'Because we're under a kind of cave roof here, that's why.'

Antsy couldn't help glancing up into what was, for him, an impenetrable gloom. He grunted his understanding. 'All right. This way.' He headed in what he believed to be the right direction.

A short time later he felt it before he heard it: a massive shuddering that threw them all from side to side. They reached out to steady themselves on the walls. Stones fell all around them, shattering. Orchid let out a panicked cry. Wreckage within the buildings about them shifted and crashed anew. It felt like every earthquake Antsy had experienced – only in this case a Spawnquake.

Then, slowly, ponderously, the entire structure around them rolled slightly, forwards and backwards, like a titanic ship. They tottered and fought to keep their balance just as one would on any vessel. In the slow, almost gentle rocking Antsy thought he sensed a new equilibrium in the massive artefact's balance. Thankfully a poise slightly closer to upright than before.

'What is it?' Orchid whispered, fierce.

'I do believe we just lost a chunk of our island.'

'Are we sinking?' Corien asked, dread tightening his voice.

Antsy scratched the bristles of his untrimmed beard. 'It's possible . . . course, we might just rise some, too.'

'Rise?' Orchid scoffed. 'How could that be possible?'

Antsy took a breath to explain but both had moved on, obviously uninterested in anything too technical. He cleared his throat, muttering, 'Well – it's just a theory.'

They came to where walls of stone bordered the town. Some sections of the rock had been left naked, others smoothed. Some bore mosaics depicting scenes of a great river of brightness running through darkness, others of an immense city of towers. Antsy wondered if such a city were somewhere within this gigantic mountain of stone. Tracing round the edge of the town they came to a set of three broad staircases leading upwards. A strong breeze blew into their faces down out of the shafts.

'Definitely rising,' Antsy said. Corien and Orchid just eyed one another, uncertain. Corien, Antsy saw, was walking more and more stiffly, grimacing with the effort, while Orchid looked bedraggled and exhausted. 'We'll rest here.'

Orchid was so worn out she merely gestured her acceptance and slumped down against a wall. Corien eased himself down with a hiss of pain. Antsy crouched to sort through their provisions. 'How're you holding up?' he asked Corien, just to hold back the darkness and the unsettling, watchful silence.

'Bed rest would have been better,' he answered with a grin. 'But I'm much improved. Thank you, Orchid.'

A non-committal murmur sounded from where she lay on her bedroll of cloaks and blankets. Antsy gnawed on some sort of dried meat, passed a waterskin to Corien. 'I don't know about you, lad, but my goals have experienced a major revision.'

The aristocratic youth's answering grin was bright in the gloom. 'Getting off alive would be a good start.'

'Un-huh. I think we understand each other.' Antsy hefted the waterskin, stoppered it. *Too damned low.* 'You rest. I'll take first watch.'

The lad nodded his gratitude and eased further down. Antsy pushed himself to his feet. He set the lamp in the middle of the alcove they'd chosen, then turned his back to the light to stare out into the dimly lit adjacent street and portals. He cradled his cocked crossbow in his arms. *So many damned nights spent on sentry duty. Seems like nothin's changed. Just the venue. Same ol' same old. Still . . . there's not many as can say they've wandered the bowels of the Moon's Spawn. Thought I was gonna collect a retirement package but seems I've just bought myself a last hurrah.*

Damned stupid waste. Looks like someone on this rock is gonna be cleaning his teeth with my bones.

An' to think Blend and Picker were relieved to see me go! Not like there's so many of us Bridgeburners left, is there? Even Ferret got a proper service and remembrance. Whiskeyjack took off his helmet and said a few words with Free Cities battle magics blastin' overhead and two dragons circling. And it's not like he was a popular guy.

Thinking of Ferret he thought he could almost see the skinny hunched figure there in front of him: his pinched pale face and sharp teeth – *gods! We weren't kind to the fellow, were we?*

Then Ferret looked him up and down and said: 'What the fuck are you doin' here, Antsy? You're not dead.'

Antsy jerked a startled breath and the crossbow jumped in his hands, the bolt skittering off down the stone street.

Corien called, alarmed, 'What is it?'

Feeling that he'd, well, seen a ghost, Antsy squinted into the empty dark. 'Nothin'. False alarm.'

'Time for my watch?'

Antsy eyed the remaining fuel in the lamp. 'Naw. Bit longer.'

'Well. I'm up now.'

Antsy nodded, distracted, while he rubbed the back of his neck. 'Yeah. Fine.' *I swear this damned dark is gonna drive me rat-crazy.*

In the 'morning' – that is, when they were all up and eating a light meal of dried fruit and old stale bread – Malakai emerged from the dark. He looked much the worse for wear, was growing a beard, and his dark jacket hung torn and stained with sweat.

But then, Antsy reflected, *none of us is looking any prettier.*

Distaste curled the man's slash of a mouth as he studied them. 'What's this? You should be up the stairs by now.'

Antsy decided he'd had a stomachful of the man's command style. *He's never with us yet he presumes he's leading.* He cleared his throat. 'Ah, we had us a talk. An' we've decided we're goin' our own way in our own time.'

'Oh?' the man breathed, a dangerous edge entering his voice.

Rather belatedly Antsy glanced about for his crossbow. He saw it sitting to one side, uncocked. *Damn. Gotta think these things through before I open my stupid mouth.*

'Yes,' Orchid cut in quickly. 'We've decided.'

The dark glittering eyes shifted to her. A scoffing smile now openly stretched his lips. 'And where will you go?'

'The closest way out. We're going to get off this rock while we still have food and water and strength in our legs.'

'You'll never make it.'

Antsy cast a quick anxious glance to Orchid: that evaluation, so final, made her flinch.

'That may be so,' Corien said into the silence following Malakai's comment, 'but that's our worry.'

The man seemed to make a show of considering the idea. He gave a great exaggerated frown while his hands brushed his belt. Antsy knew all the blades the man carried at that belt, and in other places. He ached to slip a hand into his shirt to the shoulder harness where he kept a munition in reserve, but he also knew Malakai would act the moment he saw him do that. 'There's still the matter of my investment in you two,' Malakai said, and cocked an eye to Antsy.

Shit. Why didn't I load the damned crossbow when I had the chance?

'If I may . . . ?' Corien spoke up. Malakai gave the slightest dip of his head, his eyes fixed on Antsy. 'Well. It seems to me that you are already of the opinion that you've a far better chance of achieving your goal – whatever that is – without us . . . yes?'

Both Antsy and Malakai turned to eye the lad. 'Yes?' Malakai prompted.

'Well, then, cutting us free recoups your investment by improving your odds of success.'

Antsy glared his anger. *What in Osserc's dark humour is this?*

But Malakai nodded thoughtfully. Something in the proposition seemed to touch on his own private evaluation and he slipped his hands from his belt. 'Very well. On your heads let it be.'

'Yeah – right,' Antsy said, scratching his stubbled jaw, still rather puzzled.

'We'll part company here, then.' Malakai bowed to Orchid. 'I would wish you luck but I'm afraid your luck will run to the lad's pull.'

'We'll see,' she answered, firm, having regained her confidence.

'Farewell then.' And the man backed away into the darkness to disappear up a narrow side alley. Antsy listened for a time but couldn't hear one betraying step or scuff. He thought the man had gone but looked to Orchid for confirmation.

'He's left,' she said after a time.

Corien let out a long breath. 'Thank the gods.'

'He didn't ask for any of the water or food,' Orchid said, surprised.

'Maybe he knows where he can steal any he needs,' Antsy said.

'So what now?' Corien asked.

Antsy was silent, until it occurred to him that maybe that question had been asked of him. He cleared his throat. 'Well . . . I suppose we press on. Keep an eye out.'

'Good,' Orchid said, emphatic. 'I don't want him to get too far ahead of us.'

Antsy blinked in the dimming light of the lamp. 'Hunh? What's that supposed to mean?'

'I mean just that. I don't trust him. He's after something. And there are things here on Moon's Spawn that mustn't see the light of day.'

As if on cue the lamp guttered then, and went out. After a moment of surprised silence Corien laughed. Even Orchid joined in, though Antsy just swore. 'Can't see a damned thing!' he complained, and started searching through his bags for more oil.

'Would you like to see then, Red?' Orchid offered from the dark.

'Hunh? You can do that? Why didn't you—'

'I *told* you I don't trust Malakai. I don't want him to know what I can do. *If* I can, that is.'

'Well, gods yes! If you would.'

She crossed to his side. He heard her skirts rustling over the stones, felt the warmth radiating from her. He cool dry hands touched his face. The touch pleased him.

'I'm glad you managed that without violence, Red,' she whispered. 'You nudged him just the right way.'

Antsy resisted the urge to shrug, kept his head steady in her hands. 'He's been itching to drop us since we landed. I just handed him the moment. Anyway, it was Corien here who sealed the deal.'

'I just helped out.' Corien protested.

'No. How'd you know he'd buy that argument?'

The lad grunted from the dark, sitting down. 'Well . . . it's a touch embarrassing to say, but my guess is that he didn't want to face you down, Red.'

Antsy jerked his surprise in Orchid's hands and she let out an impatient hiss. 'Sorry,' he murmured. 'Lad, the man's a killer. I think he just decided he didn't want our blood on his hands.'

'Is he a killer? Think on it, Red. We actually haven't seen him use all that hardware, have we?'

'In Pearl Town he knifed plenty.'

'Certainly – scared unarmed men and women in the dark from behind. But you're a veteran, Red. You wouldn't flinch. You may not know it, but you're a rather intimidating presence.'

Antsy snorted. *Me? You haven't met the Bridgeburners, friend.*

Orchid's long-fingered hands tightened on Antsy's cheeks. 'If you've *quite* finished?'

'Sorry.'

'Fine. Now hold still. Shut your eyes.'

He obeyed. She began speaking, singing really, in that smooth quiet tongue she'd used with the guardian. He was hearing Tiste Andii, he realized, and a sort of shiver ran up his spine. *Been hunted too often by those strange people.* The language seemed to hold more silence and pauses than sounds. It was as a whispering of a distant wind and seemed so suited to the dark. After a time she stopped, or the sounds drifted away to silence. The hands withdrew, warmed now by the heat of his cheeks. Antsy remained motionless; he felt profoundly relaxed, almost asleep. It reminded him of a trick Mallet used to pull on the wounded. A few low sounds, a steady touch, and the troopers calmed right down.

But nothing happened. A profound depression gripped his chest. Now he was doomed for sure. His last hope lost. How could he be any use, blind, a cripple? Then he realized that he was so relaxed he hadn't opened his eyes.

He blinked and a world of vision jumped to life before him. He couldn't believe it. Couldn't credit his eyes because what he saw was so alien. Monochrome, it was. All shades of deepest blue. As if he was looking at the world through a shard of blue-stained glass. The darkness of deep murky mauve even gathered in the distances, just like true vision. He looked up. There, almost directly overhead, was a stone set in the wall. It was carved in the likeness of an Andii face, feline, almost, and it gave off a lantern-like blue glow. It had been there all this time yet he'd had no idea.

He laughed. It was amazing.

'So . . . it worked?'

He looked to Orchid's anxious, glistening face. The girl had never looked so beautiful to him. He quelled an urge to kiss her. 'Yeah. Worked just great. It's just . . . amazin'.'

'So you can see me then?' Corien asked. Antsy turned to where the lad sat slumped higher up on the stairs. He was squinting roughly in their direction.

'Yeah. It's like the light of a full moon. You look terrible.'

'Oh dear. What would they say in Majesty Hall?'

'Can you do him?' he asked of Orchid.

'Yes, I think so.'

Corien raised a gloved hand. 'No need. Time to see to myself.' He fumbled at his waist-pouch and withdrew a tiny wooden box. 'Now we shall *see*,' and he chuckled. He pulled off one glove and dipped the tip of a finger into the box. It looked to Antsy as if the man was about to take snuff but the finger went into one eye instead. Corien hissed his pain. After doing the other eye he peered about blinking comically, eyes watering.

'Well?' Antsy asked.

'Like pressing salt to one's eyes. I really must talk to my alchemist about this. Tell me, is that face up there really glowing?'

* * *

A presence haunted the estate of Lady Varada. It brushed against windows and pressed against locked doors. The two colourfully dressed guards it easily bypassed to enter the main rooms of the manor house. In these empty halls it hovered near door handles and latches to find each and all dusted with a white powder the presence knew to be a rare poison sifted from the pollen of a flower found only in the near-mythical land of Drift Avalii. Other rooms it quickly sped through as if sensing the drifting fumes of scents deadly to any living creature.

Eventually, after much probing and many turnings back at dead ends, it gained access to the lower floors and here the tenebrous drifting presence coiled inward, firmed and thickened into the figure of a slim young woman in diaphanous white cloth, silver wristlets and anklets tinkling musically on her limbs.

The girl descended a last set of raw granite steps to the deepest chamber to come to a halt where a figure crouched in the middle of the empty room, legs drawn up beneath her stomach, head bowed. The girl pressed a hand to her mouth to cover a smile but her eyes held a savage triumph.

'Mother,' she said. 'You're looking . . . poorly.'

The figure raised her head to peer up through tangled black hair like a sweep of night. 'Taya,' she answered, her voice tight with suppressed pain. 'I asked you to stay away.'

'You *sent* me away,' Taya snapped. 'Why, I now know.'

'You know nothing,' the woman snarled. She surged to her knees, revealing fine mesh chains at wrist and ankle that thrummed taut, and she gasped her agony as flames burst into life where the metal of the fetters clasped her flesh.

Taya nodded her appreciation. 'So that is how you managed. Otataral chains. We'd wondered. Imagine. Vorcan Radok imprisoning herself.' She pressed a hand to her lips. 'Dare I say it? How . . . ironic?'

Vorcan returned to her crouch, panting and hissing her pain. 'You've come. You've seen. Now you can go.'

The arm swept down savagely. '*No* Mother. *You* do not dismiss *me*. Not any longer. Now it is I who dismiss *you*. And seeing you now . . . like this . . . I can finally do so.' She set her hands on her hips, tsking. 'Look at you. Such a mess. And your so-called guards! I could have slain the lot had I wished.'

Head down, Vorcan half gasped, 'I would advise you not to draw any weapon on Lazan or Madrun. And Studlock . . . well, you wouldn't know where to stick your knife to slay him.'

'Where *is* that creature from?'

'Not even I know.'

Taya's mouth drew down in the small pout of a frown and she sighed her exaggerated boredom. 'Well, it has been a treat talking, Mother. But *I* have a life worth living.' She raised her hand to her mouth once more, this time blowing a kiss. 'Thank you. Your wretched failure here frees me of so much. I had come dreaming of killing you but now I see that your suffering pleases me more. Farewell! Think of me often at the court of Darujhistan's rightful king reinstated. I know I will be thinking of you.'

She backed away, climbing the steps, waving. Vorcan did not raise her head.

Some time later another figure came shambling down the stairs, long tatters of his cloth wrappings trailing behind. Studlock bowed, 'She is gone, mistress.'

Vorcan nodded heavily. 'Good. None interfered? Madrun? Lazan?'

'None. Your instructions were most precise. Only she and the other are to be allowed to pass.'

She sank lower, relaxing, the chains clattering. 'Good. Good.'

Studlock rubbed his cloth-wrapped hands together, perhaps as a gesture of worry. 'What shall we do, mistress?'

'We will wait. Wait and see. His arising will be contested. We will see what form that will take.'

'But who, mistress? Who will contend?'

'The same as before.'

The strangely jointed hands fell. 'Oh dear. *Him*.'

　　　　*　　　*　　　*

A short stout man (generous of diameter, thank you!), dapper in waistcoat and frilled sleeves, daintily crosses the mud and open sewer channel of the town of broken hopes west of the dreaming city. And what is this? Does that city now whimper and grimace in its sleep? Does the dream threaten to slide into nightmare? Does a crowned figure stalk the edges of its vision?

And where all the frustrated failed gods take it does this meandering alley lead?

Vexed hero turns aside to a file of washerwomen bent to task at nearby trickle of stream. He pauses, struck breathless for the nonce by glorious vista of said washerwomen's backsides presented. He mops brow with handkerchief, sighs wistfully. Then, remembering errand, approaches.

'Good washerwomen! Would you be so kind as to help a poor lost soul?'

The stolid women slow in their hearty slapping of wet garments and muscular wringing of alarmingly wound cloth. 'Who in Oponn's poor jest are you?' one welcomes rather undemurely.

'I am but a humble petitioner hoping to find my way to a resident of these parts.'

'Who's 'at?' another fine strapping figure of her trade asks, and spits a brown stream of chewing leaf juice.

After hastily shifting silk-slippered foot aside of striking juice our heroic quester bows gallantly. 'Why, an old woman. Living alone. A widow, truth be told, many time over. Some think her perhaps crazy and ignorantly ascribe to her charges of witchery and hexing . . . and such . . .'

Enquirer splutters to silence as all slapping and wringing of cloths cease. All eyes turn narrowed and flashing to the fine generous figure of our innocent searcher – who extends one foot to his rear, poised.

'Get 'im!'

'Slimy rat!'

'The nerve!'

Later that same evening a family of Maiten town was quite mystified to find a fat fellow in black and red silk finery, rather faded, hiding behind their goat pen. 'Yes?' the father asked, quite slowly, worried that perhaps the poor man had lost his senses.

The man straightened up, his head coming almost to the shoulders of the father. He adjusted his stained clothes, brushed soapsuds from his lapels, glanced about. 'Just admiring your handsome animals, good sir. Ah! You wouldn't by any chance happen to know of an old woman living alone hereabouts, that is about here – one whom the uncaring world unjustly ostracizes with calumny and obloquy?'

The father's brow furrowed as he attempted to make sense of the question. He motioned upriver. 'Well, there's a crazy old witch further along at the edge of town.'

The rotund fellow bowed. 'My thanks, keeper of such handsome animals.'

Later, after much dodging of roving packs of washerwomen armed with wet laundry, the out of breath and by now very hungry wanderer came across a straw-roofed wattle and daub hut upon the threshold of which sat a nest-haired old woman, pipe in mouth, busy kneading the mud with her naked toes.

He bowed in a lace-sleeved flourish. 'Ah! Queen of the dreaming city! What a privilege! I am come to pay my respects.'

The old woman peered up, eyes red and unfocused. A vague smile came and went around her pipe. 'Slippery ball of fish oil . . . do you bring offering?'

'But of course.' Another flourish and a wrapped object the size of a walnut appeared. He bowed, holding it out.

The old woman snatched it up with a speed that belied her years. She tore the paper and pinched off a piece of the dark gum within and pushed it into her pipe. Fumbling behind her at the hearth fire inside the hut, she found a smouldering stick that she touched to the pipe while pulling in long steady inhalations. After a few breaths the stick glowed and she drew long and hard. Her eyes closed in silky pleasure.

The man clasped his hands behind his back, looked to the sky, lips pursed, rocked back and forth on his muddy heels.

Eventually the woman exhaled, allowing the smoke to drift from her mouth and immediately sucking it in once more by drawing it up through her nose.

The man let out his own long breath and examined his fingernails.

Some time later a satisfied sigh returned the man's attention to the old woman. He found her peering up at him, eyes dreamy, a wicked smile at the lips. 'Oily Kruppe – what can this poor nobody do for you?'

'Nobody! Calumny in truth! You are the secret carrier of my heart! This you have known all these years.'

'Oiliness indeed . . .' But the smile broadened, became rather lascivious. 'You know my price.'

'Of course! I am all aquiver. And so, the, ah . . . objects . . . are ready then?'

'Almost now.'

'Almost. Ah . . . well. Somehow I must contain myself. More dunkings in handy chilly river for this frustrated suitor.'

'Come back again – and don't forget more offering.'

'Fates forfend! I shall come courting again, queen of my heart. You shall not be rid of me so easily. The siege has hardly begun!'

The woman leaned forward and clutched a clawed hand at the man's knee. 'Then don't forget your battering ram!'

The man shrank back, paling, his arms nearly crossing over his crotch. 'Earthy princess! Your saltiness is, and will be, a treat . . . I am sure. But I must go – ceaseless labour, twisty plottings, constant confounding, as you know.'

But the woman merely murmured, smiling dreamily, 'Almost now.' She giggled and patted her chest.

'Er, yes. Farewell! He backed away, bowing, blowing kisses. 'I shiver in anticipation.' And he turned and waddled, rather swiftly, up the mud track.

The crowd of washerwomen watched the slimy interloper disappear into the maze of Maiten town. 'Why let the wretch go?' one hissed, furious.

'Why?' another snarled, turning upon her. '*Why*? Didn't you see? He's a friend of that crazy old witch!'

*   *   *

Looking out over the night-time blue-lit streets Ambassador Aragan considered whether the city had ever been this quiet. His gaze rose to the yawning banner of green slicing the night sky and he wondered if perhaps that had much to do with the general reserve. Somehow he didn't think so.

He was out of the command loop now. The Fists had control. He'd remained as a sort of standing offer of dialogue with . . . whatever . . . was gathering power around Majesty Hill. Something that drove the Moranth off just by showing up. *And we're powerless to do anything.*

He crossed his arms, leaned against the windowsill. At least the troops will be in a position to withdraw north if need be. Gods! He'd almost prefer a plain old physical threat like the Pannion Domin. Here he felt as if he were pushing against nothing. It was unnerving in the extreme. And he had to say that it reminded him of the way the old Emperor used to operate.

Someone stepped up next to him at the window then, making him jump aside, a hand going to his throat. 'Gods, man! Don't do that!'

The newcomer merely offered a slit of a smile, hands clasped behind his back. Aragan took in the green silk shirt, dark green cloak, long thin face and cat-like, openly dismissive eyes. *Well, at least Unta is taking things seriously – sending this fellow, of all people.* He cleared his throat. 'So, what word from the capital?'

'Darujhistan is important to the throne, Ambassador. Whosoever controls this city potentially controls the entire continent. The Empress knew it, as does the Emperor.'

Aragan simply nodded, returning his gaze to the city. 'My thoughts as well. What will you do?'

'What I do best, Ambassador. I will watch and wait.'

Not sure what to make of that Aragan merely grunted, hoping his reaction would be taken as wise agreement.

The tall man turned to him. 'I understand you have hired someone to gather intelligence already. I'd like to question him, if possible.'

'Certainly. Dreshen has the particulars.'

'Very good.' The man gave the slightest inclination of his head. 'I will be in touch, Ambassador.'

Aragan nodded openly relieved that the man was going. 'Yes, of course. Until later.'

The shadowy figure backed away to cross the room to the door. He quietly shut it behind him. Aragan was rather disappointed; he had expected something much more dramatic. *Sulphurous smoke and a clap of thunder, perhaps. Still, shouldn't be disillusioned. It's few can boast of having the Master of all the Claw come up behind them out of the dark and live to tell the tale.*

*

It was the dead of night but torches and lanterns set on poles lit the long excavation trench that extended in an immense arc all round one side of the sprawling Old Palace and the assembly galleries of Majesty Hall. Work continued day and night. Cleaned polished stones were delivered by hand-drawn cart up the steep Way of Just Rulership to be delivered to the excavation for setting within the trench. Workers dug, laid gravel and sand, levelled, compressed and prepared the foundation. All under the watchful exacting eyes of the construction bosses; one a hunched fellow with large hands that appeared to have been mangled by the white blocks he was always caressing; the other tall, fierce and scowling, quick with a cuff or a strike of the staff he sometimes carried.

The stones were gently laid one by one. A moving tent enclosed the last touches of the installation and the refilling of the trench behind. 'Interment' the two overseers called this final series of hidden steps.

One worker, levelling-board in hand, often lingered close to the flaps of the heavy canvas tent. His fellow crew members frequently had to call him back to task. 'If we fall behind I'll not take a lashing for your laziness,' one grumbled to him while they tamped down a layer of fine sand.

'Walk away then,' the new fellow answered. 'There's other work.'

'Ha! Other work! Listen to this one would you? There is no other work at all! Everything's shut down. The mines, the ironworks, all road crews. It's work here or starve for all of us. Where've you been, anyway?'

The newcomer shrugged. 'Been working in a tavern lately.'

'So that's what you call working?' another of the crew said, laughing. 'I can believe that.'

The new hand pulled on the long ratty shirt he wore, mouth clamped against any comment.

The man next to him grimaced his distaste, covering his nose. 'And it doesn't cost anything to douse yourself with water once in a while too, you know.'

'Back to work!' came a barked command followed by a slap of wood against the shoulder of the newcomer, who straightened, glaring, hands fisted.

But the overseer had moved on, his back turned. Another of the crew dragged the newcomer back down to the bottom of the trench. 'Don't try it, friend. And what's your name, anyway?'

The newcomer looked startled, as if the question was completely unexpected. He pulled at the greasy long shirt. 'Ah . . . Turn— er. Turner.'

'Turner? Harmon. Well, friend, a word to the wise. There's much worse they've done to some.'

'Oh? Such as?'

They were levelling a layer of gravel over the foundation. Head down, one answered, 'A fellow dropped a tool on one of them stones and what happened to him was a terrible thing to see.'

'So? What happened?'

Eyes met to share gauging looks. 'Magery happened,' whispered a crew member. 'The tall one with the staff – he just points, he does, and the man goes down screaming in agony. Bites his own tongue off.'

'No!'

'Aye. There's Warren magics here. Maybe these two are Free Cities mages from up north.. Maybe Pale necromancers. Who knows?'

The crew had a break as more gravel was sent for. They stood, stretching and grimacing over their aches and pains. 'What're they up to?' Turner asked.

Gazes slid aside, feet were shifted, uneasy. Harmon peered right and left then edged closer. A pained look crossed his face and he backed up a step. Then, taking a great breath, he leaned in. 'Some kinda protection for the city, right? This is one o' the new Legate's improvements, right?'

'One?' grumbled another. '*Only* one I knows.'

Turner looked suitably impressed. 'Damn . . . you don't say. Must be them stones, hey?'

Harmon frowned, suddenly a touch uneasy. 'Well, I suppose so.'

'Only one way to find out, don't you think?' And Turner picked up a shovel and headed back up the trench for the tent.

'Gods, man . . .' Harmon hissed, appalled.

'Don't be a fool!' another called, voice low.

After that hammers started clanging and chisels ringing as the crew was suddenly very busy.

Spindle was damned terrified, but he bet that these two Adepts – and he knew the two as such: as far above his capabilities as any Imperial High Mage – would see only what they expected to see: an empty-headed labourer.

He pushed through the hanging flap to find himself almost blind in the shrouded darkness. *Burn take it! Didn't think of that.*

'What in the name of the Cursed Ones do you think you're doing?' a voice snarled down the length of the tent. Spindle bowed, touching his forehead repeatedly. 'Just reportin', sir. We're almost done with the—'

'I don't give a shit what you're finished with or not. Never come in here. Get out! Now!'

Spindle could just make out a hunched figure, lantern set before him, bent over the glowing white blocks, instruments in hand. He bowed again, touching his forehead. 'O' course, sir. Yes. Course. Sorry.' He backed away, bowing, feeling behind himself for the flap.

'Out!'

He scuttled backwards through the flap, turned round and ran straight into the other overseer, the tall quick-tempered one. This mage grabbed his arm, glowering murder. At his touch Spindle felt his hair shirt writhe as if it had come alive. The mage let go, obviously quite shocked. Spindle froze; he'd been found out. This Adept had him. But the tall fellow, scars healing on his face and hands, simply regripped his staff, slowly and stiffly, his knuckles white with strain. And the eyes, black pits in yellowed orbs, shifted to the side, urging him onwards. Spindle bowed again in his role of a normal labourer returning to his work, though this man had seen through his façade.

All the rest of his shift he shared in the loading, levelling, and tamping of dirt, sand and gravels, but he hardly saw any of it. Nor did any of the crew bother him. They'd marked him as either touched or irredeemably dim. Trouble to be avoided, in either case. His hands did their tasks but his mind puzzled over what he'd glimpsed inside that tent. That strange hunchback bent over the stones – and such stones! Glowing they were, as if lit from within. But what had captured his attention were the tools. Magnificent tooled iron etching styluses, and an assortment of engineering instruments any saboteur would give his left hand for. A compass for inscribing arcs, a spirit level – only the second one he'd ever seen outside the Academy in Unta – and an eyepiece of what he suspected might be part of a surveyor's instrument, one he'd only heard described: an alidade. *Gods, he'd never even touched an alidade!*

How he wished he could talk to Fiddler or Hedge about this. Those two knew more engineering than he. *With such tools you could lay down a perfect wall – straight or curved.*

And no one needs that kind of precision for a battlement!

* * *

In the auditorium of the assembly chambers Councillor Coll had lately had a great deal of time on his hands. Fewer of his fellow Councillors than ever were now comfortable being seen in his company. The faction supporting the reinstallation of the Legate was pre-eminent and the subsequent favours, funds and prestige flowed accordingly. So now Councillor Coll sat surrounded by empty seats in assembly, hands clasped over his wide stomach, tapping his fingers. He used the time to think.

That day it occurred to him that in fact it had been some time since he'd even *seen* Lim; not that this 'Legate' was legally obliged to officiate here at the Council. Around mid-morning he heaved himself out of his seat – *Ye gods but I am starting to get a touch heavy* – to walk the steps down to the debate floor. Among the councillors present he selected one clearly in the Legate's camp, one who would have nothing to risk in actually being seen talking to him. Conversation quietened in the man's group as he drew near and the three councillors sketched the briefest greetings his way. Coll bowed to Councillor Ester-Jeen, who merely arched a supercilious brow.

'Councillor Coll,' he murmured.

'Ester-Jeen.'

The other two councillors remembered pressing business and bowed their leave-taking. 'Yes?' Ester-Jeen said, his tone implying the relationship of a superior to a petitioner. Coll let that pass, in his youth such a peremptory and disrespectful greeting would have drawn a challenge from him. He noted an unusual ornament on the man's breast, a gold brooch worked in the shape of a tiny oval mask.

'I was wondering, Ester-Jeen, just where is our illustrious leader? He doesn't seem very interested in actually leading.'

The man physically paled at Coll's daring in giving voice to such disrespect. He dropped a gloved hand to the gilt rapier at his hip even though, as Coll knew, the councillor had never fought a duel. Then his eyes fluttered and the hand fell away as he seemed to remember that not only had Coll fought many duels but he was also a veteran of the Free Cities wars from years ago.

He opted for a superior frosty glare. 'The Legate is not required to sit here and be bored by the Council's unending chatter. He will grant audience in the Great Hall for any official business.'

'*Audience?*' Coll repeated, outraged. Conversations surrounding them stilled. Coll glanced about, met many hostile, even some pitying, gazes. He lowered his voice. 'Since when do we here in Darujhistan use such language as "audience"? And the Great Hall . . . we don't use that. It's considered . . .' Coll searched for the right term, 'well . . . cursed.'

Having gauged the atmosphere of the room, Councillor Ester-Jeen was now quite at ease. No one, it appeared, was prepared to offer

Coll any support whatsoever. The man was simply making a sad spectacle of his ignorance and isolation. Perhaps now, if he was very careful, he could even lure him into discrediting himself entirely. He spoke up, loudly. 'If you have any legitimate business regarding matters before the Council then of course you may approach the Legate. Otherwise, Coll, I would suggest you not waste his time.' And he offered a small shrug of embarrassment as if to say: *I am very sorry to be the one to have to tell you this.*

He was gratified by the reaction his words elicited. The big man reared up as if slapped – which of course he had been – and his eyes widened, stunned. He glanced about at the gathered councillors and Ester-Jeen saw only flat gazes answering. Then Coll spun on his heels and marched for the doors. Ester-Jeen was delighted. *He's actually going to do it – the fool.*

When Coll pushed past Councillor Orr the young woman whispered through gritted teeth: 'Don't.' But he was past listening. He could not let this stand. There was no way he could ever face any one of those present again unless he did exactly what that upstart useless popinjay wanted him to. He marched for the Great Hall.

Majesty Hall itself was in truth a maze of halls and chambers and auditoriums, all of various sizes, ages, and levels of decrepitude. The Great Hall was among the most ancient of the hill's architecture. It was sometimes used for ceremonial balls and mass assemblies. But other than that it stood empty and neglected, having a rather off-putting dusty air, quite similar to that of the equally old Despot's Barbican.

Coll found the double doors of panelled beaten copper and bronze, as tall as three men, unaccountably closed. Before them stood two city Wardens.

'Open up,' he snapped, not slowing in his headlong rush.

The two shared helpless glances. Then, bowing to the inevitable, one threw open a small clerk's door just before Coll brained himself on the polished copper panels. Coll was furious that he had to enter like some damned mouse but enter he did, ducking and stepping over the threshold. Within, he found the long hall lit by shafts of light streaming down from high openings. Motes hung in the shafts like the downy seeds of wild flowers over a sunny field. Other than that the Great Hall appeared empty. He walked slowly up its polished pink marble floor – recently dusted, he noted – his boot heels clicking loudly in the silence.

Someone, or thing, waited at the far end. Some sort of large seat had been constructed of white stone blocks and someone sat upon it. He wore a long loose cloak of rich material, a deep maroon. But what was most mystifying was the large gold mask that entirely covered his face.

The Queen-damned Legate has lost his gibbering mind.

Coll stopped short of the – what should he call it? A dais? – and squinted up at the figure. 'Lim? Is that you? What is all this ridiculous mummery?'

The figure on the dais flicked a hand and out from the side of the hall shuffled an old man in dusty frayed clothes, grey hair all askew. The man bowed to Coll, and, nervously rubbing his hands at his chest, gulped, 'I speak for the Legate.'

'What? You?' Coll turned on Lim. 'Speak for your damned self!' He drew breath to excoriate the fool but stopped; he saw that the gold mask, beaten in the design of a calm half-smiling face, had no holes in it whatsoever. None for eyes or mouth. *How in Burn's mysteries does the man breathe?*

A strange urge almost overcame Coll then to tear the mask from the fool's face but he was distracted by the emergence of a second man from the side of the hall. A tall familiar figure walking with a staff of twisted gnarled wood. His one-time employer, High Alchemist Baruk.

Relief flooded Coll. 'Thank goodness . . . Baruk, what is all this nonsense?'

The man came very close and Coll saw that the man was Baruk, yet not. A nest of pale scars skeined his face and hands and his lips were drawn back from his teeth in a savage gleeful smile. Yet only a dead sort of dismissal, if even that, animated his eyes.

And suddenly Coll knew. *He knew.* All those whispered rumours and hearsay. The T'orrud Cabal. It was *true.* Baruk had been with them all along. And now, after all these years, they'd made their move and claimed power. He flinched away from this man whom he'd thought a friend. 'You'll never succeed,' he breathed, feeling utterly empty inside. 'The Cabal will be deposed. You will see.'

Baruk shook his head, the smile broadening to become somehow even more fey. 'You still don't understand, Coll,' he whispered, leaning close. 'We're here now because the Cabal failed.'

* * *

The hamlet clinging on at the southern edge of the Dwelling Plain was on no map. Once every few years a caravan train of camels and mules passed by on its way south to Callows and Morn beyond. But other than such intermittent visitors only ill-advised travellers, the desperate, criminal, or utterly lost, ever found their way to such an isolated stretch of emptiness. The inhabitants, refugees mostly, peppered by a few hardened locals born and raised, were bent to their task of squeezing any sustenance out of the unproductive sandy soil. Those in the southernmost fields noted the strange phenomenon first: a dark snaking line coming out of the depths of the hard brush of the Plain of Lamatath to the south. A few stopped to peer, hands shading their eyes, then returned to hoeing and jabbing at the hard soil as if to beat it into submission.

When next they looked up the line had drawn nearer, taken on more dimension in the shimmering heat-glare of the sun. A double file of men jogging, it looked like, no doubt on the move since the dawn and not stopping yet. Some leaned on their hoes to watch for a time, wondering at the bizarre sight. One or two thought that perhaps they ought to sound some sort of alarm. Though what any of them could do in the face of such an unprecedented visitation they were not sure.

Close to noon, the sun at its highest, their unrelenting steady approach brought the file of men – and women – close enough now to make out details. Everyone had stopped working to watch, silent. Lightly armoured they were in leathers, those leathers now dark with sweat. All were armed with long blades, some carrying two. All lean, wiry and nut-dark. But these details were as nothing compared to their most extraordinary feature: all wore masks. And multicoloured they were too. Painted almost gayly.

They could be faintly heard now. Their sandalled feet fell un-usually light upon the dry hardpan, all in unison, like a distant drumming. The double file of men and women passed straight across the landscape, unwavering, arrow-like, pointed north-east. Without a pause each easily vaulted a heaped wall of fieldstone as they came to it. The sight made one farmer think of a stream of water flowing magically northward.

And on they passed, none even sparing a glance for the closest of the farmers who stood not an arm's reach aside. Apart from the beat of their footfalls, utterly silent. Ghost-like. Indeed, it was almost like a vision imposed by the heat. Only the dust remained to hang in the still air, the file now to the north, jogging onward, diminishing.

Yet as the dust settled it revealed a newcomer. One of the masked. He'd stopped next to one of the children: young Hireth. Who stood staring up, mouth agape, water gourd in one hand. The man knelt, held out a hand for the gourd. Hireth's father dared to edge slightly closer; the visitor seemed to ignore him. As if being shaken out of a daze Hireth snapped her mouth shut then held out the gourd. The man took it. He turned his head aside while he lifted his mask to drink, then rose and handed back the gourd. Something in his manner made her bend her knees in a curtsy. The man reached out to gently run a hand down one cheek of her bare upturned face. The father almost started forward then but something in the gentleness of the touch, its near reverence, made him stop. He watched spellbound, his pickaxe clenched in his sweaty hands. *Jogging all the day under this sun and not even breathing hard! These are demons off on some summoned errand. Go now. Do not trouble us!*

And the stranger set off, running gracefully at a league-swallowing easy pace. Hireth's father came to her. 'Did he say anything, child?'

She shook her head, as if she too had somehow been captured by the visitors' spell of silence.

He squeezed her shoulder to reassure her. So, he hadn't spoken. Somehow he didn't imagine the man, or demon, had. And he'd been different from the rest. His mask had been very pale, all creamy white it was. With only one smear of reddish dirt across the brow.

CHAPTER X

Let it be known that a number of centuries past an ambitious
and expansionist dynasty of rulers named the Jannids asserted
control over the southern city states. These rulers prosecuted
successful campaigns across the lands gaining sway all the way
north to the Pannion region. They were famous for having raised
countless stelae upon which they ordered engraved the detailed
histories of those campaigns listing their victories, together
with exhaustive compilings of treasure taken, prisoners, and
states humbled. Only in one campaign were they crushed – a
defeat that triggered their downfall. This is known because of
one unpolished boulder that lies on the western shore south of
Morn. Carved on it are a mere four words: 'The Jannids fell
here.'

Histories of Genabackis
Sulerem of Mengal

THE FIRST VESSEL LEAVING DARUJHISTAN'S HARBOUR THAT MORN-
ing was an old merchantman ferrying passengers and freight
westward around the lakeshore. Upon sighting the ancient
ship, its paint sun-faded to a uniform pale grey, sails patched and
threadbare, sides battered and scraped to naked slivers, Torvald
halted on the wharf. Passengers brushed past laden with rolled reed
mats and bags of possessions. Some drove young sucklings ahead of
them. Just about all carried fowl gobbling inside cages woven of reed
and green branches.

He turned on one of the city Wardens sent to escort him to the
docks. 'This is supposed to be a diplomatic mission,' he hissed,
struggling to keep his voice low. 'I can't go on this tub!'

One of the guards tucked a folded pinch of leaves into a cheek and leaned against piled crates. 'It's a secret mission, Councillor,' he drawled.

Torvald tried his best superior glare but the fellow was clearly indifferent. 'If it's so secret then how come you know about it? And don't call me Councillor.'

A lazy roll of the shoulders from the man. 'Orders.'

Torvald began to wonder just what those orders were. *See him from the city even if it means throwing him from the docks*, perhaps. He picked up his heavy travelling bag and slipped its strap over a shoulder. 'Fine. Secret. Tell your superiors you saw me off then,' he said, and headed up the gangway.

The small deck was crammed with goods. Pigs squealed, terrified, sheep bawled, and caged birds gabbled. All this did nothing for the state of the decking. The only available space was a suspiciously clear arc surrounding two figures sitting against the side close to the bow. Torvald could well understand the avoidance: one of them was a giant of a fellow with a massive tangle of hair and beard all unkempt together like a great mane of dirty blond and grey. His shoulders were titanic, his upper arms as massive as Torvald's own thighs, and his chest swept out like a barrel. Torvald thought him perhaps a travelling strongman. The fellow next to him was a skinny Rhivi tribesman elder looking particularly frail in such company. To Torvald the two would have appeared a far more intimidating pair if the big fellow hadn't been so clearly absorbed in studying the city, laid out pink and golden in the dawn's light, climbing in cliff ridge over cliff ridge to Majesty Hill beyond. The old fellow was clearly sick as a dog, bleary-eyed and pale.

But then Torvald had travelled for a time in the company of someone who could arguably be named the most intimidating figure these lands had ever met. He dropped his bag and leaned up against the side. 'Not going to try your luck?' he said to the big fellow.

The man's gaze swung to him and Torvald suppressed a flinch when he saw the bestial eyes, the irises oddly shaped, and felt the plain sheer weight of the man's regard. The fellow cocked one thick brow, rumbled, 'How's that?'

Torvald found his throat suddenly dry. 'The city . . . they're always hungry for new acts.'

'Acts?' the man slowly enunciated, his voice hardening.

'You know . . . bending bars, breaking chains.'

Both brows rose as comprehension dawned and the fellow eased back, relaxing. 'Ah. No.' He crooked a small nostalgic smile. 'Been a lot of years since I've had to do any of that.'

Somehow, Torvald felt immense relief. 'I'm sorry – I thought . . .'

The man raised a gnarled hand to forestall any further explanation. 'I understand.' The fierce eyes looked him up and down. 'What are you doing on a tub like this?'

My point exactly. Torvald offered an indifferent shrug. 'First boat leaving.'

'And far from the fastest,' the man rumbled.

Unformed suspicions writhed anew in Torvald's stomach and he glanced over to see the two city Wardens who, grinning, offered lazy waves of farewell.

Gods curse the Legate!

The gangway scraped up and wharf hands threw off the lines. Two of the crew pushed off with poles while others set the single lateen-rigged sail. The menagerie of animals squealed and voided anew.

Torvald threw himself down against the side, rested his arms on his knees. *Burn's love. For the price of a bright certificate and an empty fancy title did I just sell myself on to a slow boat to nowhere?* He pressed his hands to his head.

Lim has just rid himself of an irritating new councillor.

'Love or coin?' A quavering thin voice spoke up.

Torvald raised his head to see the Rhivi elder studying him from around the great bulk of his companion. 'I'm sorry . . . ?'

'Your reasons for travel – if you would speak of them. In my experience a man travels for one of two reasons. A powerful husband or a powerful debt.'

Torvald snorted a self-mocking laugh. 'No. Nothing so romantic. Just a plain old powerful political rival.'

The big fellow now eyed him sidelong, his gaze narrow. 'Really?' he rumbled.

*   *   *

The lazy silt-laden stream that ran into Lake Azur at Dhavran hardly deserved a name. Some called it the Red, others the Muddy. In any case, it was a barrier of a sorts. Over the years a crossing had been constructed of stones and garbage capped by a simple bridge of laid logs packed with dirt. Fist K'ess eyed the mud-choked channel and thought it the most pathetic crossing he'd ever seen.

'Do we defend here?' Captain Fal-ej asked. Her tone more than made clear her own disenchantment.

K'ess adjusted his seat astride his mount. He'd been too long out of the saddle and his thighs were scraped raw. For a time he eyed the troops marching on to the short causeway. *Not enough to make a stand. And Dhavran? This collection of mud and wood huts doesn't boast one defensible position.*

He sipped some water from a skin hung on his saddle then sucked his teeth. At first he'd considered heading west into the Moranth mountains to wait things out there. But then a rider had arrived from Captain Goyan's contingent: they were moving on. And why? Word had come from the Fifth. Fist Steppen moving north. Rendezvous south of Dhavran.

All very well and good. Altogether they might field close to ten thousand. Every remaining Malazan trooper south of Cat. Enough for him to finally unclench his anxious buttocks for a moment or two.

But before he could allow himself that one moment of relaxation reports arrived from loyal Barghast scouts in the eastward foothills of the Tahlyn range: a large force moving west. Rhivi tribals, apparently. Some three days out and moving far faster than they.

It was a race he knew he wouldn't win. Thus the hope of contesting the crossing here at Dhavran. And thus his disappointment.

He straightened in his stirrups for a moment to adjust the sweaty leathers beneath his mail skirting. He eyed Fal-ej while she watched the troops march. Her helmet hung from her pommel and she'd wrapped a scarf around her head in the style of her homeland, Seven Cities. A handsome woman. Damned smart. But a touch sharp-edged. Haughty, some of the officers thought her, he knew. But not he. Good wide hips on her too. Fit for throwing out sons, as his ma would've said. Woman like that ought to have someone to hold on to.

'Sir?' she said. Her gaze had moved to him, questioning.

He cleared his throat. 'We keep going. Double-time. This place is too wretched.'

She nodded her curt assent, relieved. 'Yes, Fist.'

K'ess plucked at the gauntlets he held in one hand. 'Fal-ej . . .' he began.

'Yes, Fist?' she answered quickly.

He slapped the gauntlets to his armoured thigh. 'Nothing. It's not important.' He waved towards the stream. 'Keep the sappers on that ramshackle excuse for a bridge. The last thing we need is for it to fall apart under us.'

Fal-ej saluted, kneed her mount into motion. 'Yes, Fist.'

He watched her go, frowning at himself. *Now's not the time – what with a horde of Rhivi closing in on us.* He sighed.

Captain Fal-ej urged her mount more savagely than she intended down the stream's oversized channel. *Remember your priorities, woman,* she castigated herself. *By the Seven False Gods, what's gotten into you? Hanging about like a mare in heat. It must be offensive to the man.*

She pulled up next to a bridge picket, demanded, 'Where are the damned saboteurs, trooper?'

The man saluted twice for good measure. He pointed vaguely down towards the stream. 'Thought I saw them headin' off that way, Captain sir . . .'

Fal-ej yanked the reins over, kneed the mount onward. *Has the responsibility of every solider on his shoulders, woman! Not likely to allow himself to be distracted – and hardly by a figure such as yourself! Calluses on your cheeks from the helmet. Stink of sweat always on you. Arms like some blacksmith's!*

Cresting a grassed sandbar she spotted the crew squatting around a campfire, gutted fish on sticks over the flames. She slapped her mount down towards the stream and pulled up, kicking mud over them. 'What is this?'

The marine sergeant, a great fat woman, merely peered up unperturbed. 'Just havin' a bite, Cap'n.'

'You were *ordered* to keep an eye on the bridge.'

'Bridge is good as beer, Cap'n. Nothin' there to break. Just big ol' logs.'

Fal-ej glared down at them. 'Well . . . just the same, stay on it! Something might give.'

The sergeant rubbed a large black mole on one cheek, considering. 'Such as . . . ?'

Fal-ej threw her arms out wide. 'How in the name of Ehrlitan should I know! *I'm* not the engineer. Now get going!'

Frowning her agreement, the sergeant motioned to a trooper. 'Whitey, take your team over.'

'Aw, c'mon, Sarge. Fish is almost ready.'

The sergeant's voice took on an edge. 'Get going . . . *now.*'

'Fine!' The man straightened to slap dirt off his hide trousers, motioned his team up. The sergeant turned to the captain, cocked a brow and saluted.

Fal-ej answered the salute and yanked her mount round. 'Thank you, sergeant.' She rode off kicking up more mud.

'What's gotten under her saddle,' a trooper muttered. 'Martinet.'

'Naw,' the sergeant said as she watched the woman go, a hand shading her gaze. 'Ain't nothing a good humping wouldn't cure.'

'Sarge!' one trooper groaned. 'Do you *have* to?'

'That's your answer for everything,' another complained.

The sergeant turned, rubbing her hands together. 'Yes indeed – too bad none of you poor excuses are up to it.'

'Oh, don't go on about the damned Moranth. We don't believe none o' those stories.'

*   *   *

'Now don't go and just kill everyone, okay!' Yusek snarled over her shoulder as they struggled up the narrow mountain trail.

'You exaggerate,' Sall answered calmly.

'No I do *not* fucking exaggerate! Someone raises a cooking ladle your way and you two butcher two hundred! Try to show a little respect. This is some kinda monastery or something.'

'If they are unarmed they have nothing to fear from us.'

She snorted her scorn. Pausing, she glanced further down to distant Lo making his way up after them. *No sign of sweat or labour on either of them!* No shortage of breath. Yusek, for her part, felt light-headed and nauseous with the height. *Gods. Never been this high before. They say the air is poisonous up here. Kill you as sure as a blade to the heart.*

Swallowing to wet her rasping throat she glanced ahead to the monastery walls of heaped cobbles. Tattered prayer flags snapped in the cold wind. White tendrils of smoke blew here and there from cook-fires. Overhead a clear, painfully bright blue sky domed the world. Beautiful, in its way, but for a faint green blemish across its vault – the Scimitar of a god's vengeance, some named that banner.

A monk, or acolyte, or whatever you would call him, met them at the stone arch that was the compound's entrance. Yusek took the shaven-headed slim figure for a boy until she spoke, revealing her sex. 'Enter, please, the adytum. We offer food, shelter, and peace for contemplation to all who would enter.'

'Adytum?' Yusek repeated. 'Is that the place's name?'

'The adytum is a location. The most sacred place. The inner shrine of worship for our faith.'

'What faith is that?'

'Dessembrae.' And the woman gestured aside, inviting. Nor did she blink in the face of the two masked Seguleh.

Yusek urged Sall forward. 'Well? Go on!'

By his hesitation the young man appeared almost embarrassed. 'There is a proper time for everything,' he told Yusek aside; then, to the acolyte: 'Thank you. We would rest. And any hot food you may spare would be welcome.'

The acolyte showed them to a simple hut of piled stone cobbles, almost like a cell. A fire already burned in its small central hearth. Smoke drifted up to the ceiling hole. A black iron pot was heating over the low flames. The young acolyte – no older than me, Yusek reflected – in her loose shirt over trousers of plain cloth and her bare feet, stopped at the threshold. 'You would prefer separate quarters?' she asked Yusek, who nodded. 'This way.'

The hut she showed Yusek was no different from the other. 'Listen,' Yusek told her, lowering her voice, 'those two are Seguleh.'

'I have heard of them.'

'Yeah. Well, they're here to kill someone. You have to warn him – tell him to get out of here.'

'They've come to kill someone? I doubt that very much.'

Yusek found herself clenching her teeth. 'You don't understand—'

The young woman held up a hand. 'Your concern does you credit. But there is no need for worry. The man you speak of has no interest in their challenges. They will leave empty-handed.'

Yusek wanted to grab the girl's shoulder and shake her. *You little fool! You have no idea what you are facing here!* But the girl studied her, calm, uninflected, and something in that steady regard made her uneasy. *As if she's looking through me . . . like I'm a ghost or something.*

The girl bowed. 'If that is all.'

'Yeah . . . I suppose so.'

The girl withdrew. Yusek sat on the cot, unrolled the bedding of thick woven blankets provided against the cold. In truth she was exhausted, which surprised her. Hardly a full day's journey since their last camp, she freezing her butt off, complaining the entire time, and those two maintaining their infuriating silence – not even telling her to shut the Abyss up.

She lay down, threw an arm across her eyes. Well, she was free of them. She'd brought them to the monastery and now her obligation was over. She'd take off tomorrow and leave these pathetic empty wastes behind. Maybe she'd head on north to Mengal. Who knew, maybe she'd take a ship to some rich distant land like Quon Tali or Seven Cities.

She fell asleep dreaming of that. Of getting away, far away.

When she started awake the light coming in through the shutters over the single tiny window held the pink of dawn. Normally she never woke up this early but normally she never fell asleep in the afternoon. Groaning, she stretched her stiff frozen limbs and went to her knees before the hearth to tease the fire back to life. After a hot cup of tea she felt alive enough to head out.

When she opened the door the first thing that struck her was the silence. She'd grown used to the forest with its constant background noise of the wind through the branches, the trunks groaning as they flexed. Here there was only the low moan of the wind over stone, the faint snap of the prayer flags. She found herself almost trying to soften the fall of her moccasins on the stone-flagged walk. Almost. Then she shook off the spell and went to find something to eat.

To her chagrin she found everyone up already. *What is it with these people that they get up so early? It's inhuman.* A group of the monks, or priests, were out on a central field of sand weaving through some sort of exercise or devotional movements. She watched for a time: the practice held a kind of flowing beauty. It seemed almost hypnotic. But she was hungry and so she turned away to find someone to ask for directions to a kitchen or mess.

Later, chewing on a hot flatbread, she wandered back out to the central open field to see Sall and Lo watching the monks who were now engaged in some sort of paired physical training of throws and falls.

Aha, she thought. This is more like it. She stepped up to Sall. 'Going to talk to me? Or am I a nobody now?'

Standing arms crossed, the youth's gaze did not shift from the monks. 'I will speak to you . . . for the time being.'

'Well, that's something, I suppose. What now? What will you two do?'

'Lo will challenge the – the man here.'

Yusek gave an exaggerated nod. She too watched the monks. 'So which one's he?'

A heavy breath raised Sall's shoulders. 'That is the problem. He will not identify himself. Nor will anyone else do so.' His voice took on an almost puzzled edge: 'They are simply ignoring us.'

Yusek choked on her bread. Gulping, she managed to swallow then broke out in a laugh that left her almost helpless. She bent forward resting her hands on her knees to catch her breath. She straightened, wiping her cheeks. Sall was regarding her from behind his mask, his dark brown eyes uncomfortable. She took a steadying breath. 'Aii-ya. So . . . how does it feel to be on the receiving end, hey?'

The lad had the grace to lower his gaze. Again a great breath raised his chest behind his crossed arms. 'It is most . . . frustrating,' he admitted.

Yusek gave a satisfied: 'It most certainly is.'

The lad returned to watching the monks go through their regimen of exercise and training. Yusek sat on the stone kerb surrounding the practice field. *Need five days' rations for a start. I wonder if there's any dried meat in the larder here. Probably not. This lot do not look like the hunter type.*

And she'd be on her own again. Target of any arsehole who thought he could twist her arm . . .

It occurred to her that perhaps she shouldn't be in such an all-fire hurry to get away.

Sall straightened then and Yusek peered up. Sticks were being brought out: wooden swords. *Oh-ho. Things were getting interesting now.*

The monks paired off, one practice sword per pair, attacker and defender. While Yusek watched, the swordsmen cut and thrust and the defenders threw them like dolls, or bent them to their knees, sword-arm twisted.

Ridiculous! Any real swordsman would cut an unarmed man or woman to pieces. Sall must be laughing inside – or groaning.

She gave a glance and saw him turn his masked face aside to Lo. Something imperceptible to her passed between them , and the lad unclasped his cloak. He laid it on the stone flags then placed his sheathed swords on top of the cloth and walked out on to the sands. Yusek shifted to look at Lo and jumped to find him next to her. It gave her the creeps how he did that.

The monks all stopped their exercises to watch while Sall approached the nearest pair. Bowing, he held out a hand for the wooden sword. The acolyte turned a glance to the monk leading the practice, a wiry petite woman. She nodded and the acolyte handed over the sword.

Sall faced his partner. He bowed then struck a *ready* stance, left foot shifting back behind him. Yusek rose to her feet. The acolyte, even younger than Sall, brought his empty hands up between them, one above the other, elbows bent.

Sall struck then, but not as Yusek had seen before. Slowly, gently, he brought the wooden blade down in an exaggerated overhead drop cut. The youth rolled inwards underneath the cut, somehow hooked Sall's arms, and bent, pulling the swordsman over his shoulder and throwing him to the ground. But Sall rolled easily and came to his feet once more.

The two faced off once again. This time Sall swung a horizontal slash. The youth side-stepped, took the Seguleh's arm, and somehow led him in a spinning dance then let go and sent him flying out over the sands. The performance would have appeared laughably false had not Yusek known that Sall was in no way cooperating. Next, Sall mimed a slow two-handed thrust. The youth stepped into the move, somehow pushing Sall to send him tumbling aside.

Lo stood silent at Yusek's side.

Sall rose to brush the dust from his shoulders. He bowed again and the two paired off once more. This time he raised his sword high above his head, the blade vertical. He held it there for a time, motionless, then brought it down in a slow angled strike. The youth – perhaps no younger than Sall – again stepped in close, but Sall now side-stepped himself, bringing the sword around for another sweep. The youth pursued and now the two circled faster and faster, sword arcing and the youth's arms twisting as if attempting to ensnare his opponent's. The nearest monks scrambled backwards out of the way of the match as it spun seemingly out of control.

The silence of it was the most eerie to Yusek. All she could hear was the snap and flutter of the monk's sleeves and the hiss of the wooden sword. Neither gasped nor yelled nor snarled. Even their feet shifted noiselessly over the sands. At first she'd thought this some sort of a duel, but she saw now that it was more of a sparring match – the exchange of known moves and countermoves, each now faster than the next, each testing the other.

Finally, at some signal or agreement between the two, they spun apart to face one another.

Amazingly, neither betrayed the least hint of exertion. Neither's chest rose any deeper than before; neither breathed loudly at all.

Both bowed. Sall now stepped up, his blade held low at his side, his right leg back. The monk matched his step. Swiftly, Sall thrust the wooden sword through his belt and faced the youth with his hands at his sides.

The youth's large brown eyes shifted to the woman leading the practice; she gave another small nod. The youth raised his hands again, ready.

This time when Sall moved Yusek missed it. So too did his partner. One moment Sall stood with his hands at his sides, empty. The next he held the blade one-handed against the youth's neck.

A soft grunt escaped Lo.

The young acolyte's eyes grew huge and after taking a moment to digest what had just happened he bowed to Sall.

So ends the lesson.

But apparently not. For the woman who had been leading the practice now approached Sall. She bowed and waved in an unmistakable *try that with me* gesture.

The woman, Yusek noted with interest, was no taller or heavier than herself. Her hair was cut short and her bare arms were extraordinarily lean and muscled. Sall's mask turned towards Lo who, his arms across his chest, gave a small flick of one hand. Sall bowed to the woman, accepting.

The two faced off. Sall pushed the wooden sword through his belt once more. The woman struck a *ready* pose exactly like that of her student. The acolytes stood frozen, silent, and their watchful intensity reminded Yusek of the Seguleh themselves.

Sall shifted his sandalled feet in the sand a few times, as if unhappy with his stance, then stilled. This time Yusek almost caught it. One moment Sall was motionless. Then, in the next, he was off his feet describing an arc through the air over the back of the spinning woman, who had thrown him flying high to land in a great swath of bursting sand.

Sall sprang to his feet, sword still in hand, and to Yusek every line of his body shouted of his utter astonishment.

A clenched hiss sounded from Lo and the man walked away.

Yusek looked to Sall; the youth's masked face followed Lo's retreat, then fell. Yusek did not need to see his expression to recognize the crushing shame that hunched his form. Bowing, he handed over the sword, then walked off in the opposite direction. Yusek followed.

She found him sitting on a ledge on the very lip of the cliff the monastery occupied. Before his feet the mountain swept down thousands of feet into misted emptiness. Yusek sat next to him. The frigid cutting wind buffeted both of them. Yusek's cloak snapped.

She was not used to such dizzying heights and a sickening vertigo gripped her as she clutched the stone she sat upon. 'Not *that* bad, is it?' she offered, trying to make light of things.

After a time the Seguleh youth let out a long, pained breath. 'You do not understand, Yusek.'

'Try me.'

'I lost. I have shamed Lo. I can no longer be considered among the Agatii.'

'The Agatii?'

'The Honoured Thousand. The select warriors of the Seguleh.'

'So? Have to turn in your mask or some such thing?'

At least he snorted a weak laugh at that. 'No. But . . . I will have to repaint it.'

'Well, so what? I mean, it's not like it was deliberate, or some kind of crime, or something.'

The lad sighed, his breath almost cracking in its suppressed emotion. 'You don't understand, Yusek. Lo is Eighth! He sits with Jan among the ruling Ten, the Eldrii.' He clenched his hands, held them where the mask curved to expose the mouth. 'But one other thing . . . he is my father.'

Yusek stared, speechless. *Ye Gods . . . the poor kid. What a burden! That's just fucking cruel, that's what that is.*

She selected a small stone, tossed it over the edge. She watched its stomach-turning descent for an instant then glanced away, her throat burning. She swallowed sour bile. 'Listen, Sall – so what if some woman beat you in some match. Who the fuck cares? C'mon, she wasn't even armed!'

The lad turned to study her directly through his mask. His brown eyes appeared even more pained. 'Exactly, Yusek. *She wasn't even armed.*'

'Well . . . so what? Big deal. It wasn't for real. You weren't prepared for it, were you?' She nudged his shoulder. 'It's a valuable lesson, right? Listen. I was thinking. When I head out I want to be able to handle myself better . . . won't you teach me a few moves?' She nudged him again. 'Hey? What do you say?'

If anything his masked head hung even lower. 'I'm not worthy of teaching anyone anything, Yusek. Ask that woman, if anyone.'

'Well, I'm asking you. C'mon. You know more than I do about it all, right?'

'It would be improper . . .'

'Never mind that. Just the basics, hey?'

'Not right now.'

'Naw . . . tomorrow, hey?'

He let out another long-suffering breath. 'Tomorrow, then.'

'Yeah. All right. Tomorrow.' She stood, brushed the dust off her bottom, and left him to sit alone for a time. *Poor bastard. Obviously thinks the world of his father. And to think she'd travelled with them all these days and hadn't even the first suspicion they were father and son! What an odd people.*

* * *

Personally, Krute of Talient did want to honour yet another request from this particular client, but the communication had percolated up through standard channels thereby ensuring that enough of the guild knew of it to make it impossible for him to simply ignore it. Of course as Parish Master of the Gadrobi district he had a measure of influence on which contracts to pursue – but it was a short-lived master who neglected the fundamental truth that, in the end, everyone was only in it for the treasure.

And so come the mid-night he found himself stepping carefully through the empty and eerily quiet yards of the Eldra Iron Mongers. It was an unnatural sensation; to his memory the works had never been still. The Legate, however, had commandeered all labour for his city works projects, leaving Humble Measure with no one to run his forges, furnaces and mine.

All very deliberate and calculated, of course, as a sort of unannounced war had broken out between the two: the successful political protégé and his former patron and sponsor. And this kind of falling-out always generated the most vicious and wilful vendettas. His boots loud on the scattered gravel as he peered around at the dark sheds and silent furnaces, it occurred to Krute that his reservations may all be for naught; surely even this man's legendary wealth must be exhausted by now. There could be no way the man could offer enough to tempt the guild anew. In point of fact, he wouldn't be all that surprised to turn a corner in one of these cavernous warehouses and find the man hanging from a rafter.

No such easy resolution confronted him, however, when he pushed aside a great slab-like door to enter a silent smelting shed. The tang of smoke still clung to everything and he fancied he could still feel a residual heat leaking out of the great furnaces.

Undisguised steps sounded from the front of the shed and Krute turned to see the proprietor, Humble Measure himself, at the door. The closing of his works had obviously not been kind to him. His hair was unkempt and soot marred his face. The black of the soot cast the whites of his eyes into a bright, almost fevered, glow. His clothes were likewise askew, torn and soot-blackened. It appeared as if the man was attempting the impossible, and frankly insane, task of single-handedly keeping the works going.

Krute inclined his head in greeting. 'Humble Measure.'

'Parish Master. I was beginning to suspect that the guild had lost its edge.'

'Whosoever has the coin gets our blades,' Krute observed, congratulating himself on that pointed reminder.

'Of course. That is as it should be.' The man drew a cloth from a shirt pocket and wiped his hands. Krute noted with growing unease that the cloth was just as blackened as the man's hands. Humble waved him forward. 'This way, Master.' As they walked, the ironmonger talked. 'It strikes me that you assassins represent the exchange of business reduced to its purest form. What say you, Master?'

Krute shrugged. 'Hadn't really given it much thought.' *Gabble on, man. I'm really not interested in what crazy things you have to say.*

'You do not care who you kill, or for what hidden purpose, or to what consequences. You are merely paid money to do something, and so you do it. Rather like a prostitute, yes?'

Krute frowned, eyeing the man sidelong. 'What're you gettin' at?'

'I mean that questions of morality or ethics, honour or principles – all are irrelevant, yes?'

Krute hunched his shoulders. 'Not *all* principles . . .'

The man flashed him a smile bright against his grimed face. 'Of course. The principle of greed and profit remains paramount. Utterly uninhibited, in fact.'

He led Krute to a dilapidated manor house, pushed open the front door. 'Let me provide an example, if I may.' At the back of the house the ironmonger unlocked a trap door, revealing stone steps leading down. 'Let us say there exists a city occupying a marshy lowland. The inhabitants of this urban centre are cursed by a wasting disease carried by flies that multiply like . . . well, like flies, within

305

the swamps. Then, let us propose that a learned man studies the situation and proposes a solution to said curse: move the city to the hills nearby where the scouring winds will keep the flies at bay.'

They reached a stone-walled cellar. Here Humble lit a lantern and led the way to an arched portal sealed by an iron-barred gate, which he unlocked. 'An excavation for a wine cellar here revealed much more,' he explained, pointing to a hole in the floor where a ladder led on down. 'Now, the leaders of this fair – but cursed – city, land-owners all, were naturally horrified by the idea of all their property becoming worthless and so they hired local assassins to put an end to such unwelcome talk.'

Stepping down off the ladder Krute was astonished to find himself in a corridor of brick lined by niches. 'Burial catacombs,' Humble told him, leaning close. 'They date back thousands of years.' He motioned onward. 'This way, if you please. These killers, now, all local, were themselves victims of this wasting disease, with milky eyes and withered limbs. And all had lost sisters, brothers and parents to the fevers. But – and here is where the tale demonstrates the perversity of humanity – they accepted the contract to kill this scholar.' The ironmonger turned to Krute. 'Is that not, well, so sadly predictable?'

The assassin rubbed the back of a hand against his jaw. *Won't this man ever shut up?* 'Sounds like waters too deep for me, sir.'

'Are they?' the man asked, his eyes bright in the gloom. Then he shrugged. 'Perhaps so.' He waved a hand. 'Well, just ten years later the city was an abandoned fever-infested field of ruins in any case.'

'Your point being?'

'Ah!' Humble got to his knees and began pulling bricks from the wall. Slowly, brick by brick, a small opening was revealed. He invited Krute to slither in. For a moment Krute wondered whether the man intended to kill him, or bury him alive, or some such thing. But he knew the guild would avenge his death and he also knew that Humble was aware of this. Nevertheless, he decided some measure of caution was called for and so he motioned Humble ahead.

'After you.'

A shrug. 'If you wish.'

Within, the darkness hinted at a larger room, perhaps a burial chamber. Humble edged inward, lantern pushed along ahead. Krute followed. What he saw took his breath away. A sea of gold reflected the already golden flame. Stacks of bars set out in rows crammed the tomb. A fortune countless leaps beyond any of Krute's imaginings.

'Poured by myself and a few trusted aides in the very works above our heads,' Humble murmured with a touch of pride. 'All of this is yours should you succeed in the contract.'

'And that contact?' Krute answered, distracted. He didn't move his gaze from the neatly heaped bars. *Take twenty men all day to move this mountain . . .*

'The contract, and my point, is that I still want the Legate's head. Even if his improvements or plans for the city are somehow in alignment with my own, they are not what I planned and so I want his head.'

Krute's nod was one of slow deliberate agreement. *Vindictiveness. You can always count on that. The guild practically survives on it.* He thought of Vorcan now standing behind the Legate. *No doubt she means to retake the guild – then there will be a harrowing!* 'The man has powerful allies . . .'

'Thus this astonishing price.'

Krute rubbed his stubbled cheek once more, swallowed hard. 'Speaking for the guild, ironmonger, we agree to try again. But it will take some time to prepare.'

'I understand. Time you have. This chamber will remain sealed until you succeed. And should we both die in what comes – it will remain sealed for ever.'

'We have an agreement then, Humble Measure.'

On a rooftop across the broad avenue facing the main doors of the Eldra Iron Mongers Rallick Nom lay prone, chin resting on a fist, crossbow cradled in an elbow. He'd watched while Krute entered the closed and now quiet works, and kept watch until, many hours later, the man exited as well.

So, Humble Measure wasn't a man to abandon a task half finished. Rallick could tell from the character of his old friend's thoughtful and distracted walk that he was already planning ahead, considering the coming job.

What to do? Too late to kill the client now. An agreement's already been struck. The guild will follow through regardless. A matter of reputation. And I'm in the crosshairs. Have to find a place to lie low; somewhere no one's going to come hunting. And there's only one place comes to mind . . . Hope he won't object to house guests.

Rallick pushed himself backwards along the slate-shake roof.

*   *   *

A knock at the door to his offices drew Ambassador Aragan out of his thoughts as he stood at the window overlooking the city. He'd been thinking of the troubling lack of word from the north – it wasn't like K'ess to be out of touch for this long. Nor had word come from the south, either, for that matter. It was oddly as if events outside the city were somehow unreal, or suspended in time. A bizarre sensation.

He turned at the knock, growling, 'Yes?'

A trooper, one of his personal guard, opened the door. 'Trouble downstairs, sir.'

Coming down, Aragan found a city Warden in the open doorway, the rest of his detachment waiting outside. His own guard was ranged across the bottom of the stairs, tensed, awaiting his command.

'Ambassador Aragan,' the city Warden officer called, 'you are summoned to an audience with the Legate.'

At least this Legate sent an escort of twenty . . . anything less would have been an insult.

'Stand down ranks,' he ordered. Passing the sergeant, he murmured, 'Remain until I return.'

'Sir.'

Aragan stopped before the Warden, gestured to invite the man outside. 'After you.'

The man's gaze slid over the solid front of Malazan veterans and his lips compressed. He backed up then aside to allow Aragan to exit. The detachment formed up to either side of the ambassador and the officer waved a hand. They marched off, heading, Aragan knew, for Majesty Hill.

Along the way, the only thing of interest Aragan noted was the scar of recent construction that marred the grounds atop the hill. A broad trench had been dug up and back-filled. It cut through crushed gravel walkways, ornamental hedges and beds of flowering perennials. He only caught a glimpse as they passed, but it appeared to describe an immense arc heading off round the buildings. *Some sort of defensive installation? Pits?*

Then he was hurried along through the interminable stone halls of the complex. To his surprise and growing discomfort, he was not escorted as he'd expected straight to Council. Rather, he was taken into older dusty halls where they met almost no one save for the odd harried-looking clerk. Was he to be imprisoned? Questioned?

The way led to what he recognized from formal gatherings as the Great Hall. The largest of the surviving ancient wings of Majesty

Hall. Guards pushed open one of the immense copper and bronze panelled doors and Aragan was escorted in.

The long hall was, for the most part, empty. The only light entered in long shafts from openings high up where the pale marble of the walls met the arched roof. A small scattering of people waited at the far end where one fellow sat on a large seat, or throne, of white stone blocks: the Legate. As Aragan had heard rumoured, the man had indeed taken to wearing a gold mask. However, a few of the gathered coterie also sported gold masks – slim things that encircled their eyes and covered only the upper half of their faces.

The escort stopped Aragan directly before what he guessed he ought to consider a 'throne'. He crossed his arms, waiting. In time the Legate ceased his low conversation with an old man – a rather jarring figure in his old tattered clothes amid the glittering finery and riches on display among the coterie. This fellow stepped forward, hunched, hands clasped to his chest as if hugging himself.

'Ambassador Aragan,' he began, almost cringing, 'I speak for the Legate.'

Aragan ignored the ridiculous figure and addressed the Legate. 'You speak to the Imperium when you speak to me . . . you should show proper respect.'

The old man glanced backward to the Legate – like a dog to its master, Aragan thought. 'Invaders, thieves and murders deserve no respect,' he said, gulping as if in horror of what he'd just announced.

'Darujhistan was more than eager to cooperate with us in the crushing of the Pannions,' Aragan observed as drily as he could manage given his growing anger.

'Self-interest guided us both in that,' the old man said. 'Now, that same self-interest should guide your diminished forces north to Cat in a withdrawal and complete abandonment of the lands of South Genabackis.'

'That is your demand?'

'Such is our generous offer.'

Aragan couldn't help himself; he had to drawl, 'Or what?'

The figure on the throne gave one lazy flick of a hand. 'Or they will be annihilated,' the old man said, disbelief in his hoarse voice.

A number of the gathered crowd hissed their anxiety at that announcement; clearly it was far beyond anything they anticipated. All faces, masked and otherwise, now turned to study Aragan. He squinted his scepticism and opened his hands. 'With what? By whom? You have no army worth the name.'

'We need no army,' said the old man, rubbing his chest. 'We merely speak for all the peoples of the south. It is they who will throw off
your foreign yoke.'

'Or trade a new one for an old one, I suspect,' Aragan answered,
now eyeing the masked figure with new suspicion.

'We merely advise and guide . . . just as a caring parent wishes the
best for his children.'

Aragan cocked a bow. 'What?' *Where did that come from?*

One of the masked followers – a tall fellow with a great mane of
salted hair – motioned curtly then, and the spokesman bowed. 'The
audience is at an end. You have our terms. Follow them or many will
die.'

The Wardens urged Aragan back. He retreated, eyeing the masked
Legate who sat so immobile on his throne. Was that even the Lim
in truth, he wondered. Yet he'd recognized a number of councillors
among the crowd. *They would know him. Surely they would not put
up with some impostor.*

His thoughts elsewhere, Aragan allowed himself to be ushered out
and back down Majesty Hill. So, it was all out in the open now. War
had been declared. Yet a war against what, or whom? He felt as if
he was facing a ghost, a shadow. *Who is our enemy? This masked
would-be king? If Darujhistan wants a king in all but name then
that is up to them – we never controlled the city.*

But if the army is attacked . . . well, that is another matter entirely.

Back in the manor house Aragan entered his offices to find the
emissary from the Imperial Throne sitting on his couch, legs outstretched, waiting for him.

In the plain light of day he saw more clearly whom he faced: the tall
thin frame, the oddly shaped eyes, silvered hair. So this was Topper –
true to his descriptions. The once and returned Clawmaster.

'You witnessed? Aragan grunted, and headed to a sideboard to
pour a drink.

'From a distance, yes.'

'A distance?'

'There are some very powerful magi gathered together on that
hilltop.'

Aragan gulped down his drink, studied the lanky, unnerving man.
'Too much for you?'

A thin humourless smile. 'Let's just say it would be counter-
productive for me to tip my hand as yet.' The man's gaze roved about

the room as if uninterested in him. 'And what ridiculous demands were made?'

'Very ridiculous ones. We're to withdraw to the north. Relinquish all territory south of Cat.'

'Including Pale?'

A sombre nod from Aragan. 'Yes. Including Pale.'

'That would not go down well.'

'No. I imagine it wouldn't.'

The man cocked his head like a grackle, watching him. 'And what would you recommend?'

It occurred to Aragan that he was angry. He felt insulted. As if he, and by extension the entire Empire which he represented, had been accorded none of the respect they warranted. He sucked his teeth then finished the last few drops of the rare Moranth liqueur. 'It seems to me that so far whatever it is that now squats on Majesty Hill has done all the pushing. It's long past time someone pushed back.'

The thin slash of a smile drew up, revealing sharp white teeth. 'Mallick chose well in you, I think, Ambassador Aragan.'

'Most of my promotions were under Laseen.'

The smile faltered and the man sat up, leaning forward. The mention of the former Empress seemed to have stung him. Ah yes, Aragan realized. His failure in averting her assassination. 'Yes. A lesson there for all of us.'

'Lesson?' Somehow Aragan could not help probing; it pleased him to be able to penetrate the fellow's irritating manner.

Elbows on his knees and hands hanging loose, the master assassin said, 'That in our line of work we all die alone, Ambassador.'

Aragan didn't know whether to laugh or snort his scorn. What the devil did he mean by that? What line of work? *He* served the Throne.

Topper stood. 'I will begin making my arrangements, then.'

'You've located our assets?'

'Oh yes. And it's time I paid a visit. They will be none too pleased.'

'Is there anything I can do?'

'See to our regular forces, Ambassador. Leave the rest to me.'

Aragan nodded. 'Very good. May Oponn favour you, Clawmaster.'

A clench of pain crossed Topper's face. 'Let's leave those two out of this, shall we?'

*

'I'm tellin' ya it's some kinda foundation . . . but for what I got no idea.' Spindle sat back in his chair and frowned his confusion. 'Seems too flimsy for a wall.'

At the table Picker sent a glance to the historian, Duiker. The man was unaware of her regard, his thoughts obviously distant as he pursued the problem. *Good. May it rouse the man even further.* 'Guards?' she asked Spindle.

'Hardly any. City Wardens, that's it.' The mage drummed his fingers on the table. 'Naw, it's them mages you gotta watch for. Plenty scary, them. Remind me of the Old Guard cadre, Hairlock and Sister Chill.' He rubbed a hand over his greasy shirt. 'You know, I swear one had me cold to rights. But damned if he didn't let me go.'

'Which?' the old man asked.

'The tall one – scholarly look to him.'

The historian grunted, returned to studying the tabletop.

'There's more than them to worry about,' the bard, Fisher, said from the bar.

Picker cocked a brow. 'Oh?'

'Sadly, Envy supports this Legate.'

Blend, behind the bar, let out a long drawn out '*Damn* . . .' The front door opened and a customer entered. Blend sent a cursory glance over then froze, her eyes bulging. 'Look out!' she bellowed and disappeared behind the bar.

Fisher just stared his puzzlement.

Picker knocked over the table to duck behind. Spindle threw himself into a booth. The historian remained in his chair. He eyed the newcomer first with surprise, then distaste. He raised a hand for a halt. 'He came in the *front* door, Blend,' he called.

Blend straightened from behind the bar, a cocked crossbow trained on the man at the door. 'You've got some nerve showing yourself here, y'damned snake.'

The tall fellow held up both gloved hands. 'Now, now. I come in peace.'

Spindle emerged, hand on the shortsword at his side. 'What d'ya want?'

'Just a chat. Let us sit down together over drinks. Reminisce and tell lies of the old days.'

'I'd rather fall into a privy,' Picker said, standing, twin long-knives out.

'Who's this?' Fisher asked Blend.

'Topper. Clawmaster. The Empire's found us.'

Topper looked to the ceiling. 'We never lost track of you, Blend.'

'Everyone relax,' Duiker said. 'If Mallick wanted your heads he wouldn't send *this* one.'

Topper squinted, edging forward. 'Do my eyes deceive me? Not Imperial Historian Duiker?'

'Ex.'

Blend raised her crossbow, pulled out the bolt. Picker sheathed her long-knives and righted the table. 'What're you after?' she grumbled.

'We have a common enemy.'

Blend, Picker, and Spindle shared quick looks, then Picker snorted, 'No we don't.'

Topper pulled a chair to the table. He undid his dark green silk-lined cloak and hung it over the back, then sat. The shirt beneath was a fine satiny forest green. He drew off his gloves and peered round innocently at everyone. 'A drink, perhaps?'

Blend drew a pint from the bar and ambled over. 'Whatever you're sellin' we don't want any,' she growled.

The Clawmaster took the earthenware pint and sipped. He made a face. 'Are you trying to kill me?' Spindle started up from the table and Picker flinched. Topper raised a placating hand. 'A joke.'

Spindle's mocking smile was sickly. 'Very funny.'

Duiker eyed the Clawmaster, his lined face stony behind his grey beard. He steepled his hands on the table. 'What is your proposal? And bear in mind – these soldiers are retired.'

Topper hooked an arm over the top of his chair. He turned the pint in circles before him. 'Retired? Is that what you call it? According to the lists you are all deserters. Except for our honoured historian here.'

'Not according to us,' Picker ground out.

'Dujek told us—' began Spindle.

'He was not in a position to offer anything,' Topper interrupted.

'Don't push that line,' Blend warned from where she now stood behind Topper's chair. 'That dog won't hunt.'

Topper gave a small shrug. 'Fair enough. I understand you've already accepted a contract to collect intelligence. What would it take for you to sign on for something a little more . . . direct?'

'As free agents?' Picker said.

'Yes. Free agents.'

Picker opened her mouth to name something, a price perhaps, but Duiker took hold of her arm, silencing her. He whispered into her ear and her tangled brows rose. She cuffed the old man's shoulder. 'Our price, Clawmaster, is the formal decommissioning of the Bridgeburners.'

Topper's slit gaze glanced aside to the historian and his lips pursed. After turning the mug in circles on the rough slats of the table he gave a slow nod. 'Agreed. It will be arranged.'

'And the job?' Spindle asked nervously.

An easy shrug from the slouched Clawmaster. 'Well . . . it seems for reasons known only to himself this Legate wants a wall built . . . therefore, we should do our best to interfere with that.' His gaze rose to Spindle. 'I take it you have munitions?' The saboteur-trained mage gave a jerked nod. 'Excellent. Then you lot can do what you're best at.'

'And you?' Blend demanded, her chin stuck out.

'I'll provide cover in case there are any . . . complications.'

Picker snorted. 'Somehow I'm not so relieved by that.'

The Clawmaster laid his hands flat on the table. His smile was now supremely assured. 'You should be.'

*　　*　　*

At their servant's table in the kitchens of the Lim estate, Leff let out a long loud sign. Scorch, opposite, roused himself, blinking. 'You say somethin'?'

Leff shook his head. He tucked his hands up under his arms, sighed again. 'You know, Scorch, I don't think anyone's comin' back. I'm gettin' the distinct feeling that we've been handed our hats.'

Scorch's puzzled frown deepened even further. 'Howzat? Hats? I ain't got no hat.'

Leff glared his disapproval. 'It's an expression, man. Means we're fired.'

Scorch goggled at his partner. 'What? Fired? We ain't even been *paid* yet!'

Now Leff banged his chair forward, gaping. 'Ain't been paid yet? How can that be? You're supposed to be in charge of all that.'

Scorch's consternation creased his forehead until his brows met between his small darting eyes. 'I thought you were supposed to be handlin' that.'

Leff pressed a hand to his brow. 'I distinctly remember me saying that you should do it.'

'Oh. Well, we could take it up with the scholar.'

Now Leff's brow wrinkled in bewilderment. 'The scholar? What in the Queen's name does he have to do with any of this?'

'He's with the Legate. I seen him.'

Leff dropped his hand, amazed. 'Burn protect us! Why didn't you say so?'

'You didn't say it was important.'

Leff pushed himself up from the table, stretched his numb legs, wincing. 'Gods, man. You have to learn to think for yourself! I can't be expected to keep doin' all the thinking for us.'

Scorch hung his head. 'Sorry, Leff.'

'Well I should think so!'

City Wardens stopped them at the gate to the Way of Justice leading up Majesty Hill. The two Wardens gripped their wood truncheons. 'You're carrying weapons,' one called, accusing.

Leff and Scorch glanced to their peace-strapped swords, the crossbows over their shoulders. 'Looks like it,' Leff answered and attempted to brush past. The thick wooden portal was closed, however, and he pushed against it to no effect. 'Open up,' he shouted. 'Official business.'

The two Wardens shared smirks. 'Official? You two?'

'Go squat your official business off in the bushes,' the other suggested.

Scorch drew himself up, offended. 'I'll have you know we're all certified, listed and official. I'd go ahead 'n' check if I were you. Otherwise could be consequences.'

'That's right,' Leff put in, though with much less certainty. 'Consequences.'

One of the Wardens banged his truncheon on the rough timbers of the door. A small communicating slit opened. 'Names?' someone demanded from behind the slit.

'Leff and Scorch,' Leff shouted, mouth to the slit.

'All right, all right!' the hidden clerk grumbled. 'You don't have to shout.'

One Warden leaned against the door, arms crossed, shaking his head. Leff adjusted the weight of the crossbow against his shoulder. Scorch dug a finger into his ear and twisted it round.

The heavy door slid backwards and the Warden almost fell with it. He jerked, wildly surprised, and received a superior look from Leff as the latter pushed through. Scorch ambled after, crossbow held behind his neck, arms draped over it. 'Consequences,' he murmured, and winked.

As they wandered their slow way up the twisting path Leff rubbed his unshaven jaw, casting narrowed wondering glances Scorch's way. Finally an idea occurred to him and he gave an exaggerated knowing nod, saying, 'Ah! I get it now . . . good ol' Captain Soen. Ever conscientious, that one. Good guess, Scorch.'

Scorch's permanent scowl of resentful confusion took on an even greater perplexity. 'What're you talking about? I just said that, that's all. Sounded like the kinda thing important persons say.'

Leff used his crossbow to brush aside a clerk who was waving papers at him. 'Sometimes I wonder about you, Scorch. I really do.'

But his partner was ambling down another hall. 'Got us in, didn't it?'

Eventually, after being shooed out of a number of chambers and offices, they found the guarded doors to the Great Hall. Leff approached the city Wardens standing guard, and as one opened his mouth to challenge them bellowed, 'Message for Captain Soen!' The Warden snapped his mouth shut and exchanged an uncertain glance with his fellow. Leff pushed open the small clerk's door and strode in.

'Message for Captain Soen!' Scorch echoed as he stepped through.

'You don't have to say it again!' Leff hissed, pushing him aside.

Scorch pushed back and Leff nearly dropped his crossbow. '*I* got us in, didn't *I*!'

'We're already . . .' Leff tailed off feeling the weight of numerous eyes. He turned.

A great crowd of nobles and councillors filled the length of the Great Hall. All were dressed in rich finery. Many wore masks, as was traditional for the various city religious ceremonies and fetes. Leff bowed, cuffing Scorch, who bowed as well. Dismissing them, the many eyes turned away. Leff scanned the crowd. 'There he is.'

'Who?'

'Soen, dammit! Who else? C'mon.'

They tramped forward. The clank and clatter of their weaponry almost downed out the low murmured conversations. A figure sat motionless on a raised seat of white stone at the far end of the hall. Before Scorch and Leff were halfway across Soen intercepted them, a sharp grip on the forearm of each. He steered them aside into the shadows of a colonnaded walk along one wall of the hall.

'What in the name of the Queen of Mysteries are you two doing here?' he hissed, furious.

Scorch looked to Leff. Leff saluted. 'Reporting in, sir.'

The big man's salted brows clenched. 'What? Reporting? Why?'

A panicked look gripped Leff's lined features, as if he'd reached the end of his gambit and hadn't realized more may be required. 'Ah . . . reporting that the manor house is all secure, sir!'

'*What*? Secure? Who gives a—' The captain bit back his rising voice, peered round, anxious. 'You two are fired,' he said, his voice low and fierce. 'Get out of here and never come back.'

'Fired?' Scorch echoed, outraged. 'What for? Guild rules—'

'Guild rules require justification, I know. Deserting your post. How's that?'

The two shared a pained look. Leff pulled at his lower lip. 'Well . . . I suppose that would kinda do it.'

'It most certainly does. Pay can be collected at the guild office. Now leave – or must I escort you out?' The captain didn't wait for an answer but beckoned others of Lim's private guard over.

'Wait!' a voice called. Captain Soen turned and immediately bowed to one knee. 'Sir.'

Scorch and Leff were astonished to see their old employer, the scholar Ebbin. Something like wonder was on the man's face as he gazed upon them. 'I . . . know . . . you,' he breathed, as if awed by the realization.

Leff knuckled his brow. 'Yes, sir. Been working for you for some time now, sir.'

The old man's gaze seemed to wander as he stood, brows furrowed in concentration. 'Yes. I remember. I . . . remember you.' He glanced to the captain. 'These men work for me, Soen. They are my guards.'

The captains' brows climbed almost all the way up to the rim of his helmet. He shot a glance to the immobile and silent figure on the throne, blew out a breath. 'Well . . . if you say so . . . sir.'

'They may remain.'

Soen was obviously still very confused, but as a good private soldier he accepted his employer's dictates – no matter how stupid in his estimation. He saluted. 'Yes, sir.'

Leff saluted too. Then he cuffed Scorch, who also saluted.

But the scholar had wandered off. He'd pulled out a cloth and was wiping his sweaty strained face, the other hand rubbing his chest. Captain Soen scowled down at the pair; then he nodded to himself. 'I see it now. Friends in high places. Looks like I'm stuck with you.'

He eyed them up and down again, his disgust increasing. 'At least get yourselves cleaned up.'

Scorch straightened, outraged. 'I washed just a few weeks ago!'

'Your clothes and armour, man! Clean them up.'

Leff saluted. 'Yessir. Right away sir.'

The captain just shook his head, jerked a thumb to another of his guards. 'Willa here will kit you out. Come back when you're presentable.'

'Yes sir! With pleasure, sir!'

Soen answered with half salute, half dismissive wave. 'Whatever. Get out of here – *now*.'

* * *

They travelled at night once they entered the desolate hills of the Dwelling Plain. Despite this, and all Fist Steppen's many precautions in water conservation, they still lost irreplaceable mounts and dray animals. Even a few men and women collapsed under the unrelenting pace. Some died; others recuperated in the wagons trailing the column.

That pace was nightmare for Bendan. Never having had cause to walk for longer than one bell – *what in Fanderay's name for? There was never any need* – he couldn't believe what was being demanded of them. What in all the Lost Lands could be so important? He managed to keep up, but barely. He walked in a daze and knew he'd be no use in a fight. Not that there'd been any raids. But still, he felt defenceless, hardly able to stand.

This day their scout, a Rhivi exile named Tarat – word was the young woman had killed a relative – raised her hand and crouched, studying the dry dusty ground. Sergeant Hektar joined her, and, bored, Bendan staggered over.

'What is it?' the giant Dal Hon rumbled.

'The column has crossed this trail,' she answered, a hand indicating a line northward.

'So?'

'It's like nothing I have ever seen before.'

'So?'

The girl blew out a breath and pushed the unruly kinked hair from her freckled face. 'Malazan. I know every spoor on the face of these lands. If I see something new it is a strange matter. Still . . . this trail reminds me of something. Something from an old story . . .'

Bendan simply took the opportunity for a breather; and he didn't mind standing looking down at the tribal girl, either. Fine haunches she had. Too bad she also had a knife for anyone who got too close.

He pulled out his skin of water and took a pull. He was about to take another when Hektar pushed the skin down.

'That's enough, trooper. You know the water rules.'

'I know I'm damned thirsty.'

'You'll be even more thirsty two days from now when you run out.'

Both of them jumped when the Rhivi girl let out a shout of alarm and scrambled back from the trail as if it was a snake that had reared at her. 'What is it?' Hektar demanded.

Tarat's gaze swung to them, her eyes huge with wonder. 'I have to speak to the commander.' Almost the entire column had passed now. Hektar drew off his helmet to wipe his dark sweaty face. 'She's with the van . . .' he began.

'I must. Immediately.'

Hektar sighed his disgust. He wiped the leather liner inside the helmet then pulled it on again. 'All right. Let's go.'

'I'll tell Little,' Bendan said.

'No – you're comin' with us. Let's go.'

'What for? You got her. You don't need me.'

'You seen it too. Now c'mon.'

'Aw, for Hood's sake . . .' But the big sergeant crooked a finger and started after the scout. Bendan dragged himself along behind.

The van was a damned long way ahead. First, they were all mounted, something which irked Bendan no end. Why should they be mounted when the rest of them had to plod along? And second, they were all so much cleaner and better accoutred than he. Something that also never failed to stir his resentment. Why should they wear such superior armour – cuirasses of hammered iron and banded hauberks – when all he wore was a hauberk of boiled leather faced with ring mail, with mailed sleeves? It was his general view that anyone with better equipment than his, or with greater wealth, just didn't deserve it.

In response to a signal from the sergeant a messenger rode over, spoke to him briefly, then wheeled off to take his request to the Fist. Shortly thereafter a small mounted body broke off from the van to return to them. It was Fist Steppen, accompanied by a small guard and her inner staff. They parted around the three waiting troopers. Sergeant Hektar saluted the dumpy sunburned woman in her sweat-stained riding trousers and loose shirting, and noticed that the skin of her forehead was peeling.

'Fist Steppen.'

'You have a report?'

Hektar gestured to Tarat. 'Our Rhivi scout has news.'

Tarat saluted, quite smartly. Steppen nodded to her. 'The trail the column passed just back—' the girl began, but was interrupted.

'We all saw it,' an officer put in. 'A band marching double-file, north. Bandits, perhaps.'

Tarat's hand snapped closed on the bone-handled knife at her side and she glared at the man.

Steppen raised a hand for silence. 'Continue,' she said to Tarat.

The girl did so, but still glared murder at the officer. 'No bandits – or even soldiers – have the discipline to maintain such a straight trail. Look to our own meandering track if you don't believe me. Men and women pause to adjust gear, to relieve themselves, to remove stones from their sandals. Only one people are capable of moving across the land in this manner. It is said they can march for four days and nights without a single pause.'

'It is said?' Steppen asked, cocking her head.

Tarat lost her glare, removed her hand from her blade. 'In our stories, Fist. Among us Rhivi are told stories of these people. Most speak darkly of them.'

'And they are?'

Tarat was clearly unwilling to say just who she was talking about, but asked directly she hunched slightly, as if expecting scorn, and said, 'The Seguleh.'

Bendan laughed out loud. Hektar glared for him to shut up but he couldn't help it. The Fist arched a brow. 'You have something to add, trooper? I see you too are a local. What is your opinion?'

He waved a hand in apology. 'I'm sorry, ma'am. It's just . . . the *Seguleh*? Scary stories for children only, ma'am.'

'I assure you they are quite real.'

'Oh yes. Real enough. Down south. I'd say they're damned good all right – damned good at puffing up their reputation, if you follow me, ma'am.'

Leather creaked as the Fist leaned forward on to her pommel. 'You are from Darujhistan, yes?'

'Yes, m'am.'

'And the opinion you express regarding these people . . . this would be typical of the city, would it?'

'Oh, yes. Just a lot of tall tales.'

'I see. Thank you. Very informative.' She turned to Tarat. 'Thank you for your report. That is all.'

The troop edged their mounts aside and cantered off to return to the van. Tarat whirled to face Bendan. 'Laugh at me again and I'll slit you open like a weasel. Yes?'

Bendan held out his arms. 'Yeah. Fine. Whatever.'

The tribal girl stalked away on those fine haunches.

Gods! So damned prickly!

CHAPTER XI

We are the freemen privateers.
We sail the forested isles
from Callows to far Galatan!
We have thrown off the chains
of yoke, coin and tyrant.
So join us who dare to be free!

The Freemen Privateers
Author unknown

BARATHOL HAD TAKEN TO SLEEPING IN HIS WORK TENT. DURING THE late afternoon he'd drop in on the house to make sure little Chaur was fed and clean. He didn't blame Scillara for her lack of maternal instincts – he was resigned to it. Perhaps it balanced what he admitted might be was his own over-developed nurturing instinct.

This night he was bringing up the heat of the forge, readying for another shift, when heard a strange sound. It seemed to be coming from the excavation trench. Outside the tent, the work crew was on break and all should have been silent, yet intermittent clanging or thumping reached him. He stepped out into the dig, listening.

He thought it came from the exposed stone blocks themselves. Kneeling, he placed an ear close to the cold smooth stone. Shortly, he heard it: a clanging or banging reverberating down the stones. It sounded as if someone was digging somewhere along the now nearly completed arc of set blocks. He stood to peer about; no one was around. The mages who oversaw the installations never arrived until much later. Frowning, he picked up a crowbar and set off to walk the circuit.

He sensed nothing strange until halfway round the nearly completed circle. Here the arc cut through a patch of woods dense in underbrush, part of an artificial park planted on the hilltop. Damn good cover, it occurred to him, and he immediately ducked down to take advantage. Edging forward, he found another excavation, this one much smaller. A pit had been dug over the arc of the stone ring. Even as he watched, dirt flew up to land in the brush. *What in the Twins' name was this?*

Then he sensed someone behind him. He spun, gripping the crowbar horizontally. Steel rang from the heavy tool and a wide burly figure readied for another thrust. Barathol fell, swinging the crowbar; it glanced from a shin and the figure grunted her – *her?* – pain, tumbling. As the assassin fell her foot caught him across the throat. Both rolled in the dirt, gasping. Barathol rose just in time to block another stab then readied the crowbar for a swing but stopped, astonished. His attacker also froze.

'Barathol?' she said, amazed.

'Blend?'

'What in the Queen's name're you doing here?' she snarled, wincing and holding her shin.

'What are you marines up to?' he demanded.

A needle-point pricked his back and a voice whispered from behind, 'The Legate has declared war on Malaz, friend. Time to choose sides.'

'Don't do it, Topper,' Blend warned.

Topper? Where had he heard that name before?

Blend straightened, tested her weight on her leg. 'Stand aside, Barathol. This is nothing to do with you.'

'Barathol?' said the one named Topper. 'Mekhar? Kalam's brother?'

'Yes.'

The knife point pressed harder for an instant, as if its holder were of a mind to finish him quickly then and there. He wasn't the type to go quietly and he almost moved rather than just stand and be slaughtered but the thought of little Chaur without stopped him and he froze, tensed, his limbs twitching.

'Don't,' Blend urged Topper. 'He's a friend.'

The blade withdrew – slightly. 'Are you, Barathol . . . a friend?'

'This is just a job. I have rent to pay. A family to feed. I'm lucky to have any work.'

'If it's just a question of coin – you'll have it.'

'On your word?'

'Yes.'

Barathol allowed himself a small shrug. 'Then I'll be on my way. This isn't my business.'

'Very well. On your way. But I'll be watching. One word to anyone and you'll die. Understood?'

'Yeah. I know the drill.'

The blade pricked him to urge him on. He nodded to Blend and headed off. A few steps later he tossed the crowbar into the woods and continued along the path.

At the trench the work crew had returned to prepping the foundation. Barathol made a show of straightening his trousers as he descended into the trench. He pushed aside the tent flap and ducked in. The tall mage was there waiting for him, staff of old wood in one hand.

'Where were you?' he growled.

'Call of nature.'

'Took your time.'

'I'm not eating right these days.'

'How much do you think I care about the state of your bowels?'

Barathol held a hand over the coals, thrust in a bar to stir them. 'You asked.'

'Don't leave the forge again. We are on a timetable. There can be no delay.'

Over his shoulder Barathol studied the strangely lean angular fellow. 'Oh? To accomplish what?'

The man's eyes seemed to flare and he clasped the staff in both hands. The wood creaked in the fierce grip. 'That is not your concern,' he ground out.

Barathol shrugged. He gestured to the wood and leather bellows. 'Work those for me then.'

The mage sneered. The fresh scars on his face twisted in disgust. 'Find another to do that, imbecile.'

Barathol threw down the bar. 'Fine. More delay.'

He impressed a worker from the crew to help on the bellows. The entire time, the mage paced the narrow confines of the tent. The work might have gone as usual, but for Barathol it seemed to flow as slowly as the silver melting in the glowing ceramic crucible. He kept suppressing the urge to peer over his shoulder, and he hunched at particularly loud bangs and crashes of dropped equipment in the trench.

All the time, he felt the gaze of the mage on his back like the twin impressions of heated dagger-points. Finally, the work was done. Both moulds were poured, and the mage shouldered him aside to inspect the cooling bars. 'These appear acceptable,' he growled, bent over them. A flicked hand dismissed Barathol, who straightened his back with a murmured 'You're welcome'.

He pushed aside the heavy canvas flap and stepped out into cool dawn air. He drew a cloth from inside his shirt and wiped his face and hands, then stood still for a moment, enjoying the caress of the wind. Walking up from the trench he paused, glanced back towards the distant woods hidden behind a wing of the rambling complex of Majesty Hall. *No alarm as yet. Not even a peep. Reconnoitring? Investigating the stones? Or . . . no, they wouldn't dare try* that, *would they?*

Best to be far away in any case.

He headed for a twisting walkway down the hill.

Halfway down he flinched as a boom creaked over the hillside, echoing and rolling into the distance. It sounded eerily like broad sails catching a brisk wind. He turned in time to see a great cloud of dirt and dust billowing up over the tiled rooftops of the various buildings crowding the hilltop. He could even make out the clattering of rocks as they tumbled down the cliffs. Distant shouts and screams sounded. He hung his head. *Damn! Now I have to go back for a look – it would be strange if I didn't.*

He turned round to climb the walkway.

City Wardens had already formed a cordon holding everyone back from the crater smoking in the pocket forest. He identified himself as a worker on the installation and so was let through. He found his two bosses – the hunchback and the hooknose, as he thought of them – investigating the site. The hooknose caught sight of him and waved him closer. He edged his way down into the pit. The loose dirt was hot beneath his sandals.

The hooknose rose from studying the arc of exposed blocks. To Barathol the stones looked to be discoloured and scorched, but otherwise intact. The mage eyed him sourly. 'What do you think?' he asked.

Barathol allowed himself a shrug. 'Moranth munitions, I imagine.'

The hooknose, ever in an ugly temper, looked to the sky. 'Obviously, fool! No, the blocks. The links – how are they?'

'I'll have to examine them, I suppose.'

'Well do so!' and the man swept aside, curtly waving him forward.

Suppressing his own temper, Barathol knelt next to the course of blocks and began brushing away the dirt. He found the twin pins and used his shirt-tails to clean them, spitting and wiping. Leaning close, he studied the silver for cracks, the hair-line skein of shattering, or other surface distortions such as stress from flexing. He studied four in all, two exposed sets, but saw no damage that he could make out. Throughout the entire examination the two mages hovered close, shadowing his every move.

He leaned back, motioning to the exposed course. 'There's no damage that I can see. Amazing, that. The blast must have been enormous.'

Over Barathol's head the two mages shared looks of savage satisfaction. 'So we conclude as well,' said the hunchback.

The hooknose waved him away. 'That is all – you may go.'

He inclined his head then clawed his way up the steep side of the blast pit. The Malazans must have back-filled it to contain the force, he thought to himself. Yet the explosion had failed to mar the stones at all. He could only conclude that the blocks were ensorcelled against such attacks.

News to pass on to the Malazans. But no doubt they'd discover the failure of their opening move soon enough.

*

Blend, Picker, and Duiker were playing cards. Or at least pretending to. None seemed to have their mind on the game. Spindle paced, stopping on every lap of the common room to peer out of the window. Fisher was at the bar plucking out a composition.

'Do you think he talked?' Spindle asked of the room in general.

'Topper's watching,' Blend said, irritated.

''Cause he might've.'

'Shut up, Spin. We'll hear all about it.'

Spindle rubbed his shirt. 'Should've gone by now,' he murmured.

'Don't trust your own work?' Picker asked, cocking an eye.

'It's been a while, okay?'

'Like *never*.' Picker smirked at Blend.

'I'm trained!'

'So you keep claiming, Spin. So you claim.'

'Well . . . I am. Okay?'

Then a sound like a loud booming gust of wind passed over the bar and everyone stilled. The empty bottles on the bar rattled.

Blend and Picker both eased back in their chairs, letting go long breaths. 'There you go,' Picker said, lifting a glass. Blend clacked hers with Picker's and they tossed back the liquor.

Spindle raised his fists. 'There! I *told* you. Two cussers! There ain't nothing left. Ha!'

'Good job,' Duiker told Spindle. 'Now have a seat, will you?'

Spindle pulled up a chair. 'What are we playing?'

Before mid-day a knock sounded at the door. Spindle pushed himself from the table. 'That couldn't be Topper, could it?' He headed across.

Before Spindle reached the door Picker's head snapped over and she dropped her cards. 'Get away from there!' she shouted.

Spindle turned. 'What?'

The door burst from its hinges in a blast of light and heat that knocked Spindle flat. Blend and Picker upturned the table, cards flying, and ducked behind pulling Duiker with them. Fisher leapt over the bar.

Dazed, Spindle raised his head to see the crab-like figure of the hunched mage in his loose layered rags lumbering into the room. The man's arms hung unnaturally long and the hands seemed grotesquely oversized and warped. He gestured savagely and the table protecting Blend and Picker punched backwards. 'Too obvious, Bridgeburners!' he bellowed. 'Too damned obvious!'

In answer Spindle rolled aside, shouting, 'Clear!'

Blend and Picker appeared from behind the table, threw in unison.

Twin explosions tore into the mage, lacerating his already tattered clothes. The blast threw him back into a wall. Fisher stood up behind the bar, a crossbow levelled. He fired and the bolt took the invader in the chest. Spindle had crawled to a far corner. Now he stood, reaching for the one munition he always carried for just such an end-game.

An arm in a rich brocaded silk sleeve grasped his arm and twisted it painfully backwards. Spindle looked up into the snarling features of the tall mage. The man shook him like a dog. 'Do not make me do what I might otherwise avoid doing, Bridgeburner,' he hissed through clenched teeth. Spindle reached for his shortsword but remembered he wasn't wearing it. *Twins take it! You drop your guard for one moment* . . . 'Now we shall see – she will not tolerate this insult,' the man said, scanning the common room.

A girl appeared next to Fisher. She wore the airy white clothes of a dancing girl but brandished a wicked slim dagger. The bard smashed the crossbow into her, sending her staggering back. The shocked outrage on her face was almost comical to Spindle. Fisher threw aside the mangled weapon and raised his empty hands.

Great Osserc! The man broke a crossbow over her!

The girl darted in once more. Somehow the bard grasped her wrist. He twisted the arm in a tight circle and Spindle heard the snap of the joint clear across the room. The girl voiced her agony in an inhuman guttural snarl.

Ye gods, who is this man?

Even the fellow holding Spindle by one fist eyed the bard, unease wrinkling his brow.

A shape appeared before the table behind which Blend and Picker were crouching once more and Spindle's hair shirt writhed with agitation. It was a haunt, a ghost. It snatched them both by the necks. 'I have them,' it announced. Duiker rose, slashing with a long-knife, but the blade passed harmlessly through it.

'Just kill them,' snarled one who had taken the crossbow bolt. He straightened brushing at his smouldering rags, then took hold of the bolt and yanked on it. 'At least we've cleared out this rats' nest early on.' He cocked his lopsided head to Fisher. 'Stand aside, bard. We've no quarrel with you.'

'*No quarrel?*' the girl snarled, furious, cradling her broken arm.

Fisher inclined his head in greeting to each. 'Aman. Barukanal. Hinter.' He raised a brow to the girl.

'Your future killer,' she said, baring her teeth.

Despite Blend's and Picker's struggles the revenant maintained his grip. He slammed them into the wall, yet their blows and tearing hands swept through him as if he were smoke. Duiker backed away, calling, 'Spin!'

Spindle gaped. *What? Set my Warren against these mages?*

'Perhaps questions are in order,' Hinter said.

The stairs leading from the upper floors creaked and everyone stilled. All knew that no one else was present within the old building. All eyes moved to the open portal where the stairs rose. A hunched figure stepped out, cloaked, a large hood down. Her thin hair shone silver. Her face was deeply tanned and weathered. Black glittering eyes settled on Hinter and Spindle was shaken to glimpse their depths.

'Begone,' she said, and waved. The shade of Hinter faded away, astonishment on its face. Blend and Picker fell to the floor, gasping in breaths.

The girl backed away towards the door. Aman raised his hands. 'What can these be to you?' he demanded as he too edged to the door.

'They are not important,' the old woman said, slowly advancing. 'What is important is that I did not give you leave to enter my house. Therefore, you must go.'

'*Your* house?' Aman said. 'Not for ages.'

'Blood has been shed. What has been done is done.'

Aman threw down the crossbow bolt and hurried to the door with his limping shambling gait. He waved to the girl. 'Come. *He* must be apprised of this.'

The old woman turned on the one Fisher had named Barukanal. The mage released Spindle's arm, bowed ever so faintly. 'Foolish, to make things all so clear.'

'I am taking no one's side but my own. And there is nothing any of you can do about it.'

The tall hatchet-faced mage bowed again, thoughtfully. 'Perhaps not *us* . . .' he allowed. He peered down at Spindle. 'Your gambit of Moranth munitions was inspired, but ineffective. The . . . structure . . . is proofed against *their* alchemy.' The man glared then, holding Spindle's gaze, as if meaning to say more.

'Go,' the old woman commanded.

The mage winced, the scars across his face rippling. 'I have no choice but to obey,' he murmured, his voice thick. Bowing, he backed away to the door.

Picker crowded the smoking doorway after him. 'And don't come back!' she yelled. She turned to the room. 'Our thanks, old . . . where'd she go?'

Spindle looked up from rubbing his numb elbow. Blend was righting the table. She peered about as well. 'She's buggered off.'

'She's still here,' Duiker said. Fisher was setting out glasses on the bar, and the historian watched him fill them with Free Cities white wine. 'This is her house. We can all use a drink, I imagine.' Everyone took a glass. 'To our host,' Duiker announced. 'K'rul.'

Spindle, who had started drinking already, spluttered his mouthful down his shirtfront. 'The hoary old one himself? Not just some city mage who's taken up residence? Well, why doesn't she just curse these wretches to the Abyss? Or snap her fingers?'

'Because she's under assault everywhere,' Fisher said. 'I'd wager her direct influence extends only to these four walls.'

The old historian was nodding. 'I didn't like Barukanal's – Hood,

Baruk's – comment. They'll send soldiers next. Regular mundane agents.'

Spindle winced. *Just us mortals. K'rul wouldn't be able to help them out then.*

'Or assassins . . .' Picker snarled.

Blend slammed down the empty glass. 'I hope so. I want their blood.'

Spindle peered round. 'Yeah – and speakin' of them, just where's Topper, anyway?'

Blend sneered. 'The useless blowhard! Looks like four of them is four too many.'

*　　*　　*

She spent her days turning pots. A fever of work seemed to have taken hold of her. As if Darujhistan suffered from a crushing lack of pots, urns, and amphorae that she alone could answer.

And why would there be such a shortage?

Because all the rest are broken.

The malformed mass of clay squashed in Tiserra's hands and she threw herself back, panting, pushed sweaty hair from her face with a forearm. She stopped working the pedals of the wheel with her bare feet.

A time of great shattering.

She cleaned her hands in a basin of water and walked through the empty house as she dried them. *Gone again.* She could not stop that niggling question: *Fleeing her?*

No. He had his life just as she had hers.

She stopped at one particular place in the floor. Kneeling, she tapped, listening. *Had he?*

She went to her shop to return with a clawed bar. With this she attacked the floorboards, found the dug-out space below. Empty. He'd never taken them with him before.

All those strange Moranth items, gone. Why this time?

She hammered the floorboards back into place, and, standing, pushed up her sleeves. *Best get back to work. There will be a great need soon.*

*　　*　　*

They climbed the stairs single file. Antsy led, crossbow freshly reassembled and cocked. Orchid came next, followed by Corien. They made much better time now they all could see. Granted, it was not the clear vision of daylight, but it was far better than total blindness. And Antsy thought his vision was even improving as he got used to discerning the subtle shadings of blues, mauves and deepest near-black.

The majestic circling stairwell ended at a wide arch-roofed hallway. Chandeliers of glowing blue crystals hung at intervals, floating like clouds of fireflies. Trash littered the polished stone floor: shards of smashed vases and pots, ornate alien sculpture and broken stone statuary. Yet there was no cloth, leather or wood. Nor anything of obvious value such as jewellery or gold or silver artwork. In the distance one chandelier had fallen, leaving a patch of darkness and a jumble of the blue crystals bright on the floor like a scattering of coals. There was no sign of Malakai, though Antsy was sure he must be ahead of them.

Again he was surprised by just how empty the place was. Where was everyone? Hundreds must've taken boats out over the months. They couldn't all be dead . . . could they? The memory of those clawing hands and desperate starved faces in Pearl Town returned and he wanted to spit but he couldn't draw enough saliva.

'Anyone?' Orchid asked, her voice pitched so low as to be almost inaudible.

'No. But someone may be around.'

'Oh?'

'Yes,' Corien said, 'all the combustibles are gone.'

'Uh-huh,' Antsy seconded. 'Picked clean. Which way?' he asked Orchid.

She edged further up the hall, stepping carefully over the scattered debris, she sighed, a hand going to her mouth.

'What is it?' Antsy asked.

She glanced to him then lowered her gaze, embarrassed. 'This hall. Beautiful, even yet. The Curtain Hall of the Hunter.'

'What?'

'This could be it. One of the Twenty Halls . . . one for each of their ancient zodiac. Each has its own name, architecture, history. There will be temples, cloisters, living quarters. A lot of rooms.'

'Fine,' Antsy cut in. 'Just which way?'

She turned back, glaring, but sighed again, adjusting her skirts. 'Straight, for now.'

'Okay. Take this.' He handed her the crossbow. It yanked her arms down.

'I can't use this. What am I supposed to do?'

'Fire off a shot at any hostiles.'

'Oh, certainly.'

Antsy waved Corien to the right then drew his long-knives. Orchid followed, the heavy crossbow braced in both arms. They advanced along one edge of the wide hall. Far ahead awaited a tall set of double doors, ajar. Darkness lay beyond. They passed portals that opened on to smaller side halls and chambers. Some were dark, others were lit by the glowing feline faces that Antsy figured to be stylized representations of the Children of the Night themselves. From his own memories of those faces he was glad none remained on the Spawn.

Short of the tall doors the air currents brought a new draught to his face and he raised his hand for a halt. People. The unmistakable stomach-churning miasma of latrine-stink mixed with sweat and cooking odours. He motioned to a nearby portal and they slipped inside.

Watching intently, he could now see a shifting brightness flickering from the right side of the hall. Firelight, and people moving. And above the constant groans and rumblings that reverberated through the rock around them came the murmur of voices and the occasional clatter of gear.

'Now what?' Corien mouthed.

Orchid motioned to the left. Antsy shook his head. She made an impatient face demanding explanation. Antsy leaned close. 'They're ignoring it. Therefore, there mustn't be any route up or down that way. Yes?' She appeared unconvinced, but subsided. He motioned Corien close. 'We need to find a way round.'

'I'll have a look.'

'No—'

He stood up but Antsy pulled him back: a bright light was approaching. A man appeared walking up one of the right-hand halls. He was carrying the smallest of lanterns yet to Antsy's dark-adjusted vision the light seemed as intense as the sun. The man stopped at a side opening, threw something in that clattered amid debris, then set down the lantern and started undoing the ties at the front of his trousers.

Orchid turned her face away.

A stream of urine hissed against the stone floor.

Wonderful. They were skulking in the cesspit

Finished, the man hawked up a great mouthful of phlem and spat, then picked up the lantern and headed back up the hall. Embarrassed, Antsy did not look at Orchid when he motioned them across. He'd chosen the darkest of the right-hand halls, hoping that it would perhaps lead to a way round the camp. Once within it was obvious to Antsy that it was indeed dark, even to him. There was no source of the blue night-light in the hall. A side portal beckoned just beyond and he had started towards it, for it meaning to talk things over with Orchid – perhaps she could provide some sort of light – when he stepped on someone.

The woman shrieked to crack open the very rock and Antsy leapt backwards. 'Shit!'

Many voices arose around them, clamouring, shouting. *Sleeping quarters? They'd stumbled into the fucking sleeping quarters?* He waved Orchid and Corien back.

Pounding feet sounded from a number of the side corridors. Antsy pushed Orchid back across the main hall into the maze of left-hand passages. She thrust the crossbow at him and he sheathed his longknives to take it. 'What are we doing?' she hissed.

'Hiding. Now, c'mon.'

He led them up a side corridor, turned a corner and stopped dead. Now he knew why the left-hand side of the complex was being ignored. The corridor was blocked by heaped rubble. They'd stopped up the route. *Hood take it!* He motioned for a reverse through another chamber. After just a few further twists and turns, the inhabitants of the encampment yelling and rushing about behind them, they came to yet another blocked doorway. *Shit! There's no other way!* He led them back towards the main hall. *Have to double back, hope to find a different route.*

They came out on to the main hall close to the tall double doors. Antsy stepped out first, crouched, crossbow ready. The hall appeared empty. He listened for a time. All the noise seemed to be coming from elsewhere. He motioned Orchid to him. He didn't want to have to do it, but back down the main hall was the only exit he could be sure of.

When Corien edged out, sliding along the wall, a lantern was unhooded further down the wide hall and a voice ordered: 'Halt or we fire!'

He and Corien exchanged despairing glances and it was Orchid who said, 'The doors . . .'

Antsy felt his shoulders fall. *Burn take it! The very way he was avoiding.* He motioned her on. 'Go.'

'Fire!'

They ducked. Crossbow bolts slammed into the stone walls around them. It occurred to Antsy that they must be at the very limit of the lantern light. He and Corien backed up, covering Orchid, who ran first through the tall yawning doors. They followed her in and took up positions covering the opening. From the echoing sounds around him he knew the room they'd just entered must be immense but he had no time to think about that just then.

Feet slammed and the light bobbed as lanterns neared. Antsy levelled the crossbow and Corien braced himself, sword and parrying gauche at the ready. But their pursuers did not enter. Instead, the doors began grinding shut. Antsy and Corien exchanged further uncertain looks. What to do?

'You've run to your deaths!' someone laughed.

'Fools!'

Antsy dropped the crossbow to grab an edge of one door. '*What's in here?*' he yelled.

Laughter answered and a blade chopped at his fingers. He yanked his hands away. The doors slammed shut, cutting off the light.

Antsy stood frozen in the darkness. To one side Corien panted his tension. 'Orchid?' he whispered into the black. Even this faint murmur raised echoes from distant walls. *A damned large open space here.* 'Orchid?' Silence.

'Corien?' Antsy said.

'Yes?'

'I'm coming to you. Don't move.' Arms out, Antsy edged his way towards Corien's loud breathing. His hand brushed a blade and Corien gasped in surprise. 'It's me.'

'Yes. Sorry. Where's Orchid?'

'Don't know.'

'You have the lantern?'

'Yeah. In my bags. I'll try and light it.'

'Okay. I'll cover you – though I can't see a thing.'

Antsy knelt and yanked off his bedroll and bags. Rummaging, he found the small metal box then dug out his tinderbox. 'Pray Oponn's with us,' he murmured, and readied the flint and iron.

He tapped down into the gathered tinder and kept at it until a glow betrayed itself. He blew gently, hands cupped. Between blows a tiny flame climbed to life within his hands. He held the wick to the tinder, turning it slightly to catch the fibres. A yellow-orange flame grew to life. Antsy carefully handed the box over to Corien then repacked.

'Well, at least there's no wind,' the lad offered, his smile bright in the strengthening light.

'Just like a gods-damned mine,' Antsy grumbled, drawing a single long-knife. He took the lantern. 'Let's have a look.'

The weak flickering flame hinted at an immense room. Fat pillars of black stone serried off into the distances. He could just be made out an arched ceiling. The polished stone of the floor appeared to be inlaid with what looked like a near infinity of gems. *An unguessable fortune – yet none have claimed it.*

He didn't want to find out why but was afraid he was going to anyway.

Carefully advancing, they found Orchid standing motionless at the far end of the chamber. She stood before a chair – a huge seat carved from black stone. Antsy raised the lantern to see her staring upwards, seemingly enraptured.

'Orchid,' he whispered. 'Are you all right?'

Blinking, she glanced at him as if not seeing him then smiled, motioning all about. 'Isn't it wondrous?'

'Orchid,' he began gently, 'we can't see a damned thing.'

'Oh. I'm sorry . . .' She clapped her hands and gave a command, a single word in Tiste Andii. An ice-blue glow arose from the gems at her feet and expanded in all directions, the set gems coming to life all about the huge chamber, on the floor, the pillars, even the ceiling, until it was as if they stood suspended among an infinity of stars.

Antsy and Corien turned full circles, stunned. Antsy blew out the lantern.

'The Sacristy of Night. Perhaps,' Orchid supplied.

Most of the lights were mere tiny diamond-like pinpricks. Just like stars at night. But some were large pale blue balls suspended just overhead like moons. The room was now fully lit, but it was the cool silvery light of a full moon on a clear starry night. There was no sign of any sun anywhere in the sky.

'It is said that this is a representation of what one would have seen from the homeland of the Andii,' Orchid explained. 'Perhaps. I don't know for certain, of course.'

'And this?' Antsy motioned to the seat. 'Is this . . . some kinda throne? Is this like a throne room?'

'I don't think so. More like a temple to Mother Dark, I should think. Sacred—' She broke off.

Antsy had seen them as well: shapes approaching. Like rippling cloths of pure black darkness. They'd seen one just like them before: the guardian who'd tried to kill them. He moved back to back with Corien. *Damn it to Trake! What could they do against these?*

One addressed Orchid in a whispered breathless version of Andii. She answered, then translated: 'They say we are polluting sacred ground and that they will cleanse us.'

'Ask for the way out and tell them we'll go right away.'

She spoke again and the same one answered. Orchid translated: 'It says the way out is the way we came in.'

'Perhaps there is a back door?' Corien asked, raising his sword and gauche.

The shapes were crowding very close now, almost a solid sheet of impenetrable black surrounding them. Orchid spoke again and was answered.

'What did it say?' Antsy asked.

'You don't want to know,' Orchid said, her hands falling.

'Try that incantation thing again,' Antsy told her.

'That won't work here. We really *are* trespassing.'

The scrap of elemental night gestured then, an unmistakable sign of dismissal or end of debate, and Antsy wondered whether munitions would have any effect upon them.

Suddenly a new voice rang out, loud and firm, in the Andii tongue and the shapes stilled and edged away slightly. A man stepped through the ring. He was obviously Tiste Andii with his night-black skin, but there were differences from other Andii Antsy had seen. His eyes were the same almond shape but more lifeless-looking, being black on black. His hair was dark as well, and very long. He wore it braided and hanging forward over one shoulder. His clothes were dark yet rich: a shirt, vest and open robes all of a velvety cloth. He was also rather heavier-set than most Andii Antsy had met.

The man faced an amazed Orchid, looked her up and down, and smiled. 'I was meditating . . . saying my goodbyes if you will . . . when whispers reached me through the night of the True Tongue spoken by a young woman. At first I could not believe it. All were sent away. Yet here you are speaking the Noble Language. I cannot tell you how pleasing it is to me to hear it once more.' He bowed, smiling even more broadly. 'Forgive me, but it has been a *very* long time.'

One of the shades spoke and the man frowned. He gave a curt answer but the shape replied firmly. The man turned from Orchid, crossed his arms. He spoke again, and while his tone seemed light enough Antsy sensed the iron beneath the words. It also seemed suddenly rather cold in the chamber. Antsy edged away from the man and noted that the gems beneath his boots no longer gave off light. As if they were dead, or had had all the light sucked from them.

Then, raising the hair on Antsy's neck, the entire ring of shades bowed to the man, murmuring. Orchid paled, a hand going to her throat as if to cut off what she almost blurted out.

The shades withdrew and the man turned once more to Orchid. 'My apologies. They have their duties. One mustn't blame them for being true to their assigned tasks.'

Antsy sheathed his long-knives. 'Well, thanks for intervening. Do you know if there is another way out of this place? If there is, we'll be on our way.'

It was as if he'd not spoken at all. The man continued to study Orchid, his chin pinched between his fingers. 'What is your name, child?'

'Orchid.'

'Orchid? In truth? That is an Andii name. Did you know that?'

Orchid's face darkened even further in a blush. 'No, sir. That is, no. I did not.'

'And what's your name?' Antsy asked loudly. Corien set a hand on his elbow.

The man's unnerving black eyes slid to him. 'You may call me Morn.'

'Morn? Right. Well, you just point us in the right direction and we'll leave you in peace.'

The eyes slid back to Orchid. 'Perhaps you should remain here. You would be safe and welcome.'

If anything the girl paled even more to a sickly near-grey. 'We must be moving on.'

'What is it you seek?'

'The Gap. We just want to get out of here.'

The man frowned almost as if hurt. 'Really, child? Don't you wish to remain? To learn more of your inheritance?'

Swaying, she barely whispered, 'What do you mean?'

Morn spread his arms wide to indicate the entire chamber and perhaps also everything beyond. 'I mean, Orchid . . . welcome home, Child of the Night.'

Her eyes rolled up then and she fainted. She would have smacked her head on the stone floor had not Antsy jumped forward to ease her fall.

*

The place wasn't so bad, Antsy reflected, once you got used to the wraith-like beasties occasionally wafting forward to look you over – perhaps searching for the best place to bite. In any case in terms of his own personal philosophy he couldn't complain: he wasn't dead yet.

He and Corien saw to their weapons and armour. Corien morosely inspected what was left of his brocaded jacket. Orchid walked the chamber hounded by the creature Morn who seemed determined to persuade her to stay. Antsy hoped she wouldn't be beaten down, despite the possible truth of this revealed ancestry of hers. Which may or may not even be true. And frankly he had his doubts. He doubted everything until it betrayed him or bit him or tried to kill him – and then he knew he'd been right about it all along.

And the old squadmates called me a pessimist. Given the state of the world I'm the realist!

He and the lad then had a few practice sparring matches. Corien was still weak on one side but other than that Antsy knew he faced a duellist vastly more skilled than he. 'You Darujhistani fellows all seem to be pretty damned good with the sword,' he told him as they sat resting after a long bout. 'Why's that?'

The lad's shrug said he didn't rightly know. 'We have a tradition of swordsmanship that goes back a long way.'

Antsy grunted his understanding. 'Like where I'm from. We've been fighting each other for so long that forming line and taking orders is second nature.'

Corien gave an easy admiring laugh. 'That's where we tend to fall short. On that forming line and taking orders part.'

Orchid approached followed by her new shadow. Antsy pulled out a strip of dried meat and cut a bite off, chewing. 'What's the verdict?' he asked around his mouthful.

'We have to go. This place is still a deathtrap. The longer we remain . . . well. I'm afraid it will finally get us.'

Antsy shoved home his knife. 'I'm with you there.'

Morn stepped forward, hands clasped behind his back. 'If you must go, allow me to guide you.'

'We make for the Gap,' Orchid warned, firm.

'If that remains your wish.'

'Do you know another way out of this place?' Antsy asked.

'Yes.'

'Okay. Lead on.'

The shade, or Andii, or whatever he was, bowed. 'Very good.'

They gathered together their gear. Orchid was also firm about carrying the remaining waterskins and shoulder bags of food and supplies – including Antsy's pannier. He and Corien tried to talk her out of it but fared no better than Morn had in changing her mind.

When they were ready she gestured Morn to go ahead. Antsy fell in next to her. He had the crossbow readied once more. 'Will we still be able to see?'

'I think so.'

'Good.' He cleared his throat, eyed Morn where he walked in front of them. 'So . . . what do you think about his claim? You bein' part Andii and that.'

The tall girl bit her lip – she appeared terrified by the idea. 'I don't know. Part of me feels that it is right. But . . . I can't be sure.' Her gaze shifted to Morn. 'Part of the reason I can't be sure is I don't know if we can trust this one.'

Prudently, Antsy merely nodded his agreement.

'He is more than he pretends to be,' she continued. 'The shades . . . maybe I misheard, or mistranslated, but when they bowed . . . they called him *Lord*.'

Antsy's brows rose in appreciation. *Really? Some kinda Andii high muckety-muck. Or the ghost of one. Who knew?* He joined Orchid in studying the man's back and wondered: had they just made a bad trade . . . Malakai for this fellow?

Morn led them through a maze of chambers and halls. What they found cluttering these rooms made Antsy regret his vow not to stop to loot. Obviously no one had ever reached these precincts and the riches revealed made him almost whimper. The collected treasures of uncounted centuries lay sprawled at his feet like the wreckage of a siege. Shattered delicate glass artwork, fragments of precious ceramics, paintings, busts carved in precious stone. Even upended tables and furniture that were themselves beautiful works of art. He winced as his sandalled feet ground priceless fragments into the stone floor.

The deep aquamarine monochrome mage-light made it impossible to distinguish one gem from another, or gold from other metals, but he wasn't above picking up the odd stone or small piece of metal-work to study it more closely. Ahead, Morn studiously ignored his darting and stooping like a scavenging bird at a battlefield.

'Look here,' Orchid murmured, awed. She'd stopped at an immense tapestry that hung fully five paces from floor to ceiling. It was the representation of a city hugging the coast of a lake. Galleys plied the waves. Men and women crowded the waterfront dressed in unfamiliar archaic costume. They were busy at markets, buying and selling fruit, birds, carpets, finely wrought furniture, even horses. One immense pale blue dome dominated the city's skyline. Pearl white, Antsy guessed it would be, in the light of day.

'That is Darujhistan,' Corien announced, surprised. 'Or looks like it. There's no dome like that.'

'Darujhistan more than two thousand years ago,' Morn supplied. He had returned to them, utterly silent. 'During the age of the Tyrant Kings. It is said none could match their mastery of sorcery.'

'I know of no dome like that,' Corien said, dubious.

Hands clasped at his back, Morn raised and dropped his shoulders. 'I understand much was lost during the cataclysm of their fall.'

'How do you know all this?' Antsy demanded.

Corien winced and Orchid sent a glare, but the Andii seemed unruffled. 'It is true. I have been . . . away . . . for some time. But I was scrupulous in questioning everyone I met for news. There was little else to do where I've been all this time.'

Antsy snorted his scepticism. Morn merely gestured ahead. 'This way, if you please. There is a light in the next corridor.'

Antsy gaped. '*What?* Why didn't you say so?'

'You didn't ask.'

'And all this time we've been—' He clamped his mouth shut and signed to Corien in the hand signals he'd been teaching the lad. *Scout ahead.*

Corien nodded, jogged off.

Antsy shouldered his crossbow, gestured that Orchid should stay behind him, and followed.

He found the lad waiting at a corner. Corien pointed ahead and held up one finger. *One. A sentry.* Antsy motioned him aside, glanced round the corner. One fellow, sheathed swords at his sides, standing straight in the middle of the corridor with a lamp behind, facing their way. *Canny, that. Not facing the light.*

He raised the crossbow, nodded to Corien, who slowly drew his weapons. He took three short breaths, steadied his arms, then stepped out from the corner training the crossbow on the man. 'Don't move!' he commanded. 'You're covered.' Corien stepped out with him, weapons bared.

The figure didn't even flinch; his hands remained at his belt. The head turned slightly and one word was called in some language Antsy didn't recognize. 'Don't move!' he ordered again. The fellow appeared to be wearing the lightest of armour, leathers only, but also some sort of helmet. He'd made no move to his sheathed weapons.

As they came closer, a gasp sounded from Orchid and Corien straightened, grunting his surprise. His weapons fell slightly. The barbed point of Antsy's bolt didn't waver from the man's chest. 'Who're you?' he challenged.

'Red . . .' Orchid began, a warning in her voice.

The fellow didn't answer. Closer, he saw in the dim light that the man was in fact a woman, and that she wore a simple small mask that hid the upper half of her face. *A mask? Who did she think she was? A fucking robber?*

Another fellow came jogging up the corridor and Antsy swung his crossbow. 'You're covered!' he called.

Orchid touched his arm. 'Red . . .'

'Get back, dammit.'

Corien suddenly sheathed his weapons.

'What the fuck are you doing?' Antsy snarled.

'It's all right, Red.

'*What?* Tell me why this is all right.'

The newcomer stepped forward, hands at his sides. He too wore some sort of multicoloured mask.

'No further!' Antsy barked. 'Or you are a dead man.'

'Who are you?' the man called in oddly accented Daru.

'Who am I?' Antsy couldn't believe what he was hearing. 'I'm holding the crossbow here! Who are you?'

'My name is Enoi. Please step forward and let us speak.'

Orchid tightened her grip on his arm. 'Red. It's okay. Lower the weapon.'

He spared her one quick glance. 'Why? Why the name of dead Hood should I lower my weapon?'

'They are Seguleh,' Corien said.

'Seguleh? Really?' He'd heard the stories, of course. But he'd never thought he'd ever actually meet one. He lowered the crossbow, slightly, to study them, curious. *So, Seguleh are they? Everyone says just three of them defeated the entire Pannion army.*

Not true, of course. But it made for a great story around the camp-fire. When neither went for their weapons Antsy set the crossbow butt to his hip. 'What do you want?' he called.

The man, or youth, judging from his clean chin, stepped forward. A multitude of shades swirled across his mask – all variations of blue to Antsy's mage-sight. 'You wish to pass through to the upper galleries, yes?' he said.

'What of it?' Antsy said.

The masked face shifted to study Morn. 'You do not impress us,' he said. 'We do not fear ancient shades.' Morn provided the ghost of a smile. The youth looked back to Antsy. 'You may pass. All we ask is that you swear a vow to us.'

'Swear a vow? To you?' Antsy laughed his disbelief.

'What is it?' Orchid asked, very quickly.

'That should you find one particular object you will relinquish it to us before you leave this rock.'

Antsy laughed again. These fellows were the most naïve idiots he'd ever met! 'And this thing? What is it?'

'A piece of artwork stolen from my people long ago. It is a legacy of ours. We believe it to be somewhere within the Spawn, as it is our belief that its master, Blacksword, either took it, or acquired it. It is of little monetary value but important to our religion. A plain white mask. Of little value to any but us.'

'I do so swear,' Morn said immediately, sounding even more solemn than usual.

'And I,' Orchid echoed.

'I also swear,' Corien said, enacting a Darujhistani courtier's bow.

Antsy eyed the lot of them. 'Just what in the Abyss is going on? Some masked clown walks up, tells you to swear, and you bow to him?'

Orchid glared her fury, urging him to cooperate. He raised a hand. 'Just a minute. Now, if this thing is so important to you, why aren't you searching for it yourself?'

The youth drew himself up straight, offended. 'We do not scramble through ruins like common thieves. Someone has it, or in the course of his or her looting will find it. And when he comes down we will be waiting and he will relinquish it. If he does not, he will be killed.'

Antsy turned to the others, crossbow still resting on his hip. 'Is it just me or doesn't that sound like stealing too?'

'Red . . .' Corien warned.

'No – c'mon.' He waved to the two Seguleh. 'Here they are pretending to be so superior to everyone yet what they're doing is no better than any highwayman threatening travellers in the woods.'

'Just swear,' Orchid ground through clenched teeth. 'You're being an ass.'

'No. Let's hear their answer.' He turned back to the young Seguleh. 'What do you say? You're the ones with the masks, after all.'

The youth glanced back to the short wiry female sentry. She yanked a bag from her belt and tossed to him. He upended it, sending a cascade of gems bouncing and clattering over the stone floor. 'We've been here for some time,' he said airily. 'We've collected many of these gems for their beauty. Yet whoever brings the mask may have them all.'

Antsy stared at the scattered stones: the dark ones must be rubies, the pale ones possibly sapphires or emeralds. He saw countless pearls as well, white and black. *Ye gods! A king's ransom!* With this he could purchase lands, a title. He cleared his throat. 'Ah . . . well. Why didn't you just say so . . .'

The youth crossed his arms. 'Few have challenged our terms.'

Orchid jabbed Antsy in the side. 'Right. Well, fine. I swear too, then.'

Both Seguleh inclined their heads fractionally. 'We thought so. You may pass.'

Morn led them on. A few turns and lengths of corridors later Antsy noted that all the scattered riches were now gone. These halls had been picked clean.

'Why didn't you just swear back there?' Orchid demanded. 'What's it to you? This thing they want has probably just sunk to the bottom by now anyway.'

'Matter of principle,' Antsy answered, distracted. The inlay of blue stones and the chandeliers and glowing faces still lit their way, but a side portal ahead remained dark. As if no light could penetrate it. He motioned ahead. 'You see that?'

Orchid peered and frowned. 'It's utterly dark to me – and that's strange.'

Antsy signed *caution* to Corien then noted that Morn was nowhere to be seen. 'Where's—'

There was a rustle of heavy cloth being thrust aside and blinding yellow lanternlight burst from the opening, dazzling Antsy's vision. 'Don't move!' a voice bellowed in accented Daru.

Shit! Wincing and blinking, Antsy tried to see through his slitted eyes. 'Who's there?'

'Drop your weapons or die!'

Dammit! He lowered his crossbow, raised a hand. 'All right!'

'Hands up!'

'Yes,' said Corien.

Antsy could now make out some eight crossbowmen crouched in two ranks within the room, all aiming their weapons at them. He knelt to set down his. *Goddamned ambushers!*

'Drop your weapon belts,' the voice ordered.

Antsy undid his to set it down with its sheathed long-knives and heavy dirk. Corien let his fall as well. A man pushed forward through the crossbowmen. He wore a slashed long jupon over a banded iron hauberk. His sleeves and leggings were mail and a blackened helmet, visor raised, rode high on his full head of dense brown curls. A thick beard was braided and tied off with strips of leather, lace and cloth. Antsy thought there was something vaguely familiar about him.

He hooked his thumbs in his wide belt and looked them over. 'So who's in charge of this sorry ass group?'

'I am,' Corien said.

The man shook his head. 'No, mister fancy-boots. I don't believe you are. Not that it matters any more. Turn round and put your hands behind your back.'

'There's no need for that,' Antsy said.

'Oho! I know that accent. A damned Malazan spy!'

Antsy just ground his teeth. Orchid turned round and clenched her hands behind her back. Corien followed suit. Teeth almost cracking, Antsy snarled and lurched round as well.

They were marched through a sprawling, well-lit complex of living quarters, halls, guard chambers and large assemblage rooms. Antsy counted some fifty armed and armoured men and women, though their equipment was all mismatched and ill kept. Looted and scavenged from one dead fortune-hunter after another, no doubt. He wondered, idly, just how many had worn the hacked mail or used the battered blades around him. Also present were obvious slaves: dressed in rags, carrying out errands, fanning fires, cooking, mending. They passed one very pregnant woman cooking at a fire.

The collected loot of an entire section of the Spawn glittered here as well: heaped gold artwork and plates, silver jewellery. Statuettes of semi-precious stone cluttered the corners of rooms; circlets of gems hung at the necks and wrists of almost all. Antsy recognized this for what it was, having seen its like in every war. Call these people what you would – raiders, scavengers, bandits, looters – they were the jackals who gather wherever laws break down, or never reach.

Just as below, in Pearl Town, this lot had simply moved into living quarters now empty of their prior owners. The three of them were pushed into one such narrow cell. Two guards remained at the opening. A simple cloth hanging was yanked across the portal.

'Are you all right?' Corien asked Orchid. She nodded, rubbing her wrists. 'Where's—' he began, but Orchid signed for silence. He nodded his understanding.

'Now what?' she whispered to Antsy.

He sat on a plain stone ledge that might, or might not have been intended as a bed. 'An interview of a kind, I suppose. They either need us or want us, or not.'

'If not?' Corien asked.

Antsy shook his head.

'Well, shouldn't we—'

Antsy held up a hand. 'Sleep, for now. There's nothing else we can do.'

Disbelieving, Corien looked to Orchid for support but she nodded her agreement. 'Yes. We need to rest. Who knows how long it's been – or will be?'

Sighing, Antsy lay back and threw an arm across his eyes.

Malazan spy. He didn't like the sound of that.

CHAPTER XII

A tale is told of a distant city where, when its exalted ruler
wishes to travel, it is the custom of its inhabitants to lie down
in the dirt before him so that his feet need not be sullied. When
travellers ask the why of this custom they are told that the
inhabitants willingly and gladly lay themselves down for their
ruler as he protects them from the countless threats of raiders
and bandit armies surrounding their peaceful settlement.

And these travellers go their way shaking their heads, for all
those surrounding the city have no interest in such a wretched
place.

A History of Morn
Author unknown

C OLL WALKED THE EMPTY UNLIT ROOMS OF HIS MANOR HOUSE,
gloriously drunk. He carried a cut crystal decanter loosely in
one hand. It was late in the night, long past the mid-hour, and
he was waiting to be killed.

How better, it was his considered opinion, to die than carefree and
thus beyond the reach of all pain? For it had always been care that
brought him pain. He stopped, weaving, before one particular stretch
of empty whitewashed wall. He knew what used to hang here . . .
during that all too short anomaly in his life he knew as *happiness*.

He wiped a sleeve across his face, sloshing wine. *Damn her. Damn
him!* He'd been such a fool! And paying for it all his life. Was it
pride? Masochism? That he cannot forget, cannot let go? He let his
arms fall. Well, perhaps that was just the way he was.

He lurched on, inspecting the main-floor rooms. But not upstairs.
No, not there! Never there! He leaned against the long formal dining

table, pulled the sweaty linen shirt from his chest. Humid tonight. Warm. The summer doldrums when tempers are short and passions run hot.

He could have remarried. Plucked some daughter of a rich merchant house, or respected artisan. Someone grateful enough, or hungry enough, for a noble family name. And yet . . . he would always wonder: *what's she doing now?*

He raised the decanter for a drink. And any smirk or whisper among the young bloods! Gods, he could see the contempt in their eyes now! What could they be insinuating? Did they know something he did not? Eventually, he knew, it would've ended in a humiliating mismatch on the duelling grounds.

At least this is private. The blade across the throat or through the back. Quiet and without witnesses. Much better than a ring of uncaring faces. Some shred of dignity may be kept . . .

Gods. Who am I kidding?

He slammed down the decanter, slumped into a chair. *Was that it, then, that kept me alone all these years? Fear? Fear that I could never trust again and would thus make some good woman's life a misery? Fear of my own weakness? Was that pathetic . . . or just sadly accurate?*

He blinked in the greenish light of the night sky streaming in from the colonnaded walk that led to the rear grounds. Someone stood there, cloaked, tall. *Their chosen blade. Fanderay's tits, they wasted no time about it.*

He threw his arms out wide. 'Here I am, friend. May I call you friend? We are about to share an intimate moment – surely that permits me to call you friend.' He reached for a tall wine glass, raised it. 'Drink? No, I suppose not. Well, I believe I will.' He poured a full glass.

The man walked to the other end of the long table, regarded him from the darkness within his deep hood. Coll raised a hand for silence. 'I know, I know. Quite the sight. In the old days I understand just a note was enough. Something like "save us the trouble". We live in a decaying age, so they say.' He emptied the entire glass in one long pull.

The man closed further, coming up along one side of the table. He ran a gloved hand over the smooth polished surface as he came. Coll eyed him all the way, swallowed his mouthful. 'Liquid courage, some would say, hey? But no – not in my case. I have courage. What I need is liquid numbness. Liquid oblivion.'

The figure raised a hand to his hood while the other slipped within his cloak. 'What you need,' the man growled, throwing back his hood, 'is balls.'

Coll yelped and flinched backwards so hard he upended the chair and fell rolling. He came up clutching at his chest. 'Gods, Rallick! Don't *do* that!' He righted the chair. 'I thought you were . . . you know . . .' He froze, then straightened to eye his friend. 'You're not . . . are you?'

Rallick selected a plum from the table, sat. 'No, I'm not.'

'Well . . . is there . . . someone?'

'I wouldn't know.' He took a bite of the fruit, threw a leg up on the table. 'But I suspect not.'

Coll sat. 'You suspect not? Why?'

Rallick chewed thoughtfully, swallowed. 'Because you're old and ineffectual. Useless. Unimportant. Marginalized and sidelined . . .'

Coll had raised a hand. 'I get it. Many thanks.'

'Well, isn't that just what you've been moping around these rooms about?'

Coll would not meet his friend's gaze.

Rallick sighed. 'Isn't it about time you married someone? Sired another generation to carry on the family name? It's your duty, isn't it?'

Coll sat back, waving a hand. 'I know, I know. But what if she . . .'

'I assume you'll choose more wisely this time. And in any case, so what? Life's a throw of the bones. Nothing's guaranteed.'

'How reassuring. And you are here because . . . ?'

Rallick finished the plum. 'I'm under a death sentence from the guild.'

Coll stared from under his brows. 'And you come here.' He gestured angrily to the grounds. 'What if they're following you? You've led them here! They could be coming any moment!'

Rallick held up his hands. 'I thought you were expecting them.'

Letting out a long breath Coll leaned forward over the table to massage his temples. 'What do you want?'

'I want that *thing* up on Majesty Hill gone.'

The fingers stilled. He sat back, eyed his friend anew. 'What's this? A civic conscience? Rather belated.'

The lines around the lean man's mouth deepened as his jaws tightened. 'Think. Who have we done work for all these years?'

'Baruk. But Baruk has been taken – or has fallen, or failed. There's nothing we can do.'

'Then it falls to us. We are all that's left. Us and Kruppe.'

'Gods!' Coll looked to the ceiling. 'You almost had me, Rallick. Then you had to go and mention that greasy thief.' He waved to the grounds. 'Where is he? Have you seen him? The man's halfway to Nathilog by now.'

'No he's not. He's in hiding. I'm seeing his hand in things more and more.' The man looked down, frowning. 'I wonder now if all along I was nothing more than his hand and ear in the guild. As Murillio was among the aristocracy, and young Crokus may have been on the streets. While you were a potential hand and ear in the Council.'

'Happenstance only, friend. You're looking backwards and inventing patterns. You give him too much credit. I grant you he's some sort of talent – but he uses it to do nothing more than fill his stomach.'

'Does he? I heard he faced down the Warlord.'

Coll frowned, uneasy. He reached for the decanter then thought better of it. 'Brood just sort of . . . missed him.'

'Exactly. I'm thinking no one has ever managed to get a firm grip on that fellow. Including us.'

Coll knit his fingers across his gut. 'So? You have a point?'

'We should stay in this card game. Play the waiting hand. They want you out, yes? Well, all the more reason to remain.'

Platitudes. A tyrant is closing his fist on the city and this man offers me platitudes. He raised his gaze to the immense inverted mountain that was the chandelier hanging, unlit, above the table. *She always liked that monstrous thing. Gods, how I loathe it.* He lowered his eyes to the man opposite. The harsh monochrome light painted the angular face in even sharper planes of light and dark. *The man is serious. A serious Rallick should not be discounted.*

He took a deep breath that swelled his stomach against his entwined fingers, let it out. Beyond the walls, all over the neglected estate grounds, the crickets continued their songs to the night. He cocked his head, thinking. 'Is the guild under their control?'

'No. I believe not. In fact, I believe they may have just reopened their contract against the Legate.'

Coll sat up, amazed. 'What? Why didn't you say so, man?'

'Because I believe they will fail as they did before.'

'Anyone can be killed,' Coll mused. 'If recent events in the city have taught us anything they have taught us that. It's just a matter of finding the right way.'

Rallick swung his leg down, stood. 'Very good. I'll shadow the guild. You shadow the Council.'

'It's no longer a Council,' Coll said, sour. 'It's become a court of sycophants and hangers-on.'

'One more thing,' Rallick said.

Coll peered up, brows raised. 'Yes?'

'Do you have an extra room? I need a place to sleep.'

Coll fought down a near-hysterical laugh. 'Here? Gods, man, this is the first place they'll look for you.'

'No. You're still a Council member. They won't move against you unless they're offered a contract.'

'How can you be so sure they won't act anyway – unilaterally, so to speak?'

Rallick smiled humourlessly and Coll reflected that even the man's smiles resembled the unsheathing of a knife. 'Guild rules,' he said.

*   *   *

Under the clear summer night sky the long banner of the Scimitar arced high and the moon cast its cold, emerald-tinged silver light upon the empty Dwelling Plain. A lone figure, dark cloak blowing in the weak wind, walked the dry eroded hills. His features were night dark, his hair touched with silver. He wore fine dark gloves and upon the breast of his dark green silk shirt rode a single visible piece of jewellery: an upright bird's foot claw worked in silver, clutching an orb. The Imperial Sceptre of the Malazans.

Topper had only been to Darujhistan a few times. Personally, he did not understand its prominence. He thought it too vulnerable, relying as it did on such distant market gardens and fields to feed its populace. Yet he did detect among the dunes and wind-swept hills straight lines and foundations which hinted that things had not always been this way. Logic, however, rarely guided such choices. History and precedent ruled. His names for such forces in human activity were laziness and inertia.

He came across yet another wind-eaten ring of an abandoned well, and dutifully he knelt to examine the stones. Nothing here. That report had better be accurate or he'd have the head of that useless mage for wasting his night. He moved on.

Frankly, nothing of what he'd found here interested him over much. He was glad of the recent carnage to the south. In his opinion such disarray and expending of resources opened the way for Malazan expansion. So too here in Darujhistan. Anomander gone.

The Spawn ruined. In all, things could not have worked out better for the Throne.

What worried him was his absence from Unta. Who knew what idiocy Mallick might be initiating? Like that adventurism in Korel. It had better work out, or the regional governors might start to wonder if perhaps they'd made a mistake in backing the man . . .

He reached another dry well and knelt to examine it. This time he grunted his satisfaction and turned his attention to the lock blocking its top. Under his touch it opened easily. He threw aside the wooden lid and jumped in. A hand lightly touching the side slowed his descent. As the bottom approached he spread his feet to either side and stopped himself. Here he noted the faintest remnant glimmers of ancient wards and Warren magics. To his eye the work appeared to bear the touch of an Elder's or Other's hand. In either case, not plain human Warren manipulation. This fit with what he knew of what he faced.

All simply more intelligence to help him build the profile that would guide him in his own possible action against this Legate. *If it should come to that.*

And he rather hoped it would. For it would allow him to indulge in a bit of personal vindication. For the description of this young female servant – the filmy white clothes, the bangles and long hair – resembled someone else. Someone he hoped to have the excuse to confront.

He launched himself into the slim tunnel and pushed himself along on elbows and knees to where it emptied into a larger chamber. Here he dusted himself off then peered about. Empty. Side vaults empty as well. He examined the skulls decorating the floor, the empty stone plinth. Then he found the one occupied side vault. Here he paused for a long time.

The lingering magery flickering about this corpse interested him the most. He rested his hands on the stone ledge the carcass lay upon to lean closely over the remains. Why had this one alone resisted, or failed, reconstitution and escape? It seemed a puzzle. A trap within a trap within a trap. Subtle weavings. Yet who was trapping whom? And could he be certain? According to those cretin marines there could be only one witness. Only one individual emerged from the well before this masked creature appeared. The one others called a scholar, a small-time potterer here among the ruins.

He leaned back, brushed his fingertip across his lips. As before: one set apart. Why? There must be some significance. He simply couldn't get a tight enough grip upon it yet. The lineaments of the castings held a cold sharp edge. They whispered of non-human origins. Not Tiste – he knew his own. Certainly not K'Chain nor Forkrul. That left Jaghut. So, the legends of the ancient Jaghut Tyrants. Returned? Didn't the Finnest house finish that?

Reason enough for any other to be wary.

He brushed his gloved hands together, climbed from the narrow alcove. Too *many players for things to be straightforward and clear. Have to watch and wait.*

At least until the inevitable frantic recall to the capital comes.

*   *   *

While the cargo scow was slow, it made steady progress all through the day and on through the night and so far sooner than Torvald expected they drew up next to the sagging dilapidated pier at Dhavran. His travelling companions, he knew, would be disembarking here. He was saddened to see them go. They'd been extraordinarily informative regarding the political situation among the Free Cities and the Malazans to the north. From hints and details he gathered that the big fellow, Cal, had once been some sort of military commander far in the north.

In the dawn's light, alongside all the other passengers preparing to leave, the two put together their meagre travelling gear. At the rail Torvald waited to say his farewells. Sailors readied the gangway.

'Sorry to say goodbye,' he told the old man, Tserig.

The fellow glanced up to his huge companion, who peered down at Torvald from amid his wild mane of blowing hair and beard, a half-smile at his lips, and rumbled, 'Haven't you been listening? You're coming with us.'

Torvald blinked. For an instant he had a flashback to another of his travelling companions, one similarly large and abstruse. 'I'm sorry?'

'There is no longer at Pale anything of any relevance to your master in Darujhistan. Here at Dhavran, however, will soon arrive something of great significance.'

'And that is?'

'The Rhivi nation is invading the south, meaning to crush the Malazans. Don't you think you should discuss the matter with them? You are, I gather, a duly appointed city councillor, yes?'

Torvald coughed to clear his throat. 'You are not serious, I hope?'

'Very serious.'

Tserig gummed his nearly toothless mouth, nodding his agreement. 'We are here to try to talk them out of it.'

The gangway slammed down, rattling the dock. The crowd on the deck hefted their bags and rolls while babies cried, pigs squealed, and caged fowl gobbled. Torvald shouldered his own bag. 'Well . . . I suppose I ought to accompany you, then.'

'Very good,' Cal said. 'They should be here shortly.'

They waited until all the other departing passengers had shuffled down the gangway. Tor watched families reunited amid hugs and tears; travelling petty traders set down their wares and immediately start haggling; and local merchants fuss over the unloading of ordered goods. This was the stuff of normal life – the daily round of trying to build a better future. This was what people wanted. Really, in the final accounting, they just wanted to be left alone to get on with things.

Once the way was clear they hefted their bags and tramped down the planking. Tor noted that it bowed alarmingly beneath Cal's weight.

They set up camp close to the muddy riverside where a meagre bridge made a crossing. Here they waited. 'It will only be a few days,' Tserig assured Torvald. In the meantime Torvald questioned Cal. It turned out the man knew an incredible amount regarding general history and politics. Torvald, who had been away from the region for some time, suddenly found himself very well informed.

Just a few days later the first of the Rhivi outriders arrived at the broad shallow valley that this creek, the Red, meandered through. Cal, Tserig and Torvald went to meet them at the bridge.

The riders trotted up to the bridge, dismounted. Cal awaited them with his hands tucked into the wide leather belt of his travel-stained trousers. Old Tserig leaned on a large walking stick. Torvald stood just behind. He keenly felt that he was intruding.

The two outriders knelt before Cal. 'Warlord,' they said.

Torvald slapped a hand to his mouth. *Great gods! Warlord? Cal – Caladan – Caladan Brood!* He heard a roaring in his ears and his vision darkened, narrowing to a tunnel. The old man grasped his arm with a grip like the snaring of a root, steadying him. The riders bowed to Tserig as well, murmuring, 'Elder.'

'I would treat with Jiwan,' Caladan said. 'If he will receive my words.'

'We will carry your message.'

'One more thing.' The Warlord motioned aside to Torvald. 'I also have with me an emissary from the ruling council of Darujhistan, Torvald Nom. He too would speak with Jiwan.'

The two bowed again, then returned to their mounts. Caladan watched them go. After a time he turned to Torvald. 'We should have an answer soon enough.'

Tor struggled to find his voice. 'Why . . . why didn't you tell me . . . ?'

'I could hardly announce it there on that boat, could I?'

'Well . . . I suppose not. But . . . why aren't you . . .' Tor swallowed, realizing his indelicacy, and finished lamely, 'you know.'

'With them?' the big man supplied, arching a bushy brow. 'I argued against any further war but I was outvoted. The young bloods want to prove themselves, and being the aggressive faction they won the day.' His hands knotted at his belt. 'At least that is how it had better have been. Otherwise . . .' He shook the great mane about his head and gestured to the creek. 'In the meantime let's try and catch some fish.'

After an evening meal of fish skewered over flames, the noise of hooves announced the approach of riders. Rising, Caladan pulled his hands through his thick beard then wiped them on his trousers. Torvald helped Tserig to his feet. 'My thanks,' the man murmured. 'My joints are not what they used to be. Though I'll have you know my prick is just fine.'

Torvald clamped his teeth together against a choking laugh. 'That . . . is . . . encouraging news, Elder.'

The old man gummed his mouth, nodding. 'It should be!'

The riders were Rhivi warriors finely accoutred in mail and enamelled leather armour with skirtings that hung down the sides of their mounts. Torvald recognized these men and women as the cream of the Rhivi's leading clans. The foremost rider drew off his helmet to nod to Caladan. His thin beard was braided, as was his long black hair.

'Warlord. To what do we owe this honour . . . again?'

'Jiwan. I am here to ask you one last time to put down the spear. No good will come of it, only suffering and tears. Think of your people – the lives that will be lost.'

The young commander nodded thoughtfully, frowning. 'I hear your words, Warlord, and I honour you for your past leadership and wisdom. But these words are not those of a war leader. They are the words of an old man who has lost a great friend. A mourning elder who looks at life only to see death. Such a dark vision must not guide a people. We who see life, who look ahead to the future. We must lead. And so, Caladan . . . I ask that you stand aside.'

'Pretty words, Jiwan,' Brood answered, unruffled by the young man's dismissal. 'I see now how you turned the heads of the Circle of Elders. But I do not think I will stand aside. I think I will block this bridge to you and all those foolish enough to follow anyone hypocritical – or inexperienced – enough to speak of life while going to war.'

Torvald's mood had fallen from uncomfortable to distinctly exposed here on the open bridge as more and more of the Rhivi cavalry, mixed medium and light, came trotting down the shallow valley. He felt like an interloper among the negotiations of a war leader who had dominated the north for decades, and had led the resistance there against the invading Malazans. Now to be dismissed in such an ignoble and off-handed manner! It grated against his instincts. To so blindly dismiss the hard-learned wisdom of centuries!

The young war leader's gaze now found Torvald. He raised his chin. 'You are this Darujhistani emissary, Torvald, Nom of Nom?'

Torvald bowed from the waist. 'I am he.'

'What think you of this man's position here?'

'I think it . . . rather unassailable.'

A scornful smile drew back the youth's lips. 'Strange words from an emissary of Darujhistan when all the others are so eager for Malazan blood.'

'What's that?' Caladan growled, his voice suddenly low and menacing.

The war leader seemed to believe he had scored a point and he nodded his assurances. 'Oh, yes. The city is with us. We have the fullest intelligence from them. For example, the remnant fleeing just before us number less than twelve hundreds, while our numbers swell with every passing day. Soon we shall reach thirty thousands! And your Legate, Nom of Nom, promises aid during the engagement. Obviously he too recognizes the threat these Malazans pose.' Jiwan sat up taller in his saddle. He raised his voice to be heard by the surrounding riders. 'Now is our chance to rid our lands of the invader! They are weak. Leaderless. Few in number. Now is our best chance and perhaps our only chance! We must strike now! While we

355

are assembled! The gods have handed us this opportunity. We must not let it slip away out of fear.'

'Your words lack respect!' Tserig called suddenly. 'They displease the ancestors.' The Elder pointed to Caladan. 'This man sheltered Silverfox the Liberator! The gift of the Mhybe!'

The war leader bowed his head in acknowledgement. 'True. But where is the miraculous Silverfox now?' He turned in his saddle to shout: 'She has abandoned us!'

'*Enough!*' Caladan bellowed. So strong was the yell that Torvald felt the bridge judder beneath his feet. 'Enough talk. Jiwan, this bridge is closed to you.'

Exaggerated regret drew the war leader's mouth down. He shook his head. 'Caladan, it is sad to see you reduced to such petty gestures.' He pointed to the shallow waterway. 'You accomplish nothing. We will merely ride through the creek.'

Caladan crossed his arms. 'You are welcome to do so. You are much overdue, I think, for getting muddy.'

Jiwan merely clamped his lips shut. Yanking on his reins he waved for the cavalry to go round. Torvald watched while the columns passed to either side of the bridge. Some refused to acknowledge the Warlord or glance his way, while the lingering eyes of others held sadness, regret, and even guilt.

It was many hours before the last of the riders passed. Above, the mottled moon and the Scimitar cast bright competing shadows while threads of clouds passed between them. Caladan finally let out a long breath. 'A large force,' he admitted. 'Every clan represented.'

'They smell blood,' Tserig agreed.

'Malazan blood.'

'What will you do now?' Torvald asked.

The huge man uncrossed his arms and shifted his stance. The logs of the bridge creaked beneath their feet. 'I warned your Legate not to interfere in this. But he has defied me. Whipped the Rhivi on to the Malazans. All Jiwan sees is the glory of being the war leader who defeats the Malazans. He doesn't see that Rhivi blood is simply ridding this creature of his enemies for him.'

'I'll go back, then,' Torvald said, certain of what he should do. 'Speak against this.'

The man's tangled brows rose. 'Great Burn, no, lad. You'll be killed out of hand. No. I'm going. I intend to take this Legate by the neck and let him know of my displeasure.'

Suddenly Torvald felt rather afraid for his city. There were stories of this man – this Ascendant – levelling mountains in the north. 'You won't . . .' he began, only to pause as he realized he wasn't sure what he intended to say. *Won't destroy the city?*

The man smiled his reassurance. 'Only this Legate troubles me. I am sorry, Torvald Nom, but all is not as you think in your home. I suspect something is controlling Lim, or he has struck a bargain where he should not have.'

Something strange going on? What is strange about Lim's having resurrected an ancient reviled title? Or started wearing a gold mask? There is nothing strange in that.

'Tserig,' Caladan continued, 'would you re-join Jiwan's forces? If things go badly there will be a need for your voice.'

'I understand, Warlord.'

The man regarded Torvald, stroked his beard. 'Perhaps if you accompanied me you would be safe enough.'

Tor thought about the offer but realized that there might be something else he could do. Something perhaps *only* he could do. 'No.'

Caladan stopped to turn, frowning. 'No?'

'No. The Moranth withdrew when they sensed something was happening. And here we are in the shadows of their mountains. I'll . . . I'll go to them.'

'Torvald Nom, that is an extraordinary offer. But no one has ever succeeded in reaching them in their mountain strongholds. They speak to no one. I've heard that only the Emperor and Dancer ever managed to sneak into Cloud Forest.'

'They will speak to me.'

The Ascendant eyed him while he pulled at his beard. He was obviously curious as to the source of Torvald's certainty, but refrained from challenging it. He grunted instead, nodding. 'Very well. I wish there was some help I could offer.'

'Well – I could use a horse.'

The big man smiled behind his beard. His gaze shifted to the south where a galaxy of campfires now lit the plain. 'I think I might be able to produce one.'

*   *   *

Leoman sat with his arms draped over his folded knees. He watched the titanic shadow of Maker high against the horizon where the giant continued his labour while the stars wheeled and the waves of glimmering Vitr worked their eternal erosion.

He sighed and glanced over to where Kiska stood high on the strand, facing the Sea of Vitr. Day after day she stood in plain view of Tayschrenn, or Thenaj, and his cohort of helpers while they carried out their rescue mission of dragging unfortunates from the burning energies of creation and destruction. Her goal, he believed he understood, was that somehow, eventually, the sight of her would trigger some memory within the archmagus and the man would come to his senses.

He thought it a forlorn hope. He stretched then sat back, his elbows in the black sand. Was he loosing weight? Wasting away? Would he fade to a haunt doomed to wander the shores of creation wringing his hands or searching for a black button he'd dropped?

Kiska nudged his leg – he'd been wool-gathering. He'd been doing a lot of that lately. She peered down at him then away, screwing up her eyes. 'You don't have to stay,' she said.

He nodded. 'True.'

'You *should* go. There's no need for you to be here.'

'One does not return empty-handed to the Queen of Dreams.'

'She's not vindictive.'

He snorted. 'This is all assuming we *can* return.'

'She wouldn't have sent us to our deaths.'

'She said she couldn't see beyond Chaos.'

Kiska set her hands on her hips. 'Well . . . so, you're just going to lie around watching?'

He peered about as if searching for something else, then returned his gaze to her. 'Looks like it.'

'Well . . . you're making me uncomfortable.'

'Oh – I'm making you uncomfortable?'

'Yes! So go away.'

He pointed one sandalled foot to the beach. 'I'm sure our friends feel the same way.'

'That's different.'

'It is? Shall we ask them?'

Kiska's lips tightened to almost nothing. 'They won't talk to me.'

Fine lips they are for kissing. Too bad there's been precious little of that. Now there's *a reason to go back.* He squinted up at her. 'That's because you're making them uncomfortable.'

She waved curtly, dismissing him – 'Gods, I don't know why I bother' – and marched away.

Well . . . that didn't work. What now? Bash her on the head and drag her back to the Enchantress? Here you are, your ladyship – one troublesome agent returned safe and sound. Are we even now?

He eased back into studying the horizon. Time for that yet. Best wait a touch longer. See if she works this out of her system all on her own. As he'd learned from experience – it's always easiest simply to set out the bait and wait for them to come to you.

*   *   *

The old witch who lived at the very western edge of the shanty town that itself clung to the western edge of Darujhistan seemed to spend all her time whittling. That and incessantly humming and chanting to herself. People whose errands happened to bring them wandering by sometimes considered telling the hag to shut up. But, after reconsidering, none ever did so. It was after all asking for trouble to insult a witch.

This afternoon, as the sun descended to the west, where just visible was the top of the great hump of the tomb of the Andii prince – uncharacteristically unlooted as yet, as, again, it would be asking for trouble to attempt to rob the tomb of the Son of Darkness – this afternoon the witch's head snapped up from her sticks and she stuffed them away into the folds of her layered shirts. She stood, peering narrowly to the south. Out came her pipe in one hand and in her other a pinch of mud or gum that she rolled between grimy thumb and forefinger.

She brought the lump up to her eyes, squinting. Brought it even closer, so close that her thumb touched the bridge of her nose and her eyes crossed. Then she grunted, satisfied, and jammed the lump into the pipe. This she lit, puffing, before returning to studying the south, an arm tucked under the one holding the pipe. Passers-by noted her attention and stopped to look as well. But, seeing nothing but the dusty hills of the Dwelling Plain, they shook their heads at the woman's craziness and moved on.

'Almost,' the woman muttered aloud as if conversing with someone. She blew twin plumes of smoke from her nostrils. 'Almost.'

*   *   *

Barathol was in the back building a crib. Little Chaur, he'd noticed, was now as long as the basket he currently slept in. It was late afternoon and the work was going slowly; he kept forgetting where he was in the process – which piece to cut and how long to make it. He was, frankly, dead on his feet. His hands were clumsy crude gloves, his thoughts glacial.

Glancing up he noticed Scillara at the back door, watching, arms crossed over her broad chest. 'Asleep then?' he said.

'Aye. A feed and a nap – practising being a regular man, he is.'

'Our needs are simple.'

'Bar . . .' she began slowly.

'Yes?'

'I'm . . . sorry. I was – I am – angry that you took that work. I'm scared that . . .'

He set down his handsaw. 'Yes?'

She raised her eyes to the darkening sky as if not believing what she was about to confess. 'I'm scared. Scared that I'm going to lose you.'

He sat back, resting his hands on his thighs, and gave her a crooked smile. 'You'll never lose me so long as you have Chaur, yes?'

'I'm sorry, Bar. All I see is a lump of need that looks at me with hungry eyes. I don't like that look, Bar.

'In time then, Scil. As he grows you'll see more and more of you and me in him.'

She was looking to the north, picking at the cracked wood of the jamb. 'I don't know. It's you I chose – not him. Maybe . . . maybe we should go. Leave tonight while we can.'

'There's work for me here. Enough for us to get by on.'

'And this other work? When will it finish?'

'Soon. Very soon. They're almost done now.'

She watched him carefully, as if studying him. 'What've they got you doing up there anyway?'

'Nothing important, Scil. Nothing important.'

*   *   *

Grisp Falaunt was lord of one row of turnips. That and a shack that really wasn't a shack being as it was more of a lean-to of broken lumber and canvas cobbled from the remains of what once was a shack. But from the shade of his wholly-owned domicile he could look south to the shimmering images of orchards, fields and groves covering the hills of the Dwelling Plain. All that had almost been – and rightfully ought to have been – his. For in the absence of all other claims was he not the lord and master of all the vast plain? Who could dispute that? Why, none, o' course.

Again he reached down next to his chair where his hand encountered nothing and he growled and adjusted the cactus spine held between his teeth from one side to the other. Damned trespassing devil-dogs. Broke his fine cabin and burst the heart of his last loyal friend, fine Scamper, buried now among the turnips.

Ought to fence his property. That's what he ought to do. *Then* them fancy nobles in Darujhistan would come a callin'. Why, then—

Grisp leaned forward, the front legs of his chair thumping in the dust. What in the name o' dried up Burn was *that*? More trespassers?

A file of men had emerged from a gulch, or draw, or gully, or whatever it was you called a damned depression out there on the plain. A great cloud of dust was following them. In fact, they was running like the very devil-dogs was after them.

And they was headed right for him.

Or not. Maybe not *quite* right for him. More like . . . His slit gaze shifted aslant to his last remaining row of turnips. The spine clamped between his lips stood straight up. *Oh no.*

Hood's bones! They was headed for his turnip plantation!

Chair thrown aside numb bare feet tangling with staked rope ties of canvas roof much cursing and flailing to stand bony chest thrown out athwart limp brown leaves defiant!

The jogging twin files of men and women – masked, for all sakes! – parted to either side, their sandalled feet trampling the row into flattened dirt and bruised turnip flesh.

Upraised fists fell. Screwed-up features twisted into puzzlement, then despair.

Grisp landed on the tattered rear of his trousers while the yellow ochre dust of the Dwelling Plain blew about him. There, between his feet, brown leaves intact, lay his last undamaged turnip.

'Fair enough,' he croaked, waving the dust from his face. '*This* time, Scamper m'boy. *This* time I mean it. Time for action. Time for pullin' up stakes and movin' on. Fer . . .' He eyed the limp bug-gnawed specimen before him and slumped even further into the dry dirt. 'Aw, t'Hood with it.'

*

Not long after that, the guards of Cutter Road Gate, newly reconstructed, let go of the robes of the dealer in rare woods from the plains of Lamatath as the alarm from the watchtower sent up its strident warning. Both peered down the length of Cutter Lake Road over the heads of the crowd of farmers and petty traders held up behind the tottering wagon of the dealer in rare woods.

The elder guard noticed that the wagon blocking the gate. 'Get moving, you damned fool!' he bellowed at the man. The other guard, staring south, mouthed something like 'Ghak!'

Ghak?' the elder wondered, then an arm slammed him backwards into the wall of the gatehouse and he slid down the gritty stones, dazed and breathless, while a file of men and women jogged by, hands resting near the grips of sheathed swords as they passed without so much as a glance down.

After the last of the file had gone the man pulled himself up, wincing and gasping and rubbing his chest. Masks, he wondered? Why in Beru's name were they wearin' masks? He and his partner shared helpless stricken looks across the wagon. The dealer leaned to one side to spit a stream of thick brown fluid across the dusty road.

'You all are in big trouble now,' he commented with great satisfaction, and flicked the reins.

On a street in the Gadrobi district a boy coming into adolescence ran up to a heavyset woman standing in the entranceway to the open hall of a school of swordsmanship. 'Masked men!' he cried excitedly, his eyes shining. 'Masked men running through the streets!'

'What's that?' the woman answered sharply.

'Some say Seguleh!' He waved her out. 'Come.'

'Inside,' she demanded.

'But . . .'

'Harllo . . .'

His shoulders slumped and he brushed in past her. 'Yes, Mother.'

The woman slowly closed the door on people running past, on yells sounding from the distance. Inside, she lowered a heavy bar across the door then pulled a crossbow from where it hung on the wall. She flexed its band, testing it, and nodded.

Sulty handed out the plates of hot goat skewers on couscous then paused, tilting her head – marching feet, double-time. Been a long time since she'd heard *that* sound. Her gaze caught Scurve at the bar and he shrugged; evidently he knew nothing of it.

Moments later a man ducked inside, breathless, red-faced. 'Seguleh!' he shouted. 'On the Way!'

As one the patrons surged to their feet to charge the door.

'You ain't paid!' Jess bellowed. Then the three women were left alone in the room amid fallen chairs and steaming food. Sulty blew hair from her face. Jess motioned the others outside. 'Might as well have a look.'

They joined the crowd eyeing the distant Second Tier Way. But there was nothing to see. Whoever, or whatever, had passed, and only the witnesses remained. The patrons gathered round those who claimed to have seen. The two women rubbed their aching chapped hands in their aprons, shrugged, and went back inside.

It had nothing to do with them.

In the common room, Sulty eyed the table with its steaming plates and skewers and wondered – hadn't there been five?

The clerk posted at the gate to the Way of Justice heard the marching echoing up the walls enclosing the Way. Puzzled, he picked up his scrolls and stepped outside. No notice of procession had been filed for this day. Who were these fools?

A double file of men and women came jogging round a corner and the clerk stared, squinting. *Great Fanderay . . . were they . . .* Before he could complete his thought they sped past to either side, leather jerkins stained wet with sweat, limbs glistening, eyes hidden behind masks riveted straight ahead.

One by one the scrolls slid from the clerk's hands. Kicked and trampled they flew, wind-caught, to flutter over the wall of the Second Tier, wafting towards the glimmering waters of Lake Azur.

After the last had passed the clerk quickly finished his sums and came to an astounding number that kept him from discovering his empty hands. *Five hundred. Great Ancient Mother of the Hearth! Surely they cannot be real!*

He crossed to one of the city Wardens who guarded the Way. The man was staring off up the rising cobbled path, a gourd of water half-raised to his mouth. 'Do something,' the clerk demanded.

The man swallowed, his face as pale as the finest vellum. 'Do what?'

'Warn them! Warn the Council!'

The man slammed the wooden stopper home. 'I'll just trot along behind, shall I?'

The clerk raised his hands to shake a finger, then realized. He started, gaping. 'Great Mother of Pain!' He threw himself to the stone lip of the wall to peer over and down. 'I'm ruined!'

'You're ruined?' The guard flicked the truncheon at his side and snorted. 'I think we're all fucking ruined.'

The journey had been a strange experience in double vision for Jan. All the landmarks, major features and place names remained as handed down through the ancient lays and stories of his people. And yet all was different. Gone were the orchards, groves and fields of the verdant Dwelling Plain. All was dust and desolation. The great network of irrigation canals and the artificial lakes sand-choked and buried; the many brick towers, the leagues of urban dwelling, all gnawed to the barest foundations and scatterings of eroded sun-dried brick. A population collapse – just as described in the catastrophe of their exile.

And the city itself, fair white-walled Darujhistan. White-walled no more. Oh, it appeared large and wealthy enough. But gone were the soaring towers of translucent white stone so clear one could see the sun through their walls. Gone the great Orb of the King, the Circle of Pure Justice. All destroyed in the Great Shattering and Fall.

Many of the inhabitants carried weapons, as well. There appeared to have been a proliferation of those willing to place themselves under the judgement of the sword. But that could wait. Ahead lay the Throne and the one who sent out the call. What would it be? The fulfilment of the long-held dream of his people? It seemed unreal that this should be achieved, now, in his lifetime. The last First had never spoken of it, had always deflected Jan's probes. It was this uncharacteristic *reluctance* that troubled him now as he jogged up the Way of Justice. Such guardedness had all been too much for one Second, the one whose name had been stricken. Slaves to tradition, he had denounced them, as he threw away his sword.

And it was said the man had subsequently taken up a sword in the service of true slavery. But such were tales outside the testing circle and thus beneath attending.

In any case, they would soon know. Jan led the way. He hardly noticed the figures he brushed aside as he entered the Hall of Majesty. The body of their handed-down songs and stories contained many descriptions of the approach to the Throne, although it took a moment to sort through the subsequent alterations and additions to the rambling complex. That done, Jan directed those of the Fiftieth to guard the path, then walked up to the tall panelled doors – not even noting the two guards who stood ashen-faced to either side – and pushed them open.

It was dusk now, and the golden light of the sunset shone almost straight across the Great Hall, illuminating the gathered crowd in flames of argent. Jan paused, disconcerted to find a sea of plain golden masks directed his way. Though not all, he noted, wore them. And among those who did some now fell limp to crash to the floor.

He ignored them all as beneath his direct attention and strode for the Throne. His escort, the Twenty, followed him in. The crowd parted like torn cloth. Two of those insensate were dragged across the floor to clear the way.

The one on the throne rose to meet him.

He wore the template upon which all these others were obviously patterned. Jan recognized the power and authority radiating from it as if from the sun itself – but it was not the mask he had come all this way to meet. Halting, he met the man with his own masked head slightly inclined, eyes a shade downcast: the posture of uncertainty regarding rank.

The masked figure gestured, arms open, his thick burgundy robes wide.

'Greetings, loyal children.' A voice spoke from one side, quavering and breathless, almost choking. 'You have answered the call of your master. Soon all shall be restored to what it was. The Circle of Perfect Rulership is near completion.'

The golden Father? First guide me! Was this the source of your silence? Ancestors forgive me . . . which do I choose? The knee or the blade? Which will it be? All now are watching, waiting upon me, the Second, to show the way. And yet . . . there it is. For am I not Second? And did not the last First ever instruct – the Second has but one task.

The Second follows.

And so he knelt before their ancient master reborn, his mask bent to the floor. And, leathers shifting and hissing, all the Twenty knelt in turn.

In the crowd yet another of those assembled crashed to the floor.

CHAPTER XIII

And the truth is not yet revealed
With the fall of the first gossamer veil
Nor does the second drifting shroud
Sent curling to the gold-dusted tiles
Bring the unthinking one step closer
To the necessary awareness of how
Close wafts the third clinging cowl
Troubling those fascinated as pure
White flashes yet promise and allure
Distracting the unwary from the
Fourth sheet unwound enlightening
All too late that only Death could
Dance so seductively

Song of the White Throne
Mad Ira Nuer

ANTSY AWOKE TO A HAMMERING ON THE WALL OF THEIR ROOM. 'UP and on your feet,' someone growled. 'Let's go.' The feeble yellow light of a lamp glowed through the burlap hanging. He sat up, stretched, and set to pulling on his gear. He and Corien stepped out first to give Orchid more privacy to squat over the chamber pot.

The motley crew in their mismatched armour, men mostly, all chuckled at the loud hiss of the liquid stream against metal that came echoing out from behind the hanging. In charge of this detachment was the fellow boasting the huge thick beard tied off in tails and the tattered dirty jupon over the banded iron hauberk, its heraldry rendered murky and indistinguishable. When Orchid stepped out he gestured them impatiently. 'This way.'

They were led through narrower and narrower private passages – what might have once been a large private dwelling – to a guarded room where tables stood crowded by scrolls and vellum sheets held down by countless statues of animals real and fantastic, some carved from semi-precious stone, others cast in silver and gold. Light was provided by a large candelabra so low it threatened to ignite the many sheets. A fat man sat with his boots up on one of the tables, leaning back, studying a document.

But what really caught Antsy's attention was the wonderful scent of fresh fruit and cooked meat. His stomach lurched and grumbled and his mouth, dry for days, now flooded.

'Prisoners, sir,' their captor grunted.

The man did not look up from the document. 'Very good, Lieutenant.'

The lieutenant promptly slouched into a chair, one of slung cured leather over carved dark wood that itself looked like a work of art. He helped himself to a cut crystal jug of red wine, pouring it into a cup that appeared to have been carved from jade. He waved away the guards.

The man tossed down the sheet. He was unshaven, his face glistening in the candlelight. His hair, bald on top, hung in a tangled mess. He rubbed his sunken red-ringed eyes with a pudgy hand thick with gem-studded rings. He blinked at them. 'A Darujhistan dandy, a Malazan deserter, and some rich merchant's plaything. How can any of you be of use to me?'

'Torbal Loat,' Antsy blurted, the name suddenly coming to him.

The man cocked one bloodshot eye. 'Met before, have we?'

'This fellow carved out quite the territory for himself up north during the wars,' Antsy told Corien and Orchid.

'Before you Malazans drove me out.'

Antsy raised his hands. 'Hey, I chucked that in. No percentage there.'

The man merely grunted. He raised his chin to Corien. 'You can use a blade, I assume?'

The youth bowed. 'At your service.'

The lieutenant laughed a harsh bray and raised his glass in salute. 'And you?' Torbal demanded of Orchid.

'She's a mage of Rashan,' Antsy said before she could answer.

Torbal's heavy mouth twisted his irritation. 'This true? If not, I'll kill you myself.'

'I have some small gifts, yes,' she stammered.

He grunted, unimpressed. 'Well . . . it's the usual deal. You swear to fight for me and you'll receive your fair share of food and shares in the profits. As you can see, we control the majority of the Spawn. Most of all that is worth anything is with us. Fight well and eventually your original gear will be returned. Though,' and he glared at Antsy, 'not *all* of it. Desertion is of course punishable by immediate execution,' he added, continuing to give Antsy a hard eye.

'For a share of the total profits I'm your man,' Antsy said.

'As am I,' Corien added.

'And I.'

'Now,' Torbal began, picking up a star fruit and examining it. 'Our lookouts report that there was someone else with you . . . what happened to him?'

Antsy could not take his eyes from the ripe yellow star-shaped fruit. 'He ran off.'

'Ran off? You won't mind then if we have a look for him?'

Antsy kept his face dead straight as he said: 'No. We don't mind at all.'

'Where do you get all this food?' Corien breathed, his voice thick with longing.

Torbal's expression said that he was very pleased his little demonstration had had the desired effect. He sat back and took a bite of the fruit. 'I have contacts with the Confederation boys. For a few trinkets I get regular shipments. My people eat well – remember that.' He gestured to the lieutenant.

'Get them rooms.'

The lieutenant pushed himself up. 'Let's go.'

He marched them back through the rambling living quarters. Antsy quickly became lost though he was doing his best to keep his bearings; he suspected the man was leading them in circles. Eventually he stopped before a portal covered by a hanging – a hacked portion of a tapestry that must once have been worth a fortune before such desecration. 'You have a name?' Antsy asked him.

The man pulled off his helmet and shook out long thick hair around his scarred and pitted face. 'Otan.'

'Otan of Genalle?'

'The same.'

'You gave us – ah, the Malazans – a lot of trouble.'

368

'I still do,' the man said, eyeing Antsy with obvious distaste. 'Listen . . . Torbal says you live for now, but I don't like you. Spy or deserter, whichever you are. I'll be keeping an eye on you. Be sure of that.'

'That'll keep me warm at night, friend.'

'We'll settle this. Don't worry. We'll settle up.' He ambled off, his armour rattling and creaking.

It was a plain living chamber. A side room allowed the option of privacy for Orchid. They remained together in the main room talking in low voices while Corien kept a watch at the hanging.

'What now?' Orchid asked. 'We're captives.'

'Are we at the top?' Antsy asked.

'No. According to all the descriptions I've heard there's still a way to go.'

'Thought so.'

'Why?'

He gestured back the way they'd come. 'I didn't think this lot would be in charge.'

'They have a lot of swords,' Corien pointed out.

'Yeah. But they're fighting someone for control of the rock.'

'Who?'

Antsy rubbed his slick forehead; his fingers came away greasy and sticky. He sighed. 'I think maybe Malazans.'

'Malazans?' Orchid echoed in disbelief.

'Yeah.' Antsy sat on a stone sleeping ledge. 'I heard that a while back a Malazan man-of-war bulled its way through to here. That would be maybe some two hundred fighting men. That's why old Otan there's accusing me of being a spy.'

Corien raised a hand for silence. Someone approached and he opened the hanging. It was a slave, a skinny crippled fellow with one hand and one bandaged eye. He was hugging a platter containing a hunk of cheese, dry hardtack, smoked meat, and a ceramic pot of water.

'What's your story, old man?' Antsy asked him.

The man's answer was the sad wreckage of a smile. A stream of clear fluid ran down his cheek from under the bandage. 'Came out to make out my fortune. Like a gold rush, everyone said. Jewels to be plucked from the streets of the Spawn.' With his remaining hand he gestured to himself. 'But, as I found, riches don't come cheap.'

'I hear you, old man. What about weapons?'

'When there's an attack.'

Corien swore, then apologized to Orchid.

'An attack?' Antsy continued. 'Who?'

The man shook his battered head. 'Can't say. Talk means punishment.'

'I understand. Thanks for the food.'

The old fellow bowed and padded off into the darkness. Antsy used his short eating knife to cut slices from the lump of cheese. Chewing, he squinted into the dark side room. 'I think your night vision thing is still working, Orchid.'

'Me too,' Corien affirmed.

'Good,' she said bleakly.

Antsy turned his squint on her. 'Could you give us darkness?'

'There's plenty of that.'

He cut and handed out slivers of the hard meat. Tasting it he wasn't sure what it was. Horse? 'No. Real darkness. The kind light can't penetrate – would we still be able to see in that?'

'I think so, yes. I believe you should.'

'Good. That might be enough to get us out of here.'

'Darkness?' Corien said. 'We have no weapons.'

'Then we'll bash people over the head and take theirs!' Antsy answered, a touch irritated.

Corien inclined his head. 'Of course. A sophisticated plan. When?'

Antsy scratched his own thickening beard. 'Yeah. When. Common wisdom says we should wait a while – look like we're fitting in. But I can't shake the feeling that time's not on our side. This whole rock is unstable. Who knows what might happen to it? Every day we're stuck here we're tempting Oponn and I don't like that.'

'So . . . we don't wait?'

'No.' He wrapped the food to pack it away. 'We go now.'

'But our supplies. Your munitions!'

'I'm happier keeping my head, thanks.'

Corien smiled his rueful admiration. 'You've weathered more reversals than we have, Red.'

Antsy shoved the food into a roll of the tattered blankets and tied it off. 'Aw, Hood. It ain't Red. It's Antsy.'

The youth and Orchid shared a glance of suppressed humour. 'Well,' Corien said, 'we knew it wasn't Red.'

'So,' Orchid whispered, facing Antsy. 'What do we do?'

He moved to the hanging and motioned to Corien. 'Snuff the light.'

Corien wet his fingers and pinched the wick of twisted hemp. In the bloom of utter dark Antsy waited for his vision to adjust. Eventually the faint blue glow returned and the walls and his companions slowly emerged from the gloom as if wavering into existence. He raised his hands to the Darujhistani aristocrat, who nodded his affirmation.

Orchid came up. 'Now?' she whispered.

He motioned a negative. 'Let's give it a while. Maybe they'll think we're sleeping.'

She was standing so close her thick mane of black hair brushed his ear, sending a shiver down his frame. He suddenly became very aware of the warmth of her body so close. The smell of her sweat was a pleasure to him. It reminded him of some rare spice. He turned his face away, clearing his throat. *Ye gods, man. Get a grip.*

'So,' he began, his voice thick and hoarse, 'Morn thought you part Andii. What do you think?'

Her dark eyes sought his but he resolutely kept them on the hall. 'It *feels* right. I guess I'd never thought about it until he said it. It explains a lot of things.'

He leaned back against the side of the portal. 'Never thought about it? Who raised you, then?'

'I grew up in what I know now was some sort of temple, or religious community. The priests and priestesses were my parents and teachers. I never left it. As I grew older I explored a bit and found that the temple was on an island. A very small island. After that I suppose I just contented myself with learning about the world through the stories and texts in the temple. That and my teachers.'

'Who taught you the Andii tongue, and their letters.'

'And their literature and legends and mythology.'

'That didn't make you wonder?'

She cocked her head aside in the darkness, considering. 'No. Should it have? I just thought it was normal. I thought everyone learned these things. There was nothing to compare it to. Now, I suppose that must have been a temple to Elder Dark.' She shook her head, a regretful smile at her lips. 'I'm not the first to discover that most of what I've been taught was either wrong, irrelevant, or insane.'

Antsy nodded at that. *Yeah. Parents and family work their craziness too. Gods, just look at Spindle.*

'There's more, of course,' she continued, sounding puzzled. 'Other strange things that I still can't understand. I seem to remember . . .' She shifted, uneasy.

'You don't have to go on,' Antsy murmured, keeping his gaze fixed on the dark hall. 'I understand. But maybe I can help you sort through it.'

She let out a steadying breath, her lips clenched, then nodded. 'I had many teachers. They seemed to come and go.'

'Uh-huh. And this is strange?'

'Antsy . . . They were young when they came and when they left . . . they were old.'

He forced himself to swallow to wet his suddenly dry throat. 'Ah. That is strange. You sure . . . ?'

'Yes. And I seem to remember it happening many times.'

Antsy let out a sound as if thinking that through. *Queen release me! When will I learn to keep my damned mouth shut?* 'Well . . . Andii are long-lived, right? There you go.' *Hood! This 'child' is probably more than twice my age! What's she been learning all that time?* 'Listen. Maybe that's enough for—'

The jarring clanging of metal on metal blasted through the Spawn's steady background noise of groans and clatterings. Corien leapt to his feet. Shouts sounded up the hall and quite a few screams as well. A figure stepped into the hall, shouted: 'C'mon, you lot! It's the alarm. Let's go!'

Their watcher. Antsy nodded to Orchid. 'Put a darkness here in the hall.'

She shut her eyes, murmuring, and all the faint glow of distant lights disappeared. The man peered about, panicked. 'What in the Abyss . . .'

Antsy made for him. The fellow heard his approach and went for his sword but he was obviously blind so Antsy kicked him in the groin then kneed him in the face, shattering the cartilage of his nose and possibly killing him. He took the man's weapons while he lay stunned.

'Which way?' he called to Orchid. She pointed up the other way. He gave the sword to Corien, kept a fighting dirk. 'I'll lead. Corien, watch the rear.'

As they traced halls and turned corners, it appeared to him that Orchid was attempting to lead them round the settlement. He was happy with that because occasional blasts and screams reached them from whatever was going on over at one side of the complex. But as Orchid took longer and longer to chose directions the noise steadily became louder with each length of empty hall or chamber traversed and the yellow glow of lanterns and lamps thickened. By the time she

372

came to a full halt in a narrow chamber whose only other exit was an open portal, he could make out the thumping release of crossbows, the ringing of iron from stone, shouts, and, above all, an argument of some sort between a high strident harridan's voice and a much lower, deeper and fainter man's voice.

'This is not the way!' the woman screeched.

'Let us hear what our guide has to say,' the man murmured.

'Fire!' a voice bellowed, Otan's, and volley of crossbows released, the bolts clattering from stone.

'Aiya!' the woman yelled. 'Who are these wretches?'

'Indigenes? Perhaps?'

'Indigenes? Are you brainless? These are not Andii!'

'Yet strictly speaking . . . are they not the new residents here?'

What in the name of Oponn . . . ? Antsy edged forward to peer round the lip of the opening. *What in the name of Oponn was all this?* It gave access to a large hall, what seemed a main boulevard faced by many building fronts carved from the stone of the Spawn. Bodies lay scattered among wreckage across the floor. Lanterns lay fallen, spilled oil burning to send up clouds of black smoke that obscured the high ceiling.

Two figures faced each other in the centre of the hall. One, the old woman, wore an eye-watering costume of all shades of red, complete with a headdress of fluttering crimson ribbons, and what appeared to be carmine gloves on her hands. The other was a short round ball of a man, bland-faced, in layered dark robes, his hands clasped across his broad front as if to hold it in from bursting.

So amazed by these two was Antsy that he failed to notice a third figure scuttling up the hall, staring at him, his eyes huge and his mouth open. 'Kill that man!' this fellow howled, pointing.

Antsy flinched – and met the glaring eyes of the young thief from Hurly. *Great Burn! What was that fool's name? Jallin! Yes, that's right.*

The lad ran to the squabbling pair, still pointing. 'Kill him, mistress!'

The woman took a swipe at him that he ducked. 'Shut up, fool. Does the way go on?'

'Yes,' the youth snarled.

Armour clattering announced another file of crossbowmen led by Otan crossing the hall.

Gotta give the man credit for guts.

'Hesta . . .' the fat man murmured.

373

The woman threw her hands in the air. 'Oh, cursed gods above! *More* of them?'

She lowered her arms, palms out. Orchid yanked on the back of Antsy's armour. 'Down!' she hissed. Like an upended forge, flames came billowing up the wide boulevard. Men and women screamed, dark shapes consumed by the churning yellow and orange.

A furnace's searing heat crackled at Antsy's arms, which he had thrown up to protect his head, and then with a redoubled avalanche roar the radiance disappeared, leaving him blinking, momentarily blinded. The cackle of the youth sounded in the sudden silence, followed by a slap that cut it off. 'Show us!' the woman commanded.

'Perhaps they merely wished to talk,' the man's voice reached them, retreating.

'Oh, shut up!'

Antsy dared raise his head. Flames lit a scene out of Hood's own realm. Burning corpses and furnishings sent smoke curling up into the thickening miasma choking the air. He didn't like the way it just hung there. *No outlet.*

Orchid was crushing the burnt ends of her frazzled hair. 'I'm sorry, Antsy,' she said, sounding miserable.

'Sorry for what?'

She raised her soot-smeared chin to the boulevard. 'That's the way up.'

Somehow I knew she was going to say that.

*   *   *

Bendan gave his name to everyone in the Malazan camp as 'Butcher'. His own squad didn't use it any more now that they'd reached the main rendezvous south-west of Dhavran. They'd used it for a while after that last engagement and during the march, and it had been among the happiest times of his life. It even rivalled the feeling of belonging and safety he'd known among his peers in the mud ways and alleys of Maiten town. He'd revelled in it those few years alongside his brothers and sisters, jumping rival gangs and cleaning out anyone not a local and foolish enough to wander into their territory. He'd felt untouchable then, utterly secure. Wanted and appreciated. Valued, even, it seemed to him now, looking back. He'd gone from worthless to valued. When they'd all been together on the street they could stomp on anyone's face and no one dared say anything! He remembered how Biter and Short Legs had held one kid down and invited him to lay in. And he'd kicked and kicked on and on until the kid coughed up an explosion of blood and never moved any more. How they'd all laughed! Good times then.

Now when I say 'Butcher's the name' I just get funny looks. Even outright laughs. What's wrong with everyone? There's a guy in the 10th named 'Rabbit.' What kinda name's that for a soldier?

His squad spent the days digging a big-arse ditch to surround the new fort. Other squads were dragging logs from the nearest woods, raising a palisade. It was a damned crowded camp: all the remnants of the Second, Fifth, and Sixth from Pale all jammed together in one round hilltop surrounded by a deep ditch that put the top of the palisade logs a good three man-heights above the heads of any attacker. And on top of that Fist Steppen had them sharpening a forest of stakes to set leaning out like the quills on one of them mythical spiny lizards.

It was gettin' so troops were starting to call her 'Scaredy-Step'. Bendan just called her a dumb-arse granma hiding behind her walls when everyone knew the way to win was to go break heads. He had said as much to his squaddies and Corporal Little had come back with some watery talk about how winning was control of ground, not battles. Ground? He understood that. In Maiten town he and his brothers and sisters had had theirs – and defending it meant fighting! You had to be out there every day showing those rivals you were strong and so crazy-arse violent they'd better leave you alone. That he knew and understood.

Then Corporal Little had said something really loopy. She said that the best way to win was *not to have to fight at all!* How the fuck was that possible? You had to fight to win. You had to tear the head off the other guy – otherwise it was you without a head! He was starting to suspect that maybe Little was some kinda gutless woman hiding behind her fancy book-learned ideas.

Not to mention how she slapped his hand away when he grabbed her tit. Imagine that? Turning him down? Back in Maiten town every girl he cornered went along with it in the end. All it took was a little playful arm-twisting – not like he was gonna *really* hurt them. This corporal must prefer women, not like a proper gal at all.

Then orders came for a march west. Minimal gear. The squads formed up, including his, thank the gods! And they were off even though it was near dusk. Rumours flew up and down the column as they trotted along. Some of theirs under attack to the east, apparently.

They jogged through half the night until they came over the rise of a gentle valley slope and there before them, under the bright starlight and emerald glare of the Scimitar, churned a horde of horsemen all circling a dark knot.

Sergeant Hektar slapped him on the back as they headed down without a pause. 'Now *there's* action, hey Butcher?'

'But look how fucking many there are!'

The big black fellow made a face. 'Naw – that's just an advance force. Just a few thousand. Enough for you to butcher, hey?'

'Well . . . yeah,' he answered as they picked up their pace. *I suppose so . . . but why? Just to rescue a few troopers stupid enough to get caught out in the open? What a dumb waste.*

'Ready shields!' came the order.

Bendan struggled with his big rectangular burden as he trotted along.

'Form square!'

The column thickened and slowed to a steady march. And just in time, as elements of the cavalry swung off to encircle them.

'Halt!'

Once the manoeuvring was done Bendan's squad was far back from the front rank. They would wait for their turn to cycle through to the shield wall. Dust blew up, obscuring his view beyond the square. Riders, men and women – Rhivi, he recognized – circled them firing their short-bows and hurling javelins.

What's gotten them all riled up?

Then the frantic call came: 'Merge! Merge!' and the square shuddered, shields scraping shields. Everyone shifted position as men and women came surging into the centre, many supporting others or even carrying them over their backs. All grimed and dirt-smeared, battered, and gulping down air.

Useless bastards. Gonna get killed 'cause of you. Hope you're happy.

Being near the centre he saw the captain commanding the column salute some beat-up burly fellow and heads around him craned gawking and people whispered: 'K'ess.'

'So who's this K'ess?' he asked Bone next to him.

The man gave him one of those funny looks as he struggled to keep his shield overhead. 'Served on Onearm's staff. Put in charge of Pale when the Host headed south. Now he's in charge of this whole mess. Other than the Ambassador, o' course.'

Shit! And we had to rescue him? *Piss-poor start if you ask me.*

Orders to reverse sounded and they turned to face the way they'd come. Then started the inevitable grinding march back. Bendan's squad cycled through to a turn in the shield wall. The Rhivi circled past whooping and shouting and throwing their slim javelins. He watched from over the lip of his shield, fuming. 'Why don't the order come to rush 'em?' he demanded. 'We're just hidin' here behind our shields like cowards!'

'Be my guest!' Bone laughed, and he hawked up a mouthful of all the dust they'd been swallowing.

'Hey, Tarat!' Bendan shouted to their squad scout. 'Them's your people out there, ain't they?'

'Just dumb-arsed fools tiring their horses for no good reason,' she commented, sour.

'Looks like they're havin' fun,' Hektar said, a wide smile on his face.

'What're you smiling about?' Bendan snapped.

The big man turned his bright teeth on him. 'I'm smilin' cause I see we got nothin' to worry about from these Rhivi. Another day's soldierin' under the belt, lads!' he added.

Laughter all around answered that.

What was with these fools? Why were they laughing? Couldn't they see that one of these arrows or javelins could easily take any of them?

The sun was just topping hills to the east when their slogging retreat brought them within sight of the fort. The shield on Bendan's arm seemed to weigh as much as a horse itself. His arm was screaming and numb all at the same time. Dust coated his mouth and he was stumbling on his feet. Horns sounded then, pealing from behind the palisade as if welcoming the sun and from all around amid the fields of tall grass crossbow ranks rose as if sprouting from the ground. The circling Rhivi flinched aside, their cartwheeling attack broken as wings of the cavalry swung to either side. Orders were shouted and salvos of bolts shot to either side of their square. Men and women in the formation shouted and bashed their shields, sending the Rhivi on.

Bendan rested his bronze-faced shield on the ground. *Gods almighty! It was about Burn-damned time. What a useless errand! They'd been safe in the fort – why should they have to stick their necks out for these fools? And all they did was hide behind their shields. They didn't kick anyone's head!*

New clarion calls sounded from the fort. The men and women

around Bendan searched the horizons. Sergeant Hektar, one of the tallest of them all, grunted as he peered to the west.

'What is it?' Bendan demanded.

'Company. They almost succeeded.'

'Who succeeded? At what? What'd you mean?'

A woman's voice bellowed astonishingly loud from within the square: 'To the fort! Double-time! Move out!'

The entire detachment immediately set off, jogging swiftly. Troopers ran carrying others on their backs, or supporting wounded between them.

Then thunder reached Bendan. Thunder on a mostly clear dawn. He squinted back over his shoulder to see a dark tide flowing over the distant hills. A flood that seemed to extend from horizon to horizon. *Dead god's bones! Thousands upon thousands of the bastards!*

He heeled and toed it even faster for the cover of the fort.

*   *   *

Krute heard first-hand from many in the guild the doubts raised by the arrival of these Seguleh. Their prowess was said to be unsurpassed. And perhaps it was. But he was now in agreement with Grand Master Seba. The guild in the recent past seemed to have lost its way. They were assassins. Their art was concealment and murder. To have to fight meant one had failed already. Rallick's unsanctioned storied feats of the past seemed to have convinced some that fighting ability actually had something to do with murdering people. The unromantic and ugly truth was that it really didn't.

Much as he admired Rallick – and was saddened by his betrayal – he thought the man had done this one disservice to the guild. In his opinion the best assassination was the one no one even suspected. And Rallick had succeeded in that requirement when he hid the act behind the façade of a duel. But most seemed to have misread that moment. Dazzled by the romanticism of the confrontation, they'd taken away the wrong lesson. The real lesson was not his prowess with his chosen weapons, but rather the stratagem of hitting upon one fatal weakness to reach the target, in that case the latter's over-confidence and bloated pride.

And in this case he believed they'd found the correct weakness as well. Surrounded by these Seguleh the Legate seemed to consider himself invulnerable. He slept entirely unguarded in a small chamber behind the Great Hall, or the 'throne room', as it was now officially known. Word from informants within the Wardens was that the Legate had even gone so far as to forbid anyone from entering the throne room at night, Seguleh or otherwise.

Squatting on his haunches on the roof of that selfsame hall, Krute looked to the three guild talents accompanying him as team leader. Hardly qualifying for the title mage, these two lads and one lass did have some small abilities in sensing the presence of Warren magics and powers. They nodded their approval and so Krute signed the *all clear* to the team assembled on the roof. These six tossed their hair-thin lines down the open windows and repelled down. They would execute the target within and return in a matter of minutes – should all go as planned.

He glanced back to the three guild talents. The youths exchanged looks. One pressed a hand to the roof. The second raised her face to the gusting warm wind as if sniffing for scent. The third held his hands cupped close to one eye. Krute knew that in his hands the lad held four night bugs, the sort of flying insects that light up. What do they do when a haunt's around? Dance a jig?

The wind was high this night. Thin feathery clouds did nothing to diminish the combined light from the reborn moon and the Scimitar. Light that was both a blessing and a curse, depending upon when you wanted it, and when you didn't. He studied the ropes again and saw all still slack. The sight made him uneasy. Should be climbing by now. He signed that he would go to investigate.

Closer, he saw that one of the ropes was now taut. In fact it fairly vibrated under some immense strain. As he watched, it narrowed even further to the thickness of a reed; then, instantly, it was gone. Snapped. He heard a muted thump from below.

Damn the fates! What was it? A hidden guard? Yet no alarm.

He clambered down to the window to peer in. The interior was as black as a cloudy night. But far below, in the shafting silver and jade light, he made out a figure climbing to its feet, cloaked. As he peered down, straining to see, the figure raised its face to him and revealed the bright pale oval of the mask of the Legate.

Krute was a hard man in a hard calling but even he felt a preternatural dread at the sight of that graven half-smile – hinting at so many uncanny secrets – and a hand beckoning him down. He scuttled back up the roof, his flesh cold. *Ye gods, spare him . . . what were they facing here?*

Crouched, the wind snapping his cloak, he ran along the centre line back to the jumbled tiled slopes of the Majesty Hall roof. Where not one sign remained of the three guild practitioners.

Togg take it!

Then the instinct of decades of stalking and striking screamed at him and he threw himself flat, rolling.

Twin blades hissed through the air and he stared astonished at a young girl snarling down at him, her clothes no more than diaphanous wind-whipped scarves. She raised the blades again only to jerk aside, howling, grasping at a crossbow bolt now standing from her side. She staggered down the sloped tiled roof, tumbling, and disappeared from sight.

A fist at his collar yanked Krute: Rallick. The man threw his crossbow aside, drew his twinned curved blades. 'She'll be back – or another. Go now. Run.' He shouldered Krute back.

'That's not Vorcan . . .' the assassin managed, still stunned.

'No. Go on.' The man pushed him on to the maze of canted roofs. 'Run.'

Krute needed no further urging.

Rallick slipped into the cover of a gable that offered a view of the throne room roof and squatted, arms over his knees, curved knives pointed out, ready.

A band of low clouds driven off the lake came wafting across the long scar in the night sky that was the Banner – what he'd once heard Vorcan call the Strangers. In the rippling light the rooftop was empty, then in the next instant a figure stood tall right before him, staff planted and leather shoes poking out from under thick layered robes.

Rallick slowly straightened to stand before the man who had employed him for years, who had healed his broken bones and brought him back from near death. High Alchemist Baruk. He struck a *ready* stance, blades raised, one foot back. 'Baruk.'

'Barukanal, now,' the man grated. 'Do not make the mistake of forgetting that.' His hands were white fists upon the staff. The scars that traced his face like a tangled net darkened now as blood pounded behind the man's features. The wind snagged his long unbound iron-grey hair. 'I am sent to find assassins who have made an attempt upon the Legate,' he said, his voice whip-tight. 'You haven't . . . by any chance . . . seen them. Have you?'

Rallick edged his weapons down. He cleared his throat and straightened, almost believing himself dreaming. In a voice full of wonder he managed, 'I saw some men running to the east. They looked suspicious.'

'Thank you, citizen. Tell me . . . have you also seen the new construction encircling the hill?'

'In fact I have.' Rallick noted with alarm that the flesh upon the man's face and neck was cracking and smoking along the fault lines of the scars. Baruk's frame shuddered and he staggered aside as if yanked. He spoke, grinding out every word as if each were a droplet of agony: 'There is a man in the city, a Malazan . . . He may have a unique insight into its . . . peculiar . . . qualities . . .'

'I will ask around,' he assured him. Then, sheathing his knives, he could not help reaching out to the tortured figure. 'Baruk . . . tell me . . . what can I—'

'*No!*' The staff snapped up and the man staggered backwards. '*Stay away!*' Turning, he flung himself from the roof, robes flapping, and disappeared.

Rallick leaned over the edge but saw no sign of him. Then, hunching, he ran as fast as he dared across the forest of mismatched tiled roofs.

Moments after Rallick left the roof the wavering commingled jade and silver light of the night revealed another figure that uncurled itself from a window to stand, stretching. The man wore a cloak that shone almost emerald in the light. He tapped one gloved finger to his pursed lips and whispered aloud, 'Again, some go in . . . yet none come out. The lesson being . . .' he held up his gloved hands and examined them as if the answer were written there, 'don't go in.'

He clasped his hands behind his back and set off, whistling soundlessly, tracing more or less the route taken by the ex-assassin.

When Rallick judged it safe to return to the Phoenix Inn he walked straight to the old table and sat facing the door in the seat where Kruppe usually held court. Rather disconcertingly, the empty seat was already warm and he was thinking of shifting to another chair when Sulty thumped down a tankard of beer, gave him a wink, and moved on to serve the rest of the crowd. Rallick pushed back his seat, held the tankard in both hands before him, and studied that crowd.

Guarded optimism he judged the mood. People seemed to think that things would get better now that the Seguleh had arrived to guard the city. Rumours were that the Legate had somehow contracted to have them come. Never mind the utter impossibility of such a notion to anyone who knew the least shred about those people. And to guard the city against whom? The Malazans? They hadn't the troops to pacify the city in the first place. That left . . . who? No one he could think of. The city was without threats, as it had been for decades before the arrival of the Seguleh. And so the disconcerting thought: what were they here for?

His roving eye caught a man watching him from the bar. A tall, very dark foreigner, all in green. In a gesture like a mockery of some conspirator, the fellow offered him an exaggerated wink and shifted his gaze to the rear. As usual Rallick chose to reveal no hint of his mood – which was one of extreme annoyance – and he got up to push out through the crowd to the back door.

He waited leaning against a wall, arms crossed, hands on the grips of his knives. The stranger ambled out after a moment, hands clasped behind his back. 'What do you want?' Rallick said, trying to keep his voice as flat as possible.

The man held up his gloved hands, a smirk at his lips. 'Parley, as they say.'

'Claw?'

The fellow merely shrugged.

'Say our piece.'

The man waved a hand in an airy manner and Rallick clamped down even harder on his irritation. 'Oh . . . a pooling of intelligence and a uniting of efforts.'

'I'm not with the guild. You got the wrong man.'

A smile from the man – the kind of crazy grin that Rallick had known from some as an affectation of unpredictable menace. But he now saw with a tensing of chilling certainty that from this fellow the pose was utterly genuine. *A very dangerous sort – the kind who truly just doesn't give a damn.* 'The guild, such as it is, doesn't interest me. But you do.'

'How so?'

The man leaned up against the opposite alley wall, which put him in the light of the Scimitar. He grimaced and held up a hand in the light. 'You know, there are those around the world right now who go out at night carrying parasols so that the unnatural light of our Visitor doesn't reach them. They claim it corrupts all it touches.'

'Then everything's corrupted.'

'Indeed. We are all of us slowly rotting until we fall dead.'

'Is that your message? Sounds like something from a street prophet of the Broken God.'

The man let his hand fall, frowned his exaggerated thoughtfulness. 'Indeed? I suppose so. But no. That is not my message. My point is that we have intelligence mentioning "the Eel". And in that intelligence this very inn features rather prominently. And here you are. What say you to that?'

Great Burn! Does this man think I'm the Eel? No – he must be fishing. Ha! Fishing for the Eel. Have to remember that one. But then if I told him who I thought maybe was the Eel he'd have a good laugh. No – he's just trying to provoke a reaction.

Rallick turned his face away to study the empty street and the rats waddling down the centre gutter. 'That's not much of a point.' His peripheral vision caught his reward in a first betrayal of temper from the man as his mouth tightened to a slit.

'You are being deliberately difficult. Well, I blame myself. Ought to have expected it. We are both victims of our calling, yes? Neither of us willing to place our cards on the table. So be it – for now. If you should wish to exchange intelligence then look to reach me through K'rul's bar.'

Rallick eyed the man, puzzled. 'K'rul's bar? You mean the old temple to K'rul?'

'Yes. K'rul's Bar and Temple.' The man tilted his head in farewell and ambled off up the street.

There he goes. Yet another rat on the street.

There's a bar at K'rul's temple? Since when?

*   *   *

A knock brought Barathol to the door. Little Chaur was down for the night and Scillara was in bed, sent off by that one evening pipe she allowed herself to 'ease the nerves'. He'd taken the pipe from her hand as he did every night, and pulled up the blanket.

He was downstairs making a meal when the knock came. He opened the door to find one of the Majesty Hall clerks, now known as court officials, awaiting him with hands tucked into his robes and an oddly arrogant and impatient angle to his head.

'What?' Barathol asked, his own mood not improved by the youth's superior airs.

'You are summoned to the installation. Immediately.'

He half turned away. 'In a minute. I'm just making a meal.'

'Immediately,' the young man repeated, emphasizing each syllable. Lifting his head he directed Barathol's attention to his companions. Barathol peered out to see two Seguleh standing on the road, masked, swords at their hips.

Ah. So that's how it is. The new cock of the roost. So be it. No business of mine.

He gave the clerk a slow nod. 'Very well. I'll get my gear.'

Barathol watched the faces of the passers-by as the little party walked the streets. At first there'd been jubilation. The average citizen now thought himself unassailable. Now, as the Seguleh went abroad to enforce the Legate's will it seemed to him that a few people had finally – belatedly – begun to wonder. Just who did these swordsmen protect the city from? They limited themselves to guarding within the walls, atop Majesty Hill, and in the throne room itself. Protecting the ruler from . . . whom? Well, to his mind, from the ruled, of course. Perhaps this mounting suspicion was behind the worried, even pitying, glances that followed him. *Could I be next?* some seemed to wonder.

The worksite was guard by four Seguleh. Ducking into the tent Barathol found the two mages already present, awaiting him impatiently. 'Begin at once,' the tall one, Barukanal, commanded, motioning to the forge with his staff. Barathol rolled down his sleeves and donned his thick leather apron.

And who were these two anyway? Advisers? Hirelings? Surely not servants, as some believed. Yet why should such obviously powerful mages advise a mere Darujhistani aristocrat, mask or not? Unless, as others hinted, dark pacts were sealed, deals struck, and powers granted. To Barathol's mind these more ominous speculations ran closer to whatever might be the truth of things.

He took over at the bellows from the worker who was prepping the coals. After pumping, he picked up a bar to stir the bed, testing the heat by holding his hand over the glowing pile.

'This is your last pour,' the hunched mage told him from the entrance.

Barathol eyed the man's warped puzzle-piece face. *A warning?*

'I go now to deal with those fools at K'rul's,' the hunched one told Barukanal.

'I will finish things here,' Barukanal answered.

Barathol straightened from the forge. *K'rul's? The Malazans?*

How to warn them? And finish things here? What did he mean by that?

Both now watched him, their eyes glittering in the glow of the forge. 'Get back to work,' the hunched one, Aman, told him and ducked from the tent.

Barathol reluctantly turned to nurturing the bed. Well, if anyone could handle themselves, it was those Bridgeburners. They hardly needed his help. He thought of that chaotic night not so many months ago. Antsy guiding him and his friend, poor dying Chaur, to that eerie structure on Coll's estate. *Do I not owe him more than I can ever repay?*

He turned from the forge, wiping the sweat from his face. 'I'm going for a bite,' he announced. 'The bed needs to heat yet.'

The mage did not move from the entrance. He leaned on his tall warped staff. 'You will remain until the pour is done. Such are my orders.'

'There is nothing I can do here for a while.'

A grimace twisted the mage's face and he said, his voice tight and impatient with something that might have been pain, 'The blacksmith's sand awaits. I believe you have a mould to form?'

Barathol regarded the table, turned aside. 'If I must.' *Well, I tried. After that blast they must know what to expect anyway.*

After packing and setting the mould, checking the bed's heat again, he set the ceramic crucible into the coals and heaped them up around. The bits and pieces of silver went in next. Barathol crowded his elbow through the entire process.

As the silver melted Barathol skimmed the slag of impurities from the top. It was hardly demanding work. The mould was uncomplicated, open-faced. Not like a lost-wax pour where so many little things could go wrong.

Outside in the night the picks and shovels had gone silent. The stones were set and ready for their pins.

Once the liquid silver reached the mark scratched into the glowing wall of the crucible, Barathol readied the bars he would use to lift and tilt the vessel. At that moment the mage's hand shot out like a viper to grasp his wrist. He pulled against the grip but couldn't free himself. And Barathol was a strong man; among the strongest. Not even his younger brother Kalam could beat him.

The mage's other hand came up with a short wicked blade. 'Blood from the forger of the links,' he whispered, close. 'Such will strengthen the circle immeasurably.'

385

Barathol raised the bars to smash the man across the head but the mage clenched his grip ferociously and he groaned from the agony of the grinding bones. *Ye gods, this creature could pinch my hand off like a petal!*

The mage slashed the blade across Barathol's numb wrist then held the wound over the crucible. Drops fell hissing and dancing.

'Do not be upset,' the creature murmured. 'Aman would have taken the offering from your throat.' He released him and moved to one side. 'Now pour. Quickly.'

Working his hand, Barathol readied the bars. He pinched the crucible between their jaws. Grunting, he lifted the vessel and swung it to where the moulds waited. He poured until the level of the first swelled just above the lip of the mould where surface tension kept it from spilling, then moved to the second.

Finished, Barathol set the crucible on its stand to cool and stood back to wipe the sweat from his face. Blood dripped freely from his wrist. He washed his hands in the quenching water.

From where he was bent over the smoking moulds, the mage said, 'Go now. Do not return. Your work is done.'

Barathol merely grunted. He wrapped his wounded wrist in a rag then pushed his way from the tent. In the trench the final two white stones waited end to end. The tips of the installation coming together to form one perfect infinite circle. Briefly Barathol wondered what this structure might be meant to enclose or foreclose. Was it to keep inviolate what lay within? Or was it to keep ineffective that which lay without?

No matter. It was no longer his concern. If it came to it he could simply do as Scillara suggested and pack up the family to go. He turned away, flexing his wrist. He'd had enough of all this. His concern now, was just the small circle of his family.

The uncomfortable echoes within that thought haunted him all the way down the hill.

*

Lady Envy was with her maid and dressmaker when a servant announced, 'Someone is at the door, m'lady.'

Arms held outstretched, the dressmaker measuring a length of cloth against one, her maid's hands in her freshly washed hair, Lady Envy stared at the man. 'Well – answer it, you great oaf!'

The servant bowed from the waist and shuffled backwards, head lowered.

He returned accompanied by three Seguleh.

Lady Envy beamed. She drew her dressing gown tighter about her and shooed away her servants. The three remained immobile, tensed, hands close to their weapons, their attention everywhere but on her. Envy crossed the room, a hand at her lips. 'How very thoughtful of Lim!' she exclaimed. 'Three new ones! The old ones had become rather battered.'

One turned – *her! What a disappointment!* – mask to give Envy a superior glance. *Haughtiness? Was that haughtiness being turned upon me?*

'We have been warned against you, Envy,' the Seguleh woman said. 'Your enchantments hold no more power over us. The Second has knelt and we are bound by links far stronger than any you can forge.'

Envy fiddled at the knot of her gown. 'What nonsense is this? Links?'

'Where is he, sorceress?'

Envy seemed to have just discovered her wet hair; she began twining the length. 'I'm sorry . . . where is who?'

'The renegade. We know he is with you. Where is he?'

'Renegade? Whatever are you—' But the three turned aside, dismissing her.

Oh really, this is too much!

Thurule had entered. The three fanned out facing him. The one who had spoken made a small gesture with her left hand, turning it palm up as if in interrogation. Thurule's masked face seemed to drop ever so slightly. Perhaps it was the light, but it appeared as if his dark eyes behind the mask were blinking rapidly.

'Choose!' the woman commanded.

Carefully, Thurule raised a hand to his mask and peeled it away. The face revealed beneath appeared surprisingly youthful. He released the mask to let it fall before him then raised his sandalled foot and pressed down upon it. The mask shattered into powder and painted shards. His own face seemed to splinter in the act.

Ceramic, Envy marvelled. *They are ceramic.*

The three Seguleh relaxed, hands easing slightly from their weapons. Without a word they turned and left.

Envy crossed her arms and regarded Thurule. 'Well,' she said. 'Whatever am I to do with you now?'

'Whatever you wish,' the man said, speaking the first words she had ever heard from him. He wouldn't raise his gaze from the fragments littering the polished floor.

She hugged her chilled shoulders. 'Well . . . you have rather lost that certain mysterious cachet I kept you for, I must say.' She bit at a finger with perfect white teeth. 'I'm going to have to let you go, Thurule.'

The man's brows clenched as he bowed. 'I understand. I am unworthy.'

Oh, Dark Mother! Please! She turned away, snapping her fingers. 'Palley! Where are you? My hair is drying! The court awaits me!'

Her maid rushed back into the room. When Envy glanced back the man was gone. *Thank the false gods! Really. How positively embarrassing.*

*

Madrun and Lazan Door were tossing dice against the steps of Lady Varada's estate house when four masked Seguleh entered the compound. The two shared knowing looks as Lazan scooped up the dice.

'Our taciturn kin approach,' Madrun rumbled. 'Perhaps we too should remain silent as well. We could stare at one another till the gods pack up the world and return from whence they came.'

'And these would yet remain none the wiser,' Lazan answered. 'No, reflections of themselves these understand all too well.' They straightened to meet the arrivals, the giant Madrun in his clashing patchwork clothes looming over all. 'You are bold burglars, sirs,' Lazan greeted them.

'You two are known to us,' one said. 'Cause no trouble and you may remain.'

'This is of no help,' Madrun complained to Lazar. 'Trouble has so many facets.'

'Stand aside. We are here to search the premises.'

'Does doing our job constitute trouble?' Lazar enquired, smiling, revealing his silver-tipped gold teeth.

The four spread out. The spokesman stepped forward. Olive green dominated the swirls painted upon his mask. From the pattern Madrun and Lazan Door knew him to be of the Four Hundredth. 'I shall enter,' he said calmly. 'If you interfere my companions will act. Is this clear enough even for you?'

Madrun raised his hand. 'A moment, please. If you would. Am I to understand, then, that you mean to enter while your companions wait, poised, in case we should attempt to stop you? Is that what you are trying to explain?'

The spokesman remained silent for some time. From behind his mask his gaze stabbed between the two, blazing. He drew breath to speak again, reconsidered, and clamped his jaws against it. His hand went to his sword.

'Gentlemen and lady . . .' a sibilant voice quavered from the doorway, 'may I direct your attention to what I have here?'

All turned to face the doorway where Studious Lock floated amid his gauzy layers of tattered wrap. He held in one rag-covered hand a glass sphere containing a dark mist. 'Spores of the Eventine fungus. Known as the Mind-gnawer among the clans of the northern Odhan. Inhaled, they germinate within sending fibres stealing up into the brain and releasing pathogens that render the poor victim insane . . . before killing him . . . or her. My companions have of course been consuming an inoculating chemical regularly. I myself am immune for reasons I need not expound here.'

Inoculating chemical? Madrun mouthed to Lazan.

'So, gentleman . . . and lady,' Studlock added, nodding to the female Seguleh, 'will you enter?'

The spokesman eased his hand from his sword. 'We shall not press the matter now, Studious. But we shall return.'

'Please do so. I look forward to expounding on yet another of my preparations. Or, perhaps, remaining silent and exploring the results in dissection. Always most edifying, that.'

The spokesman bowed, keeping his eyes upon Madrun and Lazan, then backed away.

Once the four had left, the gazes of the two guards swung to Studlock. The giant Madrun's carried a degree of alarm. Lazan's held grudging approval. 'Well played,' he murmured. 'That orb, I presume, holds nothing of the kind.'

Studious, who had been admiring the object, now blinked at Lazan from behind his gauzy mask. 'What's that? Nothing of the kind? Not at all. It holds precisely that.' And he threw it down to shatter on the steps.

Both guards leapt from the vicinity.

A good five paces off Madrun straightened his vest and the billowing frilled shirt beneath it and cleared his throat. 'This inoculating chemical you mentioned, Studious. It's efficacy is beyond reproach, yes?'

The castellan was examining the stone steps. 'What's that?' He waved a wrapped hand. 'Oh, that. There is no known antidote.'

'No known . . .' The gazes of the two met across the thirty feet between them. Lazan slapped his hand over his nose and capped teeth.

'Well, that should be the end of them,' Studlock announced, satisfied.

'End of who?' the giant Madrun fairly squeaked.

The castellan gazed at him, his masked head tilted. 'Why, the ants of course! What else? Even-tine spores affect only them.' He floated back inside. 'Didn't I say that?'

The two regarded one another for a time in silence. Lazan eased out his long-held breath. He raised a hand and shook it, rattling the dice. 'The bones didn't see that,' he commented.

Madrun nodded in profound agreement. 'Yes. Spores. Much too small to be seen.'

*

They took turns keeping watch at the ruined door to the bar. A barrier of a table and heaped chairs blocked it. A few of the regulars had banged on the table to be let in and Picker nearly speared one fellow who refused to believe the bar was actually closed and tried to climb in over the chairs.

Two days after the Seguleh entered town Blend was watching the street from a front window when she called out, 'Trouble!'

Spindle snatched up his makeshift spear and ran for the front. He peered out between the slats they'd hammered across the window: the hunched mage, Aman, across the way. With him were several Seguleh. Spindle glanced back over his shoulder. The historian sat at his usual place. Picker had run for the rear. The bard was out. 'Hood. We are so dead,' he groaned.

He set aside the spear to pick up one of the readied crossbows. Blend did the same. 'Raise your Warren,' she told him.

'My Warren's no use here.'

Blend sent a scornful look from her window. 'Your Warren's never of any damned use. What about your *other* help?'

He was silent for a time, considering. Blend fired through the window. 'The next one won't miss!' she bellowed. 'Stay away!'

The mage, or whatever he was, Aman, remained across the street, watching, while the Seguleh advanced. Duiker came to Spindle's side. 'I'm unarmed. Perhaps I could talk to them . . .'

'You could try,' Spindle told him; then, to Blend, 'My other help says we're not alone here.' He was forced to fire on an advancing

Seguleh. The woman knocked the bolt aside with her blade. *Gods damn! From only twenty feet away, too.*

'What are your terms?' Duiker called from the scorched doorway.

'Your heads are my terms,' the mage shouted back.

A scream of surprise and terror sounded from the rear and Blend jumped. Picker? She threw down the crossbow and ran for the door to the pantry and kitchen. Duiker took her place, thrusting with a spear. He drew the haft back, surprised, to examine its cleanly severed end.

As Blend reached the door it was thrust open to reveal a Seguleh. She swung, her blade biting into the man's chest. He responded by grasping her arm and twisting. She buckled, hissing her pain and leaving the long-knife standing from the man's leather-armoured chest.

Spindle stared, then sniffed the air. Vinegar? Blades hacked at the wooden slats behind him. 'Hey – it's them pickled fellows from downstairs!'

Picker rushed out from behind the preserved Seguleh. She twisted its grip from Blend's wrist and it moved on, ignoring them. Spindle and Duiker retreated from the front where the living Seguleh were pushing back the barrier, and watched in disbelief as three more of the slow-walking, deliberate creatures emerged from the rear and took up defensive positions with the one Bland had stabbed: two at the front and two others holding the windows. The rest Spindle assumed were covering the back. At the entrance the two attacking Seguleh thrust and cut so beautifully he could only watch, awed. But their preserved – undead? – brethren, while slower, possessed the insurmountable advantage of already being dead. And so blades sliced into leathery hardened flesh to no visible effect and the attackers could make no headway.

As the assault wore on it looked to Spindle as if their protectors would be literally hacked to pieces, so he went behind the bar to collect his kitbag. Then he jumped up on to a table in full view of the entrance, he pulled out a wrapped object, shook off the layer of insulating cloth and held over his head his last remaining cusser. 'See this?' he shouted.

The attacking Seguleh flinched back a step – they indeed recognized what he had.

'Don't press me! You come in here we all go together! Understand?'

'We won't just lay down our swords, y'damned fool,' Picker yelled out of a window.

Dragging uneven steps sounded outside and the bent figure of the mage, Aman, appeared at the doorway. He pushed aside the two Seguleh to study the tableau first through one eye then through the other, much lower one; the Seguleh ready, weapons poised; their preserved undead fellows; Blend and Picker taking advantage of the lull to wind crossbows; Duiker already holding a loaded one; and Spindle, arms upraised.

'You wouldn't dare wreck this temple,' Aman said.

'Temple?' Spindle said in disbelief. 'This is a bar.'

'A bar. You think this is a bar?'

'It's our bar,' Picker said. 'So we can blow it up if we want to.'

'Privilege of ownership,' Blend added, spitting to one side.

The mage turned to Duiker. 'And what of you, historian? Are you prepared to die?'

Duiker levelled the crossbow on him. 'I've already died.'

One of the mage's mismatched eyes twitched and he frowned his acceptance of the point. 'I see. Well argued. For now, then.' He waved the Seguleh back.

Once they were up the street Spindle couldn't help himself and he leaned out of the door to yell: 'Hey, you Seguleh boys. You heel real well. Do you roll over too?'

It seemed to him that the four with Aman all missed a step with that comment, and their backs straightened. But he couldn't be sure. He turned back to the bar to find their preserved Seguleh guardians shuffling back downstairs. Everyone watched them go then lifted their heads to stare at him.

'What?'

'You're not a proper saboteur, Spin,' Picker said, and nodded to his hand. 'Could you put that away now?'

He saw that he was still cradling the cusser in one hand. 'This?' He threw it up and caught it again to a collective gust of breaths from the other three. 'Aw, don't worry. It's a dud. Hollow.'

Blend reached up as if to throttle him. 'Well you *ought* to let us know, dammit all to the Abyss!'

'No. You shouldn't know. Don't you see? That would ruin the effect. They have to see the fear in your eyes to know its real, right?'

Picker waved him away. 'Aw, shove it.'

*　　*　　*

'Now is the time to gird one's loins for the labour ahead,' the diminutive fat man murmured as he walked the mud lane between leaning shacks of waste-wood, felt and cloth. He wiped his gleaming mournful face with a sodden handkerchief. 'Yes indeed . . . the time has come to hitch up one's trousers and be a man! Or is it to pull them down and be a man? I never could get that straight . . . oh dear, I really should stop right there!'

He paused at an intersection of two lanes where a dog eyed him, growling. No hordes of unreasonably angry washerwomen armed with dirty laundry! Excellent. And the Maiten in sight where come curling currents from the plain where fates move as they do – forward, misplacing things as they go.

Seven dogs now surrounded him, muzzles down between fore-limbs, lips pulled back from broken teeth.

Hoary old ones! Washerwomen preferable to this.

He drew a bone from one loose sleeve. 'Good doggies!' He threw. Though not nearly so far as he would have wished. He turned and ran, or jogged, puffing, in the opposite direction.

The next two corners brought him to the hut on the extreme western edge of the shanty town where he stopped, short of breath, and wiped his face.

'And here he is panting in anticipation,' the old woman sitting on the threshold observed around the pipe in her mouth.

'Indeed. Here I am yet again. Your ever hopeful suitor. Slave to your whim. Prostrate in inspiration.'

'I can smell your inspiration from here,' she observed, grimacing. 'You brought offering?'

'But of course!' From a sleeve he produced a cloth-wrapped wedge the size of a quarter brick.

The old woman raised her tangled brows, impressed, as she took it. 'Things are progressing nicely aren't they, love?' She tore a piece and moulded it in one grimed fist, warming and softening it. 'The circle complete, yes?' and she eyed him, smirking.

He ducked his head. 'Ah – yes. Spoke too quickly Kruppe did. Yet, is it not so? Was Kruppe not quite correct? There! Yes, god-like perspicacity that.'

'Back to anticipation, are we?' the old woman murmured, and she drew long and hard on the pipe. 'Suggesting . . . perspiration.'

'Yes. Well. I am dancing as fast as I can, dearest.'

'Hmm, dancing,' she purred, exhaling a great stream of smoke.

'That's what I want to see. Won't you come in?'

'Gladly. Dogs and washerwomen and whatnot. But before – you have them, yes? Ready?'

She pressed her hands to her wide chest. 'All hot and ready for you, love.'

The man passed a hand over his eyes. 'Kruppe is speechless.'

'For once. Now, come in – and think of Darujhistan.' And she disappeared within.

Kruppe wiped his slick forehead. 'Oh, fair city. Dreaming city. The things I do for you!'

Shall we draw a curtain across such a commonplace domestic scene? Modesty would insist. Yet Kruppe found the witch athwart her tattered blankets snoring to beat a storm. Well. Shall vanity be stung to no end? Shall the Eel skulk away tail between its . . . whatever? Never! The prize awaits! And he knelt over the insensate woman, reaching for her layered shirts.

To feel eyes upon him. Beady eyes, low to the ground.

He turned to find the dogs watching from the doorway, eager, tongues lolling.

Aiya! Kruppe cannot perform like this! He flapped his hands. 'Begone! Have you no decency?'

Liquid eyes begged, muzzles nudged forepaws.

Defeated, Kruppe drew yet another bone from within his voluminous sleeve and threw. The dogs spun away, claws kicking up dirt.

'Now, where were we, my love?' He wriggled his fingers above her and there from a fold of the shirts peeped the weave of a dirty linen sack.

Aha! And now to pluck this blushing blossom . . .

Kruppe walked the trash-strewn mud ways of Mainten town, and all was well. He inhaled the scent of the open sewer, the steaming waste, and sighed. He patted his chest where a bag rested still warm from another, far greater and more bountiful nook. All was music to his ears: the fighting dogs, the laundry slapped with alarming force upon the rocks, the fond taunting and rock-throwing of the playful local urchins.

And now for the city! Fair Darujhistan. Ringed round and enclosed. Yet are there not ways around all walls and gates for such as the slippery perspiry Eel!

CHAPTER XIV

It is said that once a ruler in far off Tulips hosted a great and rich banquet (Tulips then being a prosperous city, unlike now) at the end of which he invited the guests to stand and give their definition of a full and happy life – the best version of which he would reward with a heavy torc of gold. One after another the guests stood to assure the ruler that his was in fact that best exemplar of a full and happy life. A Seguleh traveller chanced to be attending the celebration and she did not rise to participate in the competition. Irked, the king bade the woman stand and deliver her, all too secretive, version of a full and happy life.

The woman dipped her mask in compliance and stood. 'Of a full and happy life I can give no accounting,' she replied. 'But we Seguleh believe that the gods give men and women glimpses of happiness only to reach again to take them away. Therefore, it seems to us that it is only at the very end, at one's death, that any such measure can be made.'

And the king bade the woman depart without any largesse or honour, for he thought it utter foolishness to withhold measure until the end. Yet it is said that afterwards all peace of mind fled the ruler as he fretted without cease over when his many advantages might slip from him and in the end he died tormented and mad.

Histories of Genabackis
Sulerem of Mengal

JAN HAD GROWN UP KNOWING AN OLD SAYING AMONG THE SEGULEH: certainty is the spine of the blade. And he accepted this, making it part of his own bones. For were they not the sword of truth?

The anvil of its testing? Yet nothing since the Call was as he thought it would be. Nothing in the shining glory of service to the First in their songs and stories had prepared him for the truth to be found here, in their original home, Darujhistan.

Doubts assailed the others. That much was obvious. Therefore the duty was upon him to shoulder the weight of those doubts. To take them all upon himself and show there need be no concern. For was he not the Second? Did not all their eyes turn to him for guidance, for assurance? Let the purity of the cut lie in the steadiness of the blade.

So shall it be. Let it not be said that the Second bent from his responsibilities.

Only the First can call. And they answered. What need be complicated in that? And what do they find but the ancient mask that is a circle of gold? As storied and as fearsome as in their legends of old. What can he do but obey?

Why, then, this need to dwell upon any of this at all?

Perhaps because they were warriors. Not guards. Not warders of people or of the peace. The transition was easily accomplished; these local authorities, these Wardens, acquiesced immediately. Challenges were minimal. Only two deaths. One, a local simpleton, the other far too stubborn to pass by unanswered.

Now, perhaps now, began the truly difficult part as mundane daily trivia intruded upon their purpose.

Such as now, confronted by these two shabby would-be guards in the hands of Palla, Sixth, here in the Court. Jan signed to Ira, Twentieth, who demanded: 'Why have you returned? The hired guards have all been dismissed.'

One knuckled his dirty sweaty brow. 'Your pardons, sirs and madams. We've not been let go that we know of.'

Jan tilted his head and Ira continued, 'The orders were given. All have been notified.'

The man saluted once more. 'That's all as you say for sure, sirs and madams. Me 'n' Leff here we don't dispute any of that.'

'Then what is your claim?' Ira demanded.

Jan gave Palla a sign and she released them. They straightened their armour.

'Well, ma'am,' began the spokesman – though not necessarily the lower of the pair. Frankly, between these two, any gradation at all was difficult to tell. 'It's just that we're not your usual run o' the mill Majesty Hall guards. No sir . . .'

'They work for me,' breathed a weak voice.

Jan peered at the bedraggled figure of the Mouthpiece of the Legate. He inclined his head in respect. 'This is so?' he asked. 'They answer to you?'

The man's eyes darted, haunted and bloodshot; his features had sunk to a sweaty pasty pallor. Clearly this fellow found his duties far outmatched the strength of his nerves. Jan's gaze shifted to the masked Legate, motionless on his throne. He appeared unaware. Yet always he demonstrated preternatural knowledge of all that went on around him. And this man spoke his will. Jan wondered at such an unlikely choice. However, again, it was not for him to wonder.

'Yes,' the man affirmed, a new certainty entering his quavering voice. 'I remember them. I hired them.'

Jan signed his assent. 'Very well. It shall be as you say.' He turned away, dismissing them from his thoughts. He scanned the court searching for potential dangers or threats and found only one. The sorceress, Envy, with her flowing green dress and curled oiled hair. How he longed to part her head from her body for the debasement she brought to his brother and two followers. But she was an honoured guest of the Legate and so must he swallow her presence.

Oh, certainly some members here of the court obviously longed to challenge the Legate. Their posture, breaths and sweat shouted it – especially one older ex-soldier councillor who looked as thought he might have been a potential threat, a decade ago. And hints had come to him of assassination attempts, which the Legate and his pet mages handled.

All very well. So why then this unease? This discomfort? Perhaps it is the loss of Cant. I miss its green mountain slopes. Peace of mind slipped away with it beyond the horizon. Soon Gall will sense this and he will challenge. Then there will be a new Second and all of this will no longer be my concern. I almost welcome it. Is this what cowardice feels like?

The Legate stood then and descended the throne of pale white stone. He gestured and Jan moved to join him. The members of the court, masked councillors, their wives and masked mistresses, aristocrats and wealthy merchants, all parted at his approach. He stopped before the Legate and inclined his masked head in obeisance.

'Second.' The Mouthpiece had come to his side. 'Our enemies await to the west. You Seguleh are my blade and anvil. Crush them and Darujhistan shall rule all these lands unrivalled, as before.'

'I understand, Legate. These invading Malazans shall be removed from our shores.'

The Legate gestured impatiently. Though the beaten gold features could not change, for ever cast into their secretive half-smile, the shifting light and shadow enlivened the lips and empty eyes with expression. Now they appeared angered.

'The invaders are but a nuisance. They mean nothing. No. I speak of the true threat. This city's eternal enemy . . . the Moranth.' The Mouthpiece let out a strangled gasp as he spoke these words and clamped a hand to his mouth as if he were about to be sick.

Jan dared glance up more fully, as if he could discern some intent from the golden oval before him. 'The Moranth, Legate? I do not understand.'

'Always they forestalled us,' the Mouthpiece began again, his voice ghostly faint. 'They alone defied us when all others fell. Now we shall finish them.'

'The Moranth wars ended a millennium ago.'

'With the fall of the last of the Tyrants and the breaking of the Circle, yes.' The oval turned to address Jan more directly. 'Now that Darujhistan arises renewed we must answer that crime against us, yes?'

And what could Jan do but bow when commanded by his First? For the gold mask was the legendary progenitor, the Father of them all. *Attack the Moranth? Bring them low? An entire people? Was this what we were forged to accomplish? Our noble purpose?*

And you in your cracked wooden mask who told me so little. Was this the burden you sought to spare me? Well do I understand it now. No wonder we hide our faces.

That burden is shame.

*   *   *

Captain Dreshen found Ambassador Aragan in the stables currying the two remaining horses. Catching his breath he reported: 'Sir! The majority of the Seguleh have marched from the city.'

Aragan straightened to peer over the back of the black bay, Doan, his favourite. He rested his hands there, a brush in each. 'Out of the city?' His gaze slitted. 'Which way?'

Dreshen nodded their shared understanding. 'West.'

'Dead Hood's own grin. We have to warn them.'

'The mounts won't make it all the way.'

'No.' Aragan wiped his sleeve across his face. 'A boat. Fastest one we can find. Then we'll ride.'

'Yes. And . . . can we count on reinforcements?'

'No. No reinforcements. No recruits. Nothing. Everything's been committed to another theatre.'

Dreshen could not believe it. 'But what of our gains here?'

Aragan threw a blanket over Doan's back. 'Seems Unta considers us overextended. And I have to say I'm inclined to agree.' He eyed Dreshen up and down. 'Now get the Sceptre and our armour, Captain. In that order.'

The Untan nobleman drew himself up straight, grinning and saluting. 'Aye, sir. With pleasure.'

The two horsemen rode to the waterfront carrying large bundles tied behind the cantles of their saddles, and led their mounts down to the private wharves. Here a grossly exaggerated price was paid in rare silver councils for immediate passage west. A gangway was readied and the mounts were guided down on to the deck of the low, sleek vessel. Hands threw off lines and picked up oars. The vessel made its slow way out of the harbour to the larger bay where the freshening wind caught the sails. The pilot threw the side rudder over and they churned a course along the coast to the west.

*

Almost within sight of the ever-creeping edge of the Maiten shanty town rose the Great Barrow of the Son of Darkness, Lord of Moon's Spawn, Anomander Rake. Here a bear of a man sat in the grass and eyed the late afternoon glow of distant Darujhistan.

The lake air had cooled his temper, and now he recognized his vow to squeeze some sense into this creature who paraded as the Legate as foolish and unrealistic in the extreme. What was he to do? Use the hammer there? In the city? Kill tens of thousands? No. And this Legate knew it. So what was he to do?

For the first time in many years no responsibilities weighed upon his shoulders. No cause to champion. He turned back to the barrow. Nearby, the pilgrims and worshippers who congregated here were erecting a tent for him. He hadn't asked. But they knew him as the one who had raised the barrow and so he shared in their worship and regard.

He was not unaccustomed to it. All who worshipped Burn knew him as her champion. Caladan Brood, Warlord of the north. Yet war was far from his chosen vocation. Oh, he revelled in the individual challenge. Wrestling and trials of strength and skill. But war? Organized slaughter? No. That was the field of cold-hearted weighers of options such as Kallor. Or the opposite, those who inspired from all-embracing hearts, such as Dujek.

And what of him? Did he have this quality? He supposed he did, but in another way. Like Anomander, he inspired by example.

So he would wait. As before, eventually someone would be needed to settle things one way or the other. That was what he did best. Have the last word. The final say. The finishing blow.

*　　*　　*

The merest nudge of Sall's hand sent Yusek sprawling to the beaten dirt of the practice yard.

'You were off-balance again.'

She looked up at the kaleidoscope pattern of his mask, the amused brown eyes behind, and knocked aside his proffered hand. 'So I noticed. I was leaning forward because I was trying to hit you. That's the whole point, isn't it?' She jumped up to face him.

'Do not sacrifice form for a possible hit. When you lean forward you bring your head closer. Not a good idea.'

'But what if I hit?'

A wave in the Seguleh hand-talk dismissed the idea. 'What if you miss?'

Fine. Be that way. Yusek struck a *ready* pose, sword before her in both hands, tip held steady angled outwards at a height about level with her nose. At first she'd resisted his insistence that she use a two-handed sword grip, arguing that daggers were quicker. But Sall had been unmoved. He pointed out that most of her opponents would be larger than her and so she would need the added leverage.

When she'd grudgingly agreed, saying it would help 'muscle them back', he'd shaken his head yet again.

'No muscles.'

'What do you mean no muscles? Everyone knows that's what you do in a fight – you smash the other guy down.'

'No. Do not strain. Do not tense until the last instant. Let the blade fall on its own. Let its weight do the work.'

It all sounded crazy to her. But she'd seen the lad cut through all the most fearsome, *and big*, hulking swordsmen she'd known, so fair enough.

Now, he circled her yet again, studying her stance. He crouched before her, tilting his masked head. 'You have the same problem I used to have. Your stance is too long – always too eager to rush in, yes?'

'That's how you finish it. Bring it to them.'

Sall gave a sad shake of his head. He unwound a leather strip from his sash and knotted it round one of her ankles. 'What's this? Tying me up?' He paused, but only for an instant, then waved her other foot closer. She edged it inward.

'Closer yet.'

She gritted her teeth but complied. He tied the length of cloth tight, straightened. 'Very good. This distance will allow you to recover more quickly in either direction. I want you to pace the length of the field in the high angle cut with each step, yes?'

'Fine.'

'Begin.'

She stepped, swinging, and almost fell as her extended foot was yanked short. She turned to stare at him, appalled. *Was I that unbalanced?* He urged her onward.

Fine. Just dandy. She concentrated on her stride and started again. The shorter stance felt uncomfortable and awkward. But then, she'd been standing however she damned well pleased all this time. No one had ever shown her any technique. She must have all kinds of bad habits.

The wind was cold but she was sweating now as she paced up and down the length of the dirt practice yard. On the far side of the field the priests were out doing their forms, which Sall explained were some sort of moving meditations. It made no sense to her. She found a rhythm, cutting side to side as she stepped, turning, and cutting again. Her arms burned. Holding an iron bar out from your body all day built up endurance and strength. Now, when she picked up her old fighting dirks, the heaviest she could find, they were like hollow sticks in her hands. And it seemed to her that with the slightest shift of her two-handed grip she could move the tip of the sword even faster than she could weave her daggers.

Leverage, Sall called that. The sword was a lever, he'd said. A lever for the application or redirection of force. Nothing more mystical than that.

When the sun set behind the western coastal peaks the air chilled quickly. Yusek dropped down next to Sall, exhausted, her shirt wet with sweat.

'Your determination is commendable.'

'Well, I have a lot of catching up to do, don't I?' She nudged him with a shoulder. 'I could really use a back rub too . . .'

But Sall's attention was on his father Lo, who had spent these last days doing nothing more than watching the various priests at their practice and exercises. Now he had climbed to his feet, his gaze fixed. Sall stood as well.

Lo began making his way through the kneeling ranks of priests, none of whom moved. Sall edged forward also.

Of all the lousy timing. 'What is it?' Yusek asked, now a touch worried. *Gods, not like at Dernan's! Please no.* Sall signed for silence. *Silence! It's always silence with these two. That's their answer for everything. Don't they see that silence answers nothing?*

Lo stopped near the middle of the assembled priests. He stood before one fellow, salt and pepper hair cut short, features very dark, but calm, eyes downcast. Sall, Yusek noticed, was fairly quivering so tense was he. She also climbed to her feet.

Then Lo's blade was out, the tip extending close to the forehead of the kneeling man. The surrounding priests coolly shifted aside, not one saying a word. *Great Burn! What was this? What was going on?* 'Sall . . .' He signed again for silence, gesturing her aside.

Lo adjusted his grip on the sword, struck a *ready* stance, and for the first time Yusek heard words pass through his mask. 'I challenge you.'

The kneeling man said nothing. He did not move. He did not even look up.

Yusek's breath caught as Lo's blade flew up and he let go a heart-stopping yell, swinging for the man's neck. She jerked her head aside; she could not help it. When she opened her eyes Lo stood frozen, his blade pressed against the man's neck. The man himself appeared to have not flinched one hair's breadth.

She and Sall ran up through the motionless priests. The man slowly raised his eyes. In the darkening afternoon light they appeared to carry the depths of the ocean within them. He mouthed one word: *No.*

Lo stepped back sheathing his blade. Then he turned and walked away. Sall stood for a time staring down at the kneeling man, then he followed his father. Yusek remained. The priests merely returned to their duties, sweeping the compound, chopping wood, readying the evening meal. While Yusek watched, a bead of blood ran from the cut across the side of the man's neck.

Shaken, she retreated to her hut. So that was him? The slayer of the Son of Darkness? How could that be? He looked like nothing to her. No bluster, no show. It was contrary to everything she'd seen among Orbern's gang, or Dernan's. Just a man past middle age. Impossible to pick out of a crowd. Yet Lo had somehow managed. Just by watching. Obviously there was much more here than she could see.

She filled a bowl at the kitchens then sought out Sall. She found him sitting before his room. She sat next to him, tore off a pinch from her flatbread and dipped it into the stew. 'Now what?' she asked, chewing.

He seemed to have been studying his open empty hands on his lap. 'We leave. No one can be compelled to accept a challenge. My father could now claim Seventh should he choose to do so. I don't believe he will, however. Not like this.'

'Going to talk to him?'

'Who?'

'*Who*? Him of course. Ask him why he's here. What he's doing. Maybe you'd learn something.'

Sall made a gesture of helplessness. 'There is no need. He has made his position clear.'

Yusek studied Sall for a time as if attempting to peer past his mask. Then she gave a disgusted grunt. 'Gods . . . how you fellows manage is a mystery to me. How do you fucking accomplish anything? Aren't you the least bit curious?'

He gave a cutting sign with his hand. 'If he wanted to speak, he would do so.'

'Oh? He'd just go on like you blabbermouths?' She stood. 'Well *I'm* going to talk to him. Even if you won't.'

'Yusek . . .'

She paused, looking down. 'Yes?'

'Thank you.'

Grunting again, she left. *Can't fucking believe this crap. Should I tuck them in, too?* Maybe this wasn't all so different from the bluster and chest-thumping she'd seen at Orbern's. Posturing. Maybe it was all just posturing taken so far no one could back down any more – even if they wanted to.

She wondered. She really wondered.

The fellow was still kneeling in the same place. Looking west into the darkening mauve and deep blood-red of the fading sunset. Above, blotting out any stars that might've been visible, arced the jade curve of the Scimitar.

She sat next to him, dipped her bread, and tore off a bite with her teeth. 'So . . .' She chewed and swallowed. 'As good as any place to hide, I suppose.'

His gaze slid round to her. He let out a long breath. *Like I'm the pebble in the shoe*, she thought.

'They send you?'

'No they fucking well didn't send me. You're the man of the world, right? You should know they wouldn't do something like that.'

His mouth quirked up and he let go something that might've been a rueful snort. His gaze slid back to the west. 'Lectured by a child. Serves me right. Well, yes. That was unfair of me. They wouldn't do something like that. I'm just tired. Tired of it all.'

'Tired of what?'

He raised his chin to the west, to the sunset and the Scimitar. 'Choices are being made even as we speak. Important choices that will affect all of us. I refuse to be part of it. I'm tired of being used.' His voice fell and it seemed to Yusek that he wasn't talking to her any longer. Perhaps he'd never really been talking to her at all. 'I did what I thought was right. Damn them all, I don't even know what the right choice *is* any more. I don't even know if one exists. Everything I do is used.'

'If everything you do is used one way or the other then why worry about it? There's nothing you can do about all that. That's beyond your control, right?' The man's gaze slowly edged back to her. 'I mean, who cares about them? They can all take a flying leap into the Abyss, right? You can only do what you think is right, yes?'

One dark brow arched up. 'That's one way of looking at things. Maybe you should get some sleep. You've got a long day ahead of you tomorrow.'

Now who's tucking who in?

'Right.' She stood. 'I heard them say you killed the Lord of Moon's Spawn. But I don't think that's right. I mean, he's an Ascendant, right? Immortal. You can't just kill someone like that.' She shrugged. 'Well, that's just what I think.'

The man's gaze followed her as she crossed the moonlit central field and remained fixed for some time where she disappeared amid the stone huts. Then his eyes slowly swung back to the west, the night sky, and the Scimitar above. He felt it there, in the west. Tugging at him. It was happening again. Another gathering.

He felt its call because he was close himself. Close, if not already there. But fighting. Refusing. As he told the girl: it was a choice awaiting him. It seemed that no matter which way he turned there it was, inevitable.

If only he knew which would be for the best. Yet perhaps it wasn't a question of choice. Perhaps it had always been merely about *doing*. Perhaps that was the better way of thinking of things.

He could not be sure and that doubt was a torment. Because he didn't think much of his choices so far.

In the morning Yusek stepped out chilled and wrapped in her blanket to see the man still there, still kneeling, the pink and amber sun's rays painting his back.

Now that just ain't human.

She shuffled to the kitchens for hot tea and a round of fresh bread. She had to jostle elbows and push herself forward just to swipe that much. These boys and girls might be priests and such, she reflected, but they sure weren't shy when mealtime came around.

At her hut she packed what few bits and pieces she owned into a roll that she tied off and threw on to her back. Her new sword she belted at her left hip. On the grounds she found Sall and Lo ready to go. The fellow Lo had challenged was there as well.

Sall greeted her. 'We are leaving.'

She couldn't help looking to the sky. 'Yeah. I guessed.'

'Where will you head?' he asked.

She shrugged, indifferent. 'I dunno. Mengal, I guess. Thanks for the lessons.'

He gave a sign she recognized as meant to dismiss the subject. 'It was nothing. You were a conscientious student. That is all a teacher can ask for.'

She knew Sall to be her age but sometimes he talked so stiffly, like he was some old guy of thirty or something.

The fellow Lo had challenged stepped forward. Sall inclined his head to the man and, incredibly, so did Lo.

So . . . Lo just indicated that he considers the man higher ranked. Even though the man refused his challenge. He doesn't want to take the rank that way. Just as Sall said. Hey! I'm starting to understand these crazy people!

But abbreviated bows only seemed to make the man's already pained face tighten even more. 'I'm sorry you came all this way for nothing,' he growled, his voice hoarse. 'But when you get to Cant, give my regards to your Second. I've heard good things of him.'

Sall turned his masked face to Lo. Something passed between them. Sall turned back to the man. 'Slayer of Blacksword, we are not returning to Cant.'

Something almost like panic seemed to claw at the man's face. 'You're not?' The lines bracketing his eyes and mouth tightened into an angry suspicion. 'Tell me where you are headed.'

'We travel to Darujhistan to join our brothers and sisters. The First has called and we have answered.'

Yusek stared. Darujhistan? They're going to *Darujhistan*!

The man was shaking his head, appalled. 'All the scheming gods – you mustn't go there. Don't you see?'

'See . . . what?'

'Don't make yourself a weapon,' he said, his voice thick with emotion. 'Take it from me. Weapons get used.'

Sall tilted his head a fraction. His eyes behind the mask appeared troubled, but he answered, 'It is our duty. Our defining purpose. It makes us Seguleh.'

The man blinked as if fighting back tears. Every word Sall spoke seemed to strike him like a blow. 'Gods, you people have backed yourselves up to the very Abyss . . .'

Lo moved slightly – a motion Yusek would never have caught before, but she understood it now as a gesture of impatience.

Sall said: 'Thank you for your words, Slayer of Blacksword. But we must go.'

'I'm going with you,' the man said.

Even masked, Sall's shock was obvious. He glanced at Lo who answered with a gesture Yusek had seen him use in regard to her very often: the *It's her life* sign.

'If you wish,' Sall said. 'You are free to travel where you will.'

'Fine.' He motioned to the hut dwellings. 'Just let me pack a few things.'

After the man had gone, Yusek faced Sall. 'You didn't tell me you were going to Darujhistan!' And she couldn't believe it when the answering shift of his shoulders said, *How is this is relevant?*

*   *   *

'How come we ain't shootin' at 'em?' Bendan said, chin on his arms as he leaned against the top of the palisade of sharpened logs. He was watching the encircling lines of Rhivi cavalry encamped so close to the hilltop fort he was damned sure he could throw a stone and hit one.

'Short on crossbow bolts and such, ain't we?' Hektar said, strangely cheerful. 'And they know it.'

'How do you know they know it?' Bendan accused.

''Cause they're camped so close – that's why.'

Bendan returned to glaring at the tribesmen and women. 'Well, don't matter. Not like they need to do anything. I mean, we're trapped, ain't we? Got nowhere to go. Encircled. Brilliant piece of planning from these Fists, hey?'

The sergeant rubbed a hand over his bald nut-brown pate. 'From the city, aren't you?'

'Uh-huh. That's right. Darujhistan.' He didn't bother clarifying that really he was from a rubbish heap next to it. 'Why?'

'Well then, you'd know that if we ain't going anywhere then neither are these fellows. And that's all to our advantage, isn't it? We just have to wait them out. They got herds to mind, families, territory to patrol. And they only go to war a few months out of the year. My guess is we're already far past that season, right?'

Bendan blinked, his mouth open. 'Yeah. That's right . . . damned right.'

Bone joined them on the catwalk behind the palisade. At least, the fellow was the right height for Bone. The man was smeared head to foot in green-grey clay that was drying and cracking even as they watched. The old saboteur winked at Hektar and cracked a smile. Even his teeth were gummed with the clay.

'You fellers done playing in the mud?' the sergeant asked.

'Yeah. We're all done.'

''Bout time. Now go get cleaned up.'

The bemired figure straightened to strike a parade-ground formal salute then grinned, his clay-caked cheeks cracking.

Bendan watched him go. 'Why'd he have to get so dirty?'

'All that mud keeps you warm at night. Didn't you know that, lad?' Hektar wandered off.

Bendan eyed his retreating back. 'Yeah – I knew that!' he called. 'I know things.'

That night officers went round all the sergeants, whispering to each to rouse his squad. Outside the tall walls of the palisade the night was bright with blazing campfires that encircled the fort. Bendan's squad was one of the ones positioned at the base of the palisade where they waited, tensed. Others jammed the catwalk, hunched down behind the sharpened log ends, shields at the ready.

One fellow signed from atop the catwalk. 'Here it comes,' Hektar murmured. He peered up the lines of squads jamming the camp. 'Ready shields.'

Bendan gaped at the huge Dal Hon. 'What? What's comin'? Ready shields? Why?'

Then a great roar shook the ground from beyond the palisade wall. A rushing and thrumming and hissing that sounded like a hungry beast lunging for them. The night sky blossomed as bright as day as a ring of fire-arrows arced up above the fort as dense as hail.

'*Mother of all the gods*!' was all the time Bendan had before something slammed his shield down on to his head, making him stagger.

'Don't look up, you damned fool,' Little snapped.

Something struck him in the chest, sloshing frigid water all down his front. 'Take it, quick!' someone shouted. 'Let's go!'

Dazed, he grasped a small wooden barrel and passed it on. Next came a leaky leather bucket already nearly empty. One-handed, Bendan passed it up the line to the squads atop the catwalk where it was emptied over the timbers and tossed back down. The troopers worked in pairs, one emptying, one holding his shield high over them both.

For what seemed half the night Bendan passed along a bizarre collection of barrels, large and small, leather satchels, earthenware jugs, even leather boots. Most held barely any water at all by the time they reached him, but on they went to contribute to maintaining the palisade wall. Meanwhile, behind him he caught glimpses of flaming tents and the infernos where their remaining wagons and carts had been left to burn. What few horses they'd kept were slaughtered that night – mostly out of mercy, as the encircling fires drove them insane with terror.

Bendan's squad was relieved before dawn. For cover they hunched under their shields at the base of the palisade. The salvos were nothing like as dense as before, but a steady fall of harassing fire was being maintained. Incredibly Hektar still carried his idiotic bright smile. Bendan was soaked and frozen, his arms and back ached as if mattocked and he hadn't gotten a wink all night. He wanted to smack the grin from the man's damned face.

'What's to smile about?' he snarled.

'Outrun 'em again, didn't we?' the man laughed. 'They thought they'd hit on the answer but ol' Steppan, she was one step ahead. Ha! Get that? One step.'

'Yeah. Ha, real funny. Now what?'

The sergeant raised his great rounded shoulders. 'Whatever. We're still in here and they're still out there. That's all that counts.' He sat up straighter to yell: 'Another day's soldiering and another of the Emperor's coins, ain't that right lads?' Laughter up and down the walls nearby answered that. 'Now get some sleep.'

Sleep? How could the man sleep knowing that at any instant thousands of these Rhivi tribals could come storming this pitiful wall? And laughter? How could anyone think this was funny? Still, that laughter . . . it had been that dark sort that if he'd heard it in a bar would've sent him reaching for his knife.

*

Midway up the scree slope of a mountain shoulder a lone rider halted his mount to swing himself from the saddle. His boots crunching on the bare rocky talus, Torvald Nom eyed the ever-steepening valley side then rested his forehead against horses flank. *Shit. Didn't look so quite so precipitous from the foothills.* Cursing the fates, he set down his pack, undid the bridle, and unbuckled the girth to let the saddle fall to the ground. He poured out the last of the feed into this hand and let the horse finish it, then gave it a slap and waved it off. He watched it make its way back down the slope heading for the valley floor, then shouldered his pack and started up the loose rocks.

The view from the ridge revealed yet another valley in front of him and he let his head hang for a moment. *Me and my stupid ideas. Still . . .* He eyed the valley head where the talus gave way to naked rock which sloped back to a higher ridge and beyond that, far beyond that, a snow-capped peak. *The Moranth occupy these high mountain valleys? What do they eat? Snow and mist? Ye gods, I'll starve before reaching them.* He started down the slope, sideways, one hand catching at rocks and low, wind-punished brush.

Come dusk he reached the thin creek of melt that ran down the centre of the valley. It was loud amid its rocks and so cold it numbed his hand when he drank from it. He set down his pack and started searching for fuel. Night came swiftly in the upper valleys and he was surprised when the sunlight was cut off so soon in the west. All he had for kindling was dry moss and a few handfuls of duff. He took out his tinderbox and set to work.

The fire he coaxed to life did little thaw his bones. He huddled over the smoky smudge and thought of home. Tis throwing pots – and not necessarily at him. Warm dinners from her hands. He hadn't appreciated that as much as he should have. A lot to be said for that. Even more than warm embraces afterwards. Not that he could remember those; still, there must've been some, certainly. Once. Consummation of the union and all that. Winking friends and a great deal of liquor. He remembered being terrified that Rallick would show up and shove his knife into his back; which hadn't exactly helped his performance that night either.

Shivering, he decided he'd had enough of climbing. He could tramp from one end of this mountain range to the other and not turn them up. If they were here it was up to them to come to him. That he'd settle tomorrow. Having reached a decision on the matter, Tor gathered his blanket about himself and lay down to sleep.

In the morning's chill he shivered awake, stretched, emptied his bladder, and shocked himself with a splash of the frigid meltwater. He prepared for a march, but left one object out of his pack: one of the Moranth Blue globes given to him long ago when, as a much younger man, he'd saved a life. *And without expectation of any payment, too.* Yet the gift was offered, and it would have been gauche to reject such gratitude, wouldn't it? At least that had been his thinking at the time.

Now, he hefted the sapphire-blue ovoid and eyed the stream. It was a gamble; possibly a criminal waste. Yet how else to get attention quickly? If they had eyes out watching these high valleys, which he assumed they did.

Very well. Enough dithering. The sun is up, visibility is clear. I may be throwing away a fortune – my nest-egg, so to speak. But here goes.

He threw. The globe splashed into the streaming flow, which was hardly deep enough to cover it, and cracked against the rocks. Tor did not know what to expect, but certainly not the explosive report that echoed and re-echoed across the valley.

At the same time, for as far as he could see, all movement in the water suddenly ceased. As did all sound. Leaning closer, he saw that the stream was frozen – frozen solid where it had eddied, splashed and curled. A monstrous icicle that ran the entire length of the valley and on for who knew how far.

Well, that was . . . impressive. If this didn't get their attention, then he had no idea what might.

410

He sat leaning back against his pack and waited. Eventually, running water came trickling down from the heights over and around the streambed and the ice floe that choked it. Eventually, Tor imagined, this unnatural manifestation would melt.

Towards mid-day, when the sun had breasted the opposite valley side, an eerie whirring noise entered the valley. Tor stood. He knew he'd heard that sound before but for the life of him he couldn't quite place it. He peered about in growing unease. It was a sort of rhythmic humming or thumping, like a horse's distant gallop, only infinitely faster.

Something roared over his head, fanning up great clouds of dust, and he threw himself to the ground. The sound returned, circling around, and Tor hesitantly climbed to his feet to see one of the monstrous Moranth mounts, their quorl, settling down not far away. Its four wings fluttered in a shimmering rainbow blur. The bulbous faceted eyes regarding him seemed empty of emotion; yet perhaps they were not, as he'd heard that these beasts, like their diminutive dragonfly cousins, were carnivores.

A Moranth dismounted from the intricately carved leather and wood double saddle that hugged the beast's thorax. Tor was astonished to see that it was a Moranth Silver. He wondered if he should bow. The Silver and the Gold were aristocracy among the Moranth. Few ever saw them.

But *he* was now an emissary, was he not? If sub-rosa. And so Tor merely inclined his head in greeting. Closer, it was actually rather difficult to look directly at the Silver. Its chitinous armour reflected the light like a perfect mirror. The effect was quite dazzling. Also engraved swirling patterns covered each plate, adding to the confusion of the shimmering.

'You are Darujhistani,' the Silver said in accented Daru. 'What are you doing here on our border marches?'

'I come as an emissary of the Legate of Darujhistan.'

That gave the Silver pause. Its armour grated as it looked him up and down. 'In truth? You come as an emissary of this . . . *Legate*. All alone. Carrying stolen Blue alchemicals.'

Tor's stomach seemed to loosen. 'Stolen? Accusations? Does this pass as manners among you Moranth? I carry those items as gifts.' *Unless that Blue stole them in the first place . . .*

'Gifts? From whom? Name him or her.'

Tor forced himself to gesture casually even though he felt as if chunks of the ice from the stream were now slithering down

411

his back. 'Not for you. I am here to negotiate in the name of the Legate.'

The Silver cocked its helmed head. 'Negotiate?' A chuckle escaped it and from its high timbre Tor recognized that he faced a female Moranth.

And that chuckle made him damned uncomfortable. But he'd travelled with far more intimidating presences than this Silver and so he raised his chin. 'Yes. Negotiate. What of it?'

The Silver answered with a wave of her own while she continued to laugh quietly. 'Very well. Attend me and we will see what will come of these *negotiations*.'

She returned to the quorl. Tor threw on his pack and followed. He stepped gingerly around the great shimmering translucent wings to reach the long thorax. The Silver had already mounted. She gestured to the rear saddle seat, pointing. 'Use the long sheaths here for your feet,' she shouted over the loud whirring of the twitching wings. 'Push them down all the way. Wrap these straps around your forearms. Cinch them tight. Then hold these sunken handles here on either side.'

Tor nodded. *Right. Push down.* His slid his booted foot into the leather sheath. It took his leg up to the knee. He swung his other foot over the beast's back and down the other sheath. *Like stirrups, but with broad boots attached.* Sitting, he examined the mishmash of strapping before him. *Which ones do I wrap?*

He'd opened his mouth to ask when the Silver snapped the jesses and the quorl leapt into the air.

Tor found himself gaping down at the receding valley floor, his arms dangling and flailing. A hard gauntleted fist gathered up a handhold of his cloak at the neck and dragged him upright. The Silver shouted something that was lost amid the roaring hum of the wings and the rushing air. Tor quickly took hold of the handles sunk into the leather of the saddle.

Well, whatever that had been it must have been pretty insulting.

He was immediately frozen in the punishing constant wind. He hunched down behind the cover of the Silver's back. The wind hurt his eyes, too, so it was through the barest slits that he watched a mountain ridge slip drunkenly beneath them as the quorl arched, turning.

Gods . . . I'm going to puke all over this Silver's back. How embarrassing.

At the last instant Tor realized he had to but turn his head and the lashing wind would do the rest. His stomach was almost entirely empty anyway and so the gorge that came rushing up in a gagging acid heave hardly amounted to anything. As they swung over the next valley Tor sensed more than heard the Silver's continuing laughter.

Here Tor was surprised to see square fields of green and the shimmering of irrigation canals. The Silver guided her quorl over a walled settlement that hugged the naked rock of the valley head. Beneath him Moranth of every hue went about their work. Tor marvelled. Never had he ever heard of such a thing. No traveller that he knew of had ever penetrated the Moranth's borders.

The quorl began to circle in an ever narrowing spiral that brought them alighting on the broad flat roof of a tower. The Silver dismounted. Tor struggled to free his legs, feeling stiff and queasy with what seemed a curious analogue to seasickness. After much yanking he managed to release himself and staggered free of the quorl. A detachment of Moranth Black had climbed the rooftop. Tor shouldered his pack, eyeing them. The Silver gestured to the Black guards, speaking in the Moranth tongue. The Black encircled him. One motioned for him to drop his gear. Tor looked at the Silver. 'What's this?'

She was already on her way to the rooftop trap door and stairs down. 'You are to be imprisoned as a spy and a thief,' she said over her shoulder.

'What?'

The Black gestured again, insistent.

Tor waved the Black guard aside. 'I'll have you know I am an emissary!' he called as she disappeared down the stairs.

The Black reached for Tor's pack. Tor shook his finger in a negative. 'I am under the protection of the Legate.' The guard motioned to his fellow on Tor's left and involuntarily Tor glanced over.

Something smashed into his head from the right and his legs lost all strength. He toppled to the flags of the roof, his last thought a self-recriminatory *oldest damned cheap trick around.*

*   *   *

When Aman led her to his old shop Taya nearly deserted him at the door. 'What are we doing here? Give me one minute and I'll have all those soldiers' heads.'

The mage was fiddling with the door's many locks. 'No no, my dear. K'rul is not to be underestimated. There is a chance she may get hold of you.' He shot her a hard glance. 'Then we'd all be at risk.'

She accepted the warning with a simmering growl. '*Fine*. So what are we – oh, just force it!'

Aman looked up, horrified. 'Certainly not!' He opened the last lock. 'That would invite thieves.'

Inside, the wreckage hadn't changed. Their steps crushed the scattered litter. 'Now what?' she sighed.

'K'rul and her adherents have obviously planned ahead. What could possibly fend off Seguleh? Why, undead Seguleh, of course!' He stroked his uneven chin. 'Quite the poetic solution when one considers it.'

Taya fanned the dusty stale air. 'Yes, yes. There is a point? Or has your head finally cracked under all this pressure?'

He raised one gnarled and bent finger. 'Ah, but I've been planning too.' He crossed to where the huge statue glimmered in the shadows, dominating the room like a gigantic squat pillar. He peered up at it admiringly, perhaps the way one might admire a tall son. 'What can beat down all obstacles before it, never resting, never relenting? An automaton, yes?'

Taya eyed it doubtfully. 'I thought you said they weren't automatons.'

Irritation twisted half Aman's mismatched face. 'Normally, yes. However, I've been making certain . . . ah . . . innovations.' He patted the statue's chest where the mosaic of inset precious stones flashed. 'This one is my own project. And now it is time to set it into motion.' He hobbled to the rear of the shop.

Taya heard pots thumping, then a rhythmic grinding of mortar and pestle. She blew out a breath and looked to the cobwebbed ceiling. *Hoary ancients! I cannot believe I am wasting my time here!*

'I do not understand why Father tolerates this feud of yours,' she called.

'Hmmm?'

'Just ignore them!' she shouted. 'Leave them barricaded in that heap of stones.'

'The Warrens are a standing threat to us, my dear. Surely that must be obvious, even to you.'

She scowled, not liking the sound of that. He emerged carrying shallow ceramic bowls containing powders, which he lined up on the counter. She watched while he upended a tall earthenware jug over the statue, straining to reach its shoulders. Some sort of thick milk-like substance dribbled down its arms and front. Taya almost asked what it was, only to reconsider at the last instant. She decided she didn't want to know.

'How long is this going to take?'

'Long?' he murmured, distracted, as he rubbed the sticky liquid into the statue's torso and arms. 'Oh, quite some time. Quite some time.'

'Well . . . I'm going.'

He turned, blinking at her. 'Really? I thought you'd be interested.'

'Well, I'm not.'

He picked up one of the shallow ceramic bowls and dipped a finger into the powder, sighed. 'Let it not be said I did not try . . . I apologize, then, for attempting to further your education. There is no need for you to remain.'

'Thank you. I will be at court.'

'Of course you will,' he murmured as she yanked open the door.

*   *   *

Barathol had been napping in the afternoon heat when he awoke to see Scillara standing over him. 'That greasy fat fellow is here to see you.'

'Fat fellow?'

'That shabby one who warms a chair at the Phoenix Inn. Count your fingers when you're done talking with that one, I say.'

He rose, stretching. Joints popped. He slipped an arm round her waist. 'A breastfeeding mother is the most sensual sight to a father.'

She rolled her eyes. 'So you keep sayin'.'

'It's true.'

'Sure it is.' She pushed him to the rear door of the row-house. 'Try to get some more work. We're not living off the fat of the hog here.'

He found the man sitting at their small table, the chair pushed far back to make room for his round stomach. 'Make yourself at home,' Barathol said.

'Why thank you! I shall and did. I could not help but also notice that your pantry possesses remarkable potential for filling . . . when might this be accomplished? Soon, I hope?'

Barathol pulled out their one other chair and sat heavily. He considered for a moment and then said, 'I do the cooking here.'

'Excellent! Then I certainly am speaking to the most important person here. I would like eggs. Poached. And a roasted bird, preferably plucked beforehand. Or a roasted bird still containing its eggs. Whichever is quicker, speed being the operational consideration here. Efficiency.' He rested his pudgy hands on his stomach, grimacing.

Barathol crossed his arms, stretched out his legs and crossed them at the ankles. They reached halfway across their narrow main floor. 'I cook over the forge I built in the yard.'

The eager moon-round face fell. 'Oh dear. How unappetizing.' A hand flew to his mouth. 'I can't believe that word passed my lips. You say you actually cook over the fire? How primal. No wonder you are favoured by Burn.'

'What's that?'

'Nothing. You wouldn't have something, though, would you?' He pinched his thumb and forefinger together. 'Just a smidgen of a biscuit or a cut of lamb? Roasted, on a stick? A kebab? Yes, a kebab would be nice. Forge-roasted, perhaps?'

'No. Nothing.'

'Aiya! You are merciless! Is Kruppe to perish? Very well! You win, O ruthless bargainer. You may have the villa.'

Barathol frowned. 'The what?'

'Why, the villa outside the city. Cliff-top, with a view over Lake Azur, of course.'

'A villa? What for?'

'Dear Soliel! Isn't that enough?' The man pressed his hands to his straining waistcoat. 'I swear I have diminished. In the name of all that is civilized, relent!'

Barathol studied the sweaty, rotund figure. His black hair was so lacquered it looked like more than a layer of pitch paint slathered across his head. Delicate curls descended on to his forehead but these too were pasted down as if glued. The man's arsenic-white pallor was almost shocking in its contrast. While he watched, the fellow wiped his heavy jowls with a handkerchief so grey and grimed it seemed to do nothing more than reapply the shine of oil.

'Is there anyone at all like you, Kruppe?' he murmured wonderingly.

'What?' The fellow sat up straighter. The curve of his stomach pressed against the table. 'Another Kruppe? Why, such excess of excellence would contravene fundamental laws of creation. Or would that rather be a case of excellent excess? Nay, sir! Think of the poor ladies alone. Imagine what it would do to their respiration. They would not know which way to turn.'

'Quite,' Barathol agreed sotto voce.

'No, such dreams will have to wait. Yet what comportment such a one would possess. What élan. It would be a rare privilege to meet such a one, yes? Although . . .' He tapped a short pudgy finger to his lips, his gaze distant. 'How infuriating this paragon would be in his habit of always being right. His insufferable good looks. His intellect and generosity! No! I would hate him immediately and scheme for his downfall, of course.'

Blinking, the little man regarded Barathol anew. 'Is that squash? I swear I smell yellow squash. Sliced thinly and roasted over a high open heat. Such as that which may be possessed by a forge. For example.'

Barathol shook his head. 'No. No squash.'

'May the gods forgive such ruthlessness. The very thought. No squash indeed. Very well.' He pushed up his loose frilled sleeves and set his hands flat on the table. 'The villa, a nursemaid, housekeeper, groom and valet. And that is my final offer.' The handkerchief daubed at mouth and brows and the fellow deflated limp in his chair as if utterly spent, eyes shut, arms dangling loose.

Barathol cleared his throat. He didn't know whether to laugh or throw the man out. He took a long breath. 'For what, Kruppe?'

One eye cracked open. 'Why, for forging something, of course. Really, if I wanted shoes I would have gone next door.'

Barathol cocked his head. 'I do shoes, Kruppe. That's mostly what I do these days. Used to do swords but fashions change. Had to move to smaller premises. You want a dent beaten out of a pot? I'm your man. You want fine expert work? Try the guild.'

Kruppe sat up, straightened his crimson waistcoat. 'I remove my own dents, thank you very much. And I do not understand why anyone would wear iron shoes. Fashion does drive us to awkward choices, however, does it not? I will send a carriage. In the meantime, here are some papers that have recently come into my care.' He laid a folded packet on the table. 'Now I must take this opportunity to escape before even greater demands are made, terms raised, or outrageous conditions imposed – squash or no squash! Good day!' He threw his chin high and marched out.

Barathol eyed the packet for some time before letting out another breath and uncrossing his arms. He broke the wax seal and scanned the papers. He couldn't read them but they certainly looked official. They might be a title. Or a bordello's taxation report. He couldn't tell. He'd have to take them to the scribe on the corner who wrote letters for everyone in the neighbourhood.

He tapped them against the table and eyed the door to the rear yard. He'd have to be damned quiet about it. He slipped the papers into his shirt.

*   *   *

So it had come to this. All her struggle. Her long journey. Failure. Abject loathsome failure once again. She leaned on her staff and ran a hand through her sweaty hair, squinting in the constant stabbing glare of the quicksilver Vitr sea. Twice with the same man. That had got to be some kind of record. She'd let down Agayla – not to mention the Enchantress. And what trouble might come of that? She dreaded to think of the possible consequences.

Yet further options existed. More extreme alternatives. Tayschrenn didn't even seem to remember he was a mage and so he would pose no trouble. The only hurdle would be the man's shadow, Korus. And she and Leoman together might be able to handle him. That left those countless little wretches, and for her there lay the problem. They would surely crowd to his defence and she would be forced to strike them down.

And that she could not bring herself to do. It would be like attacking children. She just couldn't imagine it. *Gods! Defeated by my own principles.* Well, perhaps that wasn't such a bad thing after all. The Queen of Dreams could hardly fault her for that. She tapped the butt of the staff in the black sands, then swung it up over her shoulders and went to find Leoman.

He was asleep, curled up on his side. *Just like a boy. How does he do that? Sleep so soundly? It's like he's at peace.* An idea that jarred against what she knew of the man. She tapped his foot and he jerked, then stretched and blinked up at her. 'Yes?'

'All right. You win.'

He leaned up on one elbow and arched a brow. 'Win? Me?'

'Yes. There's no point in staying. We should go.'

He stood and brushed at his clothes, picked up his armour, threw his belted morningstars over a shoulder. 'So. You're going,' he said.

'Me? What do you mean me?' She motioned to the shore. 'Might as well say goodbye.'

'Yes.'

On the way to the sea Leoman said, 'You know, I find it very relaxing here. Restful. It reminds me of the deep desert. I always felt

418

comfortable there. It was just the people who occupied it I objected to.'

The moment they drew close to where Tayschrenn stood at the shore, the tribe of shambling malformed creatures he'd rescued from the Vitr gathered around protectively. Giant Korus strode to intercept them on its odd backwards-bending legs.

'What do you intend?' it demanded.

'We've come to say goodbye,' Kiska answered. 'We're going.'

'Goodbye? Farewell? You are leaving?'

'Yes.'

The creature's finger-long fangs grated like knives as it seemed to consider such a thing. It glanced over to where Tayschrenn was approaching from the glimmering surf. 'Very well. But I will be watching.' It lumbered aside.

'What is it?' the ex-mage called. 'I asked you to trouble us no more.'

Kiska bowed. 'Yes. Just come to say farewell. We are leaving.'

'I see.' He pushed back his long grey-shot hair, crossed his arms. It seemed to Kiska that he did appear younger. The harsh lines about his mouth and eyes had eased; gone was the watchfulness and guard-ed wariness from his gaze. Reborn in truth?

'Safe journey then,' he said. 'I bear you no ill will.'

'Yes. But perhaps some time from now—'

He'd raised a forestalling hand. 'No. I will never return to that. Tell whoever sent you to leave me alone.'

'Yes.' Kiska struggled against the tightness in her chest. 'There is just this. I understand this is yours.' She held out the crumpled stick and cloth remains of their guide.

He took it into his palm and studied the dry bundle of litter. 'What is it?'

'I don't know exactly – but I was told it belongs to you.'

'I don't want . . .' His voice fell away as he seemed to lose his con-centration.

Korus leaned close, looming over them all. 'Thenaj – what is this thing? Throw it away!'

But the man's hands clenched into fists around it, his body con-vulsing. He would have crashed to the sands but for the creatures easing him down. He curled into a straining knot, shuddering and twitching.

A huge fist closed about Kiska's cloak and armour from the rear, lifting her from her feet. 'What is this?' Korus boomed. 'What have you done to him?'

419

Leoman's gear fell to the sands as he grasped the demon's arm. 'We know nothing of this!' he yelled.

Kiska stared, horrified. *Gods! Have I killed him? Was this the Enchantress's scheme all along?*

Then Tayschrenn screamed. He threw his head back and howled his agony. His back arched as if it would snap. He screamed until his breath failed and he fell limp, immobile.

Kiska did not even struggle as the hand swept her spinning through the air. She crashed into the shingle and tumbled over and over, gouging a trail. Then Leoman was there wiping the sand from her face. 'Are you all right, girl? Speak to me.'

'I killed him,' she moaned. 'Me! It was to be *me* all along.'

'We don't know . . .'

A large shadow covered them and a voice snarled, 'Take them to the caves!'

CHAPTER XV

Tyranny remains because the weak and fearful seek it.

Letters of the Philosphical Society
Darujhistan

THE PASSAGES ORCHID LED ANTSY AND CORIEN THROUGH COULD only in the coarsest sense be named tunnels. As far into the distance as Antsy could see the naked rock canopy was intricately carved to imitate a wide forest. Branches glittered with precious stones and gems which had been set as if mimicking berries or flowers. They passed rooms where wrecked furniture carved from rare woods lay like abandoned works of sculpture. Such wood alone would make Antsy wealthy beyond measure. That such riches lay about ignored within these upper reaches of the Spawn told Antsy a great deal about the character of those who occupied the place. *After different coin, this lot.*

Here Morn met them. He emerged from the gloom and waited as they advanced. At his feet lay a pile of equipment: their gear. Antsy belted his sword and long-knife then shouldered his pannier, all the while eyeing the strange entity. He'd even recovered their food bags. 'Thanks,' Antsy said, meaning it. The shade had very probably saved their lives.

The ghost bowed to Orchid. 'I could not have you going hungry.'

'We're still for the Gap,' she warned him, firm.

He gestured ahead, inviting them onward. 'Of course.'

'Here is a question for you, Antsy,' Corien said after a time, his voice low, as they walked along. 'If we're supposed to be going to this 'Gap', why are we heading up?'

'It is the only way,' Morn answered from the front.

Antsy raised his brows to Corien in silent comment. Damned unnatural hearing on that man. The lad merely hefted the crossbow and offered a shallow bow. 'Very well. Let us grant that for the moment. Why then didn't we just turn round? Go out the way we came in?'

'There would be no boats there,' Morn answered, unperturbed. 'Easier now to go onwards.'

'Well . . . *now*, perhaps, but couldn't we've . . .' His voice died off as everyone stilled, peering about. A great juddering blow had shaken the artefact beneath their feet. Stone branches snapped, falling to explode into countless shards all about them. In a deafening avalanche of rock and broken furniture and rubbish the entire structure lurched to one side like a ship broadsided by an immense wave. Antsy tottered, side-stepping to hit the trunk of a stone tree. He reached for Orchid but missed as she rolled past. The Spawn now lurched back in the opposite direction and Antsy bashed his head on the stone of the tree. Reverberations of calving rock and tons of falling rubble shook and shuddered the caves all around them.

The drunken rocking of the immense artefact eased slowly. A new equilibrium was reached with the floor pitched sideways at a rather uncomfortable angle. Gems and cups rolled between their feet to clatter off into the darkness amid the stone tree pillars.

Orchid's eyes, black and huge in the mage-light, sought and found Antsy's. 'The Gap,' she called to Morn. '*Where is it!*'

The shade led them to a large opening carved to resemble an arch in an arboretum. Orchid stared in silent wonder, obviously awed. She faced Morn. 'The Processional Way?'

The ghost bowed. 'Indeed. You are well informed.'

She turned to Antsy and he was rather shaken to see her eyes almost glowing. 'We are very close.'

'About time,' he murmured, clearing his throat. 'Maybe I should lead now.' Then he sniffed the air wafting from the broad arched way and cocked his head. *Somethin' there. Something'* . . . He pulled Orchid out of view of the opening. She opened her mouth to speak but all it took was one glance at his face for her to snap it closed. *Good. We're gettin' tight now.*

He signed *wait* to Corien then poked his head round the corner to inhale once more. And there it was as before: sweat, oil, stink of clothes and armour too long unwashed. And one other thing; fish sauce. Damned Falaran fish sauce. Once tasted – or smelled –

never forgotten. 'Let go your balls, boys and girls,' he called. 'We've decided to let you live.'

'Who's that pissing uphill there?' a man called back in Falaran.

'Antsy. The Second.'

'What's a Second loser doing here?'

'Mustered out last year. Now I got me a backpack so full o' emeralds and rubies I can't hardly lift it. Could use a hand.'

'Put 'em up, lads. Let's have a look.'

The yellow glow of lanterns bruised Antsy's eyes and he turned away, wincing. A troop of six Malazan soldiers came down the broad hall; marines. The squattest of them, as broad as a horse, wore a sergeant's torc. Antsy inclined his head in greeting.

The sergeant rubbed the beard darkening his chin and cheeks while he eyed Antsy up and down. 'Well I'll be damned . . .' he breathed. Then he cocked a questioning eye.

Antsy shook a negative. The man blew out a breath and gave a quick nod of assent. 'So,' he said, glancing about. 'You alone?'

'No.' He turned and beckoned. 'Orchid . . . Corien Lim . . . Morn.'

The sergeant nodded, then motioned back up the hall. 'This way.'

As they started off Antsy glanced round to see that once again Morn had disappeared. After a time he asked, 'What's the situation?'

'Damned ugly. Got a damned menagerie o' mages 'n' sorcerers 'n' such all ready to kill one another an' all jammed together steppin' on each other's toes an' yankin' each other's knickers. It's a wonder any of 'em's still standing, it is.'

'How's your captain holding up?'

The man spat aside. 'Captain's dead. Lieutenant's in charge.'

'How's he doing?'

'He's kept us a seat at the table. But things're heatin' up.' His gaze slide sideways. 'Could use some help.'

Antsy felt his mouth tighten. 'Can't guarantee anything, Sergeant.' He jerked his head back the way they'd come. 'And there's a whole army out there that wants in.'

The man spat again. 'Faugh! Them! Fucking also-rans. Nothing to worry about there.'

'And you boys? What do you want?'

'Us?' He snorted. 'Togg's tits, man. We just want out. Friend . . . we just want the Abyss outta here.'

The sergeant, Girth, led them to the lieutenant. They found him amidst the Malazan encampment, which occupied a set of rooms off a large high-roofed assembly chamber, like an immense cavern, where numerous halls and stairs led into darkness. Antsy caught a glimpse of the two mages they'd followed standing near the centre of the room speaking to a striking slim woman dressed in a white silk shirt, tight trousers, and tall leather boots that came up to her knees. With them was their damned guide, the gangly Jallin.

The lieutenant, it turned out, was a very young fellow with the heavy build and curly hair of a north Genabackan. After Girth spoke to him he approached to give Antsy a welcoming nod. 'A veteran, yes?' Antsy nodded. 'Good. Could use your help.' He looked to Corien. 'Darujhistani. Trained?'

Corien bowed. 'Yes.'

'Very good.'

He bowed to Orchid. 'You are Dal Hon? A talent, perhaps?'

She waved a hand, embarrassed. 'Dal Hon? No. But I do have some small skills.'

The lieutenant returned to Antsy. 'Girth reported another with you. Someone in dark robes.'

'A mage. He joined us partway up. Comes and goes as he pleases. We are not answerable for him.'

'Ah. A shame. We could use the help. Welcome, regardless. I am Lieutenant Palal. Hengeth Palal.'

They introduced themselves. Then Antsy said, 'We've come for the Gap. That's all. We just want to get out of here.'

'I understand. Truth be told so do we. Problem is, that lot bar the way.'

Antsy stroked his jaw with the back of his fingers. 'Block the way? Why're they doing that?'

The lieutenant crossed his arms. It was clear he was rather overwhelmed, but it was also equally clear that he was aware of it and accepted it. *No bluster or denial here*, Antsy reflected. *Just doing what he can.*

'What are their terms?' Antsy asked.

'Terms? Their terms are . . . frankly insane.' The young officer shook his head, mystified. 'I've told them again and again – we have no munitions. None at all. We can't blow their damned door for them.'

Orchid gasped. Or at least Antsy thought she did; he was having trouble hearing over the roaring gathering in his ears. Hands steadied him and above the wind he thought he heard someone laughing. He recognized the mad laughter: it was his own. He was having a good time at his own expense. *Forgot your philosophy, Ants. They'll get ya. In the end they'll always find a way to get ya.*

'All right?' Corien asked, his head close. Blinking, Antsy squeezed the youth's hand. 'Yeah. Just thrown. That's all.'

From the centre of the large cavern came the sharp slap of hands clapping. The explosive reports echoed from the walls and distant ceiling. A woman's voice shouted: 'A meeting! Everyone! I call a general meeting! *Now!*'

Palal uncrossed his arms, sighing. 'Well, best see what the witch wants.' He raised his chin, calling, 'Sergeant. See to their billeting.'

'Aye, sir.' Girth closed, flanked by troopers. Antsy glared.

'Thanks a lot!'

He shrugged his wide humped shoulders. 'Sorry. Got over forty men and women who want out of this trap. That's all I answer to. Maybe your friends can help.'

'They're dead.'

'Hasn't stopped others.'

'Yeah, well. That's the deal.'

The man spat again. 'Too bad. Now, let's take a walk, all of us. Nice an' quiet.'

'Him too!' the woman yelled again, pointing from the distance. 'The newcomer. The soldier. That one too!'

While he was sick inside Antsy made a point of arching a brow at the sergeant. 'Gotta go. Things to do.'

Girth snorted. 'Out of the frying pan, friend. Out of the pan.'

As Antsy walked away the man called: 'We'll just look after your friends here, right?'

Antsy raised a hand over his shoulder in a gesture that needed no explanation.

The 'meeting' was one of the oddest gatherings of fearsome individuals Antsy had ever attended. And that included a few command gatherings of Malazan Imperial mages and Claws. He took his place next to Lieutenant Palal. Opposite waited the tall slim woman who had called the meeting. Her complexion was olive-hued and her hair dark and straight, pinned up in a complex design. Her dark eyes watched Antsy with a look that seemed to enjoy his discomfort. The large loose circle also included the carmine-wearing old woman and her fat companion, together with Jallin, who glared his hatred. Antsy noted that the fat fellow seemed to spend most of his time with his gaze narrowed on the tall woman.

To one side waited the armoured figure of the blonde-haired mercenary who had preceded them on to the Spawn. He was flanked by two of his men. All still carried canvas covers over their shields. Antsy wondered if these might be members of the Grey Swords. Yet they carried no symbols of the Wolves of Winter, nor any other god that he could recognize.

An old man, his thin hair a mussed cloud around his uneven skull, came shuffling up on his slippered feet. Also emerging from the gloom came the slim dark form of Malakai.

Antsy could not believe he was seeing him again. He thought the man dead, or long escaped from the Spawn. 'Look what turned up,' he drawled, giving him a hard stare.

The thief bowed, one brow quirked. 'So you made it. Congratulations. I am *very* surprised.'

'No thanks to you, you Hood-damned piece of—'

'So you two know each other,' the tall woman cut in, loud and firm. 'How nice. Yet introductions are in order, I imagine.'

'We are not yet all gathered,' the old fellow observed in a quavering breathless wheeze.

'Did someone call a meeting?' a man's voice enquired from the dark. 'Is attendance mandatory?' The owner of the smooth voice came forward: a man dressed in expensive silks over a fine blackened mail coat that hung to his shins. His midnight hair was slicked back and a goatee beard and moustache framed his mouth. A wide heavy two-handed sword hung at his side.

The tall woman, Antsy noted, eyed this well-dressed fellow with obvious distaste.

'Introductions?' the old woman squawked. She tossed her head, her ribbons rustling. 'There need not be any introductions. I do not want introductions. Damn all of you. I care nothing for you.'

'Quite,' the fat fellow at her side supplied, like a punctuation ending her rant.

'Thank you, Hesta and Ogule.

'Ogule Tolo Thermalamerkanerat,' the fat fellow corrected. 'Do please get it right. You know our dialect, Seris.'

The tall woman, Seris, smiled revealing sharp white teeth. 'Yes. Ogule.'

'Hemberghin,' the old man sneezed at Antsy.

Antsy leaned down to him. 'What was that? Hemdergin?'

'Hemper!' the old man repeated angrily. 'Hemper. Hemper Grin!'

Antsy flinched away from the spray of spittle. He wiped his sleeve. 'Right. Hemper.'

The elegant fellow inclined his head to Antsy in an ironic salute. 'Bauchelain.' He gestured vaguely to his rear. 'My companion, Korbal Broach, is, ah, currently . . . preoccupied.'

It may have been the poor light, but it appeared to Antsy as if at the man's words everyone present turned a shade more pale. He cleared his throat in an effort to find his voice. 'Ah, Antsy. Antsy's the name.'

All this time Jallin had been whispering fiercely and pulling on the old woman's rags. Whispering and pointing. She cuffed him now and shot out a withered crooked finger. 'What is in your bag, soldier?'

'To the Paths of the Dead with you, y' damned hag.'

The woman jerked so sharply the ribbons hanging from her hair snapped like whips. Her eyes widened in disbelief then slitted almost closed. A sort of creamy smile came to her wrinkled lips. 'So . . . you wish to challenge old Hesta, do you? Scream very prettily as you burn I think you will . . .'

'Hesta . . .' Seris warned. 'Soldier. We know you carry munitions.'

Antsy glanced to Malakai. 'How in the name of all the forgotten gods would you know that?'

The woman brought her long-fingered hands together to her lips then let out a loud breath as if exhausted. 'Soldier. All of us here are close to many very great powers. Many of us have seen in the deck what you carry. We have terms to offer you for their use. For example – there are very many people here who wish to leave this crippled artefact. We will allow that . . . once our terms are met.'

'What's the job?'

Seris smiled behind her clasped hands. 'This way, if you please.' She led him across the wide assembly hall. The gang of mages followed. The one who gave his name as Bauchelain sauntered along last. Many of the others cast nervous glances back to the man.

A large scene of pastoral life decorated the polished floor they crossed. Hills, streams and mountains, all done in mosaic of coloured stones. Antsy thought it odd that such a scene should be executed here within the heart of the Moon's Spawn. It seemed all too . . . mundane.

Midway across they came to a large circular opening flush in the floor like a well or a pool. Antsy peered down only to throw himself backwards, his heart hammering. The opening sank bottomless into utter night and a cool breeze wafted up. The wind carried with it the distant lap and murmur of the sea.

They came to wide curving stairs cut from black glittering stone that led up to a tall set of double doors. The doors were cut from the same black stone, but set in panels of gold, bronze and silver. Similar vignettes of woods and fields decorated the panels. Scenes of some sort of homeland, Antsy wondered? Somehow it struck him as odd that the Tiste should possess any sort of homeland. They seemed to have simply appeared from the sky. But of course they had to have originated from *somewhere*.

'These doors are barred to us,' Seris announced, slapping a hand to a silver panel. 'We cannot broach them. Do so, soldier, and you will save the lives of your fellows – plus many more.'

Antsy nodded towards the doors. 'What's inside?'

'That is none of your business!' Hesta snarled.

'Indeed,' Ogule agreed.

'Something its master thought destroyed,' old Hemper giggled with a wheezing laugh.

'The dream of night unending,' Malakai provided as if quoting a line.

'What lies within, soldier,' said Bauchelain, drawn close now, his hands clasped behind his back, his gaze in the distance over Antsy's head, 'is nothing less than the Throne of Night.'

*   *   *

Bendan forced down a leather-like string of old horsemeat and helped it along with another mouthful of water. At least they had that: all the drink they needed thanks to the well the saboteur lads and lasses had dug up almost overnight. But that was all they had. Most of the biscuits and beans went up with the wagons during the fire attacks. There was no firewood left to cook with anyway. Just dried horse and bits and pieces left now. He wiped one soot-blackened hand on his thigh only for it to come away just as dirty as before. *Nothing to wash with neither.*

The gaminess of the cut almost made him throw it down. Almost. Growing up as he had, any meat was frankly a rare treat. One of the attractions of joining up was that the army ate a damned sight better than he ever did. Because of this he wasn't feeling the pain that a lot of men and women around him were. Soft, those ones. Not used to punchin' new holes in their belts. Or suckin' on leather.

Looked to him like Hektar was wrong and these Rhivi were just gonna starve them out. It burned his butt and wasn't what he thought soldiering was all about. But there you go. More and more he was coming round to the view that it really *was* all more about manoeuvring and positioning than any of this dirty hand to hand stuff.

He glanced aside to Corporal Little where she dozed, her shield angled over her face for shade from the low sun. He frankly could not figure her out; nor any of these damned soldiers. It was plain as day that she didn't think much of him, yet time and again it was her shield that took an arrow meant for him; and time and again she offered advice and tricks on how to handle himself in the ranks. It wasn't like anything he'd ever known before. He'd felt as if he was part of a family in his gang in their quarter of Maiten town – but that had been nothing like this. There, it had all been about clawing and snarling one's way up to top dog. It was all about who could face down who. The top dogs swaggered it and did as they pleased to whoever they pleased. The little dogs got kicked. Or worse. That was life as he knew it. Abyss, life in the entire world for all he knew.

But not here. Here in the squads nobody seemed to be a big dog. There was no facing down. The nobodies, the new hands, once they got bloodied and proved their grit, people helped them out. For the first time in his life he didn't know where he stood. He'd always had to know that. *Get your head bit off otherwise.*

Not like they was all holdin' hands and slappin' each other's backs or shit like that neither. Not like family – or at least what he'd heard family was supposed to be like. In his case he was damned relieved this wasn't like family. Worst beatings he ever got were from his da and older brothers. Till one day the old man staggered inside shit drunk and they all piled on with boards and sticks. Never was the same afterwards. Couldn't move the one side of his mouth nor that arm. Lost all his fire that night and nobody paid him no attention after that. And his sister, she run off. Got tired of his older brothers selling her for drinks and hits of durhang. So, no, he was damned glad this was no Hood-taken family.

Murmuring brought Bendan's attention to the camp. People were rousing themselves to join the posted squads on the walls. Something was up. He got to his feet and kicked Little then headed for the wall. Sergeant Hektar's towering figure was easy to spot. He pushed his way to the man's side. 'What is it?'

The big Dal Hon looked even more pleased than usual. He raised his chin to the Rhivi encampment. 'Look there. See those new boys an' girls come to play?'

Bendan squinted. Luckily the day was waning and the sun was more or less behind them, descending now towards the uneven lines of the distant Moranth mountains. All he could see were crowds of Rhivi and horses. 'No. I don't really have good eyes, have to say.' Then the milling mounts and crowding Rhivi parted for a moment and he caught a glimpse of slim figures, lightly armoured, their faces covered or hooded. 'Who's that?'

Hektar seemed to make a great show of smiling even more broadly. 'Looks like you're in luck, lad. Gonna have a lesson in butchery from the pros. Them's Seguleh. And it looks like they're workin' with the Rhivi.'

Seguleh? He thought back to Tarat's claim. Togg damn! In the flesh. But . . . *holy fuck!* 'Is it true that three of them beat the entire Pannion army?'

Hektar gave a farting noise. 'Chasing off a scared-arsed peasant horde without training or spine is one thing. Facing a solid shield wall of iron veterans is another.' Raising his voice he called: 'Ain't that right, lads and lasses?'

'Aye!' came answering shouts.

Hektar leaned his thick forearms on the blackened logs. 'You just stay down behind your shield and use short quick thrusts and you'll be right fine, lad. Keep your head low. Let 'em run around and jump up and down all they want.' And he winked.

Despite the growing dread clawing at his stomach Bendan almost laughed aloud at the advice.

*

Tserig did not know what the new Warlord Jiwan meant when he'd hinted at promised aid from his ally, this so-called 'Legate'. And so, even though pointedly no invitation had been extended to him, when the flurry of activity arose in camp he readied himself and strode out to join the reception. He knew his ears and eyes were not what they once had been (though bless the Great Mother not his prang!) but it seemed to him as he made his way through the press that all was not as expected. The young bloods were subdued, not joyous with anticipated victory. Emerging into the Circle of Welcoming he was surprised to find just three individuals facing the Warlord.

He squinted anew then rocked backwards on his staff. *Great Mother! Aid? This is the aid the creature parading as the Legate offers? No, not aid. This is the fist unveiled. The ancient curse. The Faceless Warriors. Fear them, Jiwan. Fear them!*

There were two Seguleh in their leather armour. One's mask was a kaleidoscope of colours all swirling in a complicated design; the other's was all pale white, marred only by two dark smudges, one on each cheek, as if placed there by a swipe of a forefinger. Tserig's hands grew sweaty upon his staff. *Burn look away! The Third. The Third of the Seguleh!*

The third figure troubled Tserig even more. He knew what it was, that bent and broken being, twisted under harrowing punishments inflicted by his master. One of the Twelve. The demon slaves of the Tyrant Kings. Which it was made no difference. They were all the same in serving their masters' will.

Jiwan was on his feet, his bearing far less certain than when he had faced Brood. But then he did not know all the old stories about Caladan. The most ancient tales. And Brood had been an ally of many years, seemingly harmless. Jiwan had grown up knowing him as if he were no more than an uncle. He did not seem to grasp the true danger he represented. Indeed, no one in this age seemed to understand that. Unlike himself, old Tserig, hoarder of the old knowledge.

'The invaders will be dealt with, yes,' the demon mage was saying. 'They will be swept from the field. But first,' and it raised a gnarled hand to Jiwan, 'I need to know your answer to our offer.'

The Warlord of the Rhivi cocked his head, puzzled. 'Offer? What offer is that?'

'Why, the offer of his protection, of course! My master, the Legate of Darujhistan, has graciously extended to you the guarding hand of his shelter and countenance. You will be as safe as a child in the arms of its parent under his warding, I assure you of that.'

Jiwan drew himself up straighter. He was obviously attempting to keep his face neutral, but it betrayed too much of his distaste. 'We Rhivi are a free people. This alliance is one of mutual defence. Nothing more. Thank the Legate for his concern. We have no need of his guardianship.'

The mage stroked his long chin as if puzzled. 'Do you not wish to be safe and secure? To be strong? So many in these days of trouble argue for a strong hand guiding their community, their city, their lands, or province. Within the encircling arms of the Legate you will find that. It is easy. One merely need yield all troubling matters of governance to him. He will take care of you. As a father.'

431

The Warlord was now nodding. He appeared saddened. 'Aman, I hear your words and I thank you. I believe you have just handed me a great lesson. For among us Rhivi there was one who could very easily have claimed such a role. But he possessed the wisdom, the true generosity of soul, to stand aside when we chafed under his hand. Sadly, I do not believe we will ever find another to match him. And were he here now I believe I would offer him my apology.'

The demon mage, Aman, dropped his hand from his chin. 'You are right, Warlord. That is sad. For you have chosen defiance. And for that there can be only one answer.' He looked to the Seguleh Third. The Third shifted forward, and as he did so something blurred between him and the Warlord and Jiwan's face became confused, then emptied of all emotion as if drained. Then his head slid off his neck as his body toppled.

Screaming rent the air all around. Warriors lunged, drawing weapons. The Seguleh stood back to back, their swords a blur, as Rhivi warriors, men and women, tumbled aside missing hands, arms, throats and stomachs. Roaring with immense laughter, Aman ignored the many blades that rebounded from his form beneath his rags. He reached out to grasp wrists to snap them, clenched throats to squeeze pulping bursts of blood and flesh.

All this Tserig watched, motionless, horror-struck. *Ancient gods known and forgotten deliver us. It has begun anew. The iron fist of the Tyrant reborn. Shall we be once more slave for a thousand years? No!*

More warriors closed, meaning to bring down these three murderers, only to fall to the near-invisible blades or the gore-smeared hands of the mage. Tserig threw down his staff to raise his arms high. 'Sons and daughters of the plains!' he bellowed. 'Flee! Now! Ignore this filth! Flee these lands now. An ancient curse has arisen! *North! Flee north!*'

Aman closed upon him. 'Shut up old man!' He brought a fist smashing down, breaking Tserig's skull and snapping the frail vertebrae of his neck. He fell instantly dead.

*

From the palisade wall of Fort Step, which for some reason unknown to Fist Steppen it had come to be named, she and Fist K'ess and watched while the meeting of allies that promised to sweep them from the plain all went horribly wrong.

'Looks like a falling out,' Steppen said, her propensity for under-statement intact.

'Don't it though,' K'ess echoed. Then he gestured aside. 'Look at that. An encirclement.'

Steppen squinted into the lengthening shadows. There, among the tall grass, individual figures had arisen in a broad ring surrounding the Rhivi camp. One every few tens of paces. While they watched, the figures closed in, tightening the circle.

'Gods-damned slaughter,' K'ess murmured. 'Their first mistake.'

'They think they don't need them.'

The Fists met each other's gaze. K'ess cocked a brow. Steppen gave one quick nod that bulged her double chin. K'ess leaned over the catwalk. 'Captain Fal-ej!'

'Aye?'

'An immediate withdrawal west! Over the wall! Lightest pack. Three days' water.'

'Aye, sir!'

Both Fists returned to gauging the fighting. Rhivi riders, alone and in packs, thundered off through the encirclement riding north for the lake. Many fell, but the majority bulled through. Presumably those survivors wouldn't stop for anything.

'Four squads should remain on the walls till everyone's gone,' K'ess said. 'I'll stay with them.'

'I believe you held the rear-guard last,' Steppen pointed out. 'It's my turn.'

K'ess looked the rather dumpy woman up and down. 'You sure you're up to it?'

Steppen merely looked to the sky. 'These recruits don't know what a hard march is. Not like the run to Evinor. Time they learned.'

K'ess cast an eye over the fort. 'A shame, really. Well built.'

'Have to have a word with the engineers. I was really looking for something roomier.'

The distant scream of a dying horse pierced the din of battle, making Steppen wince. She faced the east. 'Run, you poor bastards,' she murmured. 'Flee. Just mount up and ride.'

K'ess squeezed her shoulder. 'Oponn's favour.' He turned and left her.

'Toren,' she called, using his first name, and he paused on his way down.

'Yes?'

'Give them something to remember,' she said, smiling. 'Show them what they've taken on, yes?'

Fist K'ess inclined his head in agreement. 'Somewhere narrow, Shurl. I will see you there.' He offered a brief salute and bounded down the stairs. Steppen turned to the east again and the screams drifting across with the wind. *Gods. So it's true. All that she'd heard. These Seguleh. A few hundreds against some thirty thousand and it's a rout.*

Facing the gathering twilight she whispered: 'Yes, Toren. We'll meet again there.'

Crouched in the tall grass Captain Fal-ej scanned a landscape painted an unnatural sea green. Like the bottom of the sea, she thought to herself. Almost beautiful. To either side sergeants awaited her command to fire. *Damn the man. Where was he? This bravado could cost them an experienced commander.* Not to mention she hadn't yet told him all that she wanted to.

Then movement among the grass and the Fist came running up the slope. Fal-ej signed for a stand-down. She rose to meet him. 'We're on the move,' she called rather angrily. 'Where's Fist Steppen?'

'Holding the fort.'

She stared past K'ess to the distant structure. 'That's—'

'Yes,' K'ess cut in. 'She's buying us time. Now let's go. Double-time.'

Fal-ej backed away, signing a withdrawal to the sergeants. K'ess kept going. 'No rear guard or outliers, Captain,' he called. 'Just a rear watch.'

'Aye,' she answered. She raised her arm in the air to inscribe the circular *pull out* sign.

*

When dawn came Fist Steppen found herself looking out at an encirclement of Seguleh. Crows and other scavenging birds wheeled in the brightening eastern sky, or hopped obscenely among the distant trampled grass. The Seguleh facing her showed no wounds, though blood splashed some. One stepped forward insolently close given the fifteen crossbows covering him. His mask was a dizzying swirled design.

'You are surrounded,' he called. 'You do not possess sufficient forces to defend your walls. Throw down your weapons and you will be allowed to live.'

'Let us discuss terms,' Steppen answered, a hand tight on the adzed log before her. 'What assurances can you provide of our fair treatment? I request a third party negotiator.'

The Seguleh gave an odd cutting motion with his hand. 'We will not allow you to delay. You are not important.'

'Not important? You mean you would just pass us by?'

'Yes.'

'Ah. Well. In that case.' She pointed. 'Kill that man.'

Fifteen crossbows fired. The Seguleh twisted and ducked. Only two bolts struck him: one high in the leg, the other slashing the flesh of his left arm. The Seguleh charged the walls. Using their hands and feet they climbed the log palisade. Troopers backed away, dropping their crossbows as there was no time to reload. Steppen drew her slim blade. *At least we wounded one of them*, she told herself as the first appeared atop the walls. She swung again but he dropped below the blade. Another jumped cat-like over the top to land with her sword already drawn. Steppen swung again and the woman seemed to parry and counter all in the same fluid motion. Her blade slid easily through Steppen's leather armour to slash across her front, eviscerating her. The Fist tried one last attack but was off balance from the severing of so many muscle groups and she could not regain her footing. She fell off the catwalk to land in a wet tangled heap. As she lay in the dirt staring at the bark of the palisade logs her last thought was: *Not that much of a damned delay . . .*

*   *   *

Torvald Nom did not spend too long in his cell. Just two meal periods later the door ratcheted and opened to reveal a Silver flanked by two Black. Torvald's first thought was that this was the same Silver. Then he realized that he really couldn't tell at all. He wished he'd spent more time memorizing the engraving on his driver's armour. But he'd been rather busy trying not to throw up at the time. He slowly climbed to his feet and gave a shallow bow. 'Welcome. If I'd known you were coming I would have saved some of my food.'

'Torvald Nom of Nom,' the Silver said, and he recognized her voice, 'word has come from our Blue cousins affirming your story. Your credentials from the Darujhistan Council have also been deemed adequate. Our apologies.'

Torvald gave another brief bow. He suspected that this was all the contrition he was going to see. 'I am glad.' *Gods! 'I am glad.' How*

435

banal! Shouldn't I say something profound like: 'Let this meeting usher in a new age of accord between our two peoples.' Something puffed up and self-important like that?

The Silver motioned him out. 'This way, please.'

As they walked the stone passages Torvald glanced sideways at his guide. He drew a long breath and straightened his shirts and cloak. 'So . . . what is your name? If I may enquire.'

'Galene.'

'Galene? Galene. Well, where are we going? What's happening?'

'There are disturbing movements of forces in the foothills.' She paused for a time as if sorting through her words. 'I have been chosen to act as your guide.'

And you're thrilled no end. Well, we all have our rows to hoe. 'Disturbing movements? You mean the Rhivi?'

'No. I do not mean the northern tribals.'

'No? Then . . . the Malazans?'

'No. Not the Malazans.'

Tor frowned at the maddening woman. 'Well . . . then who?' She ushered him into a stone circular staircase that they climbed single-file, he second. 'Well?'

'Your Darujhistani army has been summoned, Nom of Nom.'

'Army? Darujhistan has never had an army.'

They emerged on to another of the tower roofs. Here rank after rank of quorl awaited, wings setting up a roar of commingled thrumming. The wind buffeted him. Most, he saw, carried two Moranth: a driver and a passenger. As he watched, stunned, waves of the quorl took off in file after file, peeling away in flights. From other towers more arose until the sky was darkened by their fragile silhouettes sweeping overhead like a tide rushing down valley. *An army – so swift!*

'Who?' he shouted to Galene. '*Who is it?*'

'Our old enemy,' she answered, icy fury in her voice. 'The ones who drove us from the plains. Who exiled us to these mountain tops ages ago.' She thrust a finger at him. 'Your murdering Seguleh.'

*   *   *

Just inside the unlocked gate of the Eldra Iron Mongers, Barathol cast about for someone, anyone, to greet him. It was illegal to be out this late; the Legate had lowered a curfew that was enforced by the Seguleh. And never had Barathol ever heard of a curfew so scrupulously respected.

The works were silent. For months now no black choking smoke had swirled about this end of the city and the waters of the bay lapped almost clear. He was almost of a mind to turn round – curfew breaking compounded by trespassing – when he spotted the odd little fellow himself, arms clasped behind his back, closely studying a workbench of abandoned tools. He came up behind and was about to speak when Kruppe asked: 'Was the carriage ride diverting?'

'Kruppe – I don't know what you call a carriage, but I don't call a cart pulled by an ass a carriage. I could have walked faster.'

The little man's chin pulled in, aghast. 'What! Why, the lad assured me it was a carriage. Most replete.'

'Would that be the same lad who was hitting the ass to keep it going?'

'I wouldn't know, was it? And you *do* mean the ass pulling the cart, yes?'

Barathol pulled a hand down his jowls and chin while he studied the bland-faced fellow. He appeared completely forthright. 'I'm going now.' He turned to leave.

'No no no!' Kruppe dodged around him. 'It must be you. Please. A simple job. Delicate and . . . ah, *tricky*, yes. But perfect for you.'

'Kruppe – I'm no master craftsman. I'm just an average smith. You don't want me. And I have to say I'm starting to wonder about this villa of yours.'

'Why, I am assured it is most exquisite! Airy. Charming. With enormous . . . character.'

'Sounds like an old shack missing a wall.'

Kruppe froze, surprised. 'You've seen it?'

Barathol started off again. 'Like I said. I'm heading home.' Rattling at the gate stopped him. The tall iron-barred doors had been closed and someone was approaching. It was hard to see in the eerie jade-hued light but the man appeared to be a tramp or a beggar. His clothes hung tattered and blackened. His hair was a wild nest and his face and hands glistened, soot-smeared and sweaty. He was rubbing his hands in a rag that was even dirtier.

The derelict stopped before them. He eyed Barathol up and down, said to Kruppe, 'Is this your smith?'

''Tis he.'

'I know all the smiths in the city. This one's new to me.'

'He's a smith of foreign extraction.'

A smile shone bright against the man's grimed face. 'Just as I am.' He pointed. 'This way.'

As they walked Barathol peered about the quiet ghostly yard and open silent sheds. 'There may be guards . . .'

'No guards,' said the tramp. 'Just me – the owner.'

Barathol stopped dead. 'You are Humble Measure?'

'In the flesh.'

Barathol turned to Kruppe, his gaze narrowing. 'What's going on here?'

Humble waved the rag at Kruppe. 'This man has contracted for some work. Welcome income.' He opened his arms wide to encompass his yards. 'There has been a temporary slowdown in production.'

'Fabrication,' Kruppe said. 'A delicate job.'

'Indeed,' Humble Measure agreed. He motioned Barathol onward. 'Let me tell you a story – if I may. There once was a man who was frightened. He was afraid of the rule of oppressive overlords, of marauding armies, of murderers, of bloody-handed thieves. In short, of almost everything. To defend against them and to be strong he decided to build thick walls of stone all about him. He shackled himself to these walls so that he could not be dragged off. He barred the window with thick iron rods. He secured the door with locks and crossbars and swallowed the keys. Then, one day, peering terrified from between the bars he realized that in his extraordinary efforts to be protected and unassailable he had built for himself something else entirely.'

'A prison.'

'Exactly so. In his efforts to be free of oppression he had enslaved himself.'

They had entered one of the larger worksheds. Humble led him to a metal bench cluttered with metal forging tools, tongs, hammers, and pinchers. Nearby one of the immense furnaces glowed, crackling and hissing. A wide stone box sat upon the bench.

'Never touch with your naked hand what lies within,' Kruppe warned.

Humble Measure raised a pair of fine pinchers. 'I will assist.'

Barathol waved to him. 'You do it. You're the master smith.'

'It requires your, ah, intent,' Kruppe said.

'Mine? What for?'

The little man peered to the vaulted roof as if searching for the right words. 'For a certain quality of circularity.'

'What?'

'Just that.'

Barathol eyed the two as if judging their sanity – which seemed utterly lacking. 'Just what is the job?'

'Inlay,' Humble said.

'We do not possess the, ah, *resources* to unmake what lies within that box,' Kruppe explained. 'But perhaps you can *soften* it enough for a fine bit of inlay.'

Barathol grunted. *Inlay. Well . . . that didn't seem so unreasonable.*

Kruppe entwined his pudgy fingers over his stomach. 'Very good. I'll leave you two to your trade secrets.' He suddenly thrust a finger into the air. 'But remember! The finished product must be dipped in bee's wax! That is most imperative.'

Humble waved him off. 'Yes, yes. We know our trade. Now be gone.'

'Be gone? I'll have you know sir that Kruppe was about to go! Kruppe will not be hurried or rushed off. No unseemly haste for the timely Kruppe.'

'Shall we open the box now?' Humble asked Barathol.

'Kruppe is leaving – farewell!'

* * *

As they descended the foothills, the Dwelling Plain lay before them, dun and ochre, shimmering in the day's heat, and Yusek cursed the sight of it. She could not believe that here she was yet again setting out across its damned dust-choked hills and draws. How many times had she sworn, and to how many gods and demons, that once she escaped she would never set foot upon it again?

The master of the monastery led the way. Sall followed, then she, and Lo came last. The master carried a sword on his back, wrapped and tightly tied in cloth. Other than this he was unarmed. Yusek still did not know what to call him. When Sall had asked what name they should use in addressing him he'd been silent for a very long time before drawing a ragged breath and saying in a hoarse voice, 'Grief.'

Yet neither Seguleh chose to call him that. When they needed to gain his attention they simply said, 'Seventh.'

One day as they descended towards the plain the Seventh halted, peering to the north. Everyone stopped as well and Yusek squinted, but she saw nothing. 'Large numbers on the move,' the Seventh said. 'Possibly armies.' He started off again but Sall remained still.

'Our brothers and sisters may be involved,' the youth said.

'That does not concern us,' the Seventh replied harshly. 'Our purpose lies in Darujhistan. And we must hurry. Things move apace.'

'We should not turn from them.'

The Seventh faced him squarely now. He drew a hard breath. 'Tell me, do you think I *want* to go to this cursed city? It's the last place I would ever want to go. But I *am* going – because you came to *me*. So the least you can damned well do is accompany me.'

The ferocity of the man's words almost drove Yusek back a step. Sall merely inclined his head in acquiescence. Though he did murmur, 'My apologies, Seventh.'

The man looked away, blinking. He threw himself further down the trail. 'Let's move.'

For her part Yusek couldn't believe she was actually going to Darujhistan. Never did she ever dream she would see the great city. City of Blue Flames. Wealthiest city on all the continent, from Evinor in the north to Elingarth in the south. It was said you could find cloth for sale there so sheer it was like the kiss of water. And rare fruits and birds to eat. Like duck. She'd never had roasted duck. She'd heard it called succulent. Now there was a word for food. *Succulent.* She'd like all her food to be succulent. And she'd bathe in hot water in a tub with scented soap. She'd heard of that too. Now that, as far as she could imagine, must be the height of luxury.

Eating duck in a tub. Now there's luxury for you.

And Sall here. Well, she'll talk him out of wearing that stupid mask. And with him at her back there'll be no stopping them. They'll waylay all those rich fat merchants. She'll become so famous even bearded Obern squatting in his fort in the woods will hear of her. Yes, that sounded like a plan to her. And you had to have a plan – that much she knew. You don't get anywhere without a plan.

*　　*　　*

The two figures walking down the street of the bakers in the Gadrobi district cut a colourful, if jarring, picture. One was unusually tall and dressed as if he had rolled in the cast-off scraps behind a tailor's shop. The other wore drab threadbare rags, was bald, and had a face that glimmered as if speckled in metal paint. And when this one smiled at those passing in the streets, they flinched away.

They strode nonchalantly, apparently pointing out the sights to one another. They might have been on a stroll to find an inn to pass the evening. They came abreast of a sad figure crouched down on his haunches against a wall, head bowed, and the shorter of the figures nudged his companion and they swung to stand either side of the hunched beggar. There they slid down the wall to sit as bookends.

'All is not as desolate as it seems,' the larger, bushy-haired one sighed, his gaze scanning the street.

'The sting fades and new horizons show themselves,' the other confirmed.

The larger cocked his head. 'Think of it as rigidity sacrificed for an infinity of possibility . . .'

'Well said,' his companion agreed. 'You are your own man now. You may do as you choose.'

The one between them tentatively raised his head. His long un-trimmed hair hung down over his eyes. 'Actions not dedicated to a higher purpose are meaningless,' he countered as if reciting a text.

The two exchanged glances over his head.

'Then select a purpose,' the thin bald one suggested, smiling and flashing gold-capped teeth.

'Such as?'

The big one waved expansively. 'Well . . . such as ours, perhaps.'

'And that is?'

Smiling, the thin one clasped the fellow's shoulder. 'That our every action, our very appearance, be a constant denunciation and thumb in the eye to our brethren. Now . . .' he and his companion hooked arms through the young man's, 'let us continue this discussion in more convivial surroundings.'

'I suggest Magajal's place,' the big on rumbled as they set off.

The bright metal glimmering on the bald one's face was in fact gold thread stitching. It wrinkled as he frowned. 'She waters her wine to excess. No. Dinner first at the Terrace overlooking the lake. We will consider later diversions over the meal.'

'Excellent.'

'Come, friend,' the bald one encouraged. 'Let this day be the first in an open-ended garden of companionship, adventure and extrava-gance.'

*　　*　　*

Spindle watched the street through the slats nailed over the window of K'rul's bar then sat back in his chair, crossbow on his lap. 'Looks quiet,' he called back over his shoulder. 'Maybe they've given up on us as not worth the candle.'

'Whistling in the dark,' Picker grumbled from the bar. She cocked an eye to the bard Fisher at the end of the counter where he was scratching on a sheet of vellum. She drew two tankards of beer and slid down to him, peered uncomprehending at the marks squiggled on the sheet. 'Whatcha writin'?'

'An epic poem.' He lifted one of the tankards, saluted her, and drank.

Leaning forward on her elbows, she narrowed her gaze as if struck by a sudden new thought. 'Why're you here anyway?'

'I like a quiet place to compose.'

She chuckled. 'That's a good one.' Then she frowned. 'Wait a minute . . .' She had opened her mouth to say more when a loud groaning stilled everyone. It seemed to be coming from the walls themselves, as if the building were twisting, or being squeezed.

Spindle jumped to his feet clutching his crossbow. 'What's that?'

'Don't fucking know,' Picker growled as she eased her way from behind the bar, long-knives out. 'Blend!'

'Clear,' came the answer from the rear.

'Sounded like it came from below,' Fisher said.

Picker nodded her agreement. 'Let's have a look. Spin, check the cellar.'

'What? Why do I have to check the cellar?'

''Cause I say so, that's why! Now go.'

Grumbling, Spindle tramped for the stairs.

After Spindle disappeared a sudden explosive crack of wood made everyone flinch. 'Upstairs,' Picker grunted and headed up. Fisher's hand strayed to his longsword.

'This epic poem of yours,' Duiker whispered into the heavy silence, 'what's it about?'

'The Elder Gods.'

Picker came back down, wonder on her face. She motioned upstairs. 'Timbers split in the roof and walls. Main load-bearing ones too. '

Spindle emerged looking pale and ill. Speechless, he indicated his boots. Black fluid, crusted and gummy like old blood, caked them. His feet had left a bloody smeared trail on the dirty stone floor. 'The cellar,' he managed, his voice choked. 'Awash. Somethin's goin' on, Pick. Somethin' terrible.'

Duiker turned his head to study the foreign bard straight on. 'This poem . . . How's it going?'

Fisher let out a taut breath. 'I think I'm nearing the end.'

CHAPTER XVI

Paradise would be a city where pearls cobble roads and gems
serve as playthings for children. And why? Not because all will
be so wealthy, but because its citizens will have recognized that
such things truly are toys.

Words of the Street Prophets
Compiler's name withheld

THERE WERE TIMES WHEN KISKA WAS DOZING IN THE CAVE HALF
asleep in the dim phantom light of night when she thought
she heard weeping. The sound came drifting in over the surf,
faint, wavering, and she would have dismissed it as a scrap of dream
had she not heard it more than once.

The sound grated like a blade down her spine, for she knew who
it was. If Tayschrenn was not dead as Leoman insisted, then it could
be none other. His mind was gone – or, more accurately, she had
destroyed his mind by playing into the hand of the Queen of Dreams.

The scheming bitch. She saw it all now. The elegance. All the
hallmarks of her plotting. She, Kiska, naïve agent, would find the
archmagus and deliver to him the poison supplied by *her.* And once
that happened whatever reaction it was would be unleashed and he
would be stricken.

And she the brainless dupe. *Gods!* Every time her thoughts
returned to that she bashed the heels of her hands to her forehead.
She would escape from here if only to track the damned Enchantress
down.

And Agayla? No – she too must have been ignorant of the Queen's
intent. Must have.

Gods above and below, forgotten and forsworn! When would she

443

ever *learn?* Never trust anyone. Never. That had been her mistake. She'd trusted and been used. *As it is for everyone everywhere. You are no different, woman.*

She groaned again and wrapped her head in her arms, pulling it down between her knees.

Further into the cave Leoman stirred. 'Don't beat yourself up child,' he said. 'You . . . we . . . had no way of knowing.'

'Shut the Abyss up.'

She heard pebbles striking the wall as he tossed them one by one. 'It stings now but that will pass. I should know. And it wasn't even on purpose. So never mind. What's done is done. There's no sense worrying about it.'

She raised her head to stare at him, incredulous. 'Says the man who murdered thousands in a firestorm he deliberately set!'

He shrugged. 'It was war. I was fighting for my life.'

'Why should your life be worth more than anyone else's in that city?'

The man tossed another pebble. 'It is to me.'

She turned away. 'Gods. You're beyond hope.'

'Just honest.'

From the cave mouth came the dragging uneven footsteps of the rescued creatures. Kiska and Leoman shared a glance. He rose, brushed dirt from the tattered Seven Cities robes he still wore over his mail. Kiska pushed herself to her feet.

'You may exit,' came a weak quavering voice. 'Follow us.'

She ducked from the cave, followed by Leoman. The creatures had hobbled off towards the shore. 'Come,' one called.

They descended the strand of black sand. Kiska glanced about, searching for the giant, Korus. He seemed nowhere about. The enormous faint silhouette of Maker was visible, larger than any mountain, labouring somewhere on the distant shoreline.

Then she saw someone at the shore and froze. Her heart lurched as if it had been hammered. She clamped a hand to her mouth. Him. Standing. *Standing.* Staring out at the bright Vitr sea. *Oh, my Queen – I have wronged you so.*

She ran all the way down to him only to stop just short. She reached out as if to touch him but yanked her hand back, afraid she shouldn't. Or that he might not be there. He turned to her and she flinched, catching her breath. For he was Tayschrenn yet he wasn't. Gone was the sharp questing gaze that could flense flesh from bone. And gone also was the guarded mien – immobile, almost mask-like. He smiled now, studying her in turn. Yet the sight made her heart ache even more so sad was it, so melancholy.

'You are . . . healed?' she asked, her voice catching.

'Healed? Yes, Kiska. I am healed.' He reached out to brush her hair from her face. 'And harrowed. Cut through to the core.'

'I don't understand.'

He invited her to walk with him along the shore. 'You restored me, Kiska. Though I wonder whether I should thank you for it.'

'What do you mean?'

'I mean I was – am – Thenaj still. Just as I am also Tayschrenn. And I find that I was everything Thenaj loathed. I am both still and now I must choose who to be.'

'You are both? Be both then. Who you are.'

Again the wintry smile as he walked, his long thin hair loose. 'Always the hard choice with you, hey Kiska? Easier just to deny the one or the other. Blot it out. Pretend it never was . . . but instead you counsel conciliation. The difficult third path of adaptation and growth.'

He held his long-fingered hands out in front of him, turned them over as if studying them for the first time. 'So be it. I shall be both – and neither.'

'And,' Kiska asked warily, 'what will you do?'

'Yes. What to do. I cannot return to the old now that I am not who I was . . . Yet one possibility does beckon. A possible place for me. One perhaps only I can fill . . .'

'And that is?'

He turned to face her, square on. Shook his head. 'We shall see. I may not be strong enough to take it on. For now it is enough that we will be going. I am finished here.'

'So – we are leaving? You are coming with me?'

'Yes.'

Kiska felt as if she had shed ten stone. 'Thank the gods!'

'Do not thank them,' Tayschrenn snapped in a manner something like his old self. 'Terrible, unforgivable things are stirring and it could be argued that they are to blame. They've stuck their hands into the furnace once too many times and now they find they cannot pull them out. So do not thank them. But perhaps we can find it within us to pity them.'

Kiska did not know what to make that – most of which seemed directed more at himself, in any case. But it wasn't important. She'd heard the words she'd wanted to hear. He was returning. She had succeeded. Sent on a mission across creation to find someone cast into Chaos – and she had succeeded!

And now she wondered: was *that* in truth what mattered to her? Was it that which had been gnawing at her all this time? Not concern for Tayschrenn; not fear of her own fate. Was it just that she couldn't stomach failure? Not a flattering piece of self-revelation.

Perhaps, as Tayschrenn suggested, she should just blot that one out.

He led her back to where Leoman stood waiting, hands on his belt, next to the gathered creatures.

Tayschrenn stopped before the man and frowned. 'Leoman of the Flails. You have some nerve standing here before me.'

The man gave an insouciant shrug. 'All that is the past.'

The mage's gaze narrowed, the crow's feet at the corners of his eyes deepening. 'Funny you should say that . . .'

'Thenaj . . .' one of the unformed asked, its thin voice trembling. 'What is happening?'

'I am sorry. But – I am leaving.'

'Leaving? Going?' The creatures set up a clamour of murmuring and crying.

Then Korus appeared, bounding towards them from among the dunes. 'What is this!' it bellowed. 'You are going?' Coming close, it dug in its odd clawed feet to halt, kicking up sand. 'I knew you would betray us! Look at you. I sense it in you – *mage*. Torturer! Murderer!'

'That's not fair!' Kiska shouted.

'Look at you . . . abandoning us. Does your word mean nothing? No – of course it does not, for you have been forsworn all your life!'

Undisguised hurt twisted Tayschrenn's features. He raised a hand to speak. 'Please, Korus . . . my friend . . .'

'And what are we to do?' the giant demon raged on. It thrust a taloned hand to the Vitr. 'Every day I hear them calling. Our brothers and sisters, dying! Burning into dissolution! What are we to do?' Kiska was astounded to hear true torment in the demon's cracking trembling voice.

'Korus . . . Korus. Please. Listen to me. Give me your hands.'

The huge beast flinched away. 'What?'

'Korus, trust me. I am still the man you knew as Thenaj. Truly. I am. Now give me your hands.'

The high-born demon edged its wide taloned hands closer. Its knife-like fangs ground and scraped at the strain of the gesture. Tayschrenn took the mangled fingers in his. Scar tissue that twisted up Korus's forearms marked the extent of its past suffering. After a moment Tayschrenn released it. 'There.'

'*There*? What trick is this?'

'You are now inured to the Vitr, friend. You may enter it as I did. Without fear or effect. You will take my place.'

The demon backed away. It cocked its wide mangy head as if it could not, or would not, believe. 'How can I . . .'

Tayschrenn gestured to the Vitr sea. 'Go ahead. Test it.'

Korus backed away, still wary. Then it padded down to the waves. It dipped a hand into a glimmering wash of the liquid light and raised it, letting the fluid run from its taloned fingers. Then, peering back at them, it laughed. It threw back its maned head and let go a great shaking roar of laughter. It fell to its knees splashing both hands in the Vitr as if it were no more than a tidal pool. The malformed creatures gathered nearby on the shore. They murmured their amazement while Korus chuckled on and on.

'That was a great thing,' Kiska said.

The mage shook his head. 'Was it? Few who call survive. He will suffer much failure. That will be a torment.'

'No. His helplessness was his torment.'

'Helplessness?' The mage examined his own hands once more. 'Ah. Helplessness.'

'And now?' she asked.

'Now we will go.'

'Yes,' Leoman said. 'Now you will go.'

'You?' Kiska repeated sharply. 'What do you mean? You said that earlier too.'

The man brushed his moustache, shrugging again. 'I mean I will be staying, I think.'

'You? Stay?' Kiska laughed. 'That's absurd.' She gestured to the desolate shore. 'There's nothing here for you.'

'It's peaceful, Kiska,' he answered calmly, completely unruffled by her disparagement. 'I can sleep here. And to me that means a lot.'

'I understand,' Tayschrenn said.

Kiska set her hands on her hips. 'This is ridiculous.' She gestured towards Tayschrenn. 'I just got— You're coming with us. That's all there is to it.'

'No. And who knows . . . if this place can help our friend here, perhaps it can help me.'

Kiska waved for Tayschrenn to speak. 'Say something. He can't stay here all alone!'

The mage cleared his throat, nodding. 'Maker likes stories. I was always sorry I didn't have any for him.'

Leoman groomed his moustache again. 'Oh-ho!' He smiled behind his hand. 'Have I got stories for him.'

'No.'

Tayschrenn took her hand. 'Come.'

'No!'

He pulled her along behind like a reluctant child.

'No – we can't just leave him here all alone . . .'

'He is not alone.'

'Well, yes, but . . .'

'He knows what is best for him. Now come. We have far to go.'

'Fine!' She twisted her hand free and straightened her shirt. 'Fine. Leave him exiled, then! For ever!'

Tayschrenn walked on, hands clasped behind his back. 'He is not exiled. He can leave whenever he wishes. Maker can send him anywhere he chooses.'

Kiska ran to catch up. 'Oh, well. Why didn't you say so?' She glanced back, caught Leoman's eye, and waved farewell.

Leoman answered the wave then turned away, arms crossed, to watch Korus play in the sea. And, to Kiska's eyes, he did have the look of a man at peace.

*   *   *

Noise from downstairs woke Scillara. She tensed, listening in the dark. The city had been quiet these last weeks now that the Legate had imposed his curfew. Every sound carried a sudden insistence and stood out as rare and unexpected as . . . well, as an honest man.

She reached down for the long-knife Barathol kept on the floor under the bed. She'd laughed, of course, as was her way with him – anything to dance away from the grim – for she'd spotted him long ago as one of those who could slide too easily into gloomy brooding.

Up to her to chivvy him along.

Strangely enough, her first thought had been for the babe. *Now there's a shocker. Gettin' to me after all. Just as Barathol said.*

She listened once more: now all she could hear were the babe's quick wet breaths.

Then it came again. Someone moving about downstairs. As if they had two sticks to steal! As disappointing a break-in as they come. She went quickly to the stairs and edged her way down, blade out in front. Let them chuckle at the fat woman with a knife; she'd had to cut her fair share of men turned ugly with drink and sour tempers.

A light was on on the main floor. Halfway down the stone stairs she saw Barathol at the rear seeing to the banked fire. She reached up through the trapdoor to slip the blade on to the bedroom floor and went down.

'Back already?'

He grunted and turned from coaxing the fire going. She was shocked to see that he was sodden through. 'You're soaked. Was it raining?'

'No,' he croaked, his voice ragged.

She took the sticks and tinder from his shaking hands. 'I'll see to it. What happened, then?' She blew on the embers.

He slumped into a chair. 'I washed. Washed everything. Dumped water over myself from a cistern.'

'To hide the smell of the drink?'

Not a glimmer answered that. 'No. To wash away . . . something else.' He held out his hands and turned them over. They shook like leaves. Kneeling, she reached for them but he yanked them away. Even so, she felt their chill. *Frozen!*

'A lad came yesterday with a cooked meal for us and a note sayin' you were working still.' He looked confused, blinking heavily. *Exhausted – what was this job? I'll have that fat man's head!*

'Message? I sent no message.'

'Well. You're back now. Want to see the little one?'

He straightened, lurching. 'No! Have to . . . have to wash first.'

'Wash?' She laughed lightly. 'You're cleaner than I've ever seen you!'

He merely stared at the fire. 'Heat water. Bring that cake of soap. And our smallest knife. Have to cut my nails. Scour my hands. Before – before I touch anything.'

'Barathol . . . you're clean enough—'

'No!' He pressed the heels of his palms to his eyes. 'Dammit, woman, just do as I ask for once.'

Scillara backed away. *Fine. Just this once then!* She went to fill the pot.

*

449

Chal Grilol had been a woodwright turning out spoked wheels for wagons and chests, benches, just about anything anyone required in the neighbourhood. Then the joint-ache took his hands and he couldn't hold a tool no more. He couldn't work so he lost his home; his boys were long gone and the wife was dead so he was out on the street sleeping under a wharf on the waterfront. Tonight he was out fishing using a lantern to lure fingerlings off the end of one of the longer, lower docks.

Then along came this two-wheeled cart pushed backwards up the dock by a shaggy man all dirty and wild-haired and muttering to himself. And while Chal watched, amazed, this burly fellow proceeded to toss tools and bits and pieces from the cart into the lake. He threw hammers as far as he could out into the waves. Wearing thick leather gloves he tossed handfuls of smaller tools like scatterings of stones off the dock. Then he got up on to the cart and kicked over a big anvil that fell with a resounding bang that shook the entire dock from end to end. This he pushed over and over until he tipped it off the end with a huge splash. Last, the gloves themselves followed into the drink.

Dusting his hands, the fellow turned to Chal, still sitting, pole in his hands. He took out a soot-smeared rag and wiped his face and hands then peered down, frowning. 'You might be thinking to yourself, friend: 'That lot could be worth a copper or two.' But don't consider it.' He leaned even closer and there was something in his eyes, something fierce and terrible. 'They're cursed, friend. Touched with a fearsome curse.' He glanced about as if listening to the night, the water lapping, the boats groaning against their berths. 'Even now it might not be safe.' And he patted Chal's shoulder and started up the dock with his cart. 'G'night!'

As the creaking of the cartwheels diminished up the waterfront Chal sat listening and it seemed to him that the murmur of the water had taken on a more ominous hollow moaning and that the wheels' groaning had returned to his ears – this time accompanied by the jangling of metal chain, perhaps from the nearby ships. Pole in one hand and lantern in the other, he ran. His naked feet slapped the grey boards as he went and a cold chill seemed to nip at them with each step.

*

Spindle was half awake in the bar common room, chin in hands, dredging his brain trying to figure out what that damned alchemist-mage, Baruk, had been trying to tell him. There must be something there. He was sure of it. Why else let him go? Why else hint at . . . whatever it was he meant? Something *was* there just beyond his reach; it was driving him crazy.

At the barrier they'd thrown across the door, watching the night-time street, Blend recrossed her legs and tilted back in her chair, her crossbow on her lap. Then the long stone counter of the bar exploded. There was no other word for it. It just burst with an eruption that sent Blend cartwheeling backwards, the crossbow firing, to fall on her back. Spindle fell from his chair and scooted under the table.

Feet thumped and in came Duiker wearing a shirt and trousers, sheathed sword in hand, followed by Picker in a long nightshirt. The bard, Fisher, was out: taking the mood of the city, or some damned thing like that.

'What happened?' Picker demanded. Peering up, Spindle thought the woman's heavy unbound breasts pushed out the nightshirt in a very appealing way.

'Damned bar cracked,' Blend said. 'Spin . . . Get outta there, Spin. Take a look.'

'Fell out of my chair, that's all.' He straightened, adjusted his shirt. She waved him to the bar.

The stone was cracked clean across. Dust still lingered in the air. 'More of the same,' he said. 'This place is under some kinda pressure. Like it's bein' twisted and squeezed. Just like K'rul himself.'

'Herself,' Blend corrected. 'You saw her.'

'Always thought o' K'rul as a he.'

'Always been a she – everyone knows that!'

'Not as I'd heard.'

'Doesn't fucking matter!' Picker cut in. 'Get your priorities straight, would you? Spin, we in worse trouble now? Should we cut out?'

He laid a hand on the stone counter and tried to sort through the jangling messages blaring from his Warren. *Gods! Like an over-turned anthill. Everything's running all over, frantic, hunting for cover from what they don't even know. Got the feeling it won't matter where we go . . .*

'We should stay,' Duiker suddenly announced. Everyone looked at the old man.

'Why?' Blend demanded.

'I think it helps. Us, people, being here. I think it helps.'

Blend turned to Spindle. 'Well?'

He gave a quick jerk of his head. 'Yeah. Not sure we'd be any safer anywhere else.'

'Good.' Blend peered about the place, almost possessive. 'Didn't want to be run out. Got too much invested here.' She glared at them. 'Well, get back to sleep. Excitement's over.'

Spindle watched Picker head back to the old priest cells. *Man, haven't had a woman in a long time if Picker's lookin' good.* He rubbed his hand on the smooth cold stone. *Stone. The stones. Maybe that was it. Something about the stones. Yes! Had to be it. But what? What about the stones?*

He slapped the counter. *Queen take it!* It was infuriating! He knew there was something there. He just couldn't reach it. Had to be important. It just had to be.

* * *

Jan lay in the quarters that had been set up for the Seguleh among the rambling rooms of Majesty Hall. One of the Hundredth came to let him know that the Legate required him in the Great Hall. He nodded and rose.

Required. Their new status there. Servants. Servants to the Throne. Yet it was not as if this were new. They were merely returning to their original place. Their original role. Was this not all they had yearned for during the long exile? Why then his disquiet, his unease?

Too proud for service? Too arrogant to bend the knee? Was that his trouble?

Perhaps. Yet he could not help suspecting that the cause lay deeper than that. Something more integral, more essential.

He found the Great Hall crowded with councillors, city aristocrats, court functionaries, and general hangers-on such as Lady Envy – many of whom had no actual purpose but who seemed able to behave as if they did. He ignored them all, of course, not being of the sword. Even those who did wear weapons on their hips, such as some of the councillors. He and his brothers and sisters had had to come up with a new category for those individuals: eunuchs who still retained their weapons.

Talk was a low murmur – perhaps so that everyone could eavesdrop on everyone else. Jan walked straight for the throne. Four of the Twenty guarded it. Also present were those two shabby guards. They stood off to one side among the pillars of the colonnade. Right now their crossbows hung at their sides as they ate some sort of steamed buns. It occurred to Jan that they always seemed to be eating.

The Mouthpiece approached looking as pale and haggard as always. He appeared sick, fevered perhaps, sweaty, a hand constantly at his throat. 'Second,' he greeted him. Jan bowed. 'We have a prisoner. A spy who worked against us. He must be executed.'

Jan gave the slightest of shrugs. 'Executed? Very well. Let it be done.'

The Mouthpiece wiped his brow, swallowed, and held his stomach, pained. 'You do not seem to understand. The execution is for you Seguleh to perform. You must see to it.'

Jan faced the gold-masked figure on the throne. 'There must be some misunderstanding. We are warriors, not headsmen. We do not kill prisoners.'

The gold oval edged his way. It seemed to Jan that the graven half-smile on the lips took on a cold aloofness. 'You Seguleh have always been my executioners,' said the Mouthpiece. 'That is the purpose for which I moulded you. The perfect executioners who slew any and all who opposed me. Now . . . fulfil your role.'

It was not only the speed of Jan's reflexes that had raised him to the rank of Second; it was also the quickness of his mind. And so in answer he merely inclined his mask slightly and turned to leave.

Now is not the time, nor the place. Leaping into opposition now would mean confrontation and escalation. Before entering into battle one must consider all the potential outcomes, select the most desirable, then guide the engagement to the achievement of that end.

And what is that end? At this time I have no idea what it might be . . .

When the city Warden opened the cell door for Jan and two of the Hundredth, the prisoner stood to meet them. He held his head level. His hands were bound behind his back. He was an older, rather overweight, retired city guardsman, now dishevelled from having been searched and mildly beaten.

'You are charged with conspiring to bring down the rule of the Legate,' Jan said.

The two of the Hundredth exchanged wondering glances; the prisoner seemed unaware of the extraordinary honour Jan had just accorded him.

The man shrugged as best could with his hands tightly bound. 'I am not ashamed. Nor do I deny it. I would do it again. Darujhistan can govern itself without coercion or command.'

'That would be chaos.'

The ex-guardsman appeared amused. 'Only to those who do not understand it.'

Jan gave a quick cut of his hand. 'Hierarchy must be clear.'

'You of all people I do not expect to understand such things.'

'Perhaps that is so,' Jan agreed. 'I do not pretend to be conversant with all forms of rulership.'

The older guardsman nodded. 'Ah . . . I see it now. You speak of rulership. I speak of governance.'

'I do not see the distinction.'

The ex-guardsman studied Jan closely, as if attempting to peer in behind the mask. What he saw there, or failed to see, appeared to disappoint him. 'Then that is the gulf between us.' He tilted his head as if struck by a new thought. 'Yet you are speaking to me – why?'

'I am trying to understand.'

This admission rocked the ex-guardsman and his eyes widened as he seemed to appreciate the depth of it. Then his gaze slid to the floor and he let out a heavy breath. 'If that is so, then I am saddened for you.'

Now Jan was shaken as if struck. *I am here to execute this man yet he pities me?*

Perhaps alarmed by Jan's reaction one of the Hundredth stepped forward, gripping her sword. 'Kneel,' she commanded. 'You have been condemned to die.'

Jan snapped out a hand-command. *No.* 'This is for me.'

'You are Second,' the woman dared breathe, mask held aside.

'All the more reason it must be me.' *Yes, I am Second. To me must fall this burden. To me must fall the guilt.* He slipped a hand to his sword-grip, addressed the ex-guardsman. 'It will be quick.'

'For me it will be,' the man whispered before Jan's blade flashed one-handed beneath his chin. The knees gave first, seeming to drag the body down. It fell straight down, limp, sagging.

Jan regarded the corpse and its last pumping jets of arterial blood as the heart stubbornly laboured on, refusing to admit to the end. He carefully cleaned his blade before resheathing it. The two of the Hundredth stared on, fascinated by the graphic demonstration. Jan motioned them out, rather impatiently, and remained behind. The man was right. For him this had been quick. *But I fear I will never put this behind me. I have murdered. To me now falls the guilt for this . . . and so much more. Oh, First, why did you not speak of this? Was it because your guilt was too great? And yet all that was so long ago. Can't a people change? Perhaps they can – if those around them will allow it.*

Leaving the hall of cells Jan motioned to the prison guards. They passed him, eyes downcast, sliding along the far wall. And where Jan might have once read respect, due esteem, he now saw only fear. Perhaps even a touch of distaste.

Or was that just himself?

* * *

Antsy could no longer hear the muted groaning and crack of rock echoing through the Spawn now that he was chiselling out the stone threshold under the great stone doors concealing what this crazy-eyed gang of witches, priests, mages and mercenaries were convinced was the Throne of Night.

He didn't think they led to anything remotely like that at all. Maybe the Broom Closet of Dust. Or more likely the Toilet of Crap. But that wasn't his worry. His job was to open these doors, or no one was going anywhere. Even when he rested, the sharp ringing of iron on iron twanged in his ears, and so it was a shock to glance over and see a set of fine polished leather boots right next to him. He glanced up and saw the armoured and richly attired fellow who he assumed to be a mage, who had given his name as Bauchelain.

'What do you want?' Antsy said, rather loudly because of all the ringing.

The man bent down to study him with unsettling intensity. 'You are close to death,' he said.

Antsy looked the fellow up and down very pointedly. 'I sure am.'

He shook his head, chuckling. 'No, no, no. Not me. Not at the moment, in any case. No, I mean death is watching you. You are of interest to . . . ah . . . it.'

'You mean Hood?'

'Certainly not. Hood has gone to his oh-so-poetic and appropriate end, has he not? Dying, as he did. Which itself raises all sorts of disturbing chicken-and-egg questions and other philosophical conundrums. No, what I mean is the new manifestation it has fixed on which it flails about trying to find a permanent one. Which brings us back to you.'

'Me?'

455

'Yes. The current manifestation of death is, again appropriately enough, soldiers. A certain band of soldiers, whose remains, so rumours have it, can be found on this very rock. My companion, Korbal Broach, is very eager to make their acquaintance. Quite keen he is to study them. You wouldn't happen to know their whereabouts, would you?'

Antsy swallowed hard and said, dead level, 'I have no idea what yer talking about.'

'Ah. A shame, that. Well, let's hope something turns up, yes?'

Antsy said nothing.

A reedy old man's voice called from the darkness: 'Master Bauchelain! Our, ah, *friend* is getting into trouble again!'

The fellow stroked his goatee, looking at the ceiling and sighing. 'Must go. Korbal's wandered off. Till later then, yes? Take care.'

Shaken, Antsy returned to his chiselling. *Burn's own blood!* Truth be told, he'd come here precisely to make sure nothing like what that creature was hinting at would happen, or had happened. In the back of his mind he'd known the danger existed, what with the Spawn crashing and all. Sure, a bucketful of gems and coin would go a long way. But that was just cream. All along he'd wanted to make sure things were still all squared away and proper. The thought of a broken sealed pit or whatever it was, and people messin' about with the bones of his brothers and sisters, made him too furious to even think straight—

He left off his chiselling, panting, fisted hands on his thighs. *Almost busted a thumb there.*

Someone else was standing behind him now: cracked sandals, tattered trouser legs over bony bruised shanks. The lad, Jallin. He leaned down. 'You're gonna die, soldier,' he said, matter of fact. 'My mistress. The things I seen her do. She's gonna do for you . . .'

'Shut the Abyss up,' Antsy growled. 'I'm busy.'

The lad flinched, almost hurt. Then he recovered, grinning toothily. 'Gonna die,' he mouthed, backing away.

Shaking his head Antsy returned to his work. Some time later someone banged on the stone flag of the threshold and Antsy whipped round, a curse on his lips. It was the blond-haired mercenary in his plain cloth tabard over mail armour, and canvas-covered round shield. With him were two of his guards. The other two, it seemed, hadn't made it. 'What is it?' Antsy asked, wary.

The man peered at his work from under his tangled brows. 'You are making a hole, yes? A nest?'

The accent was completely unfamiliar but Antsy nodded. 'Yeah. Sorta . . .'

'How deep?'

'About the span of a hand. Why?'

'We will help dig. You go rest. Yes?'

'You're not from Elingarth, are you?'

'No. We are from another land. Far away.' He motioned to his guards and they held out their hands for the hammer and chisel. Antsy passed them over. The two laid aside their shields and set to work with a vengeance, bashing away. Antsy backed off. He drew out a cloth and wiped his face. 'Why're you here?'

'Same as you, hey? The stories of riches we heard. We were in the south. We had a ship. We were . . . how you say . . . taxing shipping, yes? Then we came here.' He shook his head. 'Very large mistake. You get us out we owe you much.'

'Antsy.'

'Cull. Cull Heel. Now you go sleep. We dig.'

Antsy kneaded the cloth in his numb aching hands. 'Well, all right. You come get me in a little while, hey?'

The man waved him off. 'Yes, yes.'

Antsy walked towards the room off the main chamber that Orchid and Corien had taken. He caught the two mages, the old woman and the fat man, eyeing him all the way across the chamber. He tried his best to ignore them.

Within, Orchid turned quickly, asking, 'How is it going?'

Antsy lay down on a pile of gathered cloaks and odd clothing and threw an arm over his eyes. 'Damned slow.'

'They keep coming round – peering at us. Like they're sizing us up for a meal. Gives me the shivers.'

'Who does?'

'All of them.'

'Orchid,' Corien warned gently from across the room.

'What? Oh.'

A light kick woke Antsy and he blinked, squinting in the bluish mage-light. It was Corien. The lad waved him up. One of the mercenaries was there; the man gestured him out. After pulling together his gear Antsy followed. Something about the mercenaries struck him then as he walked: they were all damned big fellows, wide and tall, unusually so. And they all had the same broad heavy faces, as if they were related by blood.

The blond man, Cull, motioned to the chiselled-out gap. 'Good, yes?'

'Let's have a look.' Antsy lay on his stomach to measure the space. Still too tight for his cusser. He pushed himself up to his knees. 'A touch more yet.' He reached for the hammer.

'No, no. We do more. You watch.'

'It's all right. I should . . .'

Cull held up a bloodied hand. 'No. You need your fingers to get us out, yes? We do this.'

Hunh. How do you like that? He peered around at all the sweaty glistening faces watching from the dark walkways and portals: the tall woman, Seris; the old mage, Hemper; Hesta and Ogule. *Typical. They want out but don't even consider lending a hand. Privileged shits.* And as for the Malazans, well, at least they were standing guard down the hall.

While Antsy was crouched, watching the chiselling, Orchid emerged from the dark to come to his side. 'You should see this,' she said, sounding unusually subdued.

'We're close here, Orchid.'

'It'll only take a moment.'

He saw the wonder on her face and grunted. 'All right. But quick.'

'This way.'

She led him up an unlit side passage; his mage-sight allowed him to see here away from the lanterns in the main chamber. Through doorways and a short set of stairs down she brought him into another large cavern, this one low-ceilinged and filled with undecorated stone pillars. Crystals glistened on the uneven black rock walls and from where he stood he could see a sort of natural set of terraces descending into the distance. Dirt lay under his feet along with brown withered plant stalks. 'What's this?' he breathed, sharing Orchid's wonder.

A figure emerged from the gloom: Malakai. He carried a bunch of stalks gathered up in one hand like a bouquet. He sat on the ledge of one of the low terraces, which Antsy now recognized as a kind of planting bed. 'A garden,' the man said, inspecting the dead stalks.

Antsy stared, amazed. 'Not . . .'

'Yes,' Orchid whispered, awed. 'The legends were true. A garden.'

'There were flowers here that scholars tell had never seen the sun,' Malakai said, and he shook his head. 'Imagine what a single such blossom would have brought. All dead now. This is what Apsalar

458

sought when she came to the Spawn so long ago. The Lady of Thieves came to steal a rose. A black rose. One that poets claimed had been touched by the tears of Mother Dark herself.' Shrugging, he let the handful of chaff fall. 'And I sought to best her. To succeed where she had failed.' He motioned to encompass the wrecked cavern, the spilled soil and overturned beds. 'So much for my ambitions.'

Antsy kicked at the black dirt underfoot. 'We still need to get out, Malakai. You can lend a hand.'

The man drew a heavy breath. 'Yes. Well . . . we shall see.'

Antsy motioned to Orchid. 'I have to go,' he said, low.

She nodded and waved him out.

Back in the main chamber the chiselling had stopped. On the way to the throne room doors Antsy heard ominous popping and cracking that reverberated up through the stone beneath his feet. *Time's runnin' out, I swear.*

The mercenaries were all crouched inspecting the pocket they'd worked. They were arguing. The blond man, Cull, was cuffing the other two and shouting them down. Antsy picked up his pace.

'What's this?'

'Ah, Malazan. I tell these fools no more. We wait for you.'

Antsy pushed through them – a hard task in that each seemed as solid and immobile as the rock itself – he studied the gap beneath the stone doors. 'Looks good. Let's try the fit.' He swung his pannier forward.

The three mercenaries backed away. Antsy took a moment to study them. 'Who are you anyway? What do I call you?'

Cull thumped his broad armoured chest. 'We are the Heels!'

Antsy just stared. *Right. The Heels. Okay . . .* He waved them off and returned his attention to the pocket. The fit was too wide in places and too tight in one spot. A last few touches of the chisel fixed that. Stone chips helped keep the cusser in place, then Antsy pulled out a stone of rough unpolished granite. With this he started to abrade the keratin shell of the cusser as close to the top of it as he could reach.

Fiddler and Hedge had perfected this technique – skimming. They used it to time charges. Problem was, he'd never actually had call to do it himself. But they'd all talked it over pretty thoroughly. All the squad saboteurs. Come to think of it – none of them had ever done it themselves neither!

Shit.

He pulled away the granite grinding stone. *Well then*, he decided.

Maybe that's good enough. Lying on his stomach he turned back to the chamber, yelled: 'Seris! Get your people ready!'

The tall woman emerged from the gloom. 'Now? You are prepared?'

'Yes.' And he shouted louder. 'Munitions! Ware!'

He pulled out a small hard case, opened it. Inside rested a glass tube. This he unstoppered, and, reaching awkwardly under the lip of the door's bottom, let three drops fall into the scar he'd scraped into the shell of the munition.

He pushed himself away as quickly as he could and ran. Across the chamber he spotted Orchid and Corien behind a thick pillar and joined them.

'How long?' Corien whispered.

'Don't know. Shouldn't be too—'

The entire structure juddered around them, groaning and snapping in an agony of tortured rock. A stone arch burst overhead sending shards pattering down. The Spawn began to tilt. Equipment, rubbish and broken rubble slid across the floor. Antsy grabbed hold of the pillar together with Orchid and Corien.

He watched, horrified, as something came tumbling out from the tilting threshold before the doors and rolled down the shallow stairs. The cusser. *Sweet Soliel, no!*

Even as he stared it bounced once, twice, three times, then slid down the polished smooth stone floor to disappear into the great yawning hole in the middle of the chamber.

Hood's laughter!

Everyone was screaming and shouting and cursing. A piece of what looked like expensive travelling baggage came sliding out of the darkness to follow the cusser down the well. An old man yelled his despair.

Then the stone of the Spawn kicked Antsy. At least that's what it felt like. The floor jerked, punishing his ankles and knees. A great gust of air came shooting from the well. It stank of the acrid smoke of expended munitions and was heavy with water vapour.

Ponderously, among bursting and grinding complaints of stone, the Spawn began to tilt back in the opposite direction, righting itself. The old woman, Hesta, came staggering out of the dark. Her ribbons and hair had gone, revealing a wrinkled bald scalp. With her pale head and scrawny body she more than ever resembled a vulture.

'You fool!' she shrieked, pointing. 'You've killed us all!' Wordless with fury, she threw her hands up and howled in a cracking, hoarse voice. Then she swung those hands down to Antsy. 'Die!'

A wall of blindingly bright flame came billowing and churning across the chamber for him.

A stupid *Damn* was all he managed as he stood there fully expecting to die.

A hand grasped him by the neck of his leather hauberk and yanked him backwards.

*

Antsy found himself lying in darkness. Gradually his mage-sight gathered itself and he saw that he was in an entirely different room. This one was long, low-roofed, and contained stone sarcophagi. Sitting on one of those stone coffins was a familiar figure eyeing him and scowling his disapproval. Mallet.

Antsy carefully stood and dusted himself off. He nodded to Mallet. 'Thanks.'

'You shouldn't be here,' the dead squad healer said.

'That's what Ferret said.'

'You should've listened to him.'

'Nobody ever listened to Ferret.'

Mallet nodded. 'That's what I said.'

Antsy walked the room, peered at the sarcophagi lined up in double rows. *As if marshalled at attention.* 'So this is it, hey?'

The big man shrugged his meaty shoulders – and he was big, just not tall. Squat and solid enough to swing that heavy two-handed weapon of his. 'Yeah. Last resting place.'

'I was worried, you know . . . what with all this, maybe someone had gotten in . . .'

The healer's voice was sharp: 'Think we'd allow that?'

Antsy raised his hands. 'Hey – you're dead, right?'

Mallet ran a hand along the dust-laden top of one stone slab. 'And you ain't Antsy. Which is our point. You're retired. Go back to . . . wherever it is. Don't go looking for trouble no more.'

The Spawn rocked about them, stone grinding and moaning. Dust sifted down through the still air of the burial chamber. Antsy snorted, gesturing. 'Looks like I might as well stay. I'm dead anyway.'

Mallet shook his head. 'No you aren't.'

'Says who?'

'Says us. And we can see these things now. Whose end is near. Whose isn't. We decide. And you know what? None of us ever liked you, Antsy – so you're just gonna have to kick around for quite a while yet.'

Antsy fell on to one of the sarcophagi as the Spawn rocked around him. '*What?*'

'You heard me. All that moanin' all the time about how we're all gonna die and Hood will get us all in the end. Well, look at you and look at us. You was no fun alive – imagine how you'll be dead! We've about had it, I tell you.'

Antsy straightened to hold his legs wide against the pitching while he cursed under his breath. 'Fine! To think I was worried 'bout you. You can all rot! Get me outta here.'

'Done!' and Mallet gave a backhanded wave. The darkness closed about Antsy and he was gone.

A moment later another figure walked up behind Mallet; this one taller, bearded, wearing a helmet with wide cheek-guards. 'Think he bought all that?' he asked.

'I dunno. I think so. I mixed it up with half-truths. Never could stand his groaning. A bucket of cold water he was all the time.'

'And none of us had any faults,' the figure murmured. He waved a goodbye, like a blessing. 'Go live, Antsy. Sour doomsayer that you are. Sometimes the only thing that gives me grace is the knowledge that some of us are still out there.'

'We're going where none will disturb us now,' Mallet observed.

'Four fathoms down we will rest.'

*

Antsy stepped out of darkness into pandemonium. From all sides about the great chamber, from portals, halls and doors, the ragged army of Torbal Loat was pushing in against a cordon of Malazans aided by the foreign mercenaries, Corien, and a few others. Behind Loat's robber army pressed a further horde of surviving Spawn looters. Even as Antsy watched, more kept arriving to throw their weight against the marines. Crossbows fired indiscriminately. Tossed furniture flew back and forth.

Orchid appeared to take his arm. 'We thought you were dead!' she shouted.

'I ducked.'

'We're sinking! Everyone's gone berserk.'

'I don't blame them.'

'Malazan,' a strong voice called from the dark.

Antsy glanced over, seeing nothing, but Orchid's breath caught. 'Morn.' She pulled and Antsy allowed himself to be dragged along.

'Where have you been?' she demanded.

'These are powerful mages. I am but a reflection of a shadow. I dare not show myself yet.'

'Where is the Gap?' Orchid demanded.

'It's too late for that now. The Gap is submerged. The waters are rising.'

'Then we're lost!'

'No. There is a way out but only you, Orchid, can open it. As the last of the blood here in these halls you are the mistress of the Spawn. Those doors will open for you.'

'What?'

Antsy's gaze slitted his suspicion. 'You mean all along . . . Then why . . .'

'All alternatives had to be exhausted, Malazan. Now they will listen to Orchid. And within, child, the only exit is through Night Imperishable. And only you can open the Path.'

Antsy took hold of Orchid's arm. 'Fine. Let's go. Our thanks, shade. And by the way, my charge . . . would it have worked?'

The figure of dark shook its hooded head.

Antsy pulled Orchid after him. 'Yeah, well. That's what you think,' he muttered as he marched away.

The cordon was shrinking, giving ground before the hundreds pushing in upon it. It looked as though the last stand would take place before the great tall doors of black stone themselves, where the mages had gathered together on the raised steps. With the elegant fellow, Bauchelain, was an ugly squat man, pale and bloated, an idiotic grin on his face. And behind them hunched an old man loaded with baggage – well, perhaps not so old, just looking extremely careworn.

Antsy caught the eye of one of the foreign lads, the Heels, who waved and pushed forward, tossing people from his path to make way for them. Antsy squeezed through with Orchid, nodded his thanks, then ran for the doors.

'*You!*' snarled Hesta, her wig askew.

'Another time, perhaps,' her companion, Ogule, murmured. He pointed, and a swath of desperate Spawn fortune-hunters clutched at their throats, gurgling and flailing.

'Not quite the outcome I foresaw,' Seris shouted to Antsy over the clash of battle.

'Let Orchid here try,' he called to her.

She shook her head. 'We've all tried. Not even those two could manage.' She gestured to Bauchelain and his obese companion.

463

'What's to lose?' He helped Orchid forward.

Though obviously sceptical Seris still helped make room before the doors. Orchid turned to Antsy. 'What do I—'

'Just push,' he told her impatiently.

'*Fine!*' Piqued, she threw her weight against the doors.

They swung open smoothly and silently. The gang of mages, mercenaries and servants half tumbled tripping over each other into the throne room.

'Cover the doors!' Sergeant Girth bellowed as he brought up the rear with the remaining Malazan marines. Corien and the mercenaries backed them up.

Antsy peered about. It was a smaller chamber. Circular, domed ceiling. He'd never been in a throne room proper so he didn't know if this was how they were supposed to look. But this one had more of the feel of a shrine. It even had some sort of an inner arc of pillars surrounding . . . nothing, as far as he could make out.

'Aiiya!' Hesta screeched. 'I see no throne. We are betrayed!'

'Quiet,' Seris commanded as she scanned the room. 'You, Orchid, what now?'

Orchid did not answer. She had crossed to the rear wall behind the arc of slim stone pillars. Antsy went to her. She was studying a painting on the wall: a long broad fresco that ran all round this broad niche. He took her arm. 'Orchid.'

'Stunning . . .' she breathed, intent.

'Orchid!'

She turned to him. 'Just as the legends portray,' and she gestured to the fresco.

Antsy spared it a glance: a dark outdoor night-time scene under stars. Some sort of lit parade or procession approaching, light shafting in after it.

'The Great Union.'

'What?'

'The marriage of Night and Light.'

Antsy took a step backwards. *Fener's balls! That's . . . terrifying.*

Further shudders shook the chamber. The reports of falling rock burst from nearby. The floor canted to a slightly sharper angle.

An orange flame-like light burst to life. 'Attend!' Hesta yelled. She had raised an arm and her hand was aflame as a burning brand. 'No more delay. We must escape now! Where is . . .' Her voice dwindled away as she stared down.

Antsy pushed forward through the ring of gathered mages. At

464

their feet lay a rectangle flush with the floor at the centre of the pillars. While all the chamber was now lit this rectangle remained as utterly night black as a solid pool of pitch. Oddly enough, though the floor was angled, the surface of the darkness remained flush within its containment.

'The Throne?' Ogule offered.

'Shut up!' Hesta snapped.

'Well, *a* throne,' Seris murmured.

'A gate,' Bauchelain said.

Giggling, the man's companion, Korbal, Antsy assumed, knelt to thrust an arm in. His pudgy hand met some sort of barrier just beneath the surface of night. He snarled his frustration.

The noise of battle at the door died away and everyone turned to look. 'What is going on?' the old mage, Hemper, yelled.

'They've backed off,' Girth shouted. 'Someone's coming. Someone . . . *Sacred shit!*'

'I must open it,' Orchid said, musing, as if dreaming.

'Well – do so!' Hesta screeched.

She knelt and passed a hand over the rectangle. 'I'm not sure . . .' she began, just touching the rippling liquid-like barrier. Then she fell in. Or was grabbed. Or sucked. But she suddenly disappeared without a splash into the murk as if it were a pool of black water. Antsy stared, stunned. *Was that supposed to happen?*

'The way appears open,' Seris remarked.

'Then now is the time,' Ogule murmured, and he smiled, dimpling.

A blazing pain lanced Antsy's back. He clutched there and found the hilt of a dagger. Turning, he saw Jallin dancing away. 'Gonna die!' the youth sang as he backed off. Antsy took a step to follow him but something was wrong and he staggered, almost falling.

Behind him chaos erupted. Flames burst to life. Someone shrieked. He heard the old man Hemper bellow: 'You will not profane it!'

Whadaya know, Antsy thought as the floor came up to hit him, *the old guy's a priest of darkness . . .*

He slid down the canted floor leaving a slick of gleaming blood behind. He saw Seris enveloped in black fire writhing nearby; he saw the weeping servant of Bauchelain struggling to push a huge piece of luggage up the tilted floor to reach the Throne; he saw the Malazans retreating from the door as some half-dozen masked Seguleh pushed through. So that was what Grith had seen . . .

Corien knelt before him. 'Antsy! Who . . . ?' The lad tried to move him but the pain almost blacked him out.

'No . . . Go,' he managed through clenched teeth.

Then Malakai was there. 'I'm sorry for you, soldier. But Orchid has succeeded. We have our exit. The paths to the Warrens are open now through the Throne.' He touched Antsy's shoulder just briefly. 'And I repay my debts. Farewell.'

Gods take it! Even Malakai thinks I'm done for! How do you like that? Spend my whole life avoiding all the traps the world throws at me and now that death themselves tell me to live – I don't last five minutes! Fucking comedy that is. Sink the Spawn with my one munition then get back-stabbed by some skulking alley rat! Gods. Mallet's gonna be so damned mad at me.

He watched while Malakai helped up the very rat himself, Jallin. As he did so, he even slipped something into the lad's pack that may have fallen out. Then he climbed lizard-like up the tilting floor to reach the Throne and pulled himself in to disappear without a ripple.

Bastard! I'll kill him, I swear.

Together Hesta and Ogule managed to overpower Hemper. Some arcane magic from the fat Ogule made the fellow cough up his lungs in a bloody spray of tattered flesh. Seris gathered herself in one snarling feral leap to reach the lip of the Throne and heave herself in.

'You!' a Seguleh ordered, pointing at Jallin. 'You will surrender it now!'

The youth's eyes grew as huge as saucers and he scrambled to hide behind Hesta and Ogule. The two mages struggled to push him from them. The Seguleh drew their swords in one single hiss, following. The lad dodged behind all the mages to squeeze between the Malazans and disappear. Two Seguleh gave chase.

Antsy watched, hardly able breathe, while the pale grinning companion of Bauchelain, Korbal, actually approached one of the remaining Seguleh. He laid a hand on his arm and whispered something. A sword flashed and Korbal disappeared with a yelp that transformed into a squawk. A large black crow flew off though the doors.

Having reached the Throne, Bauchelain sighed and allowed himself to slide down the floor. He dusted himself, straightening. 'Come, Emancipor,' he called, and set off after his companion. The Malazans parted to allow them to pass.

The mercenary Heels now scrambled to Antsy. The two younger ones tried to lift him but he cried out in agony. He could feel the blade scraping his spine. He fought to hang on to consciousness.

'I'm sorry,' someone said, the lad, Corien. A squeeze of his shoulder then nothing. His last sight was of the Malazans lying flat on the polished floor, which was angled now as steep as a wall, climbing up one another for the Throne. Behind them water now swirled past the doors in a churning gyre of bodies and debris.

Then all was dark and cold.

A hand touched his cheek. He opened his eyes – or regained consciousness. His mage-vision allowed him to see the sideways chamber glowing in a blue so dark as to be almost indistinguishable from black.

Someone was with him. A shape in the night – or a shape of night itself. Her face was black, as were her eyes. Black on black, as if carved from jet.

'Just you and I, soldier,' she said.

Good, he said. Or thought he said. *They got out.*

'Yes.'

And me?

The shape slid away into the dark as if dissolving. 'You spoke with a shade,' the voice said.

Yes.

'How – how was he?'

How?

'Yes. He has been . . . away . . . for some time. Now he has returned. How did he seem?'

He seemed . . . sad.

'Sad?'

Yes. He gave his name as Morn.

'Morn? He did? Thank you, soldier. For that I bless you. Now, it is time for you to go.'

Go? Right. Face my squad.

'No. Not to them. Do not be hurt or angry. They were harsh because they feared you might long to join them. They love you, Antsy. They want you to live. For that reason I am here speaking to you. That, and for the child, Orchid.'

Orchid?

'Yes. You brought her to me. And for that you have my gratitude. Farewell, soldier.'

Cold cold waters as dark as night enveloped him. Movement then. A hand pushed at the chest of his hauberk. A glimpse of a masked face in dark swirling waters, then blackness.

CHAPTER XVII

The more laws a land has, the more corrupt it is.

Message scratched in stones of a fallen
prison wall, Darujhistan

SCORCH'S AND LEFF'S BOOT HEELS ECHOED IN THE EMPTY NIGHT-
time streets of Darujhistan. They walked the Daru district, not
far from the Third Tier Wall that demarked the estate district
containing Majesty Hill. Scorch peered about at the closed doors and
the empty walks where crowds usually discussed the latest shows, a
new dancer, or a troupe of entertainers newly arrived in the city. He
nervously licked his lips and peered sidelong to his partner.

'Where is everyone?' he murmured, suspicious.

Leff squinted his disbelief. 'It's the curfew, you idiot. No one's
allowed out after the tenth bell. We was there when the Legate
signed the law.'

Scorch shrugged his bony shoulders. 'Not my business. I must've
been busy looking for threats.'

'Threats, right,' Leff murmured, looking skyward.

'Well,' Scorch went on, 'it's not like we're gettin' out much these
days.'

Leff put a touch harder stamp into his step and thrust out his chest
even further. 'That's right. Got us important work. Guardin' the
Legate and such. Busy. Can't be loafing about.'

'Not like the old days.'

'Nope. No more drinking or chasing skirts for us.'

'Can't be doin' none o' that,' Scorch sighed, and he pulled on his
lower lip. 'Leff . . .' he said, tentative.

'Yeah?'

468

'What say you we sign on any trader leavin' tonight? Head down south. Rich pickin's down there. Everyone says so. Heard me stories of buckets of coin.'

Leff stopped. He hooked his thumbs in his belt and regarded his partner, head lowered. 'You see – there's our problem. Consistency. Stick-to-it-ness.' He drove a hand through the air before him. 'Have to hoe a straight row. See things through to the ugly bitter sticky end no matter how many tell us for gods' sakes would you just drop it! No more o' that listening to other people. Not for us, right?'

Brows cramped together, mouth open, Scorch nodded. 'Right.'

'Hey, you two!' a new voice called out.

Both turned. A detachment of the city Wardens approached. They carried lanterns and were armed with truncheons. 'It's curfew, you know,' their sergeant continued.

Leff threw out his hands, aggrieved. 'Yeah! It's curfew – an' if we see anyone out we'll arrest them, won't we!' The sergeant's unshaven face screwed up as he tried to work his way through that. 'We're Majesty Hill guards, I'll have you know,' Leff continued, and he made a show of resting his hand on the grip of his shortsword.

The sergeant's gaze followed the motion and it seemed to Leff that the man was suitably impressed. He waved them on, murmuring something that might have been: 'Say hello to the Seguleh.'

Leff stamped off, chest thrown out. Scorch followed. 'Imagine,' Leff complained loudly. 'The nerve of some.'

Scorch spotted a faded sign of a bird rising from flames, a warm yellow glow from glazed windows, a door a sliver ajar, and the noise of laughter and tankards banging tables.

'Phoenix's open,' he commented.

Leff abruptly stopped again. 'After curfew?'

'Uh-huh.'

Leff set his hand once more on his weapon grip. 'Have to 'vestigate. Might be curfew-breakers.'

Scorch's wide mouth drew up in a wet grin. 'Just doin' our duty.'

'That's right.'

Inside, the noise seemed a solid barrier. Scorch and Leff peered about, blinking at the crowd. Leff scanned for a table but the floor was jammed. An older tough-looking woman glowered at them from behind the bar. 'What do you two want?' she demanded.

'Friends!' a familiar voice piped.

Leff looked round to see Kruppe gesturing them over. 'It's all right,' he told the woman, 'we're expected.'

Kruppe was at his usual small round table hidden away near the back. He invited them to sit then clapped his hands, calling: 'Jess! Summer ale for my friends here. They thirst!'

The two exchanged suspicious glances. 'What's this?' Scorch asked.

The little man appeared offended. He pressed a hand to his stained shirt. 'What is this? Why, nothing more than drinks among friends. Mere hospitality! Why should there be anything more to this than that? Why, there is none of this or that, I assure you.'

The heavy bulk of Jess pressed up to the table. 'You again,' she accused, glaring at Kruppe.

'Yes? Me?' Kruppe blinked winningly up at her, hands pressed together under his chin.

'Nothing more for you until you pay your tab.'

Scorch and Leff shared knowing looks and pushed back their chairs preparing to leave.

Kruppe clutched at them. 'No, no! Said tab is as good as covered. I assure you I have every intention of taking care of that trivial detail. There you have it, Jess. A promissory promise. I, ah, promise. So, until such time . . . would you be so good as to put these drinks on the tab?'

Jess heaved a sigh and pushed back hair stuck to her sweaty face. 'I'll ask Meese,' she allowed, and lumbered off, hips swaying.

Leff sat again. 'Gotta admire your way with women there, friend.'

Sitting back, Kruppe slipped his hands under his tight crimson waistcoat looking quite satisfied with himself. 'It's a blessing and a curse I struggle to live with.' He eyed them up and down. 'And you two? How goes the search for gainful employment?'

'Oh, we got—' began Scorch only to break off and curse as Leff kicked him under the table.

Kruppe's oily black brows rose. 'Oh-ho! What is this? You have secured positions? You have an income? Ergo, you are able now to honour certain past debts that have heretofore been graciously allowed to languish, unpursued, by certain friends?'

'We ain't been paid yet,' Leff said, glaring at Scorch.

Kruppe slapped a hand to the cluttered table. 'As good as, I should say! This calls for celebration! Let us honour this coming plentitude with a drink now – for that is exactly what you will do once it arrives, yes? The difference being only one of inconsequential timing. Then, after that, then we can discuss your debt.'

Scorch sat with his typical expression of surprise compounded by incomprehension. 'I don't get it,' he confessed to Leff.

'Never mind,' Leff sighed as tall tankards arrived with a glass of white wine, all set down by Jess.

'Meese said it was okay,'

'My dear,' beamed Kruppe, 'you are fitting in nicely here.'

She went away rolling her eyes.

'To advances, advantage, and profitable positions,' said Kruppe, lifting his glass.

Leff and Scorch knocked their tankards together. 'Aye. Twins look away.'

*　　*　　*

The upper waters of the River Maiten flowed thick and heavy with silt, almost sluggish, like old blood. The wet silts even gave it a reddish hue. For a time they paced its course, heading north for Darujhistan. Eventually, they came to a nameless hamlet that hugged the river. Here the water allowed farming and animal husbandry. And the river offered some fishing, if only small bottom-dwellers.

Since neither the Seventh nor Lo appeared inclined to approach the villagers regarding hiring a boat, Yusek and Sall headed in to do the honours. Part of Yusek wondered why they were bothering with paying at all when they could just take one of the wretched battered old punts drawn up on the muddy shore. But another part of her understood that Lo and the Seventh had these conceits of honesty and honour that had to be observed.

'They want coin,' she told Sall. 'You have any coin?'

The Seguleh lad drew a small pouch from beneath his cloak. 'I have these. Our old currency.'

A clinking heap of shiny yellow bars, or wafers, fell into her cupped hands. 'Osserc's mercy!' she exclaimed, pressing the pile to her chest. 'Where did you get all this?'

The lad seemed unconcerned. 'As I said. It is our old currency. We don't use it any more. I keep these as mementos.'

Yusek shuffled them back into the pouch, which she then kept in her fist. 'They're gold,' she hissed.

'Yes. I know.'

'Are we going to pay gold for a crappy old boat that can barely hold all of us?'

'I see no alternative.'

'Gods. The price of boats is about to go *way* up.'

'Pay them – it is of no matter.'

No matter! By the Enchantress! This is part of my fortune I'm throwing away here. 'Sall – can't we just threaten them? Just a little?'

The mask faced her square. The hazel and brown eyes grew stern. 'I'll do it.'

'All right, all right!' Yusek stalked away. 'Can't fucking believe I'm handing gold to these stinking hamlet-dwellers,' she muttered. 'They won't even know what they've got in their hands . . .'

A short time later the Seventh pushed off one of the larger of the river boats and took the stern. Lo had the bow while Sall and Yusek sat in the middle. The boat was of hide ribbed with wood. It was without seats; one merely knelt in the fetid water that sloshed within. At first Yusek held on to a thwart, refusing to let her hide trousers touch the filth. Finally Sall reached up to yank her down.

'And what do I do?' she asked, wincing as the cold water clasped her knees.

Sall handed her a cup carved from wood. 'You bail – or we sink.'

*　　　*　　　*

Kiska walked with Tayschrenn over the featureless dunes of black sands. Soon clouds swept in from ahead, which struck her as odd, since no clouds had ever before marred the sky here at the Shores. The shadows of the clouds glided over them, obscuring her vision, and in their wake she found herself walking a night-time landscape of blasted broken rock. Suddenly it was hard going, as the ground was uneven and the sharp stones turned under her feet. She missed the smooth sands, even if they did make walking a chore.

'Where are we?'

Tayschrenn did not answer. He was peering into the sky. Suddenly he knelt behind a larger boulder, motioning her down. 'Trespassing,' he murmured. She huddled under the cover of the boulder then hissed, jerking away; it was hot to the touch.

'What is this . . .' Then she saw them wheeling in the sky and she stared, astounded and terrified. Winged long-necked beasts flying off in the distance. 'Are those . . .'

'Yes.'

'Enchantress protect us. What's going on?'

'A gathering. A marshalling. Call it what you will.'

'Is that where we're . . .'

'No. All this regards the past. I prefer to look to the future.'

'Then what are we doing here?'

The mage struck off at right-angles. 'As I said, trespassing. This is a short cut.'

A short cut? This? Hate to see the long way round.

Not long after that – at least if you counted time in paces, as she was doing – the landscape changed to a forested verge. The ground became swampy as they entered the woods, and thick vine-laden trunks and ferns blocked all view. Tayschrenn slowed, then came to an uncertain halt.

'What is it?' she asked.

'We're being deflected. This is not where I intended to come.'

The very air felt charged to Kiska, vibrating and heavy with potential. 'Something's stirring here,' she whispered. 'Something awful.'

He glanced at her, surprised. 'I'd forgotten about your natural sensitivity. Yes. I feel it too. But again, this is not what I have chosen. I could commit myself – attempt to guide things one way or the other. But would it be for the better? Would the outcome be improved by yet another set of meddling hands? No, I think not.'

Kiska used her staff to flick a snake away from the man's sandalled feet. 'Perhaps we should be going . . .'

'Yes. Let us . . . no. It is too late.' He turned to face the darkness between the roots of two immense trunks. Kiska whipped her staff crossways.

A figure arose from the dark. Kiska would have said that this person, a woman, stepped from the darkness, but that was not right. She rose as if she had been crawling. She was tall and wide, wearing layers upon layers of black cloth all dusty and festooned with cobwebs. In contrast, her long black hair hung down past her shoulders, sleek and shimmering. Her complexion was a dark nut brown, her eyes very dark.

Tayschrenn bowed to her. 'Ardata.'

Ardata? Where had she heard that before? Some sort of sorceress.

The woman stepped forward. She was barefoot and the layers of cloth trailed behind, snagging on brush and roots, unravelling in long threads.

'Magus,' she greeted Tayschrenn. Her voice was surprisingly rich and musical. 'Long have I known of you.' She circled at a distance. 'Your acts come to me like ripples in the skein of the Warrens.' The dark eyes swung to Kiska. 'And who is this?'

'She is with me.'

473

The eyes flared undisguised dismissal and contempt. 'One of *her* creatures, I see. The strings are plain to me.'

'We were just going.'

'You are? You will not stay? There is much turmoil. Much . . . opportunity. Who knows what the final outcome may be?'

'My choice is made. I will lend my strength where I believe I can do the most.'

The lips twisted into a knowing sneer. 'And not incidentally positioning yourself very neatly.'

'Or assuring my inevitable dissolution.'

The sorceress laughed and Kiska felt almost seduced by the richness of her voice. 'We both know you would not allow that. You would not commit fully otherwise.'

'No. I have found purpose, Ardata. One far beyond the mere amassing and hoarding of power.'

Kiska noted that in her pacing the sorceress had left behind a trail of black threads that now completely encircled them. Halting, Ardata cocked her head to regard Tayschrenn sidelong. 'This does not sound like the magus of whom I have heard so much.'

'That is true. I have . . . changed.'

* The woman darted out a hand, pointing to Kiska. 'And does this one have something to do with that? Is she responsible?'

Tayschrenn moved to stand before Kiska. 'She was – integral, yes.'

The sorceress held her arms wide. The black shifting cloths hung from them like cowls, spreading. 'Then I believe you should remain.'

Darkness swallowed them. Blinded, Kiska hunched, holding her staff ready. An inhuman snarl burst around them, enraged and frustrated. It dwindled then snapped away into silence. The ground shifted beneath Kiska's feet and she stumbled, almost falling. Then the absolute darkness brightened in stages to mere night, but not night as Kiska knew it. Brighter, with the moon larger and two other globes in the starry sky looking like child's marbles. One tinted reddish, the other more bluish. To her relief Tayschrenn was still with her.

'Where are we now?'

'Closer.'

'That sorceress . . . she is your enemy?'

Hands clasped behind his back once more, the mage set off through the tall grass surrounding them. Kiska struggled to catch up. A cool wind smelling of pine billowed her cloak and dried her face. 'Enemy?' Tayschrenn mused. 'No, not as such. No, her hostility was directed against someone else, yes?'

'The Enchantress.'

'Yes.'

'What is the Queen of Dreams to her?'

The mage laughed, startling her. The laughter was completely unguarded, open and uninflected. She'd never heard anything like it from him before. 'What is she to . . .' He laughed again, chuckling as if enjoying the sensation. 'My dear Kiska. Who do you think held the title of Enchantress before your patron showed up? They are rivals. Bitter rivals. Ardata is ancient. The greatest power of her age. Eclipsed now in this time of Warrens and their mastery.'

'I see. I didn't know.'

'No. And I didn't expect that you should. But the mark of the Queen is upon you, so you ought to know now.'

Yes. Her 'strings'. Kiska did not like the sound of that. She wondered whether they were knotted. She knew that she would do all she could to tear them off if that should be so.

'So, just where are we?' she asked.

'This is Tellann. We should be safe here – for a time.'

'*Tellann?* But that is Imass! How can we be here?'

The mage glanced at her, startled. 'You keep surprising me with your knowledge of these things. Why is it you never pursued magery? You could have. Thyr, perhaps?'

Kiska shrugged off the suggestion, uncomfortable. 'Too much effort.' She slung her staff over her shoulders as she walked.

'Too much effort? Yet you put yourself through rigorous physical training little different from torture . . .'

'I prefer to act.'

'You prefer to act,' the mage echoed again, musing. 'Impetuous still. Not wise.'

She shrugged beneath the staff, flexed her wrists, feeling the bones cracking. 'That's how it is.'

Ahead, a rumbling filled the plain. Beneath the night sky a darker cloud of dust approached from one side. As it closed Kiska heard animal snorting penetrating the din of countless hooves hammering the hardpan prairie. A herd thundered across their path. Great woolly front-heavy beasts, some boasting wicked-looking curved horns.

Movement brushed among the tall grass nearby and Kiska whipped her staff to the side to stand hunched, ready, staff levelled, facing two low eyes across a long narrow muzzle. She stared, fascinated, as those frost-blue eyes bored into her and through her. Then they released her, snapping aside as the beast dodged, loping off through the grass. She almost fell when the gaze abandoned her. She felt exhausted, her heart hammering as if she had been running all evening. *Is this the fear of the prey in the face of the hunter? Or an invitation?*

Tayschrenn's gaze followed the wolf as it bounded after the herd. He murmured as if reciting: 'And what are the gods but need writ large?'

'What was that?' Kiska asked, still panting. She pressed the back of a glove to her hot forehead.

'Just some philosopher's musings. The wolves, Kiska. The wolves. The gods are restless. They are charging now to their destiny, for that is their role. I sense in this a welcome. Come, let us follow. I recognize the old scent now and I accept. It is time for a long overdue reunion.'

He led the way on to the churned up trail. Kiska followed, waving the dust and drifting chaff from her face.

*　　*　　*

Picker was on watch at the front of K'rul's bar when a knock on the barricaded door made her jump, so startled that she dropped the crossbow. Spindle jerked up from where he napped on one of the benches. Glaring at him to say anything, just one thing, she picked up the weapon then peered out through the boards.

'Who're you?' she called.

A low voice murmured something. 'Yeah, he's here,' Picker answered. She looked at Spindle. 'Someone's got a message for ya.'

He pushed through to peep. He was a tall fellow, lean, hooded. The evening light made his lined face look even more harsh. Spindle raised his crossbow. 'What d'ya want?'

'I have a message that I think is for the sapper here,' he answered.

'All's we got is this fella,' Picker said.

'I'm trained!'

'Barely,' she grumbled beneath her breath.

'What is it?'

'The message is – you should consider the peculiar qualities of the white stone. That's it. The qualities of the stone.'

Spindle raised a fist. 'Yes! The stones! I *knew* it.' He punched Picker's shoulder. 'Didn't I tell you? We're on to something, I'm sure!'

She gave him an angry stare then turned to the front. 'Yeah? Who says . . . damn.'

'What?' Spindle looked: gone. He pushed himself from the barricade and heaved up the crossbow to his shoulder. 'The stones,' he murmured, musing. 'I need to take another look.'

'All buried now, ain't they?' Picker said.

Spindle snapped his fingers. 'I bet there's still some down by the mole. I'm gonna go.'

'I'll go with you,' Duiker said from where he sat towards the back.

'What? Why?'

'You're only partially trained,' the old scholar muttered as he eased himself up.

'You mean partially house-trained,' Picker sneered. 'Anyway – you're not going anywhere.'

'Why not?'

'What if those Seguleh return? And us shorthanded?'

'Faugh.' Spindle waved that aside. 'If they was going to come back they'd have done it already.' He went for the door but stopped short, staring at the nailed boards and heaped benches. He glanced back to Duiker. 'I guess we'll go out the back.'

Out on the streets Spindle felt naked armed only with his little pig-sticker. He was grateful to Duiker, though, for remembering and stopping him at the door. They'd both set aside all their weapons – no sense risking a meeting with the Seguleh.

Nervous, Spindle rubbed his shirt as he walked the street. Anyway, he reflected, he was never *entirely* helpless. Always had his magics. Not that it ever amounted to much. What use was the ability to drive animals insane? It was just embarrassing, though it seemed to have helped now and then. Saved his life, if only by accident. Like that time the camp was attacked by riders and he raised his Warren, or whatever the Abyss it was, and all the animals went crazy.

Maybe, the thought just struck, it was chaos. Maybe that was the force he raised. Kind of a mental chaos. Now that sounded a lot more proper and menacing, that did. Not just Spindle, the guy who scares rats and cats. And goats and stoats. And horses and . . . *damn, what rhymes with horses?*

At his side Duiker cleared his throat, hands hooked in his belt as he walked along. The late afternoon sun shone golden on the walls of the taller buildings. Inns and cafés were doing a brisk early dinner

477

trade with the curfew in force. 'So what happened down south anyway?' the old soldier asked.

Spindle waved all that aside. 'Ach, you don't want to know. Gates and Warrens and power up for grabs. It was ugly but it came out all right in the end. I don't rightly know exactly all what happened myself.'

'Had enough of it down there, though, did you?'

'Actually I'm thinking of heading back.'

They reached the waterfront close to the paved walk and open green where the mole began. Here the wreckage of the construction site lay abandoned like a demolished building. Spindle was surprised to see that people had moved in, putting up shacks and hanging awnings; the sort who normally would do so outside the city walls at Maiten town or Raven. Usually, he imagined, the city Wardens would've rousted them along. Things seemed to have ground down to a standstill all over the city. He searched among the shanty town for any sign of the stone blocks but saw none.

'There was a bunch of 'em,' he told Duiker.

The old man frowned at the disheartening sight of the families crouched under canopies. 'Reminds me of Seven Cities,' he said to himself.

'Here we are!' He'd found a shard. A piece of a broken block about the size of a keg.

Duiker knelt next to him to run a hand over what Spindle knew to be the smooth, almost flesh-like surface. 'Amazing,' the man murmured.

'You recognize it?'

'Yes. In fact I do. Among my studies were writings of the ancient natural philosophers.'

'Who?'

'Never mind. But I know this stone. It's not marble at all, in truth. It's a rare mineral. Usually you see it only as small statuettes or figurines. Where did anyone find so much of it?'

'Don't know. So, what is it?'

The old scholar sat back on his thin haunches, scratched his beard. 'Well – there're many names for it, of course. The name I know is *Alabaster.*'

Spindle repeated the name, trying it out. It meant nothing to him. *Damn. I thought this would be it. That we'd crack it. Hood – maybe it's nothing after all. Just a dry hunch.*

'Who would use this for construction, though?' the old man went on. 'It's useless for that. It's much too soft. Among the softest of all stones . . .'

Spindle threw down a handful of dirt to pace next to the kneeling historian. *Dammit! I'm supposed to know my materials. But this is no granite, no limestone. I never studied the rarer minerals.*

'In fact,' the historian continued, musing, 'it shouldn't have even survived submersion in the lake. Some forms of it dissolve in water, you know. It must be inured to it – to all sorts of things.' He peered up at Spindle. 'They claim it survived the blast of a cusser. It shouldn't have at all. Must be hardened to that as well. Through magics and alchemical treatments, perhaps. Yet some forms of it are reputed to be particularly . . . particularly . . .' The old man shot to his feet. 'Queen forgive me!' Spindle yelped as the historian suddenly clutched his wrist. 'The Alchemist!' he yelled. 'We have to go to his tower!'

Spindle peered anxiously around, hissing, 'Quiet.'

'Do you think it will be safe?' Duiker demanded, low and urgent.

'I don't know. He's kinda busy elsewhere, ain't he.'

'We'll have to chance it. Now, collect all the pieces you can.' He stared his insistence and gestured to the ground. 'Right now, man!'

Spindle led the way through the darkening streets. The sun was setting. A deep burnished bronze light shone over the city, marred only by the glowing arc of jade already visible in the still bright sky. He carried his cloak under his arm in a bundle wrapped around a great load of the Alabaster chips. The historian followed, walking at a much slower pace, his shirt stuffed with the shards.

He led the man to the small wrought-iron gate into the grounds of the tower of the High Alchemist, Baruk. The place looked completely neglected. Brown dry stalks stood in the various planting beds. Dirt had blown across the paving stones. Spindle noted that it revealed no recent tracks.

'This is his tower?' Duiker said, dubious.

'Yeah.'

'Won't there be wards? Protections? Guardians?'

Spindle directed the historian's attention ahead. 'Look.'

The door stood a little open. 'Ah,' Duiker said, straightening. 'Togg take it. Probably not a thing's left.'

'Well,' Spindle sighed, 'let's see.' He crossed the grounds, climbed the short set of steps and tried to peer in round the door. All he saw was dust, blown leaves and litter. 'Looks like no one's home,' he said over his shoulder. He started pushing open the door then reconsidered; he set down his bundle and reached for his long-knife only to close his hand on empty air. His shoulders fell. *Mother of Hood! How do you like that. Should I raise my Warren? Yeah – an' bring all those fiends down on me in an instant! No thank you.*

Instead, he rubbed his chest. *What say you, Ma? What should I do? Should I go in? What's waitin' in there for your little boy?*

No answer. Nothing.

Fair enough. No new is good news.

He pushed open the door and stepped in to give Duiker room. The historian quickly closed the door behind him. It was dark; the day's fading light barely reached from distant windows. From what Spindle could see from the entrance foyer Duiker's prediction was correct: the place was mess. Looted and wrecked. He set down the bundle. 'Well, maybe there's still—'

A demon jumped out of a doorway, waving its arms and snarling.

Spindle swung the bundle of stones, knocking it flying back up the hall where it lay groaning. He exchanged glances of surprise and disbelief with the historian. 'Smallest demon I've ever seen,' Duiker murmured.

The little pot-bellied fiend climbed unsteadily to its feet. It held its head and weaved from side to side. It felt at its mouth. 'My toof! You broke toof!'

Spindle marched up to it. 'I'll do more than that, you wretched excuse for a guardian. 'Now – take us to your master's workroom.'

The creature stilled, a hand over its jagged teeth. 'Worroom? You wan' worroom?'

'Yes! Workroom! Where he keeps his chemicals and stuff.'

The guardian eyed the bundle. 'Wha in tere?'

'Why in Fener's arse does that matter?'

The little red-skinned fiend touched at its mouth and groaned. 'Prife. Is prife. Show me.'

'I think he means "price",' Duiker said.

'Oh, for . . .' Spindle threw down the bundle and undid it. He held out one of the chips. The little beast snapped it up and eagerly licked and bit, tasting it. It smiled, revealing needle teeth, then popped the chip in and munched happily.

Spindle and Duiker shared another amazed glance.

The fiend flinched, wincing, and hopped in circles, clawed hands clapped to its mouth. 'Arrgh! Toof! Oh, foor toof! Foor me!'

'Well?' Spindle said.

It waved them forward. 'Yef, yef. Fis way. Fome!'

* * *

As soon as the vessel bumped up against the sagging pier Aragan and Captain Dreshen led their uneasy mounts by short reins across the gangway and up the pier. They saddled the horses then set off westward for the foothills of the Moranth mountains. They rode for two days, angling south. Early on the second night Captain Dreshen woke Aragan and nodded towards a large band of riders approaching under the bright jade light of the Scimitar.

The Rhivi band encircled them, peering down expressionless from their mounts.

'Yes?' Aragan challenged, belting on his sword.

One dipped his spear to urge his mount a few steps closer. 'Come with us, Malazan,' was all he would say.

Aragan and Dreshen shared a resigned look and set to readying their mounts. Almost immediately after heading further west they encountered more Rhivi outriders. An ever enlarging band of horsemen gathered around them as the night deepened. They were guided to a fresh encampment where elders, horsewives and shouldermen tended wounded laid out in the bloodstained grass. The sight of so many slashed and crippled tore at Aragan's heart and he had a difficult time finding his voice.

'So, I'm too late,' he said to a nearby old woman. 'I'm your prisoner.'

She rose and came to him. A blood-spattered hand clutched his leg. The horror of what she had seen was still in her gaze and he had to look away. 'No, Malazan,' she said. 'We hope there is still time. See to your people. Even now the Seguleh hunt them.'

'The Seguleh! They did this?'

'No one else is so . . . precise. Few are killed, most are sorely wounded. So they would burden us.'

'I see . . . I am sorry.'

'Save your pity for your own.'

'Yes. You will ride north, then?'

The woman flinched away as if slapped. 'No! We will answer this insult. How little they know us. We are not to be brushed aside.'

'Yet . . . they are Seguleh.'

'Irrelevant. We must be who *we* are. That is what has been thrown down here before us. And we will answer it!'

'I understand. I should ride, then.'

'Yes. Of course.' She raised her blood-wet arms to shout: 'All who would bring the spear to our enemies ride now! Go! Bring blood and terror! Ride them down!'

Answering ululations and shouts grew to an enraged roar that engulfed Aragan. The ambassador rose tall in his saddle, circling an arm in the air. Kicking, he reared his mount even taller and charged off throwing dirt high behind. Rhivi warriors all around, men and women, old and young, ran for their mounts. He, the captain and their escort rode on, knowing that all who wished to follow would soon catch up.

*   *   *

'Takin' their own sweet time about it, ain't they?' Bendan complained.

Sergeant Hektar chuckled and motioned to all the soldiers surrounding them in line, some twenty soldiers deep, across the narrow valley mouth. 'Butcher's back with us,' he laughed. 'Brave as a mouse in his bolthole now, hey?'

'What d'ya mean?'

'I mean you was runnin' just as fast as the rest of us last night!' and he chortled again.

Bendan rolled his neck to crack the bones stiff from his constant watching. 'I just mean they ain't showin' us the proper respect. They're actin' like we don't matter.'

'Like they can take their time,' Corporal Little added.

'They got that right,' Bone muttered darkly.

Bendan laughed at the suggestion. 'C'mon, man. There's near ten thousand of us!'

'And a good four hundred of them.'

'Malazan iron will stop them,' Hektar said loudly and shouts arose from nearby in the ranks affirming that.

'Aye, aye, Sarge,' Bone assented, sighing.

'Here come our playmates now, anyway,' Hektar said, pointing one great paw of a hand.

The lines grew quiet as the Seguleh came jogging up out of the morning mist. Ghostly silent, they spread out to right and left in a line. That line, only a single body deep, held a fraction of the Malazan numbers. Seeing this, Bendan nudged Bone. 'We should encircle them, hey?'

The old saboteur looked astonished. 'Are you an idiot? We want them to run away.'

Bendan studied those slim figures. He'd thought them blowhards good at milking a reputation. Then he heard veterans tell of the Pannion campaign. Then he saw them rout the entire Rhivi army. He now had the sick feeling that he was facing the top dogs and he was the trespasser. They stood immobile; couldn't even be seen to be breathing. They could have been statues but for the steaming plumes leaving their masks. None had even drawn a weapon yet.

'Prepare arms!' the call went up and down the ranks. The scraping of iron on leather and wood hissed preternaturally loud in the cold morning air. Shields rattled as the ranks tightened. Far down the Seguleh line Bendan spotted one whose mask appeared much plainer than the rest. He recalled the rumours that had been flying around the camp. *That's him. Third best among 'em all.* For a moment he fantasized about bringing that one down. What a coup! He'd get some kinda medal for sure. Be famous.

What he'd get is his head cut off.

He noted how many of the warriors seemed to be peering far off into the distance past the Malazan shield wall. Perhaps studying the rising mountain slopes. Or perhaps the sky. What were they damned well lookin' at? The fucking weather?

Even squat Corporal Little shifted uncomfortably, stamping her feet to warm them. 'What're they waiting for?' she muttered under her breath.

The two lines faced one another, each motionless, watchful. The light brightened, burning off the mist. The sun was behind the Seguleh, more or less, but Fist K'ess had chosen high ground and so the Malazans were slightly above them.

None of this might have factored into the thoughts of the Third as he stood unmoving, masked head slightly tilted, his gaze seeming to search the western sky. Finally, as the morning warmed, he brought his hand up in a cutting motion and all four hundred suddenly charged.

Bendan was almost caught off guard. His attention had wandered to fix on the weight of the shield dragging down his arm. Damned fucking pain it was. Whoever made these monstrosities certainly never had to hump them cross-country. Then he flinched with everyone as the Seguleh seemed to erase the distance between them in just a few quick paces. They closed utterly silent without bellow or howl. Only the whispered hiss of swords unsheathing sounded before the first slashes clashed against shields. And the screams. Immediate shrieks of wounded howling. And sergeants bellowing: 'Close up! *Close up!*'

Bendan shuffled over with everyone. The lines shrank towards the short front of the few Seguleh as if it were a maw sucking down all the men before it. Wounded came staggering back, slipping between shields. He glimpsed severed wrists, faces slashed to the bone, hands pressed to throats with blood pulsing between the fingers.

Ye gods! They're chewin' us up!

Still the call rose up on all sides: 'Close up! Tighten ranks!'

Then his turn came. He hunched behind the shield, shortsword blade straight, ready to thrust. To one side Sergeant Hektar grunted as he reached the front line. The ground was soft and wet beneath Bendan's sandals. The noise was nowhere near what it had been in any of his earlier battles. Just clattering shields, hissed breaths and the fierce outraged screams of the wounded. Something slashed his shield yet wasn't hard at all. More like a snake slithering across the surface hunting for a gap. He poked his head up for a look and something flashed across his vision and his helmet flew off over the lines. He ducked, thrusting. Wet warmth soaked his neck and front. *Cut me – the bastard!* And he thrust again, pushing with his shield. *Bastard!* The bright tongue licked around the lip of his shield, grating against the bone of his arm, and he snarled. His neck and side were now cold and numb.

Hands grasped him, pulling him back. *Fuck! No! I'll have that bastard. I swear!*

'Easy lad,' someone soothed, urging him backwards. 'You're a right mess.'

'What?' Bendan glanced to his side. Bright wet blood soaked his armour down to his legs. 'Damn!' He touched the side of his head and barked a yell at the pain. His shield arm hung numb, blood dripping from his fingertips. 'Damn.'

He reached the rear and slumped down in the grass with the other wounded waiting for one of the bonesetters. When the cutter came alongside him she shook her head as if disgusted. 'Sliced half your scalp right off. Ear's gone, too. All I can do is stop the bleeding and wrap you up.'

'Good enough. I want back in there.'

'If there's time.' The young squad healer's gaze skittered aside as she unwound a rag.

A short while later Bendan felt the reverberation of many hooves through the ground and calls went up: 'Rhivi! Cav!'

He staggered upright and did his best to see over the heads of the shifting jostling lines. Rhivi cavalry were sweeping across the fields behind the Seguleh. Some lowered lances, others fired their short-bows. The Seguleh responded by doubling up to face both ways. The slaughter was appalling: horses' necks and stomachs slit, riders spilling right and left.

Bendan spotted Hektar standing to one side and hobbled over. 'Sarge.'

'What's going on?' the big man asked.

'You got a better view than I.'

'No I don't.'

Bendan looked up: blood and gore crossed the man's face in a slit where the bridge of his nose and his eyes once lay. His front was smeared in blood as well where it had been roughly wiped. Bendan quickly turned away, his gorge rising. *Ye gods!*

'Healers stopped the bleeding,' Hektar said. 'Other than this nick I'm fit.'

Bendan swallowed to steady his stomach and to ease a burning that was tightening across his chest. 'Yeah. Me too.' Shouting pulled his attention to the lines. The Seguleh had broken contact and were now chasing the Rhivi from the field. 'They're after the Rhivi,' he told Hektar. He saw a mounted lad hardly no more than a boy charge a Seguleh and the warrior sidestep the lance and swing and the lad topple from his saddle, his leg hanging from a few ligaments as he tumbled limp. Bendan flinched and winced his own pain at the sheer cold exactness of it.

Then a bellowed call came: '*Retreat!* Move out! Up valley!'

'Damn,' Hektar murmured, stricken. 'I can't see nothing.'

Though feeling strangely weak and a touch dizzy Bendan took the man's elbow with his one good hand. 'I'll guide you, Sarge. Don't you worry. C'mon, this way.'

*

The quorl carrying Torvald and the Silver Galene had set down just behind a sharp mountain ridge. What Torvald had glimpsed in the next valley over drove him to immediately scramble the last few feet up the slope to peer down. Watching the slaughter below, he felt as if he would vomit. 'Do *something* – now!' he begged Galene, behind him. 'They're being torn to pieces . . . can't you *see?*'

'Not yet,' she answered. 'They're too close together.'

'Too close together? What do you mean? Well, I'm not waiting.' He lurched forward to descend. An armoured hand yanked him back.

'Do not alert them.'

He pointed back to the ranks of landed quorl and the waiting Black and Red among the rocks. 'Join them! Together you can—'

'Together we would likewise be cut down by the Seguleh,' she interrupted, harsh. 'As we were before. But that was long ago. We are not the people we once were. Now we have much less . . . patience for all this. Ah – look.' She raised her helmed head to the valley. 'Good. Yes.'

*

Aragan kicked his lathered mount right up to the Malazan shield wall then threw himself from the saddle. He slapped the horse to send it off and pushed his way through the troopers. He realized he had no idea who was in charge, and grabbed a trooper, shouting, 'Who's ranking officer here?'

'You, sir,' the man drawled.

'*Other than fucking me!*'

The regular smiled as he wrapped bloodied rags over a hand that was no more than a fingerless stump. 'You must be that Aragan fellow. It's Fist K'ess.' He inclined his head to indicate further along the lines.

Aragan nodded. 'Oponn favour you, man.' He waved Captain Dreshen to follow.

When he found K'ess the Fist stared his disbelief before belatedly saluting. 'Ambassador – you shouldn't be here. I suggest you withdraw—'

'None of us should be here, Fist. What's the butcher's bill?'

The Fist exchanged bleak glances with the aides and staff surrounding him. 'First estimate is fifty per cent incapacitated,' he reported, his voice hoarse. 'Wounded or otherwise.'

Aragan's chest constricted like an iron band. He couldn't draw breath. *Burn deliver them! Fifty per cent! This was . . . unimaginable. What were these Seguleh?* The noise of the nearby fighting faded to a dull roar. He blinked away the darkness that seemed to be clawing at him from the edges of his vision and forced in a deep steadying breath. 'Fist. The Rhivi have bought us time. We no longer have the troops to hold this line. I suggest we withdraw to the head of the valley, among the rocks.'

Fist K'ess saluted. The man's face was a lifeless mask, shocked beyond expression, beyond feeling. 'Yes, Ambassador.'

*

After the scramble higher up the slope, Bendan found himself and Hektar among the front ranks. Not believing his terrible luck, he glanced to the slashed limping and crippled troopers on his left and right and swallowed his outrage. *A gimp and a blind man – best the Empire can muster! What a Twins-cursed joke.* 'Get back, Sarge. You're no use.'

'I can still fill a slot. Hold the line.'

'You can't see a thing!'

The beaming smile returned. 'We're all just hidin' behind our shields anyways, ain't we?'

Bendan squinted down the valley to where the Seguleh had assembled. What in the name of the Queen of Mysteries were they waiting for?

'Still not comin'?' Hektar asked.

'Yeah. They're just . . . standin' there. Like they was waitin' for us to run away or somethin'.'

Someone came scrambling among the rocks. It was Bone, the old saboteur. 'Hey, Sarge! I . . .' His voice trailed away when Hektar turned to the sound of his voice. '*Damn!* I'm sorry, Sarge.'

'I'm still standing. Seen Little?'

'Yeah . . . up the lines.'

'Good.'

'What're they waitin' for?' Bendan complained yet again.

'They do not pursue,' K'ess muttered where he stood with Aragan at the centre of the Malazan lines.

'No,' Aragan answered, distracted. 'They may be giving us time to have a good think about this. And frankly, the troops deserve that . . . In fact, they deserve better than that . . .'

He stepped out before the lines and turned to face them, raising his arms for their attention. 'Rankers! You know me. Some of you knew me as Fist Aragan, some as Captain Aragan. Abyss – some of you old dogs even knew me as Sergeant Aragan! And what's my point?' He swept an arm behind to the Seguleh, now forming up in column. 'You've all heard the stories about how these Seguleh have never been beaten. How they've slaughtered everyone who've ever faced them. Well, look around . . . *We're still here!* And now – now

487

they're offerin' you a choice! All you have to do is drop your swords to surrender. That's all. But if you do that I can promise you one thing . . . You ain't gonna get another shot at the bastards! So what's it going to be? Hey? What's your answer?'

Silence. Aragan glared right and left, his heart hammering, gulping his breaths. Then at the far end of the line a hulking Dal Hon trooper drew his blade, held it out saluting, and bashed it to his shield twice. Hands went to sword-grips all up and down the lines. Swords hissed, drawing to clash in a great thunderous roar against shields, once, twice, then extending in the formal salute.

There's your Malazan answer. Aragan's vision blurred and he blinked to clear it. To all appearances the man was overcome. Inwardly he unclenched a nightmare of dread. *Thank the gods they didn't tell me to piss off.*

He rejoined Fist K'ess in the lines.

'Still not coming,' K'ess murmured. Aragan squinted down on the gathered Seguleh then up at the mountain slope, sweeping on above to the distant snow-touched peaks, then back again. 'They're waiting . . .' He cursed and slammed a fist to his armoured thigh.

K'ess glanced at him. 'What?'

Aragan raised his hands as if clutching at the air. 'We're bait! Nothing more than Hood-damned bait!'

'Bait? What do you mean?'

'They don't want us, man! They've never wanted us.' He pointed to the mountains. 'It's the Moranth! They're calling out the Moranth!'

K'ess rubbed his chin, nodding. Then he muttered, 'Knew we should've stayed at Dhavran.'

Shouts of alarm sounded and Bendan glanced up. The Seguleh had started up the valley. They came on at a slow jog, double-file. 'Would ya look at that,' Bone murmured from nearby. 'Beautiful. Done for the Rhivi and now comin' to finish us off.'

'Shut up,' Bendan snapped.

'What's that?' Bone answered, grinning. 'Thought you was all for butchery.'

'Not like this.'

'Aw. Not so pleasant when it's you gettin' pummelled, hey?'

'I mean not like this!' He thrust a hand behind them. 'What're we doin' here? There's nothing here but rocks. What's the point?'

'Point is we stood up,' Hektar answered. Then he tilted his head, listening. 'Swear I heard somethin'.'

Torvald held on for his life as the Silver sent her quorl stooping down the mountain slope, scudding over trees and stone outcroppings with barely an arm's length to spare. They turned and the valley came into his sight ahead. The Seguleh were advancing in column on the Malazans who had formed a new line, a much thinner line, along higher rough ground.

'Open the satchel,' Galene shouted over the wind tearing at them.

Arms wrapped in the leather strapping, his hands free, Tor reached for the heavy-duty leather pack tied to the saddle between them. He undid the metal clasps and opened the mouth of the pack. What he saw nestled within made him jump and the quorl jerked in answer, weaving unsteadily in its flight.

'Careful!' Galene called loudly, her voice pitched rather higher.

His gaze slit, Torvald peered down at the valley swooping up to meet them, the diminutive figures moving there, and he shook his head. 'No. I won't do it,' he shouted.

Galene turned awkwardly in the saddle to glance back at him. 'Take it out!' she ordered, fierce.

'No! How can you even consider—' and he choked, his heart strangling him, as the quorl curved sideways, turning and diving as if meaning to smash into the valley floor below. Behind them, flight after flight of burdened quorl followed, all flitting downslope in a careering' rushing stream.

'Night-damned arm,' Bendan snarled, trying to raise his shield higher.

'What's that?' Hektar asked.

'Ach – took a slash on the shield arm. Now I can't get it high enough!'

'Use your belt. Strap it and tie it off.'

Bendan grunted. 'Right. But then . . . what am I gonna do after?'

The big Dal Hon turned in his direction as if staring though his eyes were gone. Bendan ducked his head. 'Ah. Right.' Then he jerked, surprised. 'Would ya look at that!' He rose from his crouch pointing skyward where curve after curve of Moranth quorls came arching down the valley. They appeared to be swooping in on the closing Seguleh.

Bone straightened, shading his gaze. 'Oh, no . . .' he whispered.

'What is it?' Hektar asked, peering wildly about, his sword ready.

'Moranth flyin' in on their monster mounts,' Bendan told him. 'Gonna land and rush the Seguleh!' He threw up his one good arm, shouting: 'Yah!'

'No they aren't,' Bone said, his voice shaky. 'Burn forgive us . . . The poor bastards . . .'

Bendan eyed him, frowning. 'What's that?'

The grizzled saboteur was hugging himself, backing away among the tall boulders. 'Slaughter . . . Hood-damned slaughter!'

'What's the matter, man?'

The saboteur pointed to him. 'Take cover,' he ordered. 'All o' you take cover.' He ran off up the lines, shouting as he went: '*Get cover now, damn you all!*'

Yet the lines were stirring, readying shields, regripping weapons. For the Seguleh were close now.

*

Galene reached behind herself one-handed to pull the fat oblong from its pack. Ducking from the driving wind, Tor grasped it in both hands, hugging it. 'No!' he shouted. 'It's murder!'

'Let go, fool! The quorl weaved drunkenly. Treetops slashed by beneath, almost striking Tor's boots. The impossible storm of wind threatened to sweep him from the saddle. 'This is war,' she grated. 'Our survival!'

'But they stand no chance!'

She yanked the cusser free. 'Then they should not have taken up the sword.'

The quorl dived even lower now. Tor rose off his seat in the descent. Just ahead the Seguleh column was spreading out. They now appeared so close, and he was rushing in upon them at such a ferocious speed, it seemed to him that they would collide. Before him the valley head rose rocky and steep, thin streams darkening the stone wall here and there. At its foot the Malazan line stood firm in their black surcoats, shields overlapping. Tor spared one quick glance back: line after line of quorl followed, their Silver drivers hunched forward as if racing, Red and Black passengers behind cradling the fat munitions in their arms.

Galene raised the cusser in both hands. The slashing wind snapped her flying jesses and straps about her armoured form.

*

Sword in hand, Aragan turned from the panting veteran saboteur to stare down into the valley. He took in the jogging Seguleh. Then, above, the swooping Moranth. And he felt as if he would faint. *Oh, Hood, no . . . So close . . .* He staggered forward, threw his arms out, bellowing: 'Take cover now! *Cover!'*

Bendan felt himself bending backwards further and further as the Moranth quorl seemed to be coming straight for him personally. He saw riders throwing and dark objects tumbling through the air as the quorl tore overhead, so low it seemed he could stretch up and touch their delicate thrumming wingtips. He yanked Hektar down among the rearing piled talus – the only man still standing – and bellowed in his ear over the roaring: '*Shield!*'

An enormous invisible wall struck Bendan, smashing him down into the rocks. His shield bashed him in the face, stunning him. Stones and dirt and thick choking clouds of dust came billowing over him and he coughed, spitting, and shaking his ringing pummelled head. Multiple blasts punished him, driving him down into the surrounding broken rocks, punching the breath from him.

He didn't know if he lost consciousness, but at one point he realized that it seemed to be over. He'd been waiting, tensed, curled into a ball beneath his shield for yet another concussion that never came. He dared to raise his head. Dirt and gravel tumbled from his back. He shook it from his hair and staggered up. All was obscured in hanging drifting smoke and swirling dust. He could hear nothing over the punishing ringing in his ears. He spat again, blinking, holding his chest where his ribs ached from the concussive waves that had battered him.

A huge shape shambled upright nearby, dirt sifting from him: Hektar, arms out, blindly searching about the rocks. Bendan clasped his arm. 'I'm here,' he croaked.

The Dal Hon wiped his face where a wetness had caked dirt to his mangled flesh. 'Poor bastards,' he was saying. 'Poor fucking bastards.'

It occurred to Bendan that the man was crying.

Torvald had pressed himself to Galene's back, one arm around her, the other clasping one of the saddle grips. He squeezed his eyes closed to miss the dizzying near vertical climb scudding over the naked rock face of the valley head. He felt the pressure wave of the multiple eruptions behind him. It was like a hand pressing him into the Moranth Silver and rushing the quorl along like a great tidal push.

Cold wetness chilled his cheeks in the slashing wind and he knew that he was weeping. Galene shifted in the saddle and adjusted the jesses and the quorl tilted, arching backwards. It seemed that they were turning round.

While the smoke and dust swirled and hung in curtains over the blasted slope Bendan patted Hektar's arm. 'It's all right, man. They woulda done for us.'

'Ain't right,' the sergeant was saying over and over. 'What was done here. Ain't right. It's a fucking tragedy is what it is.'

Horrified shouts sounded from the lines and Bendan turned, squinting into the clouds of settling dust. He almost fell then, his knees weakening, a hand going to his throat. 'Oh no . . . Hood no . . . Don't do this . . .'

'What is it?' Hektar demanded, peering blindly about.

They came out of the hanging smoke and dust. Some limped, some staggered. Others stayed upright only by virtue of their swords dragging along over the rocks. Still they came onward, advancing.

All around, troopers retreated, backing up the rising slope, edging past boulders. 'Stop!' Bendan shouted to one tattered figure making for him. 'Please – stop!'

It was a woman, one arm shattered, bone glistening white through the flesh. Her mask was broken, half gone, that side of her face a blackened red ruin. Still she raised her sword, pointing.

Bendan backed away, a hand on Hektar's arm.

'Where is he?' the Dal Hon whispered.

'She's on your left.'

The Seguleh came on. A trooper scrambled down to her, hunched, sword in one hand, reaching out with the other. 'Let's put it down, lass,' he urged, gently. 'Drop your sword. It's all over now.'

Lunging, she slashed one-handed and he fell, eviscerated in a great gout of splashing innards. She straightened again, weaving slightly, blade pointing straight at Bendan.

'Tell me when she's close,' Hektar ground out.

Two more regulars charged her, swinging. Both were weeping as they attacked. She sidestepped, parrying, her sword sliding easily over the first to slash his throat then quickly blocking the other, twisting in a blur round and under his shield, taking the man's leg off at the knee. He fell shrieking.

It seemed to Bendan that the woman would have fallen at that moment but for leaning her weight on a stab into the crippled man's chest. She recovered then, her mouth writhing in agony beneath its caked dirt and blood. The sword snapped up again, the point inhumanly steady.

He let go Hektar's arm. 'Ready now,' he whispered beneath his breath, crouching, shortsword raised.

Two quick paces from the woman closed the gap. Bendan hunched even further, eyes barely peeping over his shield. Her blade slashed across the top and he flinched. Warmth ran down his nose. Behind his shield Hektar cocked his head as if listening; then he suddenly launched himself forward with a roar, throwing his arms out.

The woman slashed and a forearm flew but the man's enormous weight bulled her over and they fell together. Her slim blade somehow licked up between them even as they crashed among the rocks and Bendan jumped after them. He stabbed at the woman, piercing her hip, his blade grating down the pelvis bone. Lancing burning pain erupted in his leg and he glanced down to see the woman's blade twist free from high in his thigh. Then more troopers crowded him, all thrusting, crying, cursing, weeping. He slumped down against a rock, his leg completely numb. He sat in a cold shaky sweat of pain, shock and panic.

One of the troopers turned Hektar over to reveal the man's chest slashed open. Pink foam blew at his mouth as he laboured to breathe. Bendan slid down to cradle the man's head on his lap. Hektar's wide smile returned but the teeth were bright red with blood now. 'Got one,' the big man smiled.

'Yeah. You got one.'

'All . . . done . . . now.'

'Yeah, Sarge. All done now.'

Bendan sat for a long time holding the dead man. Squad cutters came and tied off his cuts and stopped the bleeding. When they gently pulled at the corpse he batted them away. Having seen it before the healers moved off without objecting. The hot sun beat down and still Bendan rocked him. Carrion birds gathered, circling over the blasted field of kicked-up dirt and scattered torn bodies. A shadow occluded the sun over Bendan and he looked up, squinting. It was Corporal Little.

She crouched on her haunches at his side, rested a hand on Hektar, then looked to him.

'Don't you say it,' he croaked. 'Don't you fucking say anything.'

She looked away, blinking back tears. 'No,' she managed, her voice barely audible. 'I guess not.'

*

'Sir?' Fist K'ess said, clearing his throat. Ambassador Aragan did not turn away from where he had stood since the attack, his gaze steady on the shattered field. K'ess himself was not insensate to the horror: the drifting smoke, the broken bodies lying in droves around craters blasted into the loose talus of the slope. He almost turned away, imagining that firestorm of blasts and the fragmented rock chips lancing like shrapnel through unprotected flesh. What disturbed him the most, however, was the silence. How eerie it was; nothing like any of the many fields of battle he'd known. No cries or moans of wounded echoed over the slopes. No calls for water. No outbursts or hopeless cursing.

Indeed, all the murmured sounds of stricken awe, all the curses, the moans and quiet weeping sounded now around him among the Malazan troops. And he wondered; what was worse? To have died in that ill-fated charge, or to have to live now having witnessed it?

It took a strong effort of will to tear his gaze from that appalling field of slaughter and he glanced back to Captain Fal-ej, the woman's arm and chest bloodied and wrapped in stiff drying cloth. She signed to him to speak again. 'Sir,' he repeated, a touch louder. 'The Moranth have landed. A contingent awaits.'

The ambassador appeared to gather himself. He turned, blinking and wiping at his eyes. He cleared his throat against the back of his hand. 'Yes. The Moranth,' he said, his voice shaking with emotion. 'Thank you, Fist. Let's go and see what they want, shall we?'

As they clambered down the rocks K'ess was surprised to see a man alongside a Moranth Silver and a battered Red. What was more, the ambassador and the Red actually embraced.

'Fist K'ess, Captain Fal-ej,' said Aragan, 'may I introduce Torn, our attaché.'

Torn gestured to the Silver. 'Galene, an Elect. What you might call a priestess. And this is Torvald, Nom of Nom, member of the Darujhistan Council.'

K'ess and Fal-ej bowed. 'Councillor, an honour.'

494

The Darujhistan aristocrat grimaced. He looked shaky and sickly pale. 'Well, it would seem the Council has been suspended.'

'None the less,' Aragan murmured. He gestured aside to another officer, calling, 'Captain Dreshen!'

The young officer jogged up, bowing. Aragan held out a hand and the man dug in his shoulder bag to pull out an object about the size of a mace, wrapped in black silk. He handed it to Aragan who held it in both hands, studying it, lips pursed in thought. He looked up. 'Attaché Torn, Councillor Nom. I believe we need to negotiate.' He gestured towards the woods. The Moranth Red bowed.

'Yes, Ambassador.' He turned to Torvald. 'Councillor . . .'

The three walked off into the forest. Fist K'ess faced the Silver, Galene. 'What of the prisoners?'

The Moranth female tilted her bright helm. 'Prisoners?'

'Some of the Seguleh survived. Badly wounded, but alive. Some few threw down their swords.'

'Surprising, that.'

K'ess rubbed an arm as if cold. 'Well – it might just have been the shock.'

'Perhaps. What of it?'

'Well . . . we could hold them until such time as they can be re-patriated.'

'I doubt they will be, Fist. But, yes, if you wish. We have no interest in them.'

'Very good.' He bowed. *Elect, Torn named her – one of those who guide their people?*

When the Silver had gone K'ess introduced the two captains, then eyed the woods. *Negotiate? Aragan, you've got balls.*

Captain Fal-ej cleared her throat. 'Fist. Forgive me . . . but we're in no position to negotiate anything.'

'Yes, Captain.'

'Then . . . ?'

K'ess raised his chin to the blasted field of craters and thrown dirt. 'Look . . .'

Malazan rankers were silently spreading out among the fallen torn bodies, collecting around the mangled corpses. Out came cloaks and blankets and other odds and ends to wrap the bodies. Then saboteur shovels and picks, and individual shallow graves were hacked out of the thin rocky soil. Some even took advantage of the craters the munitions had blasted to site their pits.

Then one by one, respectful hands clenching the tied-off cloth at head and feet and sides, the bodies were laid in their graves. Only the noise of shovels clattering from stones sounded from the valley. Each pit was covered and the troopers stood still.

K'ess wondered at their thoughts. *Thank the gods that ain't me? Damn you to Hood's lost Abyss?* Or what he himself felt as a knife point in his heart: *No one should die like that. If this is war then I want no more to do with it.*

To one side the captured Seguleh, a bare handful out of the four hundred, sat or stood, unarmed, still masked, watching while their dead were buried. K'ess could not even imagine what was going through their minds.

Clearing his throat, he turned to the officers. 'Captain Fal-ej . . . I believe what Aragan is hoping to do is stop the Moranth from doing to Darujhistan what they just did here in this valley. Reducing the entire city to smoking rubble.'

'By the Seven,' Fal-ej murmured, falling back on her old faith. 'That would be unforgivable. We cannot allow that.'

K'ess let out a long pained breath. 'It looks as though we no longer have much say in the matter.'

'But Fist . . . over a half-million live there.'

'Yes, Captain . . . Yes.'

BOOK III
Throne

CHAPTER XVIII

The contempt of the cultured elite of Darujhistan for the manners and customs of the Seguleh of the far south is well known. One Council member famously remarked that what these Seguleh fail to understand is that words are the most powerful weapons of all.

A Seguleh informed this argument responded: 'Then when he is silent he is useless.'

Histories of Genabackis
Sulerem of Mengal

LIKE SMALL BLESSINGS MOMENTS OF CALM OCCASIONALLY DESCENDED unbidden into the punishing windstorm of Ebbin's thoughts. During these respites he was able, at least briefly, to gather his scattered identity and reconstitute his thoughts.

Sometimes he would find himself in a recurring dream of the gold-masked figure standing at the edge of Majesty Hill overlooking Darujhistan. Either the ancient terror allowed him to join him there in reviewing these memories, or he was simply too insignificant to matter. Each time Ebbin was unwilling to creep up to the overlook, for he knew what would confront him there: the city in flames, screams, mass murder, carnage. The fall of a civilization.

After many of these dreams, or waking nightmares – having wandered here, or been drawn, or allowed to discover him here – Ebbin finally dared speak: 'Why do you always come here?'

'Lessons learned,' the masked and cloaked figure answered.

'You seek to avoid this.'

'I seek to avoid a paradox. Escape the inescapable. I wish to complete the circle without suffering its fate.'

'Each time it has ended this way.'

'So far.'

'So many would-be tyrants,' Ebbin breathed, saddened.

The graven gold face turned his way. 'Still you do not fully understand.'

Emboldened, Ebbin ventured: 'What is there to understand? You failed once, you shall fail again.'

'Once? No, scholar. Evidently the truth is even more difficult for you to swallow than that. In truth, I have failed countless times.'

'What?'

The taunting secretive curve carved on the lips of the mask seemed to be verging on a full smile. 'Each time it has been me, scholar. In truth, there has been but one Tyrant.'

The raging winds of Ebbin's mind crept closer. Walls of impenetrable black closing in. 'But . . . that cannot be. What of Raest? What of him?'

'Ah, yes. Raest. Too crude in his methods. I have refined and perfected his tools. Lessons learned, scholar.'

Ebbin clenched his skull as if to hold it from flying apart. 'Why tell me this?'

'Give up, scholar. Yield. There can be but one outcome.'

'No! Never. I . . . never.' And he fled. Hands pressed to his skull, he ran from the ledge and laughter chased him. The laughter melded with the howling of the winds that came sweeping in to toss him spinning and flying into countless shattered fragments.

* * *

Jan could not get used to being confronted wherever he turned by hundred of replicas in miniature of the Legate's gold mask. The ladies of the court held theirs on long gold stems that they raised to their faces. The men's rested on the bridges of their noses, held there by fine thread that ran behind their heads.

Part of Jan wished to slap them all off. Just as he still could not help twitching upon meeting so many directly challenging, even haughty, stares from armed men.

These are no longer your people, his inner voice said to him. *These are no longer your ways.*

Across the court Palla, the Sixth, signed to him: *Any word?*

None.

It has been long.

The mountains are vast.

The Moranth have never been shy.

True. A tentative throat-clearing at his side. Jan turned knowing who to expect: the Mouthpiece. 'Yes?'

'A word, Second.'

They crossed to the edge of the court where a pillared colonnade stretched all along one wall. It was the favoured locale for much whispering. 'Yes?'

'Send a runner to your people in the south. Have them all relocate here to the city.'

Jan snapped his gaze to the masked figure on his throne, hands resting lightly atop a white stone armrest to either side. 'All?'

'Yes. All. It seems strange notions and distortions have crept into your teachings over the years. It would be best if I took over all future training.'

'You,' Jan said, his gaze fixed on the broad oval mask.

'Yes.'

Jan nearly fainted in the animal urge to draw and slice. *No! The burden is yours! Endure!* He allowed himself a shuddering intake of breath while his eyes slitted almost closed. 'Very well,' he grated through clenched jaws. 'It shall be as you order.'

'Of course.' The Mouthpiece, Jan noted, appeared more sweaty and pallid than ever before.

He turned his back, signing to Palla: *We must talk.*

At a side entrance he came to the two private guards. Seeing him they jumped to attention, saluting. 'Don't you worry there, sir,' one said, 'we'll keep a watch out. Ain't that so, Scorch?' He elbowed his companion.

'Yessir,' the other winced, blinking his bloodshot eyes.

Jan swept past without answer. Odd that the Legate should want these two here. But, as he had read, every court has its fools.

He waited in his quarters for Palla to find a moment to excuse herself. Eventually the door quickly opened and was just as swiftly shut. *What now?* she signed.

'He would have us all here. All our people,' he whispered.

'That cannot be allowed,' she answered, her mask averted.

'No. It cannot. We do not belong here.' Something shook him then. Something arising from the base of his spine and low in his stomach. He shuddered as it clenched his throat and he fought it with hands clamped to his sides. *Was this weakness? Is this the gathering wail of despair?* 'I am so sorry.' The words seemed to escape of their own accord. 'This is all my doing.'

She drew close, almost raising her mask to gaze up at him. 'No! You did as any Second would have. The call came and you answered. There is no error in that. It is this place,' she went on, fierce. 'Here. Darujhistan. It is no longer worthy of us.'

Jan groaned. *Oh, the loftiness of pride! No longer worthy of us? Or are we simply . . . obsolete?*

'What should we do?'

'When the others return I will reinstitute the Exile.'

'Gall will challenge.'

'That is his right.'

'We must not allow that. He must be stopped before he can—'

'*Palla!* Listen to yourself. And we worry about perversion of our ways?'

She touched his arm, lightly, as if frightened that he would brush her hand aside. 'But what if he . . .'

'What if he wins?'

She whispered a faint '*Yes*'.

He crooked his lips. 'Is your estimation of my abilities so low?'

She ducked, genuinely hurt, and he winced inwardly. 'I see how all this weighs upon you,' she breathed.

He touched her arm. 'I only jest. If he should best me then he deserves the victory.'

Her grip tightened. 'Then do not force me to wade through the Fourth and Third to reach him.'

'I will go peacefully knowing you would avenge me, Palla.'

'You know,' she said, after a brief silence, 'the others will note our absence, and . . .'

'. . . there will be much wagging of tongues in the dormitory.' He allowed his fingertips to trace a line down her taut arm. 'Another reason to hope for better times, Palla.'

She returned the gesture, sending a shiver through his flesh. 'Let us hope, then.'

'Yes.' He opened the door. 'In the meantime . . .'

Stepping out to the hall she murmured low, 'We delay.'

*   *   *

Antsy came to, coughing up a great gout of water followed all too swiftly by the contents of his stomach. On his side, his face pressed

502

into dirt, he groaned, his stomach still cramping. A great shout of surprise sounded then and hands grasped at him.

'You're alive!' Orchid shouted.

'We thought you dead,' Corien said, amazed.

He merely groaned again, dry-heaving. 'What in the Abyss happened?' he managed, spitting.

'You ought to ask these gentlemen,' Corien said.

Antsy peered up. It was still as dark as the inside of a barrel, but his mage-vision allowed him to see that they occupied what appeared to be a meadow surrounded by a thick forest, its boughs windswept. Starry night arched above, empty of any greenish glow.

With him were Orchid and Corien, yes, but also the three mercenaries, the Heels, and about ten or so Malazan marines including Sergeant Girth. But what captured his attention were the six Seguleh standing about him, water dripping from their leathers.

'Where's the Hood-damned menagerie of mages?'

'All fled as soon as they could,' said Orchid.

'Even Malakai?'

Corien nodded. 'Even him.'

'Well . . . how do you like that. Not even a by your leave.' He eyed the Seguleh. 'Who's the spokesman here?'

'I,' said one.

'Right.' He gestured for Corien to help him up. 'So, what happened?'

'We returned to the Throne as soon as we were able. You were in our way so we merely pushed you through with us.'

'Well . . . my thanks.'

'We did not intend to save your life – we thought you dead.'

Antsy waved a hand. 'I said thanks!' He held his head, grimacing. 'Leave it at that. Gods.'

He faced Orchid. 'So. Where are we?'

'Isn't that obvious?' She turned a full circle, arms raised to the night sky. 'Kurald Galain. Elder Night.'

'We shouldn't be here. We have to go. Right away.'

'And go where?' Girth demanded, pushing forward blindly. Antsy realized that none of the others could see a thing. 'Just where would you suggest? And how? And who's gonna send us? All the mages have scarpered. We're no better off now than where we were.'

Antsy pointed. 'We have her.'

The Malazan sergeant peered about. 'Who?'

'Orchid – the girl!' Antsy barked then held his head again, groaning.

Girth pulled at his beard. 'Fine. So – question still stands. What's the marching orders?'

'Well . . . I don't know quite yet,' Antsy admitted. He rubbed his neck, feeling where the dagger had entered, and found only slit cloth and throbbing pain.

'I would suggest Darujhistan,' said a new voice, and Orchid gasped.

'Morn! You escaped.' She ran to him.

The hooded figure of dark wavered, translucent. 'I am barely here at all, Orchid,' he said, his voice hollow. 'In truth I am very committed elsewhere.'

'You're fading!'

'I'm sorry, child. This sending has done its duty. Now it must disperse. All I can say is that these men ought to go to Darujhistan. You have given me much hope, child. It was a pleasure, this time I spent with you. I found it . . . renewing.'

'Don't go!'

'I must. I cannot stay. It is too . . . painful. May Night bless you. Farewell.'

The hooded figure faded away like smoke.

'Well – that was no damned help,' Girth complained after a moment of silence. 'And I still can't see a Togg-farting thing!'

Antsy went to Orchid's side, whispered, 'We should go, lass. These Warrens are dangerous.'

'I believe it may be too late,' Corien said, pointing to the woods.

Some sort of party or procession was approaching through the trees. They carried torches on tall poles, but to Antsy's eyes the torches burned with black flames that gave off black light that seemed to aid his mage-vision. The strange inversion made him dizzy.

The Malazan marines were linking up, he noticed, weapons out, sweeping the blades through what to them must be utter dark. 'Form circle!' Antsy barked, and set to helping organize them. When he reached for Cull Heel the man brushed his hand aside, making him jump. 'You can see?'

'Aye,' the man ground out, his narrowed eyes on the approaching party. 'We can see a little – someone's coming.'

Antsy had no time to wonder about that at the moment. 'Form up with the soldiers. Help them out.'

'Aye.'

Aside, the Seguleh formed their own small circle round one of their number as if to protect him. His mask was mostly pale; only a handful of lines marred it. Three crossed the forehead and three each cheek. One crossed the bride of the nose. While Antsy studied him the man's hand strayed to a cloth-wrapped package thrust into his waist sash and rested there for a time as if making sure of it.

Antsy and Corien shifted to stand before Orchid at the centre of the circled marines and Heel mercenaries.

'That's close enough,' Antsy shouted. The party halted. It consisted of a double file of female Tiste Andii. From their flowing dress and rich jewellery he thought them priestesses of some sort. One at the forefront advanced slightly closer. She held high a torch of the liquid pitch light.

'There is no need for such suspicion,' she called in accented Talian . . . herself understood through magery.

'What do you want?' Antsy called.

She gestured towards him. 'Our daughter.'

A gasped breath sounded from Orchid. 'I think that's up to her,' Antsy said.

'Indeed. Then let it be so.' The Andii woman's black on black eyes swept past him. 'Child,' she called, 'we have been bereft, in mourning. For we have lost a Son of Darkness. Yet behold. We rejoice! For just as precious and rare are the Daughters of Tiam.'

Orchid's weight fell on Antsy, and he grunted. The girl was much more solid than she looked. He clasped her arm. 'What's this, lass? What's she goin' on about?'

She steadied herself, blinking rapidly, a hand on Antsy's shoulder. 'If what she says is true—'

'It is,' the Andii woman asserted.

'—then I am part Andii, yes. But also part – *Eleint*.'

Antsy jerked away a step. 'Eleint!' But that's . . .'

'Yes,' the Andii woman shouted. 'That is so. Child, whoever hid you and protected you all these years has taught you also, I see. Very good. Now join us. It is time to continue your education.'

'Orchid,' Corien murmured, 'you don't have to go with these witches . . .'

'I *need* to know,' she answered just as low, fierce. 'I want to.'

Antsy nodded. ''Tis true – we can't stop you. But what of us?'

She shot him an insulted look. 'I'm not an *utter* fool, Bridgeburner.' She raised her chin to the Andii woman. 'I have terms!'

They barely made it to shore before the hide boat became too heavy with water to be manoeuvrable. Crouched, Yusek hugged her knees, warming herself, watching the flooded thing slowly drift away. It was no more than an oval rim now, like a squeezed ring laid on the smooth dark surface of the river. She was soaked and shivering but had to admit that she missed the damned thing. *Beat walkin', that was for sure.*

The Seventh merely shouldered his meagre roll of gear, waterskin and such, and set off. Sall and Lo followed. Yusek bent her head back to send an entreating look to the sky and all the gods, but bit back any complaint knowing it would be entirely useless. *Well,* she suddenly realized, *seem to have finally understood* that *lesson at least.*

She pulled up her own roll and shoulder bag of wet gear and followed. It was many hours before dawn. She was exhausted. It had been almost impossible to sleep in the damned boat what with the constant bailing and the sloshing water. Now they were expected to march on? What was the rush? It's not like the city was goin' anywhere.

She pushed herself to reach Sall, and announced: 'I'm beat! I ain't going another step. We need to sleep.'

Sall hesitated, glanced ahead to the others. 'They will not stop.'

Yusek sank to her knees. 'Well – what's the use of arriving on your last legs? Too tired to be of any use? Aw, fuck it,' and she glared at the river making its sluggish way north, gleaming beneath bands of clouds.

Sall jogged ahead.

Some time later the three returned. They sat without a word. A few scraps of food were handed out and the waterskins made the rounds. Someone must have kept watch but Yusek didn't know who because she immediately fell asleep.

Late in the morning they set off again, following the Maiten's east shore. Here they climbed small hills and narrow gullies the sides of which seemed too steep to be natural. It occurred to Yusek that they were crossing the remains of large channels that might have once carried water from the river. The Maiten was far too low now even to reach these features, but at some time in the past it must have run much higher. And these channels, then, would have directed part of the flow eastward. To farms, no doubt. Yet now the Dwelling Plain was a dusty wasteland of dry hills and wind-scoured hardpan. Frankly that fitted quite well with her personal experience of what happened anywhere after people arrived. She'd seen it again and again as a refugee fleeing the Pannions. Their bands would come staggering into towns and settlements, and fighting would immediately break out over water and food. Homes were invaded, herds decimated, water sources bled dry. Then the whole stream would move on again, a swarm of locusts, consuming and destroying all it met. And the only way to have a hope of snatching anything, a handful of barley, or a crust of hard bread, was to be among the first to arrive. Thus the mad dash westward; the desperate effort to beat the mob; to be among the first to kick down the doors.

It had been a harrowing time. And it had left its mark upon her wiry lean limbs, her restless gaze and her constant, almost feverish, nerves. And what of the scars one couldn't see? The marks upon psyche and spirit? Well, she didn't even want to think about that.

Now Sall, he interested her. He wasn't like anyone she'd ever met on her march west, nor among Orbern's crew. All those boys forced too early to become men had ruled through muscle and viciousness, the fist and the club. But not Sall, nor his father Lo, or this fellow, the Seventh.

Their way was strange, and, she could admit, harsh. But it had clear rules, and that attracted her. She knew she wanted to be part of it.

Late in the day, from one of the higher hillsides, they saw the first hints that they were getting closer. Smoke stained the north-east sky and ahead more and more huts and rotten piers crowded the riverbanks.

They were close now. Close to the greatest city of the continent. Yusek had to hug herself to contain her yip of glee.

*   *   *

The murmurings of the arrival preceded them: doors slamming, sandalled feet stamping the stone floor; gasps and exclamations. Then the doors to the Great Hall swung open to admit a troop of Seguleh, dirty and sweat-stained, jogging up the centre.

Courtiers and aristocrats hastily flinched to the sides, making way. From near the white throne Jan watched their advance with stunned incomprehension. *What was this? Why were they here?*

Leading the troop came Gall. Soot stained his mask and black dried blood caked his side where a wound still gaped wet and open. The Third bowed to Jan.

'Speak,' Jan managed, almost breathless with wonder.

Gall straightened, weaving slightly. His chest worked soundlessly. 'The Moranth,' he grated. 'They . . . used their alchemical weapons upon us. Only we few . . . escaped the slaughter.'

Still uncomprehending, Jan glared at the man. 'That is nothing new. They have always had their strange chemistries. The smoking and bursting globes that they throw.'

The Third shook his head as if unable to find the words. 'This is different, Second. Things have changed during our absence.'

And what an understatement, Gall. Yes. It seems that just as we have changed, so too have the Moranth. It is to be expected.

The Third bowed again. 'I accept full responsibility, Second. I await your judgement.'

Jan signed for him to rise. 'No, Third. All responsibility is mine and mine alone. Our rush to engage was foolish. And obviously costly beyond measure. We must re-evaluate our strategy.'

'I concur,' put in a new voice and Jan glanced down to see the Mouthpiece at his side. 'When the rest of your people arrive, Second, then a new army will be sent to punish the Moranth. In the meantime control over the city must be enforced. You Seguleh must keep the population in order.'

Jan struggled to keep his tone neutral as he said: 'And how do you propose we do so?'

'Why,' the sickly pale man answered as he daubed a cloth to his sweaty forehead, 'are you not my sword and anvil?'

Jan turned his mask to the immobile Legate upon his white stone seat. 'I suggest, Legate, that we may not have the time.'

'Oh?'

'Yes. The Moranth have dealt us a severe blow. I would be surprised if they did not strike now while we are weakened.'

'Do not fear, Second. We are impregnable here within the protection of the Circle.'

Fear? This creature thinks I fear? Great Ancestors! The gulf between our thinking. Our mutual miscomprehension . . . beyond belief. If I fear at all, it is for the future of my people.

Yet Jan bowed, saying, 'Of that I have no doubt, Legate.'

*

A knock brought Tiserra to her door. She was reluctant to open it, expecting some damned debt collector – not that she couldn't handle such a one, but it was a distraction from her work. Finally, the persistence of the knocking, and its gentleness, persuaded her to answer.

She saw there the tall slim man that Bellam, one of her nephews on Torvald's side, had become. She opened the door fully and he bowed.

'Auntie.'

'Bellam – a pleasure. You do not come by often enough.'

'I am sorry, Auntie. I understand that the Legate has sent Torvald from the city. Some sort of political mission. So you are alone . . .'

'Yes?'

'Well, Seguleh have returned to the city from the west. Just a bare ragged handful. People think there will be trouble. We are heading out to a residence in the Gadrobi hills. Perhaps you would care to join us?'

Touched, she squeezed his arm. 'Why, thank you for the offer, nephew. But no. I will remain. Torvald will be returning and I will have to be here for him. And do not worry, I will be safe. Now go. Look after your mother and father, yes?'

Reluctant, a touch confused, the lad hesitated. 'How do you know . . .'

'Never you mind that, lad. Now go.'

He was still uncertain, but he bowed, deferring to her in any case. Sometimes, she knew, a reputation for fierceness made things so much easier.

She did not shut the door but threw on a shawl instead. *So, it shall be this night. I must warn the Greyfaces – no gas! Shut the pipes! Squeeze their throats shut just as tight if I must!*

* * *

The forest they walked gave way to a canyon. A narrow strip of starry night sky shone above. Tayschrenn led, moving confidently. Kiska kept a wary eye out. The canyon became a cave then a series of natural stone tunnels. Kiska finally ventured to ask: 'Where are we going?'

But the mage merely raised a hand for patience. Kiska subsided, grumbling.

Eventually they emerged from a cave mouth and Kiska found herself high on the steep slope of some sort of mountain. Not too far away the sea spread to the horizons, black and glimmering like the sky. The jade banner of the Visitor glared high above. They were on an island.

'Where are we?'

'Kartool.'

'Kartool!' Kiska suppressed a start of revulsion. 'Why here of all places?'

A fond, almost amused, was turned to her. 'As I said, a long delayed reunion. Come.' Kiska wasn't sure if she approved of this peculiar sense of humour the High Mage seemed to have acquired.

He led the way along the narrow stone ledge. It curved round the wall of the mountain. For an instant Kiska had a flashback to a similar path on the cliffs of Malaz Isle, no great distance from her now. *Agayla . . . are you there? Is this the Queen's intent? Is this the right path? Gods, if I only knew.*

The path stepped up on to a wide flat walkway that ran straight into the side of the mountain, to a worked cave entrance whose stone pillars were carved with the sigils of D'rek, the Worm of the World's Autumn. After a moment's stunned silence, Kiska cleared her throat. 'Ah, Tayschrenn – this is a temple to D'rek . . .'

'Indeed it is. I am glad to see your education encompasses the cult's iconography.'

Ha! 'D'rek tried to capture you!'

'Many times, yes. Capture or kill. But that is the past. A new cross-roads has been reached. It is time for a chat. Mustn't hold grudges.'

They walked the processional way, where braziers lit the tunnel between thick pillars carved from the stone of the walls. No one was about. 'Where is everyone?' Kiska breathed, her voice low.

'D'rek is still without priests, Kiska. Even here and at the temple below. This is the Holy of Holies. The most sacred shrine. Only priests and priestesses were ever allowed entrance here.'

'And these braziers?'

'We've been invited, Kiska. Here we are.'

The processional way ended at a great cavern, roughly circular. Its roof went up and up until Kiska, squinting, realized there was no roof. They stood at the base of a central vent that penetrated the mountain from its very top. A dormant volcano.

At the centre of the cavern was a pit, a black jagged hole that led down into smoke and utter night. Kiska flinched back from its lip; whatever was down there, it smelled vile.

'What now?' she asked, a hand at her nose.

'Now she and I are going to have a talk, and you mustn't interfere. Stay here, yes?'

'Well, all right,' she allowed, doubtful. 'But where are you—' Then she screamed as Tayschrenn stepped up and threw himself into the pit, diving in a long arc to disappear from sight.

Screaming still, she nearly threw herself in after him, but a strong hand grasped her cloak and yanked her away. She fell on her back and found herself looking up at an old woman, bent, hair a thick ropy nest and eyes bright circles of milky white. 'Doan do that,' the old crone snarled at her crossly, shaking a crooked finger.

'Don't do what?' she gasped, completely shocked.

'Doan yell like that to wake the dead. Hurts the ears that does.'

'Sorry.' She leapt to her feet. 'But he jumped! He—'

'Yes, yes.' The old woman waved dismissively. 'That's what the most powerful of them do. Doan worry y'self. He'll be back. Or . . . he'll be dinner for the Worm!' and she chuckled, shuffling off.

Kiska followed. 'Dinner! You mean . . . down there . . . it's down there?'

'Oh aye. Down there. Far enough. Coiling and churning eternal. The Worm of the Earth. A worm of energy it is. Fire and flame, molten rock and boiling metal. Ever restless. And a good thing too! Else we'd all be dead!'

'I'm sorry – I'm not sure what you mean.'

'Never mind. Make y'self useful. See that bucket?'

Kiska peered into the shadows. 'I think so.'

'Well, fill it and follow me!'

Against the wall Kiska found a bucket and woven baskets bursting with coal. She filled the bucket and followed.

'Keep the fires going – that's my job,' the old hag was muttering. 'Can't be neglected! It's the light and heat that keeps us all alive. Yes?' She peered about blindly.

'Ah . . . yes,' Kiska said.

'That's right!' Reaching the wall, the woman walked along tracing her way with one hand. The other hand she held up high, quavering. Nearing a brazier, she patted at the hot metal to test its heat. Kiska winced at the sight. Nodding to herself, satisfied, she moved on. 'There's precious few these days understand that, girl,' she muttered. 'Precious few understand that it's all about service. Serving!'

'Yes,' Kiska answered, understanding now that this was her role.

'No,' the old crone muttered, spitting aside. 'Nowadays it's all about *gathering* – influence and power and whatnot.' She found another brazier, patted its hot iron with her naked hand, waved. 'Low! Fill it!'

'Yes.'

'Well, that's not how it used to be. Not how it should be! Do you understand me?'

'Ah . . . yes.' *I have no idea what you're blathering on about, you miserable hag.*

'Only way to sustain anything, to build anything, is to *give*! You understand me, girl? Give and give of y'self till there's nothing left! Only then can you have something! If you take, you diminish things till there's nothing left. If you give, you provide and things grow! Yes?'

'Yes.'

'There y'go! That's right. Everyone's greedy these days. It'll only diminish the pot till there's nothing left! Then we're all in the dark, yes?'

'Ah . . . right. Yes.'

The old woman leaned back against the wall, breathing wetly. 'There we go. All done.'

'We're done?' Kiska studied the countless other braziers surrounding the chamber.

'Not us! Me. I'm done. You go on and finish.'

Kiska eased out a long low breath between her teeth, but continued. She went all the way round the cavern tossing lumps of coal into any of the braziers that were low, relighting others that had gone out. When she returned the bucket to its place she found the old woman sitting against the wall, her knees drawn up tight, a cloak wrapped around her, asleep, her mouth half open.

Tired, hungry, her nerves still jangling for Tayschrenn, Kiska eased herself down the wall to sit with her own knees drawn up and rested her chin on them. Soon afterwards she fell asleep.

She awoke to a light kick and jerked, blinking. Tayschrenn was peering down at her. He appeared to be in a good mood. He was smiling and seemed unharmed from his descent, but for his mussed hair and soot-stained cloak.

'I'm sorry if I scared you,' he said. 'But I don't think you would reacted well to my telling you what I was about to do.'

'No. I wouldn't have.' She pushed herself up, wincing and easing her back. 'So – we're done here?'

'Yes.'

'You . . . spoke to her?'

The mage eyed her sidelong. 'Sort of. That's not really how we communicated.'

'I see. Well, I had a grand old time doing chores here.'

'Chores?'

'Yes. The old woman who takes care of the place. She showed me the ropes. Gods, does she ever go on.'

Tayschrenn had been on his way to the tunnel. He stopped to turn. 'Kiska. There's no one else here.'

'Sure there is.' She glanced about. The old woman was nowhere to be seen. 'She was right here.'

'Must have been a dream, Kiska. Because we are all alone. But tell me . . . what did she have to say?'

*　　*　　*

Baruk's workroom was at the very top of the tower. On the way up the endless narrow circular stairway Spindle had grumbled to himself: *Gods, why do they always have to be at the top? Never on the ground floor. All this useless walking up and down!*

Since being guided into the room by the little waddling demon, Duiker had had him searching for all the various chemicals in their phials, globes, decanters and cups. The historian dropped samples from each liquid on to a chip of the white stone. He hadn't been happy with any of the reactions produced.

Eventually, long past midnight, they gave up for the time being and Spindle gestured for the old man to rest. He would take first watch. An old campaigner, the historian curled up on all the cloths they'd piled together as a bed and went to sleep.

From a seat beneath a window Spindle watched the city below glowing in its blue flames. Above, the green radiance of the Scimitar shone down. And it seemed to him that the two nimbuses warred over the city. Or at least that was what he fancied. The night was very quiet. In fact the city had been very quiet ever since the Seguleh arrived. Everyone hurried, reluctant to be out, constantly peering over their shoulders. People were afraid. And the Seguleh hadn't even done anything yet! He had the impression that they simply weren't welcome, weren't wanted, here in Darujhistan. Which struck him as odd since it seemed to welcome everyone, priding itself on being so cosmopolitan and all.

He supposed it was more what they represented. Or stood for, perhaps.

A few bells later he woke the historian.

In the morning nothing had changed. None of the chemicals they tested elicited the sort of reaction the historian seemed to expect. As the day waned Spindle returned to his seat at the window. A growled sigh of frustration drew his gaze to Duiker as the man pushed himself away from the worktable. He regarded Spindle through narrowed, squinting eyes. 'Nothing. I don't understand it. This should be the answer. Why is nothing reacting?'

Spindle shrugged. 'Maybe we need a new sample? Another shard?'

The historian waved his hands in a gesture of helplessness. 'Well . . . perhaps. Go get one.'

'All right.' He heaved himself from the chair and headed to the top of the stairs where they'd dropped their load of stones. Here he found the fat little demon, its head in the cloak, stuffing its great mouth with the chips.

'Hey! Git outta there!'

It raced off, dragging the cloak with it. Spindle gave chase. Its little clawed feet clicked over the polished stone floor as it ducked under tables and around furniture. Spindle swore again for leaving his shortsword behind. He almost lost his quarry amid all the furnishings and hangings but spotted a telltale corner of the cloak peeping out of a well-hidden door. Searching about, Spindle found a fireplace poker and raised it, then reached for the slim stone door.

He yanked it open, poker poised, and the little demon hissed at him then ran between his legs and scuttled off. Spindle let it go; it had abandoned the cloak. He gathered it up and gave it a shake. Just a few leavings rattled at the bottom.

Togg curse it!

Then he glimpsed something else in the narrow cupboard. A huge amphora as tall as his waist set on a wrought-iron stand. It looked to be of some sort of fired ceramic, glazed black. Its lid was sealed with wax and pressed into the liberal drippings was some kind of sigil.

He went to get the historian.

Together they carried the amphora into the workroom. Duiker studied the seal then looked at Spindle, arching one grey brow. Spindle reached outward to feel for any Warren-anchored wardings or traps. He sensed nothing and shrugged. 'What's the seal?' he asked.

'Looks like the High Alchemist's own. As far as I can deduce.'

'Should we open it?'

The historian sat back in his chair, rested his chin in one hand. 'Well, that is a question. We're inside the inner sanctum of a powerful alchemist. We find an amphora specifically hidden away and sealed and so naturally we open it. Sounds like an epitaph to me.'

Spindle nodded, pursing his lips. 'I see what you mean. Let's go get the pet.'

They lured it in with the stone chips. Spindle held one out, beckoning, backing up until they had it in the room. Duiker closed the door on it. It looked unhappy but Spindle held the chip over its head and let it have it.

Then he held out another of their rapidly dwindling supply and pointed to the amphora. 'Should we open that?' The little demon wouldn't take its beady blood-red eyes off the chip. It hissed and tried to jump. Its pot belly wobbled. 'What will happen if we open that?' Spindle tried again, pointing. It held up its skinny arms, clawing the air. Spindle sighed.

'Put the chip on the jar,' Duiker suggested.

Spindle did so, resting the piece of Alabaster on the wax. The little demon watched with narrowed eyes. It waddled over to the amphora and with scratching claws and feet tried its best to climb it. Spindle had to stop the thing from toppling over.

Duiker came up and shooed the demon off. It snatched up the stone chip and scrambled off, claws scritching. 'I guess we have our answer,' Spindle said.

'Unless the wretch has no idea what's in there – which is more than likely.'

'Ah. Well. What'll we do?'

Duiker rubbed the back of his neck and grimaced. 'I guess we have no choice. We open it.'

Using the tools and supplies available in the alchemist's workroom Spindle set up a rig. First he selected the sharpest steel tool he could find to scour a ring all the way round the neck of the amphora. Then he adjusted the height of a table so that it matched the height of the scoured line and secured the amphora to the edge. He cleared the table of everything and poured a decanter of oil all over it. Earlier he'd spotted a long iron bar and this he laid down on the tabletop so that one end touched the neck of the amphora while the other extended out over the opposite edge. Then he stood on a chair to drive a pin into the ceiling over the table. Using rope, he hung the biggest lead weight he could find from the pin. Carefully, he measured the length so that the weight – in the form of an elephant, appropriately enough – just touched the far end of the bar.

All this extraordinary effort Duiker watched, bemused, arms crossed. Finally he waved a hand. 'Why all this?'

'Don't want to be in the room when it opens, do we?'

'Well, no. I suppose not. But there has to be an easier way . . .'

Spindle paused in the act of tying off the weight so that he could pull another cord and release it to swing free, striking the end of the bar as it swung. He glared his annoyance. 'You tellin' me my trade?'

Duiker raised his hands. 'No, no. It just seems rather . . . intricate.'

'It'll work, I'm pretty sure. The point is, I can pull the cord from the door and we'll be outside when it happens.'

Duiker decided that perhaps it would be best if he said nothing more. Spindle waved him from the room, played out the cord until he stood outside with the door open a slit, then gave Duiker the high sign. He shouted, 'Munitions!' pulled the cord and slammed the door, throwing himself down on the hall floor next to Duiker.

The sound of the weight hitting the iron bar, a crash, and the metallic ringing of the bar hitting the stone floor, reached them almost simultaneously. Spindle raised a hand for a pause, waited, then carefully climbed to his feet. He edged to the door, drew a breath, and glanced back to Duiker. The historian waved him on. Shrugging, he swung open the door. They both peered in. The top of the amphora was on longer visible above the table.

Spindle cuffed Duiker's shoulder. '*Ha!* Knew it would work. What did I say?'

Indeed, the neck had snapped right off. Duiker was rather impressed; he hadn't thought the weight would strike the bar. Spindle held a hand over the open amphora neck then sniffed his palm. He wrinkled his nose: 'Sour. Acidic.' Duiker went to find a clean pot.

Spindle edged over the amphora while Duiker held the container ready. Clear liquid poured out, smelling strongly acidic. Duiker set the pot down on the table then held one chip over it. 'Ready?' he said. Spindle nodded. Duiker dropped it in and jumped backwards.

The reaction was, even by saboteur standards, impressive.

Spindle had leaned out the open window; the stink in the room was enough to turn anyone's stomach. 'What now?' he asked Duiker, who was pacing. 'Can't lug that through the streets. Might get stopped by the Wardens, or the masked boys.'

Duiker stood still. He tapped his thumb to his lips as he thought. 'Might have an answer there. Any more chips?'

'One or two.'

'Get our friend.'

Spindle went to the hall and tapped a chip to a wall, calling, 'Here, boy!' He whistled and tsked. A crimson head poked round a corner, one red eye cocked.

Duiker knelt, hands on knees, to address the demon. 'Tell me, friend. Does your master have a wine cellar?'

As the afternoon waned Spindle and Duiker walked through the city streets burdened by wooden crates of wine bottles. It was slow going. Duiker was an old man who'd been through a lot. This was more physical activity than he'd had in over a year. Spindle was patient; he knew what the man had experienced. Frankly it was a miracle the fellow was still able to function. In fact, Duiker might not be aware of it, but Spindle admired him to no end. It seemed to him that they just didn't make them that tough any more. And while the message that sent them on this errand might have been delivered to him, Spindle was of the opinion that it had really been meant for the Imperial Historian. *He* was the one who possessed the knowledge that had gotten them this far.

But it was his show from this point onward.

As the afternoon edged into a warm humid evening they reached the alley at the back of K'rul's bar. They stacked the crates in the kitchen and then, completely drained, staggered upstairs to rest.

*   *   *

The Great Hall of Darujhistan glittered with the silken finery of the city's female aristocracy vying to display the most intricate and, to Lady Envy's eyes, most cumbersome and uncomfortable dresses. Jewellery was heaped upon jewellery in a – really, quite vulgar – draping of necklaces, brooches, tiaras, bracelets and jewelled sashes.

It was all rather sadly disappointing. Not at all what she'd hoped it would be.

No one here appeared sophisticated enough to appreciate the fine subtleties she brought to the court in her exquisitely understated dress and cut of hair. It was dispiriting. Even here parochialism

517

reigned. These young beauties of the noble families: what did they know of true elegance and natural grace? Nothing at all! Empty-headed adornments they!

She'd tried engaging the Legate in conversation. 'Legate' indeed! How amusing. But only the sweaty little fellow would answer. It was almost embarrassing.

Then that young upstart approached her. Here! In front of every-one! *Mortifying!*

'You are Lady Envy,' she said, and she curtsied in her floating dancing scarves prettily enough.

'And you are Vorcan's daughter.'

'I am.'

'You . . . dance, I take it?'

A smile, revealing small sharp teeth. 'And much more.'

'I'm sure . . .'

'Had you met my mother?'

'No. But I was a great admirer of hers.'

'Oh? How so?'

'She knew her place.'

The smile disappeared into a straight colourless slit pulled back over teeth. 'Careful. This court tolerates you now but that may change.'

'I'd rather thought it was the other way around myself.'

A confused clenching of the eyes as the girl tried to work out Envy's meaning.

Oh, please! Mother Dark deliver me . . . Envy simply walked away. *Bored. I am bored. So utterly bored!*

＊　　　＊　　　＊

West of the Maiten river Ambassador Aragan called a halt to any further advance and ordered K'ess to dig a defensive line against any possible attack. Darujhistan's sapphire glow was just visible yet strangely dim, muted, and Aragan wondered if perhaps smoke obscured it. Here they would wait while their temporary allies, the Moranth, proceeded with their plans.

Negotiations had been nerve-racking to say the least. The Moranth wanted to end things with a finality that was terrifying; and Aragan was hard pressed to blame them. His heart also went out to this Councillor Nom. The poor fellow, having to stand by while the fate of his city was debated by outsiders.

After much back and forth, with Mallick himself speaking through the Sceptre, an accord was reached backed up by Malazan assurances. This was as far as they would go while the Moranth launched the fought-for compromise. But if this first gambit failed, the Moranth were firm, they would unleash a full assault. Then would come the firestorm. A city consumed. Y'Ghatan all over again.

Aragan prayed to all the Elder Gods it would not come to that. And he pondered yet again on the question that so tormented him: what would he do? If the fires should start – what would he do? Order the troops in to help the citizenry escape, thus endangering them? Or merely stand by and watch while countless thousands were consumed in flames? How could he live with himself then? How could any of them?

*

Just inland from Lake Azur, in his tent next to the barrow of the Son of Darkness, Caladan Brood, the Warlord, pushed aside the cloth flap of his tent to face the darkening evening. He frowned, revealing even more of his prominent canines, and sniffed the air. His glance went to the west, then over to the city, and a low growl sounded deep within his throat.

He ducked back within to put on his leathers and strap on his hammer.

Can't let what I think's in the air happen. No. Enough is enough. Not after all we've fought for. Have to put an end to it before it all gets out of hand. And frankly, better if I take the blame than anyone else.

*

South of the city, heading up what was named Cutter Lake Road, Yusek gaped at every building they passed. *Two storeys! Almost every building has two storeys! It's incredible.* Already they'd passed more shops and inns and stables than she'd ever imagined – and they'd not even reached the city walls!

The Seventh led though his pace was glacially slow, almost reluctant. A permanent grimace of pain seemed fixed on his face. He'd muttered that no one seemed to be about.

Yet she'd seen more people than she'd ever seen since her refugee days. And these people certainly weren't ragged drifters. Many were finely dressed. Some were even plump. Imagine, having so much to eat that you could get fat! Now *that's* damned rich. She'd be that rich one day. She could taste the duck fat already. Soon it'd be her who was fat!

Then abruptly the Seventh raised a hand for a halt. He regarded the darkening sky, the glow Yusek knew was the fabled gas lighting of Darujhistan. That glow struck her as far less than the green blaze of the Scimitar above and she thought it probably overrated. *Damned typical!* The Seventh turned to Sall and Lo. 'You Seguleh have stirred up a hornet's nest and now it's come to bite everyone. I don't know what I can do.'

'Will you challenge?' Sall asked.

The man flinched, anguished. 'No! It's not my place . . . yet something's wrong. Something's very wrong.'

'But . . . you will help, yes?' Sall asked. It was the closest the youth had come to a plea that Yusek had heard.

The Seventh's mouth worked with suppressed emotion as he looked away. 'My record isn't that encouraging,' he ground out. But he did start walking once more, his head lowered.

*

Spindle was dead asleep when he heard his ma's voice calling him down in its old familiar cadence: *Get your lazy arse out of bed!* He fell to the floor, arms and legs flailing in panic. Then he froze dead still. Something had woken him. Something that raised the hair on his head and on his shirt. A sound.

The sound of bottles clanking together.

He flew to the door, rebounded from the jamb, then threw it open and tumbled out into the hall to pound to the common room yelling: 'It's poison! Don't drink it!'

Blend spat out a great mouthful of drink over the bar and down her front. 'Gaah! What? *Poisoned?*'

Spindle hurried over to yank the bottle from her hand and sniff it.

'Fisher just brought it!' she complained, wiping her shirt. 'Kanese red.'

Spindle nodded to the bard, then examined the bottle. 'Red? Really? Sorry.' He handed back the bottle. 'Sorry.'

Blend gave him the withering glare she reserved for hopeless idiots. The one he didn't like to get. He gestured to the kitchens. 'Thought you was using those other bottles, from the back. They're not wine.'

'So they're wine bottles without wine in them.'

'That's right.'

'Paid extra for that, did you?'

'No! I mean, shut the Abyss up.' He faced Fisher and poured himself a glass of red. 'So, what's the news?'

The bard nodded. He was a tall man, rangy, yet from what Spindle had seen surprisingly strong. Even leaning on a high stool he was still taller than Spindle. Something in the mage resented that. 'I was just telling Blend,' the bard said. 'Whispers from the court. The Seguleh have been defeated out west. The Moranth. Any maybe . . . the Malazans.'

Spindle and Blend shared a look. *Damned right.* She raised her glass and they drank.

'Word is they may be expecting an attack.'

Blend waved a hand. 'Ridiculous. No one has an army big enough to enter Darujhistan, let alone pacify it.'

Fisher lifted his shoulders, conceding he point. 'That we know of . . . In any case, the Seguleh have withdrawn to Majesty Hill. Looks like they don't plan on contesting the city.'

'Why should they when the mob will do it for them? No, Aragan doesn't have nearly enough troops. And if the Moranth enter the entire city will rise against them. Always been bad blood here between them, so I heard.'

Fisher held up his hands. 'Just reporting what I heard.' He lifted his glass to Blend. 'So, what do you think's happening, then?'

The big woman – big now that she was putting on weight – swirled the wine in her glass, peering down at it. Her hair held more than a touch of grey amid the brown curls and dark circles bruised her eyes. *We're none of us gettin' enough sleep these days*, Spindle reflected. *Watchin' the streets. Too many days waitin' on edge. Waitin' for the hammer to fall. Like being back on campaign, it is. Only we're damned older.*

'So they got their noses bloodied,' she said, speculating. 'Now they'll just sit tight an' consolidate here in the city. Firm up their grip an' wait . . .' She cocked her head, eyeing Fisher. 'How many Seguleh do you think there are on that isle of theirs anyway?'

'Well, there must be several . . . thousand . . .' *Ancients, no.* 'You don't think so, do you?'

She shrugged at the uncertainty of it. 'Why not? These boys and girls we're looking at here could just be the tip of the spear. A whole army of them could be on the way. A whole people.'

Spindle felt sick to his stomach. *Togg deliver them! An entire army of these people? That was too much to imagine.* 'I need to eat somethin'. I feel faint.' He took his glass to the kitchen.

*

In a dark empty shop, its floor littered with broken wares and shattered furniture, stood a hulking stone statue inlaid with a mosaic of jade, lapis lazuli and serpentine chips. Its stone gleamed slick with oils and it was slathered in caked powders. The ash of a forest of burnt rare wood sticks lay about its feet, all now long cold. Mice scampering between its wide stone feet suddenly stilled. The bats that perched in the rafters above its head ceased their bickering. They tilted their big pointed ears, listening to the stillness.

Beneath them a grinding noise broke the silence as the statue grated its head to the left, and then ponderously to the right. At its sides further scraping of stone sounded as its fists opened and closed. In agonizing slow motion it leaned forward to grind one carved stone boot out before it across the littered floor. It paused there for a time as if testing its balance. Then it took another step.

CHAPTER IXX

We forge our weapons so that they may never be used.

> Moranth saying

ONCE MORE TORVALD GRIPPED THE HANDLES OF THE QUORL saddle and hunched behind Galene's engraved reflective back. Now that he'd grown accustomed to the noise of flight the experience seemed eerily quiet. The straps and jesses snapped in the rushing wind and the near-invisible wings hummed and hissed. Other than this constant background murmur a near serene silence reigned.

He fancied he could almost hear the waves of Lake Azur as they whipped by just beneath, so close it seemed he could reach down and touch them. For they were far out over the lake scudding over the night-dark waves, headed for Darujhistan. Scarves of cloud passed overhead obscuring the mottled reborn moon with its muted pewter glow. The jade banner of the Scimitar also loomed high among the stars. It seemed to have grown perceptibly of late. He'd heard grumbling among the troops that it was about to smash into the land in a great explosion that would mark the end of the world. Brought about, many claimed, by the hubris of the gods.

Behind and to either side flight after flight of quorl floated and darted over the waves. Each was burdened by a passenger and packs of their fearsome munitions. This was Torvald's own personal end of the world fear. He and the Malazan ambassador, Aragan, had fought hard to blunt the Moranth's intent to resolve these hostilities in one massive destructive wave. They had argued instead for this first more targeted attack.

Torvald preyed to all the gods below that it would succeed. For the alternative was just too horrific to contemplate.

Ahead, he could hardly discern the cobalt glow of Darujhistan from the lurid sea-green banner of the Scimitar arcing above. Was there a night fog off the lake? Or some trick or trap awaiting them? Never before could he remember seeing the night so dark over the city. Yet the Scimitar more than made up the difference. Their target was unmistakable. So low did the chevrons of quorl whip across the lake that tiny wakes actually glimmered in phosphor white behind. Fishing boats snapped past not below, but to Torvald's side. Men and women gaped and pointed in the light of the lanterns they hung to draw in their catch.

The night was warm, he knew, but the wind punished him. His hands were frozen numb and he could only steal quick glimpses through his slitted watering eyes. Ahead, the differing tiers of the city slowly emerged from the glow. Second Tier, and, above, Third Tier and the rambling stone complex of Majesty Hall. Galene raised an arm, signing a command. Her quorl waggled its wings. Quorls answered around them with similar signals and her flight group peeled off in tilting chevrons. Other groups flitted off in other directions, also spreading out.

Torvald leaned forward to yell: 'Why the manoeuvring?'

Galene turned her helmed head. 'This one's servants are powerful mages, Nom,' she answered, her voice low and loud. 'We will take many losses in this assault.'

Torvald didn't know what to say to that: Darujhistan was about to take many losses itself. And so he leaned back, silent, hunching from the driving wind.

'You will throw this time, yes?' she continued, relentless.

He ducked his head. 'Yes.'

'Very well. I hope so – for your sake. Ready the packs.'

With numb hands he fumbled with the clasps of the two packs strapped in before him. *Four cussers! Two in each pack. Gedderone have mercy. After this there will be no hill left!*

*

In the Great Hall, Coll was speaking to the young, and, he had to admit, very sharp and elegant Councillor Redda Orr. He was worried that she was a touch too forward in her disapproval of the powers the Legate had taken upon himself. He was constantly doing his best to counsel discretion and patience.

In return she'd taken to calling him 'Grandfather Coll'.

He answered her with 'Child'.

She broke off their verbal duelling as the murmur of conversation faded away throughout the hall. The Legate was standing before his throne. His wretched Mouthpiece came fumbling to his side. Coll pushed his way to the front of the crowd.

The Legate's gold oval was tilted up to the arched stone ceiling. Its engraved face, the half-smile, appeared now more like a sneer. 'Servants attend me,' the Mouthpiece called, and he clutched at his neck afterwards as if choking.

Baruk and the girl with the silver wristlets and see-through veil stepped up. 'Defend the Circle,' the Mouthpiece told them. They bowed, and disappeared in swirls of darkness. The gold oval turned its attention to the Second, whose mask, with its single marring stroke, rose in expectation. 'Defend the grounds. All of you.'

'All?'

'All. I am quite safe here.'

The Second bowed, then signed. The gathered Seguleh left the Great Hall.

The Legate swept back up on to his white throne. 'We are safe here,' the Mouthpiece called. 'The Orb will protect us. Nothing can get through.' The Legate placed his hands upon the armrests to either side, again utterly still and calm.

'What is this?' Redda hissed low to Coll.

He drew her aside to where the two guards stood leaning against a pillar, crossbows hanging loose, peering about as if as confused as everyone else . 'I don't know. An attack, obviously. But who? The Malazans?'

'Let's take a look.' She moved to leave.

He held her back with a touch on her arm. 'Not so easy – *he* sees everything. If you keep an eye out I'll sneak off, yes?'

She slitted her gaze as anger gathered in their hazel light. 'I can manage perfectly—'

He raised a hand for her indulgence. 'Cunning before beauty,' he murmured. He moved off, bumping into a group of chattering councillors. 'Gods I need a drink!' he told them, steadying the one he'd knocked off balance, then staggering off.

The looks of venomous derision they shot his back and the soft laughter they shared made Redda even angrier.

*

Passing a gap in the buildings of Cutter Town, Yusek paused, her breach catching. There lay Darujhistan, so close she could almost reach out and touch it. Its walls shone blue-tinted. Above them rose the dark roofs of countless buildings, and above these even taller towers jutted into the night sky. Yet, where was this much talked-up gem-like glow of the city? Hardly any blue flames shone, and these mostly confined to the walls and gates. Was this really all there was to the stories?

'Sall – it is immense, but ...'

He waved her on. 'Come. The Seventh has gone ahead.'

Together they jogged up the road. Yusek slipped next to the Seventh – a position neither Sall nor Lo was prepared to take up. 'What will you do?' she asked.

His gaze slide to her. He worked his jaws as if it were necessary to loosen them before he could speak. 'I don't know exactly,' he admitted, with what to Yusek was amazing honesty. She was rather thrown; in Orbern-town she'd become used to the absolute certainty and determined fronts fools hold up to hide behind.

'Yet you're going.'

'Yes. I can't turn away from this. Cuts too close to home.'

'Oh?'

The man just gave another sidelong glance. The jaws remained clamped tight.

Shortly afterwards the Seventh stopped to study the vista just as Yusek had herself. Sall and Lo stopped behind, patient as ever.

'What is it?' Yusek asked.

'We should take the Foss Road. Go round.'

She was outraged. 'Go *round*! Whatever for?'

It almost appeared as if the man would answer, but he bit down on the words looking as if he'd swallowed something sharp. Moving on he allowed: 'In case of a panic.'

*

In the Finnest house in the grounds of Coll's estate two strikingly differing yet oddly matched individuals played cards. The tall iron-haired one, Raest, kept raising his shattered corpse-like face to peer into the distance, as if distracted. His partner, an Imass, held his cards steady in hands no more than ligaments wrapped around naked bone.

'It is your turn, isn't it?' Raest said after a time.

The Imass's fleshless skull shifted from its fixed regard of its cards to glance up.

'Turn?' Raest said. 'Turn, yes? I did explain that, didn't I?'

The skull now shifted even further, neck crackling with dry sinew, to send a long hard glance up the hall.

Raest looked to the dim ceiling. 'Not now,' he said.

The Imass stood, nearly upsetting the table. It spoke in a creaking of leather-hard flesh: 'I smell . . . ice.'

Raest waved a dismissive hand. 'Never mind the ill-mannered neighbours . . .'

The Imass stepped from the table. Raest tutted: 'Cards . . .' It peered down as if utterly unaware it held anything in its hand, it set them face down on the table and shambled off up the hall.

Raest sat for a time, motionless, until the noise of a door slamming echoed through the house. His gaze fell on the cards opposite.

He leaned to peer up the hall; waited a little longer. Then he reached across and lifted them.

*

Ambassador Aragan flinched as a single quorl stooped their position. As it passed it waggled its wings, sending up a loud hissing and snapping of cloaks and pennants in its wake. It raced off ahead and disappeared into the darkness, making for the city. He and Fist K'ess shared taut glances. 'Any time now.' He rubbed the back of a hand to the bristles at his cheek, adding a low 'Gods forgive us'.

Fist K'ess, he saw, clutched at his neck where Aragan knew a stone representing Burn hung. Next to the Fist, his aide, Captain Fal-ej, leaned closer to whisper, 'It is very lovely.'

'You've never seen it?' K'ess said, surprised.

'No.'

He cleared his throat, his voice thickening. 'Shame, that.'

On Aragan's other side Attaché Torn sat awkward on his mount, his helmed head tilted upwards following the passing quorls.

'Twins stand aside,' Aragan offered.

Torn nodded. 'Yes. Let us hope they succeed.'

Down the lines Bendan stood with Little, now Sergeant Little, Bone and Tarat. He twisted his aching neck where the majority of his shield's weight hung. 'Don't want to see what I think we're gonna see,' he growled.

Little eyed him sidelong, her gaze re-evaluating and somehow softer. 'You're turning into a regular pacifist, Bendan.'

'Just wouldn't wish it on my worst enemy, is all.' He hawked up a mouthful of phlegm to spit.

'And that is your home, yes?' Tarat said.

Bendan shook his head in a negative. 'No. I'm from Maiten.'

*

Masts of coastal barks and merchant cargo haulers whipped past beneath Torvald's boots so close he thought he might loose a foot. Abruptly Galene yanked the nose of the quorl up and they climbed fiercely. Torvald hunched into his seat as if a great hand were pressing down upon his head. Then they broke over the lip of the Second Tier Wall and he had a glimpse ahead that disoriented him so thoroughly that he almost tumbled from his seat. 'What in Oponn's name is *that*?'

'The Orb,' Galene called over her shoulder. 'The Orb of the Tyrants.' She raised an arm, gesturing her commands in broad sweeps. 'Ready the munitions!'

Torvald reached both hands into the first pack and braced himself with his thighs against the juddering of the quorl.

*

Spindle was sitting at a table working on his third glass of wine while he thought about the mystery of when – and how! – to use the chemicals he and Duiker had collected. The damned circle was buried and there were mages keeping an eye out! How were they possibly gonna do the deed?

The historian himself was at the front keeping his own eye out. Picker and Blend were at the bar leaning together from opposite sides communicating in their one word sentences like the veterans who'd spent a whole lifetime campaigning together that they were. The bard had gone in for an early night.

He was considering his fourth glass when out front passed a noise that sent a shiver down his back and set his hair stirring: swift thrumming and hissing overhead.

He, Blend and Picker shared stunned glances.

As one they jumped to the front, knocking aside chairs and tearing boards from a window to gape up at the night sky, knocking heads and pushing at one another. Something whipped overhead obscuring the darkness for an instant. The oh-so-familiar humming and hissing of gossamer wings whispered past.

528

'A Hood-damned assault!' Blend snarled.

'A drop!' Picker barked.

'I'm on it,' Spindle declared, and he punched Duiker's shoulder. 'Let's go!'

The historian sadly shook his head. 'I'm flattered, but no – it's a young man's chase. Find a stronger back.'

'Well, who . . .' Spindle looked to Blend and Picker. They shook their heads. 'We have our post.'

'*Shit!*'

Duiker edged a hand to the back and cocked a brow. Spindle's gaze narrowed; then he smiled evilly. He ran for the rear. 'Fisher!' he bellowed. 'Get out here! We're on.'

*

Torvald's quorl now flitted over the estate district. Since reaching the city, he'd been peering all about for the gas lights but had seen hardly any. The dread gripped him that this was some sort of trap devised by these mages. Yet couldn't it also be a fantastic blessing? It may be that someone here has shown astounding forethought. He'd like to kiss whoever it was, considering all the munitions now flying over the city. Ahead, the 'Orb', as Galene called it, shone with the reflected commingled light of the moon and the Scimitar. It glowed so pale he imagined that in daylight it would be white. And he could see through it as well, as if were as thin and translucent as a bubble. Galene suddenly jerked her straps, urging her mount into a series of jerking rolls and near-spins. Torvald held on for his life.

'What's that for!' he yelled.

His answer came as something lashed from Majesty Hill to strike a chevron of the approaching quorls. For all he could tell it looked like ripples in the air, heat ripples as over a hot road. These disturbances arced out like waves and any quorl they struck tumbled from the sky, its wings shattered like crushed dry leaves. As the creatures fell spinning Torvald suddenly realized what was about to happen. He quickly looked away, yet the glaring bright flash still dazzled his vision. A thunderous roar followed, together with a great black cloud of debris kicking skyward behind. Peering back, it looked as though a block of the waterfront district had been destroyed.

'Pay attention,' Galene snarled over the wind.

Their mount now turned sharply, tilting almost sideways. The ghostly pale Orb swung into view. Torvald glimpsed the forested park grounds of Majesty Hill below, and saw masked figures running and one man, bent, his long pale arms malformed, gesturing to wreak such havoc among the quorl chevrons.

'Ready munitions!' Galene yelled above the screaming wind.

Torvald pulled out the first cusser and hugged it to his chest.

The quorl turned even more sharply now, arcing until they were riding nearly upside down. The pale lucent wall of the Orb curved directly below, as did a section of Majesty Hall.

'*Drop!*' Galene snapped.

Torvald threw. The cusser fell tumbling and spinning. He bent backwards, following its descent. As it reached the ghostly wall of the Orb he winced, blinded, as a flash jabbed at his vision. An instant later a concussive wall of force knocked their quorl sideways, sending them spinning.

Galene fought to regain control of her mount. They swung round, headed now for the waterfront. 'What happened?' she grated, turning back to confront him.

'It burst early when it struck that wall or whatever it is!'

'Elders damn that sorcerer!' She reknotted her hands through the jesses, tightening them. 'We'll go high.'

Behind them further bright flashes lit the night, followed closely by the rolling thunder of blast after blast. Torvald was thrown backwards as the quorl's nose suddenly rose straight up. They climbed and climbed, arching ever backwards until Galene had put the quorl through a complete back loop and rolled to right them. They headed back for another pass.

Torvald fought down the contents of his stomach.

*

Coll rushed back into the Great Hall to find all the councillors, aristocrats, functionaries and hangers-on jammed together in a tight circle round the raised white throne where the Legate sat still as immobile as ever. From overhead came an almost constant booming, punishing everyone. Dust sifted down from the stone ceiling.

'We cannot be harmed!' the Mouthpiece yelled, his voice cracking and quavering, rather ruining the effect of his claim.

Councillor Redda Orr pushed her way through the crowd to Coll. 'What now?' she shouted, and ducked at a particularly close punch of bursting pressure.

'That wretched weasel Mouthpiece is right,' he answered. 'None of this is getting through.'

'But what if the roof should fall?'

He squinted up at the arched ceiling and saw mortar drifting down from between the stones. 'You're right.' He glared about, searching for an answer. 'The cellars! We have to get everyone down underground.'

A pall of silence grew over all the shouting and crying around them and Coll looked over. The Legate had stood up. 'Lady Envy,' the Mouthpiece said, choking and gasping. 'Will you not demonstrate why you are the brightest jewel of this court?'

Men and women flinched from one tall woman who remained unbowed beneath the direct regard of the Legate. She crooked her painted lips in an amused smile. Then she lightly inclined her head and sauntered to the doors. All eyes followed her lazy, seemingly unconcerned exit.

Once Lady Envy had turned from sight the Legate gestured and the tall double doors of the Great Hall slammed shut.

This broke whatever spell had been holding the court together. Everyone began yelling in an instant panic, running to find exits, grabbing at one another, trying make themselves understood. Over this Coll used his battlefield bellow to roar: '*To the cellars!*'

The crowd of courtiers and councillors surged after him.

Throughout it all the Legate calmly faced the doors, hands at his sides, immobile, gold oval cocked a touch to one side. As if expecting company.

*

On the street of the weaponsmiths in the Gadrobi district, a heavy-set woman sat out on the steps of a duelling school letting the cool night air brush her face while she flexed her hand and wrist, which were numb from a long practice session.

A strange sound stilled her and she lifted her head, listening for a time. Then, dismissing the noise, she returned to rolling her wrist. She pushed back her shoulders and edged her neck from side to side, grimacing at the pain of old tight tendons.

A blast rocked her, rattling all the nearby windows and shocking her to her feet. She glared up the street to where smoke and the orange flickering of flames climbed over the city. People screamed in their rooms; others ran out on to the street to peer about.

From the north flashes lit the night, followed shortly by thunder as in a storm. But Stonny knew that sound for no storm. She ran inside and woke a sleeping boy who blinked up at her, confused.

'Gather everyone together and come to the front now,' she whispered, fierce.

'What? Do what, Mother?'

'Do it now, lad.'

'Now?'

'Yes! Go.' After making certain the boy was on his way she ran to the practice hall and strapped on two weapons. Another window offered a view of the Third Tier and Majesty Hill and here she stopped, staring, her heart now hammering. Where were all the lights?

'Fener's curse,' she whispered. Bursts of mage-fire illuminated her wide, blunt face. Then something that looked as fragile and tiny as a feather fell spinning from the sky further along in the Lakefront district and a blast rocked the school, sending her staggering back. When she returned to the window she saw that the glazing had cracked.

She ran, yelling, '*Harllo!*'

*

'There we go,' murmured Fist K'ess as a burst of light flashed over the north-east. Moments later a muted rumble sounded. Aragan nodded, realized he'd been holding his breath, and eased it out. Further multiple flashes blazed, followed by an eventual continual low rumbling.

And from the ranks came an answer. A low groan sounded up and down the lines as if every trooper felt each burst as a physical blow.

Aragan half raised his hand.

'We'll be mobbed, sir,' K'ess said, his voice soft. 'They'll blame us.'

'I agree,' Torn added.

Aragan forced his hand down. 'Yes. It's just . . . Yes.' He studied the flashes, all the while urging the Moranth on. *Get through! Get to him, damn you. Finish it!*

K'ess watched the ambassador from the edge of his vision. *Poor fellow. Hasn't seen much direct action. Always coming in behind. Yet to his credit he has that necessary compassion for his fellow soldiers. The gesture speaks well of him.*

He remembered the taking of Pale. Been a raw captain then, of the regulars. The memory of that enfilade had yet to let him go. He'd lost so many nights to those images his hope was that no similar cataclysm erupted here. *Especially after what they've already witnessed. Could be too much. Could break 'em. Hood, have to have a heart of flint not to feel it.*

Spindle tottered on the last section of the rising walk up Majesty Hill. He fell against a buttress, banging the crate so that bottles clanked, and winced, biting his lip. Stones clattered down around him and acrid smoke wafted past.

Damn close, that. Fallin' like flies everywhere, the poor bastards!

He jerked his head to urge Fisher on. The bard straightened and jogged up.

Getting this far had been simple; everyone had run off. And K'rul's hill was right next to Despot's Barbican anyway. The district was pretty much entirely abandoned. Even the streetlights were un-lit. Seemed the Greyfaces had taken the night off. Damned smart of them, considering. He peered over the wall to eye the nearest forest copse. Overhead the Moranth circled and swooped. A continuous barrage fell on Majesty Hall. Yet this magical barrier, this dome or circle, pretty much invisible up close and seemingly as delicate as a soap bubble, held back an entire war of punishment.

And Spindle knew what anchored it.

So loud were the near-continuous eruptions of munitions that he and Fisher could not speak. He caught the bard's eye then jerked his head to the woods and ran. Hunched, bottles banging, they jogged through the park forest. At least Spindle knew exactly where he was headed.

He didn't mean to slam down the crate of wine bottles but in the dark he tripped on a root and fell right on top of it. He rolled off immediately and brushed frantically at his front – which would have been a stupid thing to do if one of the bottles *had* broken and spilled on him. *Should've just started yanking off the damn hauberk.*

Through the trees he could see the Moranth arcing overhead on their quorls and tossing their charges over Majesty Hall.

Most of the cussers blew far overhead but a few landed now and then on the unprotected hilltop and shook the ground. Off to one side a crater smoked in a reminder of what might happen to them at any moment. The bard didn't know Malazan hand signs so Spindle was forced to wave and point. He'd found the site of their old exca-vation.

He threw himself to his knees and started digging in a feverish panic. Fisher joined him.

To make things even worse, through the trees he could see that the Seguleh were out as well. They were keeping to the doors and walls of the many buildings of the Majesty Hall complex. Waiting, watching, masks tilted upwards to follow the Moranth in their circling.

Spindle thought he knew what they were waiting for and he prayed it wouldn't come to that. Things would get far too crowded then.

Best to have a hidey-hole in that case. And he dug and dug.

Togg, things might get so desperate he might even have to raise his Warren! Gods, that it should come to that . . .

*

Barathol was out of bed with the first burst. He peered through the slats of the shutters.

'What is it?' Scillara asked from the dark.

A much closer blast; the house shook. A few things fell downstairs. Little Chaur set up a wail. 'Get him,' he said, pulling on trousers. 'I'll grab some food and water.'

She stood quickly, dressing as well. 'You're coming with us, yes?' she said sharply.

He paused, glancing at her shadowed silhouette. 'Yes. I'm coming with you.'

Outside, it was jarringly dark. He'd never seen the streets unlit. Now it was the Scimitar's ill-omened glow that cast shadows across the shop fronts. They joined a swelling crowd jamming the street. He peered to the east, to the higher tiers where flashes lit the night. Flames rose from much closer, however.

Then something slashed overhead, raising shrieks of fear. It hissed arrow-straight up the road, lower than the rooftops. *Moranth . . . attacking? Cover. It's using the streets to hide. Hide from what?*

Another close burst sent up a new wave of shrieks and panic through the pressing crowd.

Barathol turned to Scillara, who carried Chaur pressed against her chest. 'I'm going to—'

'No you're not!' she cut in. 'We're all going together.' She twisted a fist in his shirtsleeve, yanking. 'And we're going in *this* goddamned direction!'

He smiled at the admonishment and pressed a hand over hers. 'Yes. Let's get out of here.' He moved out in front of her and started pushing a way through the crowd.

*

Studious Lock pushed open the main front door of the Nom manor house and regarded the night. It was very dark and very noisy. There was some sort of local celebration going on nearby. Very annoying. No doubt this was what the Mistress's odd instructions regarded.

'Guards,' he called.

Three figures approached from the gloom.

Studious paused, a finger raised. *Three? Was his vision going? Seeing triples now?* He counted: 'One, two . . . three.'

He decided to fall back on the elegance of logic and biology – the process of elimination.

Let us see, now. The tall fat one, Madrun, I know. As do I the tall skinny one, Lazan. That leaves the one in the middle who is neither as tall nor as fat nor as skinny as the other two. There we have it! Logic and biology clarify all issues.

He extended a gauze-wrapped finger towards the middle guard. 'And you are, what? A polyp? A bud? Has one of you reproduced?'

'Nay, Studlock,' the fat one boomed. 'What we have here is our first apprentice.'

First? Most alarming. 'Apprentice? Apprentice in what? Guarding?'

'Our philosophy and concomitant way of life,' Lazan explained.

Ah, there you have it. All is clear now. 'Very good.' He examined the newcomer: wide loose pantaloons ballooning down to tight high leather boots. A wide gold sash over a loose silk shirt of the brightest verdant green. Studious knew himself no reliable judge of expressions and emotions, but it appeared to him as if the man standing before him was a touch embarrassed.

'Dressed appropriately, I see,' Studious commented, hoping to set him at ease. 'Now. I have instructions for you from the Mistress. Please pay due attention and enact due diligence.'

'Of course,' Madrun assured him smoothly. 'We are all seriousness.'

And the man's face is straight as he says this – humorous byplay perhaps? How quaint.

'Attend now, please.'

*

In the Eldra Iron Mongers in the far west of the city a man stood watching from the highest window of the old manor house. Leaning closer to the dirty glazing, he rubbed an even filthier rag over the glass then hunched, peering. Through the rippled glazing the bursts of munitions reached him like flashes of fireworks during any one of the many religious festivals – fireworks ironically supplied by

535

the Moranth. Beneath the barrage a broad pale dome flickered and winked in and out of sight.

Even at this great distance the window shuddered and rattled lightly.

He glanced to the card he held. So ancient. The Orb of Rulership. A white sphere held upraised in the hand of a cloaked figure.

He squeezed the card until the varnish cracked and shattered.

He only wanted to be safe. He only wanted the city to be strong. How could he have been so blind?

*

Rallick was already on the roof when the assault began. For this reason he had mixed feelings regarding the Moranth's failure to penetrate the Legate's sorcerous defences. In either case, he felt that he had the best seat in the house, as they say, standing out on the roof peering up at the blinding eruptions where the munitions struck the clear opalescent wall of the Legate's dome.

He blamed those blasts for his own failure to sense the approach of light slippered feet, and his failure to twist aside soon enough to completely avoid the blades that thrust for his back.

He rolled away but not quickly enough as blazing agony yammered down his back. He faced her now across the run of tiles, his own heavier curved blades out. She advanced, darting in and out. They tested each other's skill, she stepping lightly with a hungry smile at her lips; he slower, careful on the sloped and shifting ceramic roof tiles.

'You were a fool to return,' she shouted over the blasts that rocked them in flashing chiaroscuro.

He said nothing, tensed, waiting for her commit herself.

He did not have long to wait. She dodged in, feinting side to side, both blades spinning. A run of alternating high and low slashes backed Rallick up to the side of a gable. Here he pushed off, kicking her in the chest, throwing her back two steps. Her face betrayed open shock.

Rallick allowed himself an inward smile. Those slippered tracks at Baruk's: small but heavy. He'd struck her with all his weight, treating her like an infantryman. Her reaction told him not many ever had.

Her lips pulled back from her small pointed teeth and she readied again, raising her arms high, both blades pointing down. Rallick shuffled away from the gable to clear his retreat. Multiple shadows flashed across them and waves of concussive force popped his ears. 'There are greater threats,' he yelled, motioning to the circling Moranth.

'Their turn will come,' she answered.

Time to surprise her again, he decided, and rushed. He was right: she was taken off guard. Yet every swing was met by a parrying blade, every spin and slash avoided, every thrust turned or slid aside. His charge ended when a circling counter-parry threw one of his blades wide, opening him to a thrust he avoided only by falling backwards.

He righted himself on the narrow level run along the spine of the roof, now rather surprised himself.

'Ready?' the girl asked, grinning.

Despite the agony shooting up his back he crouched, blades out.

The girl daintily slipped a foot forward on the tiled run. To either the steep roof led down to a fall from the height of the Great Hall.

Rallick braced a foot behind, determined not to give ground this time.

She closed the distance in one leap. Blades clashed, scraping and rebounding again and again in a weaving dance of strike and immediate counter-strike until suddenly the girl pushed herself backwards. She snarled her frustration, her thin chest heaving.

'Enough,' she grated, and thrust out a hand.

A wave of pressure washed over Rallick: something like a strong wind or a splash of cold water. It passed on, leaving him untouched. The girl gaped at him. 'How . . .'

He lunged and his blade caught her front, slashing scarves and flesh as she twisted sideways, slipping and tumbling down the roof. She bellowed, spat and hissed all the way down the slope until she disappeared over the edge.

Rallick hunched his shoulders and winced at the pain slashing into his back. He knew that that was certainly not the end of the creature. Under the cover of an eave he knelt and untied a pouch, pulling out a shallow dish that contained a thick honey-like salve. This he scooped up in his hand and, reaching behind under his leather jerkin and shirting, rubbed into the warm wetness smeared there.

Almost immediately the pain lost its cut-glass sharpness and his breath came more easily. Some would think it ironic, he knew, using the alchemist's offerings while engaged in a battle against him. Rallick wondered whether the term *just* was more appropriate. He remembered using another alchemical product on a rather similar night a long time ago: dust of the magic-deadening mineral otataral. And on both nights it saved his life.

*

They circled high above the complex of Majesty Hall, over the flickering dome that so far seemed to have absorbed every munition dropped upon it. So tightly did they circle that Torvald sat sideways while the wide waist straps of the saddle harness held him tight. Below, the majority of the swooping quorls continued their runs. Blasting up to meet them came the magics of these mage-slaves who the Moranth claimed served the returned Tyrant himself. Torvald had a hard time accepting that, but what he had witnessed so far this night convinced him that *something* terrible had happened – perhaps deals had been struck with these mages themselves. Exactly what, he didn't know for certain yet.

Ducking down from the wind he peered into the packs. 'Last one!' he called to Galene.

She nodded and adjusted the jesses. They swooped anew and Torvald was thrown backwards, scraping his lower back yet again against the sharp cantle behind. The flashing pale glow of the sorcerous dome rose up to meet them.

Directly over the top Galene shouted, 'Now!'

Leaning even further over he let the last cusser go. He twisted in his saddle to follow its tumbling descent. It erupted in yet another empty blast against the opalescent curve of the dome. The pressure wave pushed the quorl sideways, slapping him and Galene over for an instant. She fought again to regain control.

'What now?' he called.

She turned back to regard him through her narrow visor. 'Now? Now we land, Councillor!'

Torvald's stomach twisted mores sharply than it had all evening.

They swooped low over the estate district, weaving between lesser hills topped by noble family manors. The coruscating counterattacks of the mages blasted over them. Quorls fell over the city, either spinning tightly or limp like dead weights, to fall in bursts of light and erupting debris of broken brick and shattered wood. He caught glimpses of pockets of fire raging through the city. Thank all the gods the lamps hadn't been lit.

'You have a quick-release,' Galene shouted. 'Pull it and jump when we land.'

'Yes,' he answered, though he had no idea what he would do after that. Re-join the council was what Galene had suggested.

She began her run, angling for Majesty Hill, jerking the quorl from side to side, rolling and swooping. Torvald gripped the sunken handles with hands almost numb. The ribbed thorax of the insectile beast was hot beneath him; the poor thing was probably worn out and couldn't have carried them much further anyway.

Galene had started to climb when an invisible fist struck them. The air exploded from him in a wet grunt. Galene's helmed head struck him in the chest. For an instant his vision went black. When he could see again they were spinning sickeningly. Galene yanked the jesses but the quorl responded only fitfully, wings hardly fluttering.

'Hang on!' she yelled.

The slope of the hill came up suddenly and they struck it a glancing blow, then slid backwards down the slope. They came to rest in a grassy parkland between the hill and the city wall.

Torvald pulled his quick-release and fell from the saddle. 'Let's go!'

Galene remained slumped in the saddle. He reached round to pull her release then dragged her down to lie in the tall grass.

'Galene!'

She moved her arms listlessly. When they had struck she had obviously taken the brunt and thereby protected him from most of it. Her poor mount was clearly dying.

The bursts and pressure waves thumping his chest lessened. He peered up to see more and more of the circling quorls now swooping down. They alighted for only the briefest pause while both riders jumped from them, and then took off again to flit away far more nimbly than they had come.

They promised a full assault. The munitions failed; now comes the old-fashioned push.

Heaving Galene up by an arm, he headed to a set of rickety stairs that climbed the slope. A sort of servants' access.

*

Jan stood with Iralt, Fifteenth, near the main front entrance of Majesty Hall, watching the circling Moranth. Personally, Jan marvelled at the accomplishments of these people: their alchemical researches, their taming, breeding, and training of their insectile mounts. An extraordinary race. A pity their ambitions and those of Darujhistan clashed. But then, is that not always the way between any two ascendant peoples?

He could not help but flinch as closer blasts sent invisible shock waves punching his chest. Now he knew something of what Gall had endured. A completely one-sided slaughter. Shameful, some of his brothers and sisters called it. But he did not share that view. Why submit to an opponent's strengths? If at all possible one must work to avoid them.

As they did now, waiting beneath the protection of the Legate's sorcery. Too bad such protection could not be removed.

The bursts lessened. The riders appeared to have exhausted their munitions.

Failure, Iralt signed. *We have won.*

No, Jan signed. *They will come at us soon.*

An assault? Iralt gestured her surprise. *Surely not. They know us – they would not be so foolish.*

Do not dismiss the enemy, Jan chided. *They are brave. Remember: a challenging opponent is a blessing to one's skill.*

Iralt bowed her head. *Thank you, Second.*

'Go now. Warn for readiness.'

Iralt ran from his side. Jan raised his mask to the circling riders, the explosions few and far between now. *So, they will land and we will win this engagement. But the war?* He looked to the great unprotected spread of the city below and the fires glowing in nearby precincts. As to the war, he knew it was already lost.

Above, a massed flight of the quorl mounts came diving in upon them.

Ah. Now it is our turn.

*

'What's that?' Yusek asked as something caught her eye from the north: a flickering and winking of lights. Like nothing she'd ever seen before. The Seventh halted, suddenly immobile. Everyone stopped as well. Then she heard it: a thunderous murmur as of a storm far away.

They were passing through another town beyond the walls and people were leaning out of upper storey windows peering at the night sky.

'A summer storm over the lake?' she wondered aloud.

'No,' the Seventh grated. 'Another kind of storm. We'll head on to Worry Town.'

Yusek was outraged. '*What?* Aren't we going in?'

'Eventually.' He headed off, striking a quicker pace.

Sall and Lo, she saw, shared a long look but followed without dispute.

She fell in next to Sall, whispered, 'What's going on?'

He answered, just as quietly, 'I believe it is fighting.'

'Fighting? Who?'

'I – should not say yet.'

Oh, this is just great! I finally get to Darujhistan only there's some kinda damned war on? Just my Twins-cursed luck! I mean, why does everything have to happen to me?

*

Spindle paused in his frantic digging. Straightening, he peered up over the lip of his and Fisher's uneven pit. He glanced to the night sky, squinting. *Yeah – looks like they've thrown the lot. Question is, what's next?*

'What is it?' Fisher whispered.

'Winding down. Gotta hurry.'

He returned to thrusting his shovel into the dirt. Good thing they'd dug here already; the backfill was nice and loose. Moments later a distant staccato popping snapped Spindle's head up again. *Sharpers?*

He peered round, keeping his eyes just over the dirt surface. He saw some way off in the grounds a flight of quorls come diving in to land and Moranth throw themselves from the saddles, unslinging heavy shields and forming small squares. In ones and twos Seguleh ran to engage with them.

Spindle flinched as salvos of tossed sharpers lacerated the charging Seguleh; but those that made it through wrought havoc among the squares.

Shit! This is not good. Not good at all. Things are gettin' too crowded by far.

He returned to his digging.

'What *are* you doing?' a girl's voice called down to them.

The hair on Spindle's neck and all across his shirt stirred and straightened at that voice. *Oh, Togg take it!* He rose, taking hold of one of the bottles as he did so and holding it behind his back. Fisher moved to help conceal the motion. He found himself staring at a damned dancing girl; one who'd been in a fight, it seemed, as her wispy clothes were slashed down the front and speckled with blood. She arched a brow at him and her come-to-me lips lifted into an amused smirk.

Her Warren swirled around her in an aural storm that nearly

blinded Spindle's mage-sight. *Inhuman. No youth could possibly be this strong. Like a damned High Mage, this one is.*

'Ah – maintenance,' he offered.

Her carmine-tinged eyes shifted, searching the pit and beyond. 'There's a witch here. I sense her. Sworn to Ardata, perhaps?'

Uh-oh, Ma's gettin' her hair up.

'Leave while you can, child,' Fisher said suddenly.

Her brow wrinkled, bemused. 'What?'

'Twelve their fell number,' he sang as if reciting, 'dragged and chained from Abyss's deepest pits.'

Her gaze slitted on him. 'Who *are* you?'

Spindle pulled the cork from the bottle and held it out. 'Don't make me use this!'

She stared, frowning. A girlish giggle escaped her. 'Is the wine that bad here?'

As an answer he shook a splash on to the roots and grass at her feet. Smoke fumed and a hissing seared the air. The girl flinched an involuntary step away. 'You wouldn't dare!'

He threatened her with the bottle. 'I don't want to – but I will! I mean it.'

She glared an inhuman fury. Her eyes flared as if aflame and she hissed a snarling gurgle of frustrated rage.

Spindle jerked the bottle, splashing more of the corroding chemical.

At that she spun blurring to disappear into her daemonic Warren.

Fisher, at his side, let out a long low breath. Spindle nodded his sincere agreement. They returned to their digging.

＊

High Priestess of Shadow Sordiko Qualm sat cross-legged on her bed, elbows on knees and chin in her hands, intently studying the silk hangings that enclosed the broad four-poster as a wind passed through the chamber, causing the candles on the far walls to cast flickering shadows across the rippling cloth. Within these shifting shadows images and vistas seemed to form spontaneously, only to dissolve away almost instantly as she watched.

From the open window came hammering and flashes as of a summer thunderstorm.

Screams pulled her attention from the shifting hangings and she blinked, shaking her head. The play of shadows dispersed like shredding gauze. She drew a long curved knife from under a pillow, its blade so darkly blued as to be almost invisible, and padded from her chamber, barefoot, her silk shift so thin as to be nearly, well, invisible too.

The inner temple was crowded with men. The priestesses had retreated to the walls, cowering. Sordiko spotted Seguleh and Malazans among the crowd.

'What is the meaning of this invasion?' she cried.

The twenty or so men all looked at her. The expressions on the faces she could see changed from suspicion and confusion to something much more familiar in Sordiko's experience. She became conscious of her rather inadequate dress. 'Have you a spokesman?'

'Aye, I suppose.' A Malazan pushed forward, short, red moustache, looking like he'd just been dragged through an entire campaign; in fact, they all looked as though they'd just finished a siege that they'd lost. 'This is Darujhistan?'

'Yes. Temple to Shadow.' She raised her chin and threw back her shoulders, demanding: 'What is your business here?'

The men stared. Several let out long sighs. 'I'm joinin' Shadow,' one murmured to his neighbour.

The moustached soldier found his voice: 'We, ah – we're . . .' He raised a hand for silence. 'What's that noise?'

Sordiko nodded to him. 'War, Malazan. The Legate has called the Seguleh and now they and the Moranth make war upon each other as in ancient times. Only now the city is caught between.'

'Legate?' one shouted, stepping forward. Youngest of them, Darujhistani by his tattered clothes and the style of his weapon. In fact . . . she squinted. 'You are of the Lim family?'

'Yes. Corien.'

'I'm sorry, Corien, but your cousin . . .'

The Seguleh started for the main exit. A priestess blocked it, shouting, 'The High Priestess has not given you leave!'

The lead Seguleh, one of the Twenty by his mask, cocked his head towards Sordiko in a silent question. She waved the priestess aside. *Unreasonable bastards.* They marched out. All of the rest of the ragtag wretches followed. *Dammit!* 'You, Malazans! Your troops are west of the city! You three others – who are you? There's something strange about you! Come back!'

The doors gaped open until attending priestesses slammed and barred them. Sordiko set her fists to her hips. *How do you like that? First time so many men have ever walked out on me . . .*

The streets were jammed with citizenry all attempting to flee at once and therefore unable to flee anywhere because the way was choked. From the steps to the temple to Shadow, Antsy glimpsed a strange darkness that hung over the city, and above this, the circling quorls, and the munitions punishing the hilltop Majesty Hall. An immense opalescent dome shimmered over the hilltop. The Seguleh seemed to be making straight for the hill. The crowds screamed and flinched aside, leaving them clear passage. Antsy urged Corien onward. 'C'mon!'

'We're headin' west,' Sergeant Girth shouted. 'Ain't our fight. Gonna get yourself kilt!'

Antsy waved the man off. *Miserable bastard. Save his skin and that's the thanks I get. Well, his duty is to get his troops back safe. Fair enough, then.*

The Heels marched with him and Corien. They had huge grins pasted to their faces and peered about like country hicks, nudging one another and pointing at buildings as if this was one big night out. Trailing along in the wake of the Seguleh they all made good time. *And just what do you plan to do, Antsy? 'Cept maybe get your fool head blown off. Still, these boys and girls had been on a mission. And now they're charging for their fellows. Something's definitely up.*

*

A richly appointed carriage careered its way down one of the switchback roads of the Third Tier escarpment. Four panicked horses drew it. The coachman whipped them between terrified glances over his shoulder to Majesty Hill, where bursts of light made him flinch and an accompanying rumbling shook the carriage beneath him.

They roared down the road sending pedestrians fleeing for the walls. 'Out of the way!' the coachman bellowed. 'Clear way for Lord Pal'ull! Clear way!'

And all the citizenry did dart aside. The carriage swung round a sharp corner, iron rims striking sparks from the flint cobbles, horses' hooves clattering. A further stretch of jammed pedestrians jumped for the walls – all but for one very tall fellow coming up against the flow.

'*Clear!*' the coachman bellowed. Then his eyes widened and he dropped the whip to yank the reins aside. The horses plunged to the right and passed the tall armoured figure, but the carriage swung sideways and slammed into him in an eruption of splintering wood and bending, wrenching iron. The coachman was thrown from his seat over the road wall while the horses continued down the way, dragging the shattered fore-section of the carriage behind them in a shower of trailing sparks and falling splinters.

The armoured figure, bright reflections flashing from it in emerald and sapphire, hadn't shifted a fraction. It lifted one heavy foot to crunch down on the broken wreckage, snapping and flattening the siding. Lord and Lady Pal'ull lay unconscious amid the remains. It walked on without pause, crushing all the debris in its way.

After the great lumbering armoured figure had passed the citizenry descended on the wreckage in a looting horde. Ten minutes later all that remained at the scene was shattered wood and an unconscious lord and lady in their linen underclothes.

*

Aragan adjusted his seat on his mount – his arse was getting numb. He was still waiting next to Fist K'ess. A short time ago several quorls had come flitting overhead, twin saddles empty. Some limped along on damaged wings, hardly able to stay aloft. A few came soaring down out of the night sky in a sort of controlled fall to land out of sight without any sound of their crash.

He and K'ess shared looks of dread. Fearsome though the Moranth may be, both had hoped it wouldn't come to this. K'ess had offered marines for the assault but Aragan had vetoed the suggestion. They'd lost enough troops against the Seguleh; no need to lose more. They were the outsiders here. This was an ancient feud. One this Legate had reopened – perhaps to his short-lived regret. Or so Aragan hoped.

Regardless, he would watch and report. And far away, across Seeker's Deep, Command at Unta would then adjust Imperial strategy accordingly . . .

A deep murmuring rose to his attention. It hummed in his ears like a shaking of the earth. Standing water in the fields rippled as if vibrating. Aragan turned in his saddle, along with many others, peering about for the source of the penetrating din.

Then the light changed. Something intervened in the night sky between the glowing bright green Scimitar and the ground. He squinted up to look. A cloud. A wide dark cloud sweeping in from the west.

The murmuring swelled to a deafening thrumming that drowned out all other sounds. Aragan hunched beneath the punishing noise, as did K'ess and others all around. Peering up, he caught the cloud of glimmering wings. Each quorl now carried only one rider, but from every saddle hung fat double panniers fore and aft.

Aragan turned a glare on Torn. 'What is this?' he shouted.

'The alternative,' calmly answered Torn.

'Give the assault a chance!'

'We are. We await the signal.'

'Signal? What signal?'

'Success or failure.'

Aragan thrust a hand to the city. 'Gods, man! Give them time to offer terms, or call a truce!'

Torn shook a slow negative. 'There will be no terms from the Tyrant. We know him of old.'

'Torn, be careful here. You could be opening a blood-feud that will soak all these lands!'

'So it was in the old days, Malazan,' Torn answered, steel in his voice. 'The lands of Pale were once ours. We had colonies in the lowlands. Where are they now, I ask you! Annihilated. Such are *his* terms.'

Aragan opened his mouth but no words would come. And above the quorls circled, waiting, a thrumming drone promising a cataclysm of destruction for the unsuspecting city beyond. *Mortal enemies, each determined to utterly crush the other. No quarter. No survival for the fallen. These stakes are far too high. And we Malazans, outsiders, no more than impotent witnesses? Yet what can we do? What are our options? Soliel look away! Is there nothing we can do?*

CHAPTER XX

Of thy bones they have made a seat;
They have taken the orbs of thine eyes
Yet it is they who are blind

Warning carved on tomb entrance,
Dwelling Plain

T HE WOODEN STAIRCASE LEFT TORVALD AT THE REAR OF THE
rambling buildings. Paths nearby led through a slim belt of
woods and courts that encircled the top of Majesty Hill. He
half walked, half dragged the wounded Galene through the park-
like strip. It looked as though she'd twisted or broken her leg in the
crash. The blasts and echoing reverberations shook him rarely now;
through the trees he glimpsed quorls diving in to deposit their riders.
He knew that somewhere Seguleh were waiting and he dreaded what
would happen should he run into any now. But then, neither of them
had weapons drawn so he imagined at worst they'd only be captured.

His fears played out when they rounded a curve and he saw two
Seguleh standing where major paths crossed. He stopped abruptly,
his shoulders falling. One calmly waved him forward. Galene
fumbled for her longsword but he pushed her hand aside. 'No point,'
he murmured.

'I have one munition,' she whispered, reaching to her opposite side.

'No!' *They'd just kill us.* 'It's too late.'

'I won't allow myself—'

The Seguleh spun aside raising their weapons as heavy armoured
feet came pounding up another path. A column of Black Moranth
charged: the first two held their wide shields up and threw something from behind. Galene yanked Torvald down.

He fell; she yelped her pain as she bent her wounded leg.

Multiple blasts buffeted him and gravel came pattering down all around. When he raised his head he glimpsed the Moranth finishing off the stunned and lacerated Seguleh. Even then there was a ferocious exchange of blows and three Moranth were wounded.

Hands raised him and Galene. 'We saw you go down,' one Black said to her, 'and came for you.' They took her from Torvald, one to each side.

'Take me to the main entrance,' she ordered, her voice tight with suppressed pain.

The party formed up around Torvald and Galene and they headed to the front of the rambling complex. In the distance the staccato blasts of sharpers came and went in great volleys that shook the night. They had not gone far when they caught a glimpse through the trees of the main approach, and Galene groaned at what was revealed.

The walkways and flagged open courts and benches had been turned into one huge killing zone littered with Moranth fallen. As they landed they had formed squares or circles of interlocking shields, yet despite barrages of sharpers and crossbow volleys Seguleh had won through to slice their way into the formations, wreaking terrible destruction before being cut down from all sides.

And to one side further defences awaited in the form of a tall mage, watching, staff at his side, seemingly content to let the fighting proceed in its own course – for the time being.

Galene straightened. 'We cannot win through,' Torvald heard her murmur. 'Yet he cannot be allowed to succeed. Cannot.' From a pouch at her side she drew a tube about the size of a baton enamelled a deep red. She turned her helmed head to him. 'I'm sorry, Councillor.'

Torvald eyed the tube, uncertain at first, then horror raised the hair on his arms and neck and he lunged for her. 'No!' A Black restrained him. 'Don't call it! Please don't summon them. Wait! Just wait. That is all I ask!'

'Very well, Councillor. For you, a moment.'

*

It looked to Spindle as though they were getting close; damned close. The depth looked right from what he remembered of the trench. So far they'd been ignored, as the Seguleh had much more immediate worries. Wave after wave of Moranth had landed, formed up, and made for the entrances to Majesty Hall, where they were met by the

Seguleh. So far, from what glimpses he could snatch, despite their munitions it looked as if the Moranth were coming off far the worse. That meant that for him and Fisher time was running out.

He straightened once more to toss a shovelful of dirt only to see a pair of sandalled feet on either side of the pit. He looked up: the feet belonged to two Seguleh who were peering down at them, swords pointed.

'Do not move,' one commanded.

Spindle glanced to Fisher who slowly straightened, shovel in hand.

'Explain this,' the Seguleh demanded.

Spindle opened his mouth to answer then gaped, shocked, and threw himself flat yelling: 'Down!'

Fisher fell immediately. The Seguleh only had time to turn before multiple eruptions blasted about the pit sending dirt flying. Spindle held his hands over his head as stones and clots of soil struck him. Fisher recovered first; he straightened, shaking his hair and brushing dirt from himself.

'What was that?' he demanded, speaking overly loud as everyone does after enduring blasts.

'Just a hit and run,' Spindle said, picking up his shovel. 'C'mon. We're almost there.'

But attention had been drawn; only one of the Seguleh had been taken down. The other had limped off, and now more were on their way. Spindle had barely scooped up the freshly fallen dirt when another two came jumping through the low brush to glare down at them.

'Out,' one ordered.

Spindle dropped his shovel and raised his hands. Fisher followed suit.

'Out!'

'Okay, okay!' Spindle reached up to the side.

A great war whoop erupted from the woods, freezing him; it sounded like a cross between a Barghast war bellow and a death scream. Even the Seguleh flinched. Then a huge multicoloured shape jumped the pit, two swords flashing, followed by another equally bizarre-looking fellow also wielding two swords. Even more astoundingly, they drove off the Seguleh in a dazzling coordinated attack of continuous multiple strikes.

Spindle stared open-mouthed at the astonishing apparition.

'Ha ha!' the huge one announced, waving his blades. 'That is how you do it!' He peered down at Spindle and Fisher. 'Well? Go ahead, you two – dig away!' He motioned across the pit and Spindle turned to see a third man standing there.

'Ah, yes,' the newcomer said, his voice nowhere near as loud as the huge one's. 'Dig.'

Half stunned, Spindle retrieved his shovel to set to it once more. Fisher, he saw, was shaking his head in disbelief as he worked. 'You know them?' Spindle asked.

'It's Madrun and Lazan Door is who it is.'

Spindle tossed a shovelful of dirt. 'I thought those were just stories,' he hissed.

'No – they're flesh and blood. As for what's attributed to them, well . . . some of that is my fault.'

*

At the main entrance Jan watched while more and more of the Moranth gathered. Their strategy was simple but effective. They formed into tight squares of shield-walls from behind which the rear ranks threw their munitions. And those munitions: like the punishing heavier ones used earlier, these too demonstrated a far greater killing capacity than those written of in their records.

It was to be expected, he allowed. Time had passed. The Moranth had gone their way just as the Seguleh had gone theirs.

So far they had held them off. But the cost had been horrific. Any one fallen brother or sister was too much for Jan to imagine. Yet now, before his disbelieving eyes, ten, twenty, lacerated and maimed by the salvos of munitions. Each bloody cut was a slash across his heart. Each fallen a name and a face well known: Toru, Sengal, Leah, Arras, Rhuk.

I am responsible for this. On my head lie their severed futures. Their lost potential. How many possible Seconds cut down before they could display their mastery?

How can I possibly atone for this? What act could even begin to repair the damage wrought?

All this he watched and his heart bled.

A runner arrived. She bowed her head, begging to speak, and Jan signed his permission. 'They have broken through in the eastern wing, Second. We were few there.'

'I see.' He nodded to Palla. 'Watch here. I will go.'

'Take at least five,' Palla urged.

'No. You must defend these doors. Only I need go.'

'But Second . . .'

550

'No. It is for me to answer this.' He set off before Palla could speak again. The runner followed.

Jan found the doors blasted open and another fallen; Por, the Thirteenth. Yet the price the Moranth paid to achieve this breach had been high. Their slain far exceeded the few defenders. He drew his blade and stole ahead as silently as he could. With each step he loosed the fisted hold he kept upon everything driven down within his blazing chest: his self-condemnation, his self-disgust, his rage, and above all the lacerating sorrow that threatened to suffocate him. Until at last he carried no awareness at all into the rear of the ranks before him.

Horul, of the Hundredth, quickly fell behind within the maze of rooms. The Second more than ran; he charged unchecked by numbers. He did not slow no matter how many faced him; driving, spinning, slashing until only the bellows and howls of wounded Moranth led her on. And at every turn, every room, the fallen. Each bearing only a single mortal wound either to neck or to artery or to nearly severed limb. They did not know what was coming, so swift was his advance. No chance to throw their munitions or form a defence. It seemed to her he passed through them like a breeze, utterly silent but for the hiss of his two-handed blade.

She found him standing motionless deep within the east wing; listening, perhaps. She carefully stepped over the carpet of fallen choking the room: some sort of last stand. Gore limned his sleeves and legs. Bright droplets spattered his once pure mask, like seeds on snow. He seemed completely unaware of her before him.

'Second,' she breathed, almost reverent. 'Second. Never had I ever imagined . . .'

Awareness suddenly flooded his gaze, but not before she glimpsed something naked and utterly unguarded that drove her eyes away. *Horror. Horror and soul-lashing pain.*

'I . . . live,' he uttered, wonder in his voice.

'Yes. You live.'

'Not . . . today, then.'

'No. Not today.'

'Tomorrow, then.' He eased a hand from his side, releasing at the same time a hiss of suppressed pain. Horul glimpsed a penetrating thrust. His despairing smile made her turn her mask away again.

'Second!'

'Bind it, Horul,' he managed through clenched lips. 'Bind it tight.'

Now that the last of the crowd of councillors, aristocrats and court functionaries had all long since fled, the Great Hall was quiet. Scorch and Leff stood watch leaning up against the rear of one of the fat columns that ran along a wall. All was hushed now; the pounding had faded away. Only the laboured breathing and occasional muted sobs of that miserable Mouthpiece broke the silence of the hall. But listening, his head cocked, Leff could make out the distant clash of fighting.

Scorch turned to him, even more anxious and confused than usual. Then he sent a meaningful glance to a nearby exit. Leff shook his head. Scorch glared, demanding an explanation.

His voice as low as possible, Leff whispered: 'You don't really think anyone's gonna get through all them Seguleh, do ya?'

Scorch's expressive brows rose and he gave a great show of the light dawning. He winked. 'Right. What now?'

Leff hefted his crossbow. 'Well, now we gotta guard, don't we? Up to us. Last line o' defence and such.'

Scorch nodded towards the hall. 'Maybe we should, y' know, take a look . . . ?'

'Right. You go ahead.'

'Me?' Scorch ducked his head. He whispered sotto voce: 'Why me? You go – you're senior 'n' all.'

'No I ain't. Equals we are. Same rank.' He urged Scorch out. 'G'wan.'

Cursing under his breath, Scorch edged around the column. He stepped out, leaning to peer at the throne. 'Still there,' he whispered. 'Hasn't moved a muscle.'

'Fine. Good. All's . . .' Leff's voice faded away as he peered closely at Scorch. 'Wait a minute. What's that?'

'What's what?'

In the doorway, Palla ducked flying stone chips from an errant throw. She waved aside the obscuring smoke to study the blasted grounds dotted with fallen, and the Moranth squares pushing for the walls. Then she scanned the night sky, now empty of quorls.

'I believe that is all of them,' she called to Shun, the Eighteenth.

'How many?'

'I cannot be certain. Perhaps a thousand.'

'Then we have won. These last few we will finish off.'

552

'Still, they have taken too many with them.'

'It was their gamble. They—'

A dull brown blade smeared in gore erupted from the Eighteenth's chest and was withdrawn almost before Palla had registered that it was there. She leapt backwards an instant before it slashed again, striking shards of stone from where she had just been standing. As Shun fell a walking horror was revealed behind him in the doorway: carious face of dried sinew and skull brown with age, broken remnants of hide and bone armour, limbs of bare bone strung with ligaments and creaking flesh, legs oddly mismatched.

Ancestors give me strength! Imass!

'Attend!' Palla shouted, backing away as she parried sweep after sweep of the wide flint sword.

Three others of the Hundredth charged. Blows rocked the Imass in a flurry of bone chips, sliced rotten hide and bits of cured flesh, and still it came on. A downward sweep taken full on the edge of one Seguleh's sword shattered the blade and knocked the bearer to crash against a wall and slump unconscious.

Still Palla yielded ground one hard-fought step at a time. Each overbearing attack she slipped as obliquely as she dared, feeling her blade shudder and flex on the cusp of failing in her hands. Another of the Hundredth lunged close as the creature appeared to waver, but the Imass snatched the youth's arm and propelled him into a pillar to smack wetly and fall.

'It's not you I want,' it ground out. 'Stand aside.'

The third Hundredth took the opportunity to leap swinging a great blow to the creature's neck. The blade chopped but caught. The half fleshless skull atop canted but did not topple. Palla halted her own lunge as the Imass seized the lad under the chin and lifted him from the floor it knocked the blade from its neck.

How can I save the poor lad? What could I possibly . . .

Inspiration came. Palla offered the long deep bow of the ancient form, hands out from her sides. Then she struck the most traditional of the *ready* stances.

'Your challenge is accepted.'

The Imass stilled. A second later it tossed the lad through an open doorway, where he landed amid furniture. 'What is your rank?'

'Sixth.'

'Sixth? I met the First. Long ages ago. Then I wouldn't have dared face any of the champions. Let us see how things proceed

– now that I have had ample time to practise.' It grasped the naked flint tang of its sword in both bone and sinew hands, and advanced.

*

The whirling storms that scattered Ebbin's consciousness to the furthest corners of his mind had receded. And all his memories came crashing in at once, bringing with them the horrifying awareness of all that had happened caused by *him*. The one small stone he dislodged and the avalanche it precipitated. And so he wept. Arms wrapped around his head he sobbed, abject.

You see, the voice whispered within his mind, *The favour I do you? Ignorance is a blessing.*

Stung, Ebbin moved to scuttle off on all fours.

In his mind a hand clutched his neck. The monstrosity straddled him, gold mask turned to study the roiling clouds. 'Let me go!' Ebbin pleaded. 'You're finished!'

'Nay. I have won. The Moranth are defeated. They cannot touch me.'

'Your attack failed!'

'True,' the creature allowed. 'That was . . . impetuous. But live and learn, yes, scholar? I will bide my time.'

'No – you are lost. You're revealed for what you are.'

'And what is that, dear scholar?'

'A monster nightmare of our childhood.'

The hand released his neck. The Tyrant stepped away from him. Mocking laughter rose from behind the graven gold oval. The embossed lips seemed to drip it. 'Oh, scholar. If you only knew.' The mask snapped away. 'Enemies gather . . . but not the one I was expecting. Of course, the same may be said for me. We will continue this discussion later, scholar.'

The figure swirled away, but Ebbin's awareness remained. He groaned and held his head once more.

*

'There. That thing. In your crossbow.'

Scorch lifted the weapon to take a look. 'What? Nothing.'

'No – the . . .' Exasperated, Leff stepped out to tap the stock. 'Look at that bolt. Where'd you get that?'

Scorch stared. His mouth opened in amazement. 'Would you look at that!'

Leff cuffed him. 'Keep it down,' he hissed, fierce. 'Where'd you get it? You holding out on me?'

'I ain't never seen it afore in all my life! I promise.'

'You stole it, didn't ya?'

'What? Never.'

'Well – we need to give it back. Got our position to think about. Can't be wavin' stolen goods about.'

Unnoticed, the Legate stood to step down from his throne. He stopped before it, hands clasped behind his back.

Leff grabbed the stock. 'Look at that thing. All engraved. Wax on the head, too – real fancy, that. Gotta give it back.'

'No – let go. Don't . . .' Scorch knocked one of Leff's hands aside. Leff tried twisting the weapon from his partner's grip.

'Just cooperate! Let me . . .'

'Watch it!' Scorch hissed. 'Don't . . .'

The crossbow fired, jerking in their four hands.

The bolt slammed into the Legate, who spun round with the force of the impact.

Four eyes swivelled to see the Legate straightening. He touched at the feathered end of the bolt where it stood from his ribs. The mask turned their way. A hand stretched out to them.

Scorch and Leff looked at one another, eyes hugely wide at the enormity of the accident. And at the magnitude of their immediate danger.

'Fire!' they yelled in unison and Leff levelled his crossbow, noticing in passing that an identical bolt sat snugly in the channel of his stock. He aimed and fired while Scorch slipped a foot through the stirrup of his weapon and yanked ferociously.

Leff's bolt threw the Legate back another step. His knees appeared to weaken briefly as he staggered. Yet he came on. Smoke streamed from the two wounds.

'Fire!' Leff bawled again and Scorch levelled his weapon. The third bolt struck true, thumping the Legate backwards a good few weaving steps.

Leff reached into the sack at his side and was briefly surprised to see that every single one of the bolts he possessed had intricately engraved blackened shafts and gleaming iron heads encased in wax. None of this stopped him from frantically reloading.

'He's still comin' for us!' Scorch yelled, nearly bursting into tears.

'Fire 'em all!' Leff howled.

Lady Envy left a second-storey terrace overlooking the front battle-grounds. Tapping her fingertips together she crossed the abandoned darkened office. *So, an Imass. Never cared for them. Smelly unkempt things always leaving bits of themselves lying about.* She cocked her head, thinking. *Been ages since I destroyed one of them.*

She remembered impertinences recently suffered from one Imass in particular and her mouth hardened. *Yes . . . too long by far.*

She headed for the stairs.

Yet something whispered from the dark drew her to a pause. A presence. *Someone's there. In the shadows.* 'Who is it?'

'Envy.'

The barest whisper from the night.

She raised her defences. Her Warren crackled, sending papers flying and bursting into flame around her. 'Who's there! I demand that you show yourself!'

'*Still afraid of the dark, Envy?*'

That voice! So familiar. Who? 'Who are you?' she called, tentative now, a hand at her throat.

'*With reason!*'

A flash of munitions lit the room, and in a freeze-frame instant revealed a tall man all in black. Face, eyes and hair all black. Envy backed away, her hand at her mouth, and gasped choking and stammering, 'Father . . . !'

And she fainted dead away.

*

One of the Moranth guarding Galene gestured, pointing through the woods, and Torvald joined in squinting at the nearest building corner. There one of the mages had been standing – the hunched, oddly proportioned one – and now while they watched he was down on all fours attempting to get up, clutching at his chest.

'There! Look there!' Torvald hissed. He almost reached out for the Moranth Silver. 'Something's happening.'

The red tube still in her gauntleted fist, Galene shifted her attention.

The mage managed to straighten but fell backwards against the wall. Panting, in obvious agony, he hugged his chest as if he would burst. Then he disappeared.

'There!' Torvald exclaimed. 'See that! We've won!'

'Contain yourself, Councillor,' Galene said. She gestured to one of her guards. 'Check in with the wing commanders. What's going on?'

The Black trooper ran off through the woods.

*

Up hall after hall they duelled. The heavy flint sword was blur in the hands of the tireless Imass. Palla retreated step by step, yielding, slipping all blows, leaving countless gashes across the fleshless ribs and skull and hacking apart rotting furs. She struck for the joints, hoping to sever ligaments and cripple the creature, not knowing if it was even possible.

But she was tiring. Her reactions were slowing. The weakness of complete exhaustion now stood between what she wanted to do and what she could. She knew she would fall; it was merely a question of when and how.

It came unseen in the form of a closing feint from the creature, a stunning elbow to her temple and a choking grip on her neck. Blinking, Palla found herself staring into two empty eye sockets where only a low glow simmered, like distant campfires.

'You would have beaten me, Sixth,' the Imass growled, slamming her into a stone door and releasing her to fall, 'had I been alive.'

The Imass walked on.

*

Rallick watched from a window high up in the Great Hall while the two guards hammered bolt after bolt into the Legate. Then he watched them throw down their crossbows and run. Amazingly, the creature still stood. It must have fifteen bolts in it yet it remained upright. It leaned now bracing itself with one arm against a pillar.

Rallick raised the coiled fine silk rope ready to toss it down when out of the shadows came that shuffling servant, the Mouthpiece, and he knelt flat once more. The fellow came edging out the way a mouse might circle a crippled cat.

'You are done!' the Mouthpiece yelled, a fist raised. Then he flinched. 'How can you say that? It *is* over! It *is*!' The fellow was frantic with emotion, weeping uncontrollably. He backed away. 'Flee? Me? Go? Why? Why would they kill me? I have done nothing! Nothing!'

Then he jumped as if seeing something terrifying. His hands flew to his throat and chest. 'No!' he breathed, appalled. 'No – they wouldn't. They mustn't! Dear Soliel succour me . . . no!'

He fled from the chamber.

557

After a moment the Legate straightened from the pillar. The mask lowered as he seemed to inspect the many crossbow bolts studding his torso and the thin wisps of smoke arising from each wound. What could only be described as a muted chuckle shook him. The creature gestured to himself as if to say: *yet here I am!* And he laughed on and on behind the gold mask.

Rallick eased away from the open window ledge and pulled himself up to the roof again. Crouching, he brushed the tips of his fingers over his lips for a time, eyes narrowed, and came to a decision. He stuffed the coil of rope down his shirt and padded off along the roof, heading for the maze of mismatched gables and slopes of the complex.

Down in the Great Hall the main doors opened. The Legate turned to face them then rocked backwards, obviously shocked. An Imass strode within. The Legate backed away, hands raised. The Imass closed with astonishing speed on its oddly shaped legs, clasped hold of the Legate and raised its flint sword.

'Now I take your head, Jaghut,' it growled.

Then it stilled, hands falling. What dried muscle and flesh remained on its ravaged visage twisted as it frowned its uncertainty. It lowered its fleshless mien to the gold mask as if inspecting the workmanship. A low rumble shook the sinews and bone of its torso. It's jaws shifted in something like disgust. 'Faugh! Human!' It threw the Legate down and stalked from the chamber.

At the doors it met Palla, staggering towards the throne room, but it passed on ignoring her and Palla paid it no attention as its broad flint weapon was now tucked into the twisted hair rope it wore as a belt. She took in the crossbow-bolt-studded form of the Legate lying supine on the floor, and fled.

After a time the Legate managed to roll on to his side and lever himself upright. He staggered for the doors, one heavy step at a time. All the while his crossbow-bolt lanced chest convulsed in what may have been silent laughter.

The doors to the Great Hall slammed shut. The Legate pulled up short. He turned in a slow weaving and shuffling circle to scan the chamber.

Kruppe stepped out from behind the nearest pillar. He slicked back his oiled hair and adjusted his frilled shirt cuffs and crimson waistcoat. Then he made a great show of waving a handkerchief in a rather too elaborate courtier's bow. 'Never did Kruppe imagine he would be called to court!'

The Legate lunged for him.

Kruppe twisted and narrowly avoided one grasping hand. 'Come, then, Legate. Let us dance again!' Another catching hand swung, missing a sleeve by a breath. Kruppe dodged aside. 'Nearly!' he encouraged. 'Come. This way.' He waved the handkerchief. 'It strikes Kruppe that the problem with masks is one of seeing clearly.'

The Legate snapped out a clawed hand; cloth tore as Kruppe backed away. 'Oh my!'

*

'Pay-dirt!' Spindle announced, sitting back from where he'd cleared a patch of dirt from the bottom of the pit. Fisher crouched down. It was a mud-smeared flat white surface. Together they cleared as wide a space as possible.

'Hurry, my friends,' called one of their protectors from above. Spindle glanced up to see the man's gold and silver teeth bright against his face in a gleaming smile. 'We are attracting too much attention.'

'What? You? Attract attention?'

But the man was gone and the rapid clash of swordplay sounded from all sides of the pit. Spindle caught Fisher's eye and nodded to the bottles.

Together they uncorked two and upended them. Neither was prepared for the reaction that instantly engulfed them.

*

Palla met Jan at the main entrance. She groaned inwardly at his blood-spattered condition. Upon catching sight of her he demanded: 'What has happened? Where is this Imass?'

Palla waved her battered state aside. 'It is gone. It killed the Legate.'

'*What?* He is dead?'

'Or near it.'

'Why would it . . .' The Second turned away to the grounds; Palla thought he moved awkwardly, as if stiff. 'Recall everyone. Retreat to the inner halls.'

Palla bowed. 'As you order.' She ran for the open doors.

Jan turned a puzzled glance up the wide entrance foyer, and headed for the Great Hall.

Great roiling choking clouds drove the Seguleh from the pit. The smoke gnawed the tissue of the nose and seared the lungs. Coughing and gagging, Madrun, Lazan and Thurule backed away.

'They have been consumed!' Madrun announced, hand on chest.

A shadow moved within the clouds and a figure emerged: the taller of the two dragging the shorter. The three quickly rushed in to aid the man, who went to his knees hacking and gasping. The smaller of the two, the Malazan, sat up and made for the pit again. Lazan held him back. 'You'll die, man. It's poison!'

'The rest have to go!' the Malazan answered. His eyes were weeping uncontrollably and a stream of blood dripped from his nose.

'There's nothing you can do.'

'Oh yes there is!' and the fellow raised his arms to inscribe a great circle in the air. If Lazan had had one hair on his head he knew it would be prickling and he edged away. The Malazan ducked back within the dense clouds.

Madrun was thumping the other on the back. Then he raised his head to peer about. 'Am I mad, or do you hear horses screaming?'

*

In the Great Hall the Legate lurched away from reaching after Kruppe to face the doors. Something like a muffled snarl of panic sounded from his throat. He made unsteadily for the exit. Halfway there he fell to his knees, swayed, then crashed face down, crossbow belt snapping, the mask clanging against the floor.

Still wary, Kruppe edged slightly forward to peer more closely.

The Legate's limbs shifted and he fumbled at the polished stone flagging. He began dragging himself onward. Kruppe threw his arms out in vexation. *Great Elemental Forces! What more must Kruppe do?*

Sliding one arm ahead of the other, the Legate began to chuckle. As he crawled the chuckle swelled into a muffled full laugh.

Kruppe backed away. He tucked the handkerchief into a sleeve and set his hands on his hips. His dimpled cheeks pulled down in an uncertain frown.

Really now. This is quite unreasonable.

*

Torvald stood immobile, listening as intently as he could. He felt as if his nerves were as taut as those annoying high-pitched Seven Cities stringed instruments. He believed he could discern a lessening in the clash of battle. Did that mean one side or the other was winning? Exactly what was going on? From their vantage they could see only a small portion of the overall extent of the front. Galene still held the baton ready in one hand but he saw her stance shift as if she, too, sensed the change.

'Something . . .' he began, but she raised a hand for silence.

A Black trooper ran to them from the woods. Torvald pushed closer to hear the report.

'The Seguleh have withdrawn to the interior,' he announced.

Galene examined the blasted field dotted with fallen. 'Why would they . . . Our numbers?' she snapped.

'Less than three hundred of the flight remain viable.'

'*Ancestors*,' the Silver breathed, and the baton creaked in her ferocious grip. 'And they?'

'Perhaps seventy.'

'Then why . . . One last charge . . .'

'Perhaps,' Torvald observed, breaking in, 'someone could go and ask.'

And Galene turned to look him up and down.

*

'It is very quiet,' Councillor D'Arle whispered from his post next to the stairs up from the lowest of the cellars. 'Perhaps I should take a look.'

Coll rested a hand on the old man's arm. 'I'll go.' He turned back to examine all the gathered councillors, aristocrats and court bureaucrats staring from the dark. No one else volunteered. Sighing, he loosed his sword in its sheath and started up.

Halfway up he stopped as he heard footsteps behind him. Redda Orr came up round a corner. 'What are you doing?' he hissed.

'I'm coming with you.'

'No you're not. This isn't some summer jaunt. Stay below!'

'I'm trained!' She drew her slim sword in a flash of steel.

Coll shook his head. 'I'm sure you are, child. But this isn't the duelling field.'

'I could take *you*, old man . . .'

'Perhaps.' Coll motioned to one side. 'What's that?'

Redda looked. He snatched the blade from her hand. She gaped, frozen, then fury blazed in her eyes. 'What a dirty trick!'

'Yes it was.' He started up the stairs again carrying both swords.

'The world's full of them so you'd better get used to it.'

As he approached the top landing he lay flat to peer over the lip, his blade ready. He met the sandalled feet of two Seguleh. One motioned him back down the stairs.

Damn. We're prisoners. Goddamned prisoners.

What's going on? Has the Legate won?

A thought struck him on the way down and he paused, swallowing. *Gods! Were they expendable now?*

*

Madrun, Lazan, Thurule and Fisher all crouched as near as possible to the foaming roiling clouds steaming from the pit. The noisome fumes seemed to repel all the birds and bats stooping in upon them, and the dogs charging from the woods – even one mad horse that had stormed past threatening to run them down.

A dull thud sounded from nearby and Madrun observed, disbelieving, 'Did that owl just crash into a tree?'

The mist churned and out came the Malazan, a cloth pressed to his nose and mouth. He would have fallen had Fisher not lunged to support him. He hung coughing and gagging, and waved an arm weakly to the pit. 'That's the lot. But it's still there – still in one piece!'

'What is, Malazan?' Madrun asked.

Lazan had been squinting off into the woods and now he backed away to tap Madrun on the arm. The giant glanced over and visibly started, amazement and panic in his gaze. 'Holy Ancestors, I cannot believe it,' he murmured to Lazan. The two began edging away.

'Come, Thurule,' Lazan called. 'We have fulfilled our mistress's instructions – now is the time to withdraw!'

Spindle watched in stunned astonishment as the three ran off in what could only be described as a panicked flight. He even sensed his ma grow quiescent in what felt almost like respectful deference. He turned to the woods and saw something huge approaching. Clearing his throat, he spat up a mouthful of the awful fumes he'd endured and raised his Warren to its highest pitch.

Fisher, an arm under one of Spindle's, whispered, awed, 'Is that . . .'

The shape emerged from the shadows to resolve into a wide and massive figure that Spindle recognized as Caladan Brood, the Warlord. The man's narrowed gaze was turned aside, following Madrun and Lazan Door's hasty retreat. Bizarrely, he held a spitting cat by the scruff of the neck. His heavy gaze swung to Spindle.

'What are those two fools doing here?' he demanded.

'I . . . I don't know,' said Spindle.

The Warlord held out the frenzied cat. 'That's quite enough, Malazan,' he growled.

Spindle blinked. 'Oh! Sorry.' He lowered his Warren. Brood handed the cat to him; it ravaged his hand and arm escaping.

'Fisher,' Brood said. 'What are *you* doing here?'

The bard shrugged. 'You know how I feel about witnessing things.'

The Warlord grunted his understanding. 'Careful. One day you might just buy yourself too much trouble.' He studied the pit just visible through the cloud of fumes. 'Let's have a look, then.' And he walked into the cloud of poisonous steam.

Spindle watched as best he could through the mist. Peering forward, he thought he saw the Warlord down in the pit studying the stones, tapping them. The man sat back as if thinking. Then he raised both arms up over his head, clasped his hands into a great double fist and brought it down in a tremendous blow that shook the ground beneath Spindle's feet. Once more he raised his fists and swung them down. This time the air was split by an immense crack that felt almost like a knife jabbing Spindle's ears.

The Warlord pulled himself up from the pit and emerged waving the fumes from his face. He paused to glance down at Spindle. 'I warned the creature,' he said, and walked off the way he'd come.

Spindle let out a long slow breath. Fisher echoed the sentiment with a nod. Spindle gestured to the pit. 'Well – you know, we must've weakened it for him . . .'

'Oh, of course . . .'

*

Jan found the double doors of the Great Hall closed, but they opened easily at his touch. Within lay the Legate, or his body. He lay on his back, hands crossed over his chest. A forest of broken bolts stood from him at all angles. They gleaming gold oval remained fixed to his face. Yet it was marred now; a crack ran from the bottom up one cheek to just below a graven eye. Jan approached. He wanted to kneel; but to do so would possibly reopen the wound at his side. Was the man dead? He could not be sure.

A voice whispered then, within his mind: *'Servant . . .'*

He flinched away. *What was this?*

'Take the mask, servant.'

The mask?

'Yes. I sense you are wounded. Accept it and you will live for ever.'

Accept it? Wear it?

'Yes. I have been banished from this flesh – but accept the mask and together we shall live again.'

Jan retreated from the corpse. No.

'No? No! You have no choice, servant. Do as I command!'

No. Our slavery is long over. We have found our own way. We are our own masters now. I consign you to the past. I turn my face from you. You no longer exist.

'Slave! Come back! I order you! Obey!'

Jan walked away. Leaving the throne room he met one of the pet mages at the doors; the one who paraded as a dancing girl. She came staggering up, an arm across her stomach, agony on her panicked face. 'What is going on?' she gasped. 'Where are the others? What has happened?'

'To us he is as dead,' Jan said, flatly, and walked on, stiffly.

'No! Impossible!' She lurched into the room.

Within, alone, Taya edged up to the body. 'Master!' She reached out, but at the last instant she yanked back her hand as if stung. She started to her feet, flinching away. 'No . . .' she murmured, wincing. 'Please . . . not that. Anything but—'

A sound spun her around. Someone emerged from one of the pillars. He was tall, dressed all in shades of green, and his hair hung silver and black. A long snarled hiss escaped her. 'You . . .'

Topper bowed. 'As they say, all good things, et cetera. And look at you. You are a bonus. One I've been hoping to pluck for some time now.'

Taya flicked her hands and short thin blades appeared. 'I will have your head.'

'I rather doubt that.'

They charged, meeting in a maelstrom of whirling flashing blades. Competing Warrens rose together, spinning and swirling until both disappeared in a loud burst of displaced air.

*

Torvald had never felt so exposed in all his life. Unarmed, he walked across the gouged and overturned dirt and broken flags of the once-groomed grounds. Galene limped at his side supported by a single Black. They made for the group of Seguleh guarding the main entrance, the majority of whose masks, he noted, bore very few marks.

As they neared, one Seguleh signalled for them to halt. Another, who carried a single bold line across his brow, signed to a third and these two approached.

'I am Councillor Nom,' Torvald said quickly. 'I am come to propose negotiations.'

'What is it you wish?' the smaller Seguleh asked. She carried five hatch lines on her mask.

'We come to demand your surrender,' Galene said.

'Our surrender? I rather think it is you who should surrender.'

Galene held up an empty gauntleted hand then slowly reached into her shoulder bag to remove a red baton. She held it up. 'Your protective sorceries are gone, Seguleh. I merely have to signal with this and the hilltop will be reduced to rubble.'

The Seguleh Sixth motioned to Torvald. 'What think you of this, Councillor Nom?'

Torvald swallowed. His voice came faint: 'Darujhistan would consider that an act of war.'

Galene's helm shifted to face him. 'Better that than the alternative.'

'We propose,' said the Sixth, 'that you merely stand aside and allow us to return to our homeland.'

'Happily,' Galene snapped. 'We propose that you merely set down your swords and go unarmed.'

'That is unacceptable to us.'

'Then we have an impasse.'

'Not so,' the Sixth began again, a new iron in her voice. 'We could march out right now if we so chose and there are none here who could stop us.'

'Go ahead. We will chase you down like dogs and slay every one of you from above!'

Torvald loudly cleared his throat. 'What of the hostages?'

The Sixth reluctantly pulled her gaze from Galene. 'What hostages?'

'The councillors and other citizens.'

The Sixth glanced to the one with her, obviously the Seguleh Second. Torvald felt almost dizzy standing this close to the highest living ranked of them. He couldn't imagine what it must take to occupy such a position – let alone have all the others accept it as fully justified.

The Second signed something and the Sixth inclined her masked head. She turned to Galene. 'They will be released. It is not our way to hide behind hostages.'

Torvald bowed. 'Very good. My – our – thanks.'

Galene held out the red baton. 'Once the non-combatants are clear consider your final answer carefully.'

'You have it already,' the Sixth replied, and the two Seguleh turned away.

Torvald and Galene watched them go. 'Stiff-necked fools,' she ground out. 'They merely have to set aside their swords and all this would be behind us.'

'Galene, I believe you are asking for the one thing they simply cannot do.'

*

Spindle and Fisher crouched in the woods, peering through the branches.

'Looks like a parley,' Spindle whispered.

'Shh,' Fisher warned. 'We don't want—'

Bursting eruptions of munitions drove them to the ground with their hands over their heads. Feet ran past nearby. Alarms were shouted, followed by more munitions.

Spindle raised his head for a peep. He saw a handful of Seguleh dodging for the entrance, Moranth running to intercept. Another group followed in the distance and Spindle gaped, astonished, at who was among them. He put fingers to his mouth and let go a piercing whistle. The fellow he had spotted skidded to a halt, grabbing another and gesturing.

Spindle jumped to his feet, waving. The whole group made for him.

Spindle opened his arms wide and to his further amazement Antsy accepted the greeting, giving an answering hug in return. 'You dog!' Spindle laughed, cuffing him.

'What are you doin' here?' Antsy said. 'Thought you were down south.'

'You too!' He gestured to the lad with him. 'Who's this?'

'Corien,' the lad answered. 'Corien Lim.'

'*Lim!* No . . .'

'Fisher!' one of the giants with Antsy suddenly bellowed. He grabbed hold of the bard and lifted him from his feet in a great bear hug.

'Great Mother!' Fisher cursed. 'Cull? Cull Heel? What are you doing here!'

'Fisher! Come back home with us, yes? You have been gone too long!'

At that moment Moranth emerged from the woods to surround them.

*

Jan ordered the release of the citizens, then saw to the defences of the main entrance. Should the Moranth return to their aerial bombardment his plan was for his people to occupy those same deepest cellars, wait for night to return, then scatter in all directions to return to Cant in ones and twos. Undignified, but perhaps the best way of ensuring that as many as possible made it out alive. His side was completely numb and he was weak from loss of blood, but if he could he just avoid any further exertion he believed he may yet live to see this through.

It was here that the guards assigned to the west found him. They came escorting exhausted and bedraggled brothers and sisters whom he did not immediately recognize. It was not until one went to one knee before him that Jan realized who he was. With that understanding came a wave of anticipation that nearly caused him to faint. *Great Ancestors! Oru, the Eleventh, gone more than two years, assumed lost by so many, returned now, at such a time!*

Jan moved to raise him up but restrained himself, exclaiming instead, 'Oru!' He then clamped down on his breathing to observe dispassionately, 'You are returned to us. I am pleased – but you should not have come here.'

The Eleventh stood. His eyes shone now with even greater passion than Jan remembered from years ago. 'I believe it was fated that I should do so, Second.' He drew from his waist a small object wrapped in a fine black cloth. 'Just as I believed it was my fate to one day find this.'

Jan stared at the flat object held so delicately in Oru's hands. *This was it? The Unmarred? It seems so small.* His arms remained petrified at his sides. His eyes rose to meet Oru's eager, avid gaze. 'There can be no doubt?'

'None, Second.'

'Then call everyone. All must witness this.'

Oru bowed. 'Yes . . . Second.'

They assembled in the main entrance foyer, all remaining of the Five Hundred. Jan was stricken through the heart to count less than one hundred. Of the Eldrii, the Ten, only he, Gall and Palla yet lived.

He raised his chin for their attention. Through the windows the sky was lightening to the dark blue and violet of a coming predawn. *Please, all our Ancestors*, he invoked, eyes on the coming day, *allow me the strength to see this through! Grant me that and you shall have me.*

'Brothers and sisters,' he started, his voice thick with emotion – and more. 'In this time of our greatest testing, one who has been gone from us on a long journey has returned – with the thing he vowed never to return without.'

The gathered stirred, masks shifting to the Eleventh at his side. 'Oru,' Jan went on, 'hold up the Mask of our Ancestors. The Pure One crafted by the First who led us on our exile . . .' Even as he repeated the traditional words of invocation a sudden new realization came to Jan and their meaning shifted, taking on an utterly new significance. His breath caught at the truth of this new formulation. Everything made sense now: his people's fate, their exile. It came to him that this must be what others describe as a religious awakening.

He took a great breath and continued, louder, his voice rough. '. . . on our exile . . . which was in truth a deliverance. A flight from slavery and a flight from our shame. Crafted in the hope of an eventual redemption, a cleansing of our past.'

Oru pulled off the black covering and held up above his head a pure unmarred mask carved from the same translucent bright stone as the Legate's throne. In the gathering brightness of dawn it seemed to glow with an inner light. All those present stared immobile. It seemed to Jan that a great easing of some long-held breath escaped from them all, and as one they bowed to one knee, heads lowered.

'A sign,' he continued. 'A promise. An offering sent from our past to our future. One we hope to one day be worthy of. One which belongs to *all* our people and must be returned to await that future safe in the temple at Cant.'

At these words the Third, Gall, straightened. 'Nay! Take it, Second. Don it! With you at our head we will sweep these Moranth before us and return triumphant!'

'No! It must not be taken up in anger or bloodshed. That would taint it beyond redemption. No, this artefact is too important for us few here to risk its destruction. We shall accede to the Moranth demands so that we may see it brought safely home.'

'To that decision I give my fullest support.' A new voice spoke up from the back of the assembly – which parted swiftly as Seguleh drew blades against the newcomer.

Jan and Gall both peered, squinting. Jan recognized Lo first, then his son and some girl. And with them one other and as soon as he looked at this man he recognized him and knew him for what he was, and what he *could* be, all in one transfiguring instant. He knew then what he must do.

Gall turned his back on Lo, the Eighth, and the man who all knew must be the slayer of Blacksword, the presumed Seventh. He faced Jan. 'We must not put down our swords. How can we abandon what it means to be Seguleh? It is not for you to propose such a thing.'

Jan felt remarkably calm in the face of what all others present must see as an inexcusable insult. The Third's behaviour was nothing less than a direct challenge. Jan knew that was exactly what Gall intended. *Yet I am not strong enough! I will fall and all I have just glimpsed will be lost to us! Please, Gall, my old friend. Stand aside just this once . . .*

After a long bracing breath Jan's answer emerged level and strong: 'I propose it because I have seen what we could all too easily become – what we must *never* become.'

The Third reached out as if begging something of him. In his gaze Jan saw the reluctance, the torment of his position. 'Please,' he whispered. 'Do not drive me to what duty demands of me . . .'

'I have spoken, Third,' Jan said. 'It shall be as I say.'

And Gall said what Jan knew he felt he must as Third: 'Then I challenge you.'

*

After the Seguleh left to return inside, Torvald waited with Galene. She tapped the red baton in her palm, shaking her helmed head. 'I fear we have our answer,' she murmured. 'I'm sorry. But once word comes that your fellow councillors are clear, I am compelled to act.'

Gods protect us! Torvald turned away to study the vista of Darujhistan spread out below in the coming light of the east. The various fires appeared to have been mastered, the looming threat of a firestorm feeding gas eruptions circumvented. For that he gave thanks. *One miracle. Dare he hope for another?*

'Couldn't you—'

'No,' she rubbed her leg, hissing with pain. 'If it were up to me alone . . . perhaps. But I am not here on my own. I must think of my people. We cannot allow this threat to exist.'

'Then I am sorry as well, because I have no idea how the Council will take this. There may be war between us.'

'Perhaps.'

A party of Black troopers jogged up. One saluted Galene. 'A small group that contained Seguleh were allowed through the cordon.'

Galene straightened, outraged. 'Allowed through? On whose authority?'

Another of the troopers saluted. 'Mine, Commander.'

Torvald studied the last speaker. He appeared to be the oldest Moranth he'd seen yet. The chitinous plates of his armour were thick, cracked and lined. He bore the countless scarifications and gouges of a veteran of many battles.

Galene nodded to the trooper. 'Master Sergeant. Your record is beyond reproach. Why have you done this?'

The veteran bowed. 'M'lady. You know I was among the first contingent serving alongside the Malazans. I fought with them for decades. I allowed that party through because of the man who was with them. Though it has been many years, I recognized him. I would know him anywhere. He was Dassem, the First Sword of the Empire.'

Torvald couldn't believe what he was hearing. The First Sword? Here? Was this credible?

Galene's voice was barely audible: 'That is impossible.'

'Elect,' the veteran continued, a new edge in his voice, 'must I remind you that our treaty of alliance with the Malazans included Dassem as a signatory?'

'And if he lives . . .'

'Exactly, Elect. If he lives . . . then contrary to what we had assumed, that treaty is not void.'

*

Crowded within the rear of the hall, Yusek whispered to Sall, 'What's goin' on?'

'A challenge for leadership,' he answered just as low.

'If this is how things get resolved then I'm surprised there's any of you above Fiftieth.'

He turned to regard her more closely. 'Yusek – no one will be hurt. At this level it will all be over before you or I notice.'

'And if someone was hurt?'

'Then, consider. I see only the Sixth and Third with us now. That means this man, the Seventh, could be within one or two ranks of Second.'

'That's not why I came here,' the Seventh growled.

'Yet it is our way,' Sall murmured, undeterred.

Palla came to Jan's side, whispering, fierce: 'Do not accept! There is something wrong . . . I see it. You're wounded.'

'I must answer or stand aside – as you well know.' *How to salvage this? The future I foresaw mustn't be lost to us!* 'Will you second me?' he asked.

'Of course,' she answered, nearly choking.

'No challenges here!' a voice called from the crowd and a Hundredth stepped forward. Horul. 'This must wait until we return to Cant.' A strange panic filled her voice. 'Before the temple . . .'

Oru signed a negative. 'The challenge had been made. It must be answered. What say you, Second?'

Jan inclined his head to the Eleventh. 'I accept.'

Gall bowed, then looked around; by tradition the next highest ranked present or available should second him . . . the Seventh.

Lo extended a hand, inviting the dark-skinned Malazan forward. The man shot him a glare but the gathered Seguleh parted and so he reluctantly advanced.

As he passed through the ranks some reached out to the sword wrapped in rags on his back and Yusek heard them murmuring a word. 'What's that they're saying?' she whispered to Sall.

'Many say the sword on his back is the Son of Darkness's own. The very one that defeated him. They are saying what legends hold as its oldest name – Grief.'

The four gathered near the centre of the hall and all the assembled Seguleh backed away to the walls. 'Challenge has been issued,' Gall called out.

'And accepted,' Jan answered.

Palla stepped forward. 'As honour has been met I ask that said challenge be withdrawn.' And she added so low that only the four gathered could hear: 'If you proceed in this, Gall, then I will challenge you.'

'Do as you feel you must,' he answered, equally low. 'Just as I must.'

'Now you say that the challenge will proceed,' Jan prompted the Seventh.

The Seventh studied the Second. He looked him up and down. For a long time he let his gaze linger on Jans's wounded side. 'Is this what you wish?' he asked finally, uncertain.

Jan allowed himself a stiff nod. 'Yes. It is what I wish.'

'Very well.' He raised his voice: 'The challenge proceeds.'

The two seconds withdrew. Gall stepped away from Jan to make room.

Jan eased his weapon free. The moment the challenge was issued he had known what he had to do. It would be his most difficult performance ever. Weakened as he was he did not know if he could succeed. Yet he must. He would give all he had left. Even if it meant destroying a friend. 'In all the times we've fought before you've never come close,' he shouted to Gall. 'What have you planned this time?'

'What is he doing?' Palla murmured, thinking aloud. 'He's never taunted anyone before.'

'He's setting him up,' the Seventh grimly answered.

Palla turned to the Malazan. '*What?*' but then swords clashed.

The instant their swords met Jan manoeuvred Gall to his wounded side. The Third came on with more passion and power than he had ever displayed in all the years upon the practice sands. But Jan had been one of his teachers and knew what Gall would do before he knew himself. *It must be quick – already I'm weakening. No hint. He mustn't have time to pull the thrust.*

I'm sorry, my friend. In so many ways you are the most honourable of all of us. But this must be so.

Yusek stared, appalled and fascinated. Gods, it was so beautiful! So elegant. This was not the bashing and grunting she'd known. This was more like dance. A dance of nerves, flesh, and razor-sharp iron.

The time had come. Jan knew he could delay no longer; he was about to fall. Already in his parries and turns he had been preparing the way, leaving his hurt side slightly open. And now in an over-extended riposte he began a recovery that would invite the counter-thrust, and in the fraction of a heartbeat that committed Gall to making it he reversed his recovery and advanced to meet the sword that was already moving towards him and slid in as smoothly as if pushing through cloth.

Yusek could not be sure. It looked to her as if the Third deliberately thrust the Second through the side even as he was turning to him. She could not contain a scream at the ugly shock of it. Hers was the only cry in the utterly silent hall.

Palla did not move. *This is not happening*, she told herself. *Such things do not happen.* Yet the Second lay with the Third's sword through his side. Only by conscious effort could she move her legs. She and the Seventh approached. All others remained immobile, hushed. Shocked beyond all reaction, perhaps.

Gall stood frozen. He stared at his empty hands as if in disbelief. He raised his gaze to them and there through the mask Palla saw desolation. 'I didn't . . .' he groaned.

'I know,' the Seventh answered.

They knelt at Jan's side. He lived still, panting, his breath wet. 'Oru,' he rasped.

'Eleventh!' Palla called.

A crash sounded close by: Gall had fallen to his knees, his hands covering his face, rocking himself and shuddering with silent tears.

Oru ran to them. The Second swallowed hard to whisper: 'My last request, Oru.' His voice was slurred. 'Offer the mask to the Seventh.'

'What?' Palla gasped. 'No. You will live! There is no need.'

The Seventh jerked upright. 'Do not offer this thing to me.'

'You must,' the Second barely mouthed. 'You will take us . . . home.' His eyes, behind their blood-spattered mask, closed.

'Jan!' Palla grated, her lips clenched against a ferocious scream. 'Jan!'

'He is dead,' Oru said. The Eleventh straightened and turned to face the gathered Seguleh. He studied the mask he held in both hands.

After a moment he raised his head to be seen by all present, turning a full circle. 'All of you know me,' he began, his voice low. 'You know that years ago a vision came to me – a vision that I could find our lost legacy, our birthright. You also know that by tradition the mark of the First cannot be taken . . . it can only be offered. I came fully intending to offer it to our Second. But he refused. His last request was that it be offered to the Seventh . . .'

'But,' he continued, after a hard breath, 'we are Seguleh. We must not forget who we are. And with us rank is paramount. Therefore . . . I am bound by tradition. By duty. By our ancient code. To offer this mask of the Unmarred, the First, to the Third.'

He turned to where Gall crouched rocking himself in mute anguish. 'Third – do you accept?'

His face still covered, the man gave one savage negative jerk of his head.

Oru turned to Palla next. 'Sixth. Do you accept?'

Throughout, Palla had not taken her eyes from the dead Second. Without looking up, she shook her head.

Oru turned to the Seventh. 'It has come to you, Seventh. Do you accept?'

The man raised a hand. 'A moment – there is one here who may choose to dispute this.'

Oru cocked his head, thinking, then turned to the entrance. 'Eighth,' he called. 'Will you approach?'

Lo started forward. Sall moved to follow then stopped to point a finger at Yusek. 'You, stay here.'

'No fucking kidding,' she answered under her breath.

Lo came to Oru's side. The Seventh faced him. 'Tell me, Eighth. If this mask came to you what would you do?'

The lean man gave an indifferent shrug. Behind his mask his eyes were half lidded, almost lazy. 'Challenge has been issued. It must be met.'

Aside, Sall started forward, drawing breath, but a sign from Lo checked him.

The Seventh let out a ragged breath. 'Gods – they say never gamble with the Seguleh and now I know why.' He glared at the Eighth. His deep blue eyes shaded dark as his hands worked at his sides. 'Damn you, Lo. You're determined not to leave me any room . . .' Lowering his voice even more he growled, 'I'm of half a mind to call your bluff.'

'But you won't.' The Eighth motioned Oru closer. The Eleventh held out the mask.

Wordless, the Seventh snatched the sword from his back and shook the rags from it. Hissed breaths escaped from a hundred throats as the blackwood sheath was revealed, the hilt all blued to night black, and the sable stone orb that was its pommel. The Seventh tied it to his belt then raised his face to the gathering. 'I do not claim to be unmarred myself,' he began, and emotion cracked his voice, stopping him. After a moment he continued: 'Far from it. However, I accept this honour in the promise that perhaps one day I will prove worthy of it.'

He took the translucent white stone mask from Oru's hands and raised it to his face.

'Damned quiet in there,' Torvald murmured aloud just to hear someone speak – the Moranth were utterly silent. Pink and gold bands now brightened the undersides of clouds to the east. Dawn was coming. The Moranth remained battle-ready. They appeared to fully expect the Seguleh to come charging out at any moment. And if that did happen, from what he'd seen he personally didn't think anything would stop them.

A Black messenger came jogging up to Galene and saluted. 'Non-combatants captured on the grounds, Elect.'

'Who?'

'A citizen, Malazans, and other foreigners.'

'Malazans and foreigners? What are they doing here?'

'They looked to have come to help fight.'

'Well, release them and warn them off.'

The Black saluted. 'Very good.' He moved to leave.

'Where are the councillors?' Torvald asked.

The messenger looked to his commander. Galene waved to allow an answer. 'They have been escorted off the hill.'

'Thank you.'

Galene faced Torvald. She crossed her arms, the red baton still in one hand. 'I'm sorry, Councillor. I can't delay much longer. We will withdraw and then I will be forced to signal.'

'I'm damned sorry as well. This will destroy our relations for ages to come.'

Galene nodded her understanding. 'You are sounding more and more like a councillor, Nom of Nom.' She turned to an aide and signed. He ran off, signalling to others as he went. The Moranth Black troops stirred, readying to withdraw. 'We will be last,' she told him.

Together, they watched the troops back away, making for stairs and twisting roadways down Majesty Hill. Torvald's gaze kept re-turning to the blasted main entrance. *What are you bastards doing in there? Do you mean to hide it out?*

Then movement caught his eye and he shouted, near panicked, 'Galene! Someone's coming!'

She spun to the entrance, a hand going to her sword.

A small party of Seguleh approached – not the all-out charge they'd been fearing. From their masks these men and women represented the top leadership of the people. One fellow, however, carried a far heavier build and was far darker of skin, as dark as many Malazans, in fact. And the mask he wore blazed white in the dawn's light as if glowing. Torvald squinted even more closely at it: *was it . . .*

He turned to Galene. 'That mask! It's—'

'Yes. I see,' she answered, her voice tight. She crossed her arms, awaiting the party.

The four Seguleh, three men and one woman, stopped short of Galene. The lead one, not even of their stock it seemed to Torvald, matched Galene's crossed arms. 'You are the Elect in charge of this assault group?' he asked, speaking barbarously accented Daru.

'I am Galene.' Then she bowed to the man. 'Greetings, First. This is an unlooked-for honour.'

First, Torvald wondered? Then was this the man, then? But *which* First? And still Torvald did not know him, as the mask obscured his face.

'I propose to lead the Seguleh south, to Cant. You have my word that we shall never return. What say you?' His gaze slid aside to another of the Seguleh, one bearing ten hatch marks on his mask, and he continued: 'Shall there be any challenge between us, Elect?'

Galene uncrossed her arms. Her armour gleamed mirror-like in the gathering light. 'There can be no challenge between us, First.'

He gave the slightest dip of his head in salute. 'Very good. We will leave by the Worry Town gate. Notify your forces.'

Galene saluted. 'Done. First . . .' she called as he turned away.

'Yes?'

'I am . . . relieved.'

The man bowed briefly again. 'As am I.'

Torvald watched them go. *Wondrous gods! Was that it then? Done? Finished?* Wordless, suddenly exhausted, he watched Galene exchange the red baton for one of gold. This she held skyward and twisted. Some sort of munition shot from it, launched into the still deep-blue sky where it burst into a sizzling amber flame. Torvald watched it drift like a burning flower, smoking and popping.

*

To the west of Darujhistan Captain Fal-ej nudged Fist K'ess who looked then nudged Ambassador Aragan who jerked, blinking, and squinted to the city. He then turned to Attaché Torn.

'What is it?'

'A signal.'

Aragan bit back a sharp reply; instead he examined the quorls filling the fields around them. Hours ago they'd swooped down and landed in order to conserve their strength and wait out the night. None stirred now. No orders were shouted to mount.

'Which?' he asked, dread choking in his throat.

Torn turned his helmed head to Aragan. 'It is the call to stand down. It seems, Ambassador, that the Elect has met with some sort of victory.'

Victory? Against nearly a hundred Seguleh? He didn't think that possible. But then, they would hardly have surrendered, would they? 'Now what?'

'Now?' Torn indicated the quorls, now readying, rising to flight, all unburdened, carrying only single riders. 'The assault group will be extracted. And then we shall have a report.'

Aragan watched the quorls lifting off and flitting away, making for the glow and drifting smoke over Darujhistan. Twin wakes followed some passing low over flooded fields nearby. *And what a report that will be . . .*

Not far off Sergeant Little nudged her squad awake to motion to the disappearing quorls. 'Looks like a pick-up,' she said. 'Must be what those officer types call 'a cessation of hostilities'.'

'Sounds so pretty when you say it, Little,' one trooper called out.

'Music to my ears,' Bendan murmured, half awake. 'We gonna move out?'

Little shifted where she lay on one elbow. 'Don't know.'

'We'll pull back to Pale,' Bone opined while he picked at his teeth. 'Re-garrison. Won't they be happy to see us.'

'Pale! That pit,' someone grumbled. 'Nothing there.'

'Don't matter,' Bendan sighed. 'All the same to us.'

Little eyed him where he lay with an arm over his face. 'That's right, trooper. All the same to us.'

CHAPTER XXI

And did we not know the sweetest lassitude there
bathed in such silken glow?
How sad we must part, for the stars command
and none can forestall their turning upon the great
immutable orbs

Love Songs of the Cinnamon Wastes

SINCE SHE HAD THE DAWN WATCH BLEND MADE AN EARLY BREAKFAST of fried rashers, eggs, the butt-end of a loaf of heavy black bread and a pot of herb tea, and sat down near the front to eat.

The smell of cooking roused Picker, who was asleep on a bench. She sat up and rolled her neck to get the kinks out. 'Save me some tea.'

'Course.'

Picker groaned, rubbing her face where she sat. 'You know – I really expected something last night under cover of all that mayhem.'

'Me too. Haven't heard from Spin or Fisher neither.'

'True. Can't believe those Moranth dropped in to take on the Seguleh.'

'Must've had munitions up the you-know-what.'

Blend washed down a mouthful of bread then set down her cup. 'You hear somethin'?'

'What?'

'Out front . . .' She pushed back her chair.

The barrier at the door exploded inward with an eruption of flung splinters and boards. The heavy oak table upended to hold up heaped benches slid backwards, grating on the stone floor. Blend tripped on her chair. Picker threw aside the table before her and made for the bar.

A giant fought to force his way through the shattered timbers of the door.

Blend drew her long-knives and closed in a leap, arms drawn back to thrust. Both weapons hit home in the armoured giant's chest. One rebounded while the other shattered into fragments. A sweep of one thick arm knocked her flying backwards.

Picker fired a crossbow from the bar but the bolt glanced off the creature's inlaid armour. It stepped forward, pushing back the heaped benches and broken timbers. Blend ran for the kitchen. Picker reloaded. Duiker appeared from the hall then ducked away.

Picker fired again but the second bolt rebounded from the creature's closed full helm. She threw down the crossbow and headed out from behind the bar.

The giant batted aside benches and took another step. Blend came in from the kitchen; she carried their massive log-splitting axe. This she raised over her head in both hands and ran across the room loosing a blood-searing war howl. The axe crashed home against the creature's chest and flew free of Blend's hands. A great shower of stone chips clattered to the floor and the thing lumbered a heavy single step backwards. A crack now showed in its broad chest armour.

'It ain't human!' Blend yelled.

From the hall Duiker appeared carrying a great two-handed broadsword. He shook it free of the sheath and advanced. Blend searched for the axe. Picker lifted one of the benches and swung it at the thing in an attempt to beat it back. It groped clumsily for the bench.

The broadsword hacked stone chips from arms and torso, yet still it advanced. It appeared to be making straight for the stairs down to the cellars. Picker hammered at it using the bench as a battering ram while Blend and Duiker chopped at the limbs. Nearing the top of the stairs it managed to get hold of the haft of the axe to wrench it from Blend's hands. It snapped the thick haft in two and tossed the pieces aside.

'Spindle's munition!' Picker suddenly yelled.

'Right!' Blend dodged one awkward grab to run for the bar.

Both Duiker and Picker gripped the bench and fended the thing off by butting it in the chest. Blend reappeared behind it, cut off. 'Now what?'

'Dive!' Picker yelled.

She hugged the munition, hunched, then threw herself forward, sliding between the thing's wide braced legs and almost tumbled down the stairs. Duiker stopped her. The thing took its first step on to the cellar steps. The three looked at each other, their close quarters. 'Now what?' Picker asked again.

'I don't—' Duiker began, and then a skeletal hand grasped his shoulder and shoved him aside. A file of undead Seguleh came climbing the stairs, unsheathing their swords. Duiker, Picker, and Blend slid down along the walls, dodging the swinging weapons.

The guardians, or whatever they were, held the giant off for a time. Their weapons hacked great gouges out of its armour, which appeared to be layered plates of solid stone or fired clay. Its finish of inlaid multicoloured stones had long been scraped and bashed away. Yet it was destroying them; the clumsy stone hands grasped arms to wrench them from sockets; closed over heads to crush skulls like blood-fruit. The guardians were falling one by one. Their torn limbs and mangled bodies cluttered the stairs.

Down in the darkness of the first cellar level the three eyed one another. Duiker motioned to the cusser in Blood's hands. She nodded.

They waited until the last of the pickled Seguleh fell. Duiker took a torch, then he and Picker lay down on the much narrower rough stone staircase leading down to the lowest cellar – the one they never used. From the top of this staircase Blend watched for the giant to make its appearance.

Its heavy leaden steps announced it. Each shook the stone beneath them. It turned the corner of the landing. Blend yelled, 'Munitions!' and threw, then jumped for the stairs.

They heard the cusser crack like a dropped pot. Then the giant took another step.

Duiker cursed under his breath.

'How do you like that!' Blend snarled. 'It really *was* a dud!'

Another step sounded and the rock beneath them creaked as if under immense pressure.

'Now what?' Picker whispered, fierce.

'Let's get out of here,' Duiker said.

Picker climbed to her feet. 'Damn right.'

They scrambled up into the upper cellar only to find that the giant had reached the narrow aisle that led through barrels stacked ceiling tall. They were cut off.

'*Shit!*' Picker exploded, and she reached for her sheaths only to find them empty. 'Now what?'

Exhausted, Duiker wiped his hot slick face. 'We back up. It might widen out down below.'

'That's a plan,' Blend growled and she motioned them back.

The stairs were uneven, roughly hewn and overgrown with mould – even something that felt like a kind of moss or thick lichen. Duiker hoped the thing might lose its footing and come tumbling down in a heap of wreckage. Then he thought – *lichen?* Growing on these cut stone stairs? Then that would mean . . . *Burn preserve them . . . thousands of years!*

The stairs lost definition until Duiker found himself sliding backwards down nothing more than a stone chute. Roots hung, clawing their hair. It had become hotter and far more humid.

'We ain't never come this low,' Picker whispered, hushed. 'I don't know if I can go down any more!'

Duiker, leading the backwards descent, came up against a hard flat surface. In the dimming light of the torch he could just make out a rough-hewn granite slab. 'End of the way,' he called. 'Looks like the entrance to a tomb.'

In the gloom Picker punched a dirt wall. 'Fener take it! I can't fucking believe it. What a goddamned place to die. Break it down!'

'No! I think that's what it's here to do,' Duiker said. 'If we all charged it and hit it high we might trip it up. One of us might get by.' He glimpsed movement up the narrow tunnel. 'Here it comes.' He jabbed the end of the torch high into a wall. 'Let's go.'

'I'll lead,' Picker growled, and turned sideways, hunching a shoulder.

They ran back up the sloped tunnel. Picker and Blend let out bellowing war howls as they went. They jumped up at the last instant to smash into the creature's battered chest only to tumble together at its stone feet. It rocked backwards but did not fall.

Lying in a heap before it they peered up, bruised and puzzled. It remained immobile, like the statue it perhaps had been in truth. A sudden sharp crack split the air like the eruption of a flawed pot in a kiln and an arm fell off it to thump on to them then roll down the tunnel floor, bursting into shards. The other arm split and fell too, bursting like a pot.

They all scrambled up and backed away. A great crack shot in a jagged diagonal across its torso and the halves slid in opposite directions to crash into countless shards. Its lower torso and legs fell forward, shattering as well.

The flickering torch revealed standing behind the wreckage a man with long straight greying hair wearing a dirty threadbare shirt and trousers. A young woman hovered close behind him, all in dark clothes and carrying a stave. Blend took one look at the man, gaped, then went for her empty sheaths once more. 'Fucking Tayschrenn!'

Picker snatched a dirk from her belt.

'Hold!' Duiker bellowed. He pushed forward, and a strange sort of half-smile touched the newcomer's lips.

'Duiker,' he said. 'If there was one man I did not expect to run into right now, that would be you.'

The old Imperial Historian looked him up and down. 'It is you,' he breathed, amazed. 'Yet not – you look different.'

'We grow older. Things change. You are right . . . I am not the man I was.'

Picker snorted at that. 'What do you want?' She raised her chin in defiance. 'We're retired. It's all official now. On the books.'

The High Mage shook his head, frowning now. 'I understand your anger and suspicion, Bridgeburner. You have every right to it. All I can say is that I'm sorry for what happened. I regret it greatly.'

'Sorry?' Picker echoed, derisive. '*You're* sorry?'

Tayschrenn glanced over his shoulder. 'Let's back up, Kiska.'

In the cellar the three still warily eyed the High Mage. 'What are you doing here?' Duiker asked.

The High Mage motioned to the tunnel. 'I've come to attempt something long overdue. Something that should have been done years ago.'

Picker and Blend shared puzzled glances. Duiker eyed the tunnel then his gaze shifted back to Tayschrenn. He pulled at his black and grey beard. 'If I'm right in what you're suggesting, then I think no one has ever been strong enough – or willing enough – to risk it. If you fail you'll probably be destroyed.'

At that the young woman at Tayschrenn's side started her surprise and turned a savage glare on him. 'What's this?' she hissed.

The High Mage raised a hand for quiet.

'No! I'll not be hushed. You never said anything about this.'

Duiker caught Blend's eye and motioned to the stairs. She nudged Picker and they started up.

Alone now, Tayschrenn took Kiska's shoulders. 'I'm sorry. But it has to be this way. This is something only I can do.'

Kiska wrenched free of his hands. She stamped the butt of the stave to the cobbled floor in a crashing report. 'For this I drag you from the ends of the earth? So you can throw your life away on some damned fool attempt – at what?'

The High Mage leaned back against a barrel. He eyed the darkness as if studying something hidden deep within its depths. 'Think, Kiska. Think of all those who nudged and manipulated and plain lied to bring you and me here to this place at this time.' He raised a finger, 'Your Aunt Agayla for one. The Enchantress. That priest of Shadow you mentioned – so Shadowthrone himself schemed for this. Even D'rek has given me her blessing. And so it must be.'

She threw out her arms. 'Oh, certainly! Better you than *they*, yes? Why haven't they stepped up if it is all so vital?'

He pressed his hands together before his lips and studied her over them. 'It is hard, I know. But right now at this moment all those I just mentioned, and many others, are utterly enmeshed in a struggle that spans the world. All their strength is already committed in a confrontation manifesting across countless fronts. And K'rul may fail. Wounded, poisoned, weakened – the effort may prove beyond her. That we cannot allow to happen.'

'But why *you*?'

He crooked a chiding smile. 'Tell me, Kiska. If Maker were here – what would he do?'

She drew a great shuddering breath, then her shoulders fell. 'He would do his job,' she granted, looking away, her lips clenched tight.

'Very good.' He crossed to her and touched his lips to her brow. 'Kiska – you saved me and you have made me whole. For this I will always be grateful.' He caught her gaze and held it. 'But now it is your turn. Be whole. Live now not for me or any other. But for yourself.'

Her answer was hardly audible. 'Yes.'

'Very good. Farewell. And, my thanks.' He walked away down the tunnel.

Upstairs Blend gave a great shout of surprise and Picker and Duiker ran up to find the wrecked K'rul's bar crowded. Antsy and Spindle were there, as was Fisher, plus three huge fellows, shields leaning up against their table, busy emptying tall tankards of ale.

Antsy shouted from the bar, 'Did you see . . .'

Picker crossed to the bar and gave a sombre nod. 'Yeah. We saw 'im.'

'Just about crapped my pants, I tell you,' Antsy muttered.

'I need a drink.' She fished behind the bar to pull out a bottle, eyed him up and down. 'So, you're back. You look awful. No big bags o' gems?'

He ducked his head, glowering. 'The go-down, get-rich, come-back plan got upended. Long fucking story. At least I didn't die.'

Picker snorted a laugh. 'Same old Antsy. Who're these huge bastards?'

'Old friends of Fisher.' He lowered his voice, 'Not too pleased to see 'em, though.'

'No kiddin'?'

Spindle came to the bar and poured a glass from Picker's bottle.

'So what was all this trouble in the city anyway?' Antsy asked him.

'Long story,' Spindle grumbled. He leaned back against the bar. 'Just my stupid luck too. I come here to avoid all the trouble down south, then this happens!' He studied the glass, took a sip. 'I'm headin' back south.'

Careful slow steps sounded from the rear, crackling and shifting through the broken stone and wood. All eyes turned to the noise and conversation died down to a heavy silence.

The young woman came up from below. She wore a once stylish dark shirt under leathers that were tattered, scraped and grimed. Her long black hair hung unwashed and mussed but pretty oval features did much to make up for all that. She held her stave crossways, a touch defensive, and peered around at everyone, her eyes puffy as if she had been crying. She wiped her face. 'This supposed to be a bar, then?' she asked of the room in general.

'Yeah . . .' Blend admitted guardedly.

'Got any wine? I could use a glass.'

Blend nodded. 'Take a seat.'

'Who's the gal?' Spindle asked, his voice low.

'She's a Claw,' Picker murmured.

Spindle choked on his drink.

*

Studious Lock was in the kitchen experimentally poking at a burlap bag of potatoes and thinking to himself: *Dear Unknowable Ancients . . . They eat these growths?* A crash sounded from the main chambers, followed by furniture breaking, gasping, flailing limbs thumping the floor, and a man's roar of outraged pain.

Guests!

He hurried out. A man – *half Andii!* – in a torn green shirt, blood-spattered, blades in each hand, was climbing to his feet among the broken wood of an ornamental table. He drew the back of one hand across his face leaving a smear of bright fresh blood.

'You are in need of dressing!' Studious announced, eager.

Seeing him, the man flinched away, almost falling again. 'Don't you touch me!' He ran off, following a trail of bare bloody footprints that led to stairs to the lower levels.

'I have unguents!' Studious called after him.

Then he sniffed the air and his mouth moved in what might be called a smile. *Ah! The Mistress's daughter has returned! Perhaps I should find some pretty live plants and pull them up to kill them. As is the barbaric custom here for celebrations.*

The lowest cellar was all one empty roughly octagonal room. At its centre a single figure sat cross-legged. She occupied a series of concentric circles inscribed in the floor, which was dotted with wards and sigils and symbols in languages spoken by no human. Her head was bowed and long black hair hung in a curtain that touched the ground before her.

Taya came down the wide staircase sliding along a wall. She clutched her side, blood a smear down that leg. Her gauzy scarves hung in tatters. She threw herself down before the crouched figure, a hand reaching, entreating.

'*Mother! Protect me!*'

The figure's head rose.

Topper came bounding down the stairs. He caught sight of the two women and stuttered to a halt. He raised his blades out from his sides, head cocked.

The woman within the centre of the wards stood. Chains rattled, running from her wrists to rings set in the floor at her sides. She wrapped a hand round one of these chains and yanked. Metal screeched and the chain snapped. She did the same with the other.

Topper's brows rose in silent appreciation. A feral smile twisted his lips and he flicked the blades, shaking droplets of blood across the floor.

The woman advanced out of the concentric circles dragging the chains behind her. She lashed one, sending a scattering of sparks flying. 'Clawmaster,' she said from behind the curtain of hair. 'Do *we* have a quarrel?'

Topper eased his left leg slightly further back. 'Vorcan. I'm here for that one. She must answer for a crime against the Empire.'

Vorcan glanced back to the prone figure. 'Leave her to me.'

'To *you*?' A puzzled frown creased his brow. He tapped one bloody blade to his lips, thinking. After a moment the feral grin returned and he offered a mockingly elaborate courtier's bow. 'Very well. For now. However . . . if I see her again I will take her head.'

Vorcan pointed to the stairs. Remaining half bowed, Topper backed up them, all the while keeping his eyes on her. At the top he disappeared in a swirl of darkness.

Vorcan turned back to Taya.

She lay on her side, still panting, drenched in a sweat of pain and exhaustion. She stared up at Vorcan, her brows crimped in puzzlement. 'All this time . . .' she breathed. 'You could have . . .'

'Yes. Had I chosen to – of my own free will.'

Taya shook her head in mute rueful incomprehension. Then she grimaced, hissing. She struggled to rise. 'Well, thank you. I knew you would help me, Mother.'

A metal click sounded and Taya jerked up an arm. One of the chains now hung from it. 'What is this?' Vorcan gripped the other wrist and transferred the second chain. '*No!*' Taya reached for a fallen knife. Vorcan kicked it aside, then took her daughter's neck in a vice grip. While she held her in the choking throttle she reattached the chains to their rings. Then she tossed her down and backed away.

Taya lunged but the chains rang and grated, restraining her. She lay rubbing her wrists. 'You cannot do this to me! I'll have your heart!'

Vorcan continued backing away up the stairs.

'Mother? You're not really . . . ?'

Vorcan disappeared. An unseen door closed heavily and a lock ratcheted.

'*Mother!* Don't leave me like this!'

She collapsed to curl into a tight foetal ball at the centre of the concentric rings. She wrapped her arms around herself and laid her head on the cold hard floor.

'Mother . . .'

*

Rallick found his man sitting on a bench in the grounds of Majesty Hill. He was facing the east. The sun's warm light was a golden wash across him. He sat next him; the man did not stir from studying the sunrise over the distant Gadrobi hills.

'You were supposed to run,' Rallick said after a time, his hands clasped on his lap.

Scholar Ebbin nodded, almost distractedly. He pressed a bunched cloth to his forehead.

'He wanted you to. He drove you off.'

The man nodded again. He let out a long sigh.

'But you didn't.'

Ebbin shook his head.

'Why not?'

Slowly, the scholar turned his head to face him. He swallowed to speak. 'I don't want to die.'

Rallick looked away. His mouth tightened. 'I'm sorry.'

Ebbin studied the sunrise once more. He tapped a finger to his temple. 'He's inside right now. Raging. But only a voice. Just a voice. He's harmless now, I swear. Couldn't I just—'

'No.'

Ebbin pressed the cloth to his watering eyes. 'I've hurt no one! I didn't mean this to happen. It isn't right!'

'I'm sorry,' Rallick said again. His voice was now much softer.

'I could have run, you know! Could've. But I didn't!'

At that Rallick's gaze tightened as if pained. 'I know.'

'Couldn't you just . . . ?'

'No.'

'Please . . .' Ebbin whispered.

Rallick motioned to a copse of woods. 'Come with me.'

'No . . . I don't . . .'

Rallick put an arm round his shoulders to raise him from the bench. 'This way, scholar. Only one thing left.'

*

A fist wrapped tight in the scholar's shirt, Rallick banged on the door of the Finnest house. Ebbin stared, taking in all the details of the bizarre structure. 'Is this . . .' he murmured, awed. 'Then there really was . . .'

The door swung open and there stood a horror. Ebbin jerked to scream but Rallick slapped a hand to his mouth. The scholar slumped, fainting in his arms.

'A sign,' Raest announced. 'That is what I need. Something like – Keep off the Mounds.'

'Can't you take him?'

'We already have a boarder.'

'That sleeping fellow?'

Raest shuffled back up the hall. Rallick followed, dragging Ebbin with him. The Jaghut motioned to a huge man lying on the floor, snoring. 'Our boarder. Quiet. Undemanding.'

Rallick studied the sprawled man. Now he thought he recognized him; in fact, he knew where he'd seen him. He'd been with that foreign blacksmith. He adjusted Ebbin in his arms. 'Well, perhaps he'd like to leave now . . . Can he?'

'Can he what?'

Rallick studied the Jag's dead scarred face. He cleared his throat. 'Can he – I mean, is he hale? Whole?'

'Physically, yes. As for his mind – it is the same as when he came to us.'

Ebbin roused in Rallick's arms. He peered about, frowning. 'Where am I?'

'Could you wake him?' Rallick asked.

'No.'

'No?'

'No. I cannot. You, however, may.'

Rallick struggled to conceal his irritation. He leaned Ebbin up against a wall then knelt over the big fellow. He touched the back of a hand to his cheek. It was as warm as a child's.

'Is this . . .' Scholar Ebbin gasped. He pointed to Raest. 'Are you . . . ? By all the gods! I have a thousand questions!'

Standing above Rallick the Jaghut let out a long low growl.

*

In the grounds of the High Alchemist Baruk's estate a small pot-bellied demon anxiously edged out of the tower's open door. As the rich amber morning sunlight struck its knobbled head it hissed, ducking and writhing from side to side. Then it shaded its gaze, blinking, and continued along on its uneven gait.

It stopped before a man lying prone halfway up the walk. Smoke curled from his shredded robes and blood matted his torn scalp. He appeared to have been in an explosion. The demon took hold of his shoulders and began attempting to drag him up the walk.

After much gasping and flailing, with the man himself weakly pushing, the demon managed to pull him in through the door. He leaned him up against a wall and waddled off. A short time later he returned with a silver flask that he opened and offered to him.

The man just peered up through pained eyes, breathing wetly, his jaws clenching against his agony. Anger appeared to be gathering in those eyes.

The demon slapped a hand to his forehead then leaned over to carefully tilt the flask to the man's mouth. The fellow drank as much as he could then gasped, choking and coughing. After a time he managed to lift an arm to take the flask. Blinking, he peered around at the rubbish, the strewn wreckage and broken furniture. 'Chillbais . . .' he began, weakly, and coughed again.

'Yes, master?'

He waved the flask to the surroundings. '. . . what have you done to the place?'

*

The brightening light cascading in through the windows woke Envy. A hand went to her forehead, pressing there, and she groaned. She rose unsteadily to her feet and staggered to a window. There she tensed, straightening, and glared about.

'No . . .' she breathed. She gripped the sill, cracking its stone under her nails. '*No!*'

She threw herself back from the window as if to dash from the room, but halfway across she raised both hands and came to a halt. She spent some time adjusting her dress and hair, then let out a long, calming breath. 'Very well. What's done is done. Can't be helped. It has all been rather a disappointment, after all.' She set her hands on her hips. 'Yes. Not what I'd hoped at all. Not at all. Perhaps a change in scenery.' She tapped a finger to her pursed lips. Her arched brows rose as an idea struck. 'Yes . . . perhaps the Empire. Hmm. *They* may be sophisticated enough . . .'

She waved a hand as if dismissing the rooms, Majesty Hall, the entire city, and walked out.

Across the city a burly foreigner drove a wagon into the yard of the Eldra Iron Mongers and shut the gates behind him. The master of the works himself, Humble Measure, met him as he brought the wagon to a halt before one of the cavernous shops.

Barathol dropped the reins, peered down at Humble. 'Ready?'

Humble Measure raised a long-handled pair of iron tongs. 'Ready.'

They went to the rear of the wagon and lowered the gate. A metal casket filled the bed. Barathol grabbed hold of a rope handle and yanked it out. It fell with a crash amid the black clinker and slag. He looked to Humble again. 'Furnace ready?'

'Iron's roiling white hot.'

'All right. Let's get it done.'

Humble set the tongs on the lid and took the other handle. Together they carried the casket into the shop, where an orange and yellow glow flickered and smoke once more billowed out to hang over the city.

Afterwards, as they walked back to the wagon, Humble Measure wiped his blackened hands in a filthy rag. 'Until next time, then.'

Barathol gave a harsh laugh. 'I know what you mean – but let's hope not, yes?'

'Yes. Quite. Twins favour you, then.'

Barathol nodded and shook the reins.

Humble Measure watched the man go. *Yes*, he agreed: *let us hope there will be no further call.* Yet in the meantime one must remain vigilant. He had his cause now. He'd been misguided before. Sought answers in the wrong directions. But now he understood. And he would apply all his resources just as ruthlessly as before. He knew where the true threats lay now and he would keep watch.

He would await the slips of paper inscribed with the broken circle.

For Torvald the farewells had been swift and without ceremony. The quorls arrived to pick up the survivors of the Moranth assault group and they had flown off, swooping to the east around the city. Galene left last. As if in salute she offered the slightest tilt of her engraved helm. He answered with his best awkward effort at a formal bow.

He stood for a time watching them disappear into the sun's glare. A mannered cough brought him round to see a young Darujhistani aristocrat in much-damaged finery. 'Yes?'

The lad bowed. 'I understand you are the new Councillor Nom.'

'I am.'

'Permit me to introduce myself – my name is Corien. Corien Lim.'

Torvald could not keep his brows from rising. 'Ah . . . I see. Well . . . I am sorry for your loss.'

The lad bowed again. He rubbed at his grimed nose, grimacing. 'You are most courteous, sir. I take this liberty because given the circumstances I believe we may be seeing much more of each other.'

Torvald had no idea what to say to that so he nodded sagely. 'Really. That is . . . most interesting.'

The Lim scion bowed again, taking his leave. 'Until then, sir.'

Torvald turned on to a path down the hill. He walked in silence, deep in puzzled thought. Had he just received his first overture of recognition from an aristocrat – a possible future councillor? If so, things were looking up for Torvald Nom. Then he recalled what lay ahead and he lost even that thin shred of optimism: homecoming awaited.

What should it be this time? Pirates? Invasions? Slavers? Stomach troubles?

As he walked the district he passed patches of fire damage. A few city blocks had burned but overall the harm was not nearly so terrible as he had feared. And everywhere, on every corner, lay pots in heaps, abandoned or broken. Some still held water – no doubt drawn from wells, troughs, and even the lake itself.

He frowned, eyeing them: something familiar about those pots.

He paused before the door to his own house. Once more wiped his hands on the thighs of his trousers. As he reached for the handle the door was yanked inward. Tiserra stood in the threshold. She cocked an eye.

'Greetings, fair wife!' He moved to step in but she blocked the way.

'And what was it this time?' she demanded.

'Ah! Well . . .' Torvald pulled a hand down his unshaven cheek. 'You may not believe this good wife . . . but I was sent on a secret diplomatic mission to the north only to be kidnapped by Moranth. And, in negotiation with them, I managed to save the city!'

'Oh, really? *You* saved the city, did you?'

He pressed a hand to his heart. 'Gods' own truth! That's exactly what happened. If I may come in I'll tell you all about it.'

'Indeed?' She edged slightly to one side. 'I can't wait to hear. Does it bear upon this non-paying job of yours?'

He slid in around her. 'Ah . . . odd you should mention that. In fact it does.'

She shut the door and brushed drying clay from her hands. 'Well then. It's a good thing that I'm owed for a great many pots.'

Councillor Coll walked the empty rooms of his manor house. Reaching the wide base of the ornate curved staircase he paused to rest a hand on the balustrade. After a time he set a booted foot on the first stair. Jaws tight, he leaned forward until he had to raise his rear foot to place it upon the second. He eased a breath out between clenched teeth, then continued on.

The bedroom door was open. He entered to stand by the low dresser. Thick curtains hung closed before the terrace doors holding the room in gloom. The air smelled of dust and stale perfume. He crossed to the curtains and drew them apart. A shaft of light played across the room: dust motes spun and danced.

He yanked the thick cloths to the sides and then pulled the double doors open. A gust of wind sent the dust swirling from the bedcovers. Taking a deep breath of the air, he turned to the door. Passing the dresser cluttered with its tiny glass bottles he ran a finger through the thick grey layer upon it. He examined his finger, then dusted his hands together and left.

Outside, his carriage-driver asked, 'Destination, Councillor?'

'Destination?' Coll answered, outraged. 'Why, Majesty Hall of course!'

The carriage-driver rolled his eyes to the sky as he gave the reins a tug.

Far outside Darujhistan, on the western edge of Maiten town, an old woman staggered from her straw-roofed shack. She held her head, groaning and blinking in the light. She wrenched at her great mane of matted frizzy hair to examine a handful. She let out a great yelp of horror and batted at the curled mass, raising a cloud of dust and dirt.

Then she worked her mouth as if having tasted something vile. She spat in the street, wiping her mouth and grimacing her disgust. She caught sight now of her mud-caked tatters of skirts and grabbed fists of them, twisting them back and forth. 'May the gods die of crotch-rot! What's happened to my dress?'

'Watch yer mouth, y' damned drunken witch,' a passers-by growled.

'How would you like—' She held her head and groaned anew. 'Oh gods! Wait till I get my hands on that slimy toad!' She reached for the wall of her shack. 'Oh, my head. My poor head. Where's Derudan's hookah off to?' She stumbled inside and began searching amid the rubbish.

*

West of the Maiten River the Malazan army broke camp to march. Fist K'ess was packing his travel panniers of orders and records when Ambassador Aragan entered. The Fist saluted, then motioned an invitation to a stool where a tray of tea waited.

Aragan waved a negative. 'I'm off for the city.'

K'ess paused in his packing. 'With respect, Ambassador. Perhaps you should wait . . .

The big man tucked his hands into his tight weapon belt. 'No, no. I'll have my honour guard, of course.'

'Come to Pale with the Fifth.'

The Ambassador tilted his balding head. 'Generous offer, Fist, but the embassy hasn't been formally closed. We'll see what the final decision is from whoever ends up in control there.'

'Very well.' K'ess saluted once more. 'A pleasure, Ambassador.'

Aragan seemed almost embarrassed as he turned away, clearing his throat. 'You're too kind, Fist.' He walked off with his splay-legged rolling gait.

K'ess watched him go. *A soldier who just wanted to be a soldier but ended up a politician.*

Captain Fal-ej paused at the open tent flaps to salute.

'Yes?'

'Outriders ready.'

'Send them off.'

'At once.' She turned to go.

'Captain,' K'ess called quickly.

She turned back, blinking, 'Yes?'

'We'll stay close to the lake shore, Captain.'

'Very good, Fist.'

K'ess pulled a hand down his unshaven chin. 'And perhaps – as we ride – you might tell me all about Seven Cities. I never did make it there.'

Captain Fal-ej's thick dark brows rose very high and she smiled broadly. 'That would please me a great deal, Fist.'

*

That evening Kruppe sat once more at his usual table near the back of the Phoenix Inn. Jess was on duty that night and when she caught sight of him she marched right over. 'You again! You've some nerve showing your oily self here. I've half a mind to call Scurvey to toss you out right now.'

Kruppe threw up his hands. 'Good Jess! What ire! What passion! I am overcome. Indeed, I am overcome with famishment. A bottle of red if you would be so kind. With two glasses, for Kruppe is in a bountiful munificent mood. And a touch of that gorgeous mutton I smell. And the pear tart for afters.'

Jess set her fists on her wide hips. 'And how are you going to pay for all this?'

Kruppe pointed past her. 'Oh, look! 'Tis Meese herself there at the bar. She'll speak for me, I'm certain.'

'Oh, I'll have a word with her about you all right, you can be sure of that.'

Jess crossed to the bar and spoke to Meese. Kruppe watched,

eyes narrowed, nervously tapping his fingertips together. The older woman waved Jess close and whispered something in her ear. Jess's eyes widened in surprise and she appeared to mouth *Really?*

The older woman gave a serious nod.

Jess straightened. Her wondering frown seemed to say: *who would have thought it?*

She returned to Kruppe's table. Here she bent down to him with a wide smile, and pushed back her hair. 'Was that two glasses you asked for, sir?'

Kruppe's gaze darted left and right. His fingertips halted their tapping. 'Why . . . yes, good Jess. If you would be amenable?'

'Certainly, sir. Right away.' She turned to go but paused for a moment to adjust the lie of her skirt over one broad hip. Then she walked off, swinging those hips like two great warships.

Kruppe's brows climbed very high indeed and his gaze shifted to Meese at the bar. An evil smirk raised the corners of her mouth and she winked.

Great anxious gods! Whatever did the evil Meese tell the poor woman!

Later that night Kruppe sat back to wipe his enormous handkerchief across his mouth and survey the conquered plates, crusts and bones scattered before him. *Most restorative struggle to the death! Kruppe is . . . satisfied.*

Yet the second glass remained untouched opposite and he regarded it for a moment, then poured himself more of the – slightly disappointing – red.

Two cloaked and hooded figures pulled up chairs to either side of him and leaned close.

Kruppe set his glass back down. 'Gentlemen . . . Kruppe was expecting company this night, but not you two.' He gestured to the empty glass. 'Alas, perhaps my friend's days of bachelor conviviality are done. The chains of domesticity have closed upon him and gone are the times of carefree bonhomie . . . Out of the window, as it were.'

'Whatever in the Abyss are you going on about, ya fat fool?' Leff growled. 'We're in real trouble here and we need your help!'

'My help? How can poor Kruppe be of any service to you?'

'We need to get out of town,' Scorch added urgently from the other side.

Kruppe's expressive thick brows climbed again; he clamped his handkerchief to his mouth and coughed behind it for a time. Fit over, he stuffed the cloth back into a frilly sleeve and thoughtfully stroked the tiny rat's tail braided beard at his chin. 'Really?' he managed after a time. 'Kruppe hardly dares ask what for . . . ?'

'It was an accident—' Scorch began.

'It was your fault!' Leff cut in. 'You fired!'

'You grabbed it!' Scorch yelled, nearly choking.

Nearby conversations stopped as people glanced over.

Kruppe raised his hands for quiet. 'Decorum in the bar, please, gentlemen. Now, what, exactly, are you two staggering blindly around?'

The two exchanged stricken looks. 'We killed the Legate,' they said together in a fierce whisper.

Kruppe slapped a hand to his mouth, choking once more. Once the coughing fit had passed he took a quick sip of wine to clear his throat. 'Oh dear,' he murmured. '*Most* serious. I daresay you are in a great deal of trouble.'

Leff pulled his hood lower and glared about. 'You have to help! The whole city's after us!'

Kruppe stroked the slim beard once more, shaking his head. He sighed heavily. 'Kruppe is only one man . . . This may lie beyond even his astounding abilities.'

'You have to get us out of the city,' Scorch pleaded. 'We'll do anything!'

Kruppe's hand paused upon the beard. His eyes darted once more. 'Anything . . . ?'

The two shared a glance of utter desperation and together they jerked a nod.

The little man picked up a last crust and gave it an experimental nibble. 'It just so happens that Kruppe *does* know of a job outside of the city that may be admirably suited to your, ah, unique, talents . . .'

The two sagged in relief. Leff cuffed Kruppe on the back. 'You're a true friend, Kruppe. Got no idea where we'd be without ya.'

Kruppe took a dainty sip of his wine. 'You have no idea,' he murmured.

EPILOGUE

THE NEXT MORNING ANTSY SAT LOOKING OUT OF THE STILL GAPING doorway of K'rul's Temple and Bar and sipped his tea. Sadly, once more they were all out of liquor as last night the three gigantic friends of Fisher, the Heel brothers, had been up drinking and singing until every bottle and keg was bone dry. After the not-so-discreet glowers from Blend and Picker the bard was out now seeing them off.

Antsy sipped the tea again and grimaced his disgust: damned cheap southern leaf.

Duiker came down and sat with him. The old historian rubbed his face and sighed blearily. 'Didn't sleep a wink.'

'You'd think with Fisher with 'em they'd at least be able to carry a tune.'

'See the sigil on one's shield? Black mountain on a blue field? Know it?'

Antsy shook his head. He poured Duiker some tea. 'Do you think he's still down there?' And he inclined his head to the rear.

The historian shrugged. 'Don't know. Probably not.' He looked to where the Claw sat at her own table staring out of an open window. She appeared pensive, somehow lost. He glanced around at the empty common room. 'So, Spindle's off?'

'Aye. We can breathe easily now,' Antsy laughed. The laugh died away as he squinted at something outside. 'Look there,' he murmured, and he lifted his chin to the open door. 'He's got some nerve showin' his face here.' Duiker turned in his chair. Across the street a man loitered; but not just any man. Duiker recognized him. In fact, he suspected that every Malazan in the building would've recognized him: Topper, Clawmaster to the Empire.

The woman appeared to have seen him now as well, as a hissed breath escaped her and she stood up. Antsy sent her a questioning look, which she answered with a sign: *stand down*. She picked up her stave and went to the door. On her way she paused at their table. 'Thanks for the room,' she told Antsy. She inclined her head to Duiker. 'Historian.' She crossed the road and the two appeared to talk for a time. Then they walked off more or less side by side.

Antsy sighed his regret. She'd been a fine place to rest his eyes, what with her long legs sheathed in those tall leather boots, and that challenging dark gaze she had – almost made him think maybe he wasn't as old as he knew he was. Now she walks off with the Clawmaster like they was old acquaintances, which, he supposed, they must be. Which made him glad he didn't try sittin' down next to her after all.

The streets were crowded that morning as all Darujhistan was out inspecting the aftermath of fallen Moranth munitions and the fires that followed. The damage not nearly as severe as it might have been thanks to the neighbourhood fire-fighting volunteers and no shortage of pots.

As they walked the streets Topper told Kiska: 'I was surprised to sense your presence.'

'And I yours.'

His gaze slide sideways to her. 'What, may I ask, drew you here – of all places?'

'A job. All finished now. You?'

'The same.'

'What is it you wish to talk about, then?'

The man studied his nails, then straightened the rings on all eight fingers. 'We're short personnel. Could always use an experienced hand. What say you? Ever considered teaching? The Academy at Unta perhaps?'

She pushed the too-long fringe from her eyes while she considered. *Need a damned haircut before I do anything – and a good scrubbing.* 'I'll admit I'm interested. Have to think about it, though. Got one last errand to see to. Then I'll give you my answer.'

Topper bowed, his smile sardonic as ever. 'Very good. Welcome back to the fold, Kiska.' And he cut away suddenly to walk off down a side alley. She continued on alone. *Let's not get ahead of ourselves . . .*

The tall iron-studded doors to the Varada estate hung open. Rallick entered to find that the two usual colourfully dressed guards had been joined by a third. All three now tossed dice together, arguing and grabbing at the bouncing pieces. Seeing him, one offered a faintly disturbing grin of gold and silver capped teeth. The second gave a broad lewd wink, while the third actually blushed and bowed deeply to hide his reaction.

Studlock met him at the door. 'The Mistress awaits upstairs. Perhaps you wish to freshen up before ascending? Scented oils to disguise unwelcome bodily odours? Honey for offending breath?'

Rallick paused to study the man in his gauze wrappings. 'Ah . . . no . . . thank you.' He moved to go but paused again. 'Is my . . .'

Studlock hovered close, hands raised, 'Yes?'

Rallick backed away. 'Never mind. Thank you.'

The bedroom was empty, the terrace doors open. He went out and leaned against the rail to look about, but saw nothing. Then his gaze rose to the lattices and climbing vines that rose to the tiled roof. He took hold of one and gave it a strong pull. It held.

He found her sitting on the peak looking out across the estate district to Majesty Hall atop its hill. She wore a loose armless shirt and trousers, and was barefoot. Her hair blew brushed by the wind. He sat at her side. In the distance Majesty Hall appeared no different from before. From here only the smoke rising from the ragged woods gave any sign of last night's assault.

'I'm glad you stayed away,' she said. 'Glad you weren't taken.'

'You could have told me more.'

She tilted her head, thinking, her gaze still on Majesty Hall. 'No. If I'd told you more you would have been tempted to try some sort of work-around and would have failed. This way all that uncertainty forced you to keep your distance.'

'If you say so.'

She turned a smile on him. 'I do.'

'And . . . the girl?'

The smile overturned into a tight scowl. 'Sent to her room to think things over.'

'Some things are the same everywhere, it seems.'

Vorcan nodded her slow agreement. 'That is so.' She glanced to him sidelong, pushing back her thick hair. 'And you? What of you?'

'I do not need to think anything over.'

He leaned to her and they kissed.

She bumped him with her bare shoulder and together they took in the view for a time. 'So tell me,' she said, after the silence, 'how did he escape us? What was his last trick?'

Rallick's eyes narrowed and he studied her from their very edges. He slowly shook his head. She cast him one quick look then let go a wistful sigh and rested her shoulder against his.

'Well . . . had to try.'

*

A knock brought Barathol to the door; this time he came without any reluctance as the tapping sounded hesitant, almost respectful. He opened the door to see a worker there, a teamster. The man jerked a nod. 'Was hired to deliver someone to this house,' the fellow said.

'Oh?'

The man motioned to the wagon. Someone was sitting hunched in the rear bed. A great wide figure of a man; he appeared to be studying the ground between his feet.

Barathol's breath caught in his chest and he took one hesitant step out. He approached slowly, silently, until he stood right before the big man, who caught sight of his feet and raised his gaze all the way up Barathol's figure to his eyes and a hugely wide smile broke there on his face and he said, 'Thol!'

Barathol could not answer. He reached out to gently squeeze the man's arm. Finally, he succeeded in clearing his throat to say thickly, 'Chaur . . . welcome back.'

Smiling, nodding, the big man slipped from the wagon bed. He peered around eagerly like a child.

The teamster coughed. Barathol looked at him. 'Got another job too,' the man said.

'Another?'

'Yessir. On my way here. Was stopped by an odd little fellow. He hired me to take you out to your villa, now. If you wish.'

'My . . . villa?'

'Yessir. East of the city, up in the hills.'

His hand still on Chaur's shoulder Barathol turned to the row-house to yell, 'Scillara! Get the lad! We're going for a ride!'

*

In the middle of the night south of the city on the Dwelling Plain Scorch and Leff fought to secure a heavy man-sized bundle to a tripod and barrel winch set up over an open well. They knocked each other's hands aside and fought and cursed one another as they wrestled with the heavy weight.

Every now and then the bundle, a contorted hunchbacked man wrapped in chains and gagged, exploded in a fit of writhing fury, struggling to escape and cursing them from behind the gag, his mismatched eyes bulging and his big mangled hands clawing at the chains. 'Shut up, ya evil fiend!' Leff yelled at the bound man. Then the two ducked and peered round nervously.

'Quiet!' Scorch hissed.

'I am being quiet,' Leff answered. 'You be quiet.' He yanked on the iron hook. 'Got that on secure?'

'Course!'

'Okay, so, what we do is take hold of the handles—'

Scorch pointed to the barrel. 'Have to flip the latch thing first.'

'No – you don't have to do that. You just ease off on the handles slow like . . .'

'No. The latch thingy has to be over.'

The bound man suspended over the well attempted to say something as he slowly spun. He repeated it louder and more urgently.

'No – I remember succinctly how it went—'

'Dissinctly. You mean you remember dissinctly.'

'Don't you pick apart my language – you just know I'm right.'

The hanging man yelled something unintelligible through his gag. Scorch gave him a savage push. 'Shut the Abyss up!'

The man swung and hit the side of the mouth of the well. The jerk shook the chain. The barrel winch rocked and the latch in its teeth slipped with a metallic ping.

The hanging figure disappeared with a hissing of rope as the barrel spun. A smothered roar echoed from the well, ending in a splash.

The two men had thrown themselves to the ground and now hesitantly rose to peer down into the darkness of the well. A weak groan sounded from below. They jumped to the handles and started rewinding the winch.

'Y'know,' began Scorch, 'maybe one of us should go down first and the other lower 'im down to him.'

'Sounds good,' Leff grunted, heaving on the handle. 'You go.'

'No – you.'

'Should be you.'

'Why's that?'

'Your idea.'

For a time Scorch chewed on that as he worked. Finally he grunted a curse under his breath. 'I hate bein' the idea man.'

*

The Seguleh established a camp on the coast just outside the city of Callows. The curious and the just plain gawkers from the city were so many that the mayor was forced to post guards at a respectful distance around the camp simply to keep the hordes away. The mayor was just thankful that so far no one had been killed and he hoped the vessels would be readied soon, for the disruption of the Seguleh's presence to the city's daily trade and business had been crippling.

On the third day Sall approached his father, Lo, where he stood facing the calm waters of the sheltered inlet. He bowed, requesting permission to speak.

'Yes?'

'Father . . . I have questions about what happened in the Great Hall . . .'

Lo slowly turned to face him more directly. 'Oh?'

'Yes.' Sall drew a breath to steel himself. 'Would you really have led us on a charge through the Moranth and on through the city – as you claimed?'

The tall slim man, extraordinarily slim even for the Seguleh, nodded his masked head as he considered the question. Seven hatch marks still marred the pale oval of that mask, as the First had judged that all challenges must wait until they were once more on the testing grounds at Cant. 'It was a valid option. We would have finished the Moranth then passed on unharmed through the city avoiding their fliers. Then we could have scattered into parties of two or three. Travelling only at night we would have reached the coast relatively unharmed. There was merit there.'

'It was only chance, then, that it was the very option the First least wished to pursue. And because of that the mask did not come to you . . .'

Lo nodded again. 'I merely presented the choice. Choices surround us every day, son. The test is in the choosing.'

Sall's breath caught. 'He passed your test.'

'Yes. Sall, the truth of it is that once you are competent enough in your technique, or your speed is as great as it can be – then what differentiates those at the highest levels? The truth is that unquantifiable ability to read others. To enter into their skin. To be able to understand them so completely that you know what they will do before they do it themselves. A sort of complete empathy. Jan possessed that. We could not help but love him for it. Gall worshipped him. But Gall was a traditionalist and would not have followed the road Jan had chosen. And so Jan did what he had to do to ensure that the mask would not come to him. And Palla? Well, those two might as well have been husband and wife. She may never recover.'

'And so it came to you – but you never challenged him!'

Lo's voice took on an edge. 'His entire life has been his test, Sall. That is my judgement.'

'Yes, Father.'

Each was silent for a time, facing the shore where an honour guard surrounded a canopy over a wrapped body on its stretcher. They were taking the Second home for burial at Cant. Burial in the soil of their new homeland.

Lo tilted his mask aside, to where Yusek trained now with a group of the lesser ranks. 'As for you . . . She has demonstrated endurance, spirit, speed with her knives.' He pressed a hand to Sall's shoulder. 'Good choice, son. You have my approval.' And the Eighth, perhaps soon to be the next Third, walked away.

Sall watched Yusek practising and he mused, *I'm sorry to say this, Father, but I don't think I know who made the choice – which, I suppose, is perhaps the way it ought to be.*

*

On a hill of black stone on the shore of the glimmering Vitr sea, Leoman sat with the hulking soot-black figure of Maker.

'. . . and so after Lammala was Seuthess – or was it Cora? I'm not certain. In any case, Seuthess . . . now there was a beauty. And didn't she know it. Full of herself she was. We fought like cat and dog.'

And Maker nodded his boulder-like head, a hand on his chin. 'So – these many women – this is how things work among you humans . . .'

'No, no, no!' Leoman waved his hands. 'That's what I'm tryin' to make you understand. It's very *unusual*. Why, I'm one in a thousand, I am. They just can't stay away from me. Like a curse, it is. They just can't help it.'

Maker turned his head and gestured. 'Indeed. You speak the truth, Leoman . . .'

Leoman leaned back to see a familiar figure all in dark clothes walking up. Her long black hair blew lightly in the thin wind off the

Vitr sea and she strode with her hands tucked into her belt behind her back, her head cocked slightly as if to say: *well, well . . . look who's here.*

'By the Seven Holies . . .' He climbed to his feet, dusted off his grimed robes. He set a hand on Maker's shoulder and gave him a wink and a grin. 'You see? It's all in the moustache, friend. All in the moustache.' He went to meet Kiska.

*

In his dream the short rotund man was drawn where he'd hoped he'd never need be drawn again. Out of the shaken, but recovering, city. Out past the shacks leaning as they did against its too-short walls, to the road that curved southwards leading to endless plain upon endless beckoning plain. And here to be waylaid into the stuttering light of a small fire in the dark next to a river where a single figure awaited.

And this figure! Dire and dark. Hooded and hunched. Oh dear!

Kruppe sat to pull on his thin rat-tail beard. 'Kruppe admits to some trepidation. He believed himself free of mysterious lurkers at fires. To what does he owe this visitation?'

The figure waved a hand – and a youthful fit-looking hand at that. 'Merely a social call, friend Kruppe. If I may call you that. No need for alarm.'

'Kruppe is reassured, he assures you. It is not in the least alarming that his social calls should now take the form of hooded figures in his dreams. He is positively cheered.'

'You should be. I am here to thank you – and to introduce myself.' The figure pulled back the hood to reveal a tanned sharp-featured face, a long sharp nose, and hanging silvered dark hair.

Kruppe's brows rose. 'Fearsome High Mage Tayschrenn! I am . . . surprised. Are my dreams privy to everyone?'

Tayschrenn shook his head. 'You need no longer play the innocent with me.'

'Nay! Kruppe must be Kruppe! But what of . . . the other . . . may Kruppe ask?'

'Still with me. I have much to learn yet. These things can take centuries.'

'Ah . . . Why, of course! Kruppe is no stranger to such things!'

The man warmed his hands at the fire. Yet man no longer. Near force of nature now! 'And that name,' he began after a time. 'Old names must pass away.'

'Absolutely – was about to suggest that selfsame thing. How then, pray, shall you be called upon?'

The figure studied the fire, thinking. In his dark eyes the twinned flames danced just as brightly. Reaching a decision he crooked an amused smile and shifted those eyes to Kruppe. 'You may call me T'renn.'